"FIRST-RATE."
—*People*

"FABULOUS."
—*Entertainment Weekly*

"MESMERIZING."
—*USA Today*

Praise for

FREE FOOD FOR MILLIONAIRES

"Unfolds in New York in the 1990s with an energetic eventfulness and a sprawling cast that call to mind the literary classics of Victorian England . . . It would be remarkable if she had simply written a long novel that was as easy to devour as a nineteenth-century romance—packed with tales of flouted parental expectations, fluctuating female friendships and rivalries, ephemeral (and longer-lasting) romantic hopes and losses, and high-stakes career gambles. But Lee intensifies her drama by setting it against an unfamiliar backdrop: the tightly knit social world of Korean immigrants, whose children strive to blend into their American foreground without clashing with their distinctive background. It's a feat of coordination and contrast that could kill a chameleon, but Lee pulls it off with conviction."

—*New York Times Book Review*

"A true page-turner, with a Korean American protagonist and a compelling plot involving the universal clash of cultures, adultery, and class distinction."

—*Chicago Sun-Times*

"An astounding debut from a talented writer."

—*Washington Times*

more . . .

"A sweeping story of first-generation Korean Americans . . . With very broad strokes and great detail, Lee paints colorful three-dimensional characters and outlines intergenerational and cultural struggles brilliantly."

—*Booklist*

"Impressive . . . a detailed vivid tapestry . . . offers us astute insights into the plights, challenges, and successes of a unique generation of new American immigrants."

—*St. Louis Post-Dispatch*

"Stirring . . . vastly ambitious . . . Not since Jhumpa Lahiri's *The Namesake* has an author so exquisitely evoked what it's like to be an immigrant . . . As much as this is an immigrant story, it's also an American story full of class struggle, rugged individualism, social status, and above all, the money haves and have-nots. Most of all, it's an epic meditation on love, both familial and romantic . . . in all its tenacious and painful glory . . . When the novel ends, readers will long for [more] pages so they can extend their love affair with Casey and Min Jin Lee, her amazingly talented creator."

—*USA Today*

"An expansive story . . . draws the reader with likeably human, multi-dimensional characters and a subtly shifting, unpredictable plot."

—*Washington Post*

"Featuring subtly drawn characters and sensitive to the nuances of race and class, FREE FOOD is a book you finish feeling certain the lives inside will go on long after the final page."

—*People*

"Explores the most fundamental crisis of immigrants' children: how to bridge a generation gap so wide it is measured in oceans . . . an insight into the secret world of Korean America."
—*Observer* **(UK)**

"In her noteworthy debut . . . Lee's take on contemporary intergenerational cultural friction is wide-ranging, sympathetic, and well worth reading."
—*Publishers Weekly*

"An absorbing debut novel offering an entertaining and shrewd glimpse into a stratified society . . . A measure of Lee's remarkable talent is her ability to effortlessly capture the thoughts of a range of characters . . . It is a pleasure to enter the world of this large cast of characters, to discover the ties that bind them, to witness the web of deceit that ensnares them, to watch them fall in and out of love, betray, and forgive."
—*Charlotte Observer*

"The smart, driven, quirky, fascinating child of Asian immigrants, Casey Han is Horatio Alger for the twenty-first century. Don't look back—Casey is gaining on you."
—PETER PETRE, **former editor at large,** *Fortune,* **and author of** *Father, Son & Co.*

"Complex and intriguing . . . an exquisite look at life's uncertainties. The beauty of Lee's novel is that it does not focus solely on Casey's sojourn from naïve pride to self-realization, as compelling as that is."
—**Associated Press**

more . . .

"Lee's keen eye for class concerns and her confident, muscular writing about the conflicting pulls toward one's cultural heritage and the unknowable, wide-open future make this book a pleasure."
—**MEG WOLITZER, author of**
The Position **and** *Surrender, Dorothy*

"Zips along . . . captures the great gulf between generations and cultures . . . should resonate especially strongly with young college graduates grappling with their own life choices and priorities."
—*San Francisco Chronicle*

"An immersion into a fully realized and beautifully written world . . . Lee gently but firmly pushes the genre in a more modern direction, and in the process manages to create her own niche in the literary world."
—*BookPage*

"A terrific debut novel . . . reminiscent of another ambitious New York novel about class collision, Tom Wolfe's *Bonfire of the Vanities* . . . the pleasure of reading this sprawling novel derives from the old-fashioned thrill of watching the wheel of fortune slowly turn for various characters . . . In the Victorian-inflected saga of Casey Han and her friends, Lee has given readers more than just Elizabeth Bennett tricked out in a Korean hanbok, she's tweaked venerable nineteenth-century fictional forms to suit the story of yet another new immigrant group claiming New York City as its own."
—**MAUREEN CORRIGAN,** *Fresh Air,* **NPR**

"New and fresh . . . a fantastically fun story . . . a smart, sassy, wild ride . . . reads like a mix of a slightly less frenetic Jay McInerny and an equally sardonic Tom Perrotta, all wrapped in the fast-paced genre perfected by Tom Wolfe."
—*Chattanooga Times Free Press*

"A big, ambitious first novel . . . Min Jin Lee, who is both wise and clever, deftly stage-manages a vast and varied cast of characters . . . all stumbling in their pursuit of the American dream. She makes the reader eager to discover where their errant quests will lead them."
—LYNNE SHARON SCHWARTZ, author of
The Writing on the Wall

"Echoes of Thackeray's *Vanity Fair*."
—*Sacramento Bee*

"A terrific look at the American melting pot that assimilates second generations . . . Readers will enjoy this strong character study, especially when Min Jin Lee focuses on the Americanization of Casey."
—*Midwest Book Review*

"A big, juicy, coming-of-age novel . . . definitely belongs in this summer's beach bag."
—*Entertainment Weekly*

more . . .

"Engrossing and illuminating . . . a panoramic portrait of contemporary Korean Americans and their 'white boy' colleagues, lovers, and friends."

—ALIX KATES SHULMAN, author of
Memoirs of an Ex-Prom Queen **and** *Drinking the Rain*

"A terrific writer."

—*Beverly Hills Courier*

"Assimilation. Independence. Love. Betrayal. Class. Race. Sex. It's all in there. And reading FREE FOOD FOR MILLIONAIRES will, in the words of another writer to whom Lee has been compared, be a 'far, far better thing' than you've ever done."

—KAREN GRIGSBY BATES, *Day to Day,* **NPR**

"A page-turner with a trenchant theme."

—*Washington City Paper*

FREE FOOD *for* MILLIONAIRES

✳

Min Jin Lee

GRAND CENTRAL
PUBLISHING

NEW YORK   BOSTON

Portions of this book appeared in a slightly different form in *Narrative* magazine in 2005. Book III, Chapter 14: *Crown,* appears in the May 2007 issue of *Women's Studies Quarterly.*

Grand Central Publishing
Hachette Book Group
237 Park Avenue
New York, NY 10017

www.hachettebookgroup.com

Printed in the United States of America

Originally published in hardcover by Hachette Book Group.

First Trade Edition: April 2008
10 9 8 7 6 5 4

Grand Central Publishing is a division of Hachette Book Group, Inc.
The Grand Central Publishing name and logo is a trademark of Hachette Book Group, Inc.

The Library of Congress has cataloged the hardcover edition as follows:

Lee, Min Jin.
    Free food for millionaires / Min Jin Lee. — 1st ed.
        p. cm.
    Summary: "Princeton graduate Casey Han stumbles to find a career while trying to maintain her integrity; friends, lovers, and family members also come of age."—Provided by the publisher.
    ISBN-13: 978-0-446-58108-0
    1. Korean Americans—Fiction. 2. Children of immigrants—Fiction. 3. Women college graduates—Fiction. I. Title.
    PS3612.E346F74 2007
    813'.6—dc22   2006037665

978-0-446-69985-3 (pbk.)

Book design by Giorgetta Bell McRee

For *Umma, Ahpa,* Myung, and Sang

CONTENTS

BOOK III *Grace*

Our crowns have been bought and paid for—all we have to do is wear them.

—JAMES BALDWIN

BOOK I

Works

1 | OPTIONS

*C*OMPETENCE CAN BE A CURSE.

    As a capable young woman, Casey Han felt compelled to choose respectability and success. But it was glamour and insight that she craved. A Korean immigrant who'd grown up in a dim, blue-collar neighborhood in Queens, she'd hoped for a bright, glittering life beyond the workhorse struggles of her parents, who managed a Manhattan dry cleaner.

    Casey was unusually tall for a Korean, nearly five feet eight, slender, and self-conscious about what she wore. She kept her black hair shoulder length, fastidiously powdered her nose, and wore wine-colored lipstick without variation. To save money, she wore her eyeglasses at home, but outside she wore contact lenses to correct her nearsightedness. She did not believe she was pretty but felt she had something—some sort of workable sex appeal. She admired feminine modesty and looked down at women who tried to appear too sexy. For a girl of only twenty-two, Casey Han had numerous theories of beauty and sexuality, but the essence of her philosophy was that allure trumped obvious display. She'd read that Jacqueline Kennedy Onassis advised a woman to dress like a column, and Casey never failed to follow that instruction.

    Seated in the spacious linoleum-covered kitchen of her parents' rent-controlled two-bedroom in Elmhurst, Casey looked out of place in her white linen shirt and white cotton slacks—dressed as if she were about to have a gin and tonic brought to her on a silver tray. Next to her at the Formica-topped table, her father, Joseph Han, could've easily passed for her grandfather. He filled his tumbler with ice for his first whiskey of the evening. An hour earlier, he'd returned from a Saturday of sorting laundry at the Sutton Place drop shop that he ran for Mr. Kang, a wealthy Korean who owned a dozen dry-cleaning stores. Joseph and his daughter Casey did not speak to each other. Casey's younger sister, Tina—a Bronx Science Westinghouse finalist, vice president of the Campus Christian Crusade at MIT, and a pre-med—was their father's favorite. A classical Korean beauty, Tina was the picture of the girls' mother, Leah, in her youth.

Leah bustled about cooking their first family dinner in months, singing hymns while Tina chopped scallions. Although not yet forty, Leah had prematurely gray hair that obscured her smooth pale brow. At seventeen, she'd married Joseph, who was then thirty-six and a close friend of her eldest brother. On their wedding night, Casey was conceived, and two years later, Tina was born.

Now it was a Saturday night in June, a week after Casey's college graduation. Her four years at Princeton had given her a refined diction, an enviable golf handicap, wealthy friends, a popular white boyfriend, an agnostic's closeted passion for reading the Bible, and a magna cum laude degree in economics. But she had no job and a number of bad habits.

Virginia Craft, Casey's roommate of four years, had tried to convince her to give up the habit that taxed her considerably while she sat next to her brooding father. At the moment, Casey would've bartered her body for a cigarette. The promise of lighting one on the building roof after dinner was all that kept her seated in the kitchen—her bare foot tapping lightly on the floor. But the college graduate had other problems insoluble by a smoke. Since she had no job, she'd returned to her folks' two-bedroom on Van Kleeck Street. Seventeen years earlier, in the year of the bicentennial, the family of four had immigrated to America. And Leah's terror of change had kept them in the same apartment unit. It all seemed a bit pathetic.

The smoking, among other things, was corroding Casey's sense of being an honest person. She prided herself on being forthright, though she often dodged her parents. Her biggest secret was Jay Currie—her white American boyfriend. On the previous Sunday night after having some very nice sex, Jay had suggested, his elbow crooked over his pillow and head cradled in his hand, "Move in with me. Consider this, Miss Han: sexual congress on tap." Her parents also had no idea that she wasn't a virgin and that she'd been on the pill since she was fifteen. Being at home made Casey anxious, and she continually felt like patting down her pockets for matches. Consequently, she found herself missing Princeton—even the starchy meals at Charter, her eating club. But nostalgia would do her no good. Casey needed a plan to escape Elmhurst.

Last spring, against Jay's advice, Casey had applied to only one investment banking program. She'd learned, after all the sign-up sheets were filled, that Kearn Davis was the bank that every econ major wanted in 1993. Yet she reasoned that her grades were superior to Jay's, and she could sell anything. At the Kearn Davis interview, Casey greeted the pair of female interviewers wearing a yellow silk suit and cracked a Nancy Reagan joke, thinking it might make a feminist connection. The two women were wearing navy and charcoal wool, and they let Casey hang herself in fifteen minutes flat. Showing her out, they waved, not bothering to shake her hand.

There was always law school. She'd managed to get into Columbia. But her friends' fathers were beleaguered lawyers—their lives unappealing. Casey's lawyer customers at Sabine's, the department store where she'd worked weekends during the school year, advised her, "For money—go to B school. To save lives, med." The unholy trinity of law, business, and medicine seemed the only faith in town. It was arrogant, perhaps rash, for an immigrant girl from the boroughs to want to choose her own trade. Nevertheless, Casey wasn't ready to relinquish her dream, however vague, for a secure profession. Without telling her father, she wrote Columbia to defer a year.

Her mother was singing a hymn in her remarkable voice while she ladled scallion sauce over the roasted porgy. Leah's voice trilled at the close of the verse, "Waking or sleeping, thy presence my light," and then with a quiet inhale, she began, "Be thou my wisdom, and thou my true word..." She'd left the store early that morning to shop and to cook her daughters' favorite dishes. Tina, her baby, had returned on Thursday night, and now both her girls were home. Her heart felt full, and she prayed for Joseph to be in a good mood. She eyeballed the whiskey level in the jug-size bottle of Dewar's. It had not shifted much from the night before. In their twenty-two years of marriage, Leah had discovered that it was better when

Joseph had a glass or two with his dinner than none. Her husband wasn't a drunk—the sort who went to bars, fooled around, or lost his salary envelope. He was a hard worker. But without his whiskey, he couldn't fall sleep. One of her sisters-in-law had told her how to keep a man content: "Never deny a man his *bop*, sex, and sleep."

Leah carried the fish to the table, wearing a blue apron over her plum-colored housedress. At the sight of Casey pouring her second glass of water, Leah clamped her lips, giving her soft, oval face a severe appearance. Mr. Jun, the ancient choir director, had pointed out this anxiety tic to her prior to her solos, shouting, "Show us your joy! You are singing to God!"

Tina, of course, the one who noticed everything, thought Casey was just asking for it. Her own mind had been filled with the pleasant thoughts of her boyfriend, Chul, whom she'd promised to phone that night, but even so, she could feel Casey's restlessness. Maybe her sister would consider how much trouble their mother had gone through to make dinner.

It was the water drinking—this seemingly innocent thing. For always, Joseph believed that the girls should eat heartily at the table, grateful for the food and for the care given to it, but Casey habitually picked at her dinner, and he blamed Casey's not eating on her excessive water consumption. Casey denied this accusation, but her father was on the mark. Back in junior high school, Casey had read in a fashion magazine that if you drank three glasses of water before a meal, you'd eat less. It took great effort on Casey's part to wear a size 6 or smaller; after all, she was a girl with a large frame. Her weight also shifted by five pounds depending on how much she smoked. Her mother was thin from perpetual activity, and her younger sister, who was short like her father, had a normal build, and Tina disapproved of dieting. A brilliant student of both physics and philosophy, Tina had once scolded Casey when she was on Weight Watchers: "The world is awash in hunger. How could you cause your own?"

Casey's water drinking at the table was not lost on her father.

At five feet three, Joseph was compact, yet his rich, booming voice gave him the sound of a bigger man. He was bald except for a wisp of baby fuzz on the back of his head, and his baldness did not grieve him except in the winters, when he had to wear a gray felt fedora to protect his head and large-lobed ears. He was only fifty-eight but looked older, more like a vigorous man of seventy, especially beside his young wife. Leah was his second wife. His first, a girl his age whom he'd loved deeply, died from tuberculosis after a year of marriage and before she bore him any children. Joseph adored his second wife, perhaps more so because of his loss. He appreciated Leah's good health and her docile Christian nature, and he was still attracted to her pretty face and delicate form, which belied her resilience. He made love to her every Friday evening. She had given him two daughters, though the elder looked nothing like her mother.

Casey drained her water glass and rested it on the table. Then she reached for the pitcher.

"I'm not Rockefeller, you know," Joseph said.

Casey's father didn't look at her when he said this, but he was addressing her. There was no one else in the room who needed to hear how she didn't have a trust fund. Right away, Leah and Tina moved from the counter to their seats at the table, hoping to dissipate the tension. Leah opened her mouth to speak but hesitated.

Casey refilled her glass with water.

"I can't support you forever," he said. "Your father is not a millionaire."

Casey's first thought was, And whose fault is that?

Tina knew when not to speak. She unfolded her thin paper napkin and spread it across her lap. In her mind, she ticked off the Ten Commandments—this thing she did when nervous; and when she felt particularly anxious, she recited the Apostle's Creed and the Lord's Prayer back to back.

"When I was your age, I sold *kimbop* on the streets. Not one piece"—Joseph raised his voice dramatically—"I couldn't afford to eat one piece of what I was selling." He lost himself in the memory of standing in a dusty corner of Pusan's marketplace, waiting for paying customers while shooing away the street urchins who were hungrier than he was.

Using two spoons, Leah filleted the fish from its skeleton and served Joseph first. Casey wondered why her mother never stopped these self-indulgent reveries. Growing up, she'd heard countless monologues about her father's privations. At the end of 1950, a temporary passage to the South had been secured for the sixteen-year-old Joseph—the baby of a wealthy merchant family—to prevent his conscription in the Red Army. But a few weeks after young Joseph landed in Pusan, the southernmost tip of the country, the war split the nation in two, and he never again saw his mother, six elder brothers, and two sisters, the family estate near Pyongyang. As a war refugee, the once pampered teenager ate garbage, slept on cold beaches, and stayed in filthy camps as easy prey for the older refugees who'd lost their sense and morals. Then in 1955, two years after the war ended, his young bride died from TB. With no money or support, he'd abandoned his hopes to be a medical doctor. Having missed college, he ran errands for tips from American soldiers, ignored his persistent nightmares, worked as a food vendor, and taught himself English from a dictionary. Before coming to America with his wife and two little girls, Joseph labored for twenty years as a foreman at a lightbulb factory outside of Seoul. Leah's oldest brother, Hoon—the first friend Joseph made in the South—had sponsored their immigration to New York and given them their American first names. Then, two years later, Hoon died of pancreatic cancer. Everyone seemed to die on Joseph. He was the last remnant of his clan and had no male heirs.

Casey wasn't indifferent to her father's pain. But she'd decided she didn't want to hear about it anymore. His losses weren't hers, and she didn't want to hold them. She was in Queens, and it was 1993. But at the table it was 1953, and the Korean War refused to end.

Joseph was gearing up to tell the story of his mother's white jade brooch, the last item he'd possessed of hers. Of course he'd had to sell it to buy medicine for his first wife, who ended up dying anyway. Yes, yes, Casey wanted to say, war was brutal and poverty cruel, but enough already. She'd never suffer the way he did. Wasn't that the point of them coming to America, after all?

Casey rolled her eyes, and Leah wished she wouldn't do that. She didn't mind these stories, really. Leah imagined Joseph's first wife as a kind of invalid girl saint. There were no photographs of her, but Leah felt she must have been pretty—all romantic heroines were. A lady who died so young (only twenty) would have been kind and good and beautiful, Leah thought. Joseph's stories were how he kept his memories alive. He'd lost everyone, and she knew from the fitful way he slept that the Japanese occupation and the war returned to him at night. His mother and his first wife were the ones he had loved the most as a young man. And Leah knew what it was to grieve;

her own mother had died when she was eight. It was possible to long for the scent of your mother's skin, the feel of her coarse *chima* fabric against your face; to lie down for the evening and shut your eyes tight and wish to see her sitting there at the edge of your pallet at dawn. Her mother had died from consumption, so she and Joseph's first wife were entwined in Leah's imagination.

Joseph smiled ruefully at Tina. "The night before I left on the ship, my mother sewed twenty gold rings in the lining of my coat with her own hand. She had these thick rheumatic fingers, and the servant girls usually did the sewing, but..." He lifted his right hand in the air as if he could make his mother's hand appear in place of his own, then clasped the right one with his left. "She wrapped each ring with cotton batting so there'd be no noise when I moved around." Joseph marveled at his mother's thoughtfulness, recalling sharply how every time he had to sell a ring, he'd unstitch the white blanket thread that his mother had sewn into the coat fabric with her heavy needle. "She said to me, 'Jun-oh-*ah*, sell these whenever you need to. Eat good hot food. When you return, my boy, we shall have such a feast.'" The yellowish whites of Joseph's eyes welled up.

"She unclasped the brooch from her *choggori*, then she handed it to me. You see, I didn't understand. I thought I was supposed to return home in a few days. Three or four, at the most." His voice grew softer. "She didn't expect me to sell the pin. The rings, yes, but not..."

Casey drew breath, then exhaled. It must have been the thirtieth time she'd heard this tale. She made a face. "I know. Not the pin," she said.

Aghast, Tina nudged her sister's knee with her own.

"What did you say?" Joseph narrowed the slant of his small, elegant eyes. His sad expression grew cold.

"Nothing," Casey said. "Nothing."

Leah pleaded silently with a look, hoping Casey would restrain herself. But her daughter refused to notice her.

Joseph picked up his tumbler for a drink. He wanted to stay with the memory of his mother, the leaf green silk of her jacket, the cool whiteness of the pin. He'd never forget the day he left the jeweler with the bit of money he got in exchange for the pin, his hasty walk to the herbalist to buy the foul-smelling twigs and leaves that never cured his wife.

Wanting to create some distraction, Leah removed her apron and then folded it conspicuously. "Tina, would you pray for us?" she asked.

Tina would have done anything to make Casey control herself. She brushed aside her thick black hair and bowed her head. "Heavenly Father, we thank You for this food. We thank You for our many blessings. Lead us, dear Lord, to Your good service. Show us Your will; let our hearts and minds converge with it. We pray in the name of our dear Redeemer, Jesus Christ, our Lord and Savior. Amen." Privately, Tina wanted God to tell her what she should do with Chul—how she could keep him interested in her without having premarital sex with him, or if he was the one to whom she should give herself. Tina wanted a sign; she'd been praying for guidance for the past several months, but she could discern nothing except her own pressing desire for this boy.

Leah smiled at Tina, then Casey. In her heart, she, too, was praying, Dear God, let there be thanksgiving, because at last, we are together.

Before anyone could eat, Joseph spoke. "So what are you going to do?"

Casey stared at the steam rising from her rice bowl. "I thought I'd try to figure it out this summer. No one's hiring now, but on Monday, I'm going to the library to write some cover letters for jobs starting in the fall. Sabine also said I could get more hours during the week if someone leaves. Maybe I could work in another department if she—"

"You know the options," he said.

Casey nodded.

"A real job," her father said. "Or law school. Selling hats is not a real job. Making eight dollars an hour after getting an education worth eighty thousand dollars is the stupidest thing I have ever heard of. Why did you go to Princeton to sell hairpins?"

Casey nodded again, pulling her lower lip into her mouth. The blood left her face, making it paler.

Leah peered at Joseph's expression. Was it safe to speak? He hated it when she took the girls' side.

"Graduation was just last week," she ventured. "Maybe she could rest a little at home. Just read or watch *terebi*." Her voice was faltering. She smiled at her daughter. "Casey had all those exams." She tried to shore up her voice and sound as if it were the most natural thing in the world for someone in her family to graduate from college and then to figure things out. Casey was staring at her rice bowl but didn't pick up her spoon. "Why don't you let her eat?" Leah said carefully. "She's probably tired."

"Tired? From that country club?" Joseph scoffed at the absurdity.

Leah shut up. It was useless. She knew from his face that he wouldn't hear her, nor would he let her win any points in front of the girls. Maybe Tina might say something to help the conversation along. But she looked as if she were somewhere else entirely, chewing her rice with her lips sealed. Even as a child, Tina had been a good eater.

Casey studied the white walls. Every Saturday night, it was her mother's ritual to wipe down the glossy painted walls with Fantastik.

"Why are you so tired?" Joseph asked Casey, furious that she was ignoring him. "I'm talking to you," he said.

She glared at him. Enough, she thought. "Schoolwork is work. I've always worked hard...just as hard as you work at the store. Maybe harder. Do you know what it's like for me to have to go to a school like that? To be surrounded by kids who went to Exeter and Hotchkiss, their parents belonging to country clubs, and having a dad who could always make a call to save their ass? Do you know what it's like to ace my courses and to make and keep friends when they think you're nothing because you're from nowhere? I've had kids step away from me like I'm unwashed after I tell them you manage a dry cleaner. Do you have any idea what it's like to have people who are supposed to be your equals look through you like you're made of glass and what they see inside looks filthy to them? Do you have any clue?" Casey was screaming now. She raised her right hand as if to strike him, then she pulled back, having surprised herself. She clasped her hand over her heart, unable to keep from shaking.

"What? What do you want from me?" she asked at last.

"What I want from you?" Joseph looked confused. He repeated himself. "What I want from you?" He turned to Leah. "Do you hear what she's saying to me?" Then he muttered, "I should just kill her and me right now, and be done with it." He cast about the table as if he were searching for a weapon. Then he screamed, "What the hell do I want from you?" Using both hands, he shoved the dinner table away from him. The water glasses clinked against the dinner plates.

Soup spilled over the bowls. Joseph could not believe his daughter's nerve.

"What do I want from you?"

"Dammit, that isn't what I meant." Casey tried to keep her voice from quavering, and she willed herself from dissolving into tears. Don't be afraid, she told herself; don't be afraid.

Leah shouted in Korean, "Casey, shut up. Shut up." How could the girl be so stupid? What was the point of being good at school if she couldn't understand timing or the idea of finessing a difficult person? Her older daughter was like an angry animal, and Leah wondered how it was that she hadn't been able to prevent her from becoming so much like Joseph in this way. A man could have so much anger, but a woman, no, a woman could not live with that much rage—that was how the world worked. How would Casey survive?

Joseph stood up. "Get up," he said, gesturing with his hand for Casey to rise.

Leah tried to pull him down. "*Yobo...*" She was begging him, and her fingers caught the belt loop of his slacks, but he swiped her hand away and pushed her back to her seat.

Casey rose from her chair, tucking aside the loose hair that had fallen over her face.

"You stupid girl, sit down," Leah cried, hoping that of the two, Casey might be reasonable. "*Yobo,*" she pleaded. "The dinner..." She wept.

"Come here," he said, his voice calm. "What?" he began, his shimmering eyes unblinking. "You think you know more about life and how you should live?" He'd long feared that his college-educated children might one day feel superior to him, but he would never have held them back from any height they wanted to scale. Still, he hadn't anticipated how cruel it'd be for his child to condescend to him in this way—to consider herself equal to him in experience, in suffering, in the things he had seen. He could hear his Korean accent muddying his English words, and he regretted having told them always to speak English at home. He'd done this for their benefit—so they wouldn't look stupid in front of the Americans, the way he did. Joseph regretted so many things.

Tentatively, Casey shook her head from side to side, not quite believing what an asshole he was. He was so unfair.

Tina pressed the fine features of her oval face into her folded hands. From behind her seat, she could feel the heat of Casey's long body moving toward their father. Ever since Casey was in high school, she'd fought with Joseph once or twice a year. And each year, her sister's anger toward their father grew, compacting into a hard, implacable thing. In ninth grade, Tina went on an overnight school trip to Boston, and there, at a museum, she saw a real cannonball. Tina could imagine such a thing lodged in Casey's belly, sheltered between the fingerlike bones of her ribs. But no matter what, Tina adored her sister. Even now, as Casey stood in front of their father, awaiting a painful judgment, there was an obvious grace in her erect posture. All her life, Tina had studied Casey, and now was no different. Casey's white linen shirt hung casually on her lean frame, the cuffs of her sleeves were folded over as if she were about to pick up a brush to paint a picture, and her narrow white wrists were adorned with the pair of wide silver cuffs she'd worn since high school—an expensive gift from Casey's boss, Sabine.

Tina whispered, "Casey, why don't you sit down?"

Her father ignored this, as did Casey.

Joseph lowered his voice. "You don't know what it's like to have nowhere to sleep. You don't know what it's like to be so hungry that you'd steal to eat. You've never even had a job except at that Sook-ja Kennedy's store," he said.

"Don't call her that. Her name is Sabine Jun Gottesman." She spat out each part of her boss's name like a nail but kept herself from saying, *How could you be so ungrateful?* After all, Sabine had given his daughter a flexible job, generous bonuses that helped pay for her books, for clothes—all because Sabine had gone to Leah's elementary school in Korea. Sabine and Leah had not even been friends back then—they were merely two Korean girls from the same hometown and school who'd by chance run into each other as grown women on the other side of the globe—of all places, at the Elizabeth Arden counter at Macy's in Herald Square. It was Sabine who'd offered to hire Leah's daughter for her store. And over the years, the childless Sabine had taken Casey on—the way she had with many of her young employees. She'd bought her rare and beautiful things, including the Italian horn-rimmed eyeglasses she was wearing now. The glasses had cost four hundred dollars, including the prescription lenses. Sabine had treated Casey better than anyone else had, and Casey hated her father for not seeing that.

14 | MIN JIN LEE

"I had to work for Sabine. I had no choice, did I?"

Joseph looked up at the ceiling tiles above their kitchen. He exhaled, stunned by the child's meanness.

Casey felt bad for him suddenly, because for as long as she could remember, they never had any money, and her father was ashamed of this. Her paternal grandfather was supposed to have been very rich but had died before her father had any real opportunity to know him. Joseph believed that if his father had explained to him how a man made money, things would have turned out differently. In truth, Casey had never blamed her parents for not being better off, because they worked so hard. Money was something people had or didn't. In the end, things had worked out for her at school: Princeton had paid for nearly everything; her parents paid whatever portion they'd been asked to contribute, so she didn't have any college loans. The school had provided her with health insurance for the first time in her life and, with it, cheap birth control. For books, clothes, and walking around money, she'd taken a train to the city every weekend and worked at Sabine's.

"I...I..." Casey tried to think of some way to take it back but couldn't.

Joseph looked her squarely in the face, studying her defiance. "Take off your glasses," he said.

Casey pulled off the tortoiseshell horn-rims from her face. She squinted at her father. From where she stood, not quite three feet away from him, she could still see his face clearly: the wavy lines carved into his jaundiced brow, the large, handsome ears mottled with liver spots, and his firm mouth—the only feature she took after. Casey rested her glasses on the table. Her face was now the color of bleached parchment; the only color in it came from her lipstick. Casey didn't look afraid, more resigned than anything else.

Joseph raised his hand and struck her across the mouth with an open palm.

She had expected this, and the arrival of the blow was almost a relief. Now it was over, she thought. Casey held her cheek with her left hand and looked away, not knowing what to do then. It was always awkward after he hit her. She felt little pain, even though he had used great force; Casey was in fact watching herself, and she wished the person who was watching her and the body she inhabited could merge and come to a decision. What to do, she wondered.

"You think good grades and selling hats is work? Do you think you could survive an hour out there? I send you to college. Your mother and I bring lunch from home or share one sandwich from the deli so you and Tina can have extra money for school, and all you learn is bad manners. How dare you? How dare you speak to your father this way?"

Leah wanted to stop this, and she rose again from her chair, but Joseph shoved her back down.

Joseph then struck Casey again. This time, Casey's torso weaved a bit. A sound rang in her ears. She regained her balance by firming her jaw and balling her fists tighter. Why was he doing this? Yes, he didn't want her to talk back to him. As her father, he deserved respect and obedience—this Confucian crap was bred in her bones. But this ritual where he cut her down to size had happened so many times before, and always it was the same: He hit her, and she let him. She couldn't shut up, although it made sense to do so; certainly, Tina never talked back, and she was never hit. Then, as if a switch clicked on, Casey decided that she'd no longer consider his side of the argument. His intentions were no longer relevant. She couldn't stand there anymore getting smacked. She was twenty-two, a university graduate. This was bullshit.

"Say you're sorry," Leah said, holding her breath, and she nodded encouragingly, as if she were asking a baby to take another bite of cereal.

Casey drew her lips closer still, hating her mother more.

Joseph grew calmer, and Leah prayed for this to be over.

"This girl has no respect for me," he said to Leah, his eyes still locked on Casey's reddened face. "She's not...good."

"She is sorry," Leah apologized for her daughter. "I know she is. Casey is a good girl, and she doesn't mean any of those things. She's just so exhausted from school." Leah turned to her. "Hurry. Go. Go to your room, now. Hurry."

"You spoil the children. You let this happen. No wonder these girls talk to their father this way," he said.

Tina got up from her seat. She rested her hands lightly on her sister's thin shoulders, trying to steer her away, but Casey refused to follow. Their mother wept; she had cooked all afternoon. Nothing was eaten. Tina wished to rewind time, to come back to the table and start again.

Tina murmured, "Casey, Casey, come on...please."

Casey stared at her father. "I'm not spoiled. Neither is she," Casey said, pointing to Tina. "I'm sick of hearing how bad I am when I'm not. You won the sweepstakes with kids like us. Why aren't we good enough? Why aren't we ever fucking good enough? Just fuck this. Fuck you." She said this last part quietly.

Joseph folded his arms over his stomach in shock, unable to accept what she was saying.

"And why am I not good enough right now? Without doing another damn thing?" Casey's voice broke, and now she was sobbing herself, not because he had hit her, but because she understood that she had always felt shortchanged by her father. It wasn't as though she hadn't tried.

Joseph took a breath and swung his fist, hitting her face so hard that Casey fell. Her eyeglasses ricocheted off the table and skittered across the floor. Tina hurried to pick them up. A nose pad was broken, and one of the sides had nearly snapped off. Casey grabbed the table for support, and the Formica table with its cheap metal legs toppled, and she slipped, falling amid the crash of bowls and dishes. A bright red flush spread over Casey's right eye, adding color to the handprints shadowing her left cheek.

"Get up," he said.

With her fingers splayed across the green linoleum, Casey pulled herself off the remaining dry patch of floor. Somehow she was standing in front of him again. Blood trickled inside her cut lip, the metal taste icing her tongue.

"You going to hit me again?" she asked, her tongue sweeping across her teeth.

Joseph shook his head. "Get out. Get your things and leave my house. I don't know you," he said, his speech formal. His arms hung limply against his body. Fighting was useless now. He'd failed as a father, and she'd died as someone to watch over. He left the kitchen, stepping across the broken pieces of a white ceramic water pitcher. From the living room, he turned around but refused to look at Casey. "I sent you to school. I did what I could. I'm done now, and I want you gone by morning. It makes me sick to look at you."

Leah and the girls watched as he walked into his bedroom and closed the door. Casey sat down in her father's empty chair. She stared up at the ceiling tiles, unconsciously counting them as she used to do at meals. Tina smoothed her hair in an effort to comfort herself and tried to regulate her breath. Leah sat still, her hands clutching the skirt of her dress. He had left the room; he'd never done that before. She believed that it would have been better if Joseph had stayed in the room and slapped Casey again.

2 | CREDIT

*T*HE CHILDHOOD BEDROOM Tina and Casey had shared until Casey went away to school was far smaller than any of her dorm rooms in Mathey College or Cuyler Hall. The girls' bunk beds were pushed up against the length of the room, blocking a dirty window that could not be cleaned from inside. Above the laminated headboard of the top bunk where Casey slept hung a faded poster of Lynda Carter dressed as Wonder Woman, her arms akimbo. Within the framed space of the bottom bunk, Tina had taped up a free Yankees poster from Burger King that she'd gotten when she was in primary school. Barely eighteen inches from the bed were two mismatched plywood desks and a pair of white gooseneck lamps from Ohrbach's. Above the desks, the girls had papered the walls with unframed certificates of excellence from their school years: Among their many awards, Casey had received recognition for photography, music, and social studies; Tina, for geometry, religion, physics, and BC calculus.

Casey didn't notice the awards anymore, their curled edges stuck down with yellowing Scotch tape. Nor did she notice the uncomfortable scale of the room or its lack of natural light. In the first years of visits back from school, she'd compared the glorious working fireplace in her suite in Mathey, the wood-paneled classrooms, and the stained-glass windows with the Dacron blue pile carpet in her Elmhurst bedroom and the bulletproof glass in her apartment building lobby, and she decided that she could not afford to look too critically at what was home, because it hurt.

Following the fight with her father, Casey went to her bedroom for the sole purpose of retrieving her Marlboros, and as soon as she got them and a book of matches, she walked out the front door.

She hiked three flights of stairs instead of taking the elevator because there was no other way to get to the tar-paved roof. From memory, she keyed in the security code—4-1-7-4, the birth date of Etelda, the building superintendent's only daughter. For years, Casey had helped Etelda with her schoolwork, then later tutored her for the SATs. In consideration, her father, Sandro, gave Casey free rein of the roof. When Etelda got a full scholarship to attend Bates College, Sandro bought a metal café table and two matching chairs from a hardware store in Paramus with his own money and left the gift along with a glass ashtray on the roof for its sole visitor.

But now Casey didn't pull up a café chair. She sat on the wide parapet bordering the roof, dangling her legs against the north side of the building facing the street, not caring if her white pants were dirtied by the brown brick facade. The night breezes, undetectable in her mother's airtight kitchen, brushed against her battered face. There was little light in the sky, no sign of the moon, and as for stars, Casey had never seen any in Queens. The first time she saw a black sky pierced with what seemed like an infinite number of white holes was on a trip to Newport with her roommate, Virginia, to her grandmother's house during a school vacation. What Casey felt initially was the pause in her own breathing. The sight literally took her breath away. Then she craned her neck to stare at the swirl of the Milky Way, and she could hardly be persuaded to go back into the great house despite the mosquitoes nibbling on her ankles. For the remainder of her visit, the senior Mrs. Craft pronounced Casey "that starry-eyed girl." The next day, when her mosquito bites grew fat and pink on her ankles and toes—forming their own raised constellation—Casey felt no regret whatsoever. At the age of nineteen, she'd finally seen stars.

Casey yearned for the darkened steel layer of city sky, banded by pink-and-gray ribbons of twilight, to be stripped to reveal the stars. There was no way to see them. Fine, she thought, feeling deprived. From where she sat, there were countless identical apartment unit windows brightened with electric bulbs, each covered by a square glass shade screwed into the ceiling. On both sides of Van Kleeck Street, there were attached rental apartment buildings raised in the late 1960s by the same developer—all with the same floor plans, Whirlpool refrigerators, and small closets. Inside them, lightbulbs flickered invitingly. The apartments were brick beehives—defined pockets of air, sound, and light. Casey wanted to believe that in them there could be happiness and not just droning.

Casey began to play her favorite roof game. There were hardly any rules, only one objective: to choose a window, then to study the contents in view. She had the idea that your possessions told about you: A plaid, duct-taped armchair showed a man's brokenness; a heavily gilded mirror reflected a woman's regal soul that had not yet faded; and a paper cylinder of store-brand oatmeal left out on a kitchen counter witnessed a lack of coins in a retiree's purse.

Across the street, at eye level, Casey made out a South Asian boy and girl watching television in a modest-size living room. They were perhaps elementary school age. Casey wanted to sit beside them, silent, invisible, and breathless, because their handsome, earnest faces possessed wonder about the images transmitted to them. The glow of Casey's cigarette kept her company, but she would've preferred a lamp and a book or, in her current mood, a rerun of *Mary Tyler Moore* or *The Bob Newhart Show*. Always, Casey had been a reader and a viewer. The contempt others had for television made no sense when *Alice, The Jeffersons, All in the Family, The Love Boat, Fantasy Island, The Bionic Woman, The Brady Bunch, Little House on the Prairie,* and of course *Wonder Woman* had served as guides to the Han sisters' understanding of America. The literary classics borrowed from the Elmhurst Public Library had taught the sisters about Americans and Europeans from long ago, but modern life had been extrapolated from the small screen. Joseph and Leah did not discourage television. With the girls' irreproachable report cards, television was a treat even the Hans could afford.

Casey heard Tina's wooden sandals clacking toward her.

"Don't jump," Tina said, her voice edged with teasing.

"Ha," Casey replied. "If only it were so easy." She glanced down at the concrete pavement ten stories below. Opposite the red fire hydrant, neighborhood kids crowded the stoop of the building catty-corner from hers and ate Sicilian pizza straight out of the box. Casey envied their appetite, feeling none herself.

Tina dried her wet hands on her blue jeans. She'd been on her knees mopping the kitchen floor with a fat sponge. Downstairs, their mother was still washing dishes. It had been Leah's idea for the younger one to go find her sister.

"So what are you going to do?" Tina asked.

Casey shrugged, saying nothing. Her feeble smoke ring lost its form.

"I expected a blowup some time around August. Not in the first week of our arrival at chez Han," Tina said.

"You're awfully funny tonight." Casey dragged on her second cigarette.

"Can you stay at Jay's?"

Casey nodded. "Looks that way. Virginia is in Newport for a month, then off to Italy. It must be nice to have pots of money. And time to piss it away."

"Italy sounds nice," Tina said. Neither of them had been to Europe.

"And I just got that credit card last week, and if I could score a ticket, Virginia would let me crash with her, but once I'm there, I don't know how to get work, and..." Her first credit card had a five-thousand-dollar credit limit. How much could a plane ticket cost? The notion of living in Italy sounded impressive and exciting, but it was ludicrous for her to think of such a thing.

Tina followed her sister's gaze and tried to guess which window Casey was studying. Tina had no attachment to this game; to her, the round shape of someone's dining table, the short denim skirt a woman chose to wear at home, did not seem telling. But then again, Tina was constantly being surprised by her peers at MIT—the marked difference between their appearances and tastes—whereas Casey was rarely stumped by people. Tina's boyfriend, Chul, was more like Casey in that way; he seemed to have a natural curiosity about other people's choices. Then Tina remembered she was supposed to phone Chul, but it was probably too late to phone his parents' house in Maryland where he was staying for the summer.

"Do you want to go to Italy?" Tina asked.

"Not this way," Casey answered.

"So, to Jay's, then?"

"Yes."

Tina didn't know what to say about the hitting. After one of these fights, Casey hated their family. And how could Tina blame her for that? No one knew how to stop their father when he was angry. "I have two hundred you can have. And twenty in quarters."

"I still owe you," Casey reminded her.

Four years ago, Tina had given Casey her savings to pay for an abortion. Before Casey had met Jay, she'd gotten pregnant from a one-night stand, a guy whose name and number she'd thrown away. Since then, however, when she'd had the money to pay her sister back, a sweater, a hat, or a pair of boots seemed more pressing. Casey wished now that her credit rating were better.

"I don't care about that money. If you hadn't had that"—Tina clenched her jaw—"procedure—your life would've been ruined."

Casey stubbed out her half-smoked cigarette—smoking was akin to burning dollar bills, but she enjoyed the wastefulness of it. Right away, she lit another.

Tina started, "I've seen pictures of lungs—"

"Not tonight, please. Spare me."

"You could have spared us tonight, too," Tina mumbled. Then, hearing the sharp truth of what she'd just said, she hoped Casey wouldn't pick up on it.

"He was being an asshole, Tina."

"Yes, I know that." Tina looked hard at her sister. "So what? None of this is new to you."

"And I suppose you would've handled it differently. No, brilliantly, with your excellent bedside manner, Dr. Han." Casey had called her this since they were kids.

"I didn't say he wasn't being an asshole." Tina resented Casey's persistent wish to choose sides.

"You also didn't say I was being an asshole, although that's what you're thinking. Fuck you."

"Why? Why do I bother with you?"

"Why do you?" Casey replied, furrowing her eyebrows. "Don't do me any favors."

Tina's voice grew quiet. When it came to family matters, she'd always felt as though she were the older one. "C'mon, Casey. It's me."

Casey exhaled, feeling stupid and alone. With her pointer finger, she tapped her right temple. "Hey, I just made up a rule. Wanna hear it?"

"Yes." Tina offered up her baby-sister smile; it said, *Tell me something I need to learn. Let me adore you again.*

"One fight per night." Casey beamed, raising her eyebrows dramatically. "I already had my one fight. So I can't fight with you. Maybe tomorrow I can squeeze you in."

"By all means, sign me up," Tina said, smiling.

They grew quiet. Tina swallowed, then with her right hand reached toward Casey's face, partly hidden in the evening shadow. "Let me see you."

"Don't." Casey flinched, blowing smoke in Tina's direction.

"You should take the money."

"Since I'm causing the problems, it's right that I should go." Casey said it methodically, as if she were reciting a geometry proof. Then she muttered, "I can never catch a break here."

"You'll kill each other if you stay," Tina said. "Take the money I can give you."

Casey nodded, trying to contain her disgust. "I'll pay you back. All of it."

"I don't care about the money, Casey." When they were younger, Tina felt pleasure if Casey merely looked at her.

"I'm leaving after they go to bed." Casey's face was impassive. "They can't know where I am. All right? Please do me that favor."

Tina wouldn't argue. By noting Casey's mistakes, Tina had avoided making the same ones. If she felt a duty to do better in life, it was because she'd screened the previews. She felt—what was it? A primitive loyalty? Certainly not gratitude. Responsibility? Regardless, it wasn't what she wanted to feel.

The dark street below was empty. A pair of rats dashed out of the black garbage bags near the curb.

The evening shouldn't have turned out this way. On the train ride down from school, Tina had been going through her list of questions for Casey—worries saved up from the semester. They rarely spoke during the school year. Long-distance calls were expensive and their schedules so full and out of sync. And Casey made things difficult. Her life appeared frenetic and purposeless. She was so hard to make out.

The evening grew darker, and with no moon or streetlights, Tina could barely detect the silhouette of her sister's face—the shallow-set eyes, their father's mouth, the high cheekbones, the nose that was slightly rounded at the tip. Her sister's skin color was fairer than her own, and her straight black hair turned chestnut brown in the summer. Tina's black hair had a bluish cast, and in the winter, it was raven. When they were out, no one ever suspected that she and Casey were sisters. But Tina wanted to protest that they were sisters; they were not best friends, but they'd always be each other's own.

Tina took a breath. There was always so little time.

"Can I ask you something?"

"Hmm?" Casey was almost surprised to hear a voice, having already wished Tina gone.

"What's...it like?"

"What?" Casey was confused.

"Sex. What's it like?"

"Are you going to have sex?" Casey widened her eyes, offering shock, then amusement. "Is there a boy in my sister's life?"

"Shut up."

"Well!" Casey pretended to be offended.

"There's a boy," Tina admitted—her eyes more full of worry than of pride.

"Name?" Casey asked.

"Chul."

"Korean?" Casey opened her mouth.

"Yes."

"Whoa."

"I know," Tina said. It was law: If either of them brought home a white boy, that daughter would be disowned. They were to marry Korean. But the likelihood always seemed zero, since no Korean boys ever asked them out.

"Tell." Casey leaned in.

It was easier to discuss him in the dark. Chul was a year ahead of her at MIT, also pre-med, tall, and a volleyball player. Harvey, the president of the Campus Christian Crusade, had brought him to an ice-cream social in December and had introduced him to Tina. He was serious looking and more manly than the other boys who milled about her at school. He had beautiful Korean eyes, an open brow, and a masculine nose. When spring term began and he asked her to go to a movie with him, she couldn't believe it, but he came for her as promised with twelve apricot-colored roses wrapped in white paper. After three dates, they made out in his blue Honda Accord.

When she told him she was a virgin, he pulled back. "It's sweet," he said. He'd had only one experience himself—awkward intercourse after a prom night. They agreed to pray about it. In no time, he said he loved her. "It's up to you, Tina." Five months of unclasped brassieres, erections that had initially frightened her, and being touched until she could hardly bear it—she was now worried that her beliefs no longer charmed him. She wanted to make love, but she was afraid of it and him and God, and everything looked gray. Was fellatio sinful, too? Her moral lines kept shifting. They'd done everything up to the last thing. "I...don't believe in premarital sex, you know. The Bible..."

"I know." Casey nodded dramatically. "But you think abortions are okay." She couldn't help getting in this little jab—and it was really toward herself, anyway.

"Didn't you have some newfound rule about one fight per evening?" Tina squinted.

"Oh yes. I forgot." Casey laughed.

"Well?" Tina asked, wanting Casey to talk.

"I think, it's..." Casey wanted the right word. "It's sincere...your faith. I don't know how you do it, but..."

Tina gazed at her sister intently. Sex was a thing Casey knew, and Tina envied her experience.

"I just can't imagine not having sex. I like it. I hope you like it. It's so...overwhelming. And I want to be overwhelmed. Can you imagine that?" Casey turned to face her sister, but she couldn't see her expression clearly. Casey wanted her sister to allow her own desire and not be impeded by conventional ideas. "It's good to be out of your head. To forget yourself. To just yearn for someone else."

Tina exhaled. Casey's boldness impressed her.

"Perhaps I like it too much," Casey said, feeling ashamed of saying what she believed. Perhaps she shouldn't lead her sister astray. So few people had any beliefs these days. "I'm probably not a good example for you." If Casey interpreted her sexual biography by her sister's template, she was probably a slut—having slept with eight different men, not all of them ones she'd been dating, and seven of them she'd slept with before she was nineteen. At Princeton, there'd been girls who'd had thirty to forty partners (with diaries and ranking methods) and girls who'd had one true love. And there was Tina: one of the last holdouts.

Tina wanted details, clues, advice. At MIT, where most of the students were male, few girls were virgins. Men fell out of the sky to have sex. Now that Tina had a boyfriend, she was beginning to get what the other girls had been telling her all along: There had always been boys willing to record cassettes of her favorite love songs, write her bad poetry, take her to dinner in Cambridge—all for the possibility of taking off her clothes. Her friends, especially the attractive ones, and even the plain ones in her Wednesday prayer circle, couldn't believe Tina was still a virgin.

"Why is it so overwhelming?" she asked.

"Because the sensations are so powerful. It's just wonderful being naked with someone you like—touching their warm skin, feeling their breath and bones, being close, so close, and feeling needed, urgently—and afterwards, it can be so soothing; everything else seems so secondary. And...and..." Casey had never described sex to anyone; no one had ever asked. Images tumbled across her mind. She felt alert, alive suddenly.

"It's exciting, so exciting to be wanted by someone you like. And with love, it's even more powerful because when you trust him, it's possible to surrender. Completely. I think if you love Chul and he loves you...well..." Casey stopped herself, feeling like some sort of premarriage sex advocate she didn't want to be.

"Tell me more."

"You know the first time a boy tries to kiss you?"

Tina nodded.

"It's that kind of thrill...but suspended and stretched out. It's...consummation."

Casey had liked Jay Currie the moment she'd spotted him beneath Blair Arch. He was standing there in the middle of a group of guys, telling some funny story, and he'd noticed her looking at him, too. His large blue green eyes—the color of a trout's body with shimmering gray-and-black speckles—had lighted on her, and she'd felt startled. A few days after, he'd sat next to her at Freshman Commons, but it turned out that he was a junior, a member of Terrace. Later, he'd confessed that he'd been trailing her and had snuck into Commons to meet her. She'd agreed to a date, and after *Pauline at the Beach* ended (she couldn't remember the story at all) and as the credits rolled, he'd leaned in and pressed his lips against hers, his chin slightly stubbled—his hair wavy and honey colored.

After pulling back, he'd remarked, "You are so soft," as if this quality had surprised him.

She'd laughed, saying, "Is that so?" and she'd bit her lower lip from happiness. Immediately, he'd kissed her again.

"So do you think Jay is the great love?" Tina asked her.

Casey made a face, not having considered it in such terms. "You mean like the great love of your life?" she asked, smirking. "That's cute."

"Don't be such a hard-ass. I was wondering...I mean...I don't mean to rationalize."

"Rationalize away, Dr. Han."

Tina ignored the gibe. "Listen, if Chul was the great love of my life, and I wanted to be with him forever, and I could promise that I would want only him...then..." It was hard for her to get the words out. She was trying to say that it might be okay to sleep with him before getting married.

"He's your college boyfriend. That's like saying...you'll...oh, my God...I mean...get married to someone who took you to your first formal or something. For heaven's sake." Casey had not intended to sound so dismissive, but Tina's argument was preposterous. Fantasy or, worse, orthodoxy.

"But you said that the sex was better when you love...."

"Yes, of course...but...love is not the same as a promise to be together always."

"But that's what I want. And I think that's what we all want, at least in the beginning."

"Well, yes. But I'm glad I didn't marry Sean Crowley." She mentioned the boy she gave her virginity to when she was fifteen.

"But are you glad that you...slept with Sean?"

The answer was a flat no, but then Casey didn't want to say that. "I'm glad I had that experience," she said. The reluctance in her voice was obvious.

Pleased by her modest win, Tina continued: "I know what I want. I want him to promise me that he will want only me. There should be some sort of promise." She couldn't think of a better word.

"You mean like a goddamn covenant?" Casey recoiled physically, almost repulsed by this suggestion. "Oh, come on, Tina. Get real. You're twenty. You can't get married. And what do you do if he's terrible in the sack? That's fucking ridiculous. You could be married for fifty years. Hell, with science the way it is, you could be married for seventy years. Then what?"

"But you're supposed to love...and you said that if you loved each other...that it's better....Then under your argument, how could the sex be bad? I've been thinking about this...."

"Yes, I can see that." Casey laughed.

"I think it would hurt so much if I wanted him, but he didn't want me...for...for...always. You know? And vice versa."

"Yes, it would hurt." Casey threw up her hands. "Sure. Of course it would hurt. But damn, Tina, love...is..." She stopped. "It's this naked thing. You can get screwed over...but..." Casey felt her position was weaker because she believed less in her own theories. She felt her face sting suddenly. The swelling was worsening. She touched her face, not really wanting to know how bad it was.

"You okay? Here, let me." Tina pushed the hair from Casey's forehead.

"I'm fine," Casey snapped, jerking her shoulder back. Then she saw Tina's hurt expression. "Sorry. What I mean is, with love, you have to march into the possibility of losing."

Tina nodded, thinking Casey didn't sound wrong.

"Never mind," Casey said. "Don't do what I do but what you think is right. But whatever you do, you can't keep yourself from getting hurt. The heart doesn't seem to work that way. I want love, Tina. I want that. I'll pay."

The streetlamps turned on, lighting Casey's face, and Tina gasped at the depth of the bruises. "Your face..." Tina closed her eyes, then opened them, and a rush of sympathy overcame her.

"Is it bad, Dr. Han?" Casey said with a smile, refusing to be moved by her sister's concern. She bit the inside of her left cheek, knowing from Tina's look that it must be awful.

"We have to clean that up," Tina said. She was trying to remain calm and keep from crying. "C'mon, let's go."

3 | NET

*W*HEN THE SISTERS GOT DOWNSTAIRS, Leah and Joseph were in their bedroom with the door shut. The kitchen table was bare except for the plastic napkin holder stuffed with paper napkins and a shot glass filled with wooden toothpicks; all the surfaces had been wiped down, with no trace of a meal that had been thrown on the floor. The living room, located in the back of the building, was quiet except for the occasional screech of a distant car. In the bathroom with the burble of the tap running, Tina cleaned Casey's face. Neither spoke—anxious that their father might be roused from sleep. After Tina finished, Casey put in her contact lenses. In their current state, her eyeglasses couldn't be worn. She packed a duffel and messenger bag.

Tina sent her off, giving her the money and securing Casey's promise to call later that week. The sisters parted without any hugging or kissing—the intimate gestures that came so easily to Americans. The painted elevator doors closed, taking Casey down to the lobby, and Tina turned back to the apartment.

Casey walked toward Queens Boulevard. She'd catch the N or R at Grand Avenue. She wore a wide-brimmed canvas beach hat and a pair of mirrored ski sunglasses lifted from a lost and found at Sabine's. The pin dots of blood on her collar were indiscernible, so she hadn't bothered to change her shirt. She was too exhausted to care. All she wanted was to fall into Jay's bed. She didn't want to talk, and he was likely at the office anyway. He worked most Saturday nights and Sundays.

At the subway platform, Casey rested her things on an empty bench. The duffel was filled like sausage casing with summer clothes and shoes. In the messenger bag strapped across her chest were her books: copies of *Middlemarch* and *Wuthering Heights* that she read and reread for comfort; a collection of Pritchett's stories borrowed long ago from Virginia and that she hadn't read yet; the confirmation Bible she read each morning in private and a ninety-nine-cent marble composition notebook in which she copied her verse for the day. Also in the bag, wrapped in a cotton scarf, was a mint first edition of Lilly Daché's biography that Sabine and her husband, Isaac, had given her for her graduation. Lilly Daché was a celebrity hat maker from the 1940s and 1950s whose career Sabine had modeled her own on. After Sabine gave her the book, she told Casey that she'd paid five hundred dollars for it. A retailer, Sabine couldn't help talking about the cost of things.

In her straw handbag, Casey carried cosmetics and a Vuitton wallet (another present from Sabine) with two hundred and seventy-two dollars in cash and her first Visa charge plate activated from her parents' apartment that night. At the bottom of the purse, two rolls of quarters weighed heavily.

Amazingly, the pay phone on the platform had a dial tone, but when Jay's home phone began to ring, the R train came, so she hung up and ducked into the car. Soon she reached the Lexington Avenue station and switched for the 6. Before midnight, Casey found herself in front of Jay's apartment building on York Avenue.

With her own set of keys, she let herself into Jay's cramped lobby—its walls painted a Schiaparelli pink. The lobby had just enough square footage for an upholstered stool opposite the elevator and a path for a resident to reach the six mailboxes behind the staircase. Jay's box, as she'd predicted, was jammed, including a fat alumni magazine from Lawrenceville where he'd been a day boy. Casey flipped through his heavy stack of mail. They had an arrangement where he gave her checkbooks with signed blank checks and she paid his bills. He didn't have time to sleep or spend money on a regular basis; his big-ticket items were skiing in the winter, golfing in the summer, and the repayment of school loans. In January, he'd received a hundred percent bonus and made one hundred and sixty thousand dollars in total compensation. Their point of view on money was identical: Whoever had more covered for the other. At school, when she'd had extra because her weekend job was steady, she'd paid their expenses. And now that he earned much more money, he picked up the tab.

In return, when she stayed over during weekends and vacations, while her parents had the impression she was sleeping at Virginia's, Casey did housewifey things for Jay—went to the dry cleaner for his shirts, tidied the apartment, scrubbed the bathtub, stocked the refrigerator with orange juice, milk, cereal, and coffee. She helped him select his suits, shirts, and ties—he preferred Paul Stuart over Brooks—and every night when they spoke on the phone while her parents were asleep, she reminded him to take his vitamins before saying good night. She could've cooked more but lacked real interest in the domestic arts—her repertoire was limited to baked ziti made with Ragú sauce and Polly-O cheese and a Lipton's Onion Soup mix meat loaf. Nevertheless, Jay was grateful. He was a pleasure to take care of because he had beautiful manners. For that, Casey took her hat off to his mother, Mary Ellen.

Casey's face was hurting. In the dim light from a pink glass chandelier installed by the landlord's nephew, she opened her compact to check her face. Her father's mark on her face was less distinctly a hand—more liver shaped. She put away the mirror. Jay didn't know about her father's hitting her. He knew her parents were difficult; he was aware that she wasn't meant to date white guys. But Casey never told anyone about the hitting. When she was a girl, her mother warned her and Tina that in America, if your parents disciplined you and the teachers at school found out, the state would put you in an orphanage. Consequently, Casey and Tina never told anyone anything. As they grew older, they saw their parents working yet unable to get ahead. Leah looked perpetually frightened in the streets, and both she and Joseph were treated like idiots by their customers, who cared little that the hardworking pair were fluent and literate in another language. Casey and Tina saw their parents' difficulties and believed that Leah and Joseph meant well. And they feared their parents' actions would be misunderstood. As if to confirm it, Jay called her parents bigoted: "Your silence about me is a form of collusion with their racism."

To Casey, it seemed upside down to call a minority person a rac-

ist, or a woman a sexist, a poor person a snob, a gay person a homo-
phobe, an old person an ageist, a Jewish person an anti-Semite. All
these labels were carelessly bandied about at school. But she admitted that it was possible to hate yourself and easy to hate others because you'd been hated. Hatred had its own logic of symbiosis. Her
father refused to buy a Japanese car and instead drove an Oldsmo-
bile Delta 88. Casey found this absurd, yet she'd never had a brother
shot by a Japanese soldier or experienced a hostile colonial occupation. She saw that her father's stance was a powerless person's sorry
attempt to regain some dignity. Casey wanted to believe she could
rise above her father's smallness. But the crazy thing was that her
father probably considered himself just as Casey considered herself:
broad-minded and fair.

She was no longer welcome in his house; she was no longer his
daughter, he'd said this. He might be right that she had no idea
what it was to lose everything. Had she lost everything? Life seemed
too vast, so many things to consider, and she was overwhelmed. How
would she explain to Jay what had happened? He would see the
bruises and think her father was a monster. Jay's own father had
walked out when he was three. Casey hoped Jay wasn't home. In
the morning, after sleep and coffee, she'd talk to him. The elevator
finally arrived.

Inside the apartment, Casey heard the bathroom radio that Jay
never turned off, but it didn't sound like the news. Jay preferred
the station with its spooled taped news reports because it broadcast
the weather in five-minute intervals, but also because the editorial
content was so absurd. He called it radio station bang-bang because
from listening to it, you'd think that all there was in New York was
bedlam, murder, and mayhem.

Casey dropped her bags on his Jennifer Convertible sleeper sofa,
removed her hat, and brushed her hair back with her hands. Then
she plopped down in Jay's grandmother's armchair—the only good
piece of furniture in the place. Casey planned to have it re-covered
for him one of these days; Jay's maternal grandmother, who'd recently died, had watched over him and his brother when they were
boys while their mother worked at the Trenton Public Library. Jay
was unequivocal in his adoration of her. Casey leaned back, feeling
calm, nearly overjoyed to be at Jay's. Then his voice drifted from
the second bedroom that he used as his office. Jay was likely on the

phone. Managing directors had no qualms about calling him any time of the day. Casey leaped up and rushed to him.

She saw the girls first. Jay lay across the beige wool carpet with two naked girls—one of them joined to him, straddling his hips, and the other crouched over his face, his mouth tight to her body. She was an attractive redhead with gold-colored eyes; the other was a pretty blonde. They looked like girls she and Jay could have known from school, but prettier than Princeton girls. Casey scrutinized them. They looked happy—their faces flushed. A half-empty bottle of red wine rested on Jay's white Ikea desk. A year ago, he had borrowed his mother's car, and he and Casey had driven out to Elizabeth to buy the desk and a pair of white shelves. They'd eaten Swedish meatballs in the store cafeteria. She and Jay had never had sex in this room and not on any floor in quite a while. His stereo was set to a top forty station, something he never listened to, and Casey was glad it wasn't radio station bang-bang because that was their joke. The song playing was "Lady in Red," and Casey focused on its maudlin lyrics and the rattling of the air conditioner—its chassis hanging out the casement window. They hadn't noticed her yet.

Casey stood, unwilling—or unable—to speak. In her mind, she kept repeating, Oh God. Oh God. Oh God. It seemed almost a pity to interrupt them; they were having so much pleasure. The three of them resembled gleeful children playing a game. They were youthful and attractive, and their sex looked like a sporting exercise more than anything else. Jay opened his eyes from his labor and stretched his neck upward, jostling the blond one with the spectacular breasts who was perched on his shoulders. He wondered how he would manage to satisfy both girls. He didn't want to get a weak performance review back at some Louisiana sorority house. The fantasy he'd held for years was turning out to be less than satisfying. Nevertheless, he congratulated himself, because he would never have discovered this information in any other way. No matter what, however, he could not climax—*must keep the boat afloat,* he told himself.

The girl with the long legs wrapped loosely around Jay's neck continued to thrust her pale hips toward his face. For an instant, she woke from her dreamy gaze and pulled herself away from him, adjusted her position, and then thrust on.

Casey felt herself fold inward like a dying fire—flames vanishing, the embers turning to black ash. She wondered if she could survive the moment. Her limbs wouldn't move. She felt stupid more than angry, and her pride instructed her to be composed in front of these pretty girls who were fucking her boyfriend. She inhaled deeply and looked down at her feet. She'd put on black espadrilles when she left her parents' house, and she felt ridiculous wearing shoes, because she was the only one in the room wearing any.

Yet she could hardly look away from the three bodies, their bright skin taut and shimmering in the low wattage of the desk lamp. The longer she looked, the less human they appeared, as if they were a more primeval species.

Jay turned his neck a few degrees. "Oh God. Casey. What happened? To your face? Are you all right?" He freed himself suddenly from the girls, saying, "Excuse me." He pulled on a pair of blue boxer shorts over his condom-covered erection. He was so upset about her face that he didn't think to explain the ménage.

Casey stared at him as if she had never seen him before, then turned away. It hurt to look at him. She wanted the girls to get dressed, but they were in no rush. They didn't know who she was, only that she was intruding. Why should they rush to pick up their things?

Jay combed his tousled hair with his fingers. "This is Brenda," he said of the redhead, and the blonde's name was Sheila. They smiled genially, not thinking that the Asian girl was Jay's girlfriend. They'd asked him if he had a girl, and he'd said, "No."

They were juniors from LSU who'd gone into a fancy Upper East Side bar with their sorority sisters on an annual end-of-the-year trip. After several margaritas each, the sorority sisters played Truth or Dare. Jay was a dare for Sheila, and when Brenda was also dared to find a one-nighter, the girls decided that it would be safer to do a triple rather than split up with strangers. They agreed on Jay. Brenda liked his pretty eyes and his jacket and tie, and Sheila thought he looked disease-free.

Holding Brenda's hand, Sheila approached Jay and asked if he'd oblige a couple of girls from out of town. At first Jay didn't understand. Then they asked if he'd ever done a neck shot. A tray of tequila appeared. "Observe," Sheila said. She rubbed lemon on Jay's neck, then dabbed coarse salt on it. Brenda licked the area and downed a shot expertly.

"Your turn," they chirped like twin girls. Sheila applied juice and salt to Brenda's neck and handed Jay his shot. Jay, seeing himself as a sporting fellow, did it perfectly on his first try.

"Hey, Jay, what do you say?" Sheila asked him—proud of her rhyme.

"Beats quarters," he said.

Jay's colleagues, who dragged him to the bar after closing a deal, nearly fell down at the young man's luck. "Fuck me," one of the older men cried out.

Brenda winked at him. "No, thank you, sweetie, this one will do."

Another of the men said, "Young Currie, don't be a schmuck. This is better than making a million a year. You may never ever—" he appraised Sheila, then took some air into his lungs, "ever—" he shook his head, "get this opportunity again. Carpe diem, you get me?"

Jay left the bar with a girl on each arm, hoots and hollers of applause cresting like a wave behind him. At the apartment, Sheila tuned the stereo and Brenda did a little dance while she took off her clothes. Not ten minutes into their dare, Casey walked in.

"Hey there," Brenda said to Casey in a friendly voice. It crossed her mind that maybe Casey might be Jay's roommate, girlfriend, or even just friend. She could be his adopted sister. None of it was very clear, and Brenda's buzz was fizzling out. Her best friend's cousin Lola had an adopted sister who was Chinese and looked a bit like this girl, but not so tall.

Sheila hooked her brassiere. "Hi." She smiled brightly, with some flash of concern for the girl, who looked as if she'd been mugged or something. It was a little spooky how she didn't talk.

Casey tried to smile, but moving her face hurt. She tried to pretend she was meeting people from school or Jay's work, but she couldn't stand it. She turned and rushed to the master bath in Jay's bedroom and locked the door.

She retched a bitter liquid tasting of cigarettes. With water, she rinsed her mouth quickly, then glanced up. In the three-way mirror, she saw her face. The right side was purple, and her left eye had a curved gash above a blue-green-streaked bruise. Jay knocked, and Casey opened the door to push past him as he was saying something she couldn't hear. She might have been shouting, she wasn't sure. It was as though he were underwater and she were standing on shore. She got to the living room, pulled her hat down over her head, slipped on her sunglasses, and grabbed her bags. She dashed out the door and ran down the flights of stairs, gulping air to calm her wild heart.

4 | DEFICIT

CASEY WALKED WEST TOWARD MADISON AVENUE—a street she loved for its polished glass storefronts and impossibly choice wares. It was past midnight, but safer on Madison than many streets in the world, because here the shop owners had secured their costly inventory, and by default, Casey was protected, too.

Virginia Craft lived one avenue over, on Park, but no one was home for the summer, and even if Virginia's elderly parents were in, Casey wouldn't have shown up at this hour. The elder Crafts were kind people, and they would have asked her to stay, but Casey couldn't imagine what they'd say seeing her in this condition—or, worse, what they would never say. They didn't have outward conflicts with their only child—adopted from a dark-haired Mexican seventeen-year-old who'd had an affair with a gringo ne'er-do-well who'd refused to marry her. The Crafts had gone to collect Virginia in Texas when she was two days old. Virginia once said about her adoptive parents: "I feel neutral to positive about Jane and Fritzy, who saved me from poverty and obscurity. But I sense that I've let them down." Virginia's long-limbed parents with coin-worthy profiles had a detached manner of speaking that trained you to follow them accordingly. Their mode of conversation encouraged restraint. To them, her father would be criminal. Her boss, Sabine, who lived less than five blocks away from the Crafts, would've called the police on Joseph.

Casey stopped at the Carlyle Hotel. There was no doorman in front of the revolving door. Virginia's grandmother Eugenie Vita Craft stayed here whenever she came to town. Old Mrs. Craft was a pleasure. She wore her white hair short and wild like a tropical bird. On her flat waist and narrow hips, she wound multiple scarves, and wherever she was, men sought her glance. Venetian rings with colored stones glistened on her freckled fingers. She was thrilling, but her only son, Virginia's father, was a disappointment. After years of therapy, Virginia analyzed him: "Grandmother's irrepressible nature blocked Fritzy from being a grander person. There isn't enough room for him in the world. Poor baby." Virginia speculated that to avoid repeating the mother-son dynamic, Fritzy picked Jane for his wife—a woman who disliked books, sports, art, drama, fashion, sex, and politics. Naturally, Virginia and Casey discounted Virginia's parents and worshipped the grandmother.

Casey pushed her way into the Carlyle, and at the front desk, she called on her best imitation of the old Mrs. Craft. "I find myself in New York for the night. Could you possibly spare a quiet room?"

The man tried not to stare at her face. He was originally from Glasgow, and long ago when he first came to New York, he'd tried to pick up a straight man in the Lower East Side and had gotten badly beaten up. That she was wearing a ridiculous hat and ski glasses and trying to sound posh made him feel more sorry for her. He considered asking if she needed medical assistance but instead offered her an excellent room at a corporate rate.

The next morning, Casey woke up enveloped in crisp white bedding. Her hotel room was large, with lovely striped wallpaper, a green wool mohair armchair, and, beside it, an inviting reading lamp. Beneath the Roman-shaded window, there was a lady's writing desk and, in the drawer, embossed stationery. She dashed a quick note to Virginia: "Thrown out of my parents' casa. I am pretending to be Lady Eugenie for a night at the Carlyle until Fate determines my course. Explanation(s) to follow. Will send return address." She'd post it later when she found a stamp.

Afterward, Casey realized that she hadn't eaten in nearly twenty-four hours. From the In-Room-Dining menu, she ordered Irish oatmeal, lemon ricotta pancakes, and bacon. Fresh-squeezed orange juice and a large carafe of black coffee. When the food arrived, she tipped the waiter on top of all the additional in-room charges. She told herself to disregard the cost. Casey sat down and ate with gusto. Everything tasted so wonderful.

In the bathroom mirror, she saw that the swelling in her face had worsened in spots, and the colors of the bruises had deepened. It would've been better if she'd iced it last night. Not much could be done now. It would heal, she told herself. She steeped in the deep white tub, sampling every bottle of bath gel, shampoo, and conditioner. To dry off, she went through four fat bath towels just because she could and used up all the lotion. This was her first time in such a place, and she decided she never wanted to stay anywhere else. Yet in her head, Casey envisioned a meter, like a taxi meter—clicking, clicking, clicking speedily ahead.

She dressed herself in a pair of faded linen slacks, a worn white polo shirt, and white tennis sneakers with no socks. This was what she wore when she was a guest at a summer house. Over the years, through Virginia's family and Jay's wealthy friends from Lawrenceville and his eating club, Casey had been invited to Newport, South Hampton, Nantucket, Palm Beach, Block Island, Bar Harbor, Martha's Vineyard, and Cape Cod. The visits had taught her a great deal about manners and dress.

At the writing desk, Casey read her Bible chapter for the day, and afterward, she jotted down her verse. She'd begun this practice during her freshman year after an office-hour visit with the esteemed religious studies professor Willyum Butler—an atheist who converted to Catholicism in his late thirties. Butler was a West Indian from St. Lucia who had been educated at Cambridge. He reviewed her mediocre paper on Kant and Huxley, and sensing the student's awe and fear of the subject matter, he asked her plainly, "Casey, what do you really think of what they are saying?" Casey swallowed and confessed an attraction to agnosticism. God's existence, Casey said in a stammer, couldn't be proved or disproved. It was easier to reconcile her life with Huxley than Presbyterian orthodoxy—the passionate belief of her joyless parents.

Willyum nodded encouragingly. "So you are a determined fence sitter."

"Yes, I mean... Am I?" she answered.

Willyum laughed, and then Casey did, too.

Willyum liked his student's earnest face and admired her willingness to talk about her faith. Her seriousness reminded him of his early beginnings at university. He felt compelled to give her something—to tell her a bit about his struggle. But he didn't want her to think that he was proselytizing, because he didn't believe in that, and it would have been wrong to do so in his capacity, he thought. He loathed thumpers as much as he disliked ex-smokers. But he also believed that if there was a cure for cancer, how could he withhold such a thing? "I think...if a mind can...a mind must wrestle before declaring victory. Really wrestle. Do you understand?" Willyum did not release his frown.

Casey nodded, not knowing what to say.

"It's your soul you're fighting for."

She wanted to know what he thought of the soul—obviously, he believed that it existed. But she didn't feel entitled to ask any more questions. There were other students waiting outside the closed door. At times like that, Casey felt like a bumpkin, and his kindness and humility affected her deeply. In longhand, he drafted a short reading list for her. That afternoon, she would go to the bookstore and buy Kierkegaard, Nietzsche, Chesterton, Lewis, de Beauvoir, and Daly—blowing most of a paycheck from her weekend job at Sabine's. As she gathered her things to leave, she couldn't help herself from asking: "Do you still struggle? I mean...wrestle?"

"Every day, I read a chapter of the Bible."

She nodded—her father and mother did this, too.

"And every day, I find a verse I cannot stomach, make peace with, or comprehend. I write it down on my calendar." Willyum opened his leather-bound diary and showed her his scratchy writing. That day he was reading Ecclesiastes. "I pray for clarity," he said, but did not mention being on his knees, hands folded, head bowed.

Casey rose from her chair and shook his hand good-bye, but in her mind, she was busy tucking away his proffered scrap of personal history like a jewel.

Then, in the second semester of her junior year, Professor Butler was killed in a car accident with his fourteen-year-old son, and Casey went to a memorial service attended by hundreds of mourners. Seated in a back pew with no one she knew, Casey could not stop weeping. Prizewinning poets flew in from all over the world to read in his honor. The university president and the janitor who cleaned Butler's office eulogized him. Casey regretted not having told him that each morning since their talk, she read a Bible chapter for ten minutes and took an additional minute to scribble down her verse of the day. It wasn't wrestling exactly, but more like approaching the mat. After he died, she began going to church each Sunday, though she told no one. She still didn't feel comfortable around people who identified themselves as Christians. But she discovered an unexpected dividend—her anxiety diminished for a while, and for that, she felt grateful.

In her block print, Casey wrote out her day's verse from the book of Joshua: "When I saw in the plunder a beautiful robe from Babylonia, two hundred shekels of silver and a wedge of gold weighing fifty shekels, I coveted them and took them." What was a shekel worth today? she wondered. She closed her Bible and notebook and stored them away in her messenger bag. She checked her face. There was little she could do except pull down the brim of her beach hat and wear her sunglasses. Lipstick seemed beside the point, but she applied some anyway. It was June in the Upper East Side of Manhattan—she kidded herself—perhaps the hotel staff might attribute her appearance to rhinoplasty. She decided to go shopping.

Clothing was magic. Casey believed this. She would never admit this to her classmates in any of her women's studies courses, but she felt that an article of clothing could change a person, literally cast a spell. Each skirt, blouse, necklace, or humble shoe said something—certain pieces screamed, and others whispered seductively, but no matter, she experienced each item's expression keenly, and she loved this world. Every article suggested an image, a life, a kind of woman, and Casey felt drawn by them. When things were difficult—and they couldn't get much worse—Casey went to buy something to wear. When she had very little cash, purchasing a pair of black tights or a tube of lipstick from the drugstore could help her get through a slump.

Casey and her college friends were ashamed of shopping. Smart girls who read books weren't supposed to be materialistic (her fellow economics majors pegged consumers as mollified idiots, and as for religion, they invoked Marx's phrase *the opiate of the masses*), and although female intellects cleverly discussed sensuality and tactility in art, smart women were not supposed to like culling or gathering more dresses. But Casey knew well from having been on both sides of the counter that even bookish girls liked to go to shops and be thrilled by a red tweed skirt or a black cloche. And equally true was that smart girls wanted to be beautiful in the way beautiful girls wanted to be smart. Size fourteen bibliophiles could love clothes as much as size two heiresses who shopped to fill their time. Everyone scrounged for an identity defined by objects.

That morning, Casey went to Bayard Toll, though her budget recommended Lucky's, a discount warehouse. What she wanted was an image of something to wear for a job interview, and the notion of combing through the round, bulky clothing racks of Lucky's depressed her, although at other times she'd relished the challenge of finding the treasures passed over from last season's styles. Today, she wanted luxury. She wanted to be someone else.

Bayard's third floor carried collections of modern designers. Casey shopped efficiently, and within half an hour she'd picked up a pair of black slacks—cut narrow and made from a fine summer-weight wool, a gray skirt with parallel kick pleats on the sides, a white Sea Island cotton shirt with exaggerated French cuffs, and a navy lightweight jacket that she could wear with slacks or a skirt. These were work clothes, and they were what called to her.

A petite saleswoman named Maud relieved Casey of the clothing slung over her arm. She glanced at Casey's face, the canvas hat and mirrored sunglasses, and gave her a clipped nod. Casey returned the nod. Maud's detached manner was amazing. As a fellow retail salesperson, Casey recognized that Maud's response was exactly right. Maud spoke plainly—without false intimacy. She was in her late fifties, dressed in a gray modernist sweater, slim gray pants. Her pouf of curly gray hair was streaked with even ribbons of pure white. She was a classic column. Around her neck, she wore reading glasses strung on a canvas cord, giving her an intellectual authority Casey found irresistible.

Casey normally avoided salespeople. At a store like Bayard's, the salespeople parted the pool of customers into two segments: those who wanted a best friend or those who wanted a silent servant to ring up the sales and deliver the packages to the proper address. Casey was pretending to be the latter, because she did not want to be found out. At most, she could afford to buy a garter belt on sale.

Maud brought her to a large dressing room, then hung up her selections on the forged iron rack. She looked them over.

"You've made good choices," she said. Maud's tone was deliberate, not fawning, and the comment meant something to Casey, although she heard this kind of thing often. Her taste was well developed for someone so young (Sabine's exact and slightly aggressive words), but it did not make Casey feel better about not being beautiful. She recalled Jay with the two girls and wished she were prettier, her waist narrower, her breasts fuller, her skin more luminous. Her thoughts embarrassed her.

Maud rested her pinkie on her lower lip. "I have something for you."

Casey nodded, pleased by the attention, and in no time, Maud brought her a suit by a German designer, the color of bitter chocolate—with a long jacket and a knee-length skirt. The fabric was wool, much like the material used for a man's suit. The jacket opening was asymmetrical and double-breasted; the price was four figures. Size thirty-six.

"I didn't see this on the floor," Casey said.

"It wasn't on the floor." Maud smiled. "Try it."

Crystal sconces brightened the peach-colored dressing room with a flattering light. Casey slipped off her street clothes and let the suit cover her pale figure.

There was a large-size pair of high heels kept in the room to try on with the clothes. Her hat off, but her sunglasses still on, Casey saw an impenetrable young woman in her mirror reflection, utterly shockproof. She crossed her silver-cuffed arms with her hands fisted tightly against her chest to make an X, taking her Wonder Woman stance. This used to make Tina crack up, but Casey didn't feel like smiling now.

The other pieces fit perfectly. Normally, she made a discard pile when she tried things on, but this time there was nothing on the dressing room floor. Each piece of clothing felt essential to her new life, whatever it would be. The least expensive of all was the shirt, and that was three hundred dollars.

With exquisite care, Casey hung each piece on its hanger, taking the most time with the brown suit, and she tallied the figures in her head. Not including tax: four thousand dollars. Among retail salespeople, of which Casey was a member in good standing, it was a point of honor never to pay retail—that was for the customers. The salesgirls at Sabine's termed those kinds of customers "Wilmas," short for willing mamas. You were supposed to look down on Wilma. You gave her your best advice, took her commissions, yet you hoped if you were ever in her situation, you would not be so foolish. But there wasn't a girl working the floor who didn't want to have Wilma's choices.

Casey sat on the plush tufted ottoman. She couldn't imagine starting her new life without these beautiful clothes—they were made for her. In the past, she had put items on hold, never to claim them. As she'd exit the shop, she'd think of who she was—the daughter of people who cleaned clothes for a living. She had no business at Bayard's. Maud rapped on the door quietly. Casey put on her hat.

"Would you hold these things for me?" she asked.

Maud kept her expression blank, knowing what was up. "Your name and number?" she asked with a courteous smile.

Casey gave her name, then sputtered, "The Carlyle…Hotel." She was looking through her handbag for the hotel room key—thinking there might be a phone number on the key folder—when she felt the tap on her shoulder. It was Ella Shim.

Ella was a girl she knew from her parents' church. She and Casey were born almost a year apart, but they were in the same grade. Ella's father, Dr. Shim, was an ophthalmologist at Manhattan Eye, Ear & Throat and a founding member of Casey's parents' church in Woodside. Once a month, Dr. Shim and Joseph Han, both elders, and Leah, a deaconess, served on the hospitality committee and visited bedridden and ailing congregants. Ella and her widowed father lived in a grand Tudor house on Dartmouth Avenue in Forest Hills. They played tennis Saturday mornings at the Westside Tennis Club, where he was its first Korean member. Ella had gone to Brearley with Virginia Craft, who thought Ella's dullness was proportional to her exceeding beauty. Casey disliked Ella for no good reason and resented how she was always popping up. Ella had a bone white complexion, small, unpierced ears, Asian eyes with the desired double fold, dark curving eyelashes, and a deep pink mouth. She had a charming left dimple and the innocence of an infant. Years ago, during Sunday school classes, Casey used to stare at Ella's long, tapered fingers. Ella's hair was jet colored, and she was often compared with the Chinese actress Gong Li.

The women at church pitied Ella since her mother died in childbirth, and they admired Dr. Shim, who never remarried after his wife's death—to them, he was a romantic ideal. At church, the mothers of sons rubbed their hands in anticipation of Ella's graduation from Wellesley—hoping that the pretty, reserved doctor's daughter might one day be theirs. But the sons did not feel comfortable around the silent beauty; in fact, few people sought her out. Hers was a beauty that alienated—she was not cold exactly, but she did not offer warmth or ease. She possessed a kind of eerie solitude.

"Hey," Casey said.

"Shopping?" Ella said, her voice breaking. Casey's face looked worse than it had from a distance.

"Seems that way."

"That's pretty." Ella pointed to the suit on top of Casey's hold pile.

"Yeah," Casey replied. She drew a quick breath. If it were a bar, she would have lit a cigarette. "What are you doing here?" she asked curtly.

"I..." Ella hesitated. How was she supposed to talk to Casey, the girl she'd most wanted to befriend at church? "I...just ordered my wedding dress." She cast her eyes down, not knowing what Casey's reaction would be. Her fiancé, Ted, had convinced her that they should get married after her graduation, and she'd been swept up in his enthusiasm for their future. He was very convincing, and Ella loved him. She had never loved anyone else. Her father wasn't against it but appeared annoyed—a look flickered across his eyes—whenever Ted expressed his ambition and well-laid plans. Ted had already written up a draft of their announcement to submit to *The New York Times* and to his alumni magazines at Exeter and Harvard.

"You're getting married?" Casey sighed. "With whom, may I ask?" She smiled as if Ella were a customer.

"Ted Kim." Ella shrugged. "I don't think you'd know him. He's from Alaska."

"Alaska?" Casey exclaimed.

"Uh-huh." Ella nodded.

"And where did he go to school?" It was prying and vulgar to ask, but Casey couldn't help herself.

"Harvard," Ella said nervously. "I mean, he's not our age. He finished business school a couple of years ago."

"Where?" Casey said.

"Harvard."

"Right." Casey nodded. "How old is...?"

"Thirty."

"Of course." It was no way to behave. Casey ordinarily prided herself on her manners.

Ella looked down at her sandals. "Everyone's invited. Your parents, you...I mean...if you want to come. It's at the church. You know, like the other weddings."

"God almighty. You're having it at the church. You are amazing, Ella." Casey had vowed never to have the typical Korean church wedding with about five hundred guests who showed up without having been invited, the reception with a groaning buffet of Korean food served by a team of lady volunteers in the church basement, no alcohol in sight.

Ella heard Casey's contempt and concealed her hurt feelings. She had come down the escalator and spotted Casey's bruised face beneath the khaki beach hat and had taken it as a kind of sign. She had forced herself to see if Casey was all right and if there was something she could do for her. Ella bit her lower lip, trying to figure out how to leave, sensing Casey wanted her to go away.

Casey saw the pain she'd caused and felt crummy. She smiled. "Ella, I'm in a shitty mood. Nothing related to you. I'm sorry if I sounded like a bitch. Congratulations on your wedding. Really."

"No, no, I'm sorry. I'm fine. You didn't do anything," Ella said.

"Well..." Casey glanced at her drugstore Timex. "I'm sure he's wonderful. Ted, right? Lucky bastard. We should celebrate sometime. Do lunch. Something." She felt sickened by her words. She despised lying.

Maud stood patiently watching this curious exchange between the two Asian women. At a pause, she asked Casey to spell out her name for the hold ticket.

"Never mind," Casey said.

Maud didn't understand.

"I want to take them. Here." Casey opened her wallet and handed Maud her credit card.

Maud keyed in the SKU numbers for the clothes, then swiped the card.

The total was forty-three hundred plus change. The hotel room would be four hundred or so. She had managed to max out her first credit card in one day. Maud handed her the receipt, and Casey signed it. She was now a Wilma.

Ella made no move to leave Casey's side. In all their years, they had never been alone in this way. She stared at Casey's lost expression.

"Are you free now?" Ella asked. "For lunch?"

Casey checked the girl's face, unable to believe Ella's relentlessness.

She gave Ella a brief, discouraged nod, and without missing a beat, Ella asked her the question her father asked her whenever she met him at his office after work: "Tell me, what would you like to eat?"

Their steaks and creamed spinach arrived right away, and the girls ate quietly. Casey wasn't hungry, but the idea of going to a dark steakhouse had made sense to her somehow. Thankfully, Ella didn't pry about her face. She just kept smiling, and Casey felt bad for having such a rotten attitude. She asked about Ella's work.

Ella was the associate development director of an all-boys' private school on the Upper East Side, where she also lived. "I believe in education. So I can raise money for that. You know, for scholarships and the endowment," Ella said, parroting her young boss, David Greene. "To help children who couldn't otherwise—" She stopped herself, feeling stupid suddenly. No doubt Casey had been a scholarship student. David would have known not to say that. He was natural at talking to different kinds of people and always thoughtful about a person's background. "Anyway. It's a very pleasant job. I love going to the office. And I have a great boss. He's a good friend, really."

Casey observed Ella's retreat. She wouldn't take the rich girl's philanthropic comments personally. After all, she had been the grateful recipient of Princeton's largesse. Someone with these lofty ideals had passed the hat on her behalf. She and Jay had been the equivalents of amusing and tolerated peasants whose enrollment reflected the university's noblesse oblige. She asked Ella about the wedding. The idea of marrying at the age of twenty-one seemed nutty to Casey.

"I don't get it," Casey said. "Why now?"

Ella stated Ted's refrain: "When you love someone, you make a commitment."

"Forever?" Casey raised her eyebrows.

"Uh-huh," Ella answered.

Ted had forced something of a gentle ultimatum with Ella. The primary gist of his campaign was: "If you love me, you will marry me." He'd employed the same tactics about their having sex. He'd said to Ella, "I love you, and I want to be closer to you. If we make love, we will know each other even better. I want to know you completely, Ella. Don't you want that, too? Don't you want to know me?" What could the girl say? He wanted, so Ella gave.

"I guess he makes you happy, then." Casey nodded, trying to sound as though she believed this might be a good thing.

"Yes," Ella said, searching Casey's face, wondering why she was so cynical about love.

Casey saw the question in Ella's face. "I just found my college boyfriend in bed with two girls."

"What?" Ella said.

The shock value alone of saying such a thing made the humiliation almost worthwhile.

"They were great-looking girls," Casey admitted. They really were. She couldn't let go of just how pretty they were. "Never mind." Somehow, it wasn't funny anymore.

Ella refrained from asking anything but kept nodding. She was still aghast that such a thing could happen.

"You're looking at my bruises," Casey said.

"It must hurt."

"I had a fight with my father." Casey laughed. "You should see how he looks."

Ella smiled painfully. It was impossible to think of her father ever striking her. "Are you really staying at the Carlyle?"

"Does that surprise you? Because my parents manage a dry cleaner?"

Ella shook her head. "No. No. That isn't what I meant. Casey, that's not fair."

"You're right. My inner bitch is just having a field day with you." The brown liquid around the sirloin congealed—streaks of white fat marbled the plate.

"You have found me at the wrong time, Ella. And to be honest, you're like the last person I want to look this pathetic in front of."

"Why?" Ella was surprised by this.

"Because. Forget it." Casey picked up her fork and knife and cut into the meat. She wanted Tabasco.

"I'm sure you have lots of money and…," Ella said, feeling exasperated by Casey's persistent hostility.

"No, I don't, actually. I just maxed out my credit card because I was so pissed at you."

"Me?"

"No. Not you." Casey checked herself. "Me."

Ella looked confused.

"I'm a failure. And you're like a goddamn success parade. God. I hate myself." Casey started to cry. "I'm sorry. As you can see, I'm not very good company. I better get going." She looked at her watch and picked up her things. "Thanks for lunch."

"Where? Where are you going? You can't go back home. I mean…" Ella didn't know how to say that right. She didn't actually know if Casey could go home or not.

Casey sighed and looked up at the tin ceiling painted a verdigris color. How did this happen to her? Then she knew: She made it happen. It was her own fault.

"And you have no money. Can I give you money? Do you have another place to stay? I mean…may I call someone for you? Can you—"

"Stop with the questions. I'll figure something out. This isn't your problem. I don't want your help."

"What did I ever do to you?" Ella raised her voice.

"Nothing. You've done nothing. I'm just a very small person." Casey smiled. "Trapped in a very big frame."

"You could stay with me. I have an extra bedroom. Until you sort things out."

"You have an extra bedroom?"

"Yes, you can hate me for that, too," Ella said, laughing. "All right?"

Ella was making a joke, Casey thought. Ella Shim could be sarcastic. Who knew? She smiled, then color rushed to her face and her eyes stung. "Please don't be nice to me. It's really…" She took a deep breath.

"I don't want anything from you, Casey. I want to help." Ella tried to think of a new way to explain this to Casey, who obviously didn't trust anyone at all. Ted was like this. He always thought everyone had an ulterior motive—that there could never be pure altruism.

"Maybe if I were in your situation, I could ask you for the same," Ella said. She reasoned that if Casey were like Ted—an argument based on exchange principles might be persuasive.

"You'd never be in this situation, Ella."

Ella narrowed her eyes, confounded by Casey's reply. "You are so arrogant, Casey. Anyone could be in your situation." She said this calmly. "Anyone at all."

Casey examined Ella's fine and rare features. There was a strength there she hadn't noticed before. It was the way she held her head erect, as if she had eyes in the back of her head as well and those eyes looked straight out to the other side of the steakhouse. Casey had been wrong about her. And she'd been envious of a good person who'd wished her well.

"After lunch," Ella said, "we can go and check you out of the hotel. You can come stay with me. I would love that." Ella borrowed Ted's assurance and the finality of his gestures—his convincing use of charisma and simple words.

Casey nodded. Today, she would have followed Maud the sales-person home.

Ella asked for the bill and paid it.

5 | BOND

A DOZEN YEARS OF BALLET LESSONS had given Ella Shim ideal posture. She was seated on a deeply cushioned sofa in her bright living room—her back pin-straight, her head bent slightly as she reviewed a recipe for lamb. There were four cookbooks tabbed with rack of lamb recipes on top of the coffee table and a thick one spread open on her lap. The following week was Ted's thirty-first birthday, and she wanted to re-create the dish that Ted had liked so much at Bouley, but she didn't have the exact recipe.

Ella was an accomplished cook. She loved to read cookbooks and food magazines. In high school, she'd enjoyed planning special menus for her father, who encouraged her interest by buying her Mauviel copper pots and installing wooden dowels in the kitchen walls so she could dry her hand-cut pasta. When church guests visited the Shim household in Forest Hills, Ella offered them her dense orange-flavored pound cake, candied rhubarb scones with Irish butter procured from Dean & DeLuca, or Dr. Shim's favorite: *pâte à choux* cream puffs with *hong cha*. At Wellesley, Ella had missed her windowed kitchen in Queens. Her current two-bedroom Upper East Side apartment, which her father had purchased for her after graduation and where she and Ted intended to live after they got married, had a nice-size kitchen with enough counter space to roll pie crust and to put up kimchi.

At the moment, she was absorbed in the taste memory of the lamb she'd eaten with Ted at the French restaurant on Duane Street. She felt she could create a dish close to it.

Seated near her on the wing chair upholstered with crewelwork, Ted was checking the movie schedule in the *Times*. He was annoyed at having agreed to see a foreign film that Ella's houseguest had recommended. From the living room, they could hear the sound of running water from the guest bathroom. It was Friday night, and Casey was getting ready to meet friends at the Princeton Club for Virginia's send-off to Italy.

Ella drafted a list of ingredients and cooking instructions in her loopy girls' school cursive. She was also trying to figure out how to convince Ted to help Casey get a job. His buddies from HBS dispensed favors for one another all the time.

"Ted, can't you help her?" Ella didn't look up from the orange-and-white-checkered cookbook.

Ted snapped the newspaper shut. But the sight of his pretty fiancée bent over her cookbooks made him smile. He was smitten with her delicacy.

"My dear Ella," he said, making his face stern, "your friend…" He paused. Ella had never mentioned Casey until she'd moved in. And now this so-called friend who had quite a mouth on her had been camping out at Ella's place for four weeks. "Casey isn't the least bit interested in finance," Ted continued. "I doubt she knows the difference between debt and equity."

"But… Ted, you didn't always know the difference, either." Ella looked earnestly at him. "People have to learn things. And they have to be taught. Right?"

"Your friend already interviewed on campus with the Kearn Davis investment banking program in the spring," he said.

"And?"

"And she was dinged." Ted rolled his eyes. "What was she thinking? Your friend applied to *one* firm. What balls."

He'd applied to eight banks in his senior year at Harvard and was invited to join seven. After working for four years at Pearson Crowell, a bulge bracket investment bank, as an analyst and later as senior associate, he got into Harvard Business School, where he was a Baker Scholar. Then he chose Kearn Davis, the sole securities firm that had rejected him as an undergraduate. In four years, Ted was made an executive director, and he was slated for managing director in January. He was two years ahead of his own plan.

Ella looked at him and inhaled before saying, "You have no reason to dislike her."

"I don't dislike her," he said. "I'm merely being rational, Ella. Applying to just one program shows nerve and a sense of overentitlement. These Ivy League girls," he muttered. "And it shows a lack of seriousness." He folded the newspaper lengthwise, then stared her down, half smiling. He was impressed by Ella's insistence. Normally she gave up fairly quickly, but Ted preferred challenges.

"Listen, sweetheart..." His voice dropped a pitch, and he sounded sincere. "I know you're trying to help. But, you know, I've worked hard for my good name. You can't expect me to risk my reputation by giving my word on an individual I don't know well and who seems to me preternaturally unable to stick it out."

Ella tilted her head and exhaled through her thin nostrils. Ted didn't believe in yielding any advantage unless he had to. Two years ago, he'd spotted her at the Au Bon Pain near the Citicorp building in midtown and had pursued her single-mindedly. His colleagues and HBS friends treated her as though she were a coveted prize, and she felt afraid to speak to them.

But what Ted didn't understand was that Ella had been pursued and flattered before. She loved him because he was a boy, anxious and hungry, running from Alaska. He was the son of immigrant cannery workers and had an older brother working as a mailman in Anchorage. His sister was a former professional bodybuilder who taught aerobics, and she was raising two sons as a single mother. Ella would have loved Ted if he'd had nothing but his desire. She was attracted to him because he was so clear and because he was so unflappable. But beneath all that, she saw the self-doubts that he could not concede to her or to himself—his terrors drove him. She liked all of that, too.

Ted and Ella heard the pipes shutting down as Casey's shower ended, and Ella lowered her voice. She appealed to him again, because she felt he, more than anyone else, ought to understand Casey's situation.

"She's been sending out résumés all month, and she hasn't heard a thing."

"The economy, Ella. I know you feel sorry for your friend..."

"Her father hits her. She can't go back home. You have to help her. She has no money, and she won't take any from me."

"You offered her money?" Ted made a face of incomprehension. "What is it with you, princess? You think the stuff grows on trees?"

"Ted..." Ella shut her cookbook.

"Tell her to get any job."

"That's what she's trying to do."

"Any job. Sell lipsticks or gloves, or whatever it is that she used to do in college."

"She might. But it's one thing to work in retail while you're in college, and another thing to do it full-time after." She stopped herself. "Her parents don't have any money, and her sister's applying to med school next year. Her boyfriend cheated on her."

Ted snorted. "That's what you get for dating white guys."

Ella ignored this. "But her family can't help her. And what's the point of succeeding, Ted, if you can't help others with your power?"

"I help plenty of people."

Ted sent money to his parents each month, and last year, with his enormous bonus, he bought his brother and sister their condos in Anchorage.

"I didn't mean that you don't help anyone."

"Casey and her family are not my problems, Ella. And they're not yours, either. Her sister can't take out loans for med school?" With his right hand, he pointed to his heart. He had just paid off the last of his education loans and was now putting aside money for his nephews.

"Not everyone is like you."

She gathered the cookbooks, stacking them alphabetically, and returned them to the shelf. She had no desire now to make the lamb dish. They would just go out for his birthday.

Casey entered the living room, dressed in a narrow black skirt and an ironed white shirt. Her bruises were no longer visible, and she looked pretty with her wet hair combed back sleekly, a fresh coat of red lipstick on her mouth. She hadn't put on her shoes yet, and Ted glanced at her bare feet. For a thin girl, her calves and ankles were a little thick. *Moo-dari*, he thought, legs shaped like daikon radishes.

Naturally, Casey noticed his glance and immediately crossed her ankles.

"Good evening," she said with a kind of mock cheer. She'd heard enough of the conversation and decided to pretend otherwise. Ted Kim was not the helping kind. Why couldn't poor Ella see that?

"Hey, Casey," Ted said, not caring in the least if she'd heard anything. He turned to Ella, gesturing that they should head out. "We can get tickets at the theater. I don't think everyone in town is running to see this." He pointed to the obscure ad for *Farewell My Concubine* in the *Times*.

"It's very good, Ted." Casey smiled at him. Ted was a triple-A, self-made jerk, but he was good-looking. He was five eleven and built like a runner—wiry, with long legs. His black hair was cut short, and the gel he dabbed on top made his hair look damp. The top button of his dress shirt was open, and the tendons of his neck framed a hard Adam's apple. She liked the imperiousness of his expressions. If she were interested in dating assholes, he would be an ideal candidate.

"You might even enjoy it," Casey said. "A bright guy like you—I would think you'd like cultural enrichment now and then. A good yuppie should know more than wines and resorts. Not that you need any help in the arts or leisure department," she said, grinning. "Or in any department, for that matter." She smiled, having managed to sound facetious and generous at once. Casey pursed her lips shut, waiting for Ted's riposte.

He harrumphed, and Ella laughed.

"And how's the job search going, Casey?" he said. Now he was smiling.

"Sabine said I could work accessories on Sundays starting next month, but she's got nothing for me during the week. She replaced me when I quit after graduation. And things are slow in the accessories world," Casey said. "You know, Ted. The economy."

Ted smiled and lifted his chin.

"Ella's been so good to let me stay here, but this can't last forever. I will get a job. I hope I get a job."

Before Ella could say anything to assure Casey that she could stay as long as she liked, Ted jumped in. "The economy will pick up. Cycles," he said, speaking as one economics major to another, knowing she would understand his meaning.

He picked up the paper, then dropped it on his chair. He glanced at Ella, and on cue, she rose from her seat and got her purse. She paid careful attention to him—that was what he wanted from her, and it was not hard to do.

Later, after the movie and dinner, she and Ted didn't talk about Casey, but early Monday morning, Ted phoned the Asian sales desk, where his friend Walter Chin had said they were looking for an assistant. He didn't think Ted should send in a friend for the gig. "Low pay, high abuse," Walter said. And the head of the desk had anger management issues.

Ted answered, "Not to worry; she's not a close friend."

Casey's interview was set for the following week. He had only to bring her by.

Virginia's father came by the club to sign for the night's tab. He and Jane stayed for a glass of champagne and were now heading out for a grown-up dinner, leaving behind the two dozen or so recent graduates at the Tiger Bar.

"You guys don't need chaperones anymore," Fritzy said to Chuck Raines, a lacrosse player who was working as a corporate paralegal at Skadden, Arps. Fritzy tapped the boy on the shoulder genially with his fist, wanting to feel young again. There had been a time in college when Fritzy felt like he was of the crowd. He had been a member of the eating club Ivy, as was his father, who'd died when Fritzy was twelve, though everyone agreed that he was really nothing like his father—a handsome and chatty senator from Delaware. Fritzy and Jane Craft stood side by side next to their daughter: He wearing his J.Press blazer to conceal his perpetual shoulder stoop, and Jane, six feet tall, an inch shy of her husband, in her size twelve Belle France dress with its high lace collar. The tiny lavender floral print on the black background obscured her thickening middle. Jane's build was more solid than Fritzy's—his frame being slight, like that of his mother, Eugenie. The Crafts, married twenty-six years, shared the same coloring—light hair, sky blue eyes, skim-milk complexion with cheeks that flushed easily—in bold contrast to Virginia, with her black curls and olive skin. The first thing you'd notice about Virginia's face was what she called her Mexican lashes—their remarkable length and dark color. Alone, Virginia passed for a striking white girl of the exotic variety, but beside her parents, she was markedly foreign. She'd been called Spanish, Italian, French, Portuguese, and, once in London, black Irish. Early on, she'd learned to spit out the race of her biological parents—half Mexican, half white—then let the unlucky guesser squirm with the facts of her adoption.

Before leaving the club, Fritzy kissed Virginia on the crown of her head, saying to the bartender, "Feel free to dilute their drinks." Chuck, on his third beer, laughed and raised his glass to Virginia's dad. The kids clustered in groups of threes or fours around the perimeter of the bar—its walls covered with class photographs and Princeton memorabilia—drinking and catching up on any news since June. Some ate the burgers and chicken Mrs. Craft had ordered beforehand. Casey knew everyone except for a couple of the girls from Brearley who'd come by to say hello. They were much like the girls from Ivy—cool legacy types with a casual manner and Ivory girl complexions. Expensive haircuts that didn't look fussy. All terrific at cocktail prattle. It was impossible to imagine them mixing with their fellow Brearley alumna Ella.

After the Crafts left, Virginia and Casey went off by themselves to a secluded table below the photograph of an ancient crew team. This was Casey's first vodka gimlet for the night, and it was delicious.

"How is it living with Ella Shim?" Virginia pulled her lips to the left corner of her mouth. She did this when peeved.

"It's tolerable." Casey frowned, feeling a little disloyal to Ella. "She's nice."

"And has Jay called?" Virginia, who'd always liked him, was not yet willing to give up on him as Casey's beau. Jay Currie was a dick for what he did, but it was unquestionable in Virginia's mind that he loved her best friend. It wouldn't have surprised Virginia if they got back together. "Or should I ask, how many times has he called?"

"He's called Tina, but she's not allowed to tell him where I am. Nor are you."

"Understood," Virginia said, still not getting Casey's decision to live with Ella. "You could have stayed with me. At Newport."

"You were visiting your grandmother—"

"Lady Eugenie would've been happy to have you."

"Thank you," Casey said graciously, having told Virginia about the fight but not the hitting.

"And if you want to be in the city, you could stay with Jane and Fritzy. They love you, too. But Ella Shim?" Virginia couldn't remember Ella uttering a word out loud in the six years she'd known her at Brearley. Did the girl even speak?

"She's not so bad." Casey could hear Ella's voice in her head from only a few hours ago, how she'd pleaded with Ted to get her a job.

"I've known her from Sunday school. And she has an extra room. C'mon, I can't stay with your parents." Casey made a face. "They're super, but—"

"Yeah, neither can I," Virginia said. Jane and Fritzy were a particular drink of water. They were also not young parents, both in their early sixties. Their excessive politeness could be construed as detachment or, worse, a social frigidity. They didn't mean to be that way; they just didn't know how to be intimate or talk like regular people. What also polarized their household was that they'd sent Virginia to a shrink ever since she could talk almost, so they'd raised this girl to have all these feelings when they appeared to have none. "They're very sweet," Virginia said of her parents, "but tough to live with. I'm sure my biological parents were deeply troubled individuals, highly emotional. And verbal. I bet my biological mother was a screamer." She smiled with some satisfaction.

"Hmm…" Casey fiddled with the ice in her drink. Over the years, Virginia had imagined her biological mother as everything between a hooker and a nun.

"And how are you?" Virginia asked.

"Fine. I just have to get a job," Casey replied.

"You'll get one," Virginia said, wanting to figure out what else was going on in that tough nut of hers. She'd never met anyone so proud in her life. "I mean, do you like living with Ella?"

"She's not you," Casey said. There was always a pecking order among girlfriends. "Once I get my cash flow in order, I'm moving out. Find an affordable place in Manhattan. No problem." She said all this confidently, as though it were just a matter of time.

"You can come to Italy." Virginia raised her hands enthusiastically. "How cool would that be?"

"I can go to the moon, too, but NASA won't return my calls."

Virginia smirked. "You can live with me."

"Not in the cards for this girl."

"Why not? They let Koreans into Italy the last time I checked."

"Mexicans, too?"

"Ha." This was the thing Virginia liked about Casey—she could fire back instantly.

"You should at least visit me. I'm not coming back for a long time. The degree can take two years or more. Fritzy and Jane will come to see me. You know how I hate flying."

"And phones."

Virginia sighed. "But I write all the time."

"Yes. You do." Casey loved her friend's letters. It was like receiving the pages of a genius's diary, and because of her flowery style, the letters read as if from another era. Virginia wrote in her unfiltered prose about her observations and desires, never holding back her failures or doubts. In her writing, she directed her thinking like a woman walking out of a maze, turning the corners of events and ideas. Casey admired Virginia's mind and hadn't known just how brilliant her friend was until she'd started to receive her letters. And Virginia didn't hide anything—this was the thing Casey prized most about her.

If Casey felt wild and angry compared with Tina, she was even-tempered and discreet around Virginia, who thrummed with vitality and curiosity. Even as Virginia got drunk, slept with too many men, and lost her house keys on a regular basis, Casey couldn't help but admire her friend, who didn't feel deterred by shame or failure. Virginia was not afraid of criticism—that, Casey thought, was an extraordinary thing.

"You will come visit me. Yes?"

Virginia smiled pleasantly, yet what Casey felt was the pang of being left behind. Their lives had always looked different, but after graduation, a divide had risen between them like a drawbridge sealing up a castle. From the other side of the moat, Casey had to make her own way.

"You're the one who's leaving. So why should I visit?" Casey said coldly.

Virginia looked hurt by this, and Casey felt sorry. She was Casey's closest friend from school—buddies since the second week of freshman year. Virginia was leaving for Italy the next day. It wasn't as though Casey didn't know her friend's sorrows—how she'd searched for her birth mother since she was eleven, all leads going nowhere. This was Virginia, the girl who'd written prizewinning papers at school and was getting a master's degree in Bologna because her spoken and written Italian was that good. Her French was native quality. The Romance language she couldn't learn, however, was Spanish—the language her biological mother would have spoken. Every time Virginia had tried to take lessons, she'd ended up dissolving into tears.

Virginia reached across the table to take Casey's hand. "I will miss you."

"Oh, stop. You'll be so busy chasing boys that you'll hardly have time to pick up a pen." Casey felt like crying.

"My record disputes such unfair charges."

Casey could say nothing to this. There were eight or nine ribbon-tied bundles of Virginia's letters at her parents' from previous summers.

"Come visit, Casey. There are Italian men in Italy."

Casey laughed.

"And gelato. Oh, the marron glacé gelato. You can't believe that ice cream can taste—" Virginia swooned, her face lighting up in rapture; Chuck came by to bring her a beer.

Casey waved at him, letting him cut in. Chuck and Virginia had had a semester-long thing during sophomore year. Virginia said they were good friends—reliable for annual strip poker nights and the occasional movie. Besides, Casey thought, it wasn't fair to monopolize the guest of honor. Though she had been on the verge of telling Virginia about the fight with her father and how she hadn't gone to Newport because of her face. But how would that have changed anything? The past couldn't be corrected by explanations. Virginia yearned for a rationale from her biological mother—*Why did you give me up?*—and Casey wondered how that would really fix anything. Would it satisfy? The Crafts seemed like perfectly good parents. Casey's biological parents were a mess. And what good would it do to talk about all of it? It was just as well that Chuck Raines had come by. He had a square head and a thin neck. He still had a crush on Virginia.

"Have you had gelato, Chuck?" Virginia asked him.

"Oh yeah," he said. "Italians make damn good ice cream. You gonna hook me up?"

"*Naturellemente.*" Virginia closed her eyes and shrugged like her Milanese aunt Patrizia, who'd married her mother's younger brother, the art dealer.

Casey smiled at their happiness, the mutual recognition of something enjoyed. She'd never tried marron glacé gelato. Marron was French for chestnut? Glacé was glazed? That much she got. How did you say "chestnut" in Italian? The world was so vast, and there was so much she didn't know.

6 | PROXY

*E*LLA HEADED TOWARD THE BANK OF ELEVATORS at Bayard's, by-passing the glass cases of exquisite jewelry as well as the premier fragrance counters of New York. She was oblivious to the sparkle and scent of the shop, still thinking about the funny face David Greene had made when she'd explained that she had to leave the annual fund meeting fifteen minutes early because of the dress. He rarely looked displeased with her. Yet whenever her wedding was brought up, David tended to change the topic or remember that he had to finish up something. His navy blue eyes, so full of mirth and curiosity, would darken soberly when she'd talk about Ted.

Naturally, Ted teased her about him, saying that her dorky white boss had a fetish for Asian girls. But David wasn't like that, she'd argued as best she could. He respected everyone, wouldn't reduce a person to a stereotype. Yet the more she'd defend David, the worse Ted got. So she certainly didn't tell her fiancé that each morning she walked to work eagerly, looking forward to listening to David's thoughts about the alumni or the parent body, the progress of the class fund. On Fridays, they ate sandwiches together in the park if it was mild outside or in the office if the weather wasn't agreeable. He'd tell her stories about the inmates from the men's prison where he taught writing on the weekends as a volunteer. Sometimes he'd bring along his students' misspelled rap lyrics and read them aloud to her with as much gravity and delight as if he were reading from his favorite poet, Philip Larkin. Two weeks ago, with shyness and pride, he'd shown her two poems he'd had published in *The Kenyon Review*. One was about a boy who sits patiently in his father's waiting room, and for days after, she couldn't stop thinking about his description of the heavy stack of *National Geographic*s the boy in the poem ends up reading as his father sees one client after another—the curling yellow page corners, photographs of sharp-nosed ladies wearing orange scarves on their heads, the white-capped mountain of Japan.

Casey was there, waiting for her as promised—by the four elevators located in the back of the store. Once inside the car, Casey pushed six for bridal. There was no one else besides them.

"So, tell me. What does the dress look like again?"

Ella couldn't answer the question. She frowned.

"Ella?" Casey said firmly. "The dress?"

"It's long." With her hands, Ella made an awkward sweeping gesture from her shoulders to her hips. "Off white?" She could hardly distinguish all the whites she'd seen that day. "You know, a regular wedding dress, like, what you'd expect. You know."

"Is that how they teach you to talk at Wellesley? 'Like' and 'you know'?" Casey feigned a look of disapproval.

Her teasing pleased Ella. At home, especially when Ted came around, Casey increasingly made herself disappear behind a kind of decorum, her formal manners creating an inviolable barrier. But at Bayard's, she seemed to revert to the plucky girl Ella had known at church—intimate and amused by whatever she saw or heard. Even the way she strolled with a kind of flair and bounce had come back.

Casey now raised her eyebrows, waiting for an answer, a little peeved with Ella for the absence of details. She wanted to know what Ella wanted. It was her wedding dress, after all.

The problem was that Ella could barely remember her choice. There had been so many: lace, ornaments, sleeves, straps, belts, flowers—with or without. It had been her father's office manager, Sharlene, who'd made the appointment for her and her father at Bayard's. But when Ella went to her father's office to pick him up, it turned out that one of his postoperative patients had gotten a viral infection and Dr. Shim had to return to the hospital. He'd left a scribbled note for her on the pink telephone message pad: "Go for broke." Sharlene, who felt sorry for the girl, had added, "Your dad really did say that you can get whatever you want." Ella had smiled bravely at the kind lady who'd told her only what Ella already knew, so she'd trudged off to face the snowy blur of dresses by herself. It was after purchasing the costliest dress there that she'd come down the escalator to spot Casey standing before a pile of clothes she'd intended to put on hold.

The elevator stopped at three. A pair of attractive women stepped in, chatting glumly about the troubles their husbands were having at work.

Casey ignored them and, staring intently at Ella, asked about the sleeves. Ella used hand gestures again to illustrate the style.

In her mind, Casey was filling in the blanks with words she'd picked up over the years working retail and from the dressmaking classes she'd taken during the summers at FIT: ivory satin silk, portrait neckline, A-line bodice with princess seams, tapered sleeves, no train, hem trimmed with seed pearls. Sounded all right. Just all right, however. Casey paid attention to Ella's tone of voice—brimming with a fear of rebuke.

After living with Ella for a month, Casey knew her host's safe wardrobe: Talbots, L. L. Bean, Lands' End, Bass Weejuns. Ella dressed like a beautiful preppy nun—Peter Pan–collared blouses, dark A-line skirts or pleated-front pants, Hanes nude stockings, boxy Shetland cardigans, stacked heel pumps with tassels. But Miss Zero Fashion Sense had screwed up the courage to ask Casey for help because she was terrified that Ted, a dandy extraordinaire, wouldn't approve of her dress. For fancy parties, Ted bought dresses for her. But neither felt it was right for him to help with her wedding dress.

The attractive women got off at five. As they left, Casey caught a whiff of Eau de Camille, a favorite scent of hers.

Then she got an idea. There were other ways to discern a shy customer's preferences. "You don't wear perfume, do you?"

"No, Ted doesn't like perfume or makeup."

"Really?" Casey said skeptically. "But do you?"

Ella shrugged.

"Okay. Think of smells you like."

Ella wrinkled her brow. Casey reached over to smooth the little V in Ella's forehead with her fingertips. "Don't do that." This was something Sabine had taught her to be conscious of—to prevent wrinkles.

Ella thought about it. "Oranges. And cinnamon."

Casey smiled. "Food. Colors."

"What does that mean?"

"Comfort, pleasure, warmth. Those come to mind. Yes?" Casey tried to look patient. "This isn't a science. I just try to associate ideas with whatever you choose. Then I wonder if that's how you want others to see you. If that's how you see yourself. Then, how do you put that onto something you want to wear? Do you understand me?"

It made little sense to Ella, but she was intrigued. "Maybe you can help me choose one. A scent, I mean."

"We're searching for a dress, darling."

Casey gave her one of her shop assistant smiles—full of courtesy and innocence. She felt like giving up. In her mind, she could hear Ella asking her to tell her who she was. How was she supposed to do that? How could anyone tell you who you are? The elevator stopped at six.

"What scents do you like?" Ella asked, exiting the elevator.

"Tuberose, gardenia, lilies."

"And that means what?"

"Knowing my preferences won't help you know yours," Casey replied, her annoyance undisguised. The bridal department was not ten yards away from the elevator. Casey slipped her hand in the crook of Ella's arm to keep her from walking ahead. She motioned to the empty camelback sofa parked opposite the lingerie department.

"Sit," she said, and Ella sat down. "Let me see the receipt."

Ella withdrew it from her purse and handed it to her. She stared at the mirrored surfaces of the elevator doors, fearful of Casey's response. The dress had cost eight thousand dollars.

Casey nodded impassively. This was her inured response to having been surrounded by the wealthy for so many years. She would never have asked the price, except that she had to know Ella's budget. Obviously there was none.

Casey read the back of the receipt carefully. "May I?" she asked before tucking it into her skirt pocket. "Now, for the last time." She took a breath. "How would you like to look at your wedding?"

"I never thought much of it, you know?"

"Again with the you-knows. You're giving women's education a terrible name."

Ella laughed. "What kind of dress would you wear, Casey?"

"I'm not the one getting married."

"Do you want to get married?"

Casey frowned, irritated by Ella's inability to stay on point. Virginia had often remarked that Casey thought like a man. It was Virginia's argument that women thought in branches and men in trunks. Ella's distractible nature made Casey feel masculine.

"No. I don't want to get married. I'm twenty-two years old."

"I'm twenty-one," Ella said.

Casey whistled. "I know."

Ella twisted the gold braid strap of her Chanel handbag—a birthday present from Ted—her slim white fingers fluttering across its quilted leather body. The girl needed comforting. That was obvious. Casey tried to think of what she should say. Ella had everything. Absolutely everything. Now she wanted Casey to assure her that she was making the right decision about her marriage. It seemed to Casey that despite Ella's bountiful generosity, she was almost greedy in wanting her approval, too. How was it possible to give affirmation to the winner when you were so clearly the loser?

"Go back to the dress."

"I barely remember it, Casey. I was so overwhelmed." Ella's slender neck bent as if burdened by a heavy yoke.

Casey then recalled how some women dragged girlfriends along to choose a rain hat, an item costing fifty bucks at Sabine's. Ella had chosen her wedding dress alone, and though Casey would've preferred to do that for herself if the occasion ever arose, it occurred to her that Ella had had no choice about it. Ella had no mother or sister. Ella was closest to her father and Ted, but they were useless for a number of things that women did for one another without thinking. Casey had many people who liked her but few she told anything to and fewer she asked anything of. From the outside, it looked as though Casey and Ella were opposites, but they were similar in the small number of intimates in their lives.

"Do you think I'm too young to get married?" Ella asked. David had joked once that she was nearly a child bride.

"Well, no." Casey dished out the appropriate response. She herself had entertained the idea of marrying Jay a few weeks ago, but she saw now how perfectly stupid that would have been.

Ella fidgeted with the flap of her handbag, clicking and unclicking the latch, refusing to look into Casey's eyes. Ella knew she wasn't a confident person, but when it came to her upcoming marriage, she felt more insecure than usual. It wasn't her father's style to over-rule her, not that it had ever needed doing, but he'd mentioned in a vague way that a long engagement might be nice. What would Ella have done if Casey said out loud what her father refused to say?

It was impossible for Casey not to notice the profound worry in Ella's pretty dark eyes.

"Ted's a good guy. A veritable catch. For God's sake, he's Korean even. How did you possibly manage to find one?" Casey sounded shrill at the last thing, because that fact to her was more shocking than anything. Nearly all the Korean-American women she knew were with white guys. Then Casey reminded herself that her sister had recently found a Korean to date, too. Then she wondered if Tina had gotten laid after all.

"Do you like him?" Ella asked, somewhat reassured.

"He went to Harvard twice. He can't be stupid, right? He's got an insanely well-paying gig. And he's good-looking." Casey did not mention love. Because it would've sound like crap and therefore contaminating the true things she'd tossed out. As it was, each word of praise was costing her something dear, but payment, Casey felt, was required.

Ella smiled. "I really appreciate you doing this."

"No problem."

"I mean you coming with me today. These places are not easy for me. I feel afraid of the salesladies. You coming here," Ella repeated, "this means so much—"

"Shut up, Ella." Casey tried to sound funny when she said this. "You're letting me live in your place for free, lending me your shoes even.... Thank God we're the same size." Casey had almost no cash left, no available credit, and if she didn't get that job as a sales assistant, then she didn't know what she was going to do. Her face looked normal now, so she could finally go see Sabine to ask about work; they'd only spoken on the phone since she'd left her parents, and it was always better to talk to Sabine in person. But her parents wouldn't want her to depend on Sabine anymore. Working weekends during the school year and full-time during summers for four years was more than they could tolerate. Everything with Koreans, Casey thought, was about avoiding shame. Her life was still a train wreck. And she missed Jay all the time. Every morning she wanted to bind her hands to keep herself from phoning him. "This is nothing."

Ella interrupted her. "You know, I've always wanted us to be friends. At church, for all those years, I had wanted you to like me." She smiled like a child. "And I didn't know how to get you to notice me." She blushed.

Casey didn't know what to do with all this sincerity. "Thank you," she said. She got up from the sofa, and Ella followed behind.

The red-haired sales associate met them and brought over Ella's sample dress. It was common for brides to show off their dresses to their friends. "It's good to see you again, Ella. And how do you do?" The sales associate smiled glibly at Casey. Her name was Joan. Joan Kenar, accent on the second syllable. Two strands of marble-size Kenneth pearls circled her mottled throat.

In no time, Ella popped out of the dressing room wearing the sample dress that she'd ordered. Casey sat on the white leather sofa set aside for the bridal party, her ankles crossed, spine vertical. Ella looked at her friend. Casey's face went vacant, as though she weren't in the room anymore. Ella understood then that Casey hated it. Why should it matter whether Casey liked it or not? Ella thought. But it did. It mattered so much. In fact, it was all that mattered. Then Ella knew. Ted wouldn't like it, either.

Casey was mum because she was trying to figure out how to dispose of Joan, who clapped at Ella as if she were a poodle doing tricks. There was nothing wrong with the dress per se; Ella merely looked as though she were wearing someone else's clothing. The style of it aged her, stripping the bloom from her face. The dress was generic and traditionally elegant—a pricey costume for a girl with Grace Kelly dreams. Ah, Casey thought, the dress would have suited an older blonde better. She tilted her head. She'd never thought about it much before, but a woman should be hopeful and soaked with good wishes on her wedding day. And the bride should embody a purity—if not sexually (Ted made audible sex noises from Ella's bedroom on Thursdays, Fridays, Saturdays, and Sundays), then at least romantically. Ella had a face like a white rose. She deserved to be distinct from every other woman that day and yet the same as every bride on her wedding: The bride should be the ideal for her intended, and the dress played a part in that ritual. Wasn't that right? Casey said none of this, however. She closed her eyes and waited for a picture to pop up in her mind of Ella's dress; sometimes this worked with her customers at Sabine's. One came very quickly, but it looked nothing like the one Ella was wearing.

Ella waited for Casey's verdict.

Casey shook her head no.

Ella turned to Joan. "Is it too late?"

The sales associate nodded. She pulled back her shoulders, smiled stiffly. "It's too late to cancel the order." Joan refused to look at Casey.

Joan had made a mistake. Casey noted this. Among the cardinal rules of retail marketing was never to disregard the opinions and feelings of spouses and friends who were there to advise the customer of her purchases. Joan was being arrogant to think that the deal was closed.

"It was ordered a month ago." Joan smiled with an implacable authority.

Ella was defenseless against her.

Casey almost admired Joan's dominant style. It looked so effective. Casey sighed then, amused and pleased by it all. She loved a good fight. She pronounced tartly: "But it won't do. It doesn't suit her."

"Ella looks stunning in it," Joan replied, taken aback by Casey's unflappable tone. "That's quite obvious." Her own tone of voice was far nastier than she'd intended, and she quickly regretted it. But the truth was that there was no way in hell this bride could return the order without Joan having to call in every favor in the book, and she saw no need in this case to piss off the manufacturer for a bride's friend's whim—no doubt motivated by jealousy.

"Ella would look stunning in any of these dresses." Casey waved her hand across the parade of mannequins in silk taffeta, shantung, and brocade. She kept smiling. So, you want to play tough, little girl, Casey thought. Her eyes never strayed from Joan's eyes.

Joan adjusted her pearls. The rhinestone ball clasp had shifted toward her collarbone.

"Joan." Casey extended the vowels, relishing the sound of her name in two syllables.

The sales associate rolled her eyes, then remembered herself. She wasn't used to having her opinions confronted in this way by someone like this. Perhaps it had been a mistake to sell Ella the most expensive dress she'd tried on. But the bride's buyer's remorse didn't seem to stem from the price.

"It's not her dress," Casey said.

"What do you mean?" Joan snapped.

"You know exactly what I mean," Casey said, her tone of voice growing more syrupy as Joan's grew more sour. "Look at how unhappy she looks in it."

The bride slumped in the armchair next to the dressing room, feeling certain that both women were angry with her stupidity. It was all her fault. Then, right away, as if Ella could cover her shame with her posture, she sat up and folded her hands in her tidy way. She wished she were sitting in her office at St. Christopher's.

Joan recognized that there was no winning this argument. She shut up and smiled, her lips covering her even white teeth. She studied Casey, giving her the once-over. The bride's friend wore the upcoming season's pieces from three. That gray skirt alone, by the Dutch designer whose name escaped her, must have been seven hundred dollars. Sometimes Joan hated rich people. They got everything and never stopped complaining. Joan believed in hell. As a hardworking middle-class person, she found the idea of justice comforted her.

That morning, Casey had dressed anticipating this appraisal. The image of this conflict had surfaced as soon as Ella had asked Casey to come look at the dress. Retail salespeople on the whole were the greatest snobs in the world. Virginia used to tease her about how much Casey fussed about her clothes. But after a while Casey retorted, hand cocked on her hip: "Well, gee, honey, but you never get confused for a Japanese tourist, nanny, mail-order bride, or nail salon girl when you walk into a store, do you? What the hell do you know about it?" Virginia, with her biracial looks that gave her the appearance of a beautiful dark Swede, never raised the issue again.

Casey glanced at Ella's defeated expression, and she tilted her head back. How little faith Ella had in her. Casey turned to Joan. "I'm sorry, I didn't catch your title." She smiled.

"Senior sales associate." Joan was growing more detached. She just didn't care anymore.

Casey nodded but said nothing for a few moments. Silence made people crazy.

"Would you like to speak to the manager? I'm happy to call her for you," Joan offered. In these situations, it was better to leave the kitchen before the fire went out of control. Joan wasn't actually afraid of the bride's friend.

"No need, I think. Not yet. " Casey wondered if she was angry enough to humiliate Joan. If Joan backed down, Casey would back down.

Ella then stared at Casey silently—her head lifted as if a string pulled it taut from the ceiling. She had no wish for Joan to get into trouble because she had picked poorly.

Casey pulled out the receipt from her pocket and glanced at the back of the sheet quickly, knowing full well what was written on the paper.

"There's no carve-out for custom orders or bridals at Bayard's. I know you must know that from your years here. We women, so fickle, shop at Bayard's and pay its premiums precisely because we can return anything, change our minds, and be pleased ultimately with our choices. Don't you think it is a privilege to see growth in one's aesthetic point of view, Joan, even in a month? So why are we pretending that the sale is carved in stone? Even monuments can be broken. The alternative, of course, is to cancel the order entirely and go elsewhere. And you have already been so kind. I would hate to do that." Casey smiled, not mentioning the commission, because it was implicit in everything she'd said.

"It was four weeks ago," Joan said quietly. This felt personal somehow.

"Joan. Be reasonable. A bride should feel no less than thrilled with her dress on her wedding day. You know that." Casey shifted her focus to the wall and began to point. "Ella, be a dear and try on those dresses over there." Casey crossed her legs and said in Joan's direction, "Yes?" She nodded once for emphasis.

Joan exhaled quietly, her contempt escaping her nostrils in small measure. She retrieved the samples that the friend had chosen and hung them up in Ella's dressing room.

7 | DERIVATIVE

MARY ELLEN CURRIE FOUND HER BY ACCIDENT. She'd taken the day off to work on her manuscript at the big library on Forty-second Street. Mary Ellen could never write in her house or at the Trenton Public Library, where she'd served faithfully as head librarian for nine years and staff librarian for an even dozen. At one o'clock, she'd strolled across the street—dreamy in her thoughts of Emily Dickinson, whom she referred to as "ED"—to the sandwich shop on Fifth, and there, seated on a stool reading the want ads, was Casey, her younger son's girlfriend of three years. Her face appeared more drawn than usual, her shoulders thinner.

"Casey! Hullo, hullo, hullo!" Mary Ellen cried. She raised her arms and rushed toward the girl. "My sweetie, I haven't seen you in months."

Casey looked up and let herself be folded into Mary Ellen's embrace.

"Where have you been?" She squeezed her again, then kissed Casey on the brow. "Never mind that. I wanted to go to your graduation, but Jay said he couldn't go, either." Mary Ellen chuckled. "I thought I'd hang back, wave from a safe distance." She felt happy to see Casey so unexpectedly, and she kissed her again; her hands held on to Casey's upper arms.

Casey burst into tears. It had been several weeks since anyone had actually touched her. The touch of a person she loved was almost too much to bear.

"What? What's the matter? Oh, I'm so dumb." Mary Ellen slapped her own forehead as if she'd forgotten something. "I know you wanted me to come. It's not your fault. I understand. Truly. I do. Your family—it was their day." Mary Ellen hoisted her knapsack from her sloping shoulders. She lifted Casey's chin toward her own face with her square hands. She used to do this when she talked to her sons when they were young. They'd never let her do this now.

Casey pulled away as gently as she could. It was so good to see Mary Ellen's floury face with its soft creases, her pretty hazel eyes beneath the pale, intelligent eyebrows. This face had welcomed her from the very beginning of her relationship with Jay, and his loss had been made worse because Casey had lost Mary Ellen as well.

Mary Ellen stroked Casey's hair, not paying attention to the customers in the sandwich shop who were straying from their lunches to take peeks at the sobbing girl. She rested her hand on Casey's back—so bony under her fingers. Her height was oddly diminished by her thinness. Casey seemed small. "It's all right, little one. It's all right." She'd already sensed that there was something amiss between her son and Casey, but she'd been uncertain as to what exactly. Jay was a very good son; by that, she meant, unlike her older son, Ethan, Jay had done well in school, gotten an excellent job, effectively made her proud through his achievements. He was the son who'd justified her labor and sacrifices as a mother. But Jay did not confide in her. Neither did Ethan. Mary Ellen envied mothers with daughters. With girls, it seemed possible to remain involved in their lives. Even when her boys were little, she'd ask them how school was, and they'd reply, "Good," and in their simple expressions, she saw shut doors. One of the lovely by-products of Jay's dating Casey was that she'd gotten to know her child better because Casey talked to her. As a mother of two grown men, she was still gleaning scraps. After her boys were out of school, she'd missed parent-teacher conferences and report cards, because news of her boys had become even less periodic, shrinking down to nil.

"Take a breath," Mary Ellen said, taking a dramatic one herself, as if she were reading the part of the Big Bad Wolf for the neighborhood children during story hour.

Casey did as she was told, breathing in a vast gulp of air. She swallowed the last of her cold, milky coffee, the same cup she'd been nursing for the past hour—her meager rent for occupying the stool.

"Are you all right? I asked Jay how you were last week, and he had to get off the phone because of work. So he said. And I haven't been able to reach him since then."

Casey nodded, knowing how Jay could use work as a way to avoid talking. Wasn't there always another fire to put out at the office? His job was a career, not like her temporary stint at Sabine's, where she could walk out the door at closing hour and be done until the next day.

Casey looked around the shop. No one was looking at them now.

"Are you at home with your parents this summer?"

She shook her head no.

"Where are you staying, then?"

"At a friend's on the Upper East."

"Why aren't you staying at Jay's?" Mary Ellen looked carefully at Casey. "Are you two fighting?"

Casey held up the want ads, not wanting to talk about Jay. "I'm looking for a job, Mary Ellen."

The woman who'd finished her soup and crackers got up from the stool next to Casey's. Mary Ellen sat in her spot.

"Okay. How is that going?"

"I have an interview tomorrow." Casey did not mention that it was at Kearn Davis where Jay worked. She'd yet to get a call from any of her cover letters. In her wallet, she had eight dollars, and her credit limit was tapped. That morning, she'd considered calling her sister to ask for more money.

"You look a little tired, honey," Mary Ellen said. That morning, Casey hadn't bothered with concealer. "Are you all right?"

Casey stared into her empty cup—a thin ring of coffee remained lodged in the bottom seam of the paper cup.

"Oh, Casey, what can I do? What won't you children tell me?"

"We broke up. There isn't much to say," Casey said, feeling the tears spring up again.

"What?" Mary Ellen was stunned. "Why? He loves you so much. I'm so certain of that."

Casey blew her nose on a milk-stained napkin.

Mary Ellen made a face, then she knew. "What did he do?"

Casey remained silent. Knowing Mary Ellen, she'd feel responsible. "I can't say."

"You are still talking to each other, right?"

Casey shook her head no.

Mary Ellen sighed. She'd never seen Casey like this before. The girl was utterly bereft.

"It's like someone cut off my limbs. Like I'm an ugly stump." Casey said this without intending to, then felt bad right away. It didn't seem right to say this to Jay's mother.

Mary Ellen's lower lip quivered the tiniest bit. That was precisely how she'd felt after Carl left.

"But we're still friends, Casey." Mary Ellen peered into the girl's eyes, making sure that she was being understood. "You're better than a daughter to me," she said. "We'll always be in each other's lives. We have our own bond." She pulled out a pad from her knapsack. "Tell me where you're staying."

Casey felt ashamed—by her crying, by talking to Mary Ellen about the breakup before Jay had told his own mother, for being so inarticulate. And she looped back again to that night. How could she have stopped that? Was there a way to keep a lover from ever wanting someone else? All the smart answers she had didn't seem to make that question go away.

"You're heartbroken." Mary Ellen felt angry at Jay. He'd given her no grief over the years, but she knew Casey was protecting him out of some stupid sense of loyalty or propriety. If it had been Casey's fault, she would've just confessed it. "You look so thin. Did you eat today? I hope you're not dieting again."

"I'm not dieting." She laughed at the thought of it now. Casey wiped her eyes. "I'm always hungry lately." She was starving, actually.

"Can I get you something?" Mary Ellen asked. She had no appetite herself.

"No, it's all right. I ate, actually," Casey stammered, lying poorly. The moment before Mary Ellen had walked into the shop, Casey had been debating whether or not she should spend the last of her money on a roast beef sandwich and a bag of kettle-fried chips. The sight of these things behind the glass case had made her mouth water.

"I have to go," Casey said. She wrote down Ella's number on the pad. "Promise me you won't give it to Jay." Mary Ellen nodded, then put her hand lightly on Casey's forearm.

Casey stood there, looking at the tiled floor.

"I'm just trying to understand," Mary Ellen said. The worry made her appear older than her age of fifty-one. "I know you're the one who should be upset. I should be comforting you." She blurted this out, not knowing the full story. But it was the not knowing that was making her so nuts. What could be worth this? she thought. What Jay and Casey did not know was that love was this rare thing. A connection between two people like them—Mary Ellen had marveled at the way they laughed, talked, and saved stories for each other—wasn't something to take lightly. *Can't you work this out?* she wanted to say. Looking at Casey's suffering, Mary Ellen thought, the loss was real because the love was real. She wanted to shake Jay. And Casey, too. "I'd somehow imagined us growing up together," she said. "Do you know that? I love you very much, Casey."

Casey swallowed, unable to speak. Her parents had never said anything like that in her entire life. Korean people like her mother and father didn't talk about love, about feelings—at least this was how Casey and Tina had explained it to themselves for not getting these words they wanted to hear.

"Would you take him back?" asked Mary Ellen. The heart is so full of hope, she thought.

Casey looked over Mary Ellen's shoulder and read the labeled thermoses of milk set out on the counter near the door: cream, half and half, whole, 2%, skim. Why were there so many choices? It didn't seem to make life any richer, she thought. All these things made you feel less grateful. Casey couldn't imagine talking to him ever again, yet all she yearned for was to be near him, to be held by him, to listen to the pulse of his heart—it was as pathetic as that. Why would she want the person who had carelessly humiliated her to hold her? That made no fucking sense. She wanted things to be the same—to love someone like that again, with a kind of endless trust. Then she saw that she had loved him fully. But judging from how awful she felt now, she decided that she couldn't let herself love like that again, not even him. Especially not him.

"Did he cheat?" Mary Ellen asked.

Casey found herself nodding yes.

Mary Ellen nodded sadly herself. There wasn't a day when she didn't think about Carl, about her marriage, and how on the day he left, it seemed her life was over, with no money, no job, and two little boys who had no understanding; yet in a way, there was relief, for it had been awful to live with a man who made you feel so lacking in femininity. "Mary Ellen, I just don't want to anymore," Carl had said to her one night after five years of marriage. "I don't need to," he'd said. Then a few weeks later, he took the car and left them. Nine hundred dollars in the bank account. Through Carl's parents, she'd heard that he'd moved to Oregon and that he was living with a male cousin whom he had loved since he was a child.

Her husband's departure had made her older boy, Ethan, give himself over to whatever cause angry boys took up. Jay had been different. He had worked so hard to please everyone, including her, and she had let that happen, because it had made her life so much easier.

"I'm so sorry, Casey," Mary Ellen said, her pale cheeks wet.

"I know," Casey said.

They walked out of the shop together. Mary Ellen lit a cigarette on the street, and Casey couldn't refrain from asking her for one, too, even though she had never before smoked in Mary Ellen's presence, following some Korean notion to not smoke in front of your elders. Mary Ellen handed her the pack, and Casey lit hers. The first drag was euphoric; the miasma in her head parted instantly, and Casey felt a kind of clarity she'd been missing for quite some time.

They hugged each other good-bye. Mary Ellen watched Casey walk uptown, then turned and went back to the library. At her empty space at the long wooden table in the Great Reading Room, Mary Ellen remembered that she'd forgotten to eat, and when she fumbled through her skirt pocket, she realized that Casey still had her packet of smokes. She gathered her papers for ED's biography that she'd been working on for eight years. Another day would hardly matter. She was a biographer who did not understand her own children's lives. Life was just guesswork even if you were an eyewitness. Mary Ellen searched for her cigarettes again, then planned to buy some on her way to Penn Station. She put her bare arms through the straps of her knapsack and left the library.

8 | COST

$\mathcal{J}$T WAS THE FINAL WEEK OF JULY, but still cool enough in the morning for Casey to wear her brown suit with Ella's brown pumps. Casey rationalized to herself that she was amortizing the cost of the suit with each use—avoiding altogether the issue of the credit card minimum payment she couldn't make. She was also calculating the odds of running into Jay. Four thousand employees worked at the Kearn Davis building on Fiftieth and Park. Jay and Ted worked on six at investment banking, and Casey would be interviewing on two with sales and trading.

From the lobby phone, she called Ted. His assistant told her that Ted wanted her to come up to six. In a huff, she marched into the empty elevator. Well, at least she was alone to hear the rumble in her stomach.

Casey was ravenous. That morning, Ella rushed off before finishing her breakfast, so Casey had eaten the discarded half of the toasted bagel with some butter. But eating that bit of bread had only made her hungrier. In the five weeks since she'd left her parents' house, Casey had lost eleven pounds according to Ella's bathroom scale. Her suit skirt spun around her waist, and for first time in her life, she was not happy about losing weight—it felt like a human rights violation to be this hungry all the time. And now that she couldn't afford to buy cigarettes (she'd already smoked two of Mary Ellen's packet and was rationing out the remainder for emergencies), her hunger was unbearable. The less she smoked, the more she wanted to eat, and food had never tasted better.

Every day, she went to the Mid-Manhattan Library to conduct her job search, and she couldn't stop thinking about bread, spaghetti, and hamburgers. Each night before Ella got home, she cooked one of her three-for-a-dollar ramen noodles bought from Odd-Job (occasionally filching an egg from Ella's refrigerator) with as much water as possible. The salty broth kept her going for a couple of hours. Sleeping when hungry was difficult. Once in a while, she broke her resolve not to take from Ella's larder and ate anyway. One night, she consumed a whole jar of Bonne Maman strawberry jam with a teaspoon. When Ella ordered Chinese food, Casey never asked for anything, but she ate the free egg roll or hot-and-sour soup and fried noodles in the waxed paper bag that Ella never touched. When Ella prepared dinner for Ted, Casey pretended to have other engagements. But having nowhere else to go, since meeting anyone in the city required cash and carfare—even hooking up with a college friend for a beer and pizza meant fifty bucks—Casey walked to the Metropolitan Museum, where you paid what you wanted, on the nights it closed late or lingered in bookstores that were still open, and when it was time for bed, she walked back to Ella's.

The sharp chime of the elevator pierced the hush of the sixth floor. Right away, Casey recognized the thick blue carpets and the dark wooden trim on the window jambs and door frames. The rest of the company was styled as a marble temple of finance. But investment banking on six resembled a private English men's club—mahogany paneling, silver-leaf-framed black-and-white photographs of New York's first skyscrapers, and buttoned leather wing chairs. The pert receptionist directed her toward Ted's office—only shouting distance from the larger shared office where Jay worked as a junior analyst with nineteen other Ivy grads chained to their rolltop desks.

The door to Ted's office was flung open. He was on the phone wearing a headset, his back facing her. While he was talking, his hand brushed across his black hair. Ted wore a French-cuffed shirt the color of a pale blue hydrangea, a darker blue woven silk necktie, navy silk braces, and gold love-knot cuff links that Ella had given him for Christmas.

Ted was aware that Casey was standing at his door. He could see her reflection on the glass covering the elongated engraving of the

Brooklyn Bridge. Not bothering to turn around, he motioned for her to come in. Then he drew his pointer finger across his neck to indicate that the call was soon ending.

Casey kept a respectable distance from his desk. Only after he glanced at one of the pair of empty chairs did she sit. Ted liked obedience, and she would not deny him this pleasure.

Ted pressed a button, turning off his phone.

"So, you made it." In her suit, she looked like anyone he'd gone to college or B school with. Her bruises had healed nicely, or she'd covered them up well. She wore lipstick—a shade between cinnamon and claret. He liked it. There was an expression the cannery boys used for girls with talent you didn't marry: worth fucking for practice.

Casey ignored his once-over and asked him demurely, "Shall we go now?"

"Coffee?" he asked.

"Thanks, but I thought we should get to the interview."

"It's actually in fifteen minutes. I only said ten o'clock because I didn't know if you were an on-time kind of person. Can't have you making me look bad." He smiled. His teeth were straight and even, but the lower half was stained lightly with nicotine.

"Thanks. Truly."

"Want to look up your friend?"

She acted as though she didn't understand.

Ted stuck out his left hand. "His office is just down the hall."

"Hmm." She nodded. There was a gorgeous color photograph of Ella tucked in a round silver frame. Her expression was wise and maternal, even though she couldn't have been more than nineteen or twenty at the time. Beside it was a black picture frame and, beneath the glass, a white envelope with "Teddy" scrawled on it in thick pencil like the writing of a child. When Ted caught her looking at the mounted envelope from his father, he turned it away from her sight.

"Just say a quick hello." Ted raised his left hand in a seemingly careless gesture. "Go on. I don't mind."

"I'm fine right here," she said.

"You sure?" Ted asked. "We could surprise him. Or I could phone him and ask him to swing by my office. I can make people do that."

"I bet you can."

"You think I'm an asshole."

"On occasion. Absolutely."

Ted laughed out loud. It was the first time he liked her.

"Jay Currie is not here today. He's down in Austin assisting with a roll-up."

"I was told that you did not work with Jay." It hurt to say his name. But on hearing that he wasn't there, Casey was at once relieved and disappointed.

"I haven't had the pleasure. Yet. But I did check him out."

"I'm flattered by your interest," Casey said, her voice even. "Are you done?"

"Funny. I'd never noticed him, and I'd been in that room dozens of times. Figures."

Casey exhaled through her nostrils, then held out for his verdict.

"Standard-issue white guy who dates Asian girls. Everything pale, generic looking. Not much personality there. Hmm. Heard he's some kind of stud due to some recent twin babe exploit." Ted coughed, amused with himself. "I am a little disappointed in you, Casey. I had you figured for the alpha type."

Casey looked at her watch and got up from her seat. "No, Ted. Ella likes the A types."

"You mean type A."

"No, I don't."

Ted laughed with pleasure. This was fun.

"Now, are you done?" she asked. His comments stung her, but she priced this mocking as payment for the favor. He was the sort of Korean guy who was angry about Korean girls dating white guys. She wanted to argue, however: *But it wasn't as if you or your buddies were ever asking me out. Should I have just stayed home?* To a Ted, she was too tall, too plain, and too much of a talker. Her family had no money. He had made his view of her clear. He believed that her present circumstances were justly deserved.

Ted grinned at her angry face. She was kind of sexy when she half pouted like that. He felt a little sorry for her.

Determined to behave like a good sport, she smiled at him.

"Well, I guess I've had my fun," he said.

"I am glad to be of service."

"So, Casey, let's dance," he said, getting up from his chair, his voice still whimsical. "Though you must be somewhat disheartened at not seeing your Mr. Currie today, looking so spiffy in your new suit." He stared at her suit jacket. "Aren't you hot in that? What is that? Wool? It looks warm."

"It doesn't feel very warm. In here."

Earlier that morning, she'd thought of Jay as she got dressed. In case she ran into him, she'd checked her makeup carefully on her way up to Ted's. After seeing his mother at the sandwich shop the day before, she'd longed to call Jay. He was a jerk; that was established. But she missed him intensely. He'd already tried to get her number from Tina, but under Casey's orders, Tina hadn't yielded to his pleas. So Jay had no idea where she was. But he was better off, since she knew where he was, and it was she who had to restrain herself from contacting him, when restraint was the very thing she was weakest in.

Ted walked out of his office, and Casey followed behind. She wished she could talk to Jay. He would've found it amusing that she was applying for a sales assistant position—basically, office manager work with a secretary's salary—because it was such a random thing for her to do. And Casey would've liked to joke with him. She missed laughing, and they'd always been good at laughing at themselves.

This was Casey's first time on the trading floor. It vibrated with activity. Seeing all these men in their crisp white shirts with their neckties swaying with their bodies was oddly thrilling. In contrast, Ted looked ridiculous with his Tiffany cuff links and silk braces crisscrossing his back like an X, marking him as a target. Rows and rows of men were positioned opposite computer terminals, talking, shouting, standing, and sitting down—their faces intense and kinetic.

The trading floor was nothing like a classroom or a library, an exclusive clothing store, or even the back room of a dry-cleaning shop—places Casey natively understood. There was no space for quiet reflection or planning. Energy bounced off every surface: Lights flickered across screens, fingers dashed across phone keys and computer keyboards. Here and there she spotted a woman, but the vast majority of those who filled the football-stadium-size room with its concert-hall-height ceilings were men: white, Asian, and a few blacks—under forty and presentable. Everyone sat side by side in long, parallel rows—a white-collar assembly line with Aeron chairs. It was hard not to feel propelled by the swirl of masculine power, and for the first time, Casey wanted this job. Suddenly it no longer mattered that being a sales assistant lacked prestige, money, and purpose, since she was likely going to law school after this year. Before this moment, her thinking had been that if she got the job, she'd still look for another position, then quit this gig (the very idea of remaining in Ted's debt and dominion had been offensive to her), but now she didn't want to consider her next move, and the thought of even plotting the next step seemed absurd. She'd stay for a year, then law school.

Ted remained beside Casey near the elevator and scanned the floor for Walter Chin, his pal from HBS. Reflexively, he crossed his arms over his chest, hating the noise and locker-room feel of two. He made a point never to go down here unless he had to. Even the smells bothered him—the cloying scent of street cart coffee and the lingering aftershave of the traders, whose way of talking reminded him of the men at the cannery. The guys on the trading floor seldom wore jackets. Ted disdained the untucked shirttails, the stained neckties, and the cheap haircuts. Junior analysts could look like shit since they rarely had time to shower, but brokers and traders, the company's front line, should look much better, Ted thought, as a man who cared a great deal about his appearance.

Ted wasn't budging from his spot of carpet, and Casey wanted to know why. He was taking in the scenery, too, but his face revealed contempt more than wonder. In all the busyness of the second floor, no one took notice of them. At the sight of Ted's profile, his square jaw tilted upward, his face so cleanly shaven, looking like a man who knocked down his fears on a daily basis, Casey felt humiliated having to wait for his move.

In life, it seemed that the ones who talked less, ate less, and slept less usually won. She'd picked up a factoid somewhere that said that sharks didn't sleep. Did winners have fewer needs or did they have greater desires than the losers? Ted's obvious advantage and ease in this room reminded her of what she'd once heard at a football game at school, that Harvard always won because Princeton thought they were too good to fight, and she thought, Yes, Harvard was winning again.

She needed this job, and no one understood that better than Ted. He predicted that eventually, with her qualifications, she could have gotten a far better position than sales assistant from one of the letters she'd sent out, but few companies hired a person based on sheer résumé, and it was nearly the end of July—a dead time for hiring. The girl had no cash left and no backup plans. The most hilarious thing about this girl was that she was too proud to use whatever connections she might have made. Her arrogance stunned him; he almost admired it. She was one of those Korean girls who thought she was as good as white and that the world was fair, and it tickled him to see her reduced to this position—to have to ask a member of the immigrant tribe for a patch of floor to sleep on and to ask another member to pull a favor on her behalf. *Where are all of your little white friends now?* he wanted to say to her. She was acting like a rich white girl, and Ted knew that life did not let you lie to yourself for very long. In that way, you had to admit, life was quite fair.

"Excited?" Ted faced her. "Or nervous?" He grinned.

"Let's play ball," she answered him. Ted Kim was sadistically illustrating that she'd only gone to Princeton, she was not *of* Princeton. As if she hadn't figured this out yet. She had exactly four dollars in her pocket, and after this demoralizing experience, wearing someone else's high heels, she'd walk thirty blocks to an apartment that wasn't hers, either. An Ivy League degree wouldn't get her on the subway, and she tried not to think of Virginia, who was in Bologna by now, taking a course or two for her master's degree in art history and filling out her afternoons flirting with the rich clients at her uncle's art gallery a brisk walk from the university.

Ted did not pay any mind to Casey's pout. He spotted Walter nearly half a city block from the elevator and instructed her to remain there. Casey held her back erect and her shoulders square like an athlete. This was no different from all the other times she'd pretended that she wasn't a visitor but in fact an honored guest. "Baby, when you're scared, walk round like you own the joint," Jay had once advised her, sounding more Trenton than Princeton. What the hell was he doing in Texas? And she wanted to know if he was thinking of her at all. She felt foolish and angry. And alone.

Ted's gait appeared confident and his carriage loose, but she could tell how he, too, hid his determination and anxiety about his future. She was more like Ted than Ella. He tried hard, and so did she; the difference between them was that he'd already figured out what he wanted in this life—money, status, and power—and she wasn't so sure about the things she wanted, preferring pride, control, and influence. Yet what each sought was related, much like first cousins.

Ted patted Walter on the back, and Walter looked pleased to see him. When he smiled broadly, Walter's small eyes looked shut. The two HBS alums chatted amiably, with Ted leaning his backside against an empty desk; then, a few minutes later, Walter told the men sitting on the sales desk that Ted had brought someone to interview for the assistant job. The way they talked seemed theatrical, almost funny, and Ted raised his head to look at her, his eyes still scrutinizing. He pointed to where he'd left her, and Casey smiled at them on cue. He made no other indication, so Casey didn't move. Then Walter waved her over, and she read his lips: "Come by." Grateful for his invitation, she went to the men, her head down, gaze averted. Then, like a blessing, she recalled Jay's words about acting as if you owned the joint, so she straightened her neck and looked straight ahead, trying very hard to appear more entitled.

9 | WORTH

Kevin Jennings, the antsy head of the Asian equities sales desk, had a rectangular face and the height and build of a former college basketball player. The Irish Catholic boy from the Bronx went to Georgetown, married a blond marathon runner, and now had a house in New Canaan, Connecticut, and three towheaded kids.

He trained his bright green eyes on the computer monitor, refusing to say good-bye to Ted Kim as he left. As a rule, he hated investment bankers, and as far as he was concerned, Ted would always be Walter Chin's foppy friend from HBS. This was Kevin's public sentiment: Guys who went to business school were assholes, and guys who went to HBS, bigger assholes. Walter, an American-born Chinese salesman on Kevin's desk, was a good guy—the exceptions to Kevin's rule of B schools in general and of HBS in particular.

Casey was directed to the empty chair between Kevin Jennings and Walter Chin. Ted had made the introductions briefly and then run off, saying he had a meeting across town. The desk head, Kevin, had snubbed Ted throughout—Casey noticed this, and in a way, his dislike of Ted went in his favor, but then she grew worried that she might be tainted by the association. After Ted left, Walter shared that Ted had been the presiding winner at HBS—the one to watch in section E. Casey nodded politely at this bit of Ted's biography, feeling at once annoyed and impressed. She was busy watching Kevin flick the cap of his blue Paper Mate pen. Pale freckled skin stretched across his long, bony fingers. The desk head continued to study his monitor, then abruptly started talking.

"When are you available?" he asked.

"Today, even," she replied quickly. His impatience was palpable, so she adapted her speech to follow his. This was a tactic she employed with hostile customers at Sabine's; in her experience, fawning or placating such people did not work. The only thing that made any kind of impression on people who were easily provoked was to persuade them of your efficiency and competence.

He picked up the fax copy of her résumé and whistled at her transcript. "Hmm," he said dismissively. "A schoolgirl, I see."

Kevin dropped her papers beside the stapler, then returned to the conclusion of the report he was reading off the screen. He disagreed with the research analyst's buy recommendation for the Taiwanese chip maker. Then he picked up the résumé again and turned to take a better look.

She was far too dressed up to be a sales assistant. A daddy's girl, no doubt. Princess wouldn't take this job seriously. Personal calls, lots of sick days—he'd seen it all before. People viewed being an assistant as a bullshit job, and it certainly paid a bullshit salary if you didn't count the O/T, but a clerical error could screw a lot of people and cost a fortune. In the past year, he'd fired three people in six months. His boss, the head of international equities sales, told him that it was starting to make Kevin look bad as a manager. "Buddy"—he'd been pulled aside after having fired the last one—"the next one has to work out. You know? Your guys need even support."

Hiring was a royal pain in the ass, however. Last year when he was promoted to desk head, he'd had no idea how much administrative crap came with the position. Somehow, when he was just one of the brokers, he'd been oblivious to what Owen, the prior desk head, had been doing. They used to call Owen "PT" for part-time, because he was often working from home (his gorgeous wife could not drop a teabag in boiling water, not to mention watch over their twin boys). Owen was promoted when Kevin was promoted, and he was now living in Hong Kong with a large household staff for his family. Kevin had been a phenomenal broker—one of the best institutional salesmen in the country—but as the desk head, he'd been forced to give up his biggest accounts to his guys to attend an endless cycle of management meetings. As far as he could see, these meetings made no dough for the company. He'd gone from running his own profit center to becoming a giant cost center. Instead of making his clients happy, he was now having to focus on budgets, shadow books, and safeguarding his ass from the great whites in the upper management pool.

"So, what are you doing here, exactly?" His green eyes flashed without warmth. "You really want to be a sales assistant?"

"A girl's gotta eat." Casey raised her eyebrows and smiled halfway.

She'd taken a risk. Kevin was amused, but he didn't show it. "Yeah, but a girl with your grades and degree can work anywhere. "

"But I want to work here."

He stared her down. Without saying a word, he was asking her why.

"I'm an econ major. This would be good experience for B school." Casey found herself lying with greater ease ever since she'd been thrown out of her parents' house—hardship being the mother of imagination.

"B school, huh?" Kevin frowned and glanced at his computer monitor again.

Seeing his disapproval, she replied, "Maybe."

"You know what B stands for in B school?" he asked loudly, mainly for Walter's benefit. Without giving her a chance to reply, he proclaimed, "Bullshit."

"Terribly original," said the man seated opposite Kevin. His hair was mahogany colored.

Hugh Underhill, the senior salesman on the desk, winked at Casey like an ally. She blinked in surprise. In a club or a restaurant, she might have stared right back at him. He looked familiar to her. Then she realized that his coloring and features were nearly the same as those of Jay's brother, Ethan, but this man was far more handsome—irritatingly so. Casey routinely ignored men like this, feeling in a curious way that they should not be given too much attention for their beauty.

Walter smiled at Kevin. His eyes disappeared into his gentle moon face. "Maybe Kevin should eat something. He gets so crabby when he's hungry. Did Mom pack your lunch today?"

Walter turned to Casey. "The quality and experience of your interview will improve markedly in a few minutes. I promise."

Kevin smirked hearing this. Walter wasn't wrong, and Kevin checked the conference room doors, which remained shut.

Again, Casey felt grateful to Walter. He seemed so gracious and thoughtful. Whatever she'd heard about B school or HBS or the hasty opinions she'd formed from knowing Ted were challenged by Walter, who seemed so considerate and modest in contrast. His humor had disarmed Kevin effectively. Casey was rarely if ever defended by anyone, and Walter's care made a big impression on her.

Casey wished she could find him attractive, however. When she thought about love and sex, she wanted a kind of cartoonish yellow thunderbolt to strike her—*shazam!*—to tell her that he was the one. For good or for bad, that almost never happened. As odd as this was, most of the boys she'd dated or slept with had wanted her more than she had wanted them, and their desire alone had been enough to cover her lack. Enough desire could induce her to feel enchanted for a while. With Jay, there had been a singular kind of thrill, a kind of lightning knowing. There was no wedding ring on Walter's ring finger (he was maybe thirty—old enough to be married) and no framed girlfriend's picture on his desk. Ted had told her that Walter was Chinese, but Casey couldn't always tell the difference between Chinese and Koreans just by looking. Walter was tall like Kevin—taller than Ted—and had a pudgy boyish face in a perpetually bemused state. His two-button suit in a rich gray wool was cut conservatively, and unlike the others nearby, he'd kept his jacket on. His shirt looked custom-made, each cuff buttoned thrice, a small notch found at the edge.

"You see, Casey"—Walter arched his right eyebrow for emphasis—"in a few minutes, there will be a stampede to that conference room"—he pointed to the room that Kevin had glanced at previously—"and Kevin Jennings, master of free lunches, will fill his plate, then be a tad kinder to humanity, including prospective assistants." In stereo, Hugh and Walter made loud seagull sounds. *Caw-caw-caw* filled the air. Hugh pretended to flap his wings and narrowed his eyes searchingly, looking like a scavenger. Walter acted as if he were throwing bread crumbs at Hugh. They were working hard to make her laugh, and Casey tried not to crack up.

Kevin rolled his eyes at them and returned to his screen, at least until, as Walter had predicted, the walnut-paneled doors opened for the free food. The aromas of the Indian food issuing from the room were intoxicating. He tried to read the research report. The day before, he'd told a client that the chip maker was at best a neutral, and now the bonehead analyst had changed his mind, saying buy. If Kevin called the client back, he'd look like a moron. Besides, the analyst's rationale was unpersuasive, and the friggin' charts made no sense. Fuck, he thought.

Kevin grunted, and no one paid him any mind.

This Casey Han girl didn't look as though she were going to work out. Was she working Ted? Kevin wondered. Possible. Whatever. He wanted to get rid of her so he could get the idiot analyst on the horn before lunch, but the guys were going to kill him if the parade of temp assistants didn't end soon. On a hunch, the girl appeared unsuited for Wall Street. The traders called him Kevlar Kevin because his instinctive calls were eerily bulletproof. However, the girl's résumé was unimpeachable. On paper, she was a WOW—walks on water—candidate. But he didn't like the way Hugh Underhill was looking at her. To his knowledge, Hugh had not yet bonked a sales assistant, but this one was cuter than the ones who'd been on the desk previously. If Hugh wanted a girl, he bagged her. That's all Kevin needed now, a flaky daddy's girl screwing his best broker. And if WOW ended up sinking, he'd have to fire her; as it was, they were also calling him Murphy Brown—the TV character who couldn't keep a secretary.

"B school, B school," Kevin muttered to himself, looking for a way out. "So why not be an analyst like your buddy Ted Kim? Get into the investment banking program or some"—he stopped himself from saying "shit"—"thing like that." When he mentioned the banking program, the brokers made faces as though something smelled bad.

"I don't want to make books," she said, borrowing a phrase she'd heard Jay's friends say in their complaints about the investment banking program. Hoping to sound like a sales and trading kind of person, Casey said, "I want more action."

The men who sat alongside each other laughed heartily. Casey didn't get it. Then Hugh, the one who had not yet been introduced, said, "And what kind of action are you looking for, exactly?" Then Casey closed her eyes, turning scarlet.

"So, Ted's friend wants more action," Kevin said to Walter, raising his eyebrows.

Hugh glanced at Casey, tickled by this. He stuck out his hand to introduce himself.

Casey murmured, "How do you do," unable to look him in the eye.

"Very well, thank you," Hugh answered, smiling broadly.

Walter jumped in. "Now you've got our dog all hot and bothered."

Hugh said, "Please ignore the boys. They don't get to see, much less talk to, attractive women often. You can see why."

Casey smiled, sensing that this man was a pathological seducer. And he was only flirting with her. He wasn't serious. She knew his kind. Hugh was a hound because he could be. In terms of looks and charm, he was in the majors, and, well, she played in the minors—a fact she'd accepted a long time ago. Men like him sought the Ellas of the world. Casey hadn't grieved too much for this missed opportunity, since Hughs weren't her type anyway, and she hoped this wasn't just sour grapes talking.

Casey heard the footsteps first. The conference room doors had opened. A cavalcade of brokers and traders streamed by to get their complimentary grub. Walter got up, hitching his pants; he'd recently lost twenty pounds but hadn't had a chance to replace any of his suit trousers. When Walter stood up, Hugh made the seagull sound again, then got up himself. All three sales guys—Kevin, Walter, and Hugh—were extremely tall, six three or four. Walter said, "Follow me."

Heaping trays of Indian food were laid out on the long table. A large, happy crowd gathered in clusters, piling food onto their white Chinet plates. Men made jokes about one another's love handles and spare tires—things women would never say to one another despite thinking them. Walter handed her a thick paper plate before taking his own. "Get what you like, but we gotta head back soon. Okay?" He spoke to her affectionately, as if she were a little kid.

The food made her mouth water. All around, people spooned food onto their plates, grabbing pieces of warm naan bread. There were pans of bread everywhere. The trays emptied gradually. The group dispersed.

Kevin and Hugh had already returned to the desk. Casey had managed to grab a cocktail-size Samosa and a scoop of *biriyani* but had hesitated to fill her plate during an interview. Walter's plate was crammed with a taste of everything.

"Gosh. Girls eat so little," Walter said with wonder in his voice.

"It happened so fast," she remarked, her free hand resting at her side.

Walter swept his right arm to the ceiling, gesturing like a ring-leader, and said, "It's free food for millionaires."

She wrinkled her brow, amused by his dramatic movement.

"In the International Equities Department—that is, Asia, Europe, and Japan sales—the group you're interviewing for—"

Casey nodded okay.

"—whichever desk that sells a deal buys lunch for everyone in the department. We finished a deal last week—a big power plant outside of Bombay. So today we bought Indian. Get it? If Japan sales finishes a deal, then we get sushi."

"Gotcha," she said.

"The funny thing is that if you were a millionaire like some of these managing directors shaking down seven figures a year, you'd have known to push your way ahead and fill up your plate. Rich people can't get enough of free stuff." Walter shrugged. There was no reproach in his tone; in fact, there was a wistful admiration in his voice, as if he were beginning to understand how the world worked.

"So, this is the game, Casey. You have to take what's offered." He spoke like a mentor.

"If you say so," Casey replied. But she didn't know how she felt about money or free things. Her father always said there was no such thing as a free lunch.

It had been nearly impossible for her to accept Ella's charity, and even though she loved the beautiful clothes that she couldn't afford, she couldn't imagine a life where she was working only for money just so she could get more stuff—because she sensed that somehow it wouldn't sustain her for very long. Working hard for good grades had made sense because she loved learning itself—the acquisition of new ways of seeing things and possessing new facts—but the good grades hadn't sustained her, and for her, school wasn't meant to be forever.

Casey glanced at her plate again, recalling the posters of her elementary school lunchroom: YOU ARE WHAT YOU EAT. So, how much

you ate indicated the quantity of your desire. Walter was also imply-
ing that how quickly you got your food revealed the likelihood of
achieving your goals. She was in fact terribly hungry, but she'd pretended to be otherwise to be ladylike and had moved away from the
table to be agreeable, and now she'd continue to be hungry.

Walter turned to wave back at a girl who was walking toward them.
It was hard to tell her age. She might have been about ten years
older than Casey but possessed the ideal figure of a twenty-year-old
and dressed like one. She wore no stockings. Remarkable legs. Her
plate held mostly vegetables and a large piece of bread.

"Hi, baby," she said. The men on the floor craned their necks to
check out her rear end as she passed them.

"Hello, Delia," Walter said cheerfully.

She came to a full stop to talk to him. Delia wore a short blue
linen skirt and a paler blue blouse with its shell buttons gaping
slightly across her full bosom. Her eyes were also blue, the color of
mint candy, and they shone beneath the waves of curly red blond
hair. She had a soft Staten Island accent, almost unnoticeable—it
showed up when she said "yeah" now and then. Her facial expression was alert, but it was easy to overlook the intelligence in her eyes
because of her suggestive clothing and curvy figure. There was a
lushness about her skin, a ripeness. Jay's literary friends would have
called her a fox and deemed her legs sonnet-worthy.

"And this is Delia Shannon. The brilliant and talented sales assistant on the European sales desk."

"Walter, you're brokering again." Delia smiled at Casey warmly.

"Hi," Casey said, feeling something sisterly about her.

"Casey Han is interviewing to be our sales assistant," Walter said.

Delia felt sorry for the poor kid. Kevlar wasn't a bad guy, but his
wife should blow him now and then before he left for work. That's
what uptight men needed—Delia felt sure of this. She shook Casey's
hand. "Good luck."

Casey withdrew from Delia's weak and powdery handshake. Used
to the firm, make-eye-contact masculine handshakes at Princeton,
she found Delia's grasp anachronistic and overly feminine.

"So we're just going to tell Kevin that Casey's a hire. It's a no-
brainer," Walter said.

Delia smiled knowingly.

"Maybe you'll help Casey out if she wants to take the job."

"Yes, I'd love that. I mean, if everything works out," Casey said.

Delia clasped Casey's large hands with her small white ones, saying, "Anything for Kevin's new victim. Anything at all." There was no malice or cynicism in her tone. Casey liked her.

Walter put his index finger dramatically across his lips, and Delia winked at him.

"I don't think you have to worry about Casey. Ted Kim tells me that Casey is as tough as anything," he said.

Casey tried not to look surprised.

"Oh? Is she Ted's friend?" Delia asked.

Walter nodded. "Well, I think she's Ted's fiancée's friend. A family friend."

Casey nodded, not thinking it necessary to explain. Delia winked again, then excused herself. She had to speak with someone in the mailroom about a package. The men nearby watched her stroll away. Delia's backside, shaped like a small blue heart, twitched with each gingerly step.

Delia was a perma-assistant, Walter explained. Never having gone to college, she was stuck in what was supposed to be a two- or three-year job. But apparently Delia did not complain.

The way Walter confided in her made Casey feel that she might be getting the job. Why else would he tell her these things? When they returned to the desk, Kevin curled his hand toward him, and she went to sit.

"Two years. Minimum. You're going to have to work out. I swear. You have to make hotel reservations, get airline tickets, arrange conferences, send out reports, make copies, pick up faxes and packages, and coordinate details. Perfectly. You have to pay attention to everything. Do you understand? Two years. Or else. You will not get a recommendation from me unless you fulfill that two-year mark. Get it?" Kevin was looking hard at her, making sure she understood.

Hugh put down his fork, amused by Kevin's offer. "It's hard to believe that he was once a stellar broker. A salesperson. His personal skills have deteriorated beyond recognition." He held out his hand. "Casey, welcome to our desk."

Casey shook his hand but looked directly at Kevin when she said, "Deal."

"And don't trust this guy," Kevin said, widening his eyes. "No matter how much he was fighting for you to get the job."

Hugh laughed, unfazed. "Yes, don't trust me. I'm just awful."

Walter said, "So you'll come to work tomorrow?"

"Yes, of course," Casey said.

"Two years," Kevin said sternly.

"Enough, tough guy," Hugh said. "Think of the Thirteenth Amendment."

"I'm impressed," Walter said. "I didn't know I was working with an abolitionist."

Hugh buffed his fingernails against his chest. "Anyway, can you imagine how Kevlar asked his wife to marry him?"

Walter shivered.

"Assholes. At least I got a woman to marry me."

"The kindness and goodness of the fair sex can never be underestimated," Hugh said, beaming at Casey.

"Down, boy," Walter said to Hugh, and Hugh made a halo over his head by joining his thumbs and middle fingers.

Kevin checked his screen. The chip maker had fallen by a basis point since lunch. He threw his pen at the monitor. "I knew it."

Casey jolted up in her chair.

Kevin turned to the girl, remembering to finish up with her. "See you tomorrow at five forty-five." He picked up the phone to call the analyst. His tone switched completely—earnest, questioning, and calm.

Walter noticed Casey's confused expression. She would get it soon—you didn't get to become the boss without having some versatility in style. Casey remained in her chair, not knowing if she was being dismissed. At once, the phones rang and both Walter and Hugh picked up calls. Walter motioned to Delia, who was back at her desk. He covered the receiver of his phone and whispered, "Go talk to her. Ask her to walk you to Human Resources."

Casey went to her, and Delia took over.

10 | OFFERING

ELLA'S LONG DARK HAIR was pinned up with a barrette, and she wore a lilac-colored linen dress reaching down to the middle of her slender calves. They were at home, so she had no shoes on her bare white feet. Ella tilted her oval-shaped face, peering into Casey's like a hopeful girl before a party.

"Maybe you can come with us today?" she asked.

Casey fumbled through her bag. There were exactly six cigarettes left in the packet she'd accidentally filched from Mary Ellen. The first thing she intended to buy with her paycheck was a carton of Marlboro Lights.

"I forget," Casey lied, knowing full well that church began at nine. "When do services start again?" It was already eight in the morning, and Casey had been awake, showered, and dressed for nearly two hours. Before starting her job at Kearn Davis, it had been her habit to rise well before Ella did, prepare coffee, tuck away the sofa bed, read the classifieds, and draft cover letters. She'd been working for a week now, and on this Sunday, she'd wanted to be by herself while Ella and Ted went to church and ate their brunch at Sarabeth's at the Whitney.

Ella told her the service times, then invited her again. Her innocence and vulnerability had the effect of making Casey feel hard and wizened. Ella appeared so easy to hurt, and this made Casey careful around her.

"We never celebrated your job properly..." Ella tried again.

"You keep saying that, but there's no need. Really." Casey didn't want any more kindness or charity from her. Without Casey's asking, Ella had handed her carfare and lunch money to tide her over until she got paid, bought her hosiery, and loaned her dress shoes to wear to the office. Casey's debts mounted like a heap of laundry.

"And I really want you to meet Unu. He promised he'd come today."

Casey nodded. In the past week, Ella had been mentioning her cousin who'd just moved into a rental across the street. He'd been an electronics analyst at Pearson Crowell—a second-tier British investment bank. Ella, who had no guile, couldn't hide her wish for Casey to like Unu and vice versa. Twenty-seven years old, raised in the suburbs of Dallas, St. Mark's, Dartmouth, the son of a businessman and a doctor—the last of four children. He'd just returned from a four-year stint in Seoul with Pearson Crowell before switching to a boutique firm in New York; he was also fresh from a quick marriage to and a faster divorce from a girl in Korea who had treated him badly.

Casey sat on the bench near the front door to put on her black espadrilles. She was headed to the roof for her cigarette, and slipped under her arm was the real estate section of the paper. As soon as she'd put together the security deposit and first month's rent, she'd move out. In anticipation of her departure, Ella had concocted a fantasy that Unu and Casey would fall in love and join her and Ted at church every Sunday. They'd both be couples and do things that couples do. Casey thought it was sweet but ultimately far-fetched. So when Ella got that gleam in her eye talking about Unu, Casey would answer politely, "Your cousin sounds nice."

Her shoes now on, Casey picked up her set of house keys.

"You don't like Ted," Ella said.

"Pardon?"

"That's why you won't go to church," Ella said. Casey would agree to do most anything with her on the weekends, mundane errands like grocery shopping or a trip to the dry cleaner, but when she invited her to do something, even fun things like movies or dinner, when Ted would be there, Casey declined. And Ella had not forgotten this from their confirmation class days: Despite Casey's "too cool for Sunday school" affect, Casey was the student who'd consistently asked the singular questions about God.

Casey dropped a book of matches into her white shirt pocket, pretending not to have heard what Ella said. She placed her right hand on the doorknob.

"He's not easy. I know that," Ella said.

"What are you talking about?" Casey asked. Had her contempt been so obvious? "Your fiancé got me a great job."

"It'll be fun. Please say yes. Unu's my favorite person. You'll—"

The phone rang, and guessing accurately it was Ted, Casey walked out, saying, "Ella, you know I can't make any big decisions without my morning cigarette."

It was Ted, a fellow smoker, who'd told her about the roof on Ella's building. Ella was allergic to smoke, and oddly enough, Ted and Casey were unrepentant. But they never smoked in her presence.

Unlike the roof at her parents', this one was meant to be used by all the residents. There were pink and white geranium plants in terra-cotta pots and metal patio furniture painted a racing green color set up invitingly on the white gravel-covered roof. On summer weekends, young women sunbathed with their bikini strings undone and men in baseball hats and sweatpants plowed leisurely through their swollen *Times*es while drinking lukewarm coffee in mugs brought from home.

The residents who'd shared a light at some point said "hey" when they saw Casey. She wore a white dress shirt, her gray knife-pleated skirt, and no stockings, and in her rope-soled shoes, she stood out against the Sunday morning crowd with their bed hair and sleepy looks. The brightness of the day, the young singles relaxing, reminded her of school in the spring when at the first sight of the warm sun, everyone skipped classes to laze in the open greenery. Casey wanted to stay there, smoke the rest of the pack, read the paper, and plan out her life after her first paycheck.

It wasn't that she didn't like church. She enjoyed a good sermon as much as she adored a stirring lecture. Ella had spotted the issue accurately. Ted's teasing felt aggressive and mean-spirited. Just last night, when Ella went downstairs to get her mail, he'd said to Casey, "Maybe I should tell Jay that his girlfriend works on two." Casey had wondered if this unrelenting behavior was equivalent to a sixth-grade boy snapping the bra strap of a girl he liked, but it wasn't that kind of retarded flirtation. Besides, Casey couldn't imagine anyone preferring her over Ella. What Casey understood was that Ted was jealous. He thought they were competing for Ella, and consequently, he treated her as a rival, and from never having fought with a boy, Casey was astonished by the nature of his attacks, so unlike a girl's—naked, persistent, and lethal. As nice was she was, Ella wasn't worth this.

Also, Casey didn't want to meet Ella's cousin. She was still preoccupied with Jay. Her sister had told her that he'd tried to reach her several times. In the past week, Casey hadn't bumped into him in the elevator or the cafeteria. The second and sixth floors remained separate, as if they were in different buildings.

As for her new job as a sales assistant, since Casey was by nature an organized person—adept at deadlines and details—except for learning some new software and eating both breakfast and lunch at her desk among several men, the nature of her work was not difficult. After her day ended, she walked home and reread *Middlemarch* or began another volume of Trollope borrowed from the neighborhood library. She studied an old millinery pattern book bought for a quarter from a homeless guy who sold magazines and outdated textbooks on First Avenue. In her spare time, she worried mostly about money and her future. Her salary minus a discretionary bonus and possible overtime (how much she'd get was hard to figure out at this point—though Delia said she might be able to get as much as half her base) was thirty-five thousand dollars per annum on a pretax basis. With her pay, she'd have to meet her credit card minimums, save up her rent deposit (nearly fifteen hundred dollars for two months' rent for a cramped studio) with the possibility of having to fork over 15 percent of the annual rent for the broker's fee, and furnish a new place, since she did not own even a buck-fifty drinking glass. Ella wouldn't hear of taking money from her for rent or groceries despite Casey's offers to pay her when she got her check.

Casey moved toward the edge of the roof. On its perimeter, there were boxes of white impatiens well tended to by the building's gardening committee. Although it was the first week of August, she felt a mild breeze in the air. The view—its grid of unshaded windows wasn't much different from the one in Elmhurst—was of small kitchens, dimpled glass obscuring bathrooms, L-shaped living rooms, and unmade beds in darkened chambers. It was peaceful to smoke here, leaning against the waist-high parapet. Jay used to joke that she liked roofs because that's where she parked her Wonder Woman glass plane. Casey allowed herself another cigarette. She tried to light it, but the wind blew north; she cupped the flame of her paper match, and when she glanced up, she saw an Asian man at a window studying her.

He was thin, around her height, wearing a dark two-button suit, a white shirt, and a medium-width purple necktie. She could make out his face: rounded nose, high cheekbones, black eyes tapered sharply at the ends, and softly arched eyebrows. She stared back at him and he smiled at her; then, suddenly feeling shy, she turned to take another drag of smoke. When she looked for him again, he was gone. After the tobacco was spent, she stubbed out the light and went downstairs.

Casey told Ella she'd go to church after all.

"Are you sure?" Ella asked, not knowing what she should do now. Ted had just called her. It turned out that the night before, Jay Currie had been staffed on a deal Ted was working on, and when they were finally introduced, Ted had blurted out that he knew Casey Han. "Is she all right?" Jay had asked him anxiously. Ted had ended up telling him where she was staying. Just like that. Ella had scolded him, saying, "How could you?" But he'd replied, "At least I didn't tell him that she works on two." He'd laughed out loud—in her mind, she could still hear his chortle—and she'd had to resist the impulse to hang up on him. She'd never done that before, but at that moment, it had seemed more than appropriate.

Ted was now on his way to pick her up for church. Flustered, Ella put on her shoes.

"Maybe you're tired after your first week of work. Would you prefer to go next Sunday?" Ella said.

"Nope. I'm all yours," Casey replied. "Let's go worship in the house of the Lord." She laughed, then shouted, "Hallelujah!" She felt cheery all of a sudden.

Ella smiled perfunctorily, feeling guilty, as if somehow this were all her fault.

"You think Ted will buy me an expensive brunch?" Casey put her hands on her hips.

"Yes." Ella nodded, head bobbing like a doll's. "Anything you want."

The doorman buzzed. Ted Kim was in the lobby.

When they got downstairs and met him, Ted kissed Ella's stiffening cheeks and returned Casey's surface pleasantries. They walked to church, not five blocks away, and Ella chattered about Unu to Casey. At the church entrance, Ted put his hand on Ella's back and she moved away from his hand.

Ushers directed them upstairs to balcony seating because the main auditorium was full. The church leased a college hall for worship because it couldn't handle the growing number of attendees. Ted was unimpressed by the shabby city college building. There were no pew hymnals or Bibles, and the service was printed on a flimsy staple-bound pamphlet. He would've preferred Fifth Avenue Presbyterian, which looked like a real church, but Ella was devoted to Dr. Benjamin, and even he, as a person who had hated Sunday school in Anchorage, had to admit that he paid attention to Benjamin's intelligent sermons and on occasion found himself reflecting on them. Ted believed that church was a good idea for a well-governed society, and he didn't trust anyone who didn't believe in God.

Casey coming to church had surprised him. He'd pegged her as a textbook atheist—one of those know-it-alls who had the blind faith to explain the world according to scientific theories that were disproved every day yet were unable to believe in the things they weren't smart enough to rationalize. Ted, who had no great faith in God or Jesus, could not believe in the randomness of chance, and he was arrogant enough to refuse fish or ape ancestors. If creationism sounded absurd, evolutionism insulted his intelligence, too. As much as Ted believed in hard work and self-determination, he also believed in a kind of guided order outside of man—an Adam Smith invisible hand kind of fate. But in general, he avoided discussions about religion. There was no way to win them anyway, he thought, why bother. Whichever side you fell on, you had to conclude with the statement "I believe..." rather than "I know." The minister called them to say the prayer that Christ had taught them to say, and Ted heard Casey recite it from memory, and he could hear some feeling.

Casey meant it when she said, "Forgive us for our debts as we forgive our debtors," because they were for her the hardest words to live by, and by saying them, she hoped they'd become possible.

Like Ted, Casey would never discuss her ambivalent views on re-

ligion. She was honest enough to admit that her privacy cloaked a fear: the fear of being found out as a hypocrite. Casey was keenly aware of her Christian failings: Routinely, she mumbled, "Jesus Christ," when she stubbed her toe; for a young woman, she had slept with enough men she'd had no love for or intentions of marrying; she'd had an abortion without regret; she'd tried drugs (liked some very much and feared that she had an addictive personality, and for that reason alone, she did not seek them out); she enjoyed getting drunk and acting on her passionate impulses; she loved acquiring nice things, and it was an explicit goal for her to have them; every day, she envied someone else's life; she adored gossip in any form; she'd stolen clothes from the return bin at Sabine's; she disliked many Christians—finding them dull and intolerant; and nearly two months prior, she'd told her own parents to fuck off. Her commandment violations were numerous and sustaining. She would not win any white-leather Bibles at Sunday school camp. Her awareness of a God, quotidian Bible reading, and obscure verse scribbling made no sense to her. Nevertheless, Casey could not commit to no God, either.

Ella had no doubts. In plain sight, she rummaged through her leather satchel, pulling out a black leather zip-up Bible and a fabric-bound sketchbook. She held a Waterman pen with a gold nib at the ready. She flipped open her sketchbook, its pages packed with blue-black-inked script, to find a clean sheet. Cross-referencing the program, she quickly found the Scripture on which the sermon was based. She wrote down the verse citation beneath the sermon title, "What sustains you?" with the precision of a student taking notes for chemistry lab. Ella looked fierce in her attentiveness.

She looked adoringly at Dr. Benjamin, which Casey found sort of amusing. The minister was middle-aged, no wrinkles—anywhere between forty-five and fifty-five. He kept his curly dark hair short and tidy. Silver-rimmed glasses covered his mink brown eyes. He wore a modest accountant-style suit with a crisp white shirt and mid-level banker's red necktie. No black robes. His look was more shrewd than sober. Ella had mentioned before that it was impossible to be married by him because Dr. Benjamin was booked solid. Like everything else in New York, a good minister's services required reservations and waiting. So Ella was going to be married by her father's Korean minister in Queens—a very nice man who yelled a lot about hell.

Dr. Benjamin read the gospel verse from the book of Matthew: "Jesus answered, 'It is written: Man does not live by bread alone, but on every word that comes from the mouth of God.'"

It was a curious consequence that from Casey's years of private reading and Sunday school, she knew the Bible cold. In that selection, the devil tempts Jesus, hungry after forty days of fasting, by saying that if he is in fact the Son of God, he could command the stones to become bread. Jesus replies by quoting Deuteronomy 8:3: "He humbled you, causing you to hunger and then feeding you with manna, which neither you nor your fathers had known, to teach you that man does not live on bread alone but on every word that comes from the mouth of the Lord." The Bible was endlessly referring to itself, and in college, this peculiar knowledge—peculiar, since no one she knew at Princeton read the Bible—had been helpful academically, since most of Western writings referred to it, too.

Ella nodded incessantly at Dr. Benjamin as she took meticulous notes on the sermon. Casey found Ella's devotion grating. When the sermon ended, the offering was collected by the ushers. A basket lined with gray sponge passed through. Casey opened her wallet and spotted two twenties—money Ella had loaned her to cover her till payday on Friday. Her Sunday school teacher Mrs. Novak used to say, "Test providence, give sacrificially." She dropped one of the twenties into the basket. Ted dropped in a folded check for fifty dollars that he'd prepared earlier. Ella dropped in a folded check for two hundred dollars—this amount representing twenty-five percent of her weekly salary.

Dr. Benjamin gave the benediction and dismissed them. Ella put away her Bible and notebook. Then she leaned over the balcony railing in search of her cousin. Casey had been observing the crowds, and Ella said assuringly, "He's supposed to meet us outside anyway."

Once they were on the street, opposite the college building, Ted and Ella discussed the brunch options: dim sum or Sarabeth's. Casey, who'd been half listening, shifted when she felt the light pressure of a hand on her upper arm. Ted's expression changed to surprise, and Casey spotted the hand first with its short blond hairs across its knuckles, then recognized Jay. With her right fist, she swung. Ella covered her mouth with her hands to stifle herself, and Ted burst out laughing, saying, "Ooooh."

Unu Shim gasped along with everyone else milling about who'd witnessed this. Then he realized it was Ella standing next to the woman who'd just hit the tall white guy so hard that blood trickled toward his lips.

11 | COVENANT

I DESERVED THAT," Jay said, tasting the blood on his upper lip. In his entire life, he had never once been hit; somehow, he'd managed to avoid having a fistfight even as he attended an all-boys' school, and at home, he had wisely refused to tangle with his older brother, Ethan, who had an unforgettable temper. Casey had clocked him. Even as Jay swept blood from the patch of skin beneath his nose, he couldn't believe it.

Feeling somewhat responsible, Ted moved closer to Casey, ready to pull her back in case she started swinging—nevertheless, he was amused by the possibility. Unu Shim had by this point managed to break through the crowd to get to his cousin Ella, who was herself so visibly stunned by this that she couldn't speak.

"Ella? Are you okay?" Unu asked. They hadn't seen each other since his wedding in Seoul three years before.

"Unu…" Ella stared at him in disbelief. "Hi. I'm so glad to see you."

Unu folded his arm around Ella's shoulders and patted her back gently, the way his father greeted people.

Ella rested her fingers lightly on Unu's forearm, then reflexively she thought to grab a Kleenex from her makeup bag and she offered it to Jay.

Casey watched this interaction as if she were seeing it on TV. What was Ella doing handing Jay tissues? Then Jay took the tissue from

Ella, mumbling a shy "Thank you." He stopped up his nose with it. Casey put her hands behind her back, suddenly appreciating what she had done. She was the one who'd made Jay bleed. It was as if her hand had been angry for her, formed a fist, and couldn't resist the act. Casey had never intended to hit him.

She looked upward at the cloudless sky. It was a perfect August morning without a trace of humidity; it could have been a clear day in May. In her life, she'd never struck another person, and she didn't think she'd ever do so again. Having been hit herself, she knew what that felt like: You felt dumb, ugly, and unlovable. Now that she'd hit Jay, she saw that she had diminished him. And herself. He had gotten bigger than life to her, and she'd had to punish him. Her body was shaky with feeling. The people leaving the church kept looking her way.

"Casey, can't I talk to you?" Jay asked. The woman who'd given him the tissue tapped her chin, telling him to lean his head back. She must have been Ted's fiancée, Ella.

Ted interjected, "Hey, man," and Jay nodded, smiling weakly. Ted Kim was in charge of his most recent deal and had a say in his bonus.

Casey ignored this. She looked at Jay. "I want my things." Each morning when she dressed at Ella's, she remembered something else at his apartment—a tube of expensive mascara, hosiery, her favorite lace brassieres, even drugstore-brand deodorant—items she couldn't afford to replace.

"You have things that are mine. I need them back." Casey started to cry.

Ella's eyes stung, and she could not look away.

Unu felt hot in the noon sun. The guy standing beside Ella, who was probably Ted, wore a black polo shirt and chinos. Certain no one cared now, Unu unwound his grape-colored print necktie, folded it, and socked it into his jacket pocket. Then he removed his suit jacket.

"Ella, you okay?" Unu asked. Ella nodded. "Maybe brunch is not such a good idea. Do you want me to call you later?"

"No, no, don't go." Ella grabbed his arm. "I am so sorry. This... this is Ted," she said, her head turning left to right as though she were watching a tennis match. Ted shook Unu's hand.

Ella didn't know if and how she should introduce Casey to Unu.

Casey couldn't seem to stop sobbing. Ella felt livid. Ted had made this happen. She moved closer to Casey, drew her arm around her friend's torso like a protective wing. "Are you all right? Should we ask Jay to go?"

Jay looked at Ella, more surprised that the woman knew his name than at her suggestion that he should leave.

Casey sniffled and leveled her gaze at Jay. They stood a few paces from each other. "You disappointed me," she said calmly.

Jay exhaled, unable to respond. He reached over to take her hand.

"Don't touch me, you son of a bitch." As she said this, Casey realized that Mary Ellen had told him how to find her. "You prick."

Casey's harsh words were thrown like quiet punches, and Ella found herself wincing.

Ted smiled at Unu and all the while felt sorry for Jay for this dressing-down. Ted grabbed Ella's hand, thinking that she shouldn't be listening to this kind of speech, and he patted Unu on the arm, motioning for them to leave. Unu agreed, feeling like an intruder. Ella refused to budge from Casey's side.

Unu peered at the lingering crowd. Using the voice of a college fraternity president—a position he'd once held at Dartmouth—he dismissed the onlookers: "Come on, folks, show's over. Go on home, now. Go on." He pulled up the Texas lilt in his voice, aware how a twang could soften a hard word.

Yes, Ella thought. That was kind. She then asked Casey, "Do you want us to go?"

Ella waited for Casey's word.

"I'll be okay. You should go to brunch." Casey wanted everyone to go. She herself wanted to disappear, to vanish.

"You sure?"

"Yes."

At this, Ella nodded to Ted and Unu, and the three of them walked away. Every few steps, Ella turned to check on Casey. After two blocks, she lost sight of her friend.

They were all gone. Casey stood there on the empty sidewalk with Jay.

The picture of the night with those girls came upon her again; and as before, she felt truncated—no arms, no body. Her quiet sobbing wouldn't end, no matter how many breaths she took.

Jay held Ella's tissue against his nose, the bloodstained paper shadowing his long face. He felt terrible, and having seen the rebuke in Casey's friend's face, he felt confirmed as a louse.

"If you really want me to go, I'll go, but I came by to apologize. I've been trying to see you for almost two months now. Your sister wouldn't tell me where you were because you wouldn't let her. I... I've been so worried. When you left, you looked—" And Jay stammered, "And I love you, Casey...I know—I know I hurt you. I am sorry."

How was he saying all this? Casey wondered, shaking her head. "I never imagined that you could, that you were even capable, interested in such—"

"I'm not," he nearly shouted. "It isn't what you think. I love you, Casey."

"Your mother broke her promise." It was too hard to hear Jay talk about love. "She promised not to." Casey looked at his face, and seeing him with the tissue wadded up his nose, she said, "Jay. You look ridiculous."

He pinched the bridge of his nose with his thumb and forefinger. "I don't think it's broken," he said, sounding nasal, and they both laughed out loud.

Mary Ellen hadn't told him where she was. It had been Ted, and that morning when Jay had gone to Ella's apartment to bring over a four-page letter saying how sorry he was, the doorman had mentioned that it wouldn't be long before they came back because Miss Shim and her friend Casey had gone to church, pointing to the block-long city college building. The services would let out in ten minutes, the doorman said. So Jay had gone to the church and waited for her to come out.

When they reached Jay's apartment, he unlocked his dead bolt, and Casey followed him in. She'd been letting him talk while they walked to his place, and she'd said almost nothing. She marched into the kitchen to grab garbage bags that she'd bought and felt entitled to, and as Jay continued to explain himself, she selected her novels and compact discs from the shelves in his black glass entertainment unit. She listened to him tell his whole story without interrupting his flow. He was the English major and she was the econ girl—always, she had admired his beautiful diction, but for the first time, she noticed that he sounded priggish and show-offy. When he was done, she said, "I don't give a goddamn shit if some sorority girls wanted to bang you. Frankly. I just don't give a flying fuck. You think I can't get laid whenever I want? Fuck you. I'm done. You're done. You can take your Trenton-converted-Princeton ass and shove it."

Jay raised his eyebrows. It was going to be harder to recover than he'd thought.

Casey went to the linen closet and pulled out two towels of hers, then headed to the bathroom. All of her things in the medicine cabinet were as she'd left them. Jay came and sat on the covered toilet and watched her take away her whitening toothpaste, perfume, and cinnamon floss. The middle glass shelf was now empty.

From the mirrored bathroom wall, he checked his nose. It was no longer bleeding.

Half jokingly, he muttered, "I thought Christians were supposed to forgive and all that." From her chilled expression, he instantly regretted what he'd just said. "I mean, I know you're an agnostic and...I was just kidding."

Casey was more angry than she thought humanly possible. "Why do atheists constantly harp on Christian hypocrisies? Why don't you fucking dodgers just get your own set of beliefs to critique yourselves against? I never said I was a good person or a good Christian, Jay. I never even acted like I was. I just fucking went to church this morning, for chrissakes. We're all fucking imperfect, you motherfucker. That's the whole absurd point of salvation through grace. I don't even know if I believe this. Got it, genius?" For the moment, he'd become the dumbest person alive.

"I wasn't calling you a hypocr—" Jay stopped himself. "I didn't really mean anything by that."

" 'That' being what? Fucking two girls or prodding me to do the Jesus thing and forgive your sorry ass?" Casey walked swiftly to the bedroom and pulled out the top two drawers, where she kept her lingerie and clothes. Nothing had been touched, and she stuffed the contents into the garbage bag. She stiffened her back, focusing on the rolled-up balls of socks and tights. She had missed her things.

Jay came up from behind and put his arms around her. Casey dropped her head to her chest, her chin touching her collarbone, and she breathed in. Paco Rabanne—it was the aftershave she'd bought him for his birthday. She turned around, not knowing if she'd slap him or walk away and never see him again—his soft cheeks, the ocean-colored eyes with their sparkle of black and gold, and the slight droop of his lower lids. She could imagine his face when he grew older, the receding hairline, the pouches under his eyes that would certainly grow heavier, even the blond hairs that would surely sprout from his ears. He'd resemble one of her history professors at Princeton. And at one point, she had loved that about him. His face over the years had become familiar to her—with all its expressions she found so dear; he was her lover and kin—like an older brother, a young uncle, a cousin, and a husband.

He kissed her on the mouth, and she did not pull away.

At four-thirty in the morning, she carried three half-filled garbage bags down to the lobby, where the doorman hailed her a taxi. Casey gave the doorman a buck for his service and spent eight dollars on her fare. At Ella's, she took a shower, then went to work. It was Monday again.

12 | LOSS

*D*OUGLAS SHIM WAS NOT THE TYPE of man to hold back his praise. He had always admired her singing. Nor was he shy. At Manhattan Eye, Ear & Throat, where he was a surgeon director, Dr. Shim was known for his practical jokes, his wry sense of humor, and his unconscious out-of-tune whistling. But there was something about Leah Han that made him uneasy about approaching her.

It was not one of the Sundays when Leah and her husband served on the hospitality committee, which Douglas chaired. If her solo had coincided with a committee visit, Douglas would've told her how much he'd enjoyed her singing in her husband's presence. It was a curious position to be in—that is, being an attractive widower and talking to married women, especially at church, and especially with Leah.

The Christmas Eve services had just ended, and the congregants were moving about the church basement, sipping coffee from Styrofoam cups and eating Entenmann's doughnuts bought day old from the bakery outlet. Leah was headed to the choir room to change out of her robe, and Douglas raised his hand. Leah Han was known to him as Deaconess Cho—by her church title and, following Korean custom, her maiden name. She stopped and bowed her head to him slightly.

"Deaconess Cho." He smiled. " 'How Great Thou Art' is a beautiful song." Only at church did Douglas speak his native language, and speaking Korean for only a few hours each Sunday reminded him of its formality—in its age and gender specificity—in direct contrast with the casualness of spoken English.

Leah blinked and smiled at the doctor. Elder Shim's beak nose and triangular chin were not considered by Koreans to be desirable features, but his intelligent and amiable manner softened the angles of his face. Her husband was more classically handsome than Elder Shim, but Leah liked how the doctor was always so quick to smile, showing his neat row of white teeth—the reward for a lifetime of eschewing coffee and cigarettes.

Douglas folded his arms—the position he took for making a medical diagnosis. "That song was a great favorite of my father's." He focused on the pretty deaconess, lowering his voice conspiratorially. "But in your case, the song itself doesn't really matter. You're the only real singer we've got."

Leah laughed in surprise, suppressing her guilty pleasure at the sharpness of his comment. She found herself reddening, embarrassed by the attention she'd craved; she tucked her hands and arms deep inside the billowy sleeves of her choir robe, her hands clutching her bare white elbows. Her long, elegant neck dipped, and the color in her face made her look alive and young.

Douglas tried to think of something else to say to make her stay a little longer. He liked looking at her up close. Hundreds of parishioners circled about, but Douglas sought to carve out this private moment with her. From his pew at church, he often stared at her hands, her fingers lean and strong like a pianist's. Her physical hesitations—the apparent nervousness—appealed to him strongly; she was quiet but vibrant in her feeling. And when she sang, his heart clutched at her sound. In her yellow robe with its black sleeve stripes and trim, she resembled a monarch butterfly—fluttering and resisting flight. At this proximity, her skin was the color of light cream, and there were no lines in her face. Her figure was still girlish.

"Casey must have told you," Douglas said. He would talk to her about Ella's wedding. That would be a safe topic.

"Hmm?" Leah looked at him, not knowing what to say.

"The wedding? Did Casey...?"

Leah shook her head slowly, still saying nothing. How could she tell him that she hadn't spoken to her own daughter in six months?

It was clear that she was puzzled. "We sent you the invitation for

Ella's wedding. I think Ella mailed it on Thursday, or was it Monday?" He was not good with dates. His office manager governed his schedule in a way that he could just show up and not have to recall very much of life's logistics.

Leah finally spoke. "Oh, I didn't know. That's so nice for Ella. And you. You must be so pleased. Congratulations."

Douglas waved this off. "No. It's so nice of your daughter to help Ella so much. How proud you must be of her. She's a wonderful—"

Leah frowned, denying the compliment as politely as she could. It wasn't appropriate to agree with another person's flattering assessment of your child. But why was he saying this?

"She seems to like her job," Douglas said.

"Have you seen her recently?" Leah asked, trying to sound calm.

"Yes," Douglas exclaimed. "She didn't tell you?"

Leah shook her head, hoping that the elder would believe that Casey could forget to mention something like that.

"I had dinner with Casey and Ella the other night. Tuesday?" Douglas made a face, unsure of the date. "Anyway, it was after we went to visit the wedding hall. Ted—" He stopped himself. "My future son-in-law..."

Leah nodded vigorously, wanting him to continue.

"He works with Casey. At Kearn Davis."

She'd heard of it.

"I don't think they work together, but I think they're in the same building."

"How?" she asked. How did this come to be?

"Ted helped Casey get an interview. She didn't say?" Douglas managed to sound as if he weren't judging her.

Leah cast her eyes down, pretending she'd forgotten—to make it her fault for not having said something earlier. This was in Leah's nature, to take the blame for things. "That was so kind of your daughter. To ask. To ask her fiancé to help Casey. That was so good. Thank you for helping my daughter," she said. In all the years she'd known the doctor, this was their longest conversation.

"Don't thank me. I didn't do anything. And knowing Ted..." Douglas paused, trying to think of the right way to speak of his daughter's future husband. "I don't think he would've gotten Casey an interview unless she was more than qualified."

The doctor did not like the groom. Leah could see that.

"Are you cold?" he asked her. The deaconess was hugging herself; her hands and arms were hidden inside her sleeves.

Leah withdrew her hands, feeling self-conscious and childish. She was bewildered by this news. Casey had phoned a few times to say she was fine—this was what Tina had said. When pressed, Tina had said, her voice full of resentment, "Casey's a big girl. She can take care of herself."

Douglas observed the deaconess's silence as if she were a patient coming by for an initial consultation. A patient told you things about herself more by the way she sat and in the way she looked at you than by what she verbalized. That was Bedside Manner 101. It was important to know this, because patients lied. Nearly always because they were ashamed. You had to look at a patient's face, her eyes, the way her eyelids twitched or didn't. Her hands and mouth revealed things, too. Your diagnosis depended on it and, consequently, the patient's health. Leah's face looked calm enough, but her dark eyes expressed tremendous anxiety. She hadn't known that her daughter was Ella's bridesmaid. How was that? he wondered. Why?

"Have you seen Casey's dress?" Douglas asked, watching her.

Leah shook her head no, feeling even more upset but not knowing why exactly.

"It's very pretty. Ella chose the dress, and Casey picked the color. It's the color of persimmons."

Leah could imagine Casey in a flame orange dress.

Encouraged by her smile, he said, "In the courtyard of my father's house, there was a grove of very old persimmon trees. It bore a great deal of fruit. Just delicious. I can still taste them." He closed his eyes, and his mouth watered. "After the season ended, the cook used to dry the fruit and make this drink, you know..." Douglas tapped his head to jog his memory. "It's got cinnamon, and it's very cold. My mother used to love it."

She knew the drink he was speaking of. It had been a long time since she'd tasted it.

"Do you like persimmons?"

"Yes. The small flat ones." Leah's eyes grew wet, and she blinked back her tears.

He nodded in sympathy, believing that she'd been moved by a memory of their homeland. Food could do that, he thought. He also found comfort in knowing that they liked the same kind of fruit.

But that didn't mean anything, he chided himself. How silly even to notice. Douglas had a strong wish to touch her. If she were a patient, he would be allowed to put his hands on her face.

"You know, ever since Ella was little, she's admired your daughter. She's so happy that Casey is going to be her bridesmaid. You can't imagine how much."

Leah tried to look pleased. She'd always liked Elder Shim, felt safe in his company, but suddenly she wanted to flee. None of this was his fault. He was the father of a girl getting married. He had every right to be happy.

"Excuse me..." Leah bowed. "My husband is waiting." She bowed again.

"Yes, yes," he said, "of course. Good-bye, then." Douglas felt like a fool. She was married. A deaconess. He shook his head briskly, as if he could cast off his feelings this way. Why did he never feel anything like this—a kind of stirring in himself—for any of the number of single women he was constantly being asked to meet? Then he marched to the cloakroom to retrieve his overcoat and muffler.

Two weeks later, Leah lied to her husband, saying she had a hair appointment. Ten days had already passed since she'd received Ella's wedding invitation, but it had taken as many days for her to come up with that alibi. She was headed, on foot, to the return address printed on the invitation envelope, guessing correctly that this was where Ella lived. On the way, she bought a large bouquet of white chrysanthemums and ilex branches.

A uniformed doorman stood in front of Ella's building, and in the lobby, a man in a suit and necktie sat at the concierge desk. He directed Leah to the modern leather armchairs, and she sat down—afraid to touch the magazines on the glass coffee table. Her shoulders were curved with worry; the invitation envelope and flowers rested on her lap. In the space between the chairs, she tucked away her leather purse, one of the first gifts her husband had ever bought for her. They'd been walking along the market in Myeongdong when a bag hawker called out to them. Joseph had asked her which one she liked. All her life, she'd carried bags made of heavy string and tarpaulin. After looking over the stall, she'd chosen a leather bag—square, without any trimming, and cheap. Joseph had studied it, then put it back on its hook, and Leah had felt ashamed at having chosen something so costly. But to her shock, he'd told the hawker to pull down another bag—similar in style and the most expensive one there. She'd protested, saying she couldn't possibly accept it. No one had ever bought her a present before. When she'd gotten it home, her brothers had teased her for days because she wouldn't let the bottom of the bag touch the ground. The bag, now over two decades old, still worked fine, so she couldn't throw it away or buy a new one. Its size was ideal for holding her Bible and hymnal, as well as her choral music and Joseph's newspapers. But against the backdrop of the pristine Upper East Side lobby of a luxury condominium, the bag was more a shabby briefcase than a lady's handbag. Leah picked it up again from the floor, sorry for such a thing that had served her so faithfully; then she laid it next to her on the chair, covering it with her woolen scarf.

The concierge called out to her, "Madam, Miss Shim asked you to go up. She's on twelve. Twelve G."

When the elevator doors opened, she spotted Ella standing in front of her apartment. As soon as Ella saw her, she bowed deep from the waist, the way she'd greet her father's guests at his home. Using flawless Korean, Ella invited Deaconess Cho in, accepting the flowers from her hand and thanking her.

Leah ducked into the apartment and sat on the edge of an ottoman. Right away, she pulled out the Bible from her purse. Without removing her coat or gloves, she bent her head in prayer. Her lips moved, but she made no sound. She thanked God for her safe arrival and prayed for knowledge about her daughter.

Casey's mother was enacting the ritual that the others had done at her father's house. The Korean Christians would dash into the living room, sit, shut their eyes, and mumble prayers of thanksgiving. Ella was used to this practice of devotion; it was as natural to her as taking off her shoes upon entering the house or floating pine seeds into her father's ginseng tea after adding his two teaspoons of honey. From her blue-and-white sofa, she would wait for Deaconess Cho to tell her why she had come.

Leah opened her eyes. The living room was clean and light: The fabric-upholstered furniture looked fresh, and a collection of jade plants of varying sizes in ceramic pots rested on the wide windowsill. A big kitchen was visible through the pass-through window. On the white marble kitchen counter, there were brand-new appliances

Leah had seen advertised in the Macy's Cellar circulars and different-shaped cutting boards stacked neatly against the tea green tile backsplash, a hickory block holding knives with black matching handles, and a row of cookbooks on a wall shelf. Leah, who'd never cared much for accumulating things, felt a prick of envy, but not for herself. She could never give the same things to her own daughters, who deserved these items no less than Ella.

Leah reminded herself that this child had no mother. "I didn't want to bother you, but is she here?"

"No."

Leah covered her face with her hands.

"I'm sorry." Ella bit her lip.

"Then can you tell me where my daughter is? I haven't seen her in six months."

Ella shook her head no again. Casey wouldn't have wanted Ella to tell her. Even Casey's sister wasn't allowed to tell. She glanced down at her own stocking feet.

Casey's father had hit her and thrown her out. She had not gone into the details. It had never occurred to Ella that there might be a plausible reason, or that her parents could be sorry and want her back, and since Ella had grown up without a mother of her own, she had somehow forgotten about Deaconess Cho. Casey never talked about her. Ella had not considered Leah's suffering. It was then that Ella realized she had no mother who'd search for her in this way. She was surprised by how bitterly she felt this lack—for a contingency that would never occur.

The bright, sun-filled apartment grew quiet and strained. The two women sat in mutual silence. The girl's refusal to tell her where her daughter was staying made Leah feel spurned by God Himself. Somewhere nearby, her daughter was hiding from her. She was well, as far as she knew, but somehow that made it worse. Her own child did not want her. When Casey was born, Leah remembered looking down at the wet, red face and thinking, I would die for you, and the fierce attachment that followed in being a mother had frightened her. Her love for her husband would never equal what she felt for her children. But how could this impossibly lucky girl Ella know what it was like to love that way? Ella didn't have a mother, and she had no children. Her apparent sympathy and kindness did not equal true experience, did it? Leah's sobs were low and blocked—she was ashamed to cry like this when a mother should be collected and determined in the face of life's crises. But life, for Leah, was overwhelming and terrifying—in every corner lurked greater dangers. It wasn't possible to plan or be safe: Life would not let you alone.

The mums and the red berries remained on the coffee table, with no one getting up to put them in water. Ella glided the box of tissues toward Casey's mother.

"Why?" Leah sniffled. "Why doesn't she call me?"

Ella couldn't answer her.

"What won't you girls tell me? Is there more I need to know? I'm her mother. I have the right to know." Leah was crying and shouting. The humiliation was unbearable. "Do you know what that means? I'm her mother."

How was she supposed to know? Ella didn't even have a mother. As a girl, she used to study Casey and her mother on Sundays during coffee hour. Ted had taught her that everyone fell under the categories of the Myers-Briggs personality test: Casey was an obvious Extravert, and Leah was an Introvert. Casey's younger sister, Tina, resembled her mother in her prettiness; their faces were arranged in a similar pattern. But Casey and her mother cried the same way—with a kind of elegiac heartbreak.

Could anyone see her own connection with her dead mother? Ella wondered. Her father never spoke of her mother anymore. In the third grade, when she learned the story of the birth of Athena, Ella had wanted to believe that she, too, had sprung forth from her father's head. That was a child's magical thought, but in the presence of Casey's mother, Ella felt her mother's loss far more profoundly than she'd thought possible.

Leah took a tissue, wiped her eyes, and blew her nose loudly. She smiled bravely for Ella's sake. None of this was the child's fault. She was being loyal to her friend. In a way, that was admirable.

"Would you give Casey something for me?"

"Of course." Ella wanted to be useful somehow.

Leah opened her Bible, and from the middle of the book, she pulled out a fat white envelope—the dry-cleaning store address printed on its upper left corner. Every month, along with eleven other women from her church choir, Leah put two hundred dollars into the *geh* pot. Each month, the pot rotated among them. Last month had finally been her turn. Leah had put the entire two thousand four hundred dollars in the envelope for Casey. Leah slid the envelope toward Ella. "Here. Please give this to her. Tell her that Mommy wants her to call. When she can—" Leah's voice broke again.

Ella tried not to cry herself.

"Your father said you're marrying... Ted. A nice boy who helped Casey get a job."

Ella nodded, proud of Ted's act of kindness, never having believed that he was as selfish as others saw him.

"I hope you will be blessed. With Ted. And in your life together." Leah smiled. Such a pretty girl, she thought, without question the prettiest girl at church, and so ladylike. She moved like a girl who had come from the best family—it showed in the way she walked, how she spoke, the way she looked at you. Wealth didn't make you proper, Leah thought, having seen so much evidence to the contrary, but once in a while, there was proof that there was a kind of proper breeding. Everything about Ella revealed her *yangban* home. But even in this beautiful apartment with expensive furniture with everything already paid for, Leah could see the child's loneliness, and she felt a kind of ache for her.

Leah smiled, and this time she spoke in English, even though her words were limited. "You're a good daughter to your father. Ella, try and be happy. With all your fortune—" And Leah shook her head at herself, knowing that fortune didn't have the same meaning in English that it did in Korean. "You have so much blessing."

Ella smiled at her, having been told this many times before (the word Casey's mother was searching for in Korean was *bok*—a kind of luck and blessing rolled up into one), and it did not occur to her to argue with these kinds of well-wishers that she would've given up nearly everything if her mother could have been alive. No one wanted to see how she might be missing something, too—that if Ella were to run away, she had no mother who'd search for her.

Ella fingered the white envelope, then found herself moving it near the tissue box. "Casey works in midtown. You know that already." She looked into Leah's eyes, making sure that she hadn't been the one who'd told her this.

"Your father said she works with Ted. At Kearn Davis. Nor far from me. At the store. I have a customer there," Leah said, recalling Mr. Perell, a customer who was someone important at that company, and how he liked to have his shirts hand-pressed and got very angry if the collars got smashed flat during delivery.

"Would you like to go visit her at the office?" Ella asked her, realizing the absurdity of her own question. It was hardly possible to imagine Leah—a slight Korean woman with a crown of white hair, wearing a dark woolen home-sewn coat—in the vast marble lobby of the investment bank. Even in her living room, Casey's mother looked out of place and out of time.

"During the week, I...," Leah stammered. "My husband doesn't know I'm here. He thinks I'm getting a haircut. On Saturday mornings, he can work without me for a while, so I can run errands," she explained hurriedly in Korean, thinking that a young American girl like Ella couldn't possibly understand the details that made up her life: sorting dirty shirts, darning missing buttons, and taking up hems of designer jeans for teenage customers whom she addressed as "miss"; trying to find the best cut of meat that was on special at the Key Food for dinner, scrubbing toilets on Saturday nights, cooking her husband's dinner at a set hour and making sure there was always enough beer and whiskey in the house for him; and lastly, all the places a woman like her didn't enter.

Leah looked lost. Ella felt terrible for not helping her.

"She's staying with a friend. Three blocks from here," Ella said. She got up from her seat almost mechanically, as if she were unconscious of her movements, and went to retrieve the pad and pencil kept by the phone. She jotted down the address.

Casey would be home at this hour. It was the first Saturday of January, and it was only nine in the morning. Jay would probably be asleep, and Casey would be smoking her Marlboro Lights in the living room, reading the papers or a novel. On her second cup of black coffee. Those were Casey's weekend habits; Ella had not forgotten them.

Leah stared at Ella, not knowing if this was some sort of test. She couldn't speak. She took the piece of paper and the envelope and tucked them into her Bible.

After Leah left the apartment, the only evidence of her visit was the dark red berries and the white flowers with their thin, curving petals resting on the coffee table, still wrapped in their clear cellophane. Ella went to get a vase and some water.

13 | RECOGNITION

*C*ASEY HAD GOTTEN UP AT FIVE O'CLOCK on a Saturday, because it had become habit for her to do so. They were living together now, and it was only mildly different from when she'd stay with him during the weekends when she was still in school. She had more or less agreed to marry him; this life was practice. While Jay slept in, she'd dashed through her daily Bible study and verse selection, and now she was finishing up the head size for her third attempt at the gathered beret assignment. With a cigarette hanging off her lips, she pick-stitched the belting ribbon into her homework hat.

"Shit," she said, her sewing thread having knotted up again. Once again, she'd forgotten to lick the length of it, as her teacher had instructed. With Jay never home, her workday ending at six, and her weekends free, for the first time in her life, Casey had the luxury of a hobby—she was learning how to make hats. Her first FIT classes in dressmaking, taken two summers ago, had not been as pleasurable, because the courses had been more demanding than any she'd taken at Princeton and because her efforts were scarcely reflected in her final product. Making clothes was difficult. Also, she'd been outdistanced by her peers, many of whom had been sewing clothes since they were little girls. Leah, a resourceful housewife and talented seamstress, had never wanted Casey and Tina to cook, sew, or clean. Being an ace student in reading, writing, and arithmetic, however, had almost zero value in terms of drafting an accurate skirt pattern. After getting a pair of C's, she'd decided to buy her clothes rather than create them.

But millinery was something else. Making hats was no less difficult than Dressmaking I and II; again, the majority of her FIT peers in millinery were technically superior, but Casey felt she understood instinctively the aesthetics of hats and why women wanted them. It was her intention to take all four classes and get the certificate—the night class schedule was convenient, and her deskmates were hilarious. In her few months on the trading floor, Casey felt occasionally exhausted by the dick-swinging quality of Kearn Davis, and it was a relief to spend time with women who were not mainly focused on beating one another.

As a millinery student, Casey was mediocre. Her hand stitches were crooked, her machine sewing zigzag, and her early attempts at machine welting her brims had been a disaster. Last week, the millinery sewing machine chewed up two thirty-dollar beaver hat bodies. The running joke—with her deskmates, Polly, Susan, and Roni, a police officer, accountant, and gourmet cheese seller, respectively—was: "So what was it that you'd studied at Princeton?" The name *Princeton* was almost shouted. Two of them had gone to community college, and Roni had gone to SUNY Binghamton. In the company of these vibrant women, Casey felt less lonely in the world. Virginia wrote letters every week, but her stay in Italy was indefinite; Ella and Ted were more and more of a package deal, and Tina was back at school and in the thrall of sleeping with Chul.

Privately, Casey thought it was remarkable to see a flat square of fabric become a baseball hat and a leftover piece of felt grow into a rosette. The fact that she struggled at millinery—compared with her ease at writing term papers, taking exams, selling hairpins, making hotel arrangements for brokers, and scheduling equity sales conferences—humbled her, but not in a bad way. Frieda, her millinery teacher, murmured reluctantly that although her construction grade was a C+, her design grade was a B+. "I see improvement," Frieda said. That comment prompted Casey to buy a round for her friends after class that night.

For four years, Casey had sold hats at Sabine's with price tags ranging from fifty dollars to one that actually cost twelve hundred dollars (Elizabeth Taylor's dresser had bought it for her to wear to Ascot). The prices had appalled her, but now, after spending twelve hours hand-sewing a homely denim chef's hat, which included pulling out all the uneven gathering stitches and starting again, Casey wondered how anyone ever made any money. On the first day of class, Frieda had warned all the millinery hopefuls that hats were not a growing industry—its heyday had long passed; in America, only eccentrics and religious women wore them.

The phone rang, and Casey picked up right away, not wanting it to wake Jay.

It was Ella.

"You did what? What the fuck?" Casey shouted. "Damn it." Ella was apologizing, but that was irrelevant. "Bye." Casey hung up.

She shook Jay awake. He protested, rubbing his eyes with one hand, fumbling with the other in search of his eyeglasses on the bedside. The clock-radio's green LCD letters read 9:15—the first day he'd had off in months.

"My mother is on her way. Can you please stay in the bedroom and not come out until she's gone?" She sat on the edge of the bed, her eyes wide open.

"Baby"—Jay stretched his neck out from under the quilt like a turtle—"I'm not hiding in my own house."

"Have it your way." Casey covered her mouth with her hand. If she waited in the lobby, pretending that she was heading out, she might be able to overtake her mother. Talk at the coffee shop on Second Avenue. Though naturally her mother would wonder why she couldn't come up.

Jay studied Casey's anguished expression. He felt sorry for her.

"What do you expect me to do? Hide in a closet? Sit out on the fire escape? It's freezing outside." He dropped his face in the pillow, then looked up, having thought of something else to say. "For God's sake, Casey, grow up. You just turned twenty-three years old. You're still going to lie to your mother about me?"

But Casey didn't say anything, unable to express the pain she felt. Her lips whitened at the pressure of her jaw clenching. How could he possibly understand what it would mean for her mother to find her here? She suddenly hated him for being an American and herself for feeling so foreign when she was with him. She hated his ideals of rugged individualism, self-determination—this vain idea that life was what you made of it—as if it were some sort of paint-by-numbers kit. Only the most selfish person on earth could live that way. Casey was selfish, she knew that, but she had no wish to hurt anyone. If her rotten choices hurt her, well then, she'd be willing to take that wager, but it was hard to think of letting her parents down again and again. But her choices were always hurting her parents, or so they said. Yet Casey was an American, too—she had a strong desire to be happy and to have love, and she'd never considered such wishes to be Korean ones.

She went to get her coat. Jay sank his head in the pillow. Then he sprang up and pulled on a white T-shirt and the pair of sweatpants that had been draped over the armchair. He needed coffee.

"Ten minutes. I will remain in the kitchen obscured from view for ten minutes. Then I demand a proper introduction," Jay said, adding, "I will do this because I love you."

"Thank you," Casey said, accepting his offer gratefully. The buzzer rang, and she flew to the intercom. Her mother's warbling voice rose to her—its sound broken up by the rushing wind from the street.

"It's *Umma*," Leah said, and Casey buzzed her in.

When she opened the front door, Casey found it difficult to accept that her mother was standing in that narrow foyer. She wore the navy wool three-button coat that she'd made last winter when she and Tina were home for Christmas break. The day Leah found its Vogue pattern, she'd asked the girls if they'd like matching ones. As usual, Casey said no, and Leah made one for Tina in a sturdy black wool.

Leah looked disoriented as she glanced about the living room. Casey saw her mother's disapproval. To her, the leather sofa would look vinyl, the hand-painted flea market table would show its price of fifteen dollars, and the new gray carpet that the landlord had just tacked down was pilling too much. None of this had bothered Casey before. But her mother had just come from Ella's—with cherrywood Ethan Allen furniture and upholstery in blues and creams.

Leah stood in her coat, her cheeks reddened from the cold, her hands clutched with worry. She studied the apartment sharply, trying to learn something about her own daughter.

"Why don't you sit down?" Casey asked her mother, her voice gentle and tentative.

Leah didn't budge. "I didn't know where you were."

Her dark eyes were full of hurt. As far back as Casey could remember, her mother was terrified of travel and entering new spaces.

"How long have you been here?" Leah asked. The apartment didn't seem like her daughter's. The space felt sterile, like an office. Coffee was brewing in the kitchen; the machine sputtered loudly. There was some sewing and blue cotton on the wooden table near the window. Who was sewing? she wondered. "Why didn't you come home?"

"Daddy said to get out." She was too grown up to say "Daddy," but it was too late to call him anything else.

"Why didn't you just say you were sorry? Do you know how hard your father works? Everything he ever did was for you girls." Leah shook her head briskly, upset by her daughter's stubbornness.

Casey could almost hear Jay's steady breathing in the kitchen.

Leah bent over her purse beside her shoes. She pulled out her Bible, zipped open the cover, and withdrew the white envelope. In her rush and shock, she'd forgotten to say her thanksgiving prayer when she'd reached Casey's apartment. She'd neglected to praise God when it was He who'd led her here. And she felt awful for lying to her husband. Leah wanted to leave then, get back to the store.

"Here." She handed the envelope to Casey quickly, avoiding any contact between them.

Casey stared at the thick packet. "No. It's okay. I have a job. I'm fine."

Leah turned to leave. Casey wanted to hold her back, to touch her. It amazed her how much she wanted her mother to touch her, too, and the more persistent this desire grew, the more Casey pulled back, because this need felt dangerous, as though the touch alone might burn her alive. Her mother had come to give her money (what else came in these envelopes anyway except for tidy stacks of twenty-dollar bills scrounged by immigrants?)—and Tina would need this money for tuition, and there was her father's retirement to consider.

"*Umma* will go now.... *Ahpa ga*—" Leah stopped herself.

Casey nodded. Her father didn't know about the visit. "Is he okay?"

Leah nodded. *Ahpa* is just okay. You have broken his heart. He has given up on you, and now it is your turn to fight him for his love. Don't you know, Leah wondered, that you cannot live well without your father's blessing? In Genesis, Rebekah had encouraged her younger son, Jacob, to deceive her older son, Esau, and their father, Isaac, so her favored Jacob could receive the blessing. Rebekah was wrong to use trickery, but she had understood something essential about the difficulties of life and the protection of a father's blessing.

You are my favorite, Leah wanted to say. Instead, she zipped up the Bible with care, making sure to tuck in the frayed ribbon page holder. The day she left Korea, her father had taken a bus from their distant country town to Kimpo airport to bring her this Bible. In the crowded terminal, they'd sat beside each other, knees touching on bucket-shaped seats, and he'd held her hands in his. He'd prayed for her. Once she was seated on the plane—her girls all settled in with their apple slices and sock dolls for the long trip ahead—Leah had loosened the knot of the dark blue fabric-wrapped package. The Bible's brown leather cover reminded her of her father's tanned face—wrinkled and thickly mottled, like the bark of a tree. Later that year, he died suddenly, and Leah felt that it violated nature for a child to live so far from her home.

The clatter of a dish came from the kitchen. "*Uh-muh,*" Leah said in surprise, but Casey wasn't startled. Seconds later, a young American man stepped out of the kitchen and walked toward her, wearing gray sweatpants, smiling, his wavy hair tousled, his eyes puffy from sleep. He held out his hand to greet her, and Leah didn't know what to do.

Casey had fully intended to come for him. He just couldn't wait. Her mother was stunned by his appearance.

Leah turned to Casey, hoping her daughter would calm her somehow—to explain this away. But Casey looked irritated more than shocked. Then Leah figured out that she must've been living with this American. Her daughter, who'd gone to college but never had any money, would've needed a roommate. The place wasn't fancy like Ella's, but the rent would've been at least fifteen hundred or something high like that. Her customers were always complaining about rents in the city. The man would think Casey must be some sort of whore. Was there more than one bedroom? Leah clutched her coat lapels and tried to look less disturbed than she felt.

"This is Jay. Jay Currie," Casey said. Her mother didn't have to say another word. Casey could read her thought bubble. "He's my fiancé. We are going to get married. I was going to—"

Leah nodded quickly, still unable to shake the man's outstretched hand. She turned to leave—it felt as though her shoulders were frozen, and she had to tell her feet to move.

"*Umma*, you should stay and have coffee. With us. Can't you?" Casey bit down on her molars.

Leah faced the door with her back to Casey.

Casey stared hard at her mother's long shoulder blades beneath her coat.

"I don't understand. Maybe your *umma* is not so smart, but... How? I didn't raise my daughters to—"

"What? Sleep with white men?"

"No. I didn't raise my daughter to lie to me." Leah turned to face Casey. She felt lost.

Jay rubbed his neck with his left hand. Casey's mother had white hair and possessed the face of a pretty child. She spoke Korean with a gentle dignity, and though he didn't speak the language, it was possible to comprehend that she was unhappy. He felt foolish for having forced this. But Casey's refusal to introduce him to her mother and father was offensive. His friends' parents universally adored him. "Charming" was the word most often used to describe Jay Currie by that set. He loved Casey. She had agreed to marry him. Casey was curious, bold, and smart. Quirky in her thinking. She could be very funny, sometimes petulant like a child. In bed, they were magical—it wasn't a word he would have used comfortably, not something he'd say out loud, but when they made love, the world was ordered in a better way. During sex, he believed in whatever she thought of as God. Was it adolescent to view sex as a manifestation of divinity? He could have written about that during college. Regardless, those sorority girls had shown him how unsavory it was to be that way with women. Some guys could do that without regret, fantasized of such things, but it turned out that he was old-fashioned after all. Love. Yes, he actually wanted to love a girl to sleep with her.

He looked down at what he was wearing; his feet were bare except for a sprinkling of pale hair on the knuckles of his toes. His mother called him her tall, fair hobbit. He must've made a terrible first impression. All his life he'd won people over, collecting every vote that was needed, gaining every inch of coveted territory. *I'm not a bad person,* Jay wanted to tell her. He wanted to make Casey happy. Would it be impossible for him to make Casey's mother like him?

Jay cleared his throat. "I wish you'd stay. I would love to invite you to breakfast. We can go anywhere. There's a wonderful hotel on Madison. I'd need only a minute to put on a tie."

Leah said nothing, still dazed by what she was saw. Her daughter was living with this man. Her daughter was getting married.

What do you do with silence? Casey wondered. It was easier to yell back at her father. It was impossible to beat a person who refused to fight, who'd never had a wish to win. She tried to give back the envelope, but her mother said no. Casey held on to it.

There was no obvious resemblance between them, Jay noticed, except for how intensely they stared at things. Sometimes the way Casey looked at a thing was as if she were putting an object through heat, so focused was her gaze.

"I can call now to get a table," Jay said. "The Mark has a delicious brunch."

Leah turned to him. It was only after he'd spoken for a while that she realized he was younger than he looked. There were soft pouches under his eyes. He couldn't have been more than twenty-five or twenty-six. He was probably Casey's college boyfriend.

"Thank you. I have to go back to the store. It was nice meeting you, Mr. . . ." She halted, unable to remember his last name.

She gave up trying and decided to leave. This was too much for her.

Casey stared at her mother's small white hand resting on the brass doorknob painted dove gray, trying to remember the sensation of her mother's warm palm. They must have held hands long ago. Wasn't that right? Back in Seoul, her mother used to walk her to kindergarten in the mornings and pick her up at the end of the day. Where was Tina then? There had been a yellow beret and a matching satchel with a shoulder strap for kindergartners. Funny how certain things were so clear in her mind. Yet the outline of the squat concrete school building was more shadowy. The school was behind the town clinic run by a female pharmacist who gave her Charms sour balls whenever her mother went to fill a prescription.

Her mother would drop her off at the school, then walk away hurriedly, as if she were being followed, and Casey would stand at the school gate to smell the warm scent of her mother's hand in her own palm, wishing she could run fast and catch up with *Umma*.

Leah opened the door and left. Jay sat on the sofa, still wanting a cup of coffee but feeling too exhausted to get up again. Casey couldn't speak to him, so she went to shower.

14 | HOLD

$\mathcal{S}$ABINE JUN GOTTESMAN HAD NO CHILDREN of her own. Her husband, Isaac, who was twenty-five years her senior, had four children from his two previous marriages, and although he could have afforded private school tuition fees, weddings, and legacies for many more children, he chose his third wife on the basis of her intelligence and devotion, taking into favorable consideration that for Sabine, her career was her greatest creative act. From the beginning, her policy had been no children, and at his age, he preferred to enjoy his twin grandsons during brunch on the first Saturday of the month with his third daughter and favorite son-in-law. Neither Isaac nor Sabine had ever felt comfortable around infants.

Isaac's adult children—three married girls and a boy who was taking over his business—liked Sabine. He'd anticipated some resistance about her age, but they approved of her, refraining from calling her the usual names. All four children were exhausted from years of distrusting their half-siblings from the other marriage and were merely trying to hang on to the attentions of their charismatic father, who was sensitive to criticism. They were relieved that there would be no more heirs, and to boot, Sabine possessed a fortune of her own. Their father's third wife was treated as a chic aunt who sent birthday gifts from Asprey and Hermès. They did not discuss Sabine with their respective mothers.

If young people preferred Sabine, she also preferred them and took to employees who were floating through a life in retail. She adopted their shapeless hopes, sent them through FIT, Parsons, or the School of Visual Arts, and they became buyers or managers, and a couple of them owned notable boutiques on Elizabeth Street. Tonight, Casey Han, a Korean-American and a great favorite of Sabine's, and her fiancé, Jay, were coming to dinner.

Before company came, it was Isaac's habit to check the bar—an enclosed space in the gallery-style living room behind a pair of rose-wood paneled doors. This was something he preferred to do himself, having tended bar while going to business school. Once, a comely benefactor of the ballet asked Isaac for a kir royale at his home, and after tasting it, she'd scrutinized her host, unable to believe that Isaac Gottesman—the charming mogul who owned dozens of blocks of prime Manhattan real estate and served as trustee of both the Columbia Business School and the New York City Ballet—could mix her favorite cocktail better than Yanni, the barman at the Oak Room. Isaac was a man who enjoyed knowing how to do things like that. He could pull coins out of children's ears and make a clean three-point shot.

Sabine entered the living room fresh from her shower, scented richly with her vetiver perfume. She wore a long Nehru jacket with slim matching pants. The shrimp color of the fabric made her dewy complexion even prettier. She kissed her husband's just shaved cheek and asked him for a neat whiskey. Each night, she had an aperitif before dinner, and with her meal, she drank two glasses of red wine.

In a wonderful mood, Sabine carried her drink to her reading chair near the solarium to enjoy the last bit of April dusk. She sipped her whiskey slowly and opened a book about Diego Rivera resting on the Giacometti coffee table. Before meeting Sabine, Isaac had never met anyone who actually read the text in these coffee table art books.

His wife was only forty-two, and in their marriage, she'd grown more refined. They'd met twelve years before when she came to a lease closing at his offices. That morning, Isaac overheard a young Asian woman tell the receptionist in her accented English that she was the new tenant for one of his buildings in Chelsea—a thirty-thousand-square-foot raw space on Eighteenth Street. Back then, her voice was louder and her tone more insistent. A speech therapist had since cured her of these inferior qualities. Out of curiosity, Isaac sat in on the closing, and the leasing broker who worked for the man whose name was above all the doors and engraved on the letterhead stammered, not knowing if his tack should be carrot or stick with the tenant Mr. Gottesman could not stop staring at.

At the closing, Sabine was far more intelligent than her broker or expensive lawyer. While she signed the six copies of the telephone-book-size lease, she evinced no fear at entering into a three-million-dollar, ten-year, triple-net lease with Gottesman Real Property. That morning, Isaac gave her every term she'd asked for. She was thirty years old then, he found out at the closing dinner—a meal he'd contrived—and three months later, she agreed to marry him. When he brought up a prenuptial agreement, she said without blinking, "Isaac, I have found you, and I will never leave you. I intend to make you happy. Never, ever again insult me with your talk of money." Against his matrimonial lawyer's advice, Isaac married her without one.

From the beginning, he'd been attracted to her toughness, and even now he admired no one as much as he admired her. His Italian mother had been prone to rages, and his Jewish father had been soft-spoken and muddleheaded. They had been barely middle-class, and he and his sister had never had the things they wanted. His parents died before his first divorce from Kate, a kindhearted WASP who felt at best neutral about sex, and his second marriage to Carla, a mean beauty from Venezuela who cuckolded him with his business partner. A few years shy of seventy, he wondered what they would have made of number three, his Korean wife—the retail tycoon.

True to her word, Sabine had become indispensable to his well-being. She bought him vitamins. Every morning, she snipped squares of wheatgrass they grew in a long flat pan on the sill of their sunny kitchen window. They were Park Avenue farmers, he joked. She fed the clippings into a juicer, then served him a double shot, resulting in grassy burps for the rest of the morning. His cardiologist was delighted—Isaac had shed forty pounds, his blood pressure medication was no longer necessary, and his sexual vigor was excellent. Yet he felt deprived.

Semiretired, Isaac worked only four hours a day, and he had a great deal of time to think. And in his leisure, he thought about love. In the pursuit of his ambition, he had neglected Kate; and after he became rich, he'd sported Carla around like a fine race car; and with Sabine, he saw that he did not know how to love her because she did not show him any need. Sabine was an ideal partner, and he'd never leave her, but Isaac found himself sleeping with other women. At sixty-seven years old, what he wanted more than anything was romance, and it flabbergasted him that this would never be possible with his wife. Sabine was incapable of loving him in the way he wanted to be loved—with a desperation or a sloppiness. He had married her because she would never fall apart, but he saw that all he wanted now was to care for a woman, and Sabine's self-sufficiency made him obsolete.

Casey and Jay arrived.

Sabine kissed Casey, her left cheek and then her right, and then she kissed Jay. "My darlings, my darlings," she said, her arms open like a conductor's, her fingers spread apart.

Isaac hugged Casey. When he let her go, she took in the spectacular sight of the enormous white dogwood branches in Ching vases at the opposite ends of the room.

Sabine's designer had recently made over the apartment. Long tailored sofas were upholstered in shades of white wool, and armchairs in oxblood velvets dotted the room like scarlet blooms over fresh snow. Their collection of ancient Chinese furniture was precious but inviting—the dark wood adding warmth to the cool Palladian-style interior. It was a room a person felt lucky to be invited to—this having been Sabine's goal.

"Congratulations," Isaac said.

"Thank you," Jay said promptly, and Casey smiled at Isaac warmly.

"No ring?" Sabine glanced at Casey's left hand.

"Later," Casey said, thinking it was rude of her to ask. They were planning to choose it together next weekend.

"Soon," Jay said.

Isaac went to the bar and brought them glasses of chilled Vouvray and for himself a glass of seltzer. The four of them raised their glasses. "To love," Isaac said.

"And prosperity," added Sabine.

The dinner was served by the housekeeper: spring pea soup, John Dory with salsify, cheese, and for dessert, poached pears and ginger yogurt. During the meal, Jay explained the plot of *King Lear*, which was playing at Lincoln Center, and Sabine paid careful attention to what he was saying.

"So he gave everything away before he died?" she asked. Even as a generous person, she found it hard to accept such foolishness.

Jay nodded—his wide-eyed expression matching her sentiment. He was pleased to exploit his English major for some useful purpose. At school, he'd carefully read over twenty of Shakespeare's plays and most of his sonnets. In his senior year, he'd written about Ovid's influence on Shakespeare. If prompted and encouraged, he would've recited sonnets after the coffee.

Isaac preferred ballet—introduced to him by his daughters. He'd never been much of a reader. However, he was impressed by Jay's exuberance for the play.

The coffee was served with petit fours from Bonté, and Isaac tapped his head, remembering the champagne. "Not much of a bartender, am I?"

He brought over a bottle of vintage Krug sloshing in an ice bucket and four flutes.

"So have you set the date?" he asked.

"Not yet," Jay said, turning to Casey. "I'm still waiting to hear about B schools."

"So we don't know where we'll be or our schedules exactly." Casey had no idea what kind of wedding they'd have. Neither her parents nor Jay's had any extra money. Whatever bonus Jay had would go toward housing and tuition when he stopped work. Even so, they'd have to take out loans. Also, her parents wouldn't attend anyway.

Sabine turned to Jay. "Casey said you were wait-listed at Columbia."

Jay smiled. "Yes."

Sabine raised an eyebrow at Isaac, and he nodded as a matter of course. He would make a call. As a trustee, he might be able to arrange for another interview. His son-in-law had needed calls, too. It would be easier to help Jay than his own son-in-law, which had seemed a bit pushy at the time.

They raised their glasses. Sabine drank hers quickly. She adored champagne. With her left hand, she brushed the hair away from her face. The gesture looked seductive. "Jay, have you met Casey's parents?"

Sabine's face was flushed from the alcohol. She appeared cheerful, but her gaze was unyielding. Jay had met her several times before at the apartment for dinners: Up until last year, Sabine had been Casey's boss, but now she had power over his life as the trustee's wife.

"Yes. I've met her mother," he replied, half smiling.

"Leah Han," Sabine said aloud in a kind of dreamy voice. "I went to school with her, you know."

"Yes." Jay nodded. "She looked very young."

"She is young," Sabine insisted, rapping the table softly with her fist. Leah was three years her junior. She, too, had married an older man. But Leah had married a Korean, and Sabine sensed that Joseph looked down on her for having married an American. "And so am I," she said, giggling.

"Yes, of course. But her hair was gray," Jay said.

Sabine laughed out loud, then caught herself by covering her mouth. Her hand grazed over her raven hair, cut and tinted by a celebrated stylist with a hidden shop on Charles Street.

"Leah grayed early," Sabine said, her voice filling with sympathy. "Stress."

Casey's neck reddened. Jay was complimenting Sabine at her mother's expense. A few days before, Casey had stopped by the store to have a cigarette with Sabine. There, she'd mentioned the engagement and Jay's wait-list status at Columbia. Sabine had then asked her and Jay to come to dinner. She hated Jay suddenly. He had every right to feel hurt by her parents' refusal to meet him, but it didn't seem fair for him to display his resentment at the Gottesmans' coral-lacquered dining room with its heavy silverware, the white ranunculus and lysianthus arranged in crystal globes. The fineness of the linen napkin on her lap brushed beneath her fingertips. Casey felt like a serf at the queen's table.

Isaac saw Casey tuck her lower lip into her mouth. This was the face his children made before he went on a business trip when they were small. Disappointment looked exactly like that, he thought.

"Whenever I pass by your parents' shop," Isaac said, "I see your mother working on the sewing machine, and if she sees me, she waves hello." He mimicked a shy wave. "Your mom is a very beautiful woman."

Casey smiled at him, grateful for his kindness. "Everybody says that. My younger sister looks just like her. You've never met Tina. She's studying to be a doctor." She said this last part proudly.

Sabine reached across and touched Casey's bare forearm. Her fingernails were oval shaped and buffed to a high sheen today.

"You could have the wedding here in the winter or spring or sooner in Nantucket if you want a summer wedding. Wouldn't that be fun?"

"But," Casey replied, taking a breath. "That's very generous of you...." This was classic Sabine. Her gifts were legendary. Sabine did nothing that was less than triple-mint (Isaac's term), but Casey could not imagine incurring that kind of debt.

"I don't have a daughter of my own, Casey," Sabine said, her pretty fingers still holding on to Casey's forearm. Jay glanced over at Isaac, but the comment did not seem to affect him in the least. No one mentioned Isaac's children.

"How smart of you to marry young. I got lucky with Isaac. To have found him when I was thirty. But the people back home are right. Girls should marry early. You're more flexible when you're young." She drank the last of her second glass of champagne and tried to pour another, but the bottle was empty.

Isaac spoke up. "It'd be wonderful for us to have your wedding at our house. It'd be fun for us to do it. I'm an old man with half a job. I could be your wedding planner." He laughed.

Jay looked jubilant, but Casey only smiled politely.

"If it would be all right with your parents," Isaac said. Sabine had already told him that Casey's parents would not attend, but he didn't want to disregard them for Casey's sake.

Jay couldn't believe such an offer. The idea of such a wedding thrilled him. He'd been invited to many beautiful homes in his life, but the Gottesman residences—Park Avenue, Nantucket, and Aspen—took the cake. Casey told him there was also a large flat on the Place Vendôme.

"Would it be okay with your mother? To have it here or in Nantucket?" Isaac asked Jay.

"She'd love it," he replied automatically. "Are you sure?"

Sabine and Isaac said in unison, "Of course."

"Really?" Jay asked like a child at the prospect of getting a much wanted gift.

"We can have up to two hundred people," Sabine said, recalling their last trustees' dinner. The new caterer had done a very nice job, she thought. If it was a winter wedding in a large church, Casey could get a cathedral-length veil because she was tall enough. "And we can clear the room for dancing. Or we can have it at the club." She felt cheery at the idea of a party with lots of young people. Then she yawned, sleepy and happy at once.

"If it's a summer wedding, you can serve lobster." Sabine put her left elbow on the table and rested her cheek on her hand.

It wasn't that Casey was ungrateful. Sabine was offering her something she'd never had. Sabine and Isaac had married in Maui with no one in their respective families to witness the ceremony. Her parents had disowned her for marrying someone who wasn't Korean. They had called Isaac garbage because he was the leftover of two women. Her mother and father returned every letter and gift Sabine sent them. Then her mother died, and less than a year later, her father died. They never saw Sabine's exclusive department store in Chelsea or any of her beautiful homes. Sabine had told Casey once, "I made that store for them. No one loved clothes like my mother. And my father was handsome like a movie star. He wore the most beautiful neckties."

Sabine fluttered her eyelids. "We had two hundred people here. Right, sweetie?" Isaac nodded at her indulgently, like a father.

"I don't know two hundred people," Casey replied, and Jay shot her a look.

She ignored him and drank the coffee served in the paper-thin porcelain demitasse cup. Sabine was falling asleep. Every morning she woke up at four-thirty, and at ten in the evening it was already an hour past her bedtime.

"You must be tired," Casey said, covering Sabine's soft, pretty hands with her own large, mannish one.

"I'm okay," Sabine said. Her mouth made a small O even as she suppressed her yawn.

"I better put my wife to bed," Isaac said. "You kids think about the wedding. The offer is good," he said. He laughed at himself because it had sounded like deal talk.

Everyone said good-bye in the foyer. Sabine leaned in on Isaac, and he wrapped his heavy arm around her small shoulders. She was melancholy about them leaving, and Isaac hoped Casey would let them give her the wedding. A project would cheer up his wife. Sabine loved to give big parties.

The night had been warm, so there were no coats to retrieve from the closet. Casey put on the spring hat that she'd blocked herself. She'd trimmed it with pale pink silk peonies, but no one remarked on it. Sabine was standing up but snoring quietly. Casey and Jay thanked them for the dinner. And the offer. For everything. She kissed Isaac on both cheeks. The penthouse elevator that opened into their apartment came right away, and Casey and Jay stepped in. She caught Isaac's wink good-bye. He looked older than she remembered—and kindly, like someone's virile grandfather.

They were alone, and Jay slid his large hands under her linen tunic and held her waist. She let him do this, feeling nothing warm in his touch. "Can you believe they'd throw us a wedding? In that palace?" His voice was rich with pleasure and excitement. "Wow," he remarked to himself. "They're so nice."

"Yes, they're incredible," Casey said. "So generous." She pulled herself away from him as the polished brass doors opened to the lobby.

"And Isaac might help me," Jay said. Again, sounding happy and lucky.

In the street, he kept chatting, and Casey nodded, looking straight ahead. She didn't want to ruin his good feelings. But the thought that had persisted throughout the evening was: I have parents of my own.

15 | DEFAULT

ASEY AND ELLA WAITED IN THE ROCOCO-STYLE bridal suite at the Coliseum, an upscale Korean wedding hall in Flushing. The photographer had just left them to find Ted for his before-the-ceremony shots, but the divorcée makeup lady had decided to stay for the ceremony and reception—after all, the bride's doctor father had asked so nicely. She was changing into her guest clothes from her work clothes in the attached bathroom. Ella sat very still on a gilded bench, her full profile resembling a fine marble carving—oval head veiled, lush silk skirts draped over her slim legs. On bended knee, Casey smoothed out the back of Ella's gown. She alone made up the whole of Ella's bridal party, leaving her to wonder again how a girl who went to an all-girls' high school and college could care so little about her own wedding and have only one girlfriend to call upon for her important day. The rationale Casey had come up with was that Ted's fierce monopoly and control over Ella's time in combination with the girl's unwavering shyness had built a kind of fortress around her.

In half an hour, Ella would marry Ted. Yet up through today, Casey often forgot that she herself was engaged. The date was not yet set. Jay had wanted to accept the Gottesmans' offer to give them a wedding in Manhattan almost immediately, but Casey continued to temporize. He didn't know this, but she was waiting for a sign.

Ever since she was twelve or thirteen, Casey had gotten, for lack of a better word, pictures in her head. They came every day. Some mornings it was like a slide show; on others, an allusive out-of-focus shot. They were more like clues for a scavenger hunt than previews for a feature film, because Casey rarely knew what they meant or how to interpret them. For example, the year before she took her specialized public high school entrance exams, she received a clear series of images of the interior of a school building. It wasn't until the second day of her freshman year at Stuyvesant High School that she realized she already knew the entire layout of the dilapidated building on the Lower East Side, because she'd seen it in her mind. Casey never told anyone about this, because it was crazy and spooky. Once in college when she was stoned, she'd almost told Virginia but decided against it. This weird picture thing also affected insignificant aspects of her life—a pair of dark green lace-up boots with stacked heels would bubble up from nowhere, then a few months later, she'd see them in a shop. Had she conjured them up? she had to wonder. Her pictures often actualized themselves, so Casey anticipated them privately, even though she nearly always just threw up her hands at them, baffled as ever. As of yet, a picture of law school had not popped forth. It wasn't as though Casey were hoping for an icon of the scales of justice—a stack of casebooks would've sufficed. And now, as she straightened out Ella's train, Casey had no picture of herself in a white gown or image of Jay in formal dress standing beside her. As irrational as this was, she planned to set a date and speak to Sabine about the wedding when some image ultimately presented itself. There was time. Thankfully, this was Ella's day.

Ella was a beautiful girl. Who would dispute this? But as a bride, she stopped your heart. Beneath the long gossamer veil, her white skin shimmered like the inside of an abalone shell. Earlier, the photographer hadn't been able to stop snapping his camera. He left only after shooting three rolls, when one was customary. The fit of Ella's dress—sleeveless, modern U-collar, hand-sewn out of six long panels of heavy ivory silk with no suggestion of ornament or lace— was devastating. Even the irritated saleswoman at Bayard's had ultimately conceded on the winner. Casey had chosen a simple gown with the finest sewing precisely because the spare, almost severe design would not detract attention from Ella's ideal face and frame. Regardless of her own abundant feelings of inadequacy, it never failed to please Casey to see a woman at the height of her beauty. The sublime, Casey felt, deserved its due.

There was a knock, and the girls heard Dr. Shim's voice. "Honey, it's Daddy."

"It's kinda early." Casey glanced at the wall clock. She'd removed her Timex at the apartment because it clashed with her flame-colored bridesmaid dress.

"Come in, Daddy," Ella shouted, her voice happy and singsongy.

The door opened slowly. Douglas stood at the threshold, unable to speak at the sight of his daughter. Today, it was his job to give her away. Could any man be worthy of such a good child? After Soyeon died, Ella had made his life sustainable. His infant daughter's require-ments: warming her bottles, changing her diapers, putting her down for the night—these had made him rise from his bed each morning. And each day he'd been able to go to work with the thought of her face and smile to return home to. Every year thereafter, his daughter had grown even lovelier than her appealing mother, who'd never lost her hold on his heart. Douglas looked away.

"Oh, Daddy, please don't make me cry." Ella's eyes filled with con-cern. She had never loved her father more than now. "We just fin-ished with makeup." She pointed to the bathroom.

Douglas shook his head rapidly, like a wet dog shaking water off his fur. He had to snap out of it, to shed his sadness. Ella was mar-rying the man she loved. He was supposed to feel happy for her. It wasn't a loss, he chided himself. It was her gain—what she wanted. He creased his brow, pretending to look stern—this used to make Ella giggle as a girl.

Ella crossed her eyes and stuck out her tongue.

They laughed together. Douglas felt his chin quiver again and closed his eyes.

Casey gave Ella's skirts a final brush and rose to her full height. They looked so comfortable in each other's company. She wanted the father and daughter to have a moment, but she had to march be-fore the bride and couldn't leave the room. Besides, Ella and Doug-las wouldn't have let her go anyway.

Douglas touched the edge of Ella's veil, then let go.

"Should...uhm?" Casey asked.

"No. It's not time yet. How are you, girls?"

The girls smiled at the kind doctor, whose heart was obviously grieving. Like a set of twins, they shrugged their bare shoulders and pretty arms helplessly, unable to say much of anything because if they did, they too might burst into tears.

Douglas looked down at the carpet to give himself and the girls a second to collect themselves. He tried to chuckle, remembering to feel joy at just being Ella's father. He turned to Casey.

"Well, Miss Casey Han, you look like Miss Korea. And how are you feeling today?"

"Excellent. I am excellent, Dr. Shim. And how are you?" she said brightly. "May I get you something? To drink or eat?" She pointed to the platters of sushi and fresh fruit on the other side of the room that could've easily fed ten people. On the bridal refreshment table, there were bottles of soda for as many.

He shook his head no. Dr. Shim clearly wanted to say something to his daughter, but Casey didn't know how to give them their privacy. The makeup lady was still fussing in the bathroom.

"You know, I think I'm hungry," Casey said, moving toward the refreshment table and away from them.

Douglas moved closer to Ella. "Waaaa...," he uttered in astonishment.

"Daddy, I told you, don't you make me cry."

"Oh-kay," he said in English. "You look good," he said, his hand on his hip, as if he were complimenting a nurse who'd just had her hair done at the beauty shop.

"Thank you," Ella replied quietly.

On the other side of the room, Casey placed a few pieces of sushi on a plate and poured herself a glass of seltzer. Someone had left a British *Vogue* on the windowsill, and she sat on the Louis XIV–style sofa to flip through it.

"You don't have to marry him," Douglas blurted out. He hadn't meant to say this. The words had left him without his permission.

"Daddy!"

"You can change your mind. Or take more time. You can wait. If he loves you—"

Ella realized he wasn't kidding. "Why are you saying this?"

Casey turned the page: She stopped herself from glancing up.

"Your father doesn't want to give you away."

"Oh, Daddy."

Douglas whistled the "Wedding March," messing up the first bar immediately. He felt crazy. "I think I got the last-minute jitters that you were supposed to get. I'm sorry, Ella."

"Nothing is changing." Ella looked afraid.

Douglas shook his head, dismissing her assurances. "You love him, right?"

Ella nodded and glanced in Casey's direction. Her friend was reading a magazine and eating sushi. "Everybody must be waiting," she said tentatively.

"That's oh-kay. You can still change your mind," Douglas persisted, wanting to offer her an out, guessing that she was worried about the guests or what they might say. But it didn't matter anymore what anyone said.

"That's not what I meant, Daddy. Why are you saying this now? Why?"

Douglas made a face because he had no clear reason except that Ted was not as nice as his daughter. He'd imagined a kinder man, a less ambitious man. Someone who'd make Ella his priority.

"Oh, my Ella. I wish you so much happiness. What can I do to guarantee that he will make you happy? What wouldn't I do to guarantee such a thing?" Douglas was not a violent man, but he thought if Ted ever diminished Ella in any way, he'd want to hurt him.

"Oh, Daddy, please don't worry. Ted is a good person. He does love me. And I admire him so much. Don't you think I've become more confident since I've been with him?" Why this aspect sprang up in her mind as a reason to marry wasn't clear. There were so many other things she liked about Ted, loved about him, but mainly, Ella looked up to him as someone who'd overcome difficulties. She wanted to be like that, too. "He's made me more bold. Don't you think?" she asked, her eyes crinkling in the corners—the way they did when she wasn't sure of herself.

Douglas nodded, wanting to give her this quality that she had wanted so much. Courage. Even as a girl, Ella had wanted courage, and he had told her as often as possible that she was brave and good. Ted had merely taught her to speak up. That was only one kind of bravery. From Ted, she'd learned to verbalize more and to not put herself down so much. She'd even learned how to ask for Casey's friendship. But couldn't those things have just come with time? Douglas wondered. Couldn't she have learned those things without Ted? Why did Ella credit him with so much of what she had done?

Ella reached for his hand, and Douglas took hold of it.

"Oh-kay. Oh-kay. Daddy is so sad that he's losing you. You are my angel, Ella. You are my angel."

"Oh, Daddy, I'm not going anywhere. I'm just getting married. Really, Daddy. Nothing will change. I'll always love you best," she said. "Just don't tell Ted, okay?" She laughed, wiping her cheek with her free hand.

Douglas opened his arms wide to embrace his daughter. He felt like a selfish old man.

From her seat, Casey took another sip of her seltzer. A water bead of condensation from her glass splashed onto the open magazine. She heard the electric organ playing. There was a knock—it was time. She got up to tell the makeup lady, who was still in the bathroom. Douglas let go of his daughter and went to the door.

The ceremony itself was brief enough, with only two sacred readings and one Shakespeare sonnet. After the photographer snapped the last group shot, the wedding party progressed to the banquet room. The cocktail hour had ended, but many of the guests remained camped near the raw bar, tucking away what seemed like a limitless supply of jumbo shrimp. It took some effort on the part of the wedding hall manager to corral the guests to their seats. When everyone finally sat down, the manager signaled the deejay. An artificial drumroll played from a noise sound track. The deejay shouted into the microphone as if they were at a Knicks game, "And I give you Mr. and Mrs. Ted Kim!"

The manager nudged Ella and Ted into the hall. There were four hundred guests seated in round tables of ten, eating their first course of lobster tempura. Someone tapped his champagne flute with a spoon, and others followed along. Ted kissed Ella on the mouth, and she reddened immediately. The guests whooped in delight. Glasses clinked all around them. Ted kissed Ella until her neck was scarlet.

By this time, Casey was sitting with Jay at a table near the dance floor. Their table was made up mostly of Ted's friends from Harvard Business School. The HBS men were attractive alpha types and their dates well-turned-out wives or prize girlfriends. She didn't know if any of the women had gone to HBS. From knowing what Ted thought of girls who achieved "too much," she didn't expect much female business school representation at the wedding. She knew many of the older Koreans in the room—those she'd grown up with from church—but there were surprisingly few in number from their Sunday school days. Walter Chin, another HBS grad, the one who'd helped her get the job, was seated at the other HBS table. Casey and Walter had talked during the cocktail hour, but Walter was occupied, utterly smitten by his gorgeous date—a petite Greek lawyer from Philadelphia. Penny was divorced, was older than Walter by at least ten years, and had full custody of two teenage daughters—her gleaned bio had surprised Jay and impressed Casey. At their table, Jay tried talking to the men, but the HBS guys were older and not interested in chatting with some scrub analyst a couple of years out of college. As usual, Jay was also sleep-deprived, and he wanted the wedding to be over. The women were talking to one another about their kids and schools. Nothing could be more boring to Jay.

Across the parquet dance floor, Leah and Joseph were seated at Dr. Shim's table, where everyone was an elder or a deaconess. Joseph didn't know why he was seated at such a table of honor: The only explanation he could foresee was that his daughter was the bridesmaid. A few tables over, Casey was seated next to a tall white boy whose arm was draped over her chair. Joseph looked away. Though he liked his own table, it made him feel poor. The other elders were *boojahs.* To his right sat Elder Koh, who owned a ten-thousand-square-foot deli behind Penn Station, employing eighty-five people to keep it going. To his left sat Elder Kong, who owned seven commercial buildings in the Bronx and a shopping mall, as well as a multilevel parking lot in Brooklyn. It was Elder Kong who'd told Joseph to buy the three-story brick commercial building in Edgewater, New Jersey. On his advice, Joseph had used every cent of his retirement savings to buy that building, which had a pizza parlor on the first floor, a dentist's office and accountant's office on the other two floors. The rent just covered the vast mortgage, but Elder Kong had assured Joseph that when he retired in five or ten years, the asset would've appreciated and hopefully the rental income could supplement his Social Security checks. Elder Kong, called Midas, was a thoughtful counselor to his friends. He believed that all Koreans should be more successful in this strange country and contribute to its growth. The empty chair at the table belonged to Dr. Shim, who hadn't sat down because he was busy greeting the wedding guests.

Douglas had reached Casey's table. He patted her shoulder gently, and she looked up. The other guests at the table offered their congratulations to the father of the bride. Douglas waved them away, entreating them to eat and dance a lot. "Look alive," he joked. "Presbyterians need help from you kids to have a good time. Also, I speak as a physician: Dancing is good for your digestion and cardiovascular health.

"The minister would have my head, you see," Douglas said as an explanation for why there was no booze. Church basement wedding receptions were traditionally dry, and though they were having it at a rented wedding hall as a concession to Ted—who'd wanted it at the much fancier New York Athletic Club or the Union Club, where he was a member, despite the fact that Manhattan parking would have been a prohibitive expense for the poorer Korean guests from Queens—the groom was not given a say regarding alcohol service to the largely Korean and conservative Christian crowd. After the honeymoon, Ted intended to have a smaller, private reception at the Union Club for his guests. "I'm very sorry about this. Believe me, I could've used a drink earlier today." He winked. "But did you see the sparkling apple cider?" he chortled, pointing to the champagne flutes.

Helmut, a German investment banker who'd gone to HBS, piped up, "Oh, there is no alcohol here?" With a harrumph, he put down his napkin dramatically, pretending to get up to leave. The guests laughed at this, and Helmut's wife yanked him down to his seat.

Douglas high-fived the kidder, then rested his hand on the back of Casey's chair. "So this is Jay?" he asked, his eyebrows raised. The white American seated beside Casey was tall, with square shoulders and bright, unblinking eyes. It was striking how dark bits of color shimmered through his blue green irises. He had a pale, open brow. A genial smile flashed across Jay's face at the mention of his name. He looked like a nice boy.

Jay held out his hand, and Douglas shook it warmly.

"How do you do, sir," he said.

"And I understand you will be marrying soon," Douglas said, trying to give off a kind of warm American heartiness. He was fond of Casey and wanted Jay to feel welcome.

"Yes, sir," Jay replied.

Casey felt grateful for Dr. Shim's kindness.

"Good, good. Marriage...marriage is a beautiful thing." Douglas had a lot of thoughts about marriage, but today none made much sense to him. "Casey, have you had a chance to talk to your parents today?" he asked. "Your parents look wonderful."

A small, tight smile formed across her lips. "Not yet...I will soon."

"C'mon. I should try some of this fried lobster anyway. Ted chose the menu." Douglas glanced at what the guests were eating. He shifted his feet toward the direction of his table. "Jay, you should come, too. Aren't the Hans just the nicest people? Have you ever heard Casey's mother sing? She's like heaven." He began to whistle "How Great Thou Art" to himself.

Casey opened her mouth to protest, but Jay got up and stood beside Douglas, who had already started to move away. Jay reached his left hand backward so Casey could take it, and she tried to catch up with his brisk steps.

Whatever small pleasure Joseph and Leah had felt at being seated at such a prominent table dissipated at the sight of Casey approaching them with Jay. Leah clasped her hands together on her lap. Elder Shim was talking to Jay, and he was smiling and nodding back. Casey concentrated soberly on her steps.

The table lit up, however, when Douglas appeared with the young people. The deaconesses brightened suddenly, the way women tend to when an attractive man enters the room. They wanted the bride's father—a well-regarded and kind doctor with property—to finally sit down and chat with them. The men, not missing this, teased Douglas right away about the cost of the wedding. They took their shots.

"So, how much a head?" Elder Koh asked. He was a businessman with four daughters. This was essential information.

"*Yobo*." Koh's wife batted his arm. "You're so tacky," she said in English, and everyone laughed. Deaconess Sohn, Koh's pretty Korean-American wife, had been born in the States—a Mt. Holyoke grad. You weren't supposed to talk about money. Although she was curious, too.

Douglas wrinkled his brow in amusement. It would've been just as easy for them to ask the managers of the Coliseum about the price, but they wanted him to squirm a bit or exaggerate how he was stretched by such an expenditure. But in fact, Douglas could've easily afforded a wedding at the St. Regis for the same number.

"Ah, be quiet." Elder Koh shushed his wife. "So how much?" His tone was jocular, but he wanted to know. There were four hundred guests at this location in Queens with parking—the nicest Korean wedding hall he knew of. His oldest daughter was twenty. Paying for a wedding couldn't be that far off in his future. His wife would certainly chide him for being a *ssangnom* when they got home.

Douglas folded his arms, quiet until he held everyone's attention.

"Two-fifty a head," he said. The guests gasped loudly.

"Give or take fifty. Saved a fortune on no *suhl*, though. Being a Presbyterian can be economical." Then everyone laughed. This cost wasn't hurting him at all. More than envious, they were awed by his abundance.

Casey's parents hadn't yet looked in her direction. Naturally, she'd anticipated this before she'd approached the table. They were capable of great detachment. Jay continued to grin, believing that somehow they'd ultimately fold him into their embrace. At times like this, she found his optimism delusional.

Douglas cleared his throat. "I brought the beautiful bridesmaid and her fiancé," he said. "Has everybody met Jay?"

"Whaaaaa—" the guests murmured, smiling at the Hans, who'd never mentioned this important detail. They smiled at Jay, assessing him privately and wondering how old he was. To the Koreans, he didn't look young, but a little mild, as though he wouldn't be much trouble for Casey.

"Hello there," Jay said, waving like a royal. There were nine people at the table, and it would have been impossible to shake everyone's hand. They tipped their heads, and Jay returned the gesture identically, but that was wrong. He should've bowed deeper from the waist, since he was the younger one. It wasn't his fault—Casey didn't blame him.

Jay spotted Leah. The short bald man to her left must have been Joseph. He and Casey had the same mouth.

The elders congratulated the Hans all at once, and Joseph gave them a clipped nod. All this was taking him by surprise. He could see no way to talk himself out of it.

From her seat, Deaconess Sohn reached over to clasp Casey's forearm. She had a habit of touching people forcefully.

"He's so cute." She winked at Jay, feeling more comfortable with the American than the other deaconesses. "Congratulations," she said to Jay. He shook her small, plump hand.

Again, she winked to Casey, then exclaimed, "I love your dress."

"That's very sweet of you to say." Casey laughed quietly. The deaconess kept talking about the reception, but all Casey wanted to do was excuse herself. Jay was expecting to be introduced to her parents. No one at the table seemed to know that this was the first time Joseph was meeting her fiancé.

Casey swallowed. Facing her parents, she said, "Hi."

The guests didn't think much of it. Several men returned to their conversation. Leah smiled at Casey yet said nothing. Joseph would not look her way.

Wordlessly, Joseph pushed his chair away from the table and got up. The guests turned to him. Then they understood. One elder coughed as though he had something stuck in his throat, and the others sipped their 7 Up. Douglas then remembered how oddly Leah had behaved when he'd mentioned Casey being Ella's bridesmaid. This awkwardness was his fault, but he couldn't have imagined this possibility. He'd thought it would be nice to bring Casey and Jay to the table. He'd done so to make Jay feel welcome, but he'd made it worse. Joseph was visibly furious.

Douglas moved to Jay's side, understanding that Joseph wanted to leave the wedding. He would take the boy away. Get him a soda.

Joseph smoothed down his suit jacket. He wore a two-button navy pin-striped suit, a white shirt, and a burgundy necktie—on it, a tie pin in the shape of a cross that Leah had given him when he became an elder.

Jay stepped toward him and stood right in front of him.

"Mr. Han, Mr. Han," Jay said. "Hello, sir. I'm Jay Currie. It's very nice to meet you, sir."

Joseph stared at him. The boy was pop-eyed and tall—little was remarkable about him. Smiled too much for a man. If Casey wanted to throw her life away, that was her business. He was resolved on this point.

"Excuse me," Joseph said, and tried to walk away.

Jay blocked him, continuing to smile. "Sir, sir," he said.

"Excuse me."

"No. Excuse me," Jay said, refusing to move aside. He didn't smile anymore. "I'm your daughter's fiancé." His voice was full of rebuke, reminding Joseph of his duty. At that moment, Jay hated fathers in general.

The guests looked among themselves.

"Get out of my way," Joseph said.

"Sir—"

Joseph cocked his head, and a quizzical expression crossed his face. What he felt was disbelief. He thought, This boy wants to die by my hands.

Seeing Joseph's look, Douglas moved closer to Jay and put his hand on Jay's elbow to pull him back.

"Sir—it's a privilege to meet you." Jay's voice grew louder—all pleasantness in his tone having vanished. The table stared at the boy in shock. It was not acceptable for a younger person to speak this way to someone of Joseph's age.

Joseph exhaled through his nostrils. He had to remind himself where he was. "Excuse me."

Jay remained still.

Joseph took a long breath, then raised his right hand. In one quick beat, he threw a powerful shove against the boy's left shoulder. Jay stumbled back but did not fall. The guests gasped, but Joseph was gone. If he had stayed, he would've murdered the boy.

Douglas patted Jay's back to calm him. Jay turned to Casey, but her eyes were shut; she was like a child attempting to make a room disappear. Leah covered her mouth with her hands. She didn't know if Joseph would return for her, not realizing that her husband hadn't taken the car. He was already outside, walking up Queens Boulevard toward the 7-Eleven. He went to buy cigarettes—his first pack in twenty-three years.

Ella had missed it. She'd been greeting guests herself when the banquet manager told her it was time for the father-daughter dance. She'd come to get Douglas herself. When she got to her father's table, no one was talking. The first person she saw seated was Leah, her face pale, her hands held over her nose like a mask. The deejay was playing disco music still, but for their dance he'd play "The Best Is Yet to Come."

"Daddy, we're supposed to dance," she said, glancing at Casey and Jay, who looked dumb with shock. "Hi, Casey. What's the matter?"

Casey shook her head, saying nothing.

Douglas patted Jay again, then turned to take Ella's hand.

They headed to the parquet dance floor. When their song started, he led her through a respectable fox-trot learned from an Arthur Murray dance instructor.

There was no time to apologize or explain. Casey and Jay left without eating their dinner.

During the cab ride going home, Jay kept repeating, "Unbelievable." He was hoping Casey would talk, but she didn't. Here and there she nodded, and at one point she said, "I'm sorry, Jay," but nothing more. When Casey was sad, it was impossible to pull her out of her silence. Usually he'd talk until she chimed in, but when it was something serious, he'd wait it out. He almost preferred it when she was angry because at least she'd talk—shout, even—but this quiet thing was hard. He had no clue as to what she was thinking. By nature, Casey was impulsive, and though overall she was funny and good-natured, by now he knew that she was always sorting through other things beneath whatever she was doing or saying. Casey was complicated, and most of the time, he liked it. But what did she mean by sorry?

At home, they changed out of their clothes. She removed her wedding makeup and the bobby pins in her hair. In the hot shower, she tried to think of what she could tell Ella when she finally reached her. She had wanted to see Ella in her *hanbok* for the *pae-baek* ceremony, where she'd bow to Ted's mother. She was supposed to have helped her change, too. It was awful, what had happened. Ella's friendship was valuable to Casey. Her goodness had trumped Casey's childhood envy after all. But Casey had walked out on her wedding reception. Her father had behaved like a thug, and Jay...Oh, Jay. He'd been ridiculous. When something went wrong, the first emotion Casey touched was shame. But here, the shame was below the surface. It was deep and vast. There was no way out of this, she thought.

When she came out of her shower, Jay was in bed reading Wallace Stevens. He read poetry when he was unhappy. Casey smiled at him, feeling sorry for both of them. She was sad, too. In the taxi, she had said the truest thing she felt inside. She was so sorry—about not having introduced him earlier, about her father pushing him, about all those people witnessing him being shoved around, about everything—her family's disgrace at a dear friend's important day. On top of shame, there was always remorse.

"I'm going upstairs. For a cigarette," she said.

"You're wearing your bathrobe, honey." He laughed. "And jammies."

"You're right!" She pretended to be shocked. He'd used a child's word for her nightgown. There was something boyish about Jay— even when he was being manly and responsible. This quality had made her love him, but she saw that it had also been this naive pluck of his that had convinced him it was okay to approach her father without warning when the same tactic had been a failure with her mother. Jay was convinced that he was impossible to reject as long as he was well intentioned and had a sunny manner. In a way, it was lovely, and in a way, it was stupid.

Casey turned to go.

"And it's late," he said, not wanting her to leave.

"No one will be on the roof," she replied, her voice gentle, thoughtful. "The robe will be fine. It's Saturday night. No one will be upstairs. And besides, I don't feel like putting on clothes." They were talking about what she was wearing. What did it matter?

"I don't feel loved," Jay said. He stared at her hard.

"What?" She made a face. "What are you talking about? Of course I love you."

"Then stay here," he said, and she knew he wanted to make love. But she didn't want to. She didn't feel sexy or even agreeable. The idea of his hands on her body made her feel awkward.

"It won't be but a few minutes, Jay. I really need a cigarette."

"Baby, I can give you something to smoke." He wiggled his eyebrows like Groucho Marx and laughed nervously. The innuendo had been a risk.

To be polite, she laughed along. But the suggestion had felt repulsive, though she wasn't a girl who disliked fellatio. Sometimes it could be very erotic to her.

"Darling," she said, "sometimes a cigar is just a cigar."

Jay laughed at this. Everything was going to be okay. "Fine, then. You know where I'll be. You addict."

The roof was empty. Casey sat on a bench, damp with the evening dew. She quickly smoked a cigarette, then lit another. Then one after that. Her long white T-shirt nightgown and terry robe were decent, if a bit frumpy. Most nights Casey wore pretty things to bed, but tonight she'd put on her least appealing gown. The cigarettes perked her up. In the morning, she'd phone Ella to apologize. After her fourth cigarette, she lit another. She heard the door. Jay stood there, wearing his Lawrenceville sweatshirt over his T-shirt and boxers.

"You were worried about me wearing jammies?"

"What's going on, Casey?" His voice was stern.

She was confused by his tone.

"Why didn't you come downstairs? I was waiting."

She raised her lit cigarette as the obvious explanation.

"How many?"

"Four? Five? Dunno."

"Come to bed."

Casey couldn't look at him. There was no picture, was there?

"Casey, I'm tired. Come on." He moved closer to her.

"I can't marry you."

"What?" Jay said. "What?"

Her mouth was open. Casey had surprised herself. She blew smoke out of her nostrils. "I don't think we should get married."

"What the hell are you talking about? Are you telling me that you don't want to marry me?"

She crossed her legs, her Dr. Scholl's dangling from her sole. The chipped polish on her toenails made her feel shabby.

"Say it, Casey. I need for you to say it."

Her lips felt cold.

"Say it, goddammit. Tell me you don't want to marry me." His voice quavered.

She couldn't look at him.

"I can't see the picture, Jay. I've been looking for a picture in my head. Every morning I get these pictures, and I can't see a picture of us—" She started crying, because then she knew. For sure. The picture had never come because it wasn't supposed to happen. Like she wasn't supposed to go to law school, either. And she had never told Jay about the pictures because she realized he would never have believed her. It was nuts.

"What are you talking about? I love you. You and I are incredible together. I love you more than anything, Casey Han. You crazy girl, I can't imagine living without you. You know how sorry I am about that time—"

"I don't actually care about that. That's not why—" She didn't want to talk about those girls again. And she did believe him. He wouldn't do that again. What was more troubling was how much of a pleaser he was, how unrealistic he was in his beliefs, and how he had never really understood what it was like to be her. It wasn't that a white person couldn't comprehend what it was like to be in her skin, but Jay, in his unyielding American optimism, refused to see that she came from a culture where good intentions and clear talk wouldn't cover all wounds. It didn't work that way with her parents, anyway. They were brokenhearted Koreans—that wasn't Jay's fault, but how was he supposed to understand their kind of anguish? Their sadness seemed ancient to her. But, thinking about what she'd just said, she felt terrified at the prospect of not being with him anymore. She would miss him so much. It had been hell to be without him. But it also seemed wrong to hold on to him just because she was afraid of the pain of loss. It made her feel weaker than she was to even think like this. Casey had compromised on sex, her goals, her morality, but somewhere she had set a boundary that she didn't want to compromise on love. But was she being extreme? Was no love better than a love without enough understanding? Earlier that evening when Jay had marched toward her father, she'd felt she didn't know him anymore, even though she could have predicted that he would do such a fruitless thing.

Casey stooped over to gather the cigarette stubs she'd been saving to throw away. There were no garbage cans on the roof, and she hated littering. She counted seven stubs. They couldn't have all been hers. Casey got up from the bench. She couldn't look his way.

"You're making a mistake. This is irreversible, Casey. I won't take you back." Jay looked at her dark eyes. He raised his voice. "Do you get that? You can't just leave me. I won't forgive this. I won't forgive you leaving me. I fucking will never forgive this."

"I'm sorry," she said as quietly as possible. But there had been no picture—somehow the irrational made more sense to her than his very reasonable threat.

BOOK II

Plans

1 | COMPASS

*T*HERE WAS NO OTHER CHOICE—Casey had to get a weekend job, and it was just easier for her to return to Sabine's. So Monday through Friday, she continued on as a sales assistant at Kearn Davis. But to keep up with the increases in her Battery Park studio apartment rent, her mounting clothing purchases, and the humiliating cost of a social life in Manhattan, Casey found herself behind the counter on Thursday evenings and all day Saturday and Sunday, selling hats and hair accessories. Next month in January, she'd turn twenty-five. She was holding the same part-time job she'd had when she was eighteen. This stasis was not lost on her.

As of this month, she'd worked at Kearn Davis for two and a half years; her boss, Kevin Jennings—the relentless doubter—couldn't say a peep if she decided to quit. She'd served her time. But where would she go? Columbia Law had refused to let her defer admission again. Not that she could see herself as a lawyer anyway. Hugh and Walter from her desk were encouraging her to become a broker, but Casey couldn't imagine that, either. Sometimes she considered business school. Sabine was lobbying for that one. Her parents had given up on her, or she had given them up.

Nevertheless, the world had pushed forward. Tina was starting her first year at USC medical school; Virginia was finishing her master's thesis on Sandro Botticelli while making love to as many dark-haired painters in Bologna as she had time for; Ella was eight months pregnant and put on bed rest from preeclampsia; and Delia, her closest female friend at Kearn Davis, had switched to the Events Planning Department after working as a sales assistant for nine years. As for Jay, they hadn't spoken since she'd moved out eighteen months ago.

Since then, Casey had been living in an L-shaped studio apartment at the bottom of Manhattan, took advanced millinery classes at FIT on Tuesday nights, owed twelve thousand dollars in credit card debt, and worked two jobs. In the spring, she'd briefly dated a chatty portfolio manager seated beside her at a benefit table bought by Kearn Davis, and after they had a few dinners together, she realized that he was another Jay Currie—confident, moderate in his views, and amiable. It scared her that she had a type, because she could predict the ending. She disappeared on him thereafter, and he did not seem to mind. He was attractive, young, and rich; naturally, there were fish elsewhere. The only private concession she'd made to the future was taking the GMATs—a prerequisite for B schools.

It was the first week of December and Casey's third Saturday back at the store, and although most of her friends there had moved on, her old boss, Judith Hast, the weekend accessories manager, was still working there.

Sabine's was a small department store—approximately thirty thousand square feet—with only two floors for women's clothing and a basement devoted to cosmetics and hosiery. The interior had been recently redesigned by the Japanese architect Yuka Mori. The unadorned walls were painted superwhite with a lacquer-smooth finish, and the floors were built out of restored plank wood from France and Italy. The contrast of the silky walls with the rough-hewn wood flooring had been remarked upon by noted architecture critics. The clothes for sale were displayed not much differently from the exhibits at the Metropolitan Museum of Art's Costume Institute. It was an intimidating space for even the most self-possessed of New York shoppers.

What made Sabine's singular for the fashionable women of New York was that Sabine Jun Gottesman was uncanny at discovering and nurturing brilliant designers who later remained loyal to her, because, unlike most department stores, she paid them on time. Sabine was also intimate with many fashion magazine editors, and her generosity with their favorite charities was renowned.

The store today was filled with anxious holiday shoppers with their lists, but there were no hat customers. In general, most women did not wear hats anymore for decorative purposes. They neither wanted the attention nor would ever yield to any wish for such things, claiming they could not pull it off. If the average woman bought a hat, it was for practical reasons (a shield against the cold or sun), and if there was a fanciful purpose, she was private about it. Hats and accessories were not easy sales, and though Casey had been given the option of working shoes or sportswear—with their higher-volume business and fat commissions—she'd chosen this counter because it offered her a curious sense of accomplishment. For Casey had a knack for timing—being able to intuit precisely when it was all right to approach a woman trying on a hat and when not to. Also, for women accompanied by men, it was fair to say that only the very secure husbands or boyfriends approved of hats for their wives or girlfriends. Men were drawn to women in hats but were skittish about their partners looking different from the others in the crowd. Today, it was unlikely that holiday shoppers would buy hats for themselves. Casey would peddle French hairpins or plush flower brooches for her commissions.

On Judith Hast's suggestion, Casey was rearranging the displays, and she picked up a brown fedora. She removed the hat she was wearing—a small-brimmed green beaver-felt fedora trimmed with a green grosgrain band and a vintage orange-colored feather from Paris—and she modeled the brown fedora for Judith.

"Oh-la-la," Judith said. Her accent was impressive.

"*Merci,*" Casey replied, then returned the hat to its pedestal.

Judith returned to cataloging the spring inventory. She was a reserved forty-seven-year-old divorced heiress, a single mother to a teenage daughter named Liesel, and she worked three days a week at Sabine's for the thirty-three percent employee discount. She'd grown up in West Hartford, wearing clothes appropriate for the country club, gone to Trinity College, and dropped out in her junior year to marry the handsome graduating senior who ended up leaving her for her best friend's older sister. After her divorce, Judith took her inheritance and moved to New York with her then infant daughter and stopped putting blond highlights in her hair. She lived in a sprawling Upper West Side apartment with Liesel and often invited Casey for dinners.

"Do not let me buy that hat." Casey tried to sound severe with herself.

"If you don't, you'll just obsess about it. Do you want me to put it aside for you?" Judith considered Casey's worried expression thoughtfully.

"No. But thank you." Casey tilted the hat forward on the display to show off its brim. It was like Judith to tell her to yield to the temptation. She was a generous person, but also a wealthy person. Three hundred dollars for a hat would not affect her in the least. Even with the discount or even if the designer gave it to her at cost (sometimes milliners gave Casey things to wear to the store), she could not afford that hat. Just that morning, she'd considered asking Sabine for an advance to help her get through the week but decided against it for fear of bringing on another lecture. Not to mention that Casey already owned a beautiful brown fedora trimmed with a wide blue ribbon. She owned easily fifty hats—twenty of her own, many she'd worn only once. No one would dispute that her consumption patterns were excessive. But sometimes Casey wanted to argue that a person like Judith owned at least two hundred hats. Judith could afford it and Casey couldn't, yet it didn't mean that Casey had any less desire to do so. Her heart was full of frivolous and lofty wishes.

Lately, she'd been losing sleep over her debts. Her rent was twelve hundred a month, her utilities a hundred and fifty, food and transportation four hundred dollars, and her entertainment (movies, drinks, and going out to dinners with friends, taxis at night) seven hundred dollars, and just meeting her credit card minimums took anywhere from four hundred to a thousand a month. Ever since she and Jay broke up, Casey had really been on her own. She didn't know how to balance her budget, nor could she keep herself from buying the new pretty skirt. Twelve thousand dollars' worth of dinners out, flowers ordered, boxes of French chocolates, gym memberships, a pair of pearl earrings from Mikimoto, clothes and shoes, tuition for her hat classes. The only people who knew about her debts were Hugh (because you could tell him anything and he didn't judge) and Sabine, who'd prized it out of her; but even they had no idea how bad it was. Life cost so much money. The craziest thing was that though her debts terrorized her, the desire for more—to eat at the restaurant recommended by the *Times,* to order the second glass of wine at dinner, to give costly wedding or shower presents, to see the Ring Cycle at the Met, to order an orchid for Ella when she got pregnant—only grew stronger.

"When are you taking lunch?" Judith asked, putting down her pen.

"In a few minutes," Casey replied. She hoped Judith wouldn't ask her any more questions.

"You want to eat with me? Stacy from jewelry can cover us. They have way too many people for today. Anyway, I brought food." Judith often brought large homemade salads that her housekeeper made for her in a blue Tupperware bowl, along with her own shallot dressing, made without sugar, and packets of rice cakes. Judith did not eat dairy, sugar, or meat.

"Can't, sweetie. But thank you." Casey left it at that.

"Are you eating with Sabine?" Judith's voice squeaked a little.

Casey nodded, continuing to arrange the thousand-dollar Tibetan fur hats from light- to dark-colored crowns. Sabine had worked Saturdays from the time she'd opened her first storefront nearly three decades ago. Ever since Casey had returned to work, Sabine wanted her to take meal breaks in her office whenever she was there—Saturdays and even Thursday nights if Sabine was working late. Nevertheless, Sabine was a bizarre stickler about two things: taking turns buying sandwiches and never letting any of her favorite employees take extra time for lunch or breaks, especially if the meals were with Sabine herself. On these issues of fairness, she was pathologically fastidious and immovable. It was Casey's turn to pick up the sandwiches and drinks, but she had no cash to speak of. Casey wanted to phone the credit card company to see if there was enough credit left for their lunch, but she didn't want Judith to know.

"Sabine is so great," Judith said, trying to conceal her disappointment.

"Uh-huh." Casey knew Judith was feeling unwanted. She hated this about women friendships. Someone always felt left out.

In Judith's ten years as a weekend manager, Sabine had never once asked her to eat in her office. They had a perfectly friendly and collegial relationship, but it didn't go further than that. Sabine had her favorites—the prize ponies, in a way—fast, intelligent, stylish, and brilliant at sales. Young. They were always young. Judith rubbed her arms as though she were cold.

"Tomorrow? Please?" Casey asked. "I'll bring a salad, too." She looked up, wondering if she had any vegetables in the house. "Or a can of tuna. I think I have peanut butter. Maybe canned corn. I think I have some of that." She laughed at herself.

"I know, I'll ask Daisy to make you a salad, too," offered Judith. She'd take the high road. Her mother used to say that whenever someone hurt her feelings: "Take the high road, Buttons. Always take the high road. Can't go wrong with that."

Casey glanced at Judith, feeling bad about being unable to include her in the lunch. If she only knew how ambivalent Casey felt about these meals, tucked away in the boss's office. Recently, someone had written in a stall in the staff cafeteria bathroom, "So what do Queenie and Principessa do in that office together anyway?" When informed of this development, Sabine had laughed and asked, "Oh, am I queenlike?"

However, Sabine's office was in many ways an ideal sanctuary from the noisy cafeteria and the crowded main floor teeming with holiday shoppers. To get there, you had to walk through a stark white hallway lit with halogen lights that led to a reception area where Sabine's assistant, Melissa, was perched on an uncomfortable steel chair; then you'd finally reach a pair of maple doors that hinted at the seamless wood paneling of her fifteen-hundred-square-foot office. As in her apartment living room, on each side of the office, she displayed enormous floral arrangements—her essential luxuries, she termed them. Near the flowers were a pair of abstract paintings with green and yellow swooshes made by impossibly large paintbrushes. All the furniture in the room was upholstered in cream-colored wool mohair. Sabine said the fabric cost four hundred dollars a yard. Therefore, only clear drinks were served in Sabine's office. The office was broadcasting the occupant's unimpeachable sense of aesthetic; the visitor had to bow to it. The story went that Lagerfeld had once walked into her office, surveyed it with his careful eye, sat in a slipper chair, his back straight, and pronounced it "very good."

Sabine was on the phone with a manufacturer in Hong Kong. She waved Casey in and quietly tapped her thumb and fingers together to mimic a person who talked too much. Silently, Casey set the conference table where they normally sat for lunch with their water bottles and identical chicken sandwiches on whole-wheat bread. She pulled open one of the maple-wood panels to reveal a wall-size mirror. Casey adjusted her hat, tucking her long black hair behind her ears. For the store, she dressed differently than she did for her office job. For one thing, she wore hats to the store—the styles were fairly conservative and flattering (nothing too weird, since that would frighten the customers), but she chose hat body colors and trimmings that were a touch surprising to be visually pleasurable. On her weekend subway rides to and from work, she stood out a little, but she didn't mind; it was a relief from her Monday through Friday dress. From the corner of the mirror, Sabine was studying Casey's reflection.

As soon as Sabine got off her call, she lit another cigarette. She smoked two packs a day (a pack more than Casey), and whenever Casey popped by her office, they shared a smoke. Several years back, they had tried to quit together, but it had been unbearable for everyone. Isaac threw up his hands, rationalizing that his wife was more lovable with her cigarettes and two evening cocktails. She had no real vices, he said, shrugging. Her French designer friends viewed Sabine's attempts to quit smoking as a puritanical Americanism that she should resist. A life without pleasure blocked creativity, they argued. To make their point, a few of them sent her cases of Gauloises or Gitanes Blondes.

"Is that a new hat?" Sabine asked.

"New being a relative term. Not really," Casey replied.

"Oh?" Sabine dragged deeply. "How much?"

"It's not from here."

"I know that," Sabine said. She reviewed every purchase order from each department. Her perfect recall of the store inventory shocked the buyers who initially placed the orders.

"You don't like the hat?" Casey frowned like a child.

"I didn't say that."

"You like it, then?"

"I'd like it more if you could afford to pay for it."

Casey looked at the sandwiches. "Hungry?" she asked Sabine.

"No."

"Okay." Casey lit her cigarette. "Me neither."

"Did you call for the applications?" Sabine asked. She left her desk and took a seat at the conference table. Her voice had mellowed a touch.

"Yes."

"And?"

"My life isn't so bad right now." Casey wanted to keep it light. She liked Sabine. She was cool, and even though she was older than her mother, Sabine was young to her. In a way, she was a role model, mentor, what have you—someone Casey looked up to—but it could get to be a bit much. That's why it was so tricky to accept anything from Sabine, because it was accompanied by a knotty string.

"You can't stay a sales assistant at Kearn Davis. And you certainly do not want to end up like Judith."

Casey looked up, her shoulders tightening. "What's wrong with Judith?"

"Nothing."

"Why did you say that, then?" Casey felt she should say something in Judith's defense.

"Judith is a nice person. She is a great weekend manager. She is a loser. Think of all that money she inherited. And what does she do with it?"

"Uh, make you rich by buying stuff from you?" Casey raised her hands in annoyance. "She's not hurting anybody."

"Wrong." Sabine put out her cigarette. "Wrong, wrong, wrong."

Casey picked up her wrapped sandwich and flipped it like a pancake. It made a small thud sound, so she did it again. And again. The stack of B school applications were on the card table she was using as a dining table back in her apartment. She'd already spoken to Ted briefly about B schools at one of Ella's brunches, and he'd minced no words in telling her that she had no chance at Harvard or Stanford. "The only schools that mattered," he'd said. "Maybe being female might help. Being Asian: no."

Her GMAT scores were respectable, but from the viewpoint of a business school admissions office, her actual work experience was neither interesting nor challenging. She was up against the Jay types who'd busted ass for three years at a bulge bracket firm in the banking program, and even he'd been dinged by those schools that Ted valued. After all, it had been Isaac's call after Jay was wait-listed that had gotten him another interview at Columbia, which then pushed his application over the hump to an acceptance. In two and a half years postgraduation, Casey had somehow put limits on her future. Law school was out of the picture—her dated acceptance letter was meaningless. The top two business schools were near impossible. But it was hardly a tragedy. Casey flipped the sandwich faster and faster.

"Cut it out."

"Huh?" Casey stopped, suddenly aware of her movements. "Oh. Sorry."

"So you like being poor?" Sabine rested her cigarette on her jasper ashtray.

"Love it." Casey smiled. "It suits me. It's familiar, comforting." She adjusted her hat again, crinkling her eyes in false amusement.

"Ha, ha," Sabine scoffed. Her phone buzzed, and she took the call. She raised her index finger to gesture that it would take only a moment. Business always came first.

Casey pushed the sandwich away from her. She hated looking at it. The sandwich was like everything else she ever bought on credit—it was uglier or less pleasurable when she possessed it, because the thing she'd bought reminded her that she was out of control, selfish, destructive, greedy. Despite all of Sabine's good intentions, Casey had wanted to throw the sandwich at Sabine for asking her such a mean question. Does she fucking like being poor? *No!* she had wanted to scream. But how did a person become rich anyway? The methods seemed inscrutable to her.

It was no longer acceptable to her to be so broke, to have an apartment furnished by pieces picked up from street corners and the Salvation Army. Even Ikea was too expensive. Nevertheless, not having the cash in her wallet or bank account didn't keep her from charging another round of drinks when she went out with the millinery girls or friends from school. Her debts fretted her, but there was one other thought that took chunks out of her well-being: If her parents or younger sister ever needed her support, she could not offer them carfare. There were no sons. She was the firstborn. In her current state, she was worthless to them, and there was no one to blame but herself. She'd had to turn down another of Virginia's offers for her to visit her in Bologna because she was so tapped. No one in her family had ever gone to Italy. Bologna would always be there, she supposed.

Virginia was a graduate student in a foreign country, earning no money, yet she was living quite the life. Businessmen bought her dinners, and painters furnished the sex. Here and there, boyfriends bought her clothes and took her on trips. There was no self-consciousness in the way she wrote about her life: "Marco and I left his flat in Turin because it was too quiet, and spent a week at his villa in Lake Como." Marco was the boyfriend of the month, and Sabine later explained to Casey that Lake Como was the loveliest resort town in Italy, adding that it cost lire to breathe its air. Virginia wrote about her friends, too, from Ivy and Brearley, and for some of them, especially the attractive ones, life after college was a long glamorous adventure. Casey was the first person in her family to go to college. Years ago, Virginia had argued that they were in the same camp since her biological mother probably hadn't finished junior high school—and who knew about her biological father, the white American cad dad? But whatever Virginia's genetic heritage, they were not in the same camp now, Casey thought.

For two and a half years, Casey had been trudging along the road, and here she was—at the damn fork again. What Sabine, Hugh, Walter, and her parents had tried to tell her were things she understood instinctively: Decisions had to be made, actions committed. But there was no guarantee, was there? Of getting into school, landing a job, of safety. People were also fired all the time, too. At Kearn Davis and at Sabine's, she'd witnessed countless people being let go. Let go—it sounded like freedom. But Casey had not forgotten what it was like to stay at a friend's apartment, being ashamed of grabbing an egg to thicken your thirty-nine-cent ramen noodle soup.

Sabine hung up the phone. Her expression was cold—her gaze all-knowing and silence icy. Flicking her platinum lighter, she lit another cigarette. Her frustration was palpable. She looked at her watch.

"Is it time for me to go?"

"No." Sabine winked at her. How could she help this girl? she wondered.

"You're not done with me yet."

"No."

"Okay. Lay it on me, sister."

"Are you applying to B school?"

"I don't know, Sabine. I just don't know."

"I hate it when you say 'I don't know.' It makes you sound stupid. Or depressed."

"Of course it does." Casey thought about it. She worked seven days a week. Even her immigrant parents who did not finish high school took Sundays off.

"Get off your ass already. Don't you have just a week to apply? You have to send in your applications."

"Kevin thinks B school is a place to fill your Rolodex. And that networking is for the untalented." Casey chuckled at this last bit.

"You're not Kevin."

Sabine meant that he wasn't a Korean girl from a poor family. Despite her own marriage to an American, she routinely said stuff like "Most Americans think Asians are insects. You're either a good ant, a worker bee, or a roach you can't kill." But it wasn't as if she were a Korean nationalist, either: "Ignorant Koreans. Bunch of bumpkins with designer clothes," she'd muttered after reading a magazine piece that cited Korea as having the highest number of female-infant abortions in the world. Sabine believed that in America, a kind of blended natural selection could operate: If you worked harder, thought more independently, knew who your rivals were, and had the right guides and necessary support, success was inevitable. In some ways, she was irrationally optimistic. She also thought God was bunk.

"I want you to do it this week. Come on, Casey."

"Can't we talk about how great my hat is?" Being around Sabine, a permanent grown-up, made Casey feel juvenile by contrast. At Kearn Davis, she was the young den mother, ordering brokers to get on planes, scheduling conference calls, ordering food for brokers, and snapping towels at them to get them to behave. But in Sabine's office, she felt like a teenage girl, worried about her lip gloss clashing with her hatband.

Sabine tried to smile at Casey. Was she being too hard on the girl? But did anyone ever benefit from coddling? She twisted off the cap of her green-glass bottle of water and swigged from it like a boxer readying for another round.

The look frightened Casey. She got up to turn on the radio, keeping the volume low. A woman sang, "Yeah, you're human, but baby, I'm human, too." Jay had given her that excuse at one point about the girls—he was only human. After she took him back, agreed to marry him even, it struck her how she could know that he loved her and understand that he'd made a mistake, yet she could not erase what she had seen him do, or forget it. The image was tattooed in her brain, and the colors never faded. Every time they made love, she could imagine him doing things to her that he had done to women he had no real feeling for. And she had done the same before she'd met Jay. For a few weeks, she had carried a fetus—resulting from sex with a man whose last name she did not know. She wasn't better than Jay. No. She wasn't a better person. Her back to Sabine, Casey turned off the radio and then faced Sabine again. She felt like an indulged child, and for that, she was grateful to Sabine.

"Change is easier than you think, my darling."

"Okay," Casey said.

"I want you to take care of the credit card debts, too," Sabine said.

Their sandwiches were still wrapped. Casey stared at the congealed balsamic mayonnaise between the bread and the meat. She poked around her purse for her packet of Pall Malls. The sight of the jolly cinnamon-colored package made her happy. It was like finding a candy bar.

"Aren't those unfiltered?"

"I know you aren't talking to me about—"

"Fine." The line of Sabine's mouth grew straighter. "I wish someone had taken me aside to tell me..."

Casey nodded, anticipating another dismal theory about life and humanity.

"Listen, Casey..." Sabine talked faster and louder because the girl's attention was slipping. "Every minute matters. Every damn second. All those times you turn on the television or go to the movies or shop for things you don't need, all those times you stay at a bar sitting with some guy talking some nonsense about how pretty your Korean hair is, every time you sleep with the wrong man and wait for him to call you back, you're wasting your time. Your life. Your life matters, Casey. Every second. And by the time you're my age—you'll see that for every day and every last moment spent, you were making a choice. And you'll see that the time you had, that you were given, was wasted. It's gone. And you cannot have any of it back." Sabine tilted her head, her eyes full of worry. "Oh, my darling. Do you see that?"

Casey couldn't lift her chin. She wanted to argue for her choice to work in these jobs that her parents, colleagues, and Sabine found so beneath her abilities. Damn it, it was her decision not to choose law or medicine like Tina. Why couldn't she take her time? Why couldn't she fall on her face? That's what you were supposed to do in America—find yourself, find the goddamn color of your parachute.

"I'm not hurting anyone," Casey said.

"No. You're wrong. You're hurting you. I've been saying that all along."

Sabine reached across the table to cover Casey's hand. "I'm not saying you can't fuck it up. I'm just saying you should be making the mistakes as you head toward your goals. Okay?"

That was the ending of the speech she'd give to the other salespeople who needed a hard shove out of the nest. It was the line she liked best.

Casey's head felt heavy. She longed to rest it on her forearm like a child taking a desk nap. She removed her hat, finger-combed her hair.

"I will pay for B school." A horizontal wrinkle formed in Sabine's otherwise creamy brow, as if it had been hiding there all along, waiting to reveal itself.

The offer didn't move Casey. A part of her had hardened. It felt like more pressure.

"Why?"

"I can sell you Sabine's."

Casey laughed. "You're hilarious. I can't afford this sandwich."

"I've spent a lifetime studying shoppers. You behave like a rich housewife."

"That's funny, too. You're doing stand-up during my lunch hour."

"If you made the hard choices and tried to live by them, you'd be at greater peace with yourself. All this spending is a substitute for what you really want. All this overspending is merely addiction." There was a burst of confidence in Sabine's tone of voice.

"I see your shrink has been working overtime." It was no secret that Sabine went to Dr. Tuttle, and he was supposed to have saved her marriage to Isaac when she was getting bored with him. "So you're basically a dealer. Selling poor little rich women things that won't ultimately nourish them." Casey raised her eyebrows, craving a little bit of triumph in this miserable lunch.

"For some customers, yes. But should we close all the wine shops?"

"And you want me to follow in your footsteps." Casey was suddenly enjoying the fight.

"Only if you want to. Casey, you don't have to be unhappy."

"Like it's a fucking choice?"

Sabine nodded.

"Well then, I'm happy." Casey crossed her arms. She put her hat back on. She didn't see herself as someone who was unhappy. Virginia had been on antidepressants since she was eleven and had never stopped seeing therapists for her depression and eating disorder. It was Virginia who was always commenting on Casey's even temperament, which Casey took as a great compliment. Sabine was moody, yelled all the time, and it made sense that Sabine needed a shrink. It was Sabine and Virginia who were unhappy. Her parents were joyless, poor, and stoic. They never talked about feelings. Casey was a study in composure and fun by contrast.

"I couldn't buy your store, Sabine. It's your baby." Casey felt a little stupid after saying that, because Sabine didn't have children. "Besides, you're too young to retire."

"I need to make some plans for the future. You think about it," Sabine said quietly, not used to such resistance. It hadn't been her intention really to say all this today, but once she started, she saw that she preferred Casey over everyone else to run the show. A good leader had to have a great succession plan. Sabine was young enough, only forty-four years old, and in good health despite the occasional migraines, but she wanted her legacy to thrive after she was gone. She would need time to groom her successor. There had been offers to buy her store, but the idea of a Federated or some other publicly traded company running this seemed wrong to her. *Elle* magazine had once written up her store as "Sabine's: Transgressive and True," and though she had to look it up, the word made sense to her, and she thought it was accurate, this idea of being against convention, and that it was a good thing for women, because convention ruined all the women she knew. All her life, she had done things differently from the way she'd been told, and it pleased her to no end to collect the payoff on following her wishes and instincts. Casey did not see her own promise, her genius at selling, getting along with American women, at knowing what style was—this very desirable thing that Sabine could identify but could hardly articulate.

"Let me help you, Casey."

What could she say? For three Saturdays in a row, they had eaten lunch together, and every time there had been this lecture. She had fought Sabine through evasion, deference, and sometimes direct dissent, but secretly guarding the knowledge that Sabine must have been right about absolutely everything. A part of her would not have known what to do if Sabine gave up the fight. In her life, two adults had paid attention to her in a real way, and to them, she had revealed in part some of her fears and herself. Jay's mother was now lost to her, despite her protests otherwise. Sabine was the merger of a fairy godmother, mentor, and bad cop. It was obvious that Sabine was getting tired of her, of this battle, and Casey knew her debt of loyalty was outstanding. She had never before felt so chosen and recognized by someone so important and smart, and this feeling was near impossible to walk away from. She loved Sabine, because Sabine loved her, but this language of love was incomprehensible to them both. To them, talk was nothing and action was everything.

Sabine looked at her wristwatch. "It's time, honey. Your break is up."

Casey put her sandwich and water in her bag. "Thank you, Sabine." She smiled. "I know you always mean the best for me."

"I do." Sabine nodded with self-assurance. Casey returned to her station.

2 | BINOCULARS

*B*ABY, THE BID WAS ACCEPTED!" Ted shouted, his voice gleeful. "Accepted! Can you believe it?"

Ella nodded. Not that he could see her. He was calling from the office. And for once, he didn't sound rushed.

"Well?" He was annoyed by Ella's slowness, but nothing would keep him from savoring this moment. His phone, as usual, was blinking like the white Christmas lights strung across his assistant's desk, but Ted refused to pick up the other calls.

"Hel-lo?" He took his time exhaling. If he tried to rush her, she'd reply in her girlish voice, "Ted, I'm thinking." In general, he liked his wife's quiet reticence—when they'd first started to date, he had admired it as a kind of conversational tact and goodness. She seemed incapable of gossiping or saying a single mean thing. Her silence didn't reflect her intelligence level, contrary to the American view that good talkers were smarter. Ted would never have married a dumb woman. A man who marries a dumb woman gets dumb children—everybody knew that. When Ella spoke, she was cogent, insightful. Rarely did he disagree with the precision of her logic. But sometimes he lost his patience waiting for the damn intelligence to manifest itself to everyone else and, namely, him. A week before bed rest was prescribed, they'd gone to dinner after seeing some movie she'd chosen. He'd asked her what she thought of the film, and while she was mulling it over, he'd snarled at her, "Just say it,

Ella, goddammit, I don't expect that much. Spit it out." She'd then burst into tears at Rosa Mexicano, where they often ate. Then, like a sulking child, she had refused to eat her fish tacos. The waiters who knew them had to pretend they hadn't seen him yelling at his very pregnant wife. He was so upset that he'd had to step out to have a smoke. But when he'd returned, he'd apologized and encouraged her to order the caramel flan, even though she was gaining far more weight than the doctor had prescribed.

Ted's impatience, however, only made Ella more nervous. It actually made her withdraw. Not knowing what to say now, she took another sip of prune juice, then rested the glass on the coffee table. The doctor had put her on bed rest because her blood pressure was so high. She was lying on the living room sofa, praying for her constipation to end. On her last doctor visit, one of the nurse-practitioners told her that she had hemorrhoids and recommended more fiber. Pregnancy was a kind of physical humiliation. Ella rubbed her stomach thoughtfully, because no matter, the baby was well. She loved her baby. It was a girl.

"Ella?...Ella?" Ted's phone buzzed with calls. He'd try a different tack with her. When he got angry, she got quieter or cried. "Baby, baby?" Ted deepened his voice, sounding more fatherly. "What's the matter? Aren't you happy about it?"

"It's good, Ted," she said, trying to sound chipper. Lying down was hurting her back.

Her husband was excited about the town house bid being accepted: a three-story brick house on East Seventieth requiring a gut renovation. Ted's colleagues thought they were lucky to have it offered for just north of a million dollars. But Ella liked their current apartment. She'd been there not even three years. There was plenty of room for their daughter. Her father had bought this apartment for her, and to buy the town house, they had to sell it and rent it back from the owners if the owners agreed while the lengthy renovation took place. There seemed to be an infinite number of variables simply out of her hands. She tried to raise some of the points, like how they didn't know the size of his bonus, though the year before he'd made so much money that they could almost have bought the house outright. The renovation would exceed half a million dollars. The numbers were dizzying to her. Her father had never discussed the cost of things, and whenever Ted started to draw his tables, charts, and graphs, Ella entered a kind of gray, smoky cloud. To be fair, she tried very hard to pay attention because Ted needed her to get it. He wanted her to appreciate the factors involved, to share the burden that he faced now as the sole provider of the family. She had to understand the facts of life—that's one of the things Ted called money—a necessary fact of life. Normally, it was easier to agree with Ted, but she was so tired lately. Sleep was impossible because she had to get up and pee all the time, and during the day, she found it difficult to rest her mind. Ella had gained eighty pounds by her thirty-sixth week—a lot of it was water resulting from her preeclampsia, but she had also been eating almost a pint of ice cream per day. Little else seemed to satisfy her except for the cold, smooth taste of coffee-flavored Häagen-Dazs. When her teaspoon hit the cardboard bottom, she'd walk out of her apartment and head down to the hallway garbage chute to toss the empty container so Ted wouldn't see the evidence. He didn't like her recent penchant for sweets.

"It's nice, Ted. It's good," she said.

"Nice? Good?" Ted needed her to be more excited about this. It was a big fucking deal. As big a deal as when he'd made managing director the year before—the youngest in the history of Kearn Davis. They were going to own a house in Manhattan on the Upper East Side. Didn't she get that? He rapped his black Waterman pen that she'd given him against the crystal deal toy from his last transaction.

"What's the matter?" He attempted to keep his irritation in check.

"I just don't know how I'll be able to manage the baby and the renovation. You're working so hard at the office. I know how busy you are. And you travel. I mean, you have to travel for work. I understand that. And I know you're doing this for me. And the baby. For the family. I know how hard you're working, Ted." Ella felt stupid for sounding so ungrateful. "I've never been a mother before, and..." She glanced at her protruding belly. It was so huge, tight, and round—a skin-covered igloo. The thought of it made her grow cold inside. Ella put her hands over her stomach as if she were warming the daughter within her.

"We'll get you a sitter. All my colleagues have nannies."

"But they work. I'm not working anymore." Ted had wanted her to stay home with the baby, and Ella thought that was right; but in the past month since she'd left work, she found herself missing the office, the sound of the boys running down the halls, her lunches with David. Some mornings, she didn't feel like getting out of bed. These feelings, she figured, would pass after the baby came. "What would I do if we had a nanny? Your colleagues—"

"I meant my colleagues who have wives who stay at home with the kids. They use nannies. You're going to need help, Ella. You can't do this by yourself. You have to take care of the renovation. And you might want to have lunch out with your friends." Ted shrugged, not knowing who that would be. "Or go to the gym. And we have to go to dinners. You can't always take the baby—"

"I hadn't intended on getting a nanny."

"Well..." Ted shook his head, disappointed by her general ambivalence. Ella lacked passion. He'd never noticed that before, or at least not consciously. In bed, she could be shy but seemingly pleased. She liked cuddling. Lately, however, she didn't appear enthusiastic about anything he cared about, including sex. But that made sense to him—how could she possibly feel like making love when she was as big as a house? It couldn't be comfortable for her, he thought.

"I mean, maybe a night sitter here and there," Ella offered. Her husband liked having a full schedule with parties and dinners and expected her to accompany him—to look nice and be sociable. Ted needed stimulation.

"We'll talk about it later," he answered. This would take a far longer discussion than he had time for. The lighted call buttons glared brightly.

Earlier that morning, after his broker had called with the news that the offer was accepted, Ted had phoned Ella right away, wishing only one thing from her: He wanted his wife to be impressed. He was going to buy her a house.

Ella was silent. She sipped her juice.

Ted put down his pen. "You're headed to the doctor, right?"

"Yes."

This was Ted's cue: He was asking about her plans so he could get off the call. It was meant to seem that he was interested and thoughtful. As though he were thinking of her needs. Why did he do this? she wondered. Why did he think she didn't know what he was up to?

"Okay, then. Gotta jump, baby. I'm backed up, too."

"Okay."

"Then, I'll see you at home." Ted waited for her to hang up first.

Sometimes he said, "Love ya," as his final valediction, though she would've given anything for him to say "I love you" with some measured pause between each word as though he meant it, though surely he must have, since he had wanted to marry her so badly. But Ella didn't know how to say any of this to Ted without angering him. If she asked him to change the way he said good-bye to her, then he'd be short with her or, worse, ignore her, giving her a kind of time-out as if she were a naughty child by working even later than he needed to or traveling for longer. Ted didn't mean to punish her, but she felt that he often did. He couldn't help it.

Ella stayed on the line, wanting some perfect wisdom to come. There must have been a better way to talk to her husband, whom she loved. She closed her eyes.

But, tired of waiting for her, Ted hung up the phone.

Later that morning in the examining room, the obstetrician confirmed that it was herpes. Dr. Reeson, a plump woman with a head of lustrous brown hair, told her that sometimes you can have herpes but not know it: "Practically everyone has it." Her tone was as flat as plate glass. For some, it could feel like a minor cut with hardly any discomfort. The initial onset of symptoms for some could be severe, but for others it would be mild and never detected. She could've mistaken it for a tract infection. She could have had it for years—the virus could lie dormant—then it could be activated. It was better, the doctor said, that Ella knew now, since she'd be delivering in a few weeks. She could be monitored carefully prior to delivery, because if at the delivery Ella had an outbreak (which, in her case, came and went without her noticing any pain), it was possible that a child could be infected with the virus through a vaginal birth. The child could suffer blindness, Dr. Reeson said, but the chances were extremely remote. "Awareness and preparation are the greatest defenses," she said, wishing Ella would stop with the waterworks. She liked Ella—there was nothing to dislike, really—but she had a number of other patients she had to see. "Ella, every single day, women who have genital herpes deliver perfectly healthy babies. You have absolutely nothing at all to worry about," she said, lightly tapping her patient's round shoulders. Ella quieted herself, took her feet out of the stirrups, and sat up. She pulled down the hospital dressing gown over her knees.

"How? How did I get this?" Ella asked. It was almost a rhetorical question.

Dr. Reeson hadn't asked if Ella had slept with anyone besides her husband. She didn't know her previous sexual history. She didn't think Ella had affairs, although she had been wrong with a number of her patients. People surprised you with their sexual habits. She had practiced medicine for seventeen years—now and then, there was a shock, but Dr. Reeson tried to understand that life was complicated, and sometimes the bedroom was a lab for men and women to figure things out. And as in science, there were botched trials.

Ella looked at Dr. Reeson's dark eyes, fringed with beautiful brown lashes. "How do you get herpes, exactly? Can I ask that, please?"

"Direct skin-to-skin contact with an area where the virus is active on the skin—usually sexual contact, genital-to-genital, oral-to-genital, or oral-to-oral." She pointed to the dark blue pamphlet in the caddie near the institutional-size jug of Betadine and a tray full of rolled gauze. "It'll explain a lot. Including how you should discuss it with your partner."

"You mean Ted?" Ella couldn't fully grasp the doctor's implication. "I was a virgin. I've only slept with—"

Dr. Reeson nodded, unwilling to convey any expression except for a kind of gentle detachment. She crossed her arms to tuck her fists beneath her armpits.

"Ella, you're quite fortunate to know. And I know it must be difficult for you to hear this now, but really, most Americans have some form of the virus. It's just that no one talks about it, because it isn't curable, but it's perfectly manageable. Especially for you. And for anyone else who actually gets frequent outbreaks, there's a great deal we can do to alleviate and almost eliminate the symptoms. You're fine."

It was tedious to give this lecture every day, but her job required it. No one took the diagnosis well, though herpes was hardly a big deal. She had it herself. Though she'd had only six lovers, there was no sure way of knowing how she'd been infected and by whom. It was easier to forget she had it at all because she had an outbreak maybe once every two years now. She was also the mother of three healthy children. Her husband, an epidemiologist from France, had a theory about the patient's predictable hysteria: Americans are ashamed of all things relating to sex.

"I'm not worried about me so much," Ella said, "but my baby..." She searched the doctor's face for any further sign of bad news.

"The baby will be fine." Normally, Dr. Reeson didn't indulge the need for these kinds of blanket, unscientific assurances.

Ella nodded, sensing that she was being dismissed. The doctor had to see other patients, she told herself.

"Now, I want you to rest at home, but come by to get your blood pressure checked whenever it's necessary. The nurse will speak to you about that. Okay?" Dr. Reeson peered into Ella's blurry eyes.

Without a word, the young woman nodded, and the doctor left.

When Ted let himself into the apartment, he was pleased to see Ella awake and reading. It was eleven o'clock, and he'd fully expected her to be asleep. His wife was focused on the papers inside a manila folder, likely the mortgage materials he'd faxed her that afternoon for her to review. Ella bolted upright at the jingle of the keys still in his hand. Ted smiled at his wife, then turned away to hang up his overcoat in the crammed hall closet. He'd been at her to organize it better; Ella couldn't throw anything out. But to be fair, she was tired and had been feeling unwell—in addition to high blood pressure, a countless number of difficulties attended her pregnancy: dizziness, heartburn, migraines, tinnitus, diarrhea or constipation, and now hemorrhoids. Ella didn't complain, but her suffering was obvious. Her father stopped by weekly with baskets of fresh fruit, mentioning to Ted without fail how delicate Ella was physically. Nevertheless, because she was a twenty-four-year-old in good health, Ted found it surprising that she'd have this much difficulty, in contrast to the forty-year-old investment bankers who came to work right up till their delivery without a murmur, had their babies without a glitch, and then returned to work six weeks later. Ella's mother had had two miscarriages, then died in childbirth—these facts hovered about them. But the obstetrician said Ella was doing very well despite her temporary ailments. The baby was doing great, she'd said.

Ella looked up, but without saying hello to him, she returned to her papers. Usually, she was very happy to see him, and no matter what time of day or night, she'd ask if he wanted something to eat or drink. There was always something good in the refrigerator. She was seated with her legs outstretched across the length of the sofa, her head bent over, and he noticed that her hands were clutching the pile of papers in her lap. She wore his crimson-colored Dunster House T-shirt and a dark blue pair of maternity pants. Ted went to her, bowed down to kiss her forehead.

"How's my baby?" he asked, stroking her head. Ella's hair was put up loosely with a large barrette. In her reading position, her gaze downcast, she had a double chin.

"How many times did you do it?" she asked.

Ted frowned, more stunned by her angry tone than the bizarre question itself.

She repeated herself. "How many times, Ted?"

"What? Do what?" No one talked to him this way. Certainly not his wife. Except for the excellent news about the house, the day had been unrelenting. All afternoon, he'd been going back and forth with some idiot lawyers about a filing, trying to keep some uppity analysts from fucking up, and managing nervous clients who didn't understand elementary principles of corporate taxation. This was no time for PMS-type bullshit. He had no energy for this. There hadn't been time for dinner.

"How many times, Ted?" Ella glared at him.

"What the hell are you talking about?"

"Did you fuck around? I need to know," Ella said, her voice screeching. She refused to back down or soften her tone.

Aghast, Ted froze. His mouth opened, exposing his lower teeth.

"I have genital herpes." She threw the papers at him. The sheets flew about, cascading around his black monk strap shoes. He hadn't taken them off yet. "I must have gotten it before I was pregnant. I don't know. The doctor doesn't know. She doesn't think it's my first outbreak, however. I...I just don't understand."

Ted didn't look at her. He ran his left hand through his hair. He did this when he was uncomfortable or about to tell a lie. Ella knew all his tics. If he were holding a drink, he would sip something after a lie, as though he could wash it down.

"Can you be a friend to me right now and explain how this can be? I have never been with anyone else but you. You know that."

Her first time, his penis had frightened her. She'd never seen one before. It looked alive, and she thought the thing was larger than it was supposed to be. He wanted to put it inside her—that was love-making, she had to remind herself—the natural course of it. She had wanted just the kissing and the fondling of her breasts to continue. He kept guiding her to touch him there, but she couldn't help jerking back her hand whenever he wanted that. For her first time, she went to his apartment. Ted had thoughtfully placed a yellow towel beneath her for the bleeding. She had read about the possibility of the hymen tearing for virgins but had forgotten it somehow. It had hurt. Afterward, he'd wanted her to shower with him. He'd washed her hair tenderly with the Head & Shoulders he kept in his bathroom. The scent alone of that pearly blue shampoo could remind her of that night. He ran to the deli after the shower to buy her pads, and he returned instantly, it seemed, with a packet of Kotex and a tub of vanilla ice cream, which he fed her with a wooden spoon shaped like a child-size tongue depressor. Before they fell asleep, he told her that he wanted her to be his wife, promising never to love anyone else the same way. In her mind, there was no question that she would want to have him as her only lover. Her body was his to have, to give him happiness. In the morning, he wanted to do it again, and it hurt less that time.

Ella's eyes filled with tears, but she was so tired of crying.

"Oh, shit, shit, shit," he said, clenching his fists. He wanted to hit something. Ted measured his breathing, staring at the blue-and-green diamond pattern of the living room carpet.

"It is what it is, then." Ella covered her face with her hands.

Ted sat at the edge of the armchair and leaned his head into his hands.

There was no denial, and Ella felt remarkably clear.

"You fuck. You fucker. You did this to our child." She had no idea how to use these words. She'd never liked the sound of these kinds of words, how they interrupted the flow of all the other words that didn't offend. But she found herself imitating Ted's way of talking, the way he spoke on the phone to work when he was at home. Not knowing how to sound angry herself, she had borrowed his style.

Ted couldn't move his neck. The words just kept striking him over and over again.

"My baby could be blind because of you. You fuck, you fucker." Her shoulders stiffened, but, unable to stand very well, she put her hands on her hips to steady herself. The yelling made her feel worse. What was the point of this anger? Nothing could be done.

"Blind?" Ted glanced up. He didn't know he had herpes, but it was true that he had screwed someone who'd invariably given it to him.

"Blind," Ella said. Dr. Reeson had said the odds were overwhelmingly against such a possibility. That afternoon, Ella had researched the family medical books she kept in the house for women's health issues; she had even called a herpes hotline—as it turned out, there was such a thing. She was a doctor's daughter, she had reminded herself, she had to be calm, do her homework. Dr. Reeson had told her that the baby would be okay. "It's possible." Ella pointed to all the papers scattered about his shiny black shoes. "You can read about it. I've been looking at all that. All afternoon. All night. I could write a paper on it." She chuckled. Something in Ella's laugh had turned sharp.

Ted bent to gather the papers, arranging them in the folder. The day had begun with everything he'd ever wanted being possible and true. He had wanted first place, the grand prize, the best of whatever was worth getting: education, job, girl, and house. Two points determined a line, three points determined a plane, and four made a thing that much more stable and with greater dimension. Just that morning, he'd had those things. In less than a day, they'd slipped from his grasp. His education and job were intact, but the latter two, harder to affix, were vanishing into infinity. That morning, he had called his ailing father to tell him about the town house, thinking that it might cheer him up. "How is Ella's health?" Ted's father had asked him right after saying hello, though he'd just spoken to her on Sunday night—on Ella's regular call to to his mom and dad. Would Ella tell his dad? She would not be so vindictive, he told himself, but he'd never seen Ella this way; this rage was new. Ted held the folder with both hands, sat back down on the armchair. His actions were irrevocable.

"Darling, please rest. The baby. The doctor said—"

"Shut up, Ted. Don't you tell me your concerns about the baby now."

Ted closed his lips, his jaws locked. No one had told him to shut up since he was a boy.

"Who?" Ella asked. "Who did you sleep with?"

His only chance of recovery, Ted figured, was full disclosure.

"This girl at work. An assistant."

"Casey?"

"No!" Ted looked at her, disgusted. "I would never sleep with Casey."

"Who, then?"

"This woman Delia. She's been there forever. She's screwed every-body." How could Delia not tell him? He had given herpes to Ella, the only person he had ever known who was truly kind. Truly good. "God, Ella, I am so, so sorry.... I... I never intended—"

"Are you in love with her?"

"No. No." He shook his head violently. "I am not in love with Delia." He touched his hair.

"She's a friend of Casey's," Ella mumbled out loud, recalling the name. Casey had spoken of her.

"Yes. I think so." He shrugged. "Ella, baby, I am sorry. You have to believe me."

"Why should I believe you? You know what? I hate you. I've never hated anyone before. But I know what it feels like right now. To hate. I want to die. God, I want to die."

Ella walked to their bedroom and shut the door behind her. She shouted from the room, "Don't come in here. I swear if you do, I'll jump out the window."

He had to get her, but his legs wouldn't yield. For several years, Ted had run the New York Marathon—each year with an improved time. He was also a brilliant sprinter. But his long legs were frighten-ingly immobile. In that moment, he didn't think he could flex his toes. He picked up a few pages from the carpet, but the words made no sense now. The text floated in front of his eyes. He had lost the ability to read. He rested his head on the back of the chair and shut his eyes as if it were all a bad dream. What was Ella going to do? He'd never heard her say the word *fuck*.

The first time he'd had dinner at Delia's apartment, she'd put away the dishes in the sink, then pulled out another bottle of beer for him from the fridge and said, "Don't you want to fuck me, Ted?" and he had replied, "Yes, Delia, yes. It's all I thought of all day." Delia liked that answer and rewarded him for it.

It began last year. A small deal had closed, another banker who knew Delia had invited her to the drinks party they were having at Chachi's. At the end of the evening, the group spilled out of the bar onto Second Avenue, and she turned to Ted, asking him to take her home because she felt light-headed. The taxi drove past K-bar, and she made the driver stop. She locked on his eyes, tugged his jacket, making him come in with her. The guy at the door knew her and waved them in without having them pay the cover. At the table, she ordered a bottle of red wine without opening the list. The waitress brought it to them, and they were left alone in the high-backed banquette.

Delia had incredible red hair; soft, natural curls tumbled down her shoulders. Her work clothes appeared professional enough, but her breasts, dusted lightly with freckles, overflowed from the open wedge of her white-collared shirt. She wore no stockings beneath her skirt. At the office, she'd slept with many of the men, but her choices were random. It wasn't the obvious managing directors—she had slept with several high-powered ones, but it was said that she liked Santo, a mailroom guy, and had dated him for a year. Some men claimed to have been with her but actually had not. How old was Delia? Mid-thirties? She had no wrinkles. Ted couldn't tell, and he didn't know how to ask. A married bond trader Ted knew called her "a talented girl"; she was choosy in her own way and, thankfully for all the men involved, discreet. She'd fuck only the men she wanted to. The trader had added, "I'd hand over ten percent of my bonus for her to do those things to me again. Just one night." But sadly for him, she didn't take money. She'd favored him only once. The trader had shrugged in the telling but smiled at the memory of Delia sitting on his lap, her skirt hiked up, his hands on her magnificent fanny.

K-bar was in the basement of an office building a block down from the St. Regis Hotel. It was dark inside, with red leather chairs and red tweed upholstered furniture. The seating area was dark, but the large, square-shaped dance floor was lighted. No one was dancing. The crowd was not so young, and the waitress was another pretty girl who'd tried modeling but had given up.

After the waitress left, Delia took Ted's hand and slipped it up her narrow skirt. He felt her immediately, and she guided him to give her pleasure. Before Ella, Ted had had sex with three other girls—decent sex with girls his age, where he pretended to be knowledgeable about what he was doing. It was astonishing, shocking, and thrilling to have a girl leading him. He felt gratitude. He couldn't pull away. A few moments into it, she closed her blue eyes, which seemed to grow darker with the evening, and she climaxed, then pushed his hand toward her again so that it would continue. She made a little gasp, and Ted almost passed out from excitement. His head felt both clear and hot. She opened her eyes and faced him, amused and delighted. With him. She moved closer to stick the tip of her tongue in his ear. With a free hand, he poured her a glass of wine. He wanted to give her something, for her not to stop. She pulled away, took a small sip almost for show. Delia pointed to his suit jacket, and he took it off and gave it to her. She placed it over her shoulders in a practiced way, slid under the table, and blew him. He took a lengthy breath when she was done, and he handed her a cocktail napkin. She returned to her seat, grabbed her purse, and walked steadily to the ladies' room. When she came back, he held her bony hand, which wasn't small, and they talked for the first time since the taxi. She told him silly stories about her brothers who lived on Staten Island—two cops and a building inspector. There were funny bits, too, about the other men at work. Nothing carping, but hilarious. Delia seemed to think life was humorous, and it was obvious that she enjoyed the moments that added it up. He was laughing out loud, feeling as though his shoulders could finally relax, because he was with her, and he didn't want to go home. If she were awake, Ella would be fussing with a menu for a fancy Sunday brunch, or as soon as he walked in the door, she'd jump on him to ask his opinion on the wedding photograph proofs or something like that. He wondered if what he was feeling for Delia was love.

The next day, he bought her a cup of coffee at the cafeteria, and she invited him to her apartment after work. She lived in a large, rent-stabilized one-bedroom in Chelsea. They ate Chinese take-out, and he asked her more questions about her family. She was one of four kids, the only girl and the only one to leave Staten Island. "Hard to imagine that being a sales assistant is a white-collar job, isn't it, Ted?" Her whispery voice hinted at sex. There was no other way to describe it.

"You have a very nice collar," he told Delia, staring at her neck.

Then they had sex on a bed, and he thought he had never seen a prettier girl naked, including porn, and he was amazed by the naturalness of her movements, how her lush body rose to meet his, and how she enjoyed everything about what they were doing. Delia was not reluctant.

They saw each other two or three times a week for almost a month, and one night he went to her apartment after work. He had bought her a gold bamboo bangle from Cartier to surprise her, and he couldn't wait until they were supposed to meet. At the store, it had pleased him enormously to think of it adorning her body. When she opened the door, he spotted Santo the mailroom guy sitting in the chair Ted usually sat in, the Chinese take-out cartons on the table, and he left, never calling her again. Delia never explained herself to him, and he saw that he did not owe any explanations to her, either. He returned the bracelet and bought Ella a pair of diamond-encrusted earrings that cost twice as much as the bangle.

Ted thought about her. Sometimes he thought he could smell her perfume in the elevator. She wore Fracas—a perfume that came in a square black bottle. When she switched to the Events Planning Department on the tenth floor, he was relieved. He never had reason to go there. When he jerked off at home or when he traveled, thinking of her red hair helped him to come. When he made love to Ella, he wished his wife's body were more like Delia's—the feminine hollow of Delia's narrow waist and the full S-curve of her bottom. Making love to Delia had made him feel complete. Happy. Was that what the married bond trader had been talking about? Ted was almost tempted to ask him as much. But Delia was a slut. This was what Ted reminded himself when he felt like punching her four-digit extension on his phone keys. She was a common Staten Island slut with a pretty face and a perfect ass. A whore. He had good reason to hate her, but even now he found that he could not.

Delia had taught him that it was possible to want two women, and to perhaps love two women, at once, and this knowledge terrified him, because it upset the way he thought of things. Life was easier to operate when objects were in their place.

He could hear Ella crying in their bedroom. What did she want him to do? If she told him to leave now and never return, he'd have done it, because she deserved as much. And he thought of church and God and all the things he had learned from his simple parents, who had worked in the same fucking cannery for thirty years, about never lying or stealing or wanting something that you have no right to have, to know his place in the world and to never overreach, and how he had disagreed with so many of their tenets because he didn't want to be them. But now he thought: They never hurt me. Except by their failure. Ted clutched his head with both hands. The older men at the cannery always said his father, Johnny Kim, was a man whose yes was yes and whose no was no. Ted had let himself get defiled.

He stretched his legs and got up from the chair. He stood by the bedroom door.

"Ella, Ella, please let me in," he said. "I'm sorry, baby. I'm so sorry. I haven't seen her in a year. I made a terrible mistake. I know I can't take it back. Please let me in. You are my best friend. You are my only friend. I have no one in the world. Ella—"

Ella wiped her face on the pillow and got up. She moved slowly toward the door because her steps were awkward. She twisted the latch to the open position, then returned to her spot on the bed. She laid her head on the hot, wet pillow. She could not face him and turned her body away from his. Ted lay down behind her, feeling safer there, and stroked her tangled hair. Ella let him do this, not knowing what else to do. He had killed her. Her mother had died in childbirth. Ella's life had killed her mother. And now Ted had killed her. How fair, Ella thought. How just. How symmetrical life was. How many lives did a person have to die? She felt desperate to drain her mind of anything bad, and she tried to recall happier moments. Even as short a time ago as this morning, she had felt joy even as she experienced nausea as the call car took her to the hospital for her appointment. She had talked to her daughter in her mind, saying, *I want to feel you so much, and I will take care of you forever.* Even Ella's limbs had felt hopeful or cooperative, if that were possible. She had believed that morning that her daughter was conceived in a pure kind of love. Ella believed in an infinite love—a kind of endless emotion that made life seem eternal. Ted was her heart first. You were supposed to forgive seven times seven times seven. Didn't she believe that?

Ella had read stories about adultery, heard tales of people who had cheated or had been cheated on, and although she had compassion for them—the cheaters and the cheated—now she saw how flawed her feelings had been, because she hadn't known a damn thing about it. All she felt was hatred. She felt a strong wish to disappear.

"Ella…Ella…I'm sorry. I mean it. I really am," he said. "I said I was sorry, and I am asking for your forgiveness. You have to believe how sorry I am."

Ella breathed as quietly as she could.

"Ella."

"Ted, I want this child. I want everything for this child. For her to never lack. Do you understand me?" Her voice was tender.

Ted wrapped his arms around his wife, pressing his forehead in the space between her stiffened shoulder blades. Ella felt unable to say another word.

3 | LUGGAGE

I THOUGHT YOU'D SEE IT MY WAY," Sabine said, her Cheshire cat grin spreading widely.

"Very gracious of you. Really." Casey winked. She didn't mind the comment. In many ways, she felt good that she'd finished the business school applications. No matter what happened, at least they were off her desk. So for lunch they were celebrating her completion with veal Parmesan heroes from Ray's. Thousands upon thousands of calories, Sabine had guessed with conspiratorial glee. "What the hell, send us the pumpkin cheesecake, too," she'd said, placing the order. Having accurately predicted Casey's decision that morning, Sabine had thought to bring champagne from her house for their Saturday in-office lunch, but it hadn't been chilled yet. There wasn't enough space in Sabine's office refrigerator for it, and she'd been too busy that morning to call the cafeteria for ice. The imposing bottle remained unopened on the conference table, like a festive decoration. They'd drink it next week, Sabine promised, not that Casey cared. Champagne gave her a headache, but like a child, she loved holding the slim flutes and staring at the bubbles floating up.

Neither spoke about the future of the store or where Casey might end up in the short run. She'd applied to only four schools: Columbia, Wharton, Harvard, and NYU. Her applications were decently prepared but not great. She wasn't being modest. Most of her colleagues at Kearn Davis with MBAs minced no words telling her that her professional résumé was hardly a standout. Regardless, Sabine was delighted that Casey had applied at all. When a person followed her advice, she transformed into her full-blown Lady Bountiful persona.

When they were done with their sandwiches, Sabine tiptoed to her desk and opened a drawer. She took out a black leather box the size of a hamburger container, not wrapped in the store's signature periwinkle blue paper but instead tied up grandly with a purple wire ribbon.

"For you," Sabine said, her eyebrows raised, with an impossible-to-restrain smile. She loved to give presents.

"For me?" Casey replied. "You shouldn't have."

"Shall I take it back?"

"No. Of course not. Don't you dare," Casey said, following their script.

It was a stainless-steel Rolex watch with a sapphire metal face.

"Oh, my God." Casey opened her mouth. "Oh, my God. Sabine! That's crazy! Why?"

"Who needs a reason? Nice, huh?" Sabine was so thrilled, she could burst. That morning, she'd had the idea to get it for Casey in the event she sent in her applications. It was a kind of reward. Sabine adored giving unexpected treats. Her driver had raced her across town to Tourneau, because Sabine had a meeting at ten-thirty with a prickly distributor from Germany back at the store, but it had taken her only minutes to select the gift. The men's stainless-steel bracelet with the small blue face had to be Casey's watch. The Rolex was streamlined and tough and possessed tremendous style. It was a durable luxury good—that naturally tickled Sabine.

"Put it on, put it on!" Sabine shouted, so Casey did, unable to believe what she'd been given.

She walked around the table to get to where Sabine was seated. She opened her arms wide to embrace her. "This is—it's incredible."

"I know." Sabine smiled. "It's nice, huh?" Casey liked it. She could tell.

Casey hugged Sabine, and she hugged her back.

"Thank you. I don't deserve it. I—I don't know what to say." Casey glanced at the cast-off Timex on the table. Her new watch rested perfectly on her left wrist next to her silver Wonder Woman cuff.

They stopped embracing to admire the watch.

"Do you have a headache?" Sabine asked.

"Pardon?"

Sabine draped her left forearm dramatically across her forehead. "Oh, dahling—I have a headache."

"Oh. Oh. Yes. I have a headache." Casey touched her forehead lightly with the inside of her forearm, flashing the new watch above her head.

She stopped this only to glance at her wrist again. "It goes with my cuffs. I love these—you know. Because you gave them to me."

"Of course you do," Sabine said, intentionally sounding haughty. Her tone of voice was ebullient, almost flirtatious. She lit up when she gave something away. To her, all her money made sense when it pleased the people she cared about, when she was able to support dreams. She loved this poor girl plucked out of Queens and wanted her to have everything she had herself. Sometimes abundance could repair a broken heart—Sabine believed that strongly. Even Casey's ridiculous, flamboyant impulses—at times damaging to herself—made sense to Sabine, who despised emotional restraint. In the girl, Sabine spotted the wide flash of the creative, and she yearned to nurture that piece. A spectacular failure was better than safety. Sabine wanted individuals to honor their greatest ambitions. All superior things—all things worth knowing, possessing, creating, and admiring, she'd observed—had begun with vast, impractical wishes. She hated smallness of character. Sabine hated fear. If Casey was given a chance to know her own desires, she'd go further than she herself had. There was no proof for this, but Sabine had made every decision in her life based on hunches. And she was never wrong about people—the entirety of one's personality was observable in the expression of the eyes. Her father, a successful fabric merchant, had taught her to look closely inside a face—that it was possible even to do this. You must spend a good length of time with an individual before you call him or her your friend, he'd instructed. To her father, a friend was the rare person—not everyone could be your friend. He scoffed at popular people: "A man the world loves cannot be a good lover." Words never mattered, he said, seasons mattered. Notice how people behave when they're desperate—that's who they are, he warned. Sabine ached suddenly, missing him.

"I want you to know that I meant what I said about every minute counting. Your life—the way you spend it—is precious."

"You are so kind to me. You are always so kind to me."

Sabine was crying now. It was good to cry, she thought as tears streaked down her high cheekbones.

"And I've never done anything for you."

"Nonsense," Sabine said, then took a moment. She spoke in Korean: "But if you performed some task or favor for my benefit, and I gave you a watch, then it wouldn't be a gift, would it?" She switched back to English: "Then it would be—an exchange." She said this last bit methodically, her voice full of well-reasoned conviction.

Casey paused to think about that. Somehow, hearing her words in Korean had made it more significant, more intimate.

"Yes." Casey sniffled, then laughed. "You're right. So where did you get your MBA, smart lady?"

Sabine smiled. "It's too late for me for school. But it isn't for you."

Was that true? Casey wondered. Then again, why would Sabine need an MBA?

"Are you sure?" She pointed to the watch, half expecting Sabine to change her mind.

Sabine caught the sobriety of Casey's expression. "You're my baby girl, Casey. I just want you to have a nice watch. Why would you deny me that pleasure? Enjoy the thing. It's pretty. Right?"

"Yes. It's beautiful. And it's from you. Thank you, Sabine." Casey nodded to herself and turned her face sharply toward the door. There was a *thump-thump* sound, a kind of shy knock. Casey wiped her face. "Sabine?" She needed to say one last thing.

"Yes, my friend?"

"I will be careful with my time."

"Of course you will."

The *thump-thump* sound came again.

"Come in," Sabine said in her boss voice. She felt delighted with herself. With life overall.

It was Judith Hast, the weekend accessories manager.

"I'm sorry to bother you, ladies, during your lunch." Judith noticed the bottle of champagne on the conference table. "Looks like there's a little party here." She laughed, her voice a touch chirpy and tittering.

Sabine ignored this. "How can I help you, Judith?" She gave her one of her famous CEO smiles.

"There's someone here to see Casey."

Casey wiped her eyes with the paper napkin. "Me?"

"An Asian lady."

"My sister? But she's supposed to be here after work." Casey looked at her watch and was surprised to see that it wasn't her Timex. Judith spotted the box on the table and the lavender ribbon. Casey was sporting a new watch.

"I met your sister once. I don't think it's her," Judith said. "But maybe because she's so pregnant, her face could've changed—"

"Your sister's pregnant?" Sabine exclaimed. "But she's in med school. When did that happen? "

"No, no, no. It must be my friend. I better go." Casey kissed Sabine on the cheek. "Thank you for...you know—"

"Yes, I know. Come by during your break. Eat cheesecake."

Casey ran ahead of Judith to see if Ella had come. She was supposed to be on bed rest.

It was her. Ella had on a well-worn men's coat that hung oddly across her large belly, a crimson-and-white college scarf wound around her neck, and green duck boots from Bean. She didn't look right, and it wasn't because of her makeshift ninth-month getup. Her skin was splotchy, grayish blue patches darkened her pretty eyes, and her usual ruler-straight posture was broken. Her bulging ankles spilled out of the tops of her boots. Ella was examining the fox-fur hat from Tibet as if it were alive—the one with the yellow satin silk crown. Her studious expression was of a disturbed person. Bodily present, but not quite there.

Nevertheless, Casey was happy to see her—it actually surprised her how much. Lately, maybe because it was near Christmas, Casey had been feeling rootless, lacking any sense of a past or family, except for her talks with Sabine and letters from Virginia in Italy. She received an occasional long-distance call from Tina, who'd promised to come by tonight. She hadn't been back home for the holidays since graduation. That was over two and a half years ago. There was no mention of Casey going to Elmhurst for Christmas or New Year's Day, either, from her family or from her. Casey felt uninvited, while her parents felt rejected.

"Hey, you're supposed to be in bed," Casey said cheerfully, trying not to look worried. She reached out to hug her. "How's the little mother? It's really great to see you—"

The rims of Ella's eyes reddened.

"Oh my. Hey, are you all right?"

Ella nodded meaningfully.

"What happened?... Hey? Ella? What's going on?"

Ella swallowed, trying not to burst into tears at Casey's job. "I'm sorry," she sputtered.

Judith couldn't look away. Casey glanced at her manager, and not missing this, Ella turned to Judith. "Thank you," she said, swallowing again, "uhm...for finding Casey. For me...." Ella panted. Her ears were ringing incessantly. Tracking her heartbeat, the ringing sounded as though someone were shooting a gun inside her head again and again and again. *Bang*, pause, *bang*, pause, *bang*.

"Really, Judith. Thank you. So much," Casey said. It scared her to see Ella like this. She'd speak to her quickly, then put her in a taxi. Dr. Shim had told Casey that preeclampsia was a serious danger for the mother.

"Judith, if it's okay with you, I'd like to take my break now," Casey said.

Judith squinted. "What time is it?"

Casey glanced at the Rolex. Like Sabine, Judith was a stickler about lunch and break periods. To make a point, Judith routinely docked people if they were only five minutes late.

"I realize I just had my lunch break, but this is important. Just fifteen minutes, okay? I'll make it up tomorrow. Sorry." Without waiting for Judith's reply, Casey dashed out from behind the counter, hooked Ella's arm securely with her own, and directed her to the back of the store to the employee elevator.

The glass-enclosed terrace of the employee cafeteria was freezing cold, but Ella didn't seem to mind. She was now heaving.

"Hey, none of that." Casey grew more worried. "What's going on?"

"Ted slept with Delia and gave me herpes." As soon as Ella said this out loud to another person, her breathing felt calmer.

"What?" Casey couldn't believe it. She could, but she couldn't. "Damn him."

"Isn't she your friend?" Ella stopped crying. Her eyes looked weird.

"Who? Delia?"

"Yes." Ella nodded, her concentration more intense. The gun-shots in her head grew louder, but she felt sharp.

"Whoa," Casey said, needing to stall. She couldn't talk about Delia to Ella. Delia would make any wife insane. With her right hand, she covered her eyes. "Right. Ted fucked Delia." She patted her pockets. Her cigarettes were downstairs. "What the fuck is his problem?"

Casey walked out to buy lunch with Delia nearly once a week, even after Delia changed floors. Not once had Delia mentioned an interest in Ted Kim or any other man. Delia didn't talk that much about men. It was almost too simple a topic for her. The only steady lay she'd admit to on occasion was Santo, whom she called the hot guy in the mailroom. But even Santo was sort of a done deal. He was Roman Catholic, and he and his high-school-girlfriend-turned-wife had four children together.

Casey liked Delia. Delia was cool. She was fun to talk to. They didn't hang out much outside of work, but Delia was someone you wanted on your side at the office. Despite her willingness to have sex with married men, Delia saw no contradiction or hypocrisy in the fact that she expected absolute loyalty from her friends, and she re-turned the favor. Her commitment to discretion had a lot to do with never humiliating the wives. She said, "Never make anyone's wife look bad. Really a stupid move." Casey had no intention of hooking up with a married guy, but if she did, she'd remember Delia's exege-sis on keeping a married man for the long haul: "The mistress can never truly replace a wife. The husband never stops needing the first wife's approval. The mistress can marry the husband, but the first wife is always somewhere in his head. Like his mother. And if there's kids, oh please, what a royal pain in the ass. The first wife might as well be in your bed, and she's definitely in your face. Stupid move. I don't advise it. Just fuck him. Knock yourself out."

"Casey?"

"Huh?" Casey glanced up. Ella looked terrified. "Are they still together?"

"He said it ended a year ago," Ella replied.

"That wouldn't surprise me. I mean—not that he screwed Delia, but that they're done with. You know?"

"My head hurts," Ella said. "This ringing in my head is so awful. I feel like someone is trying to kill me, over and over again—I want to die, Casey. This morning, I thought I'd jump out the window. But instead I came here. I thought maybe you can help me."

"Yes. Of course. Anything. It was good thinking. Good girl. Good, good—" Casey patted Ella's back. "That was good. Yes." She tried to figure out what to do. "I'm going to take you home now. We can kill Ted tomorrow." She smiled at her friend, who looked progressively younger in her eyes. "Today, we need to take care of you. Come on, sweetheart. Let's take you home. The doctor said you're supposed to be—"

Ella let Casey lead her out of the terrace and said nothing in the elevator as Casey murmured kind words to her. Ella nodded listlessly.

She was concentrating on her baby's blank face. For weeks and weeks, Ella had tried to imagine her baby's face, and she couldn't. After she found out that it was a girl, she wondered if the baby might have Ted's face or his mother's face. Somehow, she just knew the baby wouldn't look like her. Maybe the baby would resemble her dad. She would like that. Or her mother.

Casey was saying things, but Ella couldn't pay attention. When she thought of the baby's face, she stopped thinking of dying. She wanted a name for the child. But she couldn't think of one.

4 | HOLDING PATTERN

*T*HE DOORMAN HAD TO LET THEM into the apartment because Ella had locked herself out. He deserved a tip, but after paying for the taxi, Casey didn't have anything left but a twenty in her wallet and felt shy about asking Ella. She'd need the money to order a pizza for Tina later. "I'm sorry, I don't have much cash on me," she whispered as he headed out.

He shrugged. "No, problem, honey." The way the doorman said "honey" with a wink in his voice, as though he'd been there, too, reminded her of the grown men she'd known back home.

Once inside, Ella let Casey take off her coat and shoes. She lay down on her bed but refused to close her eyes. As she rested on her left side, her face softened and she blinked more than usual. Ella said nothing, resembling a sleepy, sad child.

"You should rest."

"Why do you think he did it?" Ella asked. "I got fat, didn't I?"

"You're pregnant."

"Is she thin?"

"You're thinner than she is when you're not pregnant. Stop this."

"Is she beautiful?"

"Ella! No one is lovelier than you. Please."

"Ted wants me to talk faster. Be more witty. I don't know how to talk to his HBS friends. I never know if they're just being polite or if they're actually interested. I should read more, go to lectures."

"Shh..." Casey placed her index finger over her lips. "You're exquisite." She paused for a moment to reflect on why Ella was significant to her. She wanted to give Ella something, and insight was a kind of gift. But Casey wanted to tell her something good, something true.

"You're an incredibly kind person—you make me feel loved. Like I'm all right. Like"—Casey took a breath—"I'm forgiven." The thought had taken her by surprise. "No one else does that. And I've never told you. And I should have."

Ella's face was unchanged, as if she hadn't heard a word of what was said.

"Delia must be fascinating. I bet she's funny. Ted loves funny people. I can't remember jokes. I'm quiet and responsible. And she's probably sexy. Why else would all those men...?" Ella closed her eyes as if she were trying to shut out a memory.

"Hey! Delia doesn't matter. Okay?"

"She's your friend, too. Everybody wants to be with her."

"No, no. You mustn't think that. C'mon."

"But you like her, too. You told me so a long time ago how much you enjoy seeing her. I was jealous, but I never told you. You can never see me for lunch."

"But Delia works in my building. We don't sit together and eat lunch. We walk to the cafeteria or the deli to grab something. Max— it's twenty minutes round trip, and she and I both eat at our respective desks." Was she actually justifying the time she spent with Delia? Casey had intentionally left out that at least once a month they met for a quick drink on the Wednesday nights before her millinery classes at FIT. It was a hoot because when she went to a bar with Delia, men sent them cocktails and business cards. Delia was the master of the quick bar kill—after she was done, carcasses littered the beer-stained floors. Casey had to admit that it was fascinating to witness a pro in play.

"I'll never speak to her again. Is that what you want?" Casey meant this even though that wasn't what she wanted. Regardless, Ella deserved that much.

"Does she have a nice personality? Is she independent? Like you?" Ella peered at Casey's face with pure wonder, as if a woman with enough compelling qualities would excuse what Ted had done.

"You're wonderful, Ella. Don't do this to yourself. Delia is irrelevant. Ted did this."

"I love him. But I hate him, too."

"Yes." The two sorority girls surfaced in Casey's mind. "You must."

"I have never loved anyone else but Ted."

"I know."

"I don't want him to leave me. How will I raise my daughter?" Ella was wide awake, her round face full of worry. She was breathing strangely.

"Ella, are you okay?"

"Yes."

"Let me know if you want me to call the doctor. Your blood pressure..." Casey tried to sound as relaxed as possible.

"I know, I know," Ella said plaintively. She tried to imagine her daughter's perfect infant body, fingers curling and opening. Her chest rose and fell at a more even pace.

Casey turned to the front door reflexively. "Where is that bastard, anyway? When's he getting home?"

"He went to a managing directors' off-site in Singapore. It was planned months and months ago. He's not coming home until Thursday night. My dad's coming later, and he's going to stay in the guest room." Ella blinked. "Do you think he's with her?"

What a selfish fuckhead, Casey thought. His wife was about to deliver, and he'd dumped her off with her dad. Fucking brilliant.

"He said he didn't want to go. Especially right now.... Maybe he took her with him," Ella wondered out loud.

Casey had no intention of defending that son of a bitch, but it wasn't helpful for her to get a pregnant woman with high blood pressure riled up.

"Honey, Ted doesn't matter. You matter. Your baby matters." Casey stroked her friend's hair.

Ella closed her dark eyes—the rush of blood still pounding in her ears.

*　　　*　　　*

From the living room, Casey phoned Judith, whom she hadn't had time to call to explain. But there was no answer. She phoned Sabine's direct dial.

"It better be good," Sabine said as a greeting.

When Casey told her what had happened, Sabine's response was eerily cold.

"It's nice of you, but this is ultimately Ella's problem," she said. "Besides, you can't fix that one. Too big." She categorized problems relationally—a knoll or Mount Everest. She also quantified the length of time projected to climb her challenges. "And thanks a lot. Judith thinks I'm playing favorites. You disrespected her. And I can't have that." Sabine abhorred insubordination of any variety.

"I'm sorry, Sabine. I shouldn't have just left, but I couldn't very well explain to Judith while Ella was standing right there. I wasn't trying to disrespect my manager. I'm not like that—"

"You've never even mentioned her," Sabine interrupted, voicing an entirely separate strand of argument. "It's not like she's a close friend."

"No. You're wrong. She's a very good friend." But there was no way for Sabine to have known this. Casey revealed very little of what went on in her life. And when there were difficulties, she burrowed into herself and tried to give a good show. The bit of Casey's heart that Sabine had managed to soften earlier—through Sabine's attentiveness and strong wish for her to do well in life—calcified again. Nothing kind or good came without expectations or demands. She checked the time. The new watch felt heavier on her wrist than her Timex. It was only three.

"Let me think about this," Sabine said. Her shrink had encouraged her to delay making decisions to curb her impulsive tendencies.

"Yeah," Casey muttered. "Do what you need to do."

"Don't get pissy with me, young lady," Sabine shot instantly.

"I'm sorry," Casey replied, catching herself.

Ella woke up, and she shuffled out to the living room. How long had she slept? For the past twenty-four hours, she'd thought about leaving Ted. But the consequences of such a thing—how could she manage? She wanted to see her father, to ask him for advice, but she didn't know how. What he'd said to her right before the wedding ceremony—the words had never left her mind. Perhaps she should've waited. There was no way she could tell her father what had happened. He'd hate Ted. Had they married too young? Was there something wrong with her in bed? That morning, she'd considered getting a video or some books. How did you get better in bed? How did you keep your husband interested in you? Her head hurt so much. The ringing in her ears had made it impossible for her to rest.

Ella stretched out on the sofa, desperate for some comfort. "Who was that?"

Casey glanced at the cordless phone in her hand. "No one."

"Was it Ted?"

"No."

"Do you have herpes?" Ella asked.

"Wow. Where did the reticent Wellesley girl go?"

Using both hands, Ella pulled a pillow over her head. Her suffering was evident.

"No, I don't have herpes." Ella's face went from pained to disappointed. "Sorry. But I had gonorrhea once. Does that make you feel better? My roommate had syphilis and a lousy case of genital warts, which had to be burned off. Another girl in my dorm got crabs. These things always seem like a bigger deal at the time. People should really get over the shame. Scientifically, it's more like the flu or mono, right?" Casey believed what she just said, but she'd never actually told anyone about having had a venereal disease.

"They're curable. Those—"

"Yeah. I also had an abortion. So pregnancy, it turns out, is curable as well." Casey shrugged, hating it when people had to compare problems. A truly unwinnable tack in life. Did Ella want her to list more embarrassing things so she wouldn't feel like the only one with rotten luck? Because if she did, Casey could oblige her easily. "What else do you want to know?"

Ella nodded thoughtfully. She had annoyed Casey. "I just can't leave Ted. I made this vow. God hates divorce. That's what Christ says in the Gospels."

"Okay. But Ted fucked somebody else and gave you the parting gift. I think there are a few escape clauses in the Bible. Adultery is the biggie." Casey was tempted to check, but she was fairly sure that the get-out-of-jail-free card could be found in Matthew.

"But you're supposed to forgive again and again. And he has repented."

"Ah. A lovely idea, and I'll remind you the next time I screw up."

Ella didn't laugh. She looked as if she were thinking very hard. "If I left him, where would I live? I don't even have a job."

"For a while you can stay with your dad. You can stay with me. I like kids. After a while, you'll be able to take care of you and the baby. Wait, you can stay here and make Ted get out. Why do you have to go?"

"To go from my husband's house to my father's house. What have I done?" There was outrage in Ella's voice, as if it weren't fair. "I majored in art history, got married, worked in development for two years. My husband got bored with me in bed after eighteen months. No, it must have been much, much less than that. Five months? Six? Oh, my God. He cheated with a woman everyone else has slept with at Kearn Davis. Why? And he gave me herpes. You know, I only had sex with one man."

Casey heard the indignation, and it irritated her. "Even if you had sex with fifty people, no one deserves to get sick, Ella. Sexual encounters should not involve discipline. I just find that hard to take. Would it be better if I got herpes? I had sex with more than one man, and I hope to have more sex. With more men. What would that prove if I got some STD? I don't know. I'm sorry Ted did this. And I'm very sorry you have herpes. But herpes is supposed to be one of those chronic things without much effect, anyway, I think—"

"That's not what I meant." Ella was frustrated, having expected more sympathy. "Never mind." But it did feel like some sort of un-warranted punishment. "I'm just pathetic. I feel like I should at least be sexy if I'm going to have this thing. Like more notches in my belt. My life . . ." Ella exhaled. "I did things wrong, or I didn't do enough things. I don't know. I'm sorry."

"Ella! You're not even twenty-five. It's not quite over, you know. I'd hang on to the towel if I were you." Casey stared hard at Ella's face, wanting her to pay attention.

The building intercom buzzed, and Casey jumped up.

"It's your father," she said. "He's coming up."

Ella's lower lip moved slightly.

"Are you okay?"

"I can't tell him." Ella wiped her eyes with her hands.

"You want me to stay? For a little while?"

"No. You have to get back. Thank you, Casey." Ella nodded to keep from crying. "Thank you for—"

"Hush. You sure you're okay?"

"I'll be good." Ella tried to smile.

"I know."

Casey took the subway down to the store. At the hat counter, she found Sabine and Judith speaking intimately. Neither seemed upset.

"Ah, the prodigal daughter has returned," Sabine remarked without much humor.

"I'm really sorry. For leaving like that." Casey then told them what she could about Ted, Ella's medical issues, and how Ella's mother had died in childbirth.

"Oh," Judith replied. What could she say?

"Anyway, I made a decision," Sabine said proudly, ready to dust her hands off of this event. She had a very strong need for closure. She turned to Judith. "Just knock the hours off her time sheet. Obviously starting from when she left and add back in her break time, which she's entitled to spend however or with whomever she wants."

Sabine straightened up to leave. Casey was supposed to have stopped by for cheesecake but had failed to call her about it. At two-thirty, when Casey usually took her break, Sabine had phoned Judith to ask where Casey was. That was when Judith had informed her that Casey had stormed off her post with a friend without giving any explanation.

Casey tried not to shake her head, unable to believe Sabine's docking bullshit. Sabine had given her a watch worth thousands of dollars, and she was quibbling about maybe fifty bucks. It was insane.

"But she ran over her break time last week, too. She owes twenty minutes," Judith said with a tinge of satisfaction.

"Thanks, Judith. You're a brick," Casey said. This used to be one of Jay's favorite expressions. "Really so helpful."

Sabine, who was about to step away, turned back instantly. "Listen, Casey, mind your manners. You cannot behave this way in front of me, your supervisor, or any customers."

Casey cocked her head. There were no customers near the counter.

"Do you understand? You can't get upset at Judith because she didn't cover for you. That isn't her job. That's not what I pay her to do."

"Don't yell at me," Casey said quietly.

"I will correct my employees when and how I deem necessary," Sabine said. At the word *employee,* Casey's jawline went from its natural curve to a bony hardness.

Judith considered mentioning that Casey's friend did sound a little bonkers but didn't know how to bring it up now.

A pair of elderly women stopped by the counter to admire the boaters trimmed with fabric roses. They looked like twin sisters, somewhere in their late eighties or nineties, spry and impeccably turned out in Mainbocher-style suits.

Judith opened her mouth, but Sabine cut her off. "Judith, take last week's break time off, too. I never want to hear about you letting her borrow against her break time. This credit issue is something Casey needs to fix."

Judith said yes, then switched to serve the older women, who now stood before her.

Casey's neck flushed scarlet.

"And you..." Sabine faced Casey, trying to smile at her. Her voice grew gentle. "Stop by my office today after work."

"Sorry. Can't do it. Tina will be here after work. I haven't seen her in over a year." Casey had missed her MIT graduation. She wouldn't keep Tina waiting. "Tell me whatever it is you want to now." She wasn't the least bit ashamed of her behavior that afternoon. If Sabine wanted to fire her, take back the offer to pay for B school, have her return the watch, Casey didn't give a rat's ass. She'd grown up without Rolexes—her friendships were not negotiable for legal tender or gifts. Casey refused to make eye contact. The more she thought about it, the angrier she grew. "I said I was sorry, Sabine. You know I wouldn't have left unless it was urgent. Ella had a genuine crisis."

Sabine didn't know whether to be insulted or impressed by the girl's fantastic nerve. "But you have a job, Casey Han. Work comes first." She felt she had to teach Casey an essential lesson in business: "Everyone, sweetheart, can be replaced."

"Fine." Casey shrugged. *Replace me* was on the tip of her tongue.

Sabine took a long breath and touched Casey's forearm. How could she break into the girl's glassy gaze?

"I'm not here tomorrow. Let's talk next week. When all of this will seem foolish." Sabine smiled at her again. "Okay, Casey? Everything all right?... Casey?"

"Yup." Casey smiled back at her boss.

As she walked away, Sabine turned once. Casey's body had grown rigid and tall, like a cornstalk. She could be heard asking one of the two women if there was something she'd like to try on.

Until closing time, Judith and Casey worked alongside each other, giving off the air that all was cheery at the hat counter. Neither spoke to the other, however, when there were no customers.

The interview for a summer research fellowship at Einstein had gone overtime, so Tina never showed up at the store. Casey had gone home, and Tina finally arrived there an hour and a half after they were supposed to have met.

Casey let her in. Tina had never been so late, but even that was okay. It felt so good to see her. The sisters hugged each other—neither able to remember the last time they'd embraced.

"What's that noise?" Tina asked, looking around.

"Oh!" Casey dashed back to her sewing machine to turn it off. The industrial-built secondhand Singer she'd bought in Chinatown for seventy-five bucks worked perfectly but made an intense whirring racket when it was on.

Tina dropped her coat and handbag on a nearby folding chair. "Wow," she said, taking it all in. The apartment was more spartan than she'd imagined, with only the most essential furniture.

In one corner of the L-shaped studio, there was a full-size futon mattress, and beside it, three stacks of books were piled on the floor. A Sony Dream Machine clock-radio sat on top of a copy of *Sister Carrie*. A naked extension cord snaked out from the base of the brass floor lamp. Near the window with a partial view of the Hudson and Jersey City, there were two different-looking sewing machines, including the one Casey had just shut off, a stumpy wooden stool, and opposite the Pullman kitchen was a white metal café table and two folding chairs. The closet—large by New York standards, almost the width of one of the shorter walls, with its shutter-style doors thrown open—was bursting with colorful clothes. On the bottom of the closet, multiple pairs of shoes and boots were strewn about—mismatched and their mates far apart. Dozens of hatboxes attached with Polaroids of their contents dominated the apartment. No sofa, coffee table, bookshelves, or rugs.

"What are you making?" Tina asked, her manner curious and thoughtful. She squinted at the sewing machine.

"I'm entering a contest." There was a juried exhibit for accessories at FIT, and she and Roni, the cheese seller, were entering as a team. They had designed a collapsible straw hat and matching handbag with a special compartment for the hat.

"Contest?"

"I know. It's weird."

Tina raised her eyebrows and shoulders simultaneously. Not much surprised her anymore when it came to Casey.

"Hey, I'm starving."

"The food's on its way." Casey had ordered the pizza right after Tina called from the station. Her sister wore a blue crewneck sweater and navy slacks. Her hair was cut in a blunt style, giving it more movement. She'd taken off her snow boots on the floor, and with her legs splayed out, she wriggled her toes in shabby black socks. The Einstein interview had gone well, and she'd accepted an on-the-spot offer.

"Sex has made you even prettier," Casey remarked, noticing the sock's thinning fabric on the balls of her sister's feet.

"Thank you." Tina's black hair swung in lovely chunks when she laughed. "I'm employed and engaged."

"What?" Casey shouted. "Are you serious?"

"About which part?"

"You know what I'm talking about. You're twenty-two. Honestly, I won't think poorly of you if you don't marry him. What's wrong with just living with him?" Ella had married her first. Chul probably wasn't like Ted. Dear God, let that not be the case, prayed the agnostic in her mind. Casey wondered if she should talk about Ella now. "Have I failed you? Taught you nothing? The first man you had sex with!"

"Correction. The first man who made love to me."

"I stand corrected. Excuse me." Casey was clutching the handbag pattern in her hand. She was wrinkling the corners of the taped-up pattern paper, so she went to place it in her black portfolio leaning against the wall.

"I thought you'd be happy," Tina said, sounding dispirited. She'd been so relieved on the way over here with a summer fellowship in hand. She hugged her knees with her hands.

"I am happy for you. Truly." Casey had looked forward to Tina after such a bizarre day. But this was a shock, too.

"Then you'll come to the wedding."

"Yes. I will come to the wedding. Of course," Casey said. Tina was still upset with her about the graduation. Casey hadn't gone because she couldn't deal with her parents and went to a Kearn Davis outing instead. It was work related, but truth be known, she could've gotten out of it.

Tina didn't want to talk about the wedding anymore.

"Now, here's the bad news."

"So that was the good news, then?" Casey laughed.

"Ha, ha. . . . Dad's building burned down last Sunday," Tina said calmly. She lifted a cover off a lone hatbox within reach. Her eyebrows arched in wonder at the wide-rimmed straw encircled with pink fabric peonies. "Pretty."

The pizza arrived, but Casey couldn't eat. She watched Tina devour her first slice while she discussed the fire and how the insurance would come through soon. Tina had dealt with all the paperwork that her parents couldn't read. Faulty wiring had caused the total loss. Nobody was hurt because it had happened on a Sunday. No one had bothered to call Casey, making her realize that she must've missed many other things and would miss more as time went on. Casey was feeling left out, but Tina was excusing her parents, because they were hurt too by Casey's withdrawal from their lives. "They didn't want to bother you at the office," Tina said. Their father wasn't the same, she added.

Three years ago, when Joseph bought the building in Edgewater, Casey had gone to the closing with him. Leah had called her at school. "Daddy is going to buy a building. Our retirement money will be the down pay. Elder Kong said it was a good investment." Leah told Casey where the closing would take place. Tina could have gone—her father might have preferred that—but she was in Boston, and it was cheaper for Casey to show up. And Casey was older. So she skipped her microeconomics class, took a train to the city, and met her dad at the bank lawyers' offices. Though her father understood almost everything, his lawyer talked mostly to Casey, and she translated whatever else was needed. After all the checks were passed out, Mr. Arauno, the seller's lawyer, handed Joseph the keys. Mr. Arauno told Joseph that he had a nice daughter. After the closing, Joseph drove Casey to the building before taking her back to school.

"I saw the building. After the closing," Casey said.

"Yeah?" Tina sprinkled garlic powder on her second slice.

That afternoon in Edgewater, the sun had glowed fiercely on the modest storefronts of Hilliard Avenue. Her father's building was a three-story brick with two shops on the ground floor—a pizzeria and a small electronics outlet. A side door opened onto a modest carpeted lobby with stairs that led to the professional offices on the second and third floors. Joseph didn't say much as the two of them walked around the building. He walked into the electronics store, and the salesman asked him if he needed any help. Joseph shook his head no, picking up a Panasonic answering machine that was on special, then putting it down. He never told them that he was their new landlord. Casey followed him when he walked out. They peered into the pizza shop. It looked clean. After they toured the two ground-floor stores and checked out the dentist's office and the accountant's office upstairs, they left the building. Casey returned to her father's blue Delta 88, which was parked not ten yards away. Not hearing his footsteps behind her, she turned and saw that he was standing beside the building; his right hand was pressed against the brick of the facade. Her father was smiling.

"How is he doing?" Casey asked.

"Lousy. What do you expect?"

"Can't he get a new one? With the insurance money?"

"Mom said he doesn't want to risk it. And you know her. She's no gambler. They'll probably put the money in a savings account."

What Casey had seen on her father's face that day was pride. Some happiness.

"He looks much older," Tina said.

"How old is he again?"

"He turned sixty in June."

"I sent him a tie," Casey mentioned. She'd bought an Hermès necktie that had cost over a hundred dollars and mailed it to him from the store, although it would've been far easier for her to just walk it over from Kearn Davis.

"Mom told me."

Casey nodded. The last time she spoke to her mother was around Thanksgiving, when she'd told her that she was working through the holidays for overtime money. For turkey, she'd gone to the Gottesmans', where Sabine was hosting a dinner for twenty of her favorite strays.

"Sixtieth birthday. That's—"

"We didn't do much for his *hwegap*," Tina said.

"Damn. That's right." Casey jerked back, sighing loudly. "Damn. Damn," she muttered, disgusted with herself. Their parents were often invited to these fancy potlatches thrown by well-off adult children to celebrate their Korean parents' sixtieth birthdays—the sum of five zodiac cycles. A person was supposed to have completed a full life cycle by living from zero to sixty.

"That was near your graduation, wasn't it?"

"Yeah," Tina said quietly.

"So in the month of June, I managed to miss both your graduation and Dad's big birthday. You can say that I have a genius for fucking up. They don't get better than me." Casey was afraid to ask what Tina had done for his birthday. No matter. She'd never had favored nation status.

"There's another big party at the seventieth, I think." Tina tried to sound hopeful.

"Yeah, I should've earned my first million by then. I'll be thirty-four. Let's just book the banquet rooms at the Plaza now." Casey was sinking in an ocean of shame.

"Shut up, Casey. It's going to be okay. This isn't a guilt session. I wanted to see you," Tina said with a smile.

She started to talk about Chul. He was likely to focus on cardiology, she said, beaming, at UCSF School of Medicine. His father was a professor and his mother a radiologist, and his three sisters were lawyers. Chul was the baby. Joseph and Leah had already met Chul's parents in New York after Thanksgiving. Everything had gone fine, Tina said with a little shrug of doubt. Casey listened to her talk, trying not to interrupt—a bad habit of hers—and she observed how Tina's face brightened when she spoke of him. Casey wanted to believe with all her heart and mind that true love could exist and that marrying young with the first man you made love to could yield a faithful bond. She wished that for her sister right then and there. She didn't mention what was happening with Ella and Ted. What purpose would that serve?

Tina had to leave at ten so she could take the subway home to Queens. They embraced before parting, and this time the gesture felt easier. Why hadn't they done this sooner?

Casey shut the front door. The apartment wasn't much, but it was tidy, and it was hers. She lived in Manhattan—it was called the city, though it was also a borough like Staten Island or the Bronx. Her first year at Princeton, a freshman from Jackson Hole, Wyoming, had asked her where she was from, and when she'd said New York, he'd said, Oh, where? When she'd answered Queens, he'd stared at her as though she'd been lying. Because only one borough counted as New York.

The night from her window was blue and black with the skyline of Jersey City twinkling far off in broken bits and pieces. Next to the sewing machine, her contest hat rested misshapen on the head block, needing more steam to block it than what her teakettle could generate, and the handbag fabric lay uncut on the stool. It felt later than ten, and Casey went to brush her teeth to get ready for bed. Tired and spacey, she stubbed her foot on the open closet door. She bent over to take care of a broken toenail. Her nail clippers were in one of the Kearn Davis gym bags that she used for storage. The Redweld folders with photocopies of her B school applications were also stuck in there.

Why hadn't she told Tina about applying to business school? Ella, Ted, and Delia, Dad's building, Tina's internship and marriage. Life was either breaking down or fusing together. She was trying to start something new. It was hard to picture what her life would look like beyond this moment. Casey couldn't tell her little sister about trying something new again. For surely it was possible to fail another time.

5 | VIEW

*Y*OU'RE WASTING YOUR LIFE," Hugh Underhill said.

"You're such an ass," Casey replied sweetly. She batted her short eyelashes for comic effect.

Hugh smiled back charmingly. Cleaned four times a year by a hygienist he'd slept with years before, his teeth were bright and attractive. "Young lady, I've been called better things."

"And you've been called far worse things."

"Thanks, Casey Cat," Hugh said. "You keep me honest."

"No problem, Hedge," Casey answered. "Somebody has to try." She continued thumbing through the rack of pastel-colored golf shirts embroidered with the logo of Bronan Resorts.

Hugh was picking on her about her future. Knowing how broke she was, he had decided that the solution was for her to make more money. Pushing her to be a junior broker was his way of showing concern. Business school decisions would be mailed out this month, but with the exception of Kevin Jennings—whom she had no choice but to ask for a recommendation since he was her direct supervisor—no one else at the office knew she'd applied.

The salesclerk who worked at the pro shop had gone downstairs to fetch Hugh a windbreaker vest, so they were alone. The cherry-wood paneling made the place look like a judge's chambers. As usual, Casey and Hugh were fifteen minutes early—one of the annoying qualities they shared. It was their macabre joke that they'd beat their deaths by a quarter of an hour. Secretly, they respected each other for it. However, Seamus, one of their foursome for today, the client they both liked, was running very late. He had missed his flight entirely. Walter was scouting about for a replacement. Otherwise, Hugh, Casey, and Brett Martin, another client, would make up a threesome. Hugh was not fond of Brett, who jangled coins in his pockets and gave unsolicited advice on your swing. Brett Martin was a nice guy, but a duffer.

Kearn Davis was hosting the Asian Technology Conference, which officially began tomorrow on Sunday after a sunrise breakfast. Yet the clients who wanted to play eighteen holes had come in that morning. Tee time was in thirty minutes.

Casey had tagged along, taking off a weekend from Sabine's since the latter two weeks of April were expected to be slow, with hardly any commissions worth sticking around for. The boys—as she called the men she assisted on the desk—hadn't known that she golfed, but when she'd mentioned in passing that she did, they'd shouted, Why the hell didn't you say so before? Frankly, it had never occurred to her in her nearly three years of working at the desk to go away on a golfing trip with them when she herself wasn't a broker. She didn't even know she was allowed, and certainly no one had ever asked. When she popped up at La Guardia with her sweet Ping clubs that Jay had bought her with his first paycheck at Kearn Davis, Hugh widened his dark brown eyes.

"And I thought you were smoking us for a free vacation."

"Maybe I am," Casey retorted.

The panoramic view from the pro shop window was dazzling. The grounds below were carpeted with kelly green grass, and the sky above the horizon was half silver and lavender. From where she stood, she could see a couple of foursomes playing—spotless white carts lolling there waiting to ferry them to their next hole. Acres upon acres of nature manicured and coiffed like a rich second wife for the enjoyment of a few entitled individuals. She'd played at the great private clubs with Jay and his eating club friends whose fathers and mothers were members—Baltusrol, Winged Foot, Rockaway Hunt, Westchester. Virginia's game was tennis, and Casey could keep up a modest rally, but without the precision and engagement she freakishly possessed in her golf game. Virginia said even her dull father thought golf was a snoozer. To the contrary, Casey wanted to say. There was a kind of geometry and physics in the game that she perceived visually yet could hardly articulate. She respected the game's difficulty—its aesthetic design.

She'd learned by playing mostly on New Jersey public courses with Jay. When they'd first started to date, they'd cut classes in the afternoons just to play. Golf and sex: That had been their thing. Sometimes before and after. When she asked herself why she never told the boys about golf, the answer hit her. She missed him still. Golf was something Jay had taught her from scratch. He was a very fine teacher. After they broke up, giving the clubs away had crossed her mind. But he'd been so proud to buy them for her with the money he'd made from his first Wall Street job, his face bright with the surprise. Right away she had kissed him, because the gift had moved her. And seeing his happiness, she'd kissed him two more times, and they had ended up in bed, being late for a dinner with friends. It was such a curious thing when you thought back to someone you loved: It was possible to remember the unspoiled things, and doing so lit up a bit of the sober darkness in your heart, and all the while the memory of the hurting cast its own shadow, dimming your head with the nagging questions of ifs and why-nots.

The clerk returned and said they were out of the large-size vests. "Sorry."

"No problem," Hugh replied. "You tried."

He made a face at the ladies' racks of polo shirts and madras pants. Hugh disliked preppy clothing on women. It made them look like square, flat-chested little men. Women should be soft to touch, curvy in the waist and hips, and delicious smelling. Skinny, small-boned blondes who sailed and were sun-wizened in their twenties were not his cup of tea. He didn't give two bits if that was old-fashioned. He liked a slim-waisted girl in a billowy dress, pearls on her throat; a little leg showing was fantastic. Matching bra and panties in a bad-girl color, even better. While her head was turned, Hugh checked Casey out. She was exceptionally feminine in her clothing. Her speech, however, was something else.

"The worst thing about women playing golf is the clothing," Hugh pronounced.

"Does that mean you're not getting me a shirt?"

"What? You want one?" he asked, irritated that Casey could disagree.

"You offering?" Casey raised an eyebrow.

"It all depends." He smiled suggestively. Hugh was an alchemist: He could transform any comment into sex.

She never took his innuendos seriously, and it took about a hot second for her to come up with a sassy rebuttal.

"I hope I price out better than"—Casey read the tag—"fifty-seven fifty."

Before he could reply, they heard Walter calling out.

"Seamus caught the later flight." Walter was panting. He repeated the message from his voice mail. "So, Hedge, you're still short one. You can play as a threesome. But I just saw Unu Shim from Gingko Tree Asset Management in the lobby. Didn't know he was here today. Want me to get him? Shim-kin's a good guy. You'd be a few minutes late, though. He's gotta get his gear."

"Isn't anyone on time anymore?" Casey glanced at her watch. Even after four months, the Rolex still tended to startle her.

Hugh nodded at Walter, trying to be agreeable. "Okay, man, you make it happen. I'll be at the first tee with sweetie over here."

Casey smiled at Walter and elbowed Hugh.

At the foot of the long patio where the carts were parked, Unu Shim turned up only a few minutes late. He was not quite six feet, slight build, almost skinny. His eyes had the double fold that Casey didn't have. When he smiled, radial lines formed near his temples. He was thirty or so. Like all the others, he wore khakis. His red shirt had come from a pro shop in Maui with a slogan embroidered on the unbanded golf sleeve. Small, knotty muscles lined the length of his arms. For a thin guy, he had Popeye forearms. His golf shoes hadn't been cleaned since the last time he'd worn them; mud streaked his laces.

There were seven fully manned carts on the patio, and Casey, the only female, sat alone in one. She was in the driver's seat, waiting to take the new guy. Seeing him approach the cart, she turned around to make room for his Callaway bag. Hugh had taken Brett and his noisy pockets in his cart. Unu ducked his head to get in.

"Casey, right?" Unu said. He held out his hand.

"Hey." She shook his hand. Decent grip, palm damp. "You want to drive?" she asked him, smiling politely.

"No thanks," he answered, puzzled as to why she didn't recognize him. She was Casey Han, Ella's friend. They'd met twice, and both times she'd barely talked to him, but especially at the wedding, where she had skipped out before making a toast. Was that almost two years ago? he wondered. The dad had some tussle with her boyfriend. Something like that—Ella had said. The boyfriend was history, but apparently she had zero interest in blind dates, although Ella was forever singing her hymns: creative, attractive, smart as a whip. Unu had figured that she was one of those Korean girls who hated Korean men. But she didn't seem like that right now.

Today, she looked relaxed and cheerful, like a girl on a college golf team. Her face was slightly tanner than the last time he'd seen her, making her look healthier. There was a faint spray of freckles across her nose and cheeks. She wore a white golf shirt and a pair of Nantucket reds. Her white golf shoes looked new. Unu couldn't have guessed that they cost four hundred dollars. She sported a Panama hat she'd had blocked at Manny's Millinery and trimmed with a dark blue ribbon and one of her better-executed tailored bows.

"Good hat," he said.

Touching the edge of her brim, she said, "It's an original." There was still some flirt in her tone left over from talking to Hugh.

"I bet," he said, laughing. She was taller than he'd remembered.

"You know, you look amazingly familiar," she said, then looked straight ahead. "I never say that, by the way." Her comment wasn't meant to sound like a come-on.

"I'm Ella's cousin. Unu. We've met. Twice," he said sheepishly.

"Oh." Her happy expression vanished.

"It's been almost two years. I was a groomsman at the wedding. And you—"

"Yes, yes. Of course. I'm sorry," she said, wishing she could bolt.

Casey turned on the ignition and started to drive, saying nothing. Yes, yes, yes, she thought to herself. Unu. His full name was Un-young Shim from Gingko Tree A.M. That was the name on the client list, which she had reviewed multiple times, but it never occurred to her that he could be Ella's cousin Unu. There were three Shims she knew of when she picked up the calls at the desk. And Walter sometimes called Unu "Shim-kin." Of course, of course. They must've at least said hello on the phone before she'd patched Walter through. This man had seen her pop Jay on the nose, carrying on like an insane person minutes after church service ended. He might have seen her dad shove Jay out of his way and would have remembered her taking off from Ella's wedding before fulfilling her promised duties. If he thought she was violent, from a bigoted family, and lacked both personal decorum and loyalty, how could she blame him? Casey wanted to fold her arms over the steering wheel and drop her heavy head on them.

This was what she deserved for lying to Judith and Sabine about why she needed the weekend off. With no compunction, she'd told them that she was helping a friend move. If only she could be back in her apartment working on the leather fez assignment for her costume headwear class, bent over a sewing machine, the radio humming nearby. If only. If she hid in her hotel room until the conference was over, Kevin would be furious with her, but after this experience, she didn't want to lie to another employer again. Casey pulled down the brim of her hat as if to shield herself from the bathing light of the Florida sun.

The first four holes passed quickly. Bizarrely, her game was brilliant. Shame could make you concentrate. Two birdies and two bogeys.

"Casey Cat is on fire!" Hugh laughed in a mixture of shock and delight after she sank another one. Both her long and short games were equally strong. Hugh was tickled by this surprise performance, not being the kind of broker who restrained his playing for the client's sake. Besides, the two clients weren't his anyway, and Casey was the assistant. Brett had been nearly struck dumb by her playing after the third hole, but his jingling had grown more persistent despite Unu's curious stares. Unu, an excellent golfer, was a touch behind Casey and right there with Hugh: one bogey, two par, and his last was two over par. He'd been studying her swing.

The arc of it was just gorgeous, Unu thought. The girl's posture when she was at rest was straighter than a club, and her profile was stiff. After he'd mentioned their prior meetings, she hadn't said anything to him except whatever was necessary to avoid making their interaction weird. When she was quiet, he could feel the grief in her expression. Something was making her really sad, as though she were easy to hurt and would be easy to hurt again.

His ex-wife, Eunah, had been this way. Something about sad girls sort of got to him. At their first meeting arranged by a relative, shortly after he'd arrived in Seoul as an expatriate employee of Pearson Crowell, Eunah had appeared self-possessed and determined, like a young woman driving straight toward her destiny. He liked that about her; it made her seem different from the other girls, who giggled too much or were prettier but too shy. Their engagement was barely five months long, and soon after their marriage, her resolve for life dissipated quietly. Eunah did everything she was supposed to do, but there was a quality of performance about her, and he was starting to feel that nothing he could do or be would make her feel joy. She was always grateful to him, but that wasn't necessarily happiness. She did not delight in his presence. Eunah thought he was a nice guy. Sometimes, desperate to make her laugh, he'd act the clown. He gave her expensive gifts, which she appreciated. His wife's regret would come and go, and it infected their happiness, but Unu also had his very busy work, and he could not attend to her as much as he'd wanted to. He'd always believed there would be more time later. When he was recruited by Gingko Asset Management for a job in New York two years back, Eunah had said she couldn't leave Korea.

"I don't want to be an American. I don't like bread." She'd said this with enormous hesitation, knowing how odd it sounded considering she had married an American-born Korean who had warned her from the very first date that he fully intended to go back.

"Eunah, I'll never ask you to give up rice," he'd said, laughing at her comment.

Unu didn't give up right away. He brought her guidebooks or videos of movies about New York like *Annie Hall.* She read them and watched the films. She tried to be enthusiastic for him and tried very hard to think about living in America. One night when they were in bed, she turned her long body away from his and told him that she still loved her college boyfriend, whom her parents had refused to meet solely because he was from Julla-do—a poor province of South Korea, where its natives were cruelly stereotyped as cheats. She had phoned him when Unu had told her about going to America, and he'd said he was still waiting for her. That he would wait for her until he died.

Unu let her go, not because he didn't love her, but because he did. After she left, there was a peculiar sense of heartache mingled with relief, because then he understood that the sense of doom in her life wasn't his fault. After the divorce, Eunah married that college boyfriend from Julla-do, and they had a daughter. And now Unu, the American-born Korean from Texas, lived alone in a two-bedroom Upper East Side apartment with rented furniture across the street from his cousin Ella, who invited him to brunch every Sunday after church. Unu didn't tell Ella that on Friday nights he drove his Volvo station wagon to the Indian casino in Connecticut and played blackjack until his eyes made him quit. In March, he'd cleared eight thousand dollars, but in February, he'd lost five.

They had just finished the fifth hole.

"So where did you learn how to play?" Hugh asked Casey.

"I told you. I picked it up in college." Casey smiled weakly. His attention made her feel self-conscious.

"Yeah?"

She was surprised herself by how smoothly it was going. "I haven't played in three years or so. I'm not kidding."

"Hmmm," Unu said, looking skeptical.

"I swear." Casey nodded to herself, because it was true.

"Shall we make this interesting?" Hugh interrupted. "A dollar per stroke."

"I thought you'd never ask," Unu answered.

They all looked at Brett, the weakest player of the four.

Not to be embarrassed, and believing earnestly that the pressure might do his game some good, he upped the ante. "Two. What the hell."

There'd been no need previously to discuss handicaps, but now, with the final scores needed, the issue presented itself. Casey didn't want to tell them her last handicap. It would freak them out. If the average course was seventy-two par, and this one was—that is, all eighteen holes could be completed by a very fine player in seventy-two strokes—then it had been her practice to finish such a course in eighty-six, thereby making her handicap fourteen. At the height of her playing with Jay, she often shot an eighty-five or eighty-six. That was a very good score for either sex. Golf was this useless hobby where she was a natural. It was especially useless and ironic since she could neither afford to be a member of a club nor have the leisure to play. She had no car and no friends or family who played who'd take her out to a course. Jay had been the only person who'd arranged these things for her, because he loved the game, and they had a great time playing together. Until recently, the idea of playing golf at all had, admittedly, hurt her heart.

Unu gave his handicap first: "Twenty."

"C'mon," Hugh said. "Really?"

"Yeah." Unu smiled. "I got nothing to prove."

Brett said, "Thirty-five? What's max here?" The others were very good players, and frankly, the assistant's playing had taken the piss out of him.

"Twenty," Casey said.

"Get out of town," Hugh said.

Unu cocked his head. "You can do better than that. You just shot two bogeys, two birdies, and one par, which was damn near an eagle except for—"

"Yeah," Brett chimed in.

"What did you shoot in college, Miss Full of Surprises?" Hugh looked amused at her.

"Fourteen," she said quietly.

"Damn, girl." Hugh laughed so hard, he had to clutch his bag trying not to fall down.

They made her take fourteen, and the game went on.

Eighteen holes passed faster and more quietly with the bet in place. Although her game was steady, the twelfth hole gave her a smidge of trouble, and the seventeenth was screwy when she lost her ball in the water. In the end, she shot an eighty-seven—a very respectable score by any measure—but because of Unu's larger handicap, Casey ended up placing third behind Unu and Hugh. She owed Unu and Hugh something like forty dollars. Everyone paid up quickly, but Casey didn't have her wallet with her, so she promised to get them later at the dinner.

Everyone went back to the rooms to shower. After cleaning up, she futzed around in her bathrobe. She tried not to think about the seventeenth hole. It irritated her to think of how she'd lost her focus and the angle of her wrist. She'd chuffed. It happened. She powdered her nose, resolving to be braver at dinner with Unu. Maybe she wouldn't have to deal with him. She wanted to believe that she could pretend not to be uncomfortable.

Casey slipped the sleeveless navy sundress over her head, twisting about to zip herself up. Wide straps, a square neckline edged in white, and nipped in at the waist. She'd brought along a pearl necklace, a high-quality fake, that skimmed above her clavicle and larger studs for her ears. She laced the ties of the linen wedge espadrilles about her ankles. The outfit cost a breathtaking eleven hundred dollars—more than half her monthly take-home pay. She'd become a card-carrying Wilma—willing to pay retail for the right look. In the side zipper of her tote bag, she had exactly sixty-seven dollars and a wallet full of maxed-out credit cards, and if she forked over the money she owed to Hugh and Unu, she wouldn't have sufficient cab fare to get back home from the airport. She had no one to blame except herself. She could've passed on dresses and shoes like these. Said no to the bet made on the fifth hole. Her clothes cost more than what women brokers, bankers, and analysts wore, though they made ten times her annual salary. But clothes made her feel legitimate in her shifting environments; tonight, in this dress, she was a girl who'd gone to Andover, not Stuyvesant, and a girl who'd lost her virginity at the Gold and Silver in New York, not at a roller rink in Elmhurst. She had always curated her identity, matching locale with dress, and why should this night be any different? When she completed a hat, she named it, and with this name, she tried to imagine what kind of lover the woman who'd own such a hat would make. Would she be shy or demanding? Would she trust his touch utterly or fight her feelings? Would her body rise to meet his? Through clothing, Casey was able to appear casual, urbane, poor, rich, bohemian, proletariat. Now and again, she wondered what it'd be like to never want to look like anything at all—instead, to come as you are.

When she got to the lobby, Hugh and a few others had beaten her. She was only five minutes early.

Hugh whistled. "Nice pearls."

She picked up a corner hem of her skirt and curtsied. "Thank you."

Hugh asked, "How old are you again?"

"You know how old I am. I am much, much, much younger than you." She laughed. They were less than a dozen years apart, but it was a running joke that she was jailbait as far as he was concerned.

The others paid them no mind. Kevin Jennings nodded at her briefly as though he approved but would never admit that he was pleased to see her. He was a grumpy person, and by this time, Casey realized that he possessed a fine character despite his refusal to be affable on a consistent basis. Kevin and Walter talked with Seamus

Donnelly, who'd finally arrived. He was a top-tier client—perhaps the most important client there—and accordingly, he received the attention he was due. Also, it should be said that Seamus was clever and amusing to talk to. Everyone would want to sit with him at dinner. As for his investment style, he was slightly more contrarian than either bull or bear—nearly impossible to predict. Walter said that in his experience, people who were independent-minded were the ones who had the potential to make serious cash and not just upper-yuppie money. Seamus Donnelly was crazy rich now, but he'd be the first to tell you that he was fifty-eight years old and his first two funds went under and that his kids had to go to state schools because he'd screwed up one too many calls.

Unu was disagreeing with Seamus about something, but they both looked pleased by the exchange. Something about manufacturing plants in Vietnam and Indonesia, Casey gathered. The crowd began to move toward the dining room, where they'd eat a steak dinner. She'd helped to plan the event, so she could recite the menu by heart. Unu was only a few paces ahead of her, wearing a white golf shirt, a pair of dress chinos, and a navy blazer. He wore a needlepoint belt with the Greek letters of his fraternity. The smells of soap, aftershave, and spray starch wafted about her. The group was mostly men—after a solid day of sun and sports, fresh from a shower, and dressed for dinner. It was like being back in college when she and her friends headed en masse to a spring formal on warm April evenings.

Unu broke away from Seamus, giving the others a crack at the great man in attendance. He waited to walk in with her.

"Hey," Casey said. "Good game. I owe you some money. Can I send you a check when I get back to the city? There doesn't seem to be a bank around the resort."

"I wouldn't have taken it from you, but Hugh's already taken care of it for you." Unu was pleased that she was talking to him at all. She didn't seem upset anymore. The girl on the college golf team was back with her sass in gear. She had a natural smile that made her eyes crinkle up in a pretty way.

Casey looked around for Hugh, and when he caught her eye, he raised his eyebrows like Groucho Marx. "Thank you," she mouthed to him. He made an okay signal with his hand.

"He didn't have to do that," she said.

"Something about how he owed you a shirt?"

She laughed out loud.

Unu wondered if Casey was seeing that guy, but he didn't think so. Hugh seemed too old for her, but he did resemble the old boyfriend a bit. Hugh was a better-looking guy, however. Not married and, according to Walter and Kevin, quite the hound.

The event planner had put out the folded place cards on one round table. She and Unu were seated at Walter's table. One broker was posted to each long banquet-hall-type table. Hugh was with Brett's crowd and his own clients, and Kevin hosted the one with Seamus Donnelly and other top-tier clients.

Unu plopped down next to her as though it had been his intention all along. And right away, he asked her to pass the breadbasket. He plucked out two rolls and put them on his bread plate.

"I'm starved, aren't you?" He tore into his sourdough roll and slathered two ribbed curls of butter on his broken piece. Walter sat on the other end of the long table and chatted comfortably with three portfolio managers. He was amazing at integrating several people into one discussion. Left alone, Unu and Casey chatted between themselves. It was fun to hear about Ella and Ted from someone else.

"He's completely full of shit," Unu remarked about Ted between bites of his bread. "But I love winding him up so he can start his canned speeches. I think I can recite them."

"Please don't."

"He's not good enough for my cousin Ella—"

"You're telling me—"

They both nodded and laughed.

"Your bracelets..." He gestured toward her silver cuffs.

"Huh?"

"I heard about those from Ella long before I ever met you."

Casey blushed. Except when she slept, she never took them off. She'd forgotten about them.

"Where's your invisible plane?" Unu chuckled, imagining Casey in the Wonder Woman outfit. Her boobs weren't as big as Lynda Carter's, but they looked good as far as he could tell. Her dress had an open neckline, but he couldn't see anything. He felt a little warm. It had been a long time since he'd felt attracted to a girl. "And where's your truth lariat?"

She laughed again. Both Hugh and Walter glanced her way. They would no doubt tease her on Monday.

The clients looked happy to play by themselves, so Hugh got up from his chair, leaving his napkin on his seat. He wanted to go to the men's room, but along the way, he passed Casey's table. He stopped and draped his long arms across the back of her chair and Unu's.

Hugh winked at Unu. "Is she still obsessing about the seventeenth hole?" He pointed at her with his thumb, his remaining fingers making a loose fist. "She's quite competitive, this one."

"I don't doubt it," Unu said.

Casey flicked her napkin at him.

"Did you know that Casey is my cousin's best friend?" Unu asked without taking his eyes off her.

Casey smiled. That's what Ella must've told him—that Casey was her best friend.

"Oh? You didn't tell me, Casey Cat." Hugh faced her. Another charming smile.

"You didn't ask," Casey replied, wincing a little at the nickname. "Besides, we Koreans all know each other. There aren't that many of us, you know."

Hugh raised his hand. "The white guy has an ethnic joke."

"Shoot," Casey said.

"Why did God invent WASPs?"

"Dunno," she answered.

"Somebody has to pay retail."

Casey raised her wineglass at him. "Well done."

Unu, the male Texan, didn't get it.

"By the way, thank you, Hugh, for paying my gambling debts," Casey said.

"I wish someone would pay mine," Unu said.

They all laughed; then Hugh headed to the john.

Casey watched Unu eat his steak. He'd coated the meat with a blanket of black pepper.

"Steak au poivre?" She wrinkled her nose.

"Needs *go-chu-jang*." He said this like a dare, waiting to see what she'd say.

It was a test of sorts, but Casey didn't flinch. "Tabasco would work nicely, too." She'd never met a Korean who added the chili pepper paste to steak, but on reflection it didn't sound so awful.

She didn't know for certain if he was attractive to her. He wasn't at all like Ted, who was traditionally handsome. Ted could have been cast in a Korean soap opera. He also had a brute quality that women liked. In contrast, Unu had a kind face, and she liked the way he looked at her with a kind of wonder and privacy. His eyes were so focused and attentive. Unu seemed fully engaged with what she was saying. She felt almost pretty near him, and she liked seeing his face, how familiar it looked to her. Especially around the brow and eyes, he resembled Ella exactly. With him there, she felt less lonely in the room. As though she had an ally. It wasn't just because he was Korean. When she spent any time with Ella and Ted, even when Ted wasn't being a jerk, she felt separate from them, as if they were members of some improved world, where every pot had a lid.

Earlier tonight, while she'd dressed for dinner, she'd had a hard time remembering what Unu's face looked like—whether his face was wide or narrow or if his nose was rounded or straight. As she listened to him talk a bit about his work, she tried to memorize his features, the way his hair fell across his tanned forehead and how when he smiled he looked joyful. She envied him all of a sudden, wanting that smile without restraint. His eyebrows were inky, and she touched her own—they were so sparse in contrast. Korean guys had always made her feel so rejected, even more so than whites (there were just so many more white guys wherever she was), but tonight there was a wonderful Korean guy talking to her, and she could barely concentrate. Then she had to admit it: He was attractive. She wanted to kiss him.

He told her that he gambled. A lot. This revelation surprised Unu himself. He rarely told anyone this, fearing rebuke, but Casey didn't seem judgmental like other girls. She didn't behave like a woman casting about for a husband, clutching a laundry list of desirable male characteristics. The prospective groom questionnaire was familiar to him: education, family background, job, earning potential, and so on. But being divorced had freed him from that racket. Unu didn't intend to get married again. He was done with romance and the idea of forever. Perhaps he told her about his Friday night gambling binges to see her reaction.

"I've never gambled in a real place," was all she said.

Casey was neither enthused nor deterred by his blackjack habit. What did it matter? It would take no effort to tell herself that any possible romantic notions between the two of them were all in her head. No Korean guy had ever asked her out. It wouldn't start now. Besides, he was a client, and he was Ella's cousin. There was something incestuous about the idea of dating him. But she wanted him to like her. As a friend. Casey had friends and acquaintances, but there were very few people she wanted to see when she had her few hours off between two jobs and classes. Because of Ella, she'd given up Delia. To her credit, Delia had understood. Perhaps Unu would fill in Delia's time slot. Drinks now and then before her classes. No one had replaced Jay.

She could have known more people more intimately, but as a young adult in the latter half of her twenties, it was harder to make friends who made a specific kind of connection, or perhaps it was just harder to try again and to be as innocent as you once were or needed to be. But she hadn't given up on herself so much. Somewhere, Casey had gotten this idea that she could make a person want her as a friend. Not that she could attract just anyone—no, that wasn't it, exactly—but if someone gave her a little time, whether it was five minutes or an hour, basically anything more than a glance or a brief appraisal, Casey believed that she could draw a person to her. It was the simplest thing in the world for her because she did it by doing one thing perfectly: She paid attention, the kind of attention that almost didn't exist anymore. This was her gift. So few people did this for each other. Giving someone your attention—with the greatest amount of care she could muster in whatever allotted time period—was far more precious than any kind of commodity. Years ago, Virginia had exclaimed, "Do you know what that's like, Casey? To have you shine your floodlights on me? It's terrifying and more compelling than I want to admit. My shrink does that sometimes. And he doesn't love me the way you love me." Then she'd burst into tears, and Casey had understood that it was something she had been doing to express her love. Jay had said when she was moving out that he didn't think he could live without her attention. But with men, somehow, after Jay, it was as if she'd turned around the sign on the shop door to CLOSED, and in the past year and a half, there'd been no reason to turn it back.

"Do you want to have a smoke?" he asked.

"How did you know?" Casey laughed.

"You muttered to yourself how you needed a ciggie in the seventeenth hole."

"I did?"

"Yes." He laughed at her. "You also muttered a few exquisite French phrases. In English, that is."

"Ah. Take the girl out of Queens, but you can't take Queens out of the girl." Casey didn't bother to apologize. She didn't give a shit.

They left the table, and no one seemed to notice except for the brokers, who waggled their eyebrows a bit. When she thought no one but Hugh was looking, she gave him the finger.

On the wraparound deck, they could hear the buzz of cicadas. Unu pointed to a small reddish green lizard attached to a window. Casey jumped back a bit. She knew pigeons, squirrels, and rats. That was wildlife as far as her experiences went.

"Look at it," he said. "C'mon."

Casey tried not to appear afraid.

"Won't hurt you, darlin'." Unu's Texas twang came out.

Casey moved closer to study it more carefully. "It's beautiful. Funny. It's an amazing, amazing color. That color would only exist in nature and be as sublime as it is. I always think that about flowers— you know? How in a flower, a color is perfect, but that same color matched in a fabric or paint can look garish. Do you know what I mean?"

"I'm going to kiss you," he said, making a face with only a thin trace of doubt.

"What?"

"Yeah." Unu nodded. "I think you like me."

She shook her head. "Uh-uh." She didn't know what to say.

"That's not my name," he said, looking at once offended and amused.

Casey burst out laughing.

Unu leaned in and kissed her, and when it was done, Casey pulled back and opened her eyes. "What was that?"

"They don't kiss in New York? Folks in Dallas do it. You Yankees are just a bunch of talkers."

"Shut up." She laughed.

"Can I call you in New York? Take you to dinner?"

"What?" She was surprised by the question, the directness of it.

"You heard me." He frowned. "You can say no if you want. Or you can take the bet." He shrugged, his expression detached. He was nervous, but he wasn't going to show it.

"Let's go back inside. I want coffee," she said, pleased but confused.

He followed behind her, and they sat down. He didn't ask again.

Unu went to the bathroom, and while he was away, she wrote down her number on a torn corner of the menu card, folding it under the table into a square the size of a quarter.

After the meal ended, they got up from their seats and he shook her hand, taking the paper from her palm. At this, he said nothing, but he smiled.

"Good night," she said.

"'Night, pretty girl."

Casey returned to her room and tucked herself in, feeling light, girlish. The phone rang, and when she picked it up, there was a click. She hung up, not having guessed that it had been Hugh who'd called to check her whereabouts.

6 | LANGUAGE

*E*LLA DIDN'T KNOW WHAT DAVID GREENE would say when she finally phoned, but he sounded so happy to hear from her that she forgot herself and wondered why she'd hesitated as long as she had. Also, it was David and not the school operator who had picked up his own phone on the first ring. For her, this seemed like a sign. Right after hello, he asked if she had her hands full with a six-month-old. Ella looked around the tidy apartment. The baby-sitter, Laurie, had taken Irene to the park, insisting that the baby needed fresh air. On nearly everything, Ella deferred to Laurie, who was intelligent and kind and had two decades of unimpeachable references. Now and then, Ella had to pump her breasts and freeze her milk so Laurie could give Irene her bottles when they were not together. The renovations for the town house were going well, and the cleaning lady came by twice a week to do the laundry and housework. Ella didn't have enough to do, frankly, and she felt worthless.

"Tell me everything. Tell me how you are," David said.

"Everything is good," she answered.

"It's so wonderful to hear your voice, Ella," he said. His ears felt hot.

Then came the surprise from her end. Ella heard herself asking David if he had any work for her. Maybe in September. Didn't he do his hiring in June? It was just a crazy thought anyway.

The idea of her coming back overwhelmed David. It filled him with panic and joy. He said nothing, though, trying to keep calm.

But his silence made her feel foolish. She shouldn't have asked, Ella thought. Would David think she was an awful mother to want an office job when Ted made pots of money? She wanted to see David's face—his wide-set eyes the color of charcoal glowing blue, the bear-colored curls, and his reticent smile that hid his lower teeth, tiny ivory piano keys. She didn't want him to think badly of her. His refraining from saying anything made her feel just awful. It doesn't matter—she told herself—Ted didn't want her to go back to work anyway. Yet Ella wished she didn't want to see him so badly all of a sudden. If she were sitting in his office on that apple green leather sofa, and she could see his face, then she'd know what he was thinking. She hated it when he was quiet. To put her out of her misery, all he had to say was there was nothing at the school. Then she wouldn't hope. She'd get off the phone, sulk privately, and try to get on with being a stay-at-home mother with a full-time sitter and a housecleaner and a husband who was never home while nearly every woman she'd meet who wasn't in her situation exactly would view her as redundant. At the last HBS dinner party, a woman who was the chief financial officer of a telecom company in New Jersey, also an attractive mother of three, said to Ella, "Oh, you don't work?" and Ella could read the thought bubble above her closely cropped black hair: "Oh, you don't matter." The woman fled from her thereafter as if she were afraid that Ella might buttonhole her for even a minute longer. If David had a position for her, Ella would take it.

"What kind of work did you have in mind, Ella?" David asked, sounding so patient and earnest that if it were possible, Ella would've crawled into his voice to hide.

"Well, I could do anything, I suppose. I don't expect to have my old job back. I'm, you know, rusty. And..." She paused. She had called to say hello. The job question had just popped out of her mouth. He must think she was stupid.

"Uhm, I don't know, David. I'd be happy to work reception at St. Christopher's." Ella shrugged. She might as well have mentioned working as ambassador to Pluto. Marie Calder, who'd worked as the school operator and receptionist for twenty-nine years, joked herself that she'd have to be carried out by the boys of the upper school when it was time for her to go. Thinking of Marie, Ella could almost hear the morning line of uniformed kindergartners marching across the cream-colored lobby, their well-shined shoes clicking noisily against the black-and-white marbled floors. It was so quiet in the apartment. Too quiet.

"Can you come by tomorrow so we can have a better chat?" David asked. His voice was tentative, fearful that she'd say no. "Sadly, I have to get off the phone because I just promised Mother that I'd drop by in a few minutes."

"Oh, of course. I mean. Uhm... I'm sorry. Good-bye."

"No, no. Please. I don't want you to rush off. It's just that she's a bit blue lately."

"Oh, I'm so sorry to hear that. Is she... is she all right?"

"She's having chemo at Mount Sinai."

"Oh."

"Liver cancer..." David nodded, his jaw firm.

"Oh God, I'm so sorry. My question was so intrusive. Forgive me. I didn't know."

"No, no, no, Ella. Not at all. I'm so pleased you called. Tomorrow? Can you come? Please?"

"Yes. Yes, absolutely. I'd love to," she said.

"Morning? Anytime before noon. Yes?" David found himself nodding encouragingly at the phone. He so wanted to talk to her again.

"Yes, yes. You should go." Ella released him, then hung up the phone herself, feeling flush and scared at once. She realized that she felt happy at the thought of seeing him for certain. That every morning she had looked forward to going to work because she would see him there. It had been so long since she had anticipated seeing somebody in this way.

She stood at his door, her fist at her mouth, uncertain if she could knock. She pulled back her shoulders a little. The brass plaque on his door read, DAVID J. GREENE, DIRECTOR OF DEVELOPMENT. Tall and thin, with a thoughtful slouch of his head and an inward curve of his shoulders. He listened with his eyes and face and, naturally, with his handsome ears that lay close to his head, leaning in with his heart toward the speaker. David was thirty-five years old, ten years her senior, and the only child of a prominent New York pediatrician and a devout Roman Catholic mother. He gave off a kind of light when he talked, never gossiping or swearing. When he laughed, he did it with his entire self, and you felt you were the wittiest person in the room. The only disagreeable thing Ella had ever heard David repeat was how poorly his deceased father had viewed development as a career choice: "A man makes donations, David. Does not ask for them. A grown man should not be working for his former elementary school." His father did not use contractions, David said. That was that.

David wasn't married yet, and as far as she knew, he didn't have a girlfriend. Mrs. Fitzsimmons, the headmaster's wife, used to tease that the young Mr. Greene (everyone was young to Mrs. Fitzsimmons) was infatuated with the beautiful Korean assistant director, but Ella tried not to mind her careless jokes.

But there were moments. Once, when she was sitting next to him on the sofa in his office, reading out loud a capital campaign letter to the class of 1972, he brushed the loose hair away from her face before she had a chance to tuck it behind her ear, and when she lifted her face in his direction, for a flash it looked as if he were moving to kiss her; and terrified that he might, and not knowing what she'd do if he did, Ella dropped the letter on the rug and bent to pick it up. The moment was lost, and when she straightened up, David had already adjusted himself to a relaxed stance, arms folded to his chest, and he'd smiled at her warmly. It was all in her imagination, she told herself later. But she wondered what it would have been like to be kissed by David. He had a lovely mouth. Not all men did, she thought.

She had only been with Ted. Casey said that was an amazing fact, almost impossible to behold. Before Ted, she'd let a few boys kiss her, cuddle her a little, and she'd liked the affection, but she had no real experience of men to compare with. Casey said if you hadn't had an orgasm with a man, then you were really a virgin in her book. Ella had never had an orgasm. Ted tried many things, and sometimes she thought she felt something, but often she felt as though she wanted to feel something just so Ted wouldn't feel he'd failed. Casey told her that she should try smoking a joint; that might help. Ella couldn't possibly. Besides, where did you get pot? Also, lately he hadn't wanted to make love, and she couldn't imagine telling him that she wanted to do that. What would she say? Or do? How did you ask your husband to make love to you? All these thoughts just made her feel embarrassed. Ted worked a lot lately, and she hadn't felt romantic in a very long while; but wasn't that normal after you'd had a baby? She'd heard a joke on television the other night: What's the best way to stop having sex? Get married. Ha, ha.

What would David make of how she looked? Ella had yet to lose her baby weight. She was about thirty pounds over her normal weight. Casey said she looked pretty, but Casey was being kind most likely. For Mother's Day, Ted had bought her a Steiff hippopotamus toy and membership at an exclusive gym around the corner from their apartment. "You have such a great figure, Ella. You just have to get back in shape. You know, for health reasons," he said. But he didn't want to touch her lately. Even when he kissed her good night when she went to sleep, it felt chaste, as if she were his child. Also, Ella was nursing, and she was hungry and sleepy all the time. She drank quarts of water because her mouth felt dry, and she craved chocolate bars and cake. Ted didn't like her to eat so many sweets, so she tried to throw away the candy wrappers and cheesecake boxes after she ate them. Laurie didn't think all that refined sugar in the mother's diet was a good idea for the baby, either.

Ella smoothed down her hair and stared at the brass name plaque. Perhaps she should go back home and call David to say she couldn't make it. She pulled down the black knitwear suit jacket that Casey had selected for her. Ella thought it looked pretty, but she placed her right hand on the thick roll of fat around her middle. That was all David would see—she was sure of it. Last night, Casey had come by after work and laid out the outfit for her: a black St. John's suit with small gold buttons, nude stockings, patent high heels, and the large Tahitian pearl earrings from her father. It had been Casey's idea that she call David Greene to say hello. When she heard that David had asked for Ella to stop by, Casey was adamant: "Listen, just go. Say hi to your friend, Ella. You have to get out of the house. The baby's doing great. Get out of the house. Ted is—Ted. You have to get a life of your own." Casey had been inflexible on this point.

Ella heard steps, and she turned around. The corridors were empty. The streams of blue-jacketed boys were away for the summer. They called her Miss Shim, and when she married, it was Mrs. Kim. School was out, but its redolent perfume of tempera paints and lunchroom had lingered, making her recall all the happy times she'd had amid the school of bustling boys—amazingly different from a lifetime of girls' schools and yet parallel in its cloistered privacy from the other sex. St. Christopher's was the first job Ella had ever had. She couldn't imagine working anywhere else.

The door opened before she knocked. The steps must have come from behind the door. The tinnitus in her ears had stopped a few weeks after she delivered Irene, but her hearing hadn't returned to its full range.

"Oh, Ella! You're here! I didn't hear you." David pulled back reflexively, not knowing if he should kiss her hello. Then, in a swift motion, he reached over and kissed her on the right cheek. His faint stubble and lips brushed against her skin. His breath was scented with wintergreen LifeSavers, and she detected the menthol of Bengay on his dress shirt, his sleeves rolled up to his elbows. David's long torso gave him intense lower back problems, and he had to use a lumbar cushion with his ergonomic chair. At the end of the workday, she'd sometimes walk in on him doing his stretching exercises on the office floor before he cycled across town to his house on the Upper West Side.

"Please come in. I'd almost given up hope—" David smiled, feeling so happy at the sight of her that he was almost worried she'd disappear.

Ella's shoulders stiffened, and she felt as if she were caught in his gaze. She'd almost gone straight home. But he'd opened the door. Remembering suddenly, she held in her stomach, hoping that the dark suit made her appear thinner. Casey swore that it made her look like a sexy nun, making Ella burst into giggles. For that was without question David's type. She so wanted him to think she was still pretty.

David gestured to the Windsor chair opposite his desk, then sat at his desk chair.

Ella sat where he'd indicated, feeling disappointed they weren't sitting next to each other on the green Chesterfield—how they used to sit when they worked together.

"You look marvelous, Ella," David said. He couldn't stop smiling.

Tears sprang to her eyes. How could he always be so kind?

"Oh dear." David got up to bring her tissues. He put his hand on her shoulder. "Whatever is the matter? Oh, I'm sorry. Are you all right?"

"Oh God. I'm sorry. I don't know why I'm crying. I think I'm just so happy to see you. Isn't that funny?" Ella caught her breath. "You must excuse me. It must be motherhood."

"You're lovely when you cry." David smiled again, wanting her to be happy. He was now alarmed; when he came to himself after her call yesterday, he grew concerned about her searching for a job. He wondered if she was okay. If things were all right at home. Perhaps Ted wasn't attentive enough, or there was trouble with money.

Ella sniffled and dabbed her nose with the Kleenex.

"I'm very pleased to see you." David turned to go back to his chair, then changed his mind. "Hey, why don't we sit on the sofa? Hmm? Like we used to. Come." He motioned with his hand for her to follow. Ella got up and sat next to him.

"There." He looked at her directly, leaning his torso in a little. "Now tell me what's going on. I'm all ears." He put his hands behind his ears and pulled them forward, this thing he did with the boys when any of them came by to have a chat. He was doing his Dumbo ears for her.

Ella laughed quietly. "There's nothing to tell, really. I thought maybe I'd look for some work. We've hired Mary Poppins. Laurie is just wonderful and smart. So smart. And I'd like to be of some use. In the fall. That's all. Get out of the house a bit." She was reciting bits of Casey's script.

"Yes, yes. Of course you'll have a job. You're very good at your work. We will find something for you. I will fire myself if necessary. But you mustn't cry. That's completely not fair." David would've done anything to take away her tears. Going to an all-boys' Catholic school up till college, and being an athlete then, too, meant for him that women were separate and mysterious. Their actions were alien to him, and he was drawn to them, but he was puzzled by their behavior. "I can't bear to watch you cry. Very unfair of you." He looked stern. "Tell me what to do, please." He put his hands behind his ears again. "Tell Dumbo."

Ella laughed. "Oh, David. You are so good."

"Do you need to start right away?" He paused. "Are you okay? For money, that is?" David was in many ways a quiet person, but it was said that his reluctance to talk about money explicitly was the key to his success as a development person. In his work, he never asked for money straight out. He'd say that the school had a need—for computers in the library, a new gymnasium for the little ones, a scholarship or salary increases for diligent teachers, a greater endowment for the poor boys who needed scholarships—then he'd wait patiently until the needs were met. Invariably, they were satisfied, and he was so visibly happy and grateful at any offer to help that donors couldn't resist writing larger checks. Ella knew David's asking her about money was not his way and wasn't easy for him. "Because if you need anything, Ella...anything at all—"

"No. Oh no, David." She was moved by his offer but kept herself from crying. She'd forgotten about his tremendous powers of sympathy, how he could care so much so quickly. "It's not money. I think I need to work. Have a career and be a mother." How could she tell him that Laurie was better at raising Irene for sixty hours a week? On Saturdays when Ella took Irene to the park, none of the other mothers spoke to her, and the idea of her and Irene being ignored was difficult. When Ella watched the baby sleep at home, she felt inconsolably sad, which made no sense to her.

"Yes, of course. It's good to have a job, too. Being a mother is difficult. My mother tells me so. Did you know I had colic? Seems very hypocritical of me to tell you not to cry, then, isn't it?" He smiled. "I should understand better than anyone if you wish to cry. Perhaps you should holler if you like."

Tears streamed down Ella's cheeks. "This isn't a very good interview, is it?" She laughed.

"We are friends, Ella. We have passed that point of an interview, I think."

She smiled and nodded.

David took her hands in his and clasped them tightly. "Finally, an Ella smile!"

She laughed just seeing his delight in her. "I must look awful," she said, feeling very self-conscious, and he shook his head no.

"Impossible." David reached over to his desk and handed her another tissue. Then Ella saw the picture frame on his desk she'd never seen before. In the photograph, David stood near a brown-haired woman, a red-painted barn, the kind found all over New England, behind them.

"She's pretty," Ella said. Her heart felt as if it were tearing up.

"That's Colleen. My fiancée," David said without smiling. "She's a nurse at Mt. Sinai."

"Oh. My father's office is near there," Ella said, not thinking. "I mean, congratulations, David. I'm—so happy for you. You deserve every happiness. Truly." This time, she reached over and kissed his cheek. Tears came to her eyes again, and she dabbed them with the tissue he'd handed her. "Now, these are tears of joy. For you. I have grown-up colic. That's it." She had so many questions but couldn't ask them. She had no right.

David smiled. He didn't let her hands go. "Are you all right? I mean, with working?" He couldn't talk about Colleen now.

Ella brightened up a little, not wanting to look jealous. She'd talk about work. Yes. She wanted to work.

"I've been so isolated, I think. Just the baby and the sitter and me. Ted's gone a lot. Work. And I thought if I could work from eight to four every day, then I might feel more—more relevant. I needn't be something like the assistant director again. I could take something less. I don't need much money or a title—"

"Your bargaining skills have improved. Dramatically." He smiled. "I'm going to have to raise more funds next year if we can hire you— the shark that you are."

David had a beautiful smile, she thought. So full of acceptance and truth. Her name was Colleen, she thought. That meant "girl," didn't it? She had known a Colleen once who'd told her the meaning. A brunette from her dorm. But she wasn't David's Colleen. David's girl. She played with the name in her head like a kitten with a ball of yarn, because she couldn't bear what this would mean. But what did it mean? She'd never had any claims on him, Ella told herself. It had been a schoolgirl infatuation on her side. David was the best person she knew.

"So this is what I know," David said. "The headmaster is desperate for a new assistant. That's not a good enough job for you, but maybe for a year. Susan, our current AD of development, will leave her position in the summer of 1997 because she is marrying her boyfriend, who is going to graduate school in Illinois. So after a year with Fitz, perhaps you can pop back here. Unless you like Fitz more." He made a grumpy face, as though he might be jealous. "I've already talked to him, and he said he'd like nothing better than to see your face every morning. Who wouldn't?" David smiled again. "I'm not insulting you, am I? I don't know how you feel about that kind of work—"

"It's perfect," Ella said. "I'd love it. I can start as soon as he wants."

"I think it's the latter half of August, when school reopens for the school session. But he wants to talk to you whenever you want."

"Thank you, David."

"Hush," he said. His long eyelashes shielded his dark blue pupils. They gave a vivid color to his pale face.

"You are a friend."

"We are friends. Yes?"

"Thank you—"

"Hush, hush," David said, letting go of her hands. "It's a beautiful day outside."

He walked Ella to the door, mentioning for no clear reason that he had to go to the bank, then pick up lunch for his mother, who had a strong wish for a turkey club on toast and Fritos. When would he see her again? he wanted to ask, but he couldn't. How could they be casual friends? Their Friday lunches had been social but also laced with work talk. Would things be different if she was working for Fitz? he wondered. Snap out of it, he told himself. She was married, for God's sake. She was the mother of a baby. But when he was with her, it was as though he forgot everything. It felt hopeless. And now there was Colleen. Dear Colleen—a nice Catholic girl with a big heart who watched her favorite programs on Thursday nights and liked to clean the house on Saturday mornings.

It was like David not to ask where she was going. He didn't like to pry. Standing on St. Christopher's marble steps, sloping inward from the weight of a century of little boys' feet, Ella didn't know what to do with herself. She kissed his right cheek to say good-bye, then pulled back quickly, embarrassed by her wish to linger near his LifeSavers breath. "I have to make a few calls. Gosh, David. It was so good . . ." She looked down at her shiny shoes. "Thank you—"

"None of that," he said. "Go on." He bobbed his head, unwilling to be the first to leave.

She hoped he wouldn't watch her walk away, not having any idea what she looked like from behind now. Worrying about this made her feel ridiculous. His mother had cancer, he was engaged to a lovely nurse, she herself was married and had a daughter. What did thirty pounds matter, anyway? It would be better for both of them if he found her backside unattractive. Yet a part of her still worried that how she looked was far worse than she imagined. The last time Ted had caught her coming out of the shower, he'd stared for a long moment as if he were worried, then looked away.

Ella dropped a quarter into the pay phone on East Ninety-fourth and Madison.

Hugh Underhill picked up. The Asian equities sales desk shared the same extension so clients never had to wait.

"Your buddy stepped out to grab a sandwich," he said. "Should I tell her you phoned?"

Ella shook her head no, then remembered to speak. She said good-bye and got off abruptly, then phoned her father's office.

Sharlene, the office manager, told her that he was doing an emergency surgery, but he'd be free in an hour or two. "Why don't you stop by, honey?" she asked. "Surprise him." And Ella said she would try her best.

Ella walked up the block. Her father would be happy for her, she thought. He'd never thought she should quit her job at St. Christopher's anyway. Ted would be angry. There was nothing he could say, though. He was hardly around. When they got married, he'd said he wanted five or six kids. Three Teds and three Ellas. That was the joke. But Ella no longer wanted any more children with this man. Compared with her father, Ted was inferior. He was never home, and she didn't believe him anymore when he said he was working. Privately, she was relieved when he didn't come home.

The herpes had turned out to be nothing, really. She hadn't experienced an outbreak since it was diagnosed. Dr. Reeson gave her a look like "I told you so" when Ella brought it up at the last appointment. And Irene was in perfect health. All that pointless worrying. Thank God. But Ella no longer trusted Ted, and in her mind, he had done so little to make her feel reassured or to recover any lost ground. As though she weren't worth the trouble. When they were together, they were polite to each other. In fact, Ted spoke more carefully to her than he ever had. He almost never raised his voice anymore or made her cry. They hadn't made love since Ella was six months pregnant. That would make nine months, Ella totted up in her head. Not that she missed it. But it couldn't be good for a marriage. When she told Casey this, she mentioned seeing a marriage counselor, but even Casey had to admit that Ted would never go to a shrink. That was for crazy people.

Ella walked briskly, ignoring the shop windows. She had no wish to buy anything for herself or for the house. Ted had given Laurie a credit card, so she did most of the shopping for Irene. Laurie frowned on fancy clothes for infants. "A complete waste of money, and it only serves the mother's vanity. The child has no idea what she's wearing. For stunted mothers who liked their dolls too much. The worst offenders, naturally, are working mothers who like to have well-dressed children to assuage their guilt." All this reserve of opinion had gushed out of Laurie like a broken spigot when Ella mentioned casually that she wasn't fond of buying clothes. Sometimes, Ella thought, Laurie believed that biological mothers were useless.

She was close to her father's office, but he wouldn't be there for another hour or so. Sharlene would be happy to see her, but she had enough work for two people, and she never let you help her. If she had something to read, she could go to the Austrian bakery. Her father used to bring her there as a girl when she came to his office on Saturday mornings.

It smelled wonderful in there. The woman Ella knew wasn't working today. In her place behind the display counter was a reedy woman with dark circles under her eyes. She had pretty brown eyes.

Ella asked her for a box of pastries and began selecting a dozen assortment. The woman's plastic tongs automatically grabbed the items Ella pointed to: fancy pastries filled with custards, fruit jams, and whipped cream, crullers, homemade jelly doughnuts. The woman expertly tied up the white paper box with a candy cane–striped string. Ella asked her for a cup of elderberry tea, then paid the woman. The bakery had two empty chairs and a table, but she didn't want anyone to see her eating.

When she stepped out of the bakery onto the street, a light breeze brushed against her face. Carnegie Hill always looked so spruced up and tidy, and standing on East Ninety-fourth and Madison, Ella felt horribly ashamed that all she wanted was to find a private spot to eat everything in the box and swallow big gulps of her sweet-smelling tea. But where could she go? If she returned to her apartment, Laurie might find her. Ella looked around and saw David walking right in her direction.

"Hey," he said, "fancy meeting—"

"Hi. I was going to bring these to my father, but he's busy in an emergency surgery—"

"My. Aren't we good children!" David held up the sandwich and Fritos he'd bought for his mother.

Ella laughed. She no longer had any wish to eat pastries. Furthermore, she realized that what she had wanted was David. To see him. To talk to him. To have him hold her hands again on the sofa in his office.

Ella covered her mouth with her left hand, shocked by her own thoughts. "I must be holding you up," she said. "I'm sorry. I'll let you go."

"Are you free?" David asked, feeling bold suddenly. "Why don't you come visit Mother. She must be dying to have a fresh face. It isn't easy just having one dull son to rely on for visits. You've never met Mother. She's wonderful. Really. Full of vinegar and life." He was proud of his spry little mother with the sparkling ocean eyes and head full of white curls. Mrs. Greene was tougher than his father, but to her, David could do no wrong.

David watched her face, trying to guess what Ella was thinking as she paid careful attention to his words. He loved looking at her. He wished he could photograph her right at this moment. Her face was fuller and softer since she'd had her child, the line of her jaw connecting smoothly to her long neck. The curve of her breasts appeared higher, and he fought to glance at her collarbone instead, resisting a wish to touch the hollow of her throat with his hand. He had been in love with her for as long as he had known her, which was almost three years. She was engaged when he had hired her, and that should have been taboo enough for him, but his feelings had only sharpened. It was cruel how love could find you at the worst time. When she told him she was pregnant, he'd never felt so unhappy in his life, because he'd entertained a fantasy—albeit not admitted to himself—of being with her someday. And a child would make that less and less likely. Ella had thought David had been upset by the pregnancy news because then he'd have to find and train another AD of development. There were a few times he'd considered telling her about his feelings (if only for the selfish reason that it would relieve him of the pressure he felt inside), but he sensed that such a confession would make a working relationship and perhaps a friendship between a man and a woman impossible. Also, he was terrified that she'd be repelled by such talk and take flight. In his mind, Ella was like a rare bird hidden from view. His mother, an avid birder before she got sick, said there were such creatures in this world whose shadows you were lucky to see—even just once in your life.

After Ella had left the school this morning, less than half an hour before, David recognized what he felt. It was happiness. They would work in the same building again. He'd see her in the lunchroom. Ella would be only a few doors down in Fitz's office. Colleen was nearly shoved out of his thoughts.

David focused on Ella's dark pink mouth, which had a natural pout. When she was concentrating on something, the pout grew more pronounced.

"Can you come? I mean, you must have so many things to do." David felt dumb suddenly for building his air castles again.

"No, I don't have that much to do right now. I'd love it if I could join you. I like hospitals. I must be the only girl in America who really likes going to hospitals."

"Oh, because of your father—" David had met Dr. Shim a few times. A lovely man.

"Yes, that must be it. I always think good things. That sounds crazy, I know. The nurses and orderlies were so kind to me when I was growing up—"

Then David remembered how Ella never had a mother, and he wondered if he'd been insensitive to invite her along. Would she think he was bragging about his being a good son?

Ella wanted the clouds in his expression to disappear. "I'd like to go with you if that's all right. Are you sure?"

David nodded emphatically. "It would please me more than you can know." He'd meant to say it would please his mother, to have company, that is, but that's not what came out of his mouth.

Ella smiled at him, not realizing his mistake.

"Let me, please." David reached out to take her package, and she let him carry it for her. She kept the tea.

"Have you ever had elderberry tea?"

"No." He shook his head.

"Try it." She handed him the paper cup, keeping the lid, then realized both his hands were full. "Oh..." Ella hesitated for a moment, feeling shy, then moved the cup toward his mouth and tipped it a little so he could have a sip.

David put his mouth on the cup and took a sip. "It's divine," he said.

"Yes," she said, taking it back. "It's not too hot?"

"No." He smiled. "Very good. Mmm."

"More, then?"

"Yes," he answered, and Ella held the cup to his lips.

Ella took back the cup, and she felt even more shy than she had before. He noticed this and began talking rapidly about the annual campaign. He related funny stories about donors and volunteers they knew in common. She felt she could listen to him talk for the rest of her life. They walked up to Mount Sinai, and in no time they reached the hospital, where they found his mother sound asleep, having taken her pain medication earlier than usual. David kissed his mother on the brow. She was snoring ever so quietly, and he felt happy that she was resting. The monitors and equipment were beeping rhythmically, and they left the room. He took Ella to the cafeteria, where they ate pastries. Neither mentioned Colleen, how it was possible for her to turn up at any time. Ella couldn't finish her cruller, feeling as though she were swooning. An hour later, she walked him back to school, then walked some more to her father's office on Park. The walking helped to steady her thinking in a way. If David married Colleen, Ella thought, her heart might break completely.

7 | JOURNEY

*G*EORGE ORTIZ, THE DOORMAN and occasional weekend porter for 178 East Seventy-second Street, had worked for most of his life. Ever since he was sixteen years old, he'd managed to keep a fat roll of twenties in his eelskin wallet. To his surprise, he was now forty-three—that seemed old to him. George was married to Kathleen Leary, a thirty-three-year-old schoolteacher with a master's in English, but before her, he had known all kinds of girls. He'd plowed through all shapes, sizes, ages, and colors before getting down on bended knee with a one-carat diamond ring bought with cash from Kravitz Jewelers on Steinway to ask Kathleen to have and to hold his pitiful high school dropout ass till death do us part. Anyway, this girl that Unu Shim—his buddy as well as resident of 178 East Seventy-second—had been dating for the past two months was a trip. Her outfits were sort of out there, like from magazines or the movies. He liked her tough-girl stroll, because it reminded him of his baby sister, but the hats were a little crazy.

Today, she was wearing a black one, like the kind that Laurel and Hardy wore, and a black dress that looked like a tight bathrobe made out of a long-sleeved T-shirt. It wrapped across her waist and hips and was secured by a belt made out of the same fabric. There was only one thing a guy could possibly think of when a girl put on a dress like that: one knot kept him from a naked girl. Damn. But George Ortiz was a married man who had danced a lot of salsa—

if you know what I mean—and he felt he was above any excessive ogling. A light-skinned Puerto Rican with a head full of wavy black hair and innocent deer eyes, he was proud of the fact that despite the number of honeys from his old neighborhood who called out to him from the street, saying, *"¿Oye, Jorge, qué tal?"* he did little except to toss out an occasional "Hey, *mami!*" George never took down the digits or touched *los regalos.* Kathleen Leary—a small brunette with sharp shoulders and an unforgettable pair of tits—was the wheel and sliced bread and Christmas rolled up into one, and he'd never fuck that shit up.

Casey was a nice-looking girl and not stuck-up, so it made sense that she and Unu got together, but what made George laugh was watching his boy Unu act as though this were no big thing. Unu claimed that he was finished with love.

"The divorce took all the juice out of me, man," Unu said to him after shooting pool one night at Westside Billiards. They'd each had four or five bottles of beer and a wine cooler that tasted like apples that the bar was handing out for free. "Women are great, but I will never be shackled again. No disrespect to Kathleen. She's an angel. The very last one. Almost worthy of my *hombre* George." Unu patted George's back. *Thump, thump.* Then a high five followed by two fist bangs—top and bottom. The alcohol had made Unu's face red and his eyes watery. When Unu, the Upper East Side resident and Wall Street guy, hung out with George, the doorman from Rockaway Beach with the perfect biceps, Unu spoke in a kind of frat-boy vernacular left over from his days at Dartmouth mixed with the street lingo picked up from riding the subways and watching television shows about New York City. George thought it was silly of Unu to try to talk this way, but he sensed that Unu wasn't mocking him but was merely trying to connect. Unu was a good guy. You could count on him.

Naturally—about women—George let Unu think what he wanted to think. There were rules in Rockaway: Don't talk shit about someone's girl, and never tell a guy who to like or dislike. Those were all what you called lose-lose propositions. You let your boy make his mistakes (everyone invariably did), then go for a beer when he says jump. His brother had been married to a skinny girl who drank too much for like way too long, but hey, that was his thing. Sometimes a man liked to suffer. Besides, Eileen made the best sausage and peppers in the neighborhood. That was another thing George had learned in his forty-three years: Everyone had their good points. Anyway, he knew what a boy in love looked like. He looked a lot like Unu.

George reached over to help with Casey's packages. She was holding a large hatbox and two tote bags, one stuffed with papers from work and the other with millinery supplies.

"Give you a hand?" he asked.

"No, no, it's okay," she answered, readjusting a long-handled cloth bag sloping off her shoulder. It was less than half a dozen steps to the elevator. "Thank you, though. You're a sweetie—but can you buzz me up?"

"He knows you're coming. The apartment door will be open. He was taking a shower about ten minutes ago. Said to send you up." George winked. "Guess he's cleaning up for you."

"Well, that's good." Casey laughed. "Soap is a nice thing. We girls like clean."

"Don't get me started." Kathleen made him scrub his nails with a little brush before dinner.

Casey smiled at him. He was a nice man.

George watched her walk away, then step into the elevator. Not enough bounce in the rear, he thought. The bigger the cushion, the better the pushin'.

Casey nudged the door open. Unu had grown up in Dallas, the youngest of four—with two brothers and a sister. He'd attended the St. Mark's school and was president of his fraternity at Dartmouth. Member of the golf team and blackjack aficionado. Walter and Hugh, who covered Unu, a buy-side analyst, said that he was crazy smart, but not very flexible in his market calls. The only thing Casey didn't get about Unu was his divorce. The other aspects of his life made sense to her. She was admittedly curious about the former wife who'd left him for her childhood boyfriend. They had no contact, but he didn't appear bitter about her.

Unu walked out of his bedroom, wet hair combed, wearing faded khakis and a clean white undershirt. His feet were bare, and short black hairs sprouted from his toes.

"You left the door open," she said.

"Baby, take whatever you want." He waved his arms out like a modest game show host before a stage filled with prizes. Unu had no regard for crime or theft, leaving valuables out in the open and bundles of cash unlocked in drawers.

Casey pretended to case the apartment. She put down her tote bags on the nearest chair and placed her free hand on her hip.

"Hello there," he said, and came over to kiss her. "Good dress."

"Thank you," she mumbled.

Casey liked the way he kissed. He had this way of putting her lower lip or upper lip between his tenderly, while his left hand would recede to the back of her neck, his fingers playing in her hair. He closed his eyes when he did this.

"Mmm. Thank you," he said. Unu removed her hat and held her close to him.

"For what?" She laughed.

"For coming by. For wearing your perfume. I looked forward to seeing you today."

Casey smiled. What was she to make of him? He wasn't her boy-friend really. They didn't call each other that. She had no idea what she was to him exactly. They never spoke about love or the relation-ship, but he'd been quite clear that he'd never marry again, and Casey, twenty-five years old, about to start B school in the fall, had no interest in marriage herself. But they had something between them, and all of their restraint and refusal to make explicit commitments had given their meetings a kind of inadvertent mystery; perhaps it could even be called romance. It was as if at any moment, each could decide to vanish. Expect nothing and never disappoint; never harm and be kind. Enjoy the moment. Those precepts seemed to govern their behavior. It was an interesting way to run a relationship and unfamiliar to both of them. Casey liked the freedom and spontane-ity of their arrangement, but at times it was downright odd and hard to explain to others (the boys at the desk were often asking their sta-tus). Also, now and then she wanted to know what to call what they had, in light of what seemed to her to be real feelings.

"What are you holding in your other hand?"

"I have a present for you." Casey lifted up the hatbox by its cord handle.

"It's not my birthday or Christmas."

"Shall I return it?"

"No." He took it from her, a big grin spreading across his face.

Casey watched him open the hatbox. She loved to give presents. If she had pots of money, she'd never be able to stop.

"It's amazing," he said. Unu put the gray fedora on his head. It had a conservative brim and an anthracite-colored, tailored-bow band. Size 7½.

"How's the fit?" Casey tilted her gaze to check his profile. He looked wonderful, like a Chinese movie star from the forties.

"Perfect. How did you know?"

"Lucky." That wasn't true exactly. Casey had a knack for estimating sizes just by eyeballing a person's head. She could do it for clothing as well. Again, she had talents that were essentially inapplicable to her life.

"Let me thank you." Unu said, and he kissed her again, and yielding to the slight pressure of his tongue, her lips opened a bit.

Using both hands, Unu untied the belt of her dress, and he let it slide off her body. "I always wanted to do that."

"And you did."

Casey didn't change her facial expression and stood there wearing her underwear and boots. He led her to the sofa.

Casey enjoyed having sex with Unu. He was lean and agile. It could be, at times, not gentle, and it was always wordless, but she could tell what he liked by the way he moved. They understood each other's responses. She wanted to please him, and he her.

It wasn't making love. Something happened after Jay and the two girls where Casey learned that she could climax without having affection for a man at that present moment. This was what men could do—make sex a physical sensation, not always emotional—and somewhere along the line, Casey realized that she could do it, too. Could all women? No one would dispute the superiority of sex with romantic feeling, but it was possible for her to enjoy the act without it. Tina would have been shocked. Casey did not think she was in love with Unu, nor he with her. And as for this thing about being in love, she was growing awfully suspicious of it.

They had started the sex with him on top, then he lifted her over him so she was propped over his slim hips. If right then Unu were to tell her that he loved her—from passion or from reason—she would not have said it back. Not to be cruel, but because she wasn't sure if love was a true and constant feeling. The next time Casey would utter those words, if ever, she wanted to say them with conviction and permanence. She missed Jay Currie, but she didn't regret their breakup. And gradually, she did think about him less and less than before. Especially after she had met Unu. The heart seemed to her fickle or forgetful, or perhaps, in an uglier way, it was hidden with possible betrayals. Was love a decision, then? Regardless, in the alternative to this feeling called love—maybe respect, kindness, and pleasure between two bodies and minds having sex were the ideals worth shooting for. As she rocked her hips over his, Casey closed her eyes and tried not to think anymore.

Unu was trying to make sure that Casey climaxed before he did. Part of it was because it seemed expedient to make sure your lover was happy, but also he liked watching her. When she came, her forearms bent while her upper arms remained still, making sharp Vs, and for a second or two, her fingers would flutter delicately like the tapered wings of a dragonfly. On the oval of her face, was it first a quiet fear and then a visible relief? Her eyes would shut tightly for two or three more seconds, then open wide as if she were waking up from an absorbing dream. Then she'd shift her body to appease his.

When it ended, that awkward moment of separation arrived, then a kind of absurd shyness would follow. Casey wanted to shower. After, they'd go to the House of Wing for dinner. It was often sex before dinner, then sometimes again in the late evening. Then Casey would leave, always refusing to spend the night. In two months, they had developed comforting routines for their Saturday nights together.

They had a favorite restaurant—a cheap Chinese noodle house two blocks from his apartment where they ordered enough dishes to cover the laminated table.

"And how was Sabine's today?" Unu asked.

Casey shrugged. She'd sold six hats, two scarves, and seven hair accessories. Two pairs of gloves. Buying Unu's hat had wiped out all of her earnings for the day, however.

"Just sent off my first tuition check to NYU," she said.

"Yeah?" Unu smiled, sensing she wasn't fully happy about it.

"Sabine said that was—nice. Her word." Sabine had not been impressed with Stern Business School at NYU. And Casey had never bothered to tell her that she'd been wait-listed to Columbia. In fact, she had made it seem as if she'd only gotten into NYU, which was technically true.

"It's none of her business, Casey."

"I lied to her."

"It's none of her business."

"I could have told her about Columbia. I don't know why I didn't."

"Sure you do." Unu served her the tofu and spinach that she liked. "You didn't want to be beholden." He stressed the last word, making it sound even stranger than it was.

"Guess so." Casey took a bite of her food. "Guess so."

"You're funny," he said.

"Why?" She stopped fiddling with the long plastic chopsticks.

"Because you could've had a free ride. Still can. She hasn't taken back her offer."

"I know." Casey bit her lip. "I'm crazy. Poor and stupid. This is the reason why poor people stay poor, you know that? They spend all their money on pride."

"I would've taken the money." Unu laughed.

Casey knocked her knee against his under the table. "Well, you're smart, then. That's why you make the dough. I just eat it, apparently." She put some brown rice on his plate.

Her defeated expression saddened him. He'd noticed how she was often arguing against herself.

"Hey, kiddo."

Casey glanced up.

"You were right, I think. I'm just teasing you. You can't contract out your life. If you took her money, she would have expected you to do things for her. It's just her way. I think you're very brave."

Casey stared at his face. He had a kind heart. And in the time they'd been together, she'd noticed that he tried to understand her point of view, even if he didn't agree. For the effort alone, she was quite grateful. They were friends. That bit, she didn't question.

When the bill came, Casey reached for her wallet. She'd cashed her check that day.

"It's my turn," he said.

"You paid last time. And the time before."

"I make like ten times what you make."

"Okay, rich guy." Casey pointed to the check. "Make my day."

"Not that I know where it goes." Unu laughed at himself as he pulled out his wallet. He made money last month at Foxwoods, but right before he met Casey in Florida, he was in the hole for ten grand.

"Thanks for dinner. I'm totally broke again anyway."

"Do I have to return my hat?" Unu looked fondly at his hat on the chair beside him.

"That would hardly make a difference. I'm sorry. I shouldn't have told you."

Unu put down three twenties on the plastic tray. Silently, he crossed his arms and made his face go blank the way he did when he played a fresh hand.

"Why don't you move in? When you start school, you can live in my place and you can use the rent money to pay off your bills. You can cook now and then—"

Casey opened her mouth. He had surprised her.

"I don't care if you do anything for me. Do your homework. Get A's. Whatever. I want to see what you look like in the morning. I've been wondering if maybe you're a vampire and that's why you flee at night. But I've been with you in Miami during the day, so—"

"Move in? With you?" She hoped that didn't sound unkind. "What—"

"You heard me." Unu's face grew stern, but a restrained smile curled up in the corners of his lips.

"Gosh, I don't know," she said. "I don't know," she said again, but quieter this time.

"Okay," Unu said. He told the waiter to keep the change.

The walk to his place was only two blocks. No matter what, she had to go back and get her tote bags. They walked down the street together, their bodies close but not touching. She felt anxious, but he appeared cool by contrast.

Casey's mind was full of questions. She hadn't known him for that long. What would her parents think? Did that matter? He didn't intend to marry, but neither did she. But living together meant commitments. Didn't it? And he was right: If she didn't have to pay rent, she could eliminate her credit card bills in a year almost.

"Are you going to come up?" They had nearly reached his building.

"I have to get my things." Casey stopped walking, but she didn't look at him.

Unu felt weird suddenly, as if he had taken this big risk and it had made everything awful. Fuck it, he thought. Why be coy? This was a piece of shared wisdom about women that used to float around his frat house when a brother wanted to get laid: Be direct or sleep alone.

"Are you going to leave right away?"

"Do you want me to?" She was staring at him now. They'd never had a disagreement before.

"No. Are you crazy? I just asked you to move in."

"I have twenty-three thousand dollars in credit card debts," Casey blurted out. She didn't know why she said it. Maybe if he saw her the way she was, he wouldn't sign up.

"Wow."

"I know." Casey rolled her eyes. "I know. It's bad. Maybe you want to take back your offer."

Unu just shook his head. "Holy shit. What the hell didn't you buy?"

"Stocks and bonds," she said, then suddenly they both started to laugh.

"Do you have a drug problem I don't know about?"

Casey started to laugh again. He didn't think she was terrible—this much she could tell.

"Hey, Casey. I have five or six thousand in the bank, and I don't know what bonuses will be like. If I keep it cool at the tables, then we'd be fine. I can pay for everything for the house. Listen, even if we weren't, you know—together—you're my friend. I can cover you for a while. When you're a millionaire, and I'm low on chips, you can cover me. Okay?"

"I don't get it," she said. "Why aren't you upset?"

"In March, I owed my bookie ten grand, and he carried me for a while until I paid him. If I hadn't made money yesterday at Foxwoods, I would have been in deep shit. I made two hundred thousand dollars last year as a research analyst, and I have five or six thousand in the bank. I don't own anything except my car. I spend nearly everything I have, and I gamble for fun. I will not think less of you because you buy fancy clothes. I didn't know a person could spend that much on clothes." Unu laughed, raising his eyebrows. "I shouldn't encourage you, but you look great."

"It wasn't just clothes," she said halfheartedly. What did she buy, anyway? Jana, a woman who worked stock at Sabine's, weighed two hundred and seventy-five pounds for most of her life, and she used to talk about how she didn't know how she got so big. She ate neither more nor less than most people who were quite skinny. Casey understood Jana a little better lately—they'd consumed and consumed, and at a certain point, it didn't matter if they tried to act normal. To be healthier, they'd have to make drastic changes.

Casey and Unu were still standing half a block from his apartment.

Casey's head hung low, and Unu put his arms around her. "Hey, c'mon. We all fuck up. Even those of us who know better. So we'll fix it."

"I like you," she said, her voice very low.

"Yeah, I like you, too." Unu took her hand and walked toward the building.

George nodded when they came into the lobby. "Evening," he said.

"Hey, man," Unu said, and Casey smiled at him.

"How was House of Wing?" George asked.

"Good." Casey nodded. "Ate too much, though."

"Working late tonight?" Unu asked him, pressing the elevator button.

"No. I'm getting off at midnight." George looked at his watch. "If you want me to hail you a cab, lemme know," he said to Casey. "I'm on the j-o-b for six more minutes."

"I'm staying," Casey said. "I'm going to move in soon, actually. Has Unu told you?"

George widened his bright black eyes. "Excellent." He smiled coolly at Unu.

Unu nodded back and smiled. The elevator came.

"Night, man. Night. My best to your angel," Unu said, pressing the elevator button to keep the door open.

Casey stepped in first, and Unu followed.

"Night, folks," George said, his eyebrows furrowed. He wanted his boy to be happy. *El amor es complicado,* his grandfather often said. George had to agree. *Sí, Abuelo. Sí.*

8 | GATE

*T*ED OPENED HIS OFFICE DOOR and stuck his head out. He'd just finished a conference call with assholes from Lewison when he heard the happy commotion coming from the normally silent halls. He hoped something good was going down. A touch Nerf football game with punchy analysts would have been ideal.

The flash of red hair was unmistakable. Delia Shannon was on the floor. Bankers had found excuses to step away from their desks, loll about in the common areas, breaking away from meetings to check her out. She had that kind of effect still. Not that Ted could look away, either. The late August weather might have justified her wearing such a sheer white blouse, her lace brassiere playing peekaboo, and the blue skirt that sliced across her slender thighs, but Ted knew better. Delia's beautiful body was her power—a rich man wouldn't leave his wallet at home, and Delia carried her well-polished weapons perfectly. Ted's male colleagues didn't hide their admiration of her gifts. The women on the floor shook their heads ever so slightly out of envy or resignation.

She was seen stepping out of John Heyson's office. Ted felt jealous for a second, but the feeling passed since no one would screw that speck of shit. John was a merger MD who'd been slow for work—baggage from the other side. He was lucky to have a job at all after Kearn Davis had acquired CBR Assets. He'd made all sorts of promises about his important relationships. Right. He was a welfare case as far as Ted was concerned.

Delia walked to the elevator, seemingly indifferent to the attention. The sight of all the men ogling her, however, made Ted a little insane. He had made love to that fantasy body and had not stopped thinking of her for at least a few moments every day. You could see why men bragged after getting laid by some gorgeous girl. It was like having won Lotto—how could you not brag about your winnings? It had been nineteen months since they'd last had sex—Ted did the calculation in his head rapidly—and eight months since Ella had found out about the herpes. He had never contacted Delia about the herpes. She's a slut, he reminded himself. Delia is a garden-variety slut who knows how to fuck better than any man could ever imagine a woman knowing how to; yes, that's it, and I hate her, he thought.

Delia hadn't seen him yet, so he was still able to observe her. Also, she didn't know where his office was. They'd never met on his floor. In fact, he'd never met her intentionally anywhere at Kearn Davis. Any married man standing next to her would risk all sorts of gossip. But Delia had to pass by his office from John's in order to get to the elevator. He had two choices: Stand there like a moron with his growing erection hidden by a door or close his door, return to his desk, and pretend he'd never seen her.

In her few steps, two MDs had already said their hellos to her. John Heyson, who'd walked her to his office door, was still standing where she'd left him, watching her rear sashay across the floor. Ted was furious, as if his private claims were being infringed upon. He strummed his fingers on the door frame, and when he put his hand on the knob to shut his door, there she was.

Delia saw him but said nothing.

"Hi," Ted said. God, she was hot.

"Hello," Delia said, a slip of a polite smile on her lips.

He could smell her scent again. He wanted to touch her. "How are you?" he asked.

"Fine, thanks."

"What brings you—"

"John asked me to come down. About the transportation conference."

"I bet." Ted then remembered that Heyson was in charge of that ridiculous event.

"What the hell does that mean?" Delia crinkled her eyebrows, and her voice fell deep.

Ted noticed a few people looking at them. They were within hearing distance. "Do you want to come into my office?"

"Aren't you afraid of the talk, Ted?" Delia kept her face blank, her blue eyes wide open without any judgment. In their brief relationship (though six weeks was a long stretch for Delia), Ted's excessive caution had made her feel cool toward him, when everything else about him had once made her excited. Ted was a wolf, she'd learned, but saw himself as a stand-up guy. He was that worst kind of married man to sleep with, because he was not going to be a man about anything, except for making sure that he got laid. To him, he was the innocent and she was the tramp. Whatever. What made Ted an asshole was that he completely believed his own lies about himself—that he was a great guy with all the right values. He had turned out to be like the others—full of crap. Delia wanted to hurt him with something heavy. She despised him.

"I can't imagine that you'd want me to sit alone with you in your office when everyone can see you. How would you explain this, Ted? Aren't you afraid—"

"Why would there be gossip?" he argued, knowing that was a lie. "There's nothing going on." He then felt pleased, because this was true, and he had no intention of sleeping with her again. "Everything is totally over between us." He wanted to reject her, to not feel this desire for her anymore.

Delia moved away from his door. "I have to go." He was a phenomenal bastard.

"Wait, Delia. I need to talk to you about something."

"I bet."

Ted smiled at her. She was so clever. He glanced at her neck, the triangle of skin from her neck down to her breasts. They were pink and caramel, he recalled—the color of her nipples. He hadn't forgotten any of it.

"Please, Delia. For five minutes."

Delia glanced at the elevator, then her watch. "Two minutes, Ted. You have two minutes."

He pointed to the empty chair and closed his office door, feeling the eyes and wonder of everyone on the floor watching Delia Shannon cross his threshold. This was crazy, he told himself, but he couldn't help it.

"It's smaller than I thought it would be," Delia said.

"What every man wants to hear," Ted said, smiling when Delia smiled.

"Your office, Ted. I was talking about your office."

"Me too."

Delia checked her watch. "One minute and forty seconds."

"Don't be like that. Don't be hard. I hate it when women—"

"It's men who make women hard. We are so fucking fed up with you lying sacks of—"

"When did I lie to you?"

"You told Casey that I gave you herpes. I don't fucking have herpes. Who else did you tell? Besides your frigid wife?" Delia's face was dark red now.

"I, I—"

"Don't lie to me, Ted. You lied to your wife, and now you're lying to me. I don't even care anymore. I have to go. But if you tell one more person that I have herpes, I will show you what pain is."

"Are you threatening me?"

"No, asshole, I'm giving you an option. Yeah, that's a word you should understand."

Delia got up and opened the door. "I don't normally say this, but I really hate you." She left, and Ted watched her close the door.

He couldn't work. There were fat deal books to review, a growing list of calls to return, and he couldn't concentrate. He pushed the four digits of her extension.

"It's me."

"I know it's you. Don't call me again."

"I didn't know that you didn't have herpes." Ted checked the door, and it was closed.

"Well, I don't."

"But I was told that most people can't really be tested for—I mean, I hadn't been with anyone else except for you—I mean, after I got married—"

"I had the bloodwork done, and I've never had any signs— What the fuck. Why am I even talking to you? Your wife could've had a tiny cold sore, given you a blow job, and that's all it takes, buddy."

Ted grew silent. Ella didn't like oral sex, but she did it occasionally if he asked. From time to time she did get cold sores; so did he if he was tired. He didn't know that it could transfer that way.

"What I want to know is, how? How did you find out? What did Casey say?" Ted got angry at just the thought of her. To think he'd gotten her a job.

"Well, my friend Casey Han stopped speaking to me around Christmas, and when I asked her why, she told me about your little wife who threw a fit about getting herpes, but then, despite her being pissed at you, she never left your sorry ass. I bet a million dollars that she stopped screwing you, and God, does that knowledge give me pleasure."

"What?"

"I've studied this very carefully, Ted. I've slept with a fair number of married men. Believe me, I'm not bragging. And do you know what happens when a wife finds out?"

Ted didn't have any guesses except for his own experience. But it was true, Ella had only put on more weight, and since Christmas, she'd more or less said no to him three times out of four. And she'd gotten a job at the boys' school where she used to work. But lately, he didn't even want to anymore. That is, have sex with her. But he figured it would pass. He'd been focusing on his work.

"What happens when a wife finds out?" His voice grew timid. He felt sure Delia knew the answers.

"She can leave, but almost none of these moron Wall Street wives leave a good meal ticket, and you make too much money— And a boy of your status isn't easily replaced. Especially if the wife has lost her looks."

"Ella isn't like that—"

"Oh, now you defend her." Delia laughed. "Listen, pal, I have to go. I have real work to do."

"No, please. Tell me what happens."

"Or she stays and takes revenge."

Again, Ted wanted to say that Ella wasn't this way. She wasn't the sort who'd exact punishment. And it was true. Ella had an exceedingly forgiving nature. She possessed a mild temperament. She'd never brought up Delia again, and she was always kind to him. Dinner was on the table whenever he was home, she took perfect care of the house and Irene. On his birthday, she'd cooked his favorite dishes. His parents adored her, and she spoke to them weekly. She and Ted never argued. He had nothing but respect for Ella. She was a wonderful person, a good mother, what a Christian woman was supposed to be like. But they did not touch anymore. They went to bed at different times—and it was easier this way, because then there was no conflict or unease.

There was silence on his end, and Delia felt bad, understanding that what she had predicted was true. His wife would never trust him again. And no doubt the bedroom door was closed. What else could a woman do to restore her dignity after her husband screwed another woman? If she wasn't the kind who'd have an affair herself, then how else would she feel better? Two wrongs didn't make a right, but when there was a wrong, it was near impossible to be right-minded.

"Ella wouldn't—" Ted began to say.

"She'll never trust you again, and she shouldn't," Delia interrupted him, her voice suddenly full of bitterness. "You were falling in love with me. I saw it. I can always tell. It wasn't just sex for you. And just think, you will have a sexless marriage for the rest of your natural life." She couldn't believe her own meanness, but she would not let him talk well of his wife on her clock. He'd never mentioned how great his wife was when he was trying to take off Delia's clothes. "So, congratulations, Ted Kim. Hopefully, you can find someone else to screw on your part-time. Good luck. Gotta go."

Ted felt as if he were talking to the devil himself, but he didn't believe in men in red suits.

"Wait," he said.

"What the hell do you want now?" Delia's voice grew quiet. It wasn't like her to be so cruel, and the effort had exhausted her.

"I didn't tell Casey to stop speaking to you."

"Casey? She wouldn't listen to you even if you paid her. She can't stand you. She's just being loyal to Ella, which I understand. But how dare you call me at my office—" Delia started to cry suddenly, and in her anger, she realized that he had never explained himself, never called her about walking in on her with Santo at her place, never told her that it meant something to him when it had. He had been jealous, and you weren't jealous unless you cared. Those six weeks had meant something to her. She had liked him. All these Wall Street hot shots, they acted as if they thought with just their trousers, but she could tell how they wanted to talk, to caress her, and so many of them had even said they loved her. But she never wanted to break up families. That wasn't what she wanted. So when she refused to commit to them, they left. One day, she wanted to meet someone to fall in love with. She had never been in love, thought it sounded like some sort of trick. After all, all the married men who had chased her so hard had said they loved their wives. What the hell did that mean, anyway, if they could love their wives and want her, too? So true love didn't exist as far as she was concerned. And what made Delia angry was that she had never asked for anything. Didn't want anything from them. The only thing she wanted was a baby. And for that reason alone, she had not used a condom with Ted, because even though she didn't expect him to stick around, she figured he was fertile and he really did seem like a good guy. A smart guy, but who like all the others assumed that she was on the pill. Someone who could at least biologically father her child.

"Can we talk tonight?" His assistant was standing at his door now. He'd been ignoring her beeps.

"There's nothing to say."

"May I please take you to dinner? Anywhere you want."

"Did I ever ask you for a meal? Do you think I could care about something like that?"

Ted shook his head no. It was true. Delia wasn't impressed by money. "I need to see you."

"No, Ted. I don't think so."

"I am sorry." He found himself apologizing to her, and it wasn't like him to do so.

"For what?" Again, her voice grew quiet.

"I'm sorry that it ended like this. You're a wonderful girl, and I miss talking to you. You tell funny stories." He didn't elaborate on how she always made him smile, and when he was with her, his shoulders and neck muscles relaxed. When he went home, he didn't feel that way. From the beginning, he had needed to impress Ella, to prove that he was winning or something like that—she hadn't asked him to do this, but something about her had made him feel less. With Delia, it felt different; she didn't seem to care about his performance.

"Hey—Delia, please?"

Delia's office was still empty. Her office mates were all at a food tasting at the Marriott. The door was closed, and she felt grateful for the privacy—so different from the trading floor. The truth was that she'd picked up his call because she wanted to hear his voice again.

"I gotta go."

"Delia, please. Let me see you again."

Delia bit her lower lip. She could hear the feeling in his voice. Men were always so much more romantic than women. She counted to ten in her head.

"You can come over tonight at eight."

"Your place?" Ted inhaled, growing worried.

"Don't flatter yourself. It's just easier for me because I'm going to the gym after work. Would you prefer that I go to your place?"

"No, no. That's fine. I'll see you there." Ted hung up after she did.

When Delia let him in, she was still wearing her gym clothes. Lycra running pants and a large hooded sweatshirt over her jog bra. She had run for an hour on the treadmill. She had just enough time to wash her face, but no shower. She waved her bottle of Gatorade toward him.

"No, thank you," Ted said, smiling. He sat on the sofa. "I missed you," he said.

Delia swallowed. She'd missed him, too, but didn't feel like saying it.

"I was thinking about what you said."

Delia raised her eyebrows.

"About being in a sexless marriage. For the rest of my natural life." He widened his eyes in a kind of sober fear.

"I'm sorry I said that." Delia made a face of regret. "Sometimes I can be so mean. I don't really know how these things truly play out. I just know some of the things I hear about right after the fact. You know. Don't listen to me. I was angry that Casey knew about us. That was private. Maybe you and your wife will work everything out. Just forget what I said." Delia wanted to take back what she'd said. Casey had said that Ella was a kind of saint. And Delia wanted to say that she herself was no saint. Far, far from it. She had done so little good in her life. "Anyway, good luck to you." Delia didn't want to talk about him and his wife anymore. She didn't even know why she'd let him come. But she'd felt guilty somehow that he had to face the music by himself with his wife.

"How are you doing?" Ted asked. He wanted to stay with her.

Delia shrugged. The only thing she thought about lately was how she couldn't get pregnant. For four years she had tried with Santo to get knocked up. Santo didn't know that she was trying to get pregnant with him. And Ted hadn't known, either. The doctors had said everything looked fine for her. She was thirty-four years old, and it seemed that for no apparent reason she could not conceive. At her age, her mother had already had three kids.

"Do you want some dinner?" he asked. "I could go out and pick something up for us."

Delia studied him. What could she say? He was lonesome. He still wanted to be with her.

"Take the key. I'm going to take a shower. We can eat after. Okay?" she said.

Ted reached for the keys on the table. "What do you want? Are you hungry?"

"Surprise me, Ted." And what she wanted was to believe in him again.

Delia went to the bathroom to wash her hair. Ted went to buy their dinner.

9 | CUSTOMS

*E*UROPEAN CLEANERS I WAS LOCATED on First Avenue between Fifty-seventh and Fifty-eighth streets. It was a large dry-cleaning store of its kind—that is, a Manhattan drop shop where dirty clothes were brought, sent to a plant in Brooklyn to be cleaned, then delivered to the customers' homes. A drop shop shouldn't have been a thousand square feet of Sutton Place real estate, yet its size was justified by the volume of work handled through there. It was the flagship store of a sixteen-location chain strung across Manhattan and Brooklyn—all owned by an aging Korean immigrant, Seung Ho Kang, who lived in a Georgian brick mansion in Alpine, New Jersey. The flagship and the crown jewel of the European Cleaners dynasty was managed ably by Joseph and Leah Han.

Years ago, Mr. Kang, a war refugee with dyed black hair and a barrel waist bisected by a Pierre Cardin belt, confided to Joseph that his sons were all good boys but with shit for brains. "Well," he said, "that's what you get for marrying a pretty face with perfect legs—stupid sons." Mr. Kang possessed a sense of humor about the world and history. "Oh well, what can you do?" He giggled loudly, as if he were getting another one of God's private jokes. "You're a blessed man, Han *jang-no,*" addressing Joseph by his church title as elder, for Mr. Kang was a man who'd found the gospel late in his life but now bought the good news wholesale. "You've got a pretty wife and two smart daughters who went to real colleges." Only one of Mr.

Kang's sons had finished community college, and three had gone straight into their father's business after high school. Mr. Kang also owned car washes and coin-operated Laundromats in Philadelphia and Bergen County. Mr. Kang's favorite mottoes were "Everybody loves clean" and "No money, no honey."

Joseph liked Mr. Kang, and the feelings were mutual. Joseph and Leah Han were the highest-paid nonrelative employees in his company. Joseph earned a thousand dollars a week (four hundred of it was reported, and the rest he was paid in cash), and Leah made five hundred (two hundred fifty was reported), though she worked as both cashier and seamstress. Mr. Kang would never pay the wife the same as the husband, though he always paid widows more than wives for the same work. Like most Korean businesses, European Cleaners offered no health insurance or paid vacations, but for Tina's wedding present, Mr. Kang had sent Joseph five thousand dollars, which Tina had asked be used for her medical school tuition. For Christmas bonuses, they got two weeks' additional pay and a large smoked ham. By paying them so well and treating their families with high regard, Mr. Kang ensured that his best managers would never be tempted to strike out on their own. "A full belly is hard to give up"—that was another of Mr. Kang's epigrams.

It was closing time—six o'clock on a Friday evening—and the delivery boy had already parked the van in the lot before going home. The young women from St. Lucia who sorted clothes in the back room had also left for the evening. Joseph shut down the cash register and went to lock the front door. He wore a two-button gray suit with side vents, a white dress shirt with French cuffs, and a red-and-blue repp tie. He'd borrowed his customer's, Mr. Walton's, gold cuff links. Mr. Walton habitually forgot to remove his cuff links from his bespoke French shirts when he sent them to the cleaners. Every week, Joseph returned them without fail in a small Ziploc bag taped to the receipt, and every Christmas, Mr. Walton rewarded his honesty by enclosing a crisp five-dollar bill in his engraved Christmas card, which always made for a good laugh between him and Leah about rich people's idea of generosity. Tonight, when he'd changed into his new suit in the store bathroom, Joseph realized that he'd forgotten his cuff links, and he didn't hesitate to wear Mr. Walton's.

Leah noticed him doing this but said nothing. She was busy checking off the guest list for Tina's wedding. She sat behind the black marble counter, her small head craned over her slips of paper. On the floor behind her were two shopping bags filled with gifts for Chul and the Baek family, including a stainless-steel Cartier watch for the groom that cost two thousand dollars. These gifts should've been exchanged during the engagement dinner back in early December, but since that had been their first meeting as families, it would've been too awkward, and though they'd meant to have another meal between the engagement and the rehearsal dinner, Chul's family had put it off. That the families were meeting for only the second time before the actual wedding day and that the family wedding gifts were being presented during the rehearsal dinner was unusual as far as Leah knew, but she hadn't known how to influence the outcome any other way. Chul's mother had been exceedingly charming on the phone the three times they'd spoken but evasive on any of the substantive issues. Tina said his mother was sort of like that—friendly but impossible to commit. Chul said his mom, a radiologist, wasn't the kind to bring cupcakes for the class on your birthday. Joseph refused to comment on the matter, recognizing the slight, but for the rehearsal dinner, he did buy a new Italian suit and an English necktie from the luxury Korean department store on Thirty-second Street.

Leah had sewn herself a new dress: a blue light-wool shift with three-quarter-length sleeves. The illustration on the Vogue pattern had shown a short-haired brunette resembling the young Elizabeth Taylor. It was a dress in the 1950s style, a dress for a modest young woman—something a professional girl who typed in the secretary pool might have worn on an important date. The dress was shown in a red wool, but Leah bought a cornflower blue fabric, never having worn red herself. It had crossed her mind to make a suit, something older—after all, she was forty-two years old, no longer a young woman—but she'd found herself irresistibly drawn to the pictures of pretty dresses in the neglected pattern bin located in the back of Steinler's Dressmaker's Shop. Her black Bandolino pumps with the two-inch heels were also brand new. This was the first pair of shoes she'd ever bought at full retail price—nearly one hundred dollars.

The store was quiet. Neither Joseph nor Leah was a great talker. At work, they didn't speak much. When they weren't with customers, they preferred to listen to sermon tapes or choral music on the tape deck. When Joseph had a free moment, he read any available Korean newspaper. Even so, Leah noticed that since Joseph's building had burned down, a different kind of silence had fallen between them like a dry mist of starch. Joseph really seemed to have nothing to say anymore, as though the fate of the building were like everything else in his life, subject to total loss. Elder Kong said the insurance money would be more than enough for the down payment of another small building, but Joseph didn't seem interested in trying again. And though he said Chul was a nice boy, Tina's marriage didn't appear to please him much. Sometimes Joseph stared at the newspaper, not turning the pages. Leah found herself missing his tut-tutting the bad news invariably found in the papers. Last Wednesday, when she came home from choir rehearsal, she found him sleeping through his favorite program on WKBS. Asleep, he looked older, and it made Leah feel afraid.

Leah lifted her head when she heard the rapping against the glass. Tina was standing outside the paneled door. Joseph got up from his metal stool to let her in.

"Hello," Tina said shyly. She'd just come from the Korean beauty parlor on Forty-first Street that specialized in weddings. Her black hair was swept up in three cylindrical rolls on top of her head, and a few tendrils hung from the side of her face. She was wearing the ivory-colored silk suit that Casey had found for her at Sabine's—a gift from Sabine herself. Tina could've been one of the pretty reporters on the television news. Leah felt a streak of pride at her daughter's beauty.

"*Wah*," Leah exclaimed proudly. "Tina, you look like a TV star!"

Joseph nodded, smiling.

Tina blushed deeply. She'd never cared about her appearance or what she wore. The girlie things Casey cared about so much had always seemed like a vast waste of time. All this fuss about hair and clothes. Seeing there was nowhere to sit, Tina went to the back of the store and grabbed two folding chairs. Casey would be there soon. She'd promised. Casey hadn't seen their parents in over two years. Her mother occasionally let it slip to Tina that Casey could be hard-hearted to stay away even for the holidays. Casey's constant excuse was work, but that didn't make sense on Thanksgiving or Christmas. Her father didn't bother to mention her name anymore. He had thrown Casey out of his home, but he had been confident that she'd ultimately apologize. And he would have forgiven her.

Casey phoned their mother on the first Sunday of the month when their father would be at Edgewater checking on his building; Tina got a call every two weeks.

"How are you, Dad?" Tina asked brightly, hoping her cheer would dispel some of his unhappiness. Her father hated socializing. He wanted to be left alone, and with her wedding, there was nowhere for him to hide.

Joseph nodded, trying to smile for his daughter. She was his wise child.

Tina deserved a nice wedding, yet he couldn't help but want this evening to be over as soon as possible. What did his boss, Mr. Kang, always say? A—SAP—yes, that was a good New York saying. His customers said it, too. "I need my shirts ASAP," they'd bark after dumping off a load of wash. The other saying was "I needed it yesterday."

In half an hour, they'd meet everyone at Mr. Chan's. Howie Chan was his longtime customer who owned the famous Shanghainese restaurant on Fifty-seventh Street where rich Americans paid top dollar for General Tso's chicken and beef and broccoli—dishes the Chinese would not touch. When Howie heard Joseph's younger daughter was getting married, right away he'd offered to arrange the best twelve-course wedding banquet for the rehearsal dinner. Howie, who was the same age as Joseph, had already married off all three of his daughters. "Girls are very, very expensive," Howie would exclaim. "But they come back home. When boys get married, you never see them again."

From the opposite side of the street, obscured by a diseased elm tree and two blue mailboxes, Casey could see her parents and Tina. Her family looked so attractive and well dressed that it almost took her breath away. If she were playing her roof game of choosing a life behind a window, she'd have paused for a long time at this one. Why was this prosperous-looking, beautiful family wearing their fine clothing and sitting on metal folding chairs at a dry-cleaning shop after closing hours?

They were waiting for her. The last time she'd seen them was at Ella's wedding. Since then, she'd spoken to her mother on the first of the month and holidays and birthdays, sending gifts and cards by mail with brief, almost cheery notes. Her alibi for staying away was work, but it wasn't as if they were asking to see her, either. Casey felt terrified to walk the thirty feet across the street to meet them.

But she couldn't miss Tina's rehearsal dinner or the wedding. Her sister had asked her to come, and Casey would control herself, no matter what her father might say. And this time, she'd have Unu by her side on both nights. He swore he got along with all Korean parents. "Just watch," he'd said.

Casey knocked on the door, and Tina let her in. Leah looked startled. Joseph glanced at her briefly, then returned to unfolding his newspaper.

Leah smiled at Casey. She'd grown thinner in the face, and the weight loss had made her small facial features more pronounced. She looked older than twenty-five. In January, her first child would be twenty-six years old. When Leah was a girl, it would have been unheard of to let the younger daughter marry before the elder, but everyone at church said America was different. So it was.

"Hi there," Casey said, trying to sound buoyant. She approached Tina and remained there. Leah kept smiling at Casey, wanting to say something but not knowing what exactly.

"Doesn't Tina look like a television star?" Leah asked.

Casey nodded yes, admiring her younger sister's prettiness. The beautician had put too much mascara on her sister, but the suit was perfect. The luster of the raw silk fabric made Tina look like a girl raised in a prosperous *yangban* family. This had been Casey's intention when she'd selected it—her sister's dress and shoe sizes in hand. Sabine had gotten the image instantly and accompanied Casey to the shoe department to help pick Tina's shoes, too. Sabine's parents had been merchants, and she knew what it was like to have *yangban* people think you were less somehow because you touched money. Chul's father was a physics professor and his mother a doctor—all three sisters were lawyers, and Chul was pursuing his medical degree. The Baeks had come from the *yangban* class and had stayed that way. Joseph was born into the *yangban* class, but he'd fallen off, and Leah was born poor. Rather unkindly, the townspeople would have called Leah's father—a poor man from the country—a *ssangnom*.

Joseph was looking at the newspaper, but he was listening to Leah talk to the girls. She had missed them. And Casey had come after all. He was relieved. She'd aged in just two years. Being on your own in the world can do that, he thought. He himself looked older than most men his age. Taking care of yourself came with a strain. And in life, there were many disappointments for which you couldn't prepare.

"You know, you look even nicer than a movie star. You could win the Miss Korea contest. The smartest Miss Korea in the world," Leah exclaimed.

"Oh, c'mon." Tina shook her head, slightly pleased but uncomfortable with everyone staring at her.

"But you look amazing, Tina. Absolutely beautiful," Casey said.

"This is all useless, stupid talk. What does it matter what Tina looks like?" Joseph said this, facing Leah. "She's going to be a surgeon. It doesn't matter how she looks or what she wears. That stuff is garbage. A surgeon has to—"

"Daddy, I'm pretty sure I'm going into endocrinology. Not surgery," Tina said quietly, afraid to look up. She hadn't meant to talk about this now, but it just came out.

Joseph opened his mouth, dumbstruck.

"My adviser thinks it's the most natural fit for me. I've no talent for something like surgery, and I'm more interested in research than clinical practice, and—"

"I thought you were going to be a surgeon. A heart surgeon or brain surgeon—"

"Well—that's when I was in junior high school and watching TV shows. I didn't know what I was saying—"

"My daughter's supposed to be a surgeon. That's what I told everybody. That's what they think you're going to be. That's what you said." Joseph was stunned by this change. Did he not understand her English? What was endocrinology? He felt as though she'd lied to him. "What do you mean?" he asked, his throat choking up.

"I, I—Daddy, I—" Tina had never seen her father like this with her.

Casey felt sorry for Tina. Their mother was already wringing her hands.

"Maybe we can talk about this later," Casey said, trying to sound as polite as possible. They had to be at the restaurant in five minutes.

Still in shock, Joseph looked at Casey; then, disgusted, he looked away. If only she hadn't changed her mind about law school, working in a stupid job on Wall Street as an assistant after graduating from Princeton and now going to NYU's business school, just throwing away a Columbia Law School acceptance—he couldn't stop shaking his head. Who'd go to business school when you could've been a lawyer? And now Tina was talking about research? Not working with patients? Was that what she meant? For years, he'd pictured Tina's medical office where she'd see her patients and her working in an operating room. Saving lives. These pictures had puffed him up with pride and happiness. It was as Tina had said, like on television, but his daughter had been the star. What was she talking about? This was her life—how could the girl be so careless about it?

Leah checked her watch. There was no time left. She got up quietly and picked up the shopping bags. Casey took the heavier one from her mother's hand. She wanted to do something, move her body somehow, to run. Outside the plate-glass window, the streets were strewn with the well-heeled residents of Sutton Place—good-looking older women with ash blond hair and men wearing polo shirts and khaki trousers being led by terriers on ribbonlike leashes. The August evening was still bright, and Casey yearned to bolt out the door and hail a taxi. She had thirty dollars in her wallet. It wasn't too late. She could be back at the apartment in five minutes, order a pizza. But then she remembered: Unu was expecting her at Mr. Chan's.

Tina edged closer to her older sister as if to block her exit.

Leah closed her eyes as if she were praying. She opened her eyes, blowing the stray hair from her forehead. "*Yobo*, we can't be late," she said, her voice cracking.

Joseph then got up from his seat and opened the door. Once outside, he leaped almost a foot off the pavement to catch the metal gate handles with his right hand, and he pulled them down with all his might. The metal gears made a churning noise, and European Cleaners I was finally closed. The Hans walked up the street to Mr. Chan's.

"Welcome, Joseph." Howie shook his hand, then patted his back. "Leah, hullo, hullo," he said, shaking her hand with both of his. A Hong Kong Chinese, Howie spoke with a heavy British accent. "My, my, my, are these your daughters?" He'd never met them before. "Could they be any more beautiful than they are?" He smiled, thinking that the girls were quite pretty, especially the younger one—remarkably so. "Then again, why should that surprise me when the mother is such a famous beauty," he said, winking at Joseph. "Forgive me. I am flirting with your wife."

Leah turned red and looked away. Howie spoke more dramatically inside his restaurant than when he stopped by now and then to chat with Joseph at the store. He was a tall, slender man with a straight carriage. She'd never seen him wearing his custom-made English suits before. Of course, she'd seen his clothes when they were brought to be cleaned or pressed. She'd sewn back all the dangling sleeve buttons on his shirts. His wife wore Chanel and Valentino almost exclusively, and she was a French size thirty-six. Leah had never met his wife but figured out that he also had a beloved mistress from Joseph's oblique comments about his friend.

After Howie greeted everyone, he turned to the alcove where guests normally waited to be seated. "There's one person here already from your party," he said.

Unu smiled at them from where he was sitting. He hadn't wanted to interrupt the greetings. Seated on the brown velvet bench, he'd been reading the *Post,* following the races that day. He dropped the paper on the bench, rose, and stepped forward.

"This is Unu Shim," Casey said.

Unu bowed deeply and greeted them in Korean. He had a slight American accent, but his pronunciation and diction were fantastic.

Joseph shook his hand and smiled politely as if he were meeting a new attendee at church. Leah bowed but didn't touch him. She'd been reared never to touch men outside her family, and the only reason she'd touched Howie's hand was he wasn't Korean. Americans were always touching. Howie was a Chinese man, but to her he was more Western than many whites.

Leah smiled at the boy warmly; he was Dr. Shim's nephew. There was some resemblance to Ella around the eyes. Dr. Shim had said Unu was a very nice boy. "It's too bad about the divorce, but—at least, no kids," he'd said.

Tina raised her eyebrows at Casey. She approved.

Leah looked straight at the young man. He had a nice face, full of warmth. A good forehead—open and generous—and handsome ears with thick lobes. And he spoke Korean, pleasing her greatly.

"You're Shim *jang-no*'s nephew. Ella's cousin," Leah said.

"Yes, I am. Uncle Douglas is my favorite uncle, and Ella's the cousin I am closest to."

Leah nodded, and Joseph gave a small smile. He'd noticed Unu's ears, too—indicating good fortune.

Joseph spotted the corner of a piece of paper peeping out from his pocket.

Unu casually tucked the racing form out of sight.

"Where do you work?" Joseph asked him.

Unu mentioned the name of the fund where he worked as a buy-side analyst.

"Do you know Chuck Shilbotz?" Joseph asked.

Tina and Casey looked at their father in surprise.

"He's my boss," Unu said. "I mean, he's the boss. Of everybody."

Joseph nodded, not explaining, and he turned back to Howie, who was finishing up with a waiter. Leah then recalled who Shilbotz was—a customer. He was a fastidious bachelor whose hobby was to buy historic town houses in New York and to restore them with period details and furnishings. He lived in only one of them, a block from Mr. Walton's town house, while owning three others. The bills for his draperies alone cost thousands, and his meticulous cleaning job required Joseph to contact both Roy, a specialist, and Kenny, the foreman at the Brooklyn plant, to make sure that nothing ever went wrong. When Mr. Shilbotz called for his curtains to be cleaned, Joseph had to accompany the delivery boy himself because the fourteen-foot draperies couldn't be lifted just by one person. Consequently, Joseph had been to all of Chuck Shilbotz's homes.

Unu remained silent, waiting for Joseph to indicate that the conversation had ended. Casey resembled her father around the mouth. She looked miserable right now. He wanted to put his arm around her, stroke her hair, but that wouldn't fly with this crowd.

The front door of Mr. Chan's burst open; a large party came in. Tina smiled at the young man, a head taller than his family. Chul was here.

In the foyer, everyone bowed uncomfortably. Casey and Leah were still holding the shopping bags. Mr. Chan ushered them to their private banquet room.

Once they had been seated, the senior waiters brought out the cold appetizers in an instant. Chul stared at Tina silently, his nervous expression barely concealed. He wanted her to rescue him, but Tina was lost herself. Though the couple was seated at opposite ends of the table, their eyes formed a straight path toward each other. Chul stared at Tina with both awe and need. He wanted to make love to her all the time. Tina felt his pull keenly and tried not to think about them being together.

His sisters were chattering loudly. They were smart looking, Casey thought, trying to recall everyone's names. The introductions had been made so quickly near the door—Heidi, Kathryn, Rose, and their respective husbands, Jun-hi, Clark, and Dean. Casey couldn't keep straight the children's names: Max or Alex—names with x's in them. The boys were the eldest daughter's sons—neither very well behaved.

"Game Boy in a minute," Heidi promised them.

Tina felt sorry for her mother, who appeared terrified by Chul's mother, Anna, who kept trying to hold Leah's hand.

"Leah, you must. You must call me Anna. Please," Chul's mother insisted in English. She had a tendency to touch you when she spoke, and Leah was confused by Anna Baek's overly familiar gestures. She even touched Joseph when she talked to him, holding on to his forearm when she complimented his necktie. He was repulsed by her. The unkind word he thought of was *yuh-oo*—a fox.

"And I'll call you Leah. Such a pretty name," Anna said. She brushed a speck of lint from Leah's shoulder.

Leah nodded at the handsome woman with the knobby cheekbones. Anna Baek's complexion was uneven, but her makeup was applied well. Leah had put on light pink lipstick herself, but much of it had already faded.

When everyone at the table had been served, Joseph and Leah bent their heads in prayer. Tina, Chul, and Casey bowed their heads. So did Unu. Except for Chul and Heidi, the Baek family weren't Christians. After the amens, the guests ate with great concentration.

Chul was adorable, Casey thought—a foot taller than Tina, thick black hair, nut brown eyes, and an open smile. He had his mother's best features, but with a great deal more kindness in his face. Chul looked like someone who'd have four or five kids and wear his simple navy suits for a dozen years, never losing his focus or good temperament.

Kathryn, the second born, a former gymnast with a fireplug body and shoulder-length hair, acted like the leader of the pack. She'd been the one who'd introduced everyone in the foyer.

"So how long have you and Unu been dating?" she asked Casey.

Unu glanced up from his plate.

"A while," Casey answered. It wasn't the question so much as the way she'd asked it that felt aggressive. Casey sat straighter.

"How long?" Heidi asked, smiling. She thought it was safe to ask this but felt a little self-conscious that everyone was waiting for Casey's answer to her question.

"Four happy months," Unu piped up. He beamed at Casey. "She's just terrific." It wasn't the Korean way to be so expressive, but it was obvious that the Baeks preferred the American ways.

Leah smiled at him.

"And will you two be getting married soon?" Kathryn asked. She'd gotten engaged after meeting her husband, Clark, in about that time.

The little boys giggled, making faces. "Like Uncle Chul!" the older one shouted.

Casey shouldn't have been surprised. Koreans could sometimes ask the most personal things, but she hadn't expected it from someone not far from her generation. Kathryn was maybe ten years older than her.

Tina smiled at Casey, hoping Kathryn hadn't upset her. Chul said even his parents were a little afraid of Kathryn, who was unconscious of her bullying ways. In the few times Tina had met them, all three lawyer sisters had been relentless in their lines of questioning.

"Will that be the next wedding? Hmm?" Kathryn raised her eyebrows as though she had amused herself.

This time Unu didn't look up. Casey knew where he stood on this and said nothing. No one there would understand that Unu didn't believe in marriage or that Casey didn't understand love lately. Only the innocent would rush to marry.

Anna read the answer in Casey's face and in Unu's silence. Joseph squinted at Unu and exhaled audibly.

"Kathryn," Anna said, her voice tinged lightly with chiding, "that's personal—"

Somehow, Chul's mother's sympathy made Casey feel worse. Tina bit her lip.

Joseph looked at Unu again. He seemed like a kindhearted child. The divorce was a strike against him, but he wanted to know too if Unu had any intention of marrying Casey. A divorced Korean boy from a nice family was still better than an American boy from Princeton who had too much arrogance. Unu and Casey were living together and no doubt sharing a bed. How could he take possession of her body and not want to care for her? It was a man's duty to protect the woman he loved. Those were the old ways, but they were the right ones. It occurred to him that if Casey were dating a man who wasn't going to marry her, then she was even crazier than he thought.

Kathryn had put down her chopsticks, unfazed by her mother's comment. She stared at the bride's older sister, but Casey merely picked up her red porcelain teacup and took a sip. Virginia, who'd done some media training, had once told Casey, "You don't have to answer every question."

"The presents," Tina said spontaneously. "We should give out the presents."

Leah nodded and fetched the parcels beside her chair. Glad to get up from her seat, Casey put a wrapped present in front of everyone in Chul's family.

"Oh, this was so unnecessary," Anna said. Then she pulled out her set of presents and Chul passed those out. Everyone opened their boxes.

Anna received a gold-and-diamond necklace-and-bracelet set, and the sisters each received gold-and-diamond earrings. The father was given a Burberry raincoat, and Chul got his Cartier watch. The brothers-in-law got V-neck cashmere sweaters from Scotland and scarves. The little boys received two-hundred-fifty-dollar savings bonds. Leah had spent six thousand dollars on the gifts. She'd given Joseph the receipts, and he'd never said anything about the expense. This money had come out of their retirement savings. Engagements could be broken off if inferior presents were given, and there were instances where daughters-in-law were beaten or resented from the memory of a bad gift. This was what Leah had wanted to avoid. For months, she'd worried herself about what to give Chul's family—how to give the most precious, luxurious thing that would make them welcome Tina.

Chul's family had given Joseph a black-and-white YSL logo necktie and a pair of electroplated silver cuff links. Leah received a red wool muffler, and so did Casey. Tina received an old-fashioned jade brooch in a gold frame. Casey couldn't help but tote up the cost in her head. Five hundred dollars? The gifts had all come from Macy's.

"It's beautiful," Casey exclaimed. She folded the oblong scarf in half, then draped it across her neck, pushing the ends through the folded loop she'd made to create what Sabine called the aviator knot.

"That color looks great on you," Anna said, trying to sound happy.

The difference in the gifts was too severe to ignore. Either the Hans had overdone it or the Baeks had done too little. It was too late. Rose, the youngest, tried to be nice about it, removing the pearls from her ears to put on the eighteen-karat-gold earrings in the shape of dogwood flowers that Leah had chosen so carefully. The earrings had cost seven hundred dollars at wholesale price. The lady who'd sold them to Leah was a jeweler in her *geh*, and she'd said those earrings were made in the same workshop in Florence that made jewelry for Tiffany's. They weren't knockoffs, she'd said; they were Tiffany earrings without the hallmarks or blue boxes. Leah had never given her own daughters such costly presents.

Taking Rose's example, Anna clasped the necklace around her neck. It looked beautiful on her.

"You are too much," she said to Leah. Her face was split in its expression—the mouth was smiling, but her brow wrinkled in a frown. "Too generous. Too, too much. So Korean to give such extravagant things. It is really so gorgeous, but—" Anna guessed correctly that her necklace-and-bracelet set had cost nearly as much as her son's watch.

Leah stroked her scarf. It was a nice lambswool. "It will be good and warm for the winter. Thank you so much," she said. It was better this way. Yesu Christo had said it was more blessed to give than to receive. Her father had taught her to take on the suffering, to donate her whole self to the interests of others, to give everything up because God would take care of your every need.

Tina smiled weakly, feeling so disappointed and hurt for her parents that she could hardly speak. Her mother had spent days going to shops and agonizing about whether or not the Baeks would be pleased. In a way, her mother had succeeded, because the gifts were beautiful. But she wished she could've prepared her parents for the fact that the Baeks wouldn't make a similar effort. The Baeks were undoubtedly rationalizing that the Hans were *ssangnom,* trying to act better than they were by giving such expensive things. There was no way to win. Generosity was always suspect. Tina picked up her chopsticks and moved the preserved duck egg from one end of the plate to the other. Chul put on his watch, and he made his sisters admire it. They oohed and aahed at him as if he were an indulged child.

Joseph looked Chul over carefully. He didn't have any resemblance to his own father except for the rounded jawline. Out of his summer earnings and savings through the years, the boy had given Tina a one-carat diamond engagement ring, which she loved. In the future, if he didn't take good care of his daughter, Joseph resolved to let her come home anytime she wanted.

"Thank you for the tie. It's very nice," Joseph said to Anna, closing the box before tucking it in their shopping bag. He'd never wear anything so hideous.

Casey had heard about the large house they owned in Bethesda, the beach house in Rehoboth, the membership at the country club in Chevy Chase, and she could've easily guessed the price of each St. John's outfit of the Baek sisters. The mother was wearing Armani. Chul's parents made seven or eight times more than her parents. These weren't people who shopped at Macy's normally, and none of them would have worn less than cashmere around their throats. They'd gone out of their way to let her family know its place. It was mean to Tina, but Casey saw that it was also mean to Chul.

Howie came by with a magnum of champagne. He picked up the change in mood.

"How is everyone? How was the jellyfish?" he asked.

Joseph smiled at him. "Great. Great."

"Champagne?" Chul's father checked the label: Moët & Chandon. Philip Baek liked to drink and was fond of good wines.

Howie filled the champagne glasses. "On the house! Anything for my good friend Joseph Han and for his beautiful daughter's wedding celebration!" he said mirthfully. Spotting the pile of discarded silver wrapping paper near the edge of the banquet table, Howie jutted his chin toward it and a busboy cleared it away.

"May you kids have lots of champagne in the future!" Howie said with a flourish, but only a few of them smiled.

When Howie had filled everyone's glass, he realized that none of the party was likely to make a toast. The sons-in-law were busy cleaning their appetizer plates. The groom's father had finished his bourbon and soda and had already picked up his champagne glass to drink. The grandchildren pulled at Anna and Heidi. Joseph appeared restless.

When you owned a restaurant, occasionally you had to become a guest and join the party. A glass was brought to Howie, and he filled it himself.

Howie raised his glass.

"For Tina's wedding. To Tina—Joseph and Leah's beautiful daughter who will one day become my favorite surgeon!" Howie Chan laughed. "And to love—" He directed his glass toward the groom, then the bride. He added, his voice lowered, "I believe in true love. With all my heart." One day, Howie planned to marry Emily Lo, his mistress of twenty-three years—his soul's true companion.

Everyone clinked glasses. Tina didn't correct Mr. Chan about her new specialization but felt bad for her father again. Everyone sipped the champagne, and Tina felt grateful for the restaurant owner's tenderness, his sincere wish to make people feel happier.

They got through the dinner—talking mainly about how good the food was, and it was very delicious food after all. There was no fight for the check. Joseph paid it, and Howie had cut it down to a third of its cost. The two families said their good-byes till the next day. Tina returned to Queens with her parents, and Chul left with his family to the Hilton Hotel in midtown where the Baeks were staying. Casey and Unu left together. They would walk home.

Tina would marry Chul the next day.

10 | WONDERS

*C*ASEY HAD A TENDENCY TO FIDGET. She had a long back, making it difficult for her to find a comfortable sitting position. Occasionally, when they were at a movie or at dinner, Unu would place his hand on her shoulder or thigh, calming her for a bit; but it didn't take long before she'd shift her torso again. In the past, people seated behind her had complained because it was distracting. At Tina's wedding, she was put in the front row with Unu, Joseph, and Leah on the bride's side of the pews. Casey could smell tobacco on Unu's suit jacket, and she wanted a cigarette. It would be impossible for her to sneak one during her sister's wedding. Her parents knew that she was sleeping with Unu but didn't yet know about her smoking. She crossed her legs again.

Tina and Chul stood at attention like wedding cake ornaments opposite the minister's podium. The Reverend Lim was twenty minutes into his homily, and he had another fifteen minutes to go.

"Again, the kingdom of heaven is like a merchant looking for fine pearls. When he found one of great value, he went away and sold everything he had and bought it." The minister quoted the verse in a thunderous voice, ill matched for his slight figure. The Reverend Lim couldn't have been more than five feet tall—his body lost in his black acetate robe. His mop of black hair was greased into place, yet it shook as he pointed his childlike index finger at the bride and groom. His diction was very good, but his accent was difficult to understand.

Nevertheless, three hundred guests paid close attention to him. It was hard not to. He pounded on the podium often to emphasize his points and was easily moved to tears.

Unu knocked on Casey's knee with his. He whispered, "I kind of like him. He's got—"

"He's crazy," she answered in a soft voice.

"No." Unu shook his head in disagreement. "He's passionate. He believes his message."

Casey was a bit taken aback by this. She'd been embarrassed by the minister's dramatic physical display and bad accent and thought Unu would be, too. She turned around slightly—the guests were listening to him raptly.

Suddenly the minister lowered his voice. "What is the pearl of great price?"

The guests lifted their heads, their necks straightening.

Casey was getting annoyed. Jesus? she thought. In Sunday school, that was usually the safe bet for everything.

The minister turned in her direction suddenly. Looking straight at her, he said, "You are the pearl of great price." Casey froze.

He continued, "I am the pearl of great price." Then he pointed to the middle of the pews. "He is the pearl of great price." The minister lowered his head solemnly. "And God, dear God Himself, sold everything He had to buy you. He sacrificed His only son—selling everything, absolutely everything, because you are His beloved, and you are the pearl of great price. Do you see that, my dear brothers and sisters? Do you feel how much He loves you?" Lim raised both hands in the air—his billowing sleeves falling to his suit sleeve elbows. Then he clapped loudly, punctuating his statement. His eyes filled with tears. "God loves you now. You are His priceless treasure." With hurried steps, the Reverend Lim approached Tina and Chul.

"Now, children, you must love each other deeply, seeing the treasure that you are to each other. As God sees the treasure in you. And each of you must help the other grow closer to God, for that is the true purpose of marriage. Whenever you feel apart from your beloved, see if you are helping your mate grow closer to God—the One who truly, truly sees your value. You are rich. Wealthy beyond measure in talents and love. You are a divine creation. And your mate is the half of another divine creation." The Reverend Lim placed Chul's hand over Tina's.

"Your value will never rise or fall with your beauty, work, or money. Your worth is priceless. You must remember that." The minister wept openly, and Casey turned away, feeling both irritated and embarrassed. She glanced at Tina and realized that Tina wasn't holding her bouquet. She whispered to Unu, "Her flowers."

"Hmm?" he replied, not understanding her.

"Tina forgot her flowers in the basement."

"Does it matter?" he asked.

Casey turned to her mother. "Tina's flowers."

"Mahp soh sah," Leah uttered in surprise. "Can you get them? They must be—" She grew distressed. "She needs them for the photographs. When she walks down the aisle," she said. "Casey, can you get the flowers?"

As quietly as she could, Casey got up and left the sanctuary. She walked out of the service just as the minister was preparing to ask the bride and groom to take their vows.

When Casey reached the choir room where Tina had gotten dressed only an hour before, she found Ted with his back turned to her. His right hand was on the handle of the stroller, and with his left, he was holding a mobile phone. His voice was tender, and initially Casey thought he was talking to his daughter, but she saw that Irene was asleep.

"I'll be there, baby. Around eleven. I can get there then, okay?... Okay?" His voice was full of love.

Casey leaned against the door frame of the choir room, its doors swung wide open. What was he thinking? The caterers were making noise as they set up for the reception in the church kitchen, but otherwise the halls were empty of guests.

"Delia," he said, "I love you. We're going to be together, please believe me—" Ted took his right hand off the stroller handle and finger-combed his hair. "You mean everything to me. It will all work out."

Casey cleared her throat out of instinct more than anything else. The cough was involuntary, as if her body hadn't wanted to hear any more of this. Ted turned around this time, his mouth agape slightly, but said nothing. Casey shook her head at him but could think of nothing to say. Tina's flowers—lily of the valley encased in their pale green leaves—were still on the chair near the mirror where Tina had left them. Casey walked steadily toward them, unable to look in Ted's direction. She picked up the bouquet and quickly returned upstairs.

In the sanctuary, they were done: vows said, rings exchanged, union blessed. Tina and Chul did an about-face to leave the church. As they began to march back down the aisle—carpeted with a white strip of cloth that the florists had put down that morning—Casey slipped the bouquet into her sister's hand. Tina smiled at Casey—she hadn't noticed its absence. She was married to Chul. For Tina, it was easily the happiest day of her life. Chul was the kindest, loveliest boy she had ever known, and she was profoundly attracted to him, interested in all his thoughts. When she was in his arms, she felt everything was good. It was true they were young, but she had found love.

Casey could see her sister's happiness, and she was pleased, but Ella had looked happy on her day, too. Casey had no wish to be a cynic in love. Losing Jay had been hard, but somehow she had trusted that it wouldn't work for them forever, and that had given her the courage to stick to her decision—to withstand the loneliness. And perhaps that fact alone was the sign that Casey was still hopeful about love, because she wanted marriage to be an eternal bond.

Unu touched her elbow. "Honey, it's time for us to walk, too."

"I just heard Ted telling Delia that he loves her. He's meeting her at eleven. Tonight." The words just tumbled out.

Unu turned around. "What an asshole."

"That's what I should have said. Damn," Casey whispered, her teeth clenched in a formal smile.

They were walking behind her parents. Joseph tried to smile at the guests, and Leah's shy gaze fell to the white fabric carpet.

Casey adjusted the strap of her dress, and Unu slowed his pace. He couldn't help recalling his own wedding every time he went to one. His wife, too, had been a beautiful bride, and she had seemed very happy. Women were just better at faking their feelings.

"Marriage. What a fucking sham," Unu mumbled.

"We're well aware of your thoughts on the institution. But what should I do?" Casey asked, annoyed by his comment.

"You gotta tell Ella." He shrugged. "You know where my loyalties lie." The fact that Ted could cheat on Ella was unbelievable to him. Ella was a saint, a beautiful, kind, and good person. How could he do that to her?

Asshole. She should've called him an asshole, Casey thought. She should've said something, anything, thrown her purse at him. Perhaps it was seeing Irene, sleeping so perfectly the sleep of an eight-month-old girl—her right fist curled softly, her Raggedy Ann checked dress—that had struck her dumb while hearing Ted telling his mistress that he loved her.

She felt like killing him. Because of him, she'd been avoiding Delia. Delia had called in January, and when they finally had that incredibly awkward talk about her and Ted, Casey had pretty much explained how Ella didn't want her to be friends with her. It was something out of junior high school with an adult flavor. But Casey missed Delia. She was a real friend, and though she knew Delia was at fault, she was far more upset with Ted because he was the married one. For some reason, Casey had never cared that Delia slept with married men. Maybe because Delia never seemed to want anything from them. In Casey's mind, it was absolutely possible that Delia was a good friend and that she could sleep with married men; there was no conflict. Now it seemed more complicated, because Delia had told her that it was over. But that conversation had been in January. And it sounded as if Ted was really in love. What would happen if Delia had fallen in love, too? And Ella and Irene? How about them? Casey felt scared for them.

Casey and Unu stopped walking as they approached the receiving line. Her arm was linked with his. The photographer snapped his camera.

"Again, please," the photographer asked.

Casey glanced at Unu and together they smiled politely at him.

The reception was not beautiful, but the food was abundant, and everyone seemed to relax in the church basement. The deejay that Chul had hired cracked jokes between playing top forty music. There was nothing lovely about the basement—the wedding lilies hardly covered the smell of insecticide and kimchi soup from prior communal church meals. Basketball hoops were stationed at opposite sides of the large room, which also served as a gymnasium. Chul and Tina danced to a Whitney Houston song, and at Joseph's request, the father-daughter dance was skipped, but Chul danced with his mother to "Wind Beneath My Wings." Chul's parents danced well, and remained on the dance floor, as did his sisters.

Casey had been seated with Sabine and Isaac, Ella and Ted, and Unu. Dr. Shim, who was supposed to be sitting with Joseph and Leah, had migrated to their table to chat with Unu. Sabine and Isaac left shortly after dinner, because Sabine had a migraine. As she'd expected, throughout the evening Casey was peppered with questions by several Korean parishioners as to when she'd marry and would Unu be the lucky fellow. There was no polite answer to this, so Casey was relieved when Tina told her that she had to pee.

There was no way Tina could negotiate the crinoline-and-hoop skirt beneath her wedding dress by herself. Tina and Chul had agreed on no bridesmaids or groomsmen, but as her sister, Casey had hosted a bridal shower at Sabine's apartment, gone to choose her wedding clothes at Kleinfeld's, and helped her to get dressed today, and now, they joked, she had the bridal bathroom duties.

They headed toward the bathroom behind the sanctuary on the main floor because it was large and private. Tina was irrepressibly happy and in her blissful state didn't notice that Casey was quiet.

After Tina finished her business, Casey held on to the hem of Tina's skirt because there was a large puddle of water near the sink.

"Wow. You're married."

"I know! Isn't it crazy?" Tina replied, turning from her own reflection, then seeing her sister's thoughtful face. "Hey, you okay?"

"I'm good."

Tina nodded, feeling foolish for being so giddy. She was ashamed of her happiness. It might have been difficult for her sister to deal with all these Koreans asking her questions about marriage and such when Unu had said he'd never marry again. It occurred to her that she was being inconsiderate. But she couldn't imagine getting married without Casey being there.

"Thanks for getting the flowers before. Can you believe I forgot them? What a moron!" Tina hit her head dramatically.

"You're allowed to forget things, Dr. Han."

Tina nodded, noticing how her sister's face could be so beautiful when it softened. "I'm really glad you're here. It means a lot to me."

Casey looked at her sister. "I wouldn't have missed it. I'm really happy for you. Chul seems like a terrific guy."

"I love him so much. He's a very good person. You know?"

"His mother, however..." Casey rolled her eyes.

"Oh, she's not so bad. Dad said she's a *yuh-oo.*"

"Yeah, he nailed that one." Casey laughed. "Can you believe the shitty presents yesterday?" She laughed again. "What did Dad say about them? Probably nothing."

"They didn't say a word," Tina replied. She exhaled loudly. "I felt so bad for—"

"Fuck 'em. They're snobs and cheapskates. Did you notice how flat-chested that mother is? I was feeling rather full-figured in comparison." Casey stuck out her 34B chest.

"Chul's not like that." Tina giggled.

"He's chesty?" Casey winked.

"No." Tina made her "little sister worried" face. "He's very generous. I haven't talked to him about it. I don't even know if I will. But I think he felt bad about the disparity between the gifts—" She looked at her hands and noticed her wedding band and engagement ring.

"They're just tight, I guess." Casey checked her reflection in the mirror, tucking the stray hairs into her updo.

"But what's funny is that they're not tight," Tina said, trying not to say the obvious thing.

"They think we're shit because we're poor. They thought they didn't need to go through the trouble—"

Tina said nothing. Casey always said what she saw, but it wasn't as if everyone wanted to hear it.

"Makes you want to be rich, doesn't it?" Casey pulled out her compact and powdered Tina's nose.

"No," Tina replied instantly. "Makes you feel rich to not behave that way."

Casey stopped unscrewing the lid for the lip gloss and looked directly at Tina. "You always get it right, don't you?" She smiled at her younger sister. "Dr. Han, you amaze me."

"Oh, shut up," Tina said, grinning.

They left the bathroom together, but when they reached the bottom of the basement steps, they ran into Ted holding an unlit cigarette. He was heading out for a smoke.

"Hey, the sisters," he said, acting as if nothing had happened before. That was classic Ted. He could not be ruffled.

"Hi, Ted," Tina said. She noticed Chul waving her over from the other side of the basement. "My husband beckons." Tina went to him.

Casey stood there for a moment, trying to figure out where to go. She tried to pass him, but he blocked her with a sidestep.

"Listen," he said.

"I don't have to listen to you. You're a fucking clown."

"She knows."

"Who knows?"

"Ella knows."

"Right," Casey said, and looked into his eyes and saw that he was serious.

"You don't know what it's like to be married and to fall in love with someone else."

"You're right. I don't know." Casey stood there, not wanting to judge him.

"I love Ella, but I am in love with Delia. And Delia is the person who—"

"Listen, pal, you don't need to sing their praises. I like both these women. I respect both these women, despite whatever positive feelings they could have for a pathetic piece of shit like—"

"Casey, you're such a hard person. And you've no right to condemn me."

"Don't give me this relativist crap. I don't buy it. Why shouldn't I judge you? You hurt Ella. She took you back after—"

"You don't understand." Ted wanted to explain how Delia was someone he felt he was meant to be with, and how Ella, who was ideal, was just that—an ideal, but not someone he wanted to love. "You don't—"

"And I don't want to understand. What the hell do people mean when they say they love? What the hell does it mean, anyway?" Casey stared at him.

"Delia and I are going to get married—"

"But you are married!" she cried. A Michael Jackson song was playing, and the dance floor was full.

"Ella wants a divorce. I'm only here because Ella asked me to do this last thing, and I said I would." Ted said all this rapidly, as if he had to spit it out of his body. When Ella had asked him last night, what she'd said was "I need to keep my word. I said we'd both be there."

"Okay, then." Casey could hardly believe him. Was he waiting for a pat on the head for being such an agreeable husband? His sense of entitlement and worldview were impossible to challenge. "Listen, it's none of my—" She put her hand on the banister. She felt physically weaker—her anger was giving way to a kind of coldness. She didn't feel like talking to him anymore. "Whatever, Ted. Bye," she said, and walked away.

Ted watched her go. It was strange, even to him, how much he wanted her to understand his decision. He climbed the stairs.

Casey went to her table and found Unu talking with Dr. Shim. Ella was seated beside them, her dark eyes looking drowsy. With her right hand, she was pushing the stroller back and forth steadily. Irene was still sleeping. The loud disco music didn't seem to affect her. The cake was cut, but over half of the three hundred guests lingered. They were having a wonderful time. Tina and Chul were dancing, too, and Casey couldn't help smiling at her sister.

Casey sat on the empty chair near Ella, who barely seemed to notice her.

"Hi," she said.

Ella glanced at Casey. "Oh, hiya, Casey." She reached over to give Casey a hug, her expression a little moony. "Where were you?"

Casey took a breath. "Ted—"

"I'm getting a divorce, Casey. Whaddya know?" Ella giggled.

"You don't look right," Casey said. "Are you drunk?" She checked the wineglass in front of Ella. It was full of red wine.

"You know, Casey? I really like my new job. Mr. Fitzsimmons is such a great guy!"

"Ella? You okay?"

"Ted got fired yesterday, and I'm leaving him. I'm leaving him. He's not leaving me. Nope," Ella said cheerfully.

Casey looked over at Dr. Shim to see if he could hear any of this, but he was talking with Unu and it was difficult even for her to hear Ella over the loud music.

"What do you mean, he was fired?"

"Well, he resigned. But basically, he was fired. Ted Kim was fired from the great Kearn Davis. Having sex with Delia on the trading floor. She had to 'resign,' too. Ha! Security had tapes of them. Isn't that hilarious?" Ella guffawed unnaturally.

"What?" Casey blinked. There were security cameras through-out the trading floor. Everybody who worked on the trading floor knew that. Why was Ted even on the trading floor? "Wait—what happened?"

"They were having sex, Casey. S-e-x. I didn't see the tapes, though. Don't need to. But I can guess what happened. I know how Ted likes it. He likes for me to sit on his lap. I read in *Cosmopolitan* magazine that men who are bossy like to be dominated in bed. Did you know that, Casey? But I don't want to dominate anyone in bed. I can't even imagine... But I'm sure Delia knows how to please a man."

"Ella?" Casey shouted. Ella was crying now. Who was this person talking? She didn't even sound like Ella. "Hey, hey, what's going on? How much wine did you have?"

"None. I'm not supposed to drink when I'm taking Tylenol."

"Are you taking Tylenol?" Casey looked closely into Ella's eyes but didn't know what to be looking for. When you were stoned, your eyes looked darker because your pupils were dilated, but she couldn't imagine Ella getting high. Tylenol wouldn't make you sound as though you were drunk. "Ella? How much Tylenol did you take?"

"Yes!" Ella answered, closing her eyes, then opening them abruptly. "I'm taking lots of Tylenol."

"Ella, how much Tylenol did you take?" Casey spoke very slowly. Tylenol couldn't kill you, she tried to tell herself.

"I don't remember." Ella smiled like a child and leaned into Casey. "Hi, Casey!" Her expression was growing more blank, and she no longer looked awake, although her eyes were wide open. Her left hand flopped off the stroller handle like a doll's. Reflexively, her hand returned to the stroller. "Ted said he'll get something else. These things die down, apparently." She sounded as if she were par-roting something he'd told her.

"What are you talking about?" Casey glanced over at Dr. Shim, wondering when she should pull him over, but she didn't want to upset Ella.

"His job. Ted said he'll get a new job." Her voice grew singsong. "He said we have lots of money in the bank. I mean, he has lots of money in the bank. I don't have any money of my—" Ella slumped over, her hand jerking the stroller away. Irene woke up with a scream.

"Dr. Shim!" Casey cried, moving toward Ella. "Dr. Shim!" Ella's head fell heavy on Casey's shoulder.

Unu grabbed the stroller as it wheeled past him and pulled Irene out. "It's okay, Irene-y, it's okay..." The baby settled down quickly, returning to sleep on Unu's shoulder. He patted her small back, not understanding what had happened to Ella.

"Ella?...Ella?" Dr. Shim repeated calmly. He pulled back Ella's eyelids. "Call 911," he said. "Right now. Someone call 911 right now. Right now. Right now."

11 | SOUVENIRS

$\mathscr{A}$ND HOW IS B SCHOOL?" Kevin Jennings asked. "Is it all that you expected?" He chuckled.

"I love school, Kevin. Of course, it isn't thrilling like working on a trading floor, and I miss you guys. So very, very much." Hands clasped over her heart, Casey bowed her head in a gesture of remorse.

A chorus of "Aaawww" rose from the men.

Casey was seated at the head of the table as the guest of honor. Her belated send-off dinner was being held at the private room of Kuriya on Fifty-sixth Street—a steakhouse known for cooking Kobe beef on hot stones. It hadn't been easy to get both the Asian and Japan equities sales teams together, but Walter Chin had arranged for eight institutional salesmen, five traders, and two assistants to attend Casey's farewell party.

Kuriya was Casey's favorite expense account restaurant in New York—a place where dinner cost approximately two hundred and fifty dollars a person. Her favorite item on the menu was the shiso rice, which you had to order separately because nothing came with your steak. The price tag for a scoop of rice tossed with Japanese mint and black sesame seeds: six dollars. She'd never been there on her own coin and didn't expect to anytime soon after tonight. There were sixteen people there including herself. It didn't help to think like this, because expensive meals were part of Wall Street culture, but it was hard for Casey to get used to despite having been served by waiters at eating clubs at Princeton and going to Virginia's house for dinner, where her mother pressed a bell under the table with her foot for the maid to bring the next course. Tonight's dinner would cost four thousand dollars, with the salesmen and traders splitting the tab (they never asked the assistants to pay), and of course, Casey couldn't help but do the math of equivalents: the tab for this send-off dinner would have wiped out a quarter of her credit card debts, more than three months of rent for her old studio apartment, more than ten months of groceries for her and Unu, four new suits from Sabine's, one month's salary for her father, and so on.

Living with Unu reduced her expenses enormously, because she didn't pay the rent or utilities, but she was always thinking about money, because she still had to pay for everything else. Casey had refused Sabine's offer to pay for business school, and Sabine, not wishing to offend Casey, hadn't pressed the issue. To pay for Stern, she'd borrowed almost forty thousand dollars from Citibank for tuition and living expenses. There were also credit card minimums to be made for her fifteen-thousand-plus consumer debts, as of late, nearly eight grand having already been paid down. She missed the guys—all of them seated around the table like grown-up boys, full of teasing and competition, and she also felt the loss of the Kearn Davis paychecks. On Saturdays and Sundays, she worked the hat counter at Sabine's, but her earnings there were just enough to give her walking-around money for carfare and lunches.

Last night, she'd been unable to sleep because she was so worried about her growing deficit. How would she pay all her bills? Her education loans would double invariably because B school was two years. What kind of job would she have to get next summer? After graduation? Interviews for summer internships would start next month. She'd watched Unu sleep, envying his calm, even breathing, then gotten out of bed and pulled out nearly all of her credit cards from her red plastic wallet emblazoned with the picture of Lynda Carter in her stars-and-stripes Wonder Woman suit. She'd dropped the cards into a Ziploc bag and tucked the sealed bag in the freezer right below the ice-cube tray. This idea had come from a personal finance magazine she'd been flipping through at the gynecologist's office. She'd decided to reserve a single Visa card in her main wallet for emergencies. Afterward, she'd returned to bed, feeling just a tiny bit less anxious.

As with other four-star restaurants Casey had been to—more free food courtesy of Kearn Davis—Kuriya had layers and layers of silent service people. The entrée dishes were cleared away swiftly, then the white-jacketed waiters pulled out silver tools from their breast pockets to sweep the crumbs of food off the linen tablecloth. Moments later, the waiters passed out menu cards listing desserts and after-dinner drinks. On the back, there were paragraph-long descriptions of cigars for sale. In lieu of dessert, most of the brokers ordered cognac or Sauternes. When the waiter asked Casey, she requested a pear eau-de-vie. This was Virginia's grandmother's drink, and Casey had always wanted to try it.

Walter, two seats away from her, had left the table earlier and now returned carrying a blue canvas golf bag filled with clubs. He propped the bag against Casey's chair.

"What's that?" she asked.

"For you, my dear," Hugh said. He was sitting to her left.

"For me?" Casey said shyly, smiling. She wanted to look happy about the gift. "You guys...thank you so much. You're the best." Casey nodded. She was moved by their generosity.

The men aaaawwwed again. One of the sales traders called out, "Well, we figure you might want to whack some balls in business school." He made a leering face.

With her right hand, Casey made an okay sign.

The gift was incredibly generous, but she felt terrible. What was the saying—Don't buy a Rolls-Royce if you can't afford the gas? She already had a very nice set of clubs from Jay, and she almost never played. It seemed like some sort of cosmic joke for her to have two sets of clubs, no club membership, and no time to play.

"And where did you get this amazing set of clubs?" she asked. Her eyes searched for tags, some telltale sign that they could be traded in for cash. "This is incredibly nice," she said. "You guys. Wow. Thank you so much. Thank you."

"I picked them out," Hugh said. Excited, he plucked out the fanciest clubs and held them up for show like an auctioneer. He'd taken off his gray suit jacket, and his white shirtsleeves were rolled up, exposing the light tan on his forearms from a recent trip to Bali. The men at the table whistled at the clubs, as if the titanium-head, graphite-shaft woods were beautiful girls.

When everyone had a drink in his hand, Kevin Jennings, who

could tell already that Casey's replacement, Hector Breed, a Cornell grad from Louisiana, would not work out, raised his glass and cleared his throat. Casey picked up her cordial glass of pear brandy, the color of water with the viscosity of thin cough syrup.

"On behalf of the Asian sales desk, Kearn Davis, and these jokers"—he gestured with his glass toward the Japan sales team—"we congratulate you on your foolish and misguided decision to attend B school." Everyone laughed. Kevin coughed again, his glass still raised. "And yet..." He smiled at Casey. "We look forward to your one day becoming a client. Do not forget us, Casey Han. Send us your trades."

Several men shouted, "Hear, hear!"

Casey clinked her glass with the people near her.

Hugh elbowed Kevin. "Kevin, man, are you crying?" He pulled out a white handkerchief from his pants pocket and waved it in the direction of his boss.

Kevin squinted at Hugh, accepted the proffered handkerchief, and dabbed his eyes playfully. He tossed it at Casey, and she, too, touched the corners of her eyes, placing the back of her right hand over her forehead as if she were swooning. Everyone returned to their drinking. Casey was praying that no one would send her shots of tequila—she had to go to Sabine's in the morning. The talk soon reverted to what brokers cared about: upgrades in airlines and hotels and Relais & Châteaux in America and Europe. Casey felt she could write a guidebook on the places she'd visited as a corporate flunky and from the conversations she'd overheard.

The brandy made her feel warm inside, its sweet taste coating her throat. She opened Hugh's handkerchief to fold it back properly. The act of concentrating on getting the corners right when she had a good buzz going in her head was somehow pleasurable. On a corner was his monogram, HEU, in block letters.

"Hugh E. Underhill," Casey said out loud.

Hugh turned to her. "Hmm?" He was also a little gone, having had a good-size bottle of cold sake by himself.

"What's the E for?"

"Edgar."

"After three years of sitting next to a person," Casey said, "there are still things I don't know about you, dear." The tone of her voice was mocking. She looked at his face. He was truly a handsome man.

He'd been a good friend to her over the years, not to mention the hundreds of lunches he'd bought for her. Whenever she'd try to pay him, he'd say, "I'm a good-looking and successful stockbroker, and you are a poorly paid gofer who went to a far better college than I did. And to think I almost never did my homework at Groton. Isn't that rich?" Of course, he said all this in this way to make sure she never paid. Hugh was a hound, for certain, but he was a kind person. He was also a hedonist and, naturally, never made her feel bad about her spending habits. Hugh believed in pleasure and luxury like a religion. He despised abstemiousness.

Hugh smiled at her. "So have you missed me terribly? How have you gotten on?"

"It's been unbearable, really." Casey tried to keep a straight face. "Sometimes these powerful feelings of loss overcome me, and I can hardly function. If I fail at school, the blame will rest on you, Hugh Edgar Underhill." She appeared as mournful as possible.

Hugh reached over and kissed her cheek, and Casey pushed him away. "Yuck. Cut it out." She laughed.

"Don't come begging for more," he said.

The waiters brought glass equipment to brew coffee table side. Each set resembled pieces from chemistry lab—glass bowl-shaped beakers with a kind of elegant Bunsen burner fitted on their bottoms and delicate tins with Sterno fuel. Another waiter carried a ceramic crock filled with coffee from Hawaii. The headwaiter ceremoniously lit a tiny blue fire under each beaker, and the water in the glass beaker boiled rapidly. The brokers and traders were hypnotized by the coffee preparation. They looked like boys more than Wall Street guys worth millions. Casey liked them suddenly this way, for their innocence and absence of cynicism at such a gimmicky contrivance. For her, the effect was lovely enough, especially the aroma of good coffee being brewed. But each cup was ten dollars. Waiters put out cream in pewter pitchers, and Casey put some in her white coffee cup. She dropped two sugar cubes in her cup, though she normally took her coffee black, no sweetener. Feeling poorer than she'd ever felt, she craved every bit of luxury and feared never having any more, and what made it worse was that she was ashamed of wanting it so much, to consume it, to incorporate it somehow into her body. She didn't want to feel poor anymore.

When she was growing up, her parents drank Taster's Choice

with Coffee-Mate, which they called "preem" after a nondairy additive they'd used in Korea. When she'd go to the grocery store with her mother, she'd finger the box of Domino Dots—sugar in perfect sharp cubes—but she'd never considered asking her mother to buy a box; it seemed so costly and frivolous compared with the store-brand white sugar in five-pound bags. From the ages of eighteen to twenty-five—she was nearly twenty-six—Casey had eaten at many different kinds of tables, some of the fanciest restaurants, private clubs, and homes in New York, but inside, she believed that she could be asked to leave at any moment, and what would she do but leave quietly with the knowledge that this was what happened to girls like her?

When the coffee was served, several men turned their heads toward the door, and Casey checked to see what they were staring at. Delia had come.

"Hey, Delia," a few guys said. Several of them waved.

Delia gave a small wave. She walked straight over to Casey and handed her a shopping bag tied with a ribbon.

"Hey there. Walter said I could drop by. I'm glad I caught you," Delia said, taking a deep breath. "I got you some—" She laughed.

Casey smiled politely, not knowing what to do. "Hi," she said finally. "Thank you." She accepted the bag and burst out laughing at the contents. It was chock-full of bath gels and soaps. Every Christmas, brokers' wives would send her and Casey bath products they bought from some suburban mall. It was the generic assistant gift that no one they knew ever used.

Casey winked. "Oh, how sad, no scented candles."

Delia laughed in relief. One Christmas, the two of them had piled up the cache of scented candles, soaps, and bath gels from the brokers' wives. It was nice of them, but did they think single women lived mostly in their bathtubs when they weren't at the office?

Delia remained standing, and when Casey looked around, there were no empty seats. Walter offered up his seat, but Delia refused. "Thanks, baby, but I have to leave soon."

Casey got up to stand with her. "Thanks for coming."

"I got balls to come to this. You think any of these guys saw the tape?" Delia rested her hand on her cocked hip. She blew the wisps of red hair from her forehead.

"It means a lot." Casey smiled at her, because it did.

Delia motioned toward the bar, wanting Casey to come with her.

The others seemed to get that the girls wanted to be alone. They stood close to each other.

"It's sweet of you. And very funny." Casey lifted the shopping bag. Then she closed her lips tight, feeling awful about everything. Just two weeks ago, Ella had come out of the hospital after overdosing on codeine. She'd taken too many Tylenol-3's and had to have her stomach pumped after passing out at Tina's wedding. For now, Ella was living in Forest Hills with her dad and the baby. As far as Casey knew, Ted was living with Delia. Casey grew somber at the thought. The happy mood between them was broken.

"I know it's awkward," Delia said, "but I wanted to explain."

"No, there's no need."

"I didn't mean to—to come between Ted and your friend. You know how skeptical I am about guys. But we fell in love. Casey, he's the right guy for me. He's flawed and selfish. I know that. But he loves me, and I think he's the one. I know that doesn't excuse everything, but—"

Delia spoke rapidly, as though she were being timed. Ella wasn't here, Casey told herself, and Delia deserved to be heard.

"—Casey, I've never been in love before. Not like this. He asked me to marry him. And I fought it. I tried to stay away, and so did he. But we need to be with each other. I don't expect you to understand completely, or for us to be friends like we were before—I mean, I understand how you feel about being loyal to your friend—but we're friends, too."

"Ella tried to kill herself," Casey blurted out, then felt worse than before.

Delia hung her head. She'd felt terrible about this ever since she'd heard.

"I'm not saying it's your fault, but I am confused by all this. Delia..." Casey looked at the gift Delia had brought. "For what it's worth, I don't think you're a bad person. I don't. And I can't believe I'm saying this, but I hope you're happy. I do. I hope it works out." She raised her eyebrows. "To be honest, I'm kind of puzzled by the great women Ted can attract. I really am. He must be something else."

"He can be an asshole. And when he is, I tell him to cut it out." Delia crossed her arms, then uncrossed them. "When I heard...she took codeine, I told him to go back to her."

Casey looked into Delia's eyes, wordless.

"But she didn't want him back."

"I know." It was true. Ella was filing for divorce, and she wanted full custody.

"I don't expect us to be friends like before...." Delia repeated this statement, wanting Casey to contradict her even as she fully anticipated a rejection.

Casey reached over to hug Delia, and Delia held her tight.

"I'm sorry," Delia said. "I'm sorry. I'm sorry for who I am."

"No, no, don't say that," Casey said. Delia's words upset her.

Each pulled back, and Casey looked at Delia.

"Listen, I want you to be happy. I'm glad you have love. I hope he's good to you. And you're right, when Ted is an asshole, you should let him know. He's probably grateful that someone is checking him," Casey said. "It must come as a relief to him that not everyone believes his show."

Delia nodded. "Ted's good to me."

Casey nodded.

"You know what Ted said, Casey? He said that he's a strategic person on every aspect of his life." Delia made air quotes when she said the word *strategic*. "And falling in love with me has been his most irrational act. But he said that being a smart and calculating person has been his way of building a strong cage around him, and doing the unexpected has freed him to be a new person. He said he feels free even though he's kind of scared. Ted admitted that he's scared." Delia appeared proud of him. "And I think when he explained it that way, I realized he wasn't just having an affair. He says...he says that winning life isn't worth it without me."

Delia had had no one to tell this to. She averted her gaze, filled with shame and happiness. She looked up. "I don't think I've been very strategic with my life." It was odd to use Ted's funny Harvard words. "I haven't trusted men, but I decided that I will make my life with Ted. I know it's crazy, but he and I make sense even though it doesn't look right. Do you know what I mean? Like I know what he thinks, what he'll do. I can't explain our connection."

Casey nodded, wanting to understand. She squeezed Delia's hand.

"I better get going," Delia said. She hugged Casey again.

"Bye now," Casey said, feeling her loss again.

Delia left them, and a few of the guys seemed sad to see her go but didn't urge her to stay. She was Ted's girl now. Unless you were living in a cave, you knew about the security tape and Ted's and Delia's "resignations."

On their way out, Hugh slung the golf bag over his shoulder. Everyone said good-bye at the table and again at the sidewalk. Kevin Jennings actually noogied her on the head. One of the traders put her in a headlock and made her say uncle, threatening to tickle her.

"I'm really going to miss you guys," she said, coughing, when she was freed. Drinking made everyone sentimental and ridiculous.

Hugh hailed a taxi and offered to take her home. They both lived on the East Side. Casey nearly fell into the cab while Hugh put the clubs in the trunk. From her seat, she could hear him telling the driver where to take them. "Two stops," Hugh said, and gave the driver her address as the first stop before his, although it didn't make much sense because she lived a few blocks north of him. Seated in the back of the yellow cab, she felt even more muddy-headed from the red wine, champagne, and brandy. Tomorrow would be a doozy.

"You don't like them," Hugh said as he entered the car, even before he sat down.

Casey didn't understand right away. Then she got it.

"No, no. I love them. I do. It was incredibly—"

Hugh cut her off. "Women like jewelry, clothes—"

"But girls also need cash."

Hugh laughed. An old girlfriend used to ask him for money to tip the bathroom attendant when she went to the bathroom, as if she were Holly Golightly or something. He'd always give her a hundred-dollar bill, and there was never any change. That was some girl, though—Hugh smiled at the thought of her significant talents.

"Real estate is good, too," Casey continued. "Even better than jewelry. The resale value on diamonds is actually quite shocking."

Hugh turned to her and kissed her on the mouth. The pressure of his mouth was strong, and Casey didn't resist. He put his right hand behind her neck, and Casey leaned her head back, letting his tongue in her mouth. Hugh took her hand and placed it on his crotch.

Casey pulled back. "Hey, hey, hey," she whispered, withdrawing her hand, realizing that she'd just touched his erection. The kissing had been good, and she'd certainly been with men who were less attractive than Hugh. But his direct come-on was fast and unexpected. In their three years, he'd never done anything but treat her like a college kid. "Cut it out, Hugh," she said quietly, not wanting to hurt his feelings.

"Yes, ma'am," he said, drawing his body away from hers. He combed his hair back with both hands. "Funny, I don't get that much." He wiped the corners of his mouth with his index finger and thumb.

"You don't get what much? Girls who say no?"

He nodded.

"Well, honey, there's always a first time," Casey said, thinking of the strange victories found in a woman's refusal. Virginia had once said men never forgot the girls who said no. This was particularly odd for her to say, because Virginia nearly always said yes. "I'd rather have good sex than pride," Virginia had claimed a moment later, to which Casey had replied, "Under your theory, you'd rather have good sex than be memorable." Virginia had ultimately won the point, however, when she'd declared, "Oh no, Casey, I make sure that the sex is so good, he can't forget it." Casey took her word for it.

Hugh sat up straight and adjusted himself. Then he reached over and took Casey's hand again and held it. Her long fingers laced with his.

Casey glanced at Hugh but imagined Unu's face instead—his dark, sad pupils, the sharp arch of his eyebrows when he joked. His first wife had been in love with someone else throughout their marriage. In the end, he'd told her to go, but even when she was there, she'd already been gone. She didn't want him to get hurt again.

Hugh rested his head against the back of the seat. He felt the buzz of the Sauternes and coffee. "Shouldn't have had the coffee," he said.

Casey didn't know what to say to Hugh. Why had he kissed her?

"So, you in love with your feller?" Hugh asked.

"Feller?" she said, imitating his inflection. "Oh yes, I forgot, your generation does have its speech peculiarities."

"You didn't answer the question, my dear."

"He doesn't believe in marriage," Casey said, not having intended to say that at all.

"You don't seem like the marrying kind, either," he said.

"You're probably right." She agreed with him, though it upset her to hear it. What girl wanted to be the unmarrying kind? She'd done some bad things in her life. She was no Ella, but she was no Delia, either. And even Delia was getting married, it seemed, to Mr. HBS. And at the office, she'd been more than competent and respected. They cared about her enough to throw this lavish send-off. What did Hugh mean by that? That he wouldn't marry a girl like her or that she didn't seem to want to get married? She turned to him. The blush of liquor stained his cheeks, and Casey glanced down at his pants, then felt ashamed at having looked.

He'd caught her doing this. "And what are you looking at, missy?"

"Not much," she said, giving him the line from her old neighborhood.

He was still holding her hand, and now he drew it closer to his torso. Casey's eyes didn't waver from his. He was trying to make her play a version of chicken, and she wouldn't let him win. Hugh inhaled, drawing in his flat stomach, then tucked her hand into his trousers. The cottony shirting fabric of boxers felt smooth and warm. Her fingers nested him.

Casey measured her own breathing. "Thanks for sharing the good news," she said. With control, she stroked him slowly upward. Hugh stopped breathing. She pulled her hand away. She smiled, feeling her power restored. The taxi driver was busy talking to his dispatcher in a language she couldn't make out, maybe Russian or Polish. She had no intention of giving Hugh a hand job.

They weren't five blocks from her apartment. "You know what, Hugh? It's late. I better go to sleep. I have to go to work tomorrow."

"Mmm. It is late. You should go to bed," he said, winking.

She shook her head no.

Hugh moved in and kissed her again, and this time she didn't fight it, letting his tongue move in her mouth, his hands roam over her brown silk blouse. He was good at this, and she was admittedly curious about his lovemaking, but this was where it would end, she told herself.

The taxi stopped in front of her building. George Ortiz, who was working the late shift, headed toward the car but stopped approaching when he saw a man in the car leaning toward Casey Han.

Casey pulled away from Hugh. She opened her purse to give Hugh some money.

"Put your money away," Hugh said, then told the driver to hang on and keep the meter running.

They both got out of the car. Hugh removed the clubs from the trunk and pulled the strap over Casey's shoulder. He moved closer to her.

"Don't kiss me," Casey said with a polite smile.

Hugh crinkled his pretty brown eyes.

"George," Casey whispered.

"Who's George? Now you live with two guys?"

"The doorman," she said. If George had seen Hugh kissing her in the taxi, he wouldn't say anything to Unu, she imagined, but he'd think less of her.

Hugh turned away and went into the car. From inside, he blew her a kiss. No one could tell him what to do. He screwed up his eyes when he looked at her, as though he were trying to make out a sign from far away. "Good night, Casey Cat."

"Good night, Hugh Edgar," she said, then turned toward the building.

George had kept a respectful distance, but he had missed nothing. He took the golf bag from her. "Thanks, George," she said without making eye contact.

The doorman nodded, the line of his lips drawn thin and straight. The guy in the cab had looked over Unu's girlfriend as though he wanted to eat her. He was not a good guy—that bit was obvious. George pulled the bag strap closer to his neck and followed behind Casey. He helped her with the elevator and let her get upstairs.

Unu was home. He'd been playing solitaire with a fresh deck of cards. The deliberate act of laying out the rows of cards, their faces down, was refreshing. That evening he'd come home, having forgotten that Casey would be out at her dinner, and the empty apartment felt keenly lonely to him. Things were not going well at work. His last calls on a few stocks had bombed, and Frank, his boss, in an act of kindness surely, had been giving him signs that his year-end bonus would be flat or even down this year. If his bonus was down, then it might as well be a Dear John letter. And the week before, he'd gone to Foxwoods when Casey was at Sabine's and lost eight thousand dollars. He owed his bookie two grand.

Casey let herself in, took off her shoes, and scanned the table surfaces for a packet of cigarettes. Unu was playing cards and didn't hear her come in. His concentration was hard to break. When he was reading, she had to physically tap him to get his attention.

"Hey there," Casey said, unloading the bag of clubs near the door. The parquet floor needed mopping, she noticed.

Unu peeled off another card from his stack and turned it over. A two of spades. He looked up from his neat lines.

"Whoa. A little shopping?" he said, staring at the clubs.

"My gold watch for being a good girl Friday."

"Check it out," he said, getting up from his seat. "Nice."

"Yes. Very." Casey tried to be dignified about her disappointment.

Unu pulled out two irons, one with each hand. He whistled, exactly the same way the guys had at Kuriya. "Gor-geous," he said.

"I have to sell them."

"What?" Unu looked hurt. "You can't do that. That's a gift." He seemed shocked by her statement.

They were Koreans, both educated in good private colleges, but he was the son of millionaires, grew up in an affluent suburb, private school from kindergarten on. On either side of his parents' family, there wasn't a single person who didn't graduate from Seoul National, Yonsei, or Ewha University. Her folks never went to college. She'd grown up in a tacky apartment building bracketed by the Maspeth gas tanks and Queens Boulevard. Her parents still lived in a rental, and their only asset had just burned down. Could he ever understand her?

"Listen up, rich boy, I need some dough. I can't afford two sets of clubs. You get me? Get real," she said, scowling.

"Rich boy?" Unu said. His eyes shrank, as if he were trying to hide them.

Normally, she'd have apologized, but Casey didn't feel like it. She spotted the Camels on the console. There was a lighter in her skirt pocket.

"What's the matter with you?" he asked.

"I'm just up to my ears in debt again. I can't stop thinking about my school loans and this idea of compounding interest. And of course, of course...there's always my credit card bills." Casey sealed her lips. "I know. It's my fault. I blame myself for this mess. Okay?" Her voice sounded more defensive than she'd have liked. But Unu hadn't accused her of anything. "And you are trying to help me on that score. I do appreciate it. Really." She shook her head, feeling angrier by the second. She hated explaining her problems. Money made her feel ashamed, angry, and afraid. And she had done it to herself. She'd dug the grave, one handful of dirt at a time. Her debts made her want to disappear in the hole.

"I'm going up. To have a cigarette." She picked up the Camels.

"Hey," he shouted, trying to keep her from walking out the door. "And how was your day, Unu?" he said sarcastically. It wasn't his nature to fight. Besides, common wisdom in the frat house held that it was worthless fighting girls because they couldn't be wrong. Their grudges became tattoos. But Casey was being unfair.

Casey stared at her shoes. When anyone got angry, she grew silent. A long drag of smoke would clear the swamp in her head. She wanted to leap up the emergency staircase to the roof two steps at a time. She inhaled deeply, unable to deal with Unu's angry face. She opened the front door and caught a whiff of the garbage piling up in the incinerator chute down the hall. Whether it was on the Upper East Side or Van Kleeck Street, apartment garbage smelled exactly the same—melon rinds and roach spray mingled in her nose like a cocktail.

"Can we please talk later?" she asked meekly.

"No," he said indignantly. "Frank says my bonus is shot this year. And I'll probably get laid off if I don't start making more reasonable stock calls. Everything I like is a long shot, it turns out. But I did the research and I know what's good, it's just that the market is filled with a bunch of fucking hedgers. No one believes in companies anymore or wants to hold 'em. Flip, flip, flip. That's all they do. Isn't that a fucking riot?" Unu laughed meanly. "And baby, the market wants some returns some of the time, but I am calling for the big time."

Unu walked away. He hadn't realized how disgusted he was by what was going on in the Asian equities market. Wall Street was about plundering and making as much money as possible. Did it even matter how? He walked back to the sofa. "The true believers have left the room," he muttered to himself.

Casey put her hand across the back of her neck. Unu had been hinting here and there that his calls were poorly received. Despite all of his research, charting, and analysis, the market was behaving irrationally, he'd mentioned at dinner last week. It happened when motives were at odds, he'd explained. Casey hadn't completely understood. She'd been tired herself, absorbed in trying to figure out the random mix of personalities in her business school assigned section. His boss, Frank, was always telling Unu how smart he was, but lately Frank was saying he was too smart for his own good. Unu's stock picks were too risky for their business or, worse, too conservative because the returns wouldn't come in for years. The company's investment philosophy varied sharply from Unu's. Frank said a lot of little bets were better than a gigantic loss or the attractive windfall. Unu railed against hedging. He called himself a true believer. When he liked a company, there was no way he'd back off his position.

Why can't you just do what they want you to do? she thought to say, but couldn't because this was something they shared: They were both stubborn. What was the worst thing that could happen? she wondered. He wasn't afraid to be poor, because he had never been poor. And Casey was poor, and she couldn't seem to make herself rich. But neither was willing to compromise on his or her fragile ideas.

Unu sat on the sofa and stared hard at his cards as if he could see through their blue backing.

Her eyes were tired, and Unu fell out of focus. She could make out the curve of his spine bent toward the coffee table, his head in his hands.

She put down the cigarettes. "I'm sorry. I didn't know. And I'm sorry—"

"It's okay," he said. "It's okay."

Casey sat close to him, and Unu dropped his head on her shoulders. She couldn't leave him now.

12 | INSURANCE

*U*NU WAS LET GO ULTIMATELY IN FEBRUARY, and two months
passed without his looking for work. Casey tried not to let it
get to her. Her mother's words buzzed in her head: "Never make a
man feel bad about his job." But what if he had no job? Casey wanted
to ask.

For ten months, they'd lived together happily, so Casey tried not
to change their routines. During the week, she went to classes and
did her homework religiously. On Saturday mornings before she
went to Sabine's, she rose early to clean the house and to work on
the occasional hat. Sabine was letting her sell them at her store, al-
lowing her to keep the profit without taking her cut. On average,
she sold one a month, netting about a hundred dollars or so. Unu
woke up with her and read his finance journals, and after Casey went
to work, he drove his Volvo to Foxwoods Casino, where he played
blackjack. Early Sunday mornings, they ate eggs and toast at home,
then attended services together. When church ended, Casey went to
work the counter at Sabine's, which opened at eleven. Unu stayed
home and researched companies for his own trades. To save money,
Casey fixed simple meals every night. Usually she did the grocery
shopping on her way home from school.

April was a busy school month for Casey, and it showed up on the
empty shelves of their refrigerator. There was very little to eat in the
house.

After scrambling their last five eggs with three slices of American cheese for their Saturday brunch, Casey grabbed her jacket and purse. "I'm going to the market," she said.

"I'll go with you," Unu said, putting away the dishes in the sink.

She had always seen it as her job to make sure there was coffee, cereal, and toilet paper in the house. When she lived with Jay, she'd taken care of these domestic details, and so also with Unu; it had never occurred to her to share these duties.

"I'll carry the stuff home, and you can go straight to—work," he said, folding his newspaper. "And I'll get to spend more time with you."

"Thank you," she said, surprised by his offer, not because he wasn't normally thoughtful—Unu was by nature a considerate man—but because it struck her as odd that she'd viewed marketing as woman's work. In romance, Virginia used to call Casey old-fashioned because she liked men to do the pursuing. Casey realized that Virginia's label wasn't too wrong for other things, too. It was the way she'd grown up, witnessing the things only her mother did at home. Casey felt backward; was that why it was so hard for her to accept that Unu didn't have a job?

When Unu and Casey got to the street, she reached for his hand and held it as they walked toward the market on Lexington. Unu talked about Ella and baby Irene living with Ella's dad. He thought it made sense for her to stay with Dr. Shim until she felt a little stronger. Casey couldn't imagine going back to her parents. Unu seemed happy just to be walking down the street. With few worries.

At the cleaning products aisle, Casey picked up the jug of store-brand bleach. It was sixty cents less than Clorox.

"I didn't know there was a store-brand version," Unu remarked.

"Makes no difference," she said a little defensively. Unu was staring at the Clorox.

"I'm sure you're right. I just didn't know." He laughed.

"Do you prefer Clorox?" Ever since Casey had left home, she'd bought Clorox herself.

Unu shook his head no. He'd never given any thought to it. He pushed the cart and followed her.

Casey pretended to be occupied by the grocery list. He'd caught her trying to save money, and she didn't want him to feel ashamed.

"I mean, I'm the daughter of people who do laundry for a living.

You should leave the wash to me." Casey thrust out her neck in mock defiance.

"Okay, Casey." He laughed. "I trust you."

They turned the corner to canned goods. They needed soup. Casey picked up six cans. Three for a dollar ninety-eight.

"I've never tried that one before," Unu said. "Do you like Manhattan clam chowder?" he asked. Casey didn't like tomatoes. The soup was meant for him.

"This company is fine. I've had it before." She put back the chowder and picked up three cans of sale-brand chicken noodle.

"I like Progresso better." He deliberately mentioned the one that wasn't on sale. He watched her. She was trying to shave off a few cents, and there was no need to do this.

Casey kept three sale cans of chicken noodle in the cart. She handed him two cans of Progresso clam chowder. "Thank you," he said. She walked ahead, studying her list.

Unu stopped pushing the cart and waited for her to notice.

When she reached the end of the aisle, she turned around. He wasn't moving. She waved at him to come to her, but he didn't budge. Casey walked back to him.

"What's the matter?" She was trying not to sound caustic.

"I don't want you to worry about money, Casey," he said. "There's enough money for Clorox and Progresso soup. You shouldn't skimp on these things. I told you I'd take care of you while you were staying with me." He felt desperate, wanting her not to doubt him.

She opened her mouth to say something but didn't know how to begin. On Unu's desk in the living room, near the bank of double-hung windows, he kept a deep rattan basket filled with unpaid bills. Many of them were marked "Second Notice" or "Third Notice." Occasionally, there were messages left on his answering machine—the speaker's tone of voice ominous and entitled: "We are calling to inquire about the January payment for the loan in connection with your automobile." When they heard the messages together, Unu would dismiss it: "I've just been too busy to take care of them." Jay Currie used to hand her a book of signed checks to pay his bills, so when Casey had mentioned this method without attributing its source, Unu replied, his voice quiet and vaguely annoyed, "No need. I'll take care of it." And in the past two months, he did occasionally empty the basket and pay them. She had no idea how much money

306 MIN JIN LEE

he had or how much of it came from his severance or from black-jack winnings. For her, hell would look like a room lined with laundry baskets overflowing with unpaid bills, message machines blaring with the voices of creditors, and she their sole debtor.

"It's just that I'd like to pay for the groceries. You already do so much," she said, her tone anxious. This was true. For the past ten months, he'd paid for the rent, utilities, and cable. "I'm sorry. About the soup. I didn't mean to make you eat sale soup. I'm the student, so I should be eating the—"

"Casey..." Unu spoke sternly. "Eat the food you want. Stop worrying about this stuff. For God's sake, I told you I'd take care of—" He caught himself and took a breath. He was losing his temper.

"Okay, okay." Casey got quiet. She didn't want to fight with him. Suddenly she felt so tired, worrying about his pride and their lack of money, and there was her stupid future to consider. She still didn't have an investment banking job lined up for the summer—the top-tier firms paid the highest internship salaries. Lots of Internet companies were looking, but she had no interest in that world. Hugh or Walter might be able to help her get a spot on the Kearn Davis banking program, but she was embarrassed to call them for a favor. It seemed like another backdoor entrance. Kearn Davis didn't bother to recruit at Stern; the only New York business school they recruited from was Columbia. Sabine had been right after all. Names mattered so much.

"I'm sorry, Unu," she said, not knowing why she was apologizing. "We will be all right."

"I know," she said, unable to look at him. "I know. I'm sure of it."

At the checkout aisle, Unu refused to let her pay for the groceries. He paid for everything with cash and kissed her good-bye on the street before she went to catch the 6. He carried four bags of groceries, two in each hand, and watched his girlfriend running to the train station.

Casey was a conscientious student and didn't find B school to be difficult. On Fridays, after her class in corporate finance ended, she met with her section to work on their group projects. The section went out for beers afterward at Mariano's, but as usual, Casey begged off. She said good-bye to her friends, then headed for Ella's house in Forest Hills to see her goddaughter, Irene.

The train ride to Queens was less than thirty minutes, making it an ideal time for her to read for pleasure. She'd begun *Middlemarch* again recently, finding comfort in the familiar world. She opened the book and found two letters from Virginia in place of a bookmark. One of them she'd read last night when she got home, and the other she had put aside to savor later.

Casey tore open the envelope. In it was a card with a Caravaggio painting on the front—a young boy with a succulent vermilion-colored mouth—and inside were folded sheets of Florentine marble paper where Virginia had continued the writing when there was no more space left on the card. At the sight of Virginia's girls' school cursive writing, so much like Ella's—full of fat loops and highly dotted i's—Casey felt happy.

She laughed out loud when she read the first line in the card— "Brace yourself"—anticipating one of Virginia's ugly-American-in-foreign-country escapades. Virginia didn't avoid scrapes, she yearned for them. At the sound of her own laughter, she remembered herself and looked about her. But none of the passengers had noticed, and none peered over her shoulder to read her card. The train—full of weary passengers heading home—trudged along its tracks unremarkably, fulfilling its usefulness. The train lights didn't flicker, the stops were smooth, and they weren't stuck in a dark tunnel listening to a sad story from a drunk panhandler passing his paper coffee cup—the predictable moments attached to a daily train ride. With a long letter to keep her company, it was cozy sitting there between a pair of commuters in light jackets, headphones over their ears. From one of their headsets, she could make out a voice that sounded like Ray Charles and piano playing. Her eyes strayed to the second line of the first paragraph: "Dearest beloved Casey, Jay Currie is to be married." Had she misunderstood Virginia's florid language? She reread the line; her eyes had lost track.

"I've gathered intelligence about the bride from friends who attended the engagement party at the Metropolitan Club," Virginia wrote. Jay, a member of Terrace, had been close with members of his own eating club as well as those of Ivy—Virginia's eating club. Their worlds had mingled often.

He was marrying Keiko Uchida, Virginia wrote—a taciturn foreign student with large brown eyes and pale lips who wore gray pearl studs in her ears. Her mother's family was crazy rich, and her father was a high-ranking salaryman who worked for Hirano, a porcelain company. Her mother's father gave something like a gymnasium to Brown University, where Keiko and her brothers later went to college. Her mother's best friend in New York was a member of the Metropolitan Club and hence the engagement fete there. The boys of Terrace and Ivy said the fiancée was pretty and congratulated Jay. The girls of Ivy found her ordinary and little.

No doubt Virginia had added the women's snipey comments to make Casey feel better, but Casey didn't mind Keiko's attractiveness. So be it. What threw her was the fact that he was with another Asian woman—as if they were cogs to be replaced on a machine. That was the problem with fetishes, wasn't it? There could be real love, but one couldn't feel certain what was the basis for attraction. It gave her some relief that she was with Unu now, a Korean, as opposed to a WASP who'd fallen off his class rung. Somewhere she'd read that when Yoko Ono was asked, "Why do white men like Asian women?" she'd apparently replied, "Maybe Asian women like white men." Well, Casey liked Unu, but she had also liked Jay. Ted had long ago remarked that Jay was the type of white guy who ended up with Asian women, as if Asian women were consolation prizes for these white guys who couldn't score high with one of their own kind. Ted was such a prick, she thought.

Casey skimmed the rest of the letter for more news about Keiko and Jay, but there was none. Virginia had written more about her love affair with Paolo. When she was in the initial throes of romance, Virginia sounded even more literary and precious than usual. In the final paragraph, she wrote, "I've given up the prospects of my degree. It is impossibly hard to remain cloistered in these glorious libraries and pretend that I care any more about my subject when I fear that it is irrelevant." What? Casey shrugged, then read the last lines: "I left Paolo in Rome, because, well, because. A love affair can die, Casey. You know that. He didn't love me enough, so I began to love him less. My heart responded less because he gave so little. He never gave me a birthday gift. That seems so silly, because I didn't want anything as much as to know that he had thought of me. I'd wanted some token to remember him when we weren't together. Oh well. Is that very American? Then I met Gio at the American Express office in Bologna. So I wrote to Paolo to say good-bye. He was devastated, and I'm not sorry. It had to end. Darling Casey, I have news. I think I am carrying Gio's child. Be happy for me."

She ended the letter just like that, and at that moment, Virginia's grandiloquent writing peeved her intensely. But maybe Casey was just mad at the messenger. Jay was gone.

The train stopped. She had missed Ella's house by two stations. She got out of the car, crossed to the other side, and boarded the train heading back to Manhattan to correct her mistake. Not five minutes later, she got off at Ella's station and walked to her house.

Casey was still holding the letter in her left hand and her second cigarette since lighting up at the station in her right, when Ella— who must've been waiting by the door—opened on Casey's first ring. Ella wore her gold-wire-framed spectacles that made her look like a pretty undergraduate; her dark hair was gathered in a topknot with a banana clip left over from her high school days, and a yellow burp cloth was draped over her left shoulder. Irene was latched on to Ella's dark pancake-size nipple. Somehow, in spite of the black jogging pants and white T-shirt with wet spots across her breasts, Ella managed to look lovely. A kind of striking prettiness had bloomed in her face again, and Casey hadn't noticed that it had been gone so long until she recognized its return.

"Your boob is showing," Casey said. She embraced her, being careful not to lean into Irene's happy round head. "When are we going to stop that?" She made a face. "Isn't she kinda old for that?"

"I'm sort of weaning her, but..." Ella shrugged. Irene was a year and four months, and though she could have stopped, it made Ella sad to think of it ending.

"Oh, I'm sorry, Ella. Why do I always have to stick my foot in it?" Casey was aware that she'd made a suggestion for which she had absolutely no standing.

"No. No. You're right. Irene is already drinking cow's milk during the day from a cup, and there's no reason..."

The coffee table was set up with a pot of tea, scones, and sandwiches, two teacups on a floral-design tray. "Wow. That's so nice." She went to her favorite spot in the walnut-paneled living room. Dr. Shim had decorated it like an English hunting lodge, except with antique Korean chests along the walls. Casey sat on the wing chair upholstered in green corduroy.

Irene had fallen asleep, and Casey took her in her arms so Ella could adjust herself. She snapped the flap of her nursing brassiere over her breast and pulled down her shirt. She scooped Irene back into her arms, then set her down to sleep on the porta-crib set up in the middle of the living room.

"He was here this morning," Ella said.

"And? How is Mr. Sex, Lies, and Videotape?"

"Irene didn't cry this time when he held her. She can say 'mama,' but not 'dada' yet. He didn't like that."

"And how is he?" The idea of him holding Irene bothered Casey.

"He seems great. He's happy," she said flatly.

Ted had looked handsome and fit when he'd come by. She had already filed her divorce papers, and now he seemed set to start his new life with Delia. He was in love. She could tell. With plenty of bonus cash in the bank, Ted was planning to look for a position after the security camera stories died down to a murmur. The grainy film had caught perhaps two minutes of him and Delia having sex: a redheaded woman—her neck arched, hair flowing, white blouse open—straddling a tall Asian man seated in a desk chair. On the actual tape, Ted's face wasn't even visible, but both he and Delia were asked to resign.

That morning, Ted told Ella that he was considering opening his own shop doing some program trading, which he knew nothing about, or starting up a venture capital fund, which he knew a lot about. His ability to attract capital was still good, and his reputation as a banker remained irreproachable. His faithful friends from HBS assured him that the stories would pass and soon there'd be hearty backslapping complete with attaboys. He asked if she was still seeing Lorraine, her psychologist, and Ella had told him she was. Since Tina's wedding, she had been seeing the therapist once a week on Thursdays after work.

"Are you doing okay?" Casey asked. "I mean, you know, with Ted visiting all of a sudden?"

"Uh-huh," Ella said calmly. "I'm happy for Ted. It's better this way. I think I can explain it to Irene that we married too young. And you know, I really like my work. Mr. Fitzsimmons is great, and David thinks I can definitely have my old development job back in the fall when the girl who took my place leaves in August."

"How fantastic," Casey said. She could hardly concentrate. "Do you think you'll move back to the city soon?" Ella had been living there for eight months now.

"I've been thinking about it more and more. I think I want the house."

"Good for you," Casey said. "I say you fleece the bastard."

"What are you holding in your hand?" Ella asked.

Casey looked at her left hand. It was the letter. "Oh my." Casey stared at the boy's face on the card, his crimson mouth pulsing. "Jay is getting married. How about that?"

"Oh, Casey. I'm . . . sorry. That can't be easy."

"I left him, right?" Casey said, blinking back her own tears. She missed him suddenly. So much—their first kiss at the movies, how he had looked at her with wonder beneath Blair Arch, the time he'd bought her the golf clubs—the pride shining in his happy eyes.

"Love doesn't end," Ella said.

Casey nodded. "I'm okay. Unu is terrific." Her friend was suffering far more than she was. It seemed unfair to bring up Jay now.

"How's his job search?"

Casey shrugged. "Get this." She tried to change the subject. "Virginia thinks she's pregnant! What is it with you Brearley girls? Getting knocked up so young. What's the rush?"

Ella let Casey divert her, wondering if she loved Unu in the same way that she loved Jay Currie. Ella had never loved anyone like Ted. She didn't believe that you could love anyone as much as your first. Whenever she felt angry about Ted, she contented herself with the belief that what Ted felt for Delia was somehow less than what they had. There had to be something for having been first.

Ella appeared distracted.

"And guess who the father is?" Casey tried to make light of it.

"The mural painter?" Ella couldn't remember the guy's name.

"No, no. Not Paolo. Someone new. He's a businessman from Milan! Crazy, huh?" Casey looked over the letter again, trying to find the references to Gio. A rich guy, something with textiles.

Ella shook her head in confusion. Irene woke up with a short cry. Ella jumped up to get her. She patted her baby's back.

"Perspective," Ella said. It had come out sounding more smug than she'd intended.

"Huh?" Casey looked at her.

"Babies. They give perspective. She'll see, I guess." Ella cooed at her daughter. "What's important."

Casey stared at Irene's flour-sack body stretched across her mother's left shoulder. Ella's comment was probably true, but it annoyed her. The length of the baby's spine was scrunched, and her small bottom rested on Ella's left forearm. But Irene hadn't changed Ted, Casey wanted to argue, or had she? Had Irene's birth made Ted fall in love with Delia? Sabine's husband, Isaac, once said that when a child was born, his birth signaled that you were dying. Grim. So instead of choosing his child and what her life required, had Ted chosen himself—his life and his pleasure? With Ted, it was never easy for Casey to be fair, to be compassionate. But she could think exactly like him, and it scared her.

"Would you like to hold her?" Ella asked.

"Yes, please." Casey reached out her arms. She was still holding Virginia's letter with her left hand. "Oh, for heaven's sake, look." She shoved the letter into her bag, then folded Irene into her arms. Ella smiled at her kindly, and in her tender expression, Jay's mother, Mary Ellen, came to mind: her clear patrician voice, her long-suffering genteel poverty, the endless supply of compassion. Both Ella and Mary Ellen had been left by their husbands. Why did men leave? Maybe if that kind of humiliation didn't make a woman furious, it made her sympathetic. Casey hoped that with all his work and earnings, Jay would alleviate his mother's disappointments. She hoped Mary Ellen would finish her biography of Dickinson and it would win a big prize instead of the volume being carted off to the dusty stacks. Why did Ted have money and choices, and Mary Ellen have to work for a dozen more years for the prospect of a librarian's meager pension? It was hard not to be cynical about Keiko—Jay's fiancée. Her family money and connections would help Jay in the world. He was marrying up. And why not? At school, he used to talk obsessively about who had family money and who didn't. It didn't surprise Casey that he'd found a girl who had a college gymnasium–giving kind of bankroll, but she couldn't help being saddened by it. Maybe Keiko's money hadn't mattered. But she knew it had. Jay had cared about the golf courses, the fancy skiing trips, and the country houses. All of it—he had always noticed all of it. Before he would earn his own, he'd use hers. Was it possible to resist the desires of your heart? Casey couldn't possibly have helped him socially or financially. Then she finally got it: On separate occasions, he'd felt no compunction about forcing himself on her mother and father, almost bullying them into an introduction, not just because he was angry with her for hiding him from them, but because they weren't important. They were nothing socially. And if her parents were nothing, she was nothing, too. But how could she be angry with him? That's just who he was. She was also someone who'd needed helping herself. On that score, she understood.

Casey kissed her goddaughter—her eyes dark as olives. A delicious scent of biscuits and toast came from her hair. That Ted could leave her made sense then. How did a person take up this kind of responsibility, anyway? To care for this beauty and perfection with fragrant black hair in tiny pink clips? Just holding her filled Casey with a sense of the child's needs. She didn't want to make her cry or to drop her, and she wasn't sure how to comfort the tiny person. In her sleepy little face, there was no similarity with either Ted or Ella. Dr. Shim had claimed that Irene looked a great deal like his own sister, an aunt of Ella's who had died young.

Her arms empty yet feeling content, Ella let out a sigh. She stretched her back, wiggling her shoulders, cracking her neck to and fro. She floated her long arms upward, then returned to sitting, her straight back in line with the plush sofa. The way Casey looked at Irene with love and pleasure made her feel cared for somehow. It was a precious gift when another person loved your child. You yourself felt loved.

Casey glanced up. Her friend's posture was erect, her smile stoic. To her surprise, she felt a kind of repulsion. How odd it was that she'd felt more love for Ella when she'd overdosed on the codeine. She'd seemed more human then. I'm being unfair, she thought. Ella was just trying to get through it, be tough for her child—Ella, the girl who'd never had a mother and was now one herself. And though Casey respected that, Ella's stance felt superior and untrue. She'd never once called Ted a bastard when he was truly that. Then at that moment, Casey felt everyone's brokenheartedness, including her own, and she agreed with Ella: Love did not end. How could it? But Jay was marrying someone else. That was reality, too.

Irene had fallen back to sleep. She breathed so quietly that Casey leaned her ear against the baby's flowery breath. She wished to make it up to her goddaughter somehow for her father's departure.

Would Ted be a good divorced father? Would he be around? In the past four years, Casey had come to understand that Ella was like a poor person in a rich person's disguise. Until a child is fully grown, parents should not die, Casey thought indignantly, and they should not go away. But her own parents—what about them? Her mother and father were alive, and they had stuck around to do their duty. No one was satisfied. Ted had split. Ella's mother was dead. Jay was marrying a rich girl.

Casey's heart weighed like a thousand pounds.

Ella got up to head to the kitchen. She'd bought several salmon steaks that morning, and her father had called to say he was working late. The two of them could cook dinner together and share a bottle of wine.

"Can you stay for dinner?" Ella asked.

"No," Casey answered right away. Why had she said that when she'd planned on staying for dinner all along? But she couldn't manage to be there much longer. "I have to get back home," she sputtered.

"But you just got here," Ella said, her eyes full of disappointment. She'd been so looking forward to seeing her and having a long visit.

"I can stay a little longer, but I should get back. I need to get started on the corporate finance project." Casey had already finished the project the day before. "I just wanted to check in with you today, and of course see your little one. And you both look great." She tried to sound upbeat.

"Oh," Ella said. She did understand. "Well, yes. You must be incredibly busy with school."

Casey nodded emphatically, not wishing to lie anymore. She picked up a scone and broke off a large piece. She slathered it with clotted cream. Ella poured her some tea.

Ella talked some more about Ted and how she was happy for him after all, and Casey listened to it. Ella wasn't lying so much as she wasn't telling the truth about how she felt as a woman. Casey remembered what it was to see Jay with those girls. And she'd believed him when he'd said they didn't mean much to him. Ella's husband had fallen in love with Delia and planned to marry her. He had lied to her repeatedly. Ted was an asshole, and Ella was a fool. Casey didn't want to sit there and listen to the pious fluff. Not much later, she took the train back home.

Back in the city, she found Unu at his desk, reading his new issue of *Foreign Affairs*.

"What happened to pool night with George?"

Unu shook his head. "Back's been hurting today, so I stayed in." Casey appeared crestfallen. "Hey, I thought you'd be eating with Ella.... What's going on with you? Is everything all right?"

"I'm hungry." She went to the kitchen. Nothing looked appealing in the refrigerator or the cupboard. The tedium of fixing another pasta or rice dinner made her want to scream. "Can we order in?" she shouted as she dug in a drawer in search of a take-out menu.

Unu turned around to the kitchen in surprise. Ever since he'd lost his job, she hadn't wanted to order in or go out to dinner. Casey stood by the wall phone and studied the menu.

"Do you have any cash in the house?" she asked.

"Yeah. Get what you want, babe," Unu said, and pulled out his wallet. He had seventy-two dollars on him.

Casey had already picked up the phone and was ordering. He counted four entrées, soup, rice, fried noodles, and a vegetable. Who would eat all that? he wondered.

Unu closed his magazine and set it aside on the coffee table. He turned on the television to the Mets game. When she hung up the phone, Casey came over and sat beside him.

"What was the total?" Unu asked, laughing. He was amused by her getting all that food.

"Dunno," she said, staring at the screen. She liked the Mets okay.

It was the middle of the eighth inning with the Mets pitcher on the mound. The pitcher walked the second player in a row. Casey yelled at the television, "Why do those assholes make so much money? They're not paid millions to lose, dammit."

Unu kissed her cheek, thinking she was funny.

Casey grew still. "They must have something, though," she said sadly. She felt defeated again by life. What was the point of being clever and hardworking and not knowing what to do?

Unu could see her disappointment. "No, no, Casey, you're right. They're not paid to walk the other team." It was better when she was trash talking. Casey could be so easily discouraged. Unu cupped his mouth and yelled at the television, "C'mon, you losers. Start playing some ball!" She wasn't cheered up, though, and he put his arm around her shoulder.

The doorman buzzed them. The order had arrived in less than twenty minutes. The order was ninety-seven dollars.

"Sorry, babe." He pulled out a credit card from his wallet, but the deliveryman wasn't authorized to take them.

"You want to take back something, mister?" the deliveryman asked. "Up to you."

Casey knew she'd ordered too much. She could've easily given back two of the cheaper entrées. Unu had said he had cash.

The deliveryman said, "You can call the restaurant and they take number, okay?"

Casey stared at the two bags of food. It was so much, but she wanted all of it—the beef, chicken, seafood combination, the tofu.

"Okay." Casey marched to the phone, dialed the restaurant, and gave her credit card number over the phone. She'd been making such great progress paying it down in the past ten months or so and being disciplined with her spending. The woman from the restaurant asked to speak to the deliveryman. After he got off the phone, he put down the bags on the floor near the door and prepared to leave. Casey handed him ten bucks from her wallet for a tip.

"Thank you, missus," he said, and left.

Casey was not a big eater. Most of the food would get put in the fridge or thrown away. Unu went to clear the dining table where they ate normally, but Casey picked up both bags and took them to the coffee table instead.

"Do you want dishes?" he asked, and she said no. She pulled out a pair of disposable chopsticks from the shopping bag and snapped its legs apart.

They ate watching the game.

13 | PASSPORT

*H*ER JOY WAS SONG.

When Leah Han was eight years old, her quiet mother died of tuberculosis. A year later, Leah received an overwhelmed stepmother prone to stomachaches. As a teenager, she found herself at the tail end of the shuffle of six older brothers and an impoverished minister father. At night, she made dinner for seven men and her infirm stepmother and spent Saturdays standing over a cold washbasin with waist-high heaps of laundry piled up beside her. For Leah, the church was her childhood embrace and God the Father her only comfort. Throughout her life, when she sang hymns, Leah felt the ecstatic communion of music with her Father, and when she sang a solo, the heavens seemed to open up and she felt the light of His praise showering softly upon her. It was at church where Leah felt most happy, almost girlish, and through sacred music, life prickled inside her, insisting on a divine love within her disappointed heart.

On Palm Sunday, as with each Sunday morning, two hours before services began, the sixty-member choir of the Woodside Pilgrim Church gathered to rehearse in the basement practice room—its floors laid with mismatched squares of red and black linoleum. But that morning, Mr. Jun, the seventy-eight-year-old choir director, took his place behind the lectern and took a few more minutes than usual to compose his thoughts. Next to him stood Dr. Charles Hong. To the choir's dismay, the younger man had come to church wearing blue jeans and a crewneck sweater. To his credit, he wore a brown tweed jacket that was well cut, but it was not new. His clear skin gave him the look of a healthy middle-aged man who neither ate nor drank in excess.

"Brothers and sisters in Christ, this is Dr. Charles Moon-su Hong. He is your new director," Mr. Jun said, his voice faltering and sad.

A murmur rose from the choir, then just as quickly, a hush fell as Dr. Jun continued to speak.

"As you know, I have had some health weaknesses." Mr. Jun coughed for effect. Everyone knew about his prostate cancer treatments. He'd been talking about retirement for the past five years but was never able to find an adequate replacement. "And though it is sudden"—Mr. Jun paused again meaningfully—"I have decided to move to California after Easter to live with my son. I will get better medical attention there." He smiled only when he said the words *my son*. Mr. Jun's son was an anesthesiologist in Los Angeles and the bright light of Mr. Jun's life.

"But enough about my poor health. There will be time enough for that later...." The aging tenor with the resilient vanity of half a dozen men of greater accomplishments coughed again. He tried to sound more uplifting.

"Dr. Hong is the brilliant son of my genius mentor and friend, Dr. Joo-Jin Hong, of Seoul University's Conservatory of Music. Dr. Hong is a graduate of Juilliard, where he received his doctorate in music." Mr. Jun articulated the name of the school with reverence. "He is an accomplished pianist and organist, as well as a gifted voice teacher. He is also a composer and is currently writing a song cycle commissioned by the world-famous Lysander Quartet. Dr. Hong has a special love of choral music, which has led him to us." Mr. Jun smiled. "What a tremendous blessing it is to have him work with us. I hope that you, my brothers and sisters in Christ, will love him and care for him as much as you have cared for me." Mr. Jun, greatly influenced by the letters of St. Paul, often tried to speak like him.

His hands behind his back, Charles bowed his head and said nothing.

The choir whispered among themselves. The bass with the double chin said to the tenor, "Young guy." Kyung-ah Shin, the attractive soprano seated next to Leah Han, smiled in his direction. "Look, honey, no wedding ring." Leah didn't want to get caught talking. Mr. Jun hated it when the choir members talked during rehearsals. She checked his hands. There was no wedding ring, but on his right hand, Dr. Hong wore a gold signet ring with an oval lapis lazuli. He wore no other jewelry. Kyung-ah elbowed Leah. "Do you think he is gay?" She pronounced the word *gay* in two syllables: geh-ee. Kyung-ah touched her earrings—black Tahitian pearls with paper white diamonds framing them. On her pale throat, she wore a matching choker necklace with a diamond clasp. Kyung-ah and her younger sister, Joanne, owned three wholesale sneaker stores in Manhattan that had grossed over 1.7 million dollars in business last year. She'd bought the jewelry for herself last Christmas, believing that she should get herself whatever she deserved.

Charles smiled politely, unaffected by the puffed-up introduction. In his own mind, he was the forty-eight-year-old son of a rich man with no money of his own. He'd failed marriage twice, received a worthless doctorate of music and obscure prizes for organ competitions. The church was paying him eight hundred and fifty dollars a month, a laughable amount of money to live on in New York, but Charles didn't need much in terms of daily maintenance. Also, his voice lessons earned him at least three hundred dollars a week. With both jobs, he wouldn't need his father's monthly allowance anymore. After his second divorce, his older brothers' persistent remarks about how their elderly father still supported the supposed "artist" in the family had become impossible to bear.

Charles had never directed a choir before, but he was a good voice coach. Mr. Jun had boasted that the woman singing the solo today, Deaconess Cho, had a finer voice than Kiri Te Kanawa and Jessye Norman. Charles looked over the seating chart on the lectern and spotted Leah in the soprano section. Deaconess Cho was a petite woman with slight shoulders, a pale face, and smooth white hair. She wore almost no makeup, in contrast with the pretty, dark-haired soprano seated next to her, whose eyes were painted like a tropical bird. Leah felt his hard stare, and she turned away, taking in a desperate gulp of breath.

Kyung-ah, who missed little, saw him observing Leah. The new director was interesting to her. A sexy woman, Kyung-ah fully expected him to notice her. She touched her black hair and checked for stray crimson lipstick in the corners of her mouth with her pin-kie. She wished the acetate choir robe she was wearing didn't hide her favorite Claude Montana suit, which cinched in her small waist beautifully, flattering her hips and shapely legs. She wasn't looking for herself so much; Kyung-ah was long married to a pleasant, hard-working man who was a little dull. But her sister was still single. She always scanned for prospects for Joanne, who was an excellent cook and good with children.

Charles went over the seating chart, matching names with faces as Mr. Jun droned on about what the purpose of a choir was. The choir was a predictable collection of fish-eyed men with jowly faces and ex-hausted mothers with dyed black hair, their eyebrows drawn in too darkly in brown pencil, wearing lipstick shades that no longer com-plimented them. They watched him like careful students, and he felt no kindred attachment to them. How could he possibly direct this ragtag bunch of immigrants who wanted to sing to their Jesus?

The week before, at his job interview, the Reverend Lim had asked Charles if he believed in Jesus Christ. Charles had replied, "The Lord is my shepherd." The nearly dwarf-size minister, oblivious to sarcasm, couldn't have been more pleased; to him, there could be no more perfect answer than this. Charles had recited a fragment of the first verse of Psalm 23, written by David, a brave warrior king and, of course, the Bible's most famous musician.

When the sermon ended, the choir rose to sing the offertory. Leah began the first verse of "A Mighty Fortress Is Our God." When she opened her mouth to sing, Mr. Jun closed his eyes for a mo-ment in relief. The others joined at the refrain, but the shadow of Leah's voice continued to track the piece. Charles, who was seated in the first pew, felt compelled to examine Leah's face closely, un-able to believe the high register of her vocal instrument. She had a rounded voice with a complicated range of feeling. It did in fact remind him of some of the sopranos that Mr. Jun had mentioned, but her exquisite sound wasn't cultivated in any traditional sense, and he could hear a raw sorrow in it. In a way, it recalled the lament of *pansori* music with its inexplicable anguish. When she stopped singing, Charles felt profoundly alone and yearned to hear her sing again. Her voice had lifted him from his stray thoughts, and he col-lected himself.

When the choir stopped singing altogether, they sat in their seats, and the congregation called out, "Ah-men, ah-men, ah-men," in sober gratitude and praise. Leah bowed her head and smoothed the robe over her folded knees. Kyung-ah tapped Leah's thigh reassuringly. She, too, was a good singer but accepted that comparisons could hardly be made between them.

At the rehearsal following the service, the second one of the day, the choir reconvened in the practice room, many of them carrying a Styrofoam cup of coffee and a piece of cake. For the members of the choir, life was organized around practice and church. In a week, there were two rehearsals on Sundays, one on Wednesday nights, and Tuesday night Bible study. Their robes off, their postures more relaxed, the singers gabbed about where to go to dinner after this rehearsal. Most of them were friendly, and many of the women belonged to a *geh*—the monthly savings pool. Even the ones with families with small children tried to figure out how they could get together for dinner at one another's homes. The mood was always lighter in the second rehearsal than the first. The men would grumble to Mr. Jun about the level of difficulty in some of the hymns, and the women gossiped, goading the director to chasten them. Charles noticed the shift in mood, too, and he wondered how he would fit in his new role. In age, he was more or less their contemporary and didn't view himself taking on the role of an eccentric father.

"It does seem abrupt, but I've already spoken with Dr. Hong about his conducting today's rehearsal. I have to meet with some people tonight to arrange my leavetaking next week. And naturally, he will be with you on Wednesday night as well." Mr. Jun appeared heartbroken. "But I will see you next Sunday at services." He smiled and paused. No one could tell if he was done or not. "You are like, like...my sons and daughters," he said, and began to cry. Charles moved closer to him and took his hand to hold it. "I am sorry," Mr. Jun said through his tears, "I am an old man, and when you are old like me, you will consider the things you care about with greater...feeling." He wiped his nose with a handkerchief, and Charles patted his back.

Kyung-ah stood up to clap for him, and the others followed. Everyone wept. It was like watching your father give his possessions away before he died. Mr. Jun was a fussy man who had served the church faithfully for over twenty years. At every opportunity, he spoke about his personal sacrifices for Jesus in terms of time, talent, and money that he could've earned doing something else. "But with our gifts, we must reflect His glory!" Yet over the years, through his dedicated service, the choir had changed their view of him from a broken fixture to the tolerated uncle, then to a kind of beloved parent who ultimately wanted the best for them.

Mr. Jun remained at his lectern, his spine rounded, head perched delicately on his stooped shoulders. Leah sobbed uncontrollably, and Kyung-ah put her arm around her shoulders. When the applause died down, Mr. Jun picked up his cordovan briefcase and tan raincoat. His jaw was clenched to keep himself from saying more and to stifle his sobs. When he got inside his brown Dodge with the pair of Jesus fish decals on the bumpers, he put his right forearm over the steering wheel and dropped his heavy head on it. Mr. Jun wept no less than when his angelic wife had died.

After Mr. Jun had closed the practice room door behind him, Kyung-ah went straight to the corner of the room and picked up a spare collection plate. She opened her wallet and dropped seven hundred dollars into the plate. She passed it to Leah, who opened her purse and put in all the cash she had with her: a hundred and sixty-seven dollars. No explanation was necessary. They were collecting Mr. Jun's departing gift. A person got sick, lost a husband, or even in happy times like a wedding or the birth of a child: A hat was passed, and soon after, a manila envelope stuffed with cash would be presented. Even if one Korean was nothing in this strange land, a church full of Koreans meant something to each other, and they intended to care for their own. Kyung-ah would see to it that a plaque was made up, and there'd be a ceremony next week. Charles was moved by this gesture, but he pretended to busy himself with the sheet music he'd brought. When the plate returned to the soprano in the black suit, he sought their attention.

Charles was nervous. He spoke in Korean; his Seoul accent was undeniable.

"We'll be following a schedule that Mr. Jun has kindly drafted for me for the next three months. I understand that next week's program is the same as last year's, so none of you will be surprised by the music in it." He did not smile, and he'd flattened his normal speaking voice, which like his tenor singing voice was mellifluous and tender. His father, the famous professor, used to say that the first day of class was the most important: "Establish your authority from the top, and never yield in the beginning. Later, you can be more flexible. Never, ever begin with softness." Life, to Charles, was a series of related acts, and those who succeeded in life seemed to understand the necessity of consistent performances at a high level. Charles was an inconsistent performer. All three of his brothers were successful professors in Seoul. All four of them had doctorates, but he was the only one who could not handle the negotiations and finesse of a life in the academy. Charles ended up quitting every teaching job he was ever offered.

Charles turned to the seating chart. He called the members one by one to the front of the room. Each person was asked to sing "Happy Birthday." Charles remained standing as he listened to the sharp tenors, the thin sounds of the baritones, the piercing shrills of the untrained sopranos. A few of the altos were passable and, thankfully, they did not shout. Some of the sopranos were altos, and some altos were really mezzos. Whatever compassion he'd felt a few moments before for Mr. Jun was fading. It was his fault that the singers didn't know their own sounds. He called Kyung-ah Shin, the woman who'd first stood up to clap and started the collection for Mr. Jun.

She took her time to get to her spot next to the piano. Her range was not developed, but she had potential. Her ripe eyes appealed to him, and the way she looked at him privately, her back turned to the choir, was sexual, and he found this amusing. Her clothes were rich-woman flashy, big shoulder pads, cockroach killer, heels, the too-dark hose. But her waist was tiny, her ass round, and he liked red lipstick on women. Lots of diamonds—likely one of these women who had husbands with cash businesses. Kyung-ah Shin's wedding ring was hard to miss. It had been a long time since he had been with a Korean woman, certainly, a very long time since a married one. His virginity had been lost to a lonely housewife in Seoul—the shy wife of his college professor. If given the opportunity, he'd have happily fucked the married soprano who was giving him the eye. There was nothing shy about this one.

Leah was next. When she stood beside him, he was taken aback by how young she looked. From afar, because of her white hair, he'd thought she was ten or fifteen years older than what she must have been. She didn't look more than thirty-five, and her smooth face looked as if lit from within. There was something so pure about her expression, as though she'd never had a bad thought in her head. If she dyed her hair, she would have looked twenty-eight, but it was evident that to do such a thing would have violated her submissive nature. She was a gorgeous woman, her features small and fine, but he didn't feel aroused by her as he had with the older woman Kyung-ah Shin. Leah was slimmer than all the others, with a narrow waist and straight, boyish hips. There was a modest swell of bosom rising from her severely cut gray dress, reminding him of a German voice teacher he'd once had in England. The only exposed skin on her body was her face, neck, and hands. Then he realized that she was built like his first wife, Sara, a tiny Italian soprano, who grew very fat at the end of their relationship.

Instead of "Happy Birthday to You," he had her sing the first verse of "A Mighty Fortress" just so he could hear her sing again. What was wrong with her? he wondered. Something about her just rankled him, despite this voice worthy of ancient cathedrals. She was too Korean. Probably dumb and quiet. In bed, she'd probably just lie there. Her downcast, overly modest expression was irritating. But as she sang, he couldn't fight the clutch in his heart, the same as it had been at the service earlier. Her unearthly sound arrested him. So rarely had he heard such good tone and range in an amateur singer. Her breath control was astonishing. If she were younger and had funds, he'd have encouraged her to enter competitions. She'd have won them, he bet. When she finished, Charles nodded and said nothing. He called on the next person. At the end of rehearsal, he'd finished up all his notes for each singer.

"Please return on Wednesday evening at seven-thirty. I expect that we will have a two-hour rehearsal. Thank you." Charles nodded uncomfortably. He grabbed his knapsack and jacket and fled the room.

As soon as he was gone, Peter Kim, the baritone, an insurance salesman for New York Life, gathered round the choir and told them about having once visited his house two years before. Peter knew one of Charles's brothers from school. Charles Hong was the fourth of four boys. His great-grandfather and grandfather had had a monopoly on the manufacture and distribution of MSG—the food flavor enhancer. His older brothers were academics like their father, but all of them were tycoons. Only Charles, the grandfather's least favorite, had gone to Europe and America to study music. If he'd stayed in Korea, he would've received a great deal of money annually. But he hadn't. All his life he'd just studied music and taken little teaching jobs here and there. He used to return home regularly until his mother died several years before. He was forty-eight years old, divorced from his Italian wife of eleven years, and divorced from his Swedish wife of four years. He lived alone in Brooklyn Heights in a large limestone town house that his father had bought for him in cash. He had no children. The women gasped at this.

"When I went to his house for the appointment that his brother had set up for me, he'd forgotten all about it. He was home alone, eating boiled rice and frankfurters with hot sauce off of a card table. In that huge expensive house, he had no furniture except for a gigantic piano and a sofa. He said he didn't need any life insurance. 'Who would lose if I dropped off?' Anyway, he gave me a beer and a CD of *Tristan and Isolde*." Peter shrugged. "He's a nice enough man. I don't even think he remembered us ever meeting when I sang today."

Peter and about a dozen of the men left to eat *kalbi*. Several others were looking for a house to play *ha-toh*—invariably, someone would have brought a deck of red cards to church in the hopes of getting in a game.

Leah had been paying attention to every word Peter Kim said. Dr. Hong seemed tragically sad to her from his description—to be so alone in the world. Yet she wondered what it would be like to study music all your life. That must have been like heaven.

"You want to go with the *geh* girls to eat *jajangmyun*?" Kyung-ah asked, breaking up Leah's thoughts of him.

"Oh no, sister, I have to go home and make dinner," she said.

"Oh, you're such a good wife. You put us all to shame," said Kyung-ah, who had no intention of going home so early. Her son and daughter were in college, and her husband was perfectly content to fix himself ramen on Sunday nights. She let him go to his men's Bible study twice a week, and she did what she wanted.

The members scattered and would return again to the same room in three days.

On Wednesday, Leah blew through her work rapidly. She finished most of the mending that needed to be done for the week and was able to help the girls sort clothes in the back room. She hummed the whole day. For dinner, she'd bought some broccoli and a piece of fish from the market near the store to prepare for Joseph's meal. He ate so little these days. She'd have a bowl of rice with *bori-cha* because her stomach had been feeling nervous all day. Their drive home was quiet, with hardly a word between them. Leah's mind was full of music and thoughts of the old choir director and the new one. As soon as they got home, she rushed to the kitchen to cook, and when it was done, she called out to Joseph, who was watching his favorite *terebi* program.

"*Yobo,*" she called out to him from the kitchen, but there was no answer. "*Yobo,*" she said again.

In the living room, Joseph had fallen asleep in front of the television set. He'd suffered from nightmares since the war and all through their marriage, but inexplicably, they seemed to occur more frequently since the building fire. Joseph tried to go to bed earlier, but he never felt rested.

"*Yobo,*" she said quietly, trying to wake him. She didn't want him to go to bed without having his dinner. Joseph didn't stir, having fallen into a deep sleep. Leah dragged the ottoman from the other side of the chair to prop up his feet. She covered her husband with a quilt she'd made from her sewing scraps. She set the kitchen table with his dinner in case he got up, and moments later, she drove to choir rehearsal.

Leah was hardly the first to arrive. Kyung-ah was already sitting in her chair, wearing a red belted dress and high heels. She crossed and uncrossed her pretty legs to adjust herself in her chair. Between giggles, she teased the nearby baritones, who stared at her as if she were a wedding feast.

Most of the choir members wore street clothes to practice, nothing close to their Sunday best, since many of them had come from their jobs—groceries in Spanish Harlem, midtown Manhattan nail salons, hair product wholesale shops in the Bronx, and dry-cleaning shops, like Leah. A few came from office jobs, but most of them owned or worked in stores. The Kim brothers, forty-year-old twins, both bachelor tenors, owned a brake repair shop in Flushing, but prior to Wednesday night choir rehearsals, they scrubbed themselves with Irish Spring soap and wore Aramis aftershave. They wore white shirts pressed and starched by their mother, whom they lived with and supported, and pleated trousers from Italy. Like the Kim twins, Mrs. Koh, a widow who worked twelve hours a day as a cashier at a fish market in Queens Village, made a deliberate attempt to erase her vocation through water and heavily perfumed soap. She was renowned at church for having sent all three of her sons to Harvard—the oldest awarded second place in the Westinghouse competition when he was a junior at the Bronx High School of Science.

Once everyone had taken a seat, Charles tapped his white baton against the black metal music stand. Today, he wore a black V-neck sweater with a white T-shirt underneath and blue jeans. His expression was again serious, no curve or softening of his lips. With his baton, he pointed to Mrs. Noh, the secretary for the choir, a tall, elderly woman wearing beige foundation from the base of her neck to the tip of her brow hairline. He gestured for her to come forward. For over two decades, she'd been in charge of attendance, choir robe cleanings, folder clearing, and photocopying of all choir business. He handed over a pile of scores for the song "O Divine Redeemer" for her to distribute.

At the sight of the familiar sheet music, the Kim brothers were delighted. Then they noticed that this arrangement was for a soprano. For the second week in a row, a woman got a solo.

Charles fiddled with the CD player. There had never been a CD player in the choir room. Without an introduction, he played the song. Mr. Jun used to talk so much that the choir expected a forty-minute rehearsal and an hour and twenty minutes of lecturing as well as his own vocal demonstration of the different parts.

The recording began with a cello playing solemnly, then the soprano sang the first line in English: "Ah, turn me not away." The singer's incantatory sound mesmerized them. When she hit an impossibly high note at the refrain, "I pray Thee, grant me pardon," many of them stopped breathing, feeling the soprano's infinite reach. They could hear the hymn's potence. Its sanctuary. When Charles turned off the recording, a bass sitting way back shouted in approval, "Ah-men!" Others thundered in agreement. None of the men were in the least bit intimidated by the new director's silent governing.

In a soft voice, Charles asked the accompanist to play the refrain. He pointed to the altos, and they sang their parts. It went this way for some time, with him saying little, the different sections being led by the point of his baton, and their singing voices moving about the room like a freight train. Under his focused direction, the singers sat up straighter, becoming more thoughtful of the quality of their sound. The choir felt proud of their voices, but Charles's disdain grew. They would take a great deal of work, far more work than he wished to do for eight hundred and fifty dollars a month.

Charles tapped his baton against the music stand.

"This would be a good time to bring in the solo. Deaconess Cho, please begin with the first line. It should begin andante—" He read his score, not bothering to look at Leah or at anyone else in the choir. He missed the confused glances.

Leah shook her head slightly. He had to mean her. Didn't he? Deaconess Cho was her church title, and the only other Deaconess Cho was an alto. But how could he mean her? She'd sung a solo the week before. She'd never had more than four solos per year, and that was the most anyone ever had. Kyung-ah had had three. Mr. Jun rotated the solo schedules from male to female—from tenor to soprano and back again, with an occasional minor part sung by a solo bass or alto. Mr. Jun was also fond of duets.

The accompanist played, but no one sang.

Charles looked up. "Andante—" Leah appeared lost.

"Sloooo-wly," he said, then turned to the accompanist, who started from the top.

Leah did not sing.

Charles tapped his baton again, his irritation unhidden.

"Are you ready?" He looked straight at Leah. "Is something wrong?"

Leah was terrified but had no idea how to protest. With his baton, Charles motioned for her to rise.

"Please come here," he said quietly, and Leah took a quick breath before getting up.

When she stood next to the accompanist, Charles said, *"Shi-jak."*

Leah wouldn't start.

"Shi-jak," he said again, this time in a much louder voice.

Leah began to sing, keeping in mind what she'd just heard on the recording, repeating the first two lines with greater feeling. She concentrated on her friend Kyung-ah, who'd bitten her upper lip and smudged her scarlet lipstick on her lower set of teeth.

For the next hour or so, Leah sang weakly. At nine o'clock, one of the mothers with younger children raised her hand to say she had to leave. In the following half hour, the others seemed itchy to leave. Charles tried to understand these pedestrian concerns. At nine-thirty, he let them go after saying, "On Sunday, please arrive precisely at seven-thirty a.m."

Mr. Jun normally dismissed the choir by acknowledging their efforts, saying, "You worked very hard today," or some equivalent, but Charles said nothing of the kind.

The choir trickled out, and Leah thought it might be safe to go. She was still fixed to the same spot near the piano.

"You can stay for half an hour to work," Charles said to her with only the mildest inflection of a question.

Leah stood there, watching the accompanist put on her jacket. She also had small children.

Kyung-ah marched to the front of the room and smiled at Charles, who nodded coolly at her. She was wrapped in a black cashmere shawl fastened by a large jade-and-gold stickpin.

"Do you want to go out with us?" Kyung-ah asked Leah, pretending Charles couldn't hear her.

"She has to practice some more," Charles answered for her.

Kyung-ah jerked her head back slightly. She stared hard at him, but Charles didn't notice.

Leah's left hand fluttered up to touch her collarbone. She felt panic at being left alone with this man. Charles went to the piano. Another soprano in their *geh*, Deaconess Chun, came up to get Kyung-ah.

"Good night," Kyung-ah said to her, slipping her arm into the crook of Deaconess Chun's arm.

They were alone, and unconsciously, Leah paced around the small perimeter of space she'd allowed herself.

"You can sit down," Charles said.

Leah tucked herself into the seat in the first row where Mrs. Noh, the choir secretary, sat. It made her feel safer to sit in her spot.

"This is where you're having trouble..." He talked to her more kindly, as if she were one of his voice students. He sat up straight on his piano bench, inhaled deeply, then sang, "Hear my cry, hear my cry, save me Lord, in Thy mercy." Without taking a pause to breathe, he sang the line again.

The words calmed her. His tenor voice was cool, like a cup of well water. For the first time that night, she felt the anxiety of the sinner's plea—the sinner would understand in his heart that he is undeserving of God's protection.

"Now, if you…" Charles turned his face from the sheet music. Leah was in tears, her face wrapped in her hands, and at that moment, he found her inexplicably beautiful. This wasn't unusual to witness a soprano crying; both his singer wives wept at the slightest provocation. If he was late coming home, his second wife, crying out of control, would throw the dinner on the floor. His first wife cried when she saw the color periwinkle or smelled lavender. But Charles was surprised to see Leah cry. In the brief time he'd observed her, her stoicism was thoroughly marked in her manner, expression, clothing, and posture.

Charles swallowed. "Are you all right?" he asked. He smiled at her. "You don't like the way I sing or play Gounod?" This was his first smile since he'd been in the practice room.

Leah didn't understand his meaning.

"The composer, Charles Gounod," he said in his respectable French accent. "He was going to be a priest, and he, too, was a choirmaster for over four years. I doubt I will last half that long." He laughed.

"I'm so sorry." Leah looked at him, sniffling. She was embarrassed by her emotions. She didn't know what brought it on exactly.

Charles was right—Leah didn't cry often, but somehow, when he'd sung just that verse, she had been impossibly moved. But this wasn't something she could say. Throughout her life, many had praised her singing, appearing startled by the sound that came from her mouth, and in her lifetime, she too had heard a number of voices that had affected her deeply. Yet she herself was unable to put into words the sentiments racing through her heart. Sometimes she wished she could sing back to them. But that would have been insane. Life was not an opera. When she heard a voice like Charles's or the one on the recording, what she wanted to say was, *I can hear God when you sing.*

"What's the matter?" he asked.

"I shouldn't sing the solo. I sang last week, and it's not fair to the others in the choir—"

Charles cocked his head. Singers did not turn down solos. This woman was ridiculous, her selflessness implausible.

"You must understand something: I'm not interested in fairness. And your God doesn't seem interested in fairness when He gives out talent. I see mediocrity or ambition most of the time. You have talent, but no ambition. That's why you're stuck here."

Leah furrowed her brow, not grasping his meaning.

"Mr. Jun has already explained to me his system of solo schedules. Everyone is pissed. I didn't miss that today. I will figure out an alternative, but next Sunday is Easter—a big-deal holiday for Christians, as you and I know. And it should have the finest music, don't you think? And your Mr. Jun is leaving. Shouldn't we send him off with a nice song? For this Sunday, I expect you to sing because you're the only voice I can bear right now." He resented like hell the way singers needed stroking—their bottomless need for confirmation of their gifts. Was he begging a singer to do another solo? Impossible.

"But—"

"Do you object to the song?"

"No, no. It couldn't be more beautiful...but, but—"

"Do you really care that your little soprano buddies are angry with you? The best is always shunned. Do you really care more about approval than about praising your God? Don't you care at all about Mr. Jun's last service? I saw you sobbing up there last Sunday when he announced the news."

"I...I—" Leah, who preferred silence over talking, and singing over everything, wished she could say something, but she had no words.

Charles was angry now, because he could tell she still didn't agree.

"You can't care about what people say or what people think, dammit."

"It's not just that I care what—"

"Don't be a sheep. You've already lost so much. If you'd only fought for your own—"

Leah stared at this man who didn't know her at all. Why was he saying these horrible things about her life? There was nothing wrong with her life. She was grateful for her hardworking husband who loved her, for her smart daughters, her good health. Her singing was this extra beautiful gift that she'd never expected. And she cared about her friends. Everyone should have a turn. She stared at the red tiles beneath her feet.

"This is why I never work with Koreans. They are so goddamn stuck. You must choose yourself over the group." Charles said these things, not caring if Leah even understood his meaning. He was angry with his family, with the immigrant communities in New York, even the artists he knew who weren't Korean who kept on wanting to compromise. An artist, a real artist, couldn't do that. An artist could not necessarily have the things other people had—a happy marriage, children, a quiet home life, a retirement account, even mental health. These were things that following convention might give you, but most great artists had been denied much of them. Both of his wives had wanted children, but he had told them no, for these very reasons. Charles had no intention of giving up his art to make room for a steady job or crying babies, because to him, a life without music was insupportable. Without it, he would have certainly put the gun in his mouth.

Charles put his head down on the piano. His life of music had been reduced to this basement practice room smelling of kimchi *chi-geh,* where a white-haired housewife who had true talent was reminding him to be fair.

Leah didn't know what to do. The new director was very upset with her.

"I'll sing it," Leah said. "I'll sing it for Mr. Jun's retirement on Sunday. And I'll practice at home," she continued, hoping the new director would raise his head from the piano and look at her. Perhaps smile again. "It's just that I didn't think it was right for me to sing for two Sundays in a row."

Charles lifted his head and shouted, "Goddamn you! Did you hear anything I said?"

Leah pulled back, her eyes blinking in terror. Joseph had never said anything so awful.

Charles took another breath. "Take the recording from the player and listen to it at home. Listen to her feeling. Think about the words, feel the music. Feel more than you want to. If you want to sing about redemption, you have to recognize the sin." He didn't know if she understood him.

Leah got up from her seat. Her hand trembled as she removed

the compact disc from the player, and she restored it to its jewel case. She walked quietly to the coat closet to get her things. She opened the door, then turned around to bow. Charles wiped tears from his face with both hands. Leah pretended not to see, wanting to protect his pride. In the church parking lot, the only car was hers, and Leah drove home slowly, wondering where he lived exactly and how far he'd have to travel tonight.

14 | HOSPITALITY

*C*ASEY FINISHED THE BREAKFAST DISHES and got dressed for work. She had an hour and a half before she had to be at Sabine's, but she couldn't stay home.

Unu didn't ask why she was leaving early, but Casey told him anyway that she had promised to meet Sabine before work. That wasn't true, and as she walked toward Madison Avenue, she couldn't figure out why she had lied to him.

She hated it when she felt sorry for herself and hoped a long walk down Madison might help her lousy mood. The first year of business school was almost over, but she still didn't have a summer internship with an investment bank, and it was making her feel horrible. Hugh Underhill had said to give him a call if she needed anything, but she hated the idea of asking for help. Most of her friends at school had summer job offers with Internet start-ups, and though Casey had interviewed with a few, nothing was even remotely interesting to her. She couldn't understand what happened when you stuck a ".com" behind a word or what these companies did. But everyone said that's where the action was. Also, a lot of the interviewers looked twelve. But she reminded herself that girls with five-figure debts couldn't be picky, so she had not turned down a summer internship offer from Sklar.com, a market research company. For the past three months, ever since Unu lost his job, her credit card debts had only gotten worse. The debts she'd been paying off steadily had crept up again. As she walked and walked, dressed in one of her Sabine's getups—hat, dress, and fancy shoes—Casey felt like escaping, but where would she go?

Most of the shops on Madison sold clothes, and strangely, Casey didn't care to look in them. Everything looked expensive and forbidding. Lately, she'd been revolted by her own clothing expenditures; she was in a perennial state of buyer's remorse. On the corner of Seventieth Street, she rested at the flashing DON'T WALK sign. A few feet away was a rare-book store.

The box air conditioner propped on the lintel of its front door hummed steadily, dripping water onto the street pavement. Sleigh bells tinkled when she opened the door. From somewhere in the shop, oboes played on the radio. Illustrations from loose book pages, framed handsomely long ago, hung on yellow-painted walls.

An older man wearing a pea green–colored golf shirt greeted her.

"Good morning." Fluffy white hair seemed to fly about the sides of his otherwise balding head. The frames of his eyeglasses were lapis blue, and the color matched the large face of his wristwatch. He was a very pale man, and the bright spots of blue on his face and wrist made him look younger, almost comic. He was perhaps seventy-five or eighty years old.

"That's a remarkable hat," he said. His voice was youthful and warm—it was a happy voice, and Casey felt comforted hearing it.

She touched her cloche—she'd hand-blocked the linen hat herself, sewn small red silk flowers on its left side.

"And your dress. My, my. Tremendous." His voice was filled with pleasure.

Casey glanced down at her ivory flapper-style dress. It had two crimson lines flowing vertically across the front and back, and draped over her shoulders was a cranberry-colored silk cardigan from a thrift store. On the weekends, her fanciful clothes resembled period costumes nearly.

"Daisy Buchanan," he said, referring to the coldhearted girl from *The Great Gatsby*.

"Yes. I guess so," she answered. His comment was like a private wink. She hadn't been aware of it, but he was right. Her hat and dress were things that a character like Daisy might wear. When Casey made up hats, she never thought of herself, but imagined a more interesting woman. It hadn't occurred to her that she'd dressed like a character from a story. "Well, if she were Korean, that is," she said, feeling self-conscious.

He looked at her quizzically. "Her ethnicity would hardly matter," he remarked sternly, as though he wouldn't back down on this point. "No doubt there must be many Korean Daisys or Beatrices or Juliets."

Casey blinked, not wanting to disagree with an old man. It seemed disrespectful. Where was Beatrice from? Was it Dante? There was so much she hadn't read. Jay used to say this often.

"Joseph McReed," he said cheerfully. "You can call me Joe or Joseph. I answer to both."

"Oh…" She smiled, feeling shy suddenly. He had her father's first name.

Joseph limped carefully across the hardwood floor with his aluminum walker. He wore faded corduroys and tan-colored Hush Puppies. His left shoe looked far too big for his withered ankle. When he finally reached one of the glass-fronted bookcases, he scanned the spines of the stacked volumes and pulled out a small, fat book. "Yes," he said, appearing pleased with himself. He pressed the book close to his chest with his long, mottled hands. Casey worried that he might fall over now that his hands were no longer on his walker. Liver spots dotted his creased brow, and the crinkles around his eyes deepened pleasantly when he smiled.

"Look, look." He waved the book like a child with a toy.

To keep him from having to walk to her, she went to where he stood.

Joseph was grateful for this. He never took any kindness for granted. He moved nearby to his library chair beside his walnut desk, piled high with books and newspapers, and with his right hand motioned her to sit on the wing chair opposite his. Casey glanced at her wristwatch, then sat down. She had some time before catching the train.

Joseph was still holding the book close to his chest, hiding the cover with his two hands as if he were playing peekaboo. He looked at her with great concentration, then sprang the book from his tight embrace.

"You're going to like this, I bet." He handed her a copy of *Jane Eyre* wrapped crisply in conservator sheeting.

"Oh..." she said with a sigh. She opened the cover, and in it was a three-by-five index card: "1st American Ed., Excellent Condition, sm. ink stain on the back cover. $5,000."

"That was my favorite book in high school." She wanted to ask, *How did you know?*

His dark green eyes had brown flecks in them. His blond eyelashes were short and feathery, and the papery skin around his eyes were heavily freckled from the sun. Maybe he was even older than eighty. He was much older than her father, but with white people she had a hard time dating them accurately, because they acted more youthful than the Koreans she knew who were about the same age.

"Every bookish girl in the world is Jane Eyre," he said. "Every girl who wants to be good, anyway."

"But I'm not bookish," Casey said. She had read some old books from a short list made up by Mrs. Mehdi, her favorite librarian from the Elmhurst Public Library, and a few that Mary Ellen Currie had recommended over the years, but the problem was that when Casey liked a book, she'd habitually reread the same one. It was hard to explain why she did this exactly, but to her, the books she liked were better on the second and third readings. Virginia Craft had read everything, including Dante in Italian and all those volumes of Proust in French. Jay had read dozens of Shakespeare's plays. He could recite Shakespeare's sonnets and chunks of Baudelaire's poetry. Casey had read only *Hamlet* and *Romeo and Juliet.* And as for poetry, which Ella and Jay adored, she understood almost none of it. She was an econ major, and she had read about twenty Penguin classics on her own without any real instruction as to how to read them. However, she enjoyed hearing her friends' opinions on books, and she admired how confident they were about their likes and dislikes. When her friends talked about books, she asked lots of questions. Those conversations were like good lessons to her. Her friends who'd gone to private schools and majored in comp lit and English seemed to possess the ideas inside books and felt free to argue with them. Before walking into this bookshop, Casey hadn't realized just how much she'd coveted her friends' authority and ease with literature.

Each morning, Casey read the Bible, and on the subway she reread her same books like a little child with a favorite storybook. She was not an intellectual or an aesthete like Virginia; she was more at home in front of a sewing machine or standing behind a counter.

At Kearn Davis and at Stern Business School, no one she knew read novels, and at Sabine's she'd met salespeople who were writers and artists, and they didn't talk to her, pegging her as a girl who liked to wear over-the-top hats and expensive shoes. And they weren't wrong, exactly. Many of the people she'd met with Wall Street jobs wanted to possess fancy things, eat in new restaurants, and go away on exclusive trips, and artists she'd known expressed contempt for those things. Casey didn't feel she belonged in either camp.

She cradled *Jane Eyre* in her hands. Her high school copy of it was somewhere in the middle of her book pile in Unu's apartment. There was no need for this old book. Yet she wished to put it in her purse, to go through it alone, the way she wished she could stare at a good painting by herself without the bustle of a museum crowd.

Joseph looked at the girl in the hat. She had such a sad expression on her face, and he wanted to make her happy. He closed his eyes and raised his arms dramatically. He waved his hands—hocus-pocus—like a circus magician in the direction of Casey's handbag.

"In your bag, you have a worn paperback of *Middlemarch*."

"What?" she said out loud. The zipper of her bag was closed. "How?" she asked.

Joseph burst out laughing, unable to contain himself. "We wait at the same bus stop on the corner of Seventy-second and Lexington. Until last fall, from Mondays through Fridays, you wore office clothes, and on the weekends, you wear sublime hats and extravagant dresses. Nowadays, I don't see you during the week. But on Saturdays when I see you on the bus, you are always reading. Sometimes I worry that you'll get hit by a car because you're not paying attention. This year, you read Thackeray, Hardy, and Eliot. Either you're a slow reader or you read the same books over and over. Last year, you read *Anna Karenina* for a long time. You've read some of the Americans: Cather, Hemingway, Dos Passos, and Sinclair Lewis. Nothing past 1945, almost. Almost never anyone French."

Casey opened her mouth but felt confused as to what to say. Was she in danger?

"I love *Madame Bovary* and *Cousin Bette*," she said finally, her statement sounding like a question.

"Very fine books," Joseph said approvingly. He felt energetic. "Though Flaubert is superior to Balzac, of course." He tipped his head to the side and adjusted his blue eyeglasses.

Casey smiled, not saying anything. She'd read only one book each by those authors.

"But you often return to *Middlemarch*. Last Saturday, you were reading it. I figured you'd probably still be in it."

"But I never noticed you," she muttered; then it occurred to her that she might have hurt his feelings. She'd been ignored before in places, and she hated to think she had not paid attention to him. She didn't feel afraid of him exactly, but this had never happened to her before. She'd never thought of herself as someone to observe.

Joseph sensed her anxiety. "You mustn't be frightened, dear. I'm a harmless old man. A cripple, really. I'm just nosy about what people read on the bus. My wife, who passed away last year, used to say that my staring was beyond rude. She said it was a sickness, can you believe it?" He giggled. "And you always catch my attention because of your beautiful clothes."

Casey glanced at her dress and high-heeled Mary Janes. "I look silly, I know. I think this is how I put up with working all the time. To amuse myself and—"

"No, no, dear. Not at all," he cut her off, seeing that she looked embarrassed, then regretted having done so, because he was, in fact, exceedingly curious about what she did for a living. Was she an actress? "You look lovely. My wife wore the most beautiful hats in the world. It was her great indulgence, and I'm very pleased when I see women wearing them."

"I...I didn't see you at the bus stop, I can't remember.... You're right, I am always reading as I wait. I have so little time to read—"

"No one notices old men," he said, smiling. This was something he'd started to understand in his early sixties: You'd be invited to fewer things, that young people didn't want to be around you, and middle-aged people didn't think you had much to offer. What humbled Joseph was that he had been no different when he was a young man.

Casey felt bad. Her oldest friend was Sabine, and she was only in her early forties.

"It's all right," he assured her. She wasn't the kind of girl who'd intentionally snub anyone. "I had plenty of lookers once. Now it's your turn." He laughed as though he'd amused himself with a litany of charming memories. Joseph crossed his arms and puffed out his chest in pride.

They both laughed.

"You can have Jane for two thousand five hundred, because you finally walked into my shop. I never thought you would. Daisy has come to my party," he said.

Casey smiled. She glanced at the yellowing index card and flipped to the back cover. The ink stain was negligible, faded to the color of wine.

"You see, I'm retiring this year, and I'm letting my inventory go slowly," he said. "I'm closing after Christmas. Seven more months."

Casey put *Jane Eyre* in her lap. She opened her purse and fished out her copy of *Middlemarch*. Feeling brave all of a sudden, she said, "Isn't Dorothea Brooke such a fool?"—denouncing Eliot's main character, whom Casey loved and disliked at the same time.

"Yes. Principled individuals often are," he said. "But Eliot lets her have it. Dorothea marries old Casaubon. Now he's the fool! I feel quite sorry for Dorothea. She's just a young girl who believes too much," he said. Dorothea's husband, Casaubon, was a pedagogue who'd spent his life researching a big book that no one would ever read.

"Yes, but Casaubon has his tragedy, too," she replied. "He had money and work, but not true love. You can't live without that," she blurted out.

"No, you can't." Joseph nodded in sympathy.

The book dealer looked hurt, and the sadness in his eyes made him look even older. What she'd said had upset him. Casey wished that she could afford to buy something.

"But Jane Eyre… she's a much better heroine, isn't she?" Casey said, picking up the rare book with her free hand.

A smile replaced his lonely expression. "Jane? Oh, she's the brightest girl there is," he said.

Casey nodded, remembering how much she'd loved the homely orphan who grew up to be a governess and fell in love with her tragically married employer, Rochester—how right Jane was to leave Mr. Rochester and how good she was to return to care for him when he was widowed and blinded. Its moral reminded her of Korean fairy tales her mother used to tell her and her sister when they were young—sacrifice and integrity were the only paths for good women.

Casey looked at the old book and stroked its cover. She handed it back to Joseph, but he didn't take it from her.

"Two thousand dollars," he said, wishing he could just give it to her, but he hadn't made a sale in a week. He didn't want to touch his retirement savings again to make rent. Summer was coming up, and sales were predictably slow then. It was his goal to have a good Christmas season to recoup his prior losses.

"That's a very good deal," he said.

"It's an awful lot of money," she said. If she'd had the cash in her pocket, she would've just given it to him. Money had always been a kind of burden to her. If she had it, she spent it, and when she didn't have it, she worried about how she should live. She wished she had enough so she wouldn't feel so anxious all the time. Would there ever be enough?

"Fifteen hundred," he said, pursing his lips. "That's less than what I paid for it."

What made him think that she could afford a rare book? she wondered. Her old boss, Kevin Jennings, used to make fun of her fancy Princeton words and expensive clothes. Now and then, when she walked into shops, the salespeople thought she was a rich Japanese. Was that what Joseph thought, too? That she waited at an Upper East Side bus stop alongside the young heiresses on their way to jobs at auction houses, reading old novels and wearing showy dresses—of course, he must have thought she had money to spare. If she could spend a couple of hundred dollars on shoes, why couldn't she buy a rare book?

No one had stopped by the store since she'd been there. The white-haired man had been kind to her, talked to her about books. She knew what it was like to have to make a sale.

"All right," she said quietly. What she ought to do, she thought, is call Hugh Underhill and ask him to help her get an interview for a banking summer job that would pay a lot more than the market research job. But the Kearn Davis investment banking program would have been filled by now—it had to be. It was already May.

Casey plucked out her charge plate from her wallet, the one that had a two-thousand-dollar credit left. This would have been impossible to do in college, when she'd had to pay for things by cash or check. Curiously enough, Casey had never bounced a check, because that seemed like lying to her. She handed it to him.

"Oh, I'm so pleased," he said. She'd gotten a wonderful deal. He liked the idea of her having it. Joseph wrapped the book in thin brown paper.

Casey took the package. "Thank you," she said.

"I hope you will visit me again," he said.

"Yes, and I'll look for you at the bus stop," she said.

Joseph checked her face. She didn't look happy.

"Are you all right?" he asked, concerned.

"Yes, of course," she answered. "I'd better be off."

Outside the shop, the sharp ridges of the concrete pavement dug through the soft soles of her shoes. Casey hailed a taxi. She'd use her lunch money, because she didn't want to be late. When she got to work, her manager, Judith, greeted her coolly. During her lunch hour, Casey went to Sabine's office as usual to eat a cup of yogurt, and sitting there, she half listened to Sabine talk about the fall collection. Privately, she resolved to return the book to Joseph. Perhaps he would understand.

But the next morning, Casey left the book by her bedside table, and when her bus drove past the shop, which was closed on Sundays, she recalled how Joseph had walked over to the shelf to pick out that book for her. During the week, she went to school, and on Saturday morning, she spotted Joseph at the bus stop. He looked so jolly. They sat together on the bus until he got off across the street from his shop. He admired the hat she was wearing and told her funny stories about his wife, Hazel. She'd been crazy about hats and gloves. Casey couldn't bring up the book.

The following Monday morning, Casey phoned Hugh Underhill at the office.

"Well, darling, hello there," he said. "It's good to hear your voice."

"Hello, Hugh..." Casey laughed. He was indefatigable, impossibly buoyant. The last time she'd seen him was at her Kearn Davis sendoff at Kuriya. Back in September, before school really got started. They'd spoken a few times since then but hadn't gotten together as they'd planned. "Can you get me an interview for the banking program?" she asked.

Hugh laughed out loud. "Well, please don't waste time on the niceties. How are you, Hugh? How've you been? The wife and kids? How's your summer shaping up?"

"You don't have any wife and kids," she said.

"Maybe I got some. It's been a while since we last saw each other."

"It hasn't been that long."

"It's been"—Hugh toted up the months in his head—"almost nine months! See, I could have a child."

"You must have missed me enormously to carry on this way." Casey counted the time elapsed herself, and he wasn't off. Was it possible that he'd gotten married? The idea that Hugh could marry at all was just too implausible. "Anyway, can you let me know if you can or cannot help?"

Hugh paused. In his head he counted eight Mississippis—his lucky number. Women hated being misled, and they hated waiting. He wanted to torture Casey. Just a little.

"It's kinda late, don't you think?" he said. "Tell me, did hubris strike again? Is that why you didn't call sooner?"

"Hedge," Casey said quietly, "can you hook me up or not? It's up to you."

"Yes, Casey Cat, of course I can. And I will. But with this snippy attitude, you will owe me big," he said.

Casey smiled with pleasure. "You're all talk."

"And you? Are you ready to take action?" The image of her in the taxicab came to mind.

"Stop flirting with me. Can you get me a spot?" she asked, unable to remain serious.

"I will call Charlie Seedham. It will be up to you, however, to get a spot." Charlie, Hugh's friend, was in charge of summer internships for B school students.

"I appreciate this, Hugh," she said, feeling relieved. "And you're right. I was too proud to call you earlier."

"Ah, that's better," he said. "Done. I'll call you back."

A few hours later, Casey had an interview set up for Wednesday afternoon. Casey missed her organizational behavior class to meet Charlie Seedham, who gave her a hard time about coming in so late for an interview. But he gave her an offer anyway, and Casey sent Hugh a bottle of wine and promised to take him to dinner.

BOOK III

Grace

1 | OBJECT

*E*LLA'S LAWYER, RONALD COVERDALE, was the only one who wasn't surprised by Ted's request. In his twenty-four years as a matrimonial lawyer, he had seen the worst the heart can inflict.

Ella was sitting in the lawyer's sunny thirty-ninth-floor corner office on Fiftieth and Park. It couldn't have been a prettier day outside. Ronald Coverdale's spacious office smelled faintly of cigarette smoke and an expensive citrus air freshener. On his glass-and-steel desk, a charger-size crystal ashtray sat empty except for a single half-smoked stub. The lawyer was trim and wore an English suit cut close to his body. Ronald's mind worked quickly, and he didn't have patience for most people. He hardly needed any new clients but had agreed to take Ella Shim's case as a favor to David Greene, the development director of his son's school. Ronald liked Ella Shim fine as a client. In fact, he liked looking at her, for she was easy on the eye—only confirming what he had learned over the years. Men left beautiful young women as well as ugly women. Romantic love was a complicated and fickle bond without much security.

For a marriage to last, Ronald believed that both partners should possess a stubborn will, a fear of failure, and a strong sense of shame of breaking from convention—mind you, this was not a recipe for a happy marriage, but it could make two people stay married. If two people had a lot of sex, that was helpful. Having many children did not keep a marriage going, despite all the for-the-sake-of-the-children talk to the contrary. In fact, the more kids there were, the more likely the man would cheat and the woman would be too busy to notice or too tired to care. Men left when the children were not so adorable and the women were too old to marry again, ensuring the Medea effect. The Kim divorce was interesting, because the man had stayed while she was pregnant, then bolted not much after. Ronald had seen it all.

"Why would he want joint custody?" Ella asked him, her hands folded ladylike in her lap.

"Why do you think he might want that?" Ronald redirected the question. There was no reason for the lawyer to speculate on these matters. The wife would know her spouse better.

"I was at my father's since August, and in the eight months I was in Forest Hills, Ted came by to see Irene six times."

"And since you've been back in the city?" Ronald picked up his pen to jot down the dates.

"I moved back into the house the first of May." It was Casey who had pushed her to take back the house. "And the past two weeks, ever since we've been back in the city, Ted hasn't come by at all," Ella said. "He knows I'd never deny his right to see his child, and I would want Irene to know her father and to see him regularly." Her voice grew more strained. "But now you're saying he could take her away from me."

"Not take away from you, Ella. He is asking for joint legal and physical custody, which means that he would have fifty percent decision-making power in child rearing, and he might want to have physical custody for fifty percent of the time. Ted's lawyer was rather insistent on this point—of custody."

"But I would've asked him for his opinion on how to raise Irene. Of course I would have, but..." Ella started to cry. "But she can't live with him for half the—" She couldn't get out the words.

Ronald pushed the box of tissues on his desk closer to her reach.

"I just don't understand." Ella swallowed her sobs.

"It's not that you don't understand, it's that you don't like it."

Ella looked at him, confused.

Ronald realized how sarcastic he had sounded. This was their fourth meeting, and he saw that it wasn't an act with her, as it was with so many women. This woman was actually softhearted, and he had to resist his instincts to protect the weak. In a divorce, the lawyer had no choice but to be wary even of his own client.

"You should never say you don't understand when you do. He is asking for joint custody. There isn't anything you don't understand about that concept. You are a smart young woman. What you really mean to say is that you don't like what he is doing; you hate it, in fact; or you disagree with it. When you tell me what you feel and what you want, then I, as your advocate, will know how to take action. Women cannot sit around while their worlds are falling apart around their ears and say they don't understand."

Ella nodded. She tried to look braver. Ronald's gaze was so forceful that it felt invasive. He was scaring her.

"Ella..." He spoke gently, as if she were waking from a dream. "Ted's actions are fairly commonplace in this stage of divorce. He also knows you well, and he will do what will tactically surprise you. Does Ted usually get what he wants?" This was a rhetorical question, because he knew the answer already.

"Yes," Ella said, thinking of all the times she'd given in to him because it took too much to fight him.

"Well, he will play this the way he has played all the other games he has won. Think about it. He will not change his playbook until it fails him. Do you understand that?"

"Yes. But I don't like it."

Ronald smiled. He liked cleverness. "Tell me why you don't like it."

"I don't like it because Ted always wins, and I always let him. He will fight harder, he will fight unfairly, and he will not give up. Ted is...You don't know what he's like."

"Oh, I have a vague idea. He's a winner profile, and they can be...tough customers." As a practice, Ronald avoided name-calling the other side.

Ella looked away, unable to imagine losing Irene half the time to a man who was never home. Would he know that Irene liked tofu mashed up in her rice and that broccoli gave her gas?

"You mustn't get discouraged, because even winners lose, Ella. And whenever you lost to Ted, you decided to lose, and that isn't really losing."

Ella turned back to him. Was he telling her there was hope?

"It's like this: I've met the Teds of the world, and they're fine."

Ronald shrugged. "But I also know that despite every study, every seemingly accurate tactic, there are surprises in these kinds of battles, because you are no longer fighting about things, but you are fighting about people and deeply rooted feelings. So in my line of work, there are a lot of surprises. And believe me, I am not a man who likes surprises."

"Okay," she said glumly with the disappointment of a child.

"Custody is the principal issue on the table, and it serves as a strategic weapon for Ted." Ronald checked her eyes to see if she appreciated the gravity of what he was saying. It wasn't that she appeared dense to him per se, but she still had that look of shock that in his experience took certain people anywhere from a year to five years to wear off. All men and women who'd been divorced aged in a different way. It helped if you were the one leaving, and it helped if you were leaving the unhappiness for someone you loved. Ronald's first wife had never remarried after he left her. Her shock took many years to lose, and for that, he was admittedly ashamed.

"Are you saying that he would use Irene to get what he wants?"

"Of course."

"I can't believe that. Ted isn't an evil person."

"I didn't say he was an evil person. He is just doing what serves him. We should feel lucky that he didn't ask for full custody."

Ella looked as though she'd been hit.

Ronald opened his eyes wide, like a professor who had finally reached a student. "Good. Good. You get it."

"He couldn't possibly—"

"Sure he could. He could do whatever he wants. Anyway, he could use custody to make you give up some of your rights to certain marital property, to pay less support, whatever. Money doesn't appear to be the issue at this moment, but many wealthy men can be ungenerous." Ronald had figured out from the lawyer Ted had hired (often an accurate reflection of the client's character) that Ted must be a true son of a bitch—Chet Stenor was a hungry dog from beginning to end.

"Or," Ronald continued, "he could have a sincere desire to be with Irene half the time of her life." What he didn't say was that many accomplished men saw children as assets and were unwilling to part with possessions they viewed as hard-won. Some men who left their wives flat had a difficult time even when their ex-wives remarried. "It could be a good thing for Irene to know her father well."

"Of course. I didn't expect her not to know him well. I just...I just can't let him...raise Irene." Ella couldn't mention Delia, the woman Ted was now living with.

Seated on the edge of his chair, Ronald leaned his body forward. "You are worried about him raising the child?"

"And..."

"The girlfriend?" Ronald just said it.

"They're going to get married."

Ronald didn't avert his gaze from her face. Ella was still obviously smarting from the adultery. Women didn't get over that one easily, though in his line of work, he'd noticed that men never got over it, while women somehow sifted through the humiliation and carried on.

"If they do get married, the woman will be in Irene's life. I suggest whatever happens with the custody issues that you will find it in your daughter's best interest to get along with this person. It will not be easy, but you will see that it will help Irene, even though it might be killing you." That was his standard speech about the second wife if there were kids involved.

Ella nodded. He was telling her to be nice.

"So, going back to the joint custody issue..." Ronald resisted looking at his watch. He had another client waiting outside for him. His assistant had already buzzed him once.

"I won't...I won't agree to it," she said. "He can see her for sure, but he can't, he can't live with the baby." She kept herself from tears. How could God let this happen? Why would Ted do this to her? How could he expect her to agree? Her world had been taken over by maybes and anything-could-happens. But God had disappointed her before. He had taken her mother away. She'd never thought that the loss of her mother could be matched, but that wasn't true. Life just kept threatening you, pushing you into harder corners, and you had to resist, otherwise hell would take over. No, she would fight for Irene. She would kill for Irene.

"I don't care about anything else. Don't you see?"

"Then do you see how effective he is? You've just given up everything except for your one issue."

"She's not an issue. She's my baby."

"Yes. Of course," Ronald said in a reassuring voice.

"I don't care about anything else. I really don't."

"All right, then. Now I know your limits. And mine." In his own divorce from his first wife, Ronald had given her full custody, because it was better for the children. Meghan was without a doubt the better parent. If he'd gotten joint custody, he would've ruined four lives, not just two. His first set of children were now well-functioning college graduates. His daughter was getting a master's in art history, and his son was in Colorado working for an environmental defense fund. He'd seen them every weekend, and he and Meghan had alternated holidays. His second wife, Jeannine, a painter, was a very good stepmother to them—approachable and never intrusive. His son and daughter got along well with Robert, the only child from his second marriage, who was as sweet-natured as his mother. He credited the success of his second marriage to the fact that he had given his first wife every term she'd asked for and more.

"Could you agree to shared decision-making powers—"

"This man had sex with a woman at an investment bank, and it is on video," she sputtered. "How can a person like this raise my child?" Ella's contempt was unhidden.

"How could you have married a person like this?" Ronald asked. The question was risky, but he decided to go with it.

"I didn't know he could be this way."

"I'm willing to bet he didn't know he could be this way, either, Ella. We are all full of surprises. The courts will not let the video influence the custody issues hardly at all. He had an affair. A lot of people have affairs. The child's need for both of her parents will supersede our conventional notions of sexual propriety."

None of us are perfect, was what Ella was hearing.

"He is still legally your husband and the legal and biological father of your child."

"Thank you," she said bitterly, certain that no one was on her side. "Somehow, I had forgotten." Ella broke into tears. She grabbed her handbag and prepared to leave his office.

"Ella, I will do my best."

"I know. I believe you."

"We'll be in touch."

Ella nodded and left her lawyer's office.

*　　*　　*

When Ella walked into the lobby of St. Christopher's, the first person to stop her was David Greene, who was on his way to a meeting. She had managed to fix her face in the bathroom of the lawyer's office and had kept from crying in the cab ride back, but as soon as David said hello, she burst into tears. She bit her lip.

"Ella, what happened?"

"Ted wants joint custody. But, David, he doesn't care about her. He's using her as a pawn—"

"What? That's crazy."

Ella wiped her face with her hands. She checked the lobby clock. No one else nearby had noticed her crying. "I have to get back to my desk. I'm okay."

"You can't go back to your desk like this." Ella's desk in front of the headmaster's office was in full view of anyone who'd pass by. "Come. Come to my office. Fitz's fine for a few more minutes."

Ella nodded. Her boss had given her most of the morning off for this meeting. "But you were stepping out—"

"Don't worry about that. Come on."

In his office, Ella sat on his green sofa, and David sat beside her.

"This is becoming old hat, don't you think?" she said of her crying jags. As soon as his office door had shut, she'd started to tear up again.

"No. This is a difficult thing." The sight of Ella's unhappiness grieved him. He didn't know how to comfort her. Two friends of his from college had recently divorced, and of the divorces he knew of in passing, the details were uncomfortably similar—overwork, bad habits, affairs, and faulty communication—yet it was never clear to him how love's alchemy turned passion to indifference.

David had met Ted a few times and fairly or unfairly believed him unworthy of Ella. It was obvious why a woman would marry a man like Ted—the clarity of his ambition, the proven intelligence and good looks—but even in their limited interactions, it seemed to David that Ted didn't have the deep-rooted kindness that defined Ella. Ted was a thoroughly expedient person. During a charity benefit dinner, Ted had remarked about the actress—the evening's honoree—who was reputed to sleep with directors to get parts: "So what? If she got on her knees, she was only doing what works. So sex is her currency. Everyone sells something." He'd tossed it off as if it were a widely shared value. David had smirked guiltily then but recognized that Ella and Ted would always negotiate the world differently. Ted was not unlike David's father—another man of the world.

Ella pulled out a tissue from her purse to clean her face. David took her in with wonder. Unworthy men got worthy girls because they believed that they deserved the best. If David were ever to get a girl like Ella, he would have to feel entitled to be with her. Top dogs got the best girls—his father used to say this at the club when he noticed attractive women with powerful men. David cared for his fiancée, but what he felt for Colleen couldn't possibly match what surged through him for Ella. Colleen was smart and kind, and his mother liked her a great deal, but David had never felt the urgency to hold her the way he wanted to hold Ella at this moment. If he took Ella in his arms, he thought he might have a hard time letting her go.

"I love you," he said.

Ella looked at him. "What did you say?"

It was too late to take it back.

"I love you, and I'll wait until you're finished with this marriage."

"David. What are you saying? You're engaged."

"I know. But it has occurred to me that she deserves someone who loves her the way I love you. I think I agreed to my mother's suggestion about Colleen because I respect my mother, and she's so ill. Colleen has taken such good care of her, and I felt grateful. And you were married, and I'm thirty-six years old. Maybe those aren't good enough reasons....I think I've been waiting for you anyway, and I didn't even let myself admit these things because it's wrong to covet someone else's wife." Once he confessed, he felt freer from his anxieties. He sat up straighter and looked at her carefully. Their relationship might have been ruined forever, he thought. She might think he was an awful person.

Ella tilted her head in disbelief. He was serious, and she looked at his wavy hair, parted in the middle, his beautiful eyes, and the upward curve of his lips. She loved him, too. There was no one else she liked more than David. She swayed her head slowly from side to side.

"But is it any less wrong now? Your words, I mean, your feelings. David, you're nearly married, and I got your wedding invitation only last week. Maybe you're getting cold feet...." She couldn't imagine being a party to hurting another person the way Ted had hurt her with Delia.

"I'm not getting cold feet. That's not it. I'm going to tell her right away. Even if you don't... don't feel the same way." David studied her eyes as best he could, but he couldn't read them properly. Did she love him, too? Ella wasn't a donor for the school or an old friend of his—he could read most people instinctively. It was different when you were attracted to someone; the reading came out fuzzy. All he could feel in the moment was his wish—his wish for her to love him—and this wish was clouding his perception. But he felt certain about Colleen.

"I can't marry her. One person shouldn't serve as a substitute for another."

Ella paused for breath. How was it possible to digest the sheer number of things that could happen in a day—the cruelty of Ted, the hardness of her lawyer, the need she felt for her daughter, the love of David. The love of David. How was that possible? No one had ever spoken to her so plainly about his feelings except for Ted. And she had believed him. There had never been anyone else except Ted. The idea of dating (Casey had mentioned it already a few times) had sounded ludicrous. And sex (Casey had mentioned that, too) seemed impossible. There was also the herpes. She hadn't had an outbreak in almost a year, but still. Herpes wasn't curable. If she had the virus, she could shed it when she had symptoms: That's what the doctor had said. How could she explain that to someone? How could she explain that to David? Why would anyone want to touch her?

"I don't know how I feel...."

"Of course." David couldn't hide his disappointment. "I picked the dumbest time to say such a thing."

"No, no, David. That's not what I meant. I've struggled with these feelings for you, too."

His eyes lit up.

"I thought what I felt was admiration. You know? And I wouldn't have admitted having a crush on you or anything like that because a woman who's married shouldn't... I mean... you're not supposed to feel anything like that, right? And—"

She couldn't tell him that she felt like a diseased person. She had a permanent sexually transmitted condition. If David had told her that he had herpes and she didn't, she wouldn't have cared. She would have understood, gotten through it. But she couldn't imagine him understanding. How could he? Ted once told her that deep down, all men wanted virgins.

"I'm not helping. I'm sorry," David said, thinking that he shouldn't have mixed her up about his feelings when she was going through this tough period.

"No, David, you're my dearest friend. I see that now. And thank you for saying what you did. It means... so much." Ella had stopped crying. She felt pulled into the stare of his enormous eyes, fringed with light brown lashes. He looked afraid. She'd never thought much of blue eyes, and Ted had said it was self-hating for a Korean person to admire blue eyes; but when Ella had pressed Casey for details about Delia, Casey had told her that Delia's eyes were blue. Why had she always believed so much of what Ted had said? *Why can't something beautiful be just that?* she wanted to say to him now. Not all blue eyes were beautiful, but David's were extraordinary. She wanted to kiss his eyelids—the silvery skin, the thin blue veins stretching beneath them like the roots of a tree.

"Close your eyes," she said to him.

David closed them, and Ella reached over to kiss his eyelids as she had just imagined doing. His eyes remained closed. The kisses had touched him like a blessing, like he had been loved, that he had been cured.

Ella covered her mouth with her hands. "Oh, my God, what did I just do?" She felt as though she'd woken up from a spell. "I'm so sorry. I don't know what came over me. I mean, I do. I wanted to—"

David opened his eyes. He had kept them closed to savor the tingling sensation.

He smiled at her. "I should go," he said. If he stayed, he felt certain that he'd try to make love to her, and that wasn't what he should do. It would ruin everything that he wanted with her. He would wait.

"But this is your office," Ella said, giggling.

David smiled and looked about him as if he needed to make sure. He actually felt light-headed. "I mean to my meeting. Can we have dinner tonight?" Then he remembered that he needed to talk to Colleen.

"I have to go home. To Irene."

"Oh yes. Of course."

"You can call me tonight. At home. After Irene goes down for the night."

"Yes. I will."

Ella nodded, feeling confused and oddly happy. They would talk tonight, and she looked forward to talking to him for many days after. She got up from the sofa, and David rose thereafter.

They were packing to leave Delia's apartment. The movers were scheduled to come on Tuesday, and Delia was in charge of handling them. The renovations on their new apartment were finally done. The three-bedroom wouldn't be as comfortable as his town house, obviously, but anything would be better than living in Delia's tiny apartment another week longer. Delia also liked the new place; she'd never lived anywhere with a view, and this one was of the East River. There was a doorman and an eat-in kitchen. Ted wanted all new furniture. She'd said yes to everything. There was only one thing she cared about.

"What did Chet say? About Irene?" she asked Ted.

"He said I had a very good shot at getting joint custody." Ted hooked the metal rod inside the wardrobe box. "I should go see her soon. I have to call Ella about that. But she's going to be in no mood..." Ted made a face. He didn't feel like dealing with her crying again.

"I'm sure she'll let you see her."

"Oh, I'm sure she will, too." Ted hung up his suits neatly in the box. He kept the one he'd wear on Monday and saved two shirts.

On the other side of the apartment, opposite the coat closet, Delia folded a red parka trimmed in white rabbit fur and tucked it into a heavy-duty garbage bag. She was pretty sure she'd give it away. Ted had started his new job at Lally & Co. last November, and he'd taken her to several business dinners where wives of colleagues or clients had been in attendance, and she'd had to think more carefully about her clothes. Ted never said anything critical, but from the looks of the other women, Delia became more conscious that her wardrobe was too bright. She often wondered what Ella wore or how Ella behaved at these functions. Ted didn't talk about Ella, and though Delia had no wish to hear anything bad about her, sometimes she couldn't help worrying if she was doing a good job as the future wife of the head of investment banking of Lally & Co. Ted had gotten a big job—that was the phrase that his HBS friends used about his new position. Lally & Co. had recently acquired Jones Hobson and was a threatening competitor to Kearn Davis in terms of assets managed and in the underwriting business.

"Ted, I think she should get the house."

"I found that house. I spent nearly a whole year getting it up to speed. Even with my bonus next year, it will take me another year or so to buy one of equal quality. And Ella doesn't even like the house—"

"You said you renovated it with the proceeds from her apartment sale."

"Yes, but I paid for the down payment and the mortgage and a good chunk of the renovation. The HVAC bill alone was—"

"You don't want your first wife to be angry with you," Delia said, walking toward him. "You just don't."

"Whose side are you on, anyway?"

"And you don't want your second wife to be angry with you, either," she said, grinning. She stood a few inches away from him and kissed him, dipping her tongue lightly in his mouth.

He smiled at her. "Don't think I don't know what you're doing," he said. "I'm smarter than I look." He raised his eyebrows. She turned him on just by talking to him.

Delia kissed him again. "I like smart men. Very much." She pressed her body closer to him, then drew back. "I have never doubted how smart you are, Mr. Kim," she said. "But you want custody, right? And you won't get everything. Nobody gets everything."

"Watch me, honey." Ted would take that as a challenge. His intention was to get everything—to win every point.

"Do you want the house?" she asked.

"I don't want to lose the house."

"Oh, Ted. I don't care about the house. We can get a better house."

"You haven't seen this house."

"I don't need to. We can stay in the new apartment, and it's so close to Irene. And when you get a new place, it will be close to the old one so we can see Irene as much as possible." Delia felt happy to say her name. She wanted to be a stepmother. She loved Ted, and of course she would love Irene. "I'd love to see her. Soon. Can't you bring Irene here?"

"I don't know. I usually just visit her when Ella is there. She's walking, but she's not potty trained yet."

"I know how to change diapers."

Ted sealed up the wardrobe box with packing tape. Ella wouldn't want Delia to be with Irene. The lawyer had said to avoid unclear behavior. The baby talked some, but would she tell Ella about Delia?

"All in good time, my love."

Delia walked back to where she'd left her work. She had more clothes to sort through.

"I didn't know you liked kids so much," he said.

"I love kids. You know I love kids." A corner of the closet was nested with dustballs. Delia grabbed a rag from the table.

"We can have kids. As many as you want. I like kids." A lot of the guys on Wall Street with big jobs had three or four kids. Their favorite complaint was the cost of private school tuition.

Delia wiped up the dustballs, trapping them beneath her rag. She threw the rag into the garbage can. "But what if I can't?" she said quietly.

"Of course you can," Ted replied, not in the least perturbed.

"Ted..." Delia looked at him.

"Yes, sweetie." He had finished his bit of packing. There wasn't much for him to do. Delia had already finished the kitchen things.

"I don't know if I can."

Ted didn't know what to say. She was serious.

"I've tried to get pregnant for years. And I can't. Is that going to work with you?" She closed her mouth and look at him straight. If he wanted to leave right now, she would let him.

"Oh," he said. Should he have asked her why? The determination in her face was not easy to take. He had actually thought they would have children together. The idea of just the two of them was a little lonely.

"We could adopt. And we'll have Irene." Delia picked up the loose plastic hangers from the floor.

Ted shrugged. Adoption seemed like taking on other people's problems. Who knew what you could get? How could you verify their backgrounds? He said nothing.

"There's all kinds of technology now." Ted felt brightened by the things he'd heard about. A few of his colleagues had had kids through IVF. He pushed the box off to the side of the room. He turned to her and saw that Delia was now seated inside her coat closet, odd pairs of shoes heaped about her folded knees, her arms clutching her legs. He went to her.

"Hey? It's okay. We'll work this through," he said. Delia wasn't crying. That was her way. His Delia was stoic, the way he was.

"I want you, Delia. And we'll have Irene."

She smiled at him. He did love her. Delia didn't bring up the town house again. She would trust that Ted would get everything he wanted. Maybe they might even have a child of their own. Who could say for sure? When she was with Ted, everything did seem possible.

2 | STEAM

$\mathcal{D}$OUGLAS SHIM REACHED FOR HIS OVERCOAT from the long row of hooks along the bumpy concrete wall of the church basement. He'd already put on his walking cap. He patted his suit pocket and felt the hand-drawn map of where Charles Hong lived.

Apparently, the choir director had the chicken pox. As chair of the church hospitality committee, Douglas traveled to the homes of the infirm and elderly each Sunday. In these visits, however, there were times he wished he weren't a doctor. Even as Elder Shim reminded the bedridden parishioner that he was an eye surgeon and didn't specialize in whatever ailed him—liver, pancreas, gallbladder, prostate, the list went on—he found himself having to play the doctor anyway and listen to the patient describe his illness and treatment in a muddled fashion. Douglas was routinely asked to render a second opinion for which he felt unqualified. Elder Joseph Han and his wife, Deaconess Cho, were accompanying him to Brooklyn today, and he scanned the room to find them.

Leah approached him by herself, as ever, her steps small. Her braided hair was pinned into a bun, and her head resembled a white flower on the stem of her neck. She wore a simple tan-colored coat.

Douglas broke into a smile. "Ah, Deaconess Cho. We didn't have a solo from you today. It's too sad, don't you think, when I have to hear your perfect voice get swallowed up by those toads in that choir of ours?" He grinned like a naughty child waiting to be chastised.

Leah was incapable of responding to his teasing. Her friend Kyung-ah would have known what to say, but she was on the other side of the basement, drinking coffee with her sister.

"Where's the elder?" he asked. Elder Han usually walked ahead of his wife, with the deaconess following closely behind.

Leah swallowed before speaking. "Tina had her baby."

"*Uh-muh.* I didn't know she was pregnant." Douglas smiled broadly. The doctor had a great fondness for children.

Leah turned a bit. She hadn't told anyone except for Kyung-ah and some of the girls in her *geh* that her younger one had gotten pregnant in what must've been within days of her wedding. Very much the time frame in which Casey had been conceived. But for Tina and Chul, the condom had broken, and they hadn't wanted an abortion.

"And she's still in medical school?" There was concern in his voice.

"She finished the first semester of her second year, but she's taking a break for now. Until things get a little easier. Chul is finishing his third, and this is an important year for him."

"It's important for both of them to finish," Douglas said with a deep nod for emphasis. The deaconess's expression grew more reticent. "So is Elder Han visiting the baby?"

"Yes." Leah anticipated the judgment. It would've made more sense if she had gone to California to help with the baby, but she would not travel. The last time she'd been on a plane was when she'd first come to America. "He went to California on Thursday. I stayed here to take care of the store. One of us had to. Stay, that is."

"Of course, of course."

"It's a boy," she offered.

"How nice for you."

"Yes, finally. A boy."

Douglas raised his eyebrows. He'd never wished for a boy. Ella was a wonderful daughter to him.

"They named him Timothy. After the young man who helped St. Paul."

"Yes, yes. A fine name.... Deaconess Chung can't come with us today," Douglas told her. He was a little nervous about this but didn't want to show it.

"Oh?" Leah blinked. She'd never been alone in the car with Elder Shim.

"She had to take her son to his chemistry tutor. Stanley's going to take his Regents exam in June, and she said he's failing everything. I thought she might start to cry." Douglas made a worried face. "He's always giving her trouble with his schoolwork. You see, sons are not so wonderful," he said.

Leah smiled. Elder Shim was being nice, because she didn't have any sons. Her husband, too, had never complained that she hadn't given him a son.

Douglas motioned toward the exit near the parking lot and paused. He wanted her to walk ahead of him, so Leah took the first step.

Douglas drove a dark green Subaru station wagon. He opened the passenger door for her. Leah smelled Japanese air freshener—something like grapefruit or orange. There was a tin of pink waxy deodorizer by the cup holder.

"What are you carrying?" he asked, buckling his seat belt. On her lap, the deaconess was holding three stacked metal containers wrapped in a large packing cloth. It had been a long time since he had seen *do-si-rak* containers—what day workers in Korea would have used to carry their lunch.

"Soup and some fish I made last night."

"How nice," he said. In the back of the car, he kept cases of canned fruit juice for sick parishioners. The choir director would get a case.

"Oh, the fish." Leah wrinkled her nose. "Should we open the window?" she asked, anxious that the smell of soy sauce and garlic from the fish might bother Elder Shim.

"It smells wonderful. The choir director will get better right away after he eats your food," Douglas said. He was humming as he shifted the gear from park to drive. "Do your daughters cook?"

"Not really. I wanted them to study for school," she said. "Ella cooks wonderfully. I remember her cookies. The ones she baked for the older parishioners. They were delicious."

"Ella is a gourmet cook. But she doesn't make much Korean food. Says the cookbooks aren't very good. But she knows how to make kimchi. She found a recipe in *The New York Times*. Isn't that funny?"

Leah nodded, feeling sorry that there had been no one to teach his daughter.

"I'll let her know. What you said about the cookies. Maybe she'll send you a batch."

"Oh no, no. I mean, I'm sure she's so busy. With...with all the work and her baby—"

She didn't know if it was okay to talk about Ella. With the divorce and all.

"Ted is a fool. An absolute fool," Douglas muttered. He looked ahead at the road. The thought of his son-in-law upset him, but he was a cautious driver, and he kept his foot light on the accelerator. He hadn't spoken to anyone at church about the divorce, not even when the minister had asked him about it. But somehow it felt all right to talk to the deaconess—perhaps it was being alone with her in the car or the fact that she, too, had a daughter Ella's age. Douglas missed his wife most when he had concerns about Ella.

"Is everything okay with your granddaughter?" She said the word *okay* in English. Her Korean words felt too specific.

"Irene is perfect. Just like my Ella." His granddaughter was a smiley baby, full of laughs and easy to please. She didn't cry except for when she needed a diaper change, was tired, or was hungry. His office desk was covered with framed photographs of her and Ella together.

"And how is Ella?" Leah finally ventured to ask.

"She's doing very well." Douglas wanted to correct the last image that the deaconess might have had of his daughter: when the ambulance had to take her away to the hospital from Tina's wedding. "She went back to work at that school, and there's a very nice nanny and housekeeper still working for her." Douglas grew quiet, having had to say out loud that his daughter was raising her child in the same way he'd had to after his wife had died—as a single working parent. "She'll be twenty-six in November."

Leah watched his face as he drove, how it softened with grief.

"She will marry again," Leah said. "Ella is the most beautiful girl and so very kind."

"Ted is a fool," he repeated.

"Then"—Leah paused before continuing—"it's good that she got rid of him sooner than later." Her sister-in-law had once told her that a woman's life was completely determined by the man she married. And in her experience, this was true. All the women she knew who were happy had made good marriages to nice, hardworking men. "Ella will find someone better. Because now she has..." Leah thought about it a bit. "Life experience."

Her words surprised Douglas, but he could tell she meant them.

"Whatever she wants to do is fine with me," he said, his tone confident. Yet that wasn't entirely true. He still regretted not having pushed her to wait to marry Ted. He could've said no. His daughter was a mild child with a gentle disposition. Even in this day and age, she would have listened to him; he felt certain of this. But things like infidelity usually didn't show up until the marriage was well under way. Douglas tried to imagine Irene's face, her pretty eyelashes and gurgly laughs—how she lit up when she heard Ella's voice. She was a year and five months, but already she was stringing words together. Irene called him *ba-buh,* short for *hal-ah-buh-jee.* If it weren't for Ted, there would be no Irene. He would focus on the good, Douglas told himself—to possess joy and peace in Yesu Christo.

Douglas rang the doorbell—a low, quiet chime. Almost pleasant. But no one answered. He pulled out the scrap paper with the map and address. They were at the right place, standing on the limestone stoop, six tall steps above street level. There was another entrance at the street below the staircase. The facade of the Federalist house was imposing. Douglas rang again.

Leah shifted her food package from one hand to the other. Would he like her cooking? she wondered. There were houses similar to this in Sutton Place, but she'd never been to Brooklyn before. She was impressed by the size of the home and understood from rumors that he came from a prominent *boojah* family, but it was oddly disappointing to see him live so prosperously. She had pictured him in a small, unheated apartment, suffering for his music. He was supposed to be a composer, and she'd imagined him sitting on a hard stool, despite his illness, writing sacred music on a makeshift desk. There were a few customers at the store who were artists—one painter who worked as a waiter had given her and Joseph a small watercolor of a golden carp because he couldn't pay to have his uniform cleaned one week. That wasn't allowed, but Joseph put money in the register from his own wallet to pay for the cleaning.

"One more time," Douglas said, pressing the bell. "Maybe he's okay after all and stepped out."

But they heard footsteps approaching. The old brass knob turned from inside. The immense wooden door opened.

Charles appeared shocked, almost as if he didn't recognize them. He was wearing a blue sweater, gray sweatpants, and no socks. His face and neck were spotted with red blisters. The living room behind him, however, was filled with the brilliant sunlight of the early Sunday afternoon. He invited them in, shaking his head.

"There was no need for you to come all this way." Charles spoke to them in Korean. He felt embarrassed to be seen like this. He tried not to look at Leah.

The door shut behind him. The piano and the stereo that the insurance broker had mentioned the day Charles had first started the job were beside the Palladian windows facing the street. The tall windows were unshaded and looked grimy. Since the broker's visit, Charles's father had come to New York and bought him two Le Corbusier sofas and a Noguchi coffee table now piled high with books and sheet music. Dustballs collected in the living room corners like miniature tumbleweeds.

"I brought the soloist. Maybe Deaconess Cho will sing for you. That might make you well," Douglas said with a straight face.

The elder couldn't be serious, Leah thought.

Charles glanced at Douglas, then Leah. "The doctor is undoubtedly right. Do you think you can give us a song?" He smiled at her.

Leah flushed from her neck to her forehead. Without removing her shoes, she rushed to the nearest chair and sat down to pray. Even in his condition, the choir director was handsome to her, and she felt guilty. Douglas smiled genially at Charles, then went to sit on the sofa. Silently, he gave thanks that he was able to serve God in this capacity, also for their safe arrival.

When Leah finished her prayers, she opened her eyes.

"May I put the food in the kitchen?" she asked.

Charles hesitated, knowing the condition it was in. But there was nothing he could do but comply. He pointed in the direction of the kitchen.

Leah picked up the food she'd brought and followed him. The kitchen smelled of cigarettes and tuna fish. The sink was full of dishes and frying pans and the counter littered with empty Vienna sausage tins and opened cereal boxes. It was a kitchen that was used every day but hadn't been properly cleaned in what might have been weeks, perhaps months. The space was enormous, however, nearly the size of her apartment minus a bedroom. The old cabinets had been painted so many times over, they looked as if there were a layer of cake frosting over them. Leah admired the expanse of the old marble counters. It would be easy to put up a dozen bottles of kimchi in a kitchen this size, she thought. The fact that the kitchen was dirty and cluttered didn't bother her—in fact, the amount of work needing to be done made her feel better, and oddly, standing there, she felt comfortable. Leah rested her package on the kitchen table and removed her coat, laying it over a chair. She started to drop the empty sausage cans and bottles on the counter into the waste bin.

The men didn't know what to say as she began to clean. It didn't seem possible to stop her, and even Douglas, who was in a better position to relieve her from this, knew better than to keep her from it. The work had to be done—that was clear enough—and growing up in Korea, men like them had had women to do it. For both of them, it had been some time since a Korean woman had been in either of their kitchens in this kind of intimate way, and in their wonder and surprise at being cared for by someone else's wife and mother, who reminded them of other women in their past lives, Douglas and Charles found that they could hardly say anything, hoping not to diminish the moment. For this was love, wasn't it? To have someone clean up after you, to think about you when you were sick, to not walk away when there was nothing to be gained for the labor required. Yet the task was also enormous; it would take a person all day to clean up this kitchen. Douglas thought he should try to help her. He took off his coat and put it over hers.

Charles spoke up finally.

"Deaconess Cho," he said quietly.

Leah was now running the water in the sink, her arms deep in the dishes. She did not answer.

"Leah," Charles said. Douglas was taken aback to hear someone call the deaconess by her American name.

"Leah," Charles said again, "you don't need to do this."

Leah turned around.

"I should be offering you tea or something. I'm sorry about the mess."

"No. You should be resting," Douglas said firmly. He'd had no idea what to expect upon visiting the bachelor choir director. He himself was a widower, but his life looked very different from this man's. Douglas was a tidy man who'd hardly tolerate such disorder. His housekeeper, Mrs. Jonas, had taken care of him and Ella proficiently for over twenty years, and when she retired, she had trained Cecilia to take over her work. "I will help Deaconess Cho clean up before we go. Why don't you lie down?"

It was hard to resist the doctor's suggestion. Charles felt itchy and hot all over. Last night, he'd barely slept. He trudged toward the living room to lie down on the sofa.

"Deaconess Cho," Douglas said loudly, trying not to shout over the running faucet. "Here, let me help you."

Leah brushed him off, smiling. "Elder Shim, you should check on the director. I'm fine right here. This I know how to do." She air-swept her hand across the dirty things on the counter as if to display her province of expertise. "I'll work better alone." She nodded pertly, tipping her head toward the living room. She looked adorable to him, but Douglas stared at her soberly to see if she was okay doing this. Ignoring his discomfort, she went to the table and pulled out two cans of mandarin orange juice from one of the six-packs that the doctor had brought in and handed them to him. She couldn't imagine finding two clean glasses and a tray nearby. Douglas went to find Charles.

Finally alone, Leah squeezed the water from the dishwashing sponge and dabbed some detergent onto it. Thankfully, there was soap for the dishes. It was better to work than to talk, she thought. What would she have said to the choir director, anyway? Typically in these visits, Elder Shim would lead the small group in prayer and ask his series of questions that he tended to ask the bedridden parishioner. Then they'd conduct a brief worship service, drink a glass of juice or eat a doughnut, then leave. In the book of James, Jesus's brother wrote about how you had to take care of your neighbor's practical needs as well as spiritual needs. Her father's favorite passage in the Bible had been "Suppose a brother or sister is without clothes and daily food. If one of you says to him, 'Go, I wish you well; keep warm and well fed,' but does nothing about his physical needs, what good is it? In the same way, faith by itself, if it is not accompanied by action, is dead." If she could locate some teabags, she would boil water in a cooking pot—there being no kettle on the stove—to serve the men something warm to drink. She glanced about and noticed the rice cooker behind the large chrome coffee machine that she didn't know how to use. At home, she and Joseph drank Taster's Choice. In her mind, Leah ordered up a list of tasks she could try to accomplish in an hour.

In the living room, Douglas found Charles sleeping on the sofa, his body curled like an S, his face reddened by the pox. The doctor crept up the stairs quietly. Charles's bedroom was the first large open chamber near the landing. The room itself was beautiful, with two enormous windows that opened like doors, shellacked hardwood floors, and a carved stone fireplace. The wide-planked floors were covered with dirty clothes and piles of newspapers. On the lone armchair, there were stacks of music scores. Douglas shook out the blanket rumpled over the bed and folded it over his arm. The bedsheets felt hardened to the touch from lack of wash. He put down the blanket to strip the beds and took the dirty sheets downstairs.

First, he went to cover Charles with the blanket. Then he snooped around the house and discovered the laundry room beside the kitchen and put the sheets into the washing machine. The stainless-steel machines were from Germany, a manufacturer Douglas had never heard of. He pressed a red button to start the load, and it was so quiet that he opened the top to see if there was water running at all. From the looks of it, the choir director didn't possess many things, but the items he owned were costly and well chosen, and yet none of it was cared for—as if the owner wished the things themselves to fall apart from neglect or disrepair.

When he stepped out of the laundry room, he saw that Leah had swept the kitchen floor and was now on her knees mopping the tiles, the way the maids of his childhood home would clean the *maru* in smooth, concentric motions. When he was growing up, Douglas's mother would chide the cleaning girls if she spotted one hair on the floor, and all the common-room floors of their enormous estate had to be cleaned twice daily. Leah was singing quietly, and he could not make out the words of the hymn. Douglas went to her. Leah, her knees tucked under her, a rag in her hand, looked up at him.

"I thought maybe I would ask Cecilia, my housekeeper, to come by tomorrow." She also lived in Brooklyn, but Douglas didn't know where exactly. He hesitated from telling the deaconess how bad the conditions of the upstairs room were. "I put his bedsheets in the wash." He gestured to the shuttered laundry room door. Leah opened her eyes wide in surprise. It was hard to imagine the doctor doing a load of wash. "Maybe you could stop now," he said. "The kitchen looks much better." Leah smiled at the recognition. "Deaconess, it's your only day of rest. Maybe we should leave after the director has woken up and we could pray for him." He bent his head forward slightly her way. Her face shone like a happy child's, and his heart fluttered a little, and he had to look away from her.

"I don't mind. Maybe I can find sheets for the bedding and make up the bed while the wash is going on." Leah tried to stand, and Douglas gave her a hand up. She took it, and when she rose, she let go of his hand quickly, never having been touched by him before.

"There's no one at home anyway, and I feel useful doing this—" Then Leah said nothing more, because she remembered that the doctor had no one at home, too. Was that why each week he served the sick and bedridden of the church? He didn't want to face an empty house on Sunday afternoons? That seemed like an unfair rationale for his dedicated service to the Lord. Leah had never had cause to think of it this way before. But this was the first time she herself had ever spent any time apart from her husband.

Douglas smiled at her. In her company, he felt almost dumb with pleasure. It reminded him of the way he felt in the presence of his older sister, who used to take him to school and who had died before Ella's high school graduation. The deaconess had the same gentleness in her expression that his sister did.

Leah bent to pick up the dustpan and went to the garbage can, filled to its capacity. She began to pull at the edges of the black garbage bag. A new one would have to be put in. Douglas moved swiftly to her side to relieve her from this.

"He's sleeping very well," Douglas said. He grabbed the two corners of the bag and knotted them to make bunny ears. Ella had liked this when she was a child.

"It must be very uncomfortable." Leah wiped her brow; a strand of hair had come loose from its bun. "I remember when Casey got chicken pox. I put Tina in the room with her right away so they would get it together. So it would be over faster."

Douglas understood. Working parents had to do these kinds of things to save time. He wouldn't have known what to do if he'd had two children.

"The choir director doesn't have any food at home. Maybe we could go to the store to pick up some things for him to eat. There's no fresh fruit or vegetables here."

"Yes, of course." Douglas tucked his hand into his trouser pocket for the car keys. His beeper vibrated. "Oh. What's this?" He studied the beeper screen, the size of a stick of gum. "The phone?" he said, wanting to make a call, and looked around.

Leah pointed to the wall beside the refrigerator. She couldn't help noticing the thick layer of dust above the freezer.

Douglas dialed the hospital. The resident had paged him because an elderly patient recovering from surgery had a very high fever and was having convulsions. The neurologist on call had advised the resident to contact him. Douglas got off the phone.

Leah stood waiting, not knowing what he'd say.

"We better go back now," he said, sucking air through his teeth.

"Oh." There was still so much left to do. "We didn't have our worship service. And he's sleeping."

Douglas opened his mouth to speak but said nothing. "You're right," he said. "And the laundry." He looked down. "I know." He raised his index finger. "I'll go to the hospital and come right back. I don't think it will take long."

"And I can stay here and clean up while you go."

"Do you mind?" he asked. "No." He shook his head as if he were disagreeing with himself. "I mean, you should come with me, and we can both come back when I'm done." Douglas felt confused. It was hard to say how long it would take. The hospital was half an hour away without much traffic, and if the medicine worked, he'd talk to the attending physicians and return in no time. "I think we could be back in two hours at most."

"No," Leah found herself saying quietly, thinking it would be a better deed for her to clean the house and fix dinner for the choir director than to wait at the hospital. "I'll keep working. I really prefer it. I was feeling bad that I'm not helping Tina. Anyway..." She made a long face, looking ashamed of herself. She was surprised by her own admission.

"But Cecilia could probably come tomorrow."

"Has she had chicken pox?" Leah asked.

"I don't know," he replied, thinking he should have thought of that.

"I'll stay. He's asleep, and I'll make up the bed and finish up. Please don't worry."

"Are you okay with that?"

Leah nodded reassuringly. The resemblance to his sister when she smiled like that was uncanny, and he had to shake it off. Douglas wrote down his beeper number and left her in the kitchen.

Two hours passed, but Douglas had not returned. Charles was still asleep. The kitchen was nearly clean, and Leah had drawn up a list using a small brown bag of all the things the house needed, like paper towels, laundry soap, lightbulbs, and basic food items like milk, juice, and coffee. He had a tablespoon of cooking oil left in the bottle and no white sugar or tea. From the moldy take-out containers in the refrigerator, it looked as if he had been ordering in; otherwise, he'd been eating out of cans or boxes. Perhaps he ate out all the time, but she had no way of knowing. Leah washed the inside and outside of the Japanese rice cooker with hot water and soap, and she opened the new bag of rice found in the corner of the pantry and made a fresh pot. She felt happier than she had in a long while. What she was doing really mattered. She carried up the clean pile of sheets and went to Charles's bedroom and discovered the mess Elder Shim had already witnessed.

She made up the bed and diligently carried down load after load of wash and sorted the piles by colors. It was six in the evening, and she hadn't heard from the elder yet. Leah didn't know where she was exactly or where the nearest subway station was located. There were no taxis outside the window, and she didn't know whom to call. The cooker beeped three times when the rice was done, and she opened the lid and fluffed the steamed grains. She was hungry herself. It would have been nice to have a cracker or an apple, but there wasn't anything like that in the house. She knew because she'd already looked. There were four cans of Campbell's Chunky soup and three tins of tuna in oil. Leah picked up the broom, dustpan, and rags and went upstairs.

After she picked up the books and scores from the floor and stacked them on the chest of drawers, she moved the scattered pairs of shoes left in his unused fireplace into his closet, then cleaned the floors as her mother had taught her to do—first sweep carefully, then wipe with a wet rag, and then last, a dry one.

"What are you doing?" Charles asked her, leaning uneasily against the doorjamb of his bedroom.

"Huh," Leah said, startled. She touched her heart with her hand. Concentrating on her work, she'd almost forgotten about him.

"Who let you up here?" he asked, his voice quiet and dazed. He wasn't angry, but he was annoyed at himself, because he couldn't honestly recall how the soloist had gotten into his house. He rubbed his upper arms, feeling the chill of the bedroom.

Leah had opened the windows to air the room. She'd heard somewhere that rooms with sick people should be aired often.

Charles marveled at the cleanliness of the room. The floors gleamed with the original polish, reminding him of the way the house had looked initially when he and his father had come by with the real estate broker.

"I came with Elder Shim," she said. Didn't he remember? "But he got called to the hospital. And I was cleaning up. I'm sorry. I was trying to help—"

"No. I mean, okay. I...I—" Charles closed his eyes, feeling dizzy.

"Are you all right?"

Charles clenched his teeth, trying to focus.

"Have you eaten today?" she asked.

"Where is Elder Shim?"

"I—he was paged, and he's coming back soon." Hadn't he heard what she'd said only a moment ago? she wondered. "I'll leave as soon as he comes. I just wanted to finish the laundry."

Charles noticed then that all the clothes on the floor were gone.

"Maybe you should lie down," Leah said, worried that he would faint. She stood up from the floor and went to him.

Charles moved toward the bed, and on his third step, he nearly crashed into her. She stayed close to him, trying to balance herself in case she needed to break his fall. He weaved a bit, and Leah slipped her hand beneath his arm to prop him up. He smelled like cigarettes and sweat.

"It's late. Shouldn't you be home?" he asked as she put the covers over his legs.

"If you can call a taxi for me, I can go, but Elder Shim is coming back to—"

"I'm not asking you to leave, I just thought your husband—"

"He's in California."

"Oh." Charles didn't ask any further.

"I think you should eat something. Wait here." In his weakness, Leah permitted herself to possess greater authority in her voice.

It took two trips to bring his soup, fish, and rice up the stairs. He drank two cans of juice and ate his food silently in steady bites. He finished his dinner, and Leah felt pleased at his appetite. When he was done, she took the dishes downstairs and began to clean the living room. Now, wide awake and fed, Charles sat up in bed, wondering what to say to her. The doorbell chimed, and Leah rushed to get it.

Douglas was breathless. The patient's infection had been serious, and the consults with the neurologist and cardiologist had taken longer than he'd expected. After the patient had settled, he had left right away, but there was traffic on the bridge. He explained himself to the deaconess, but she didn't seem to have minded the wait. The house was nearly unrecognizable.

"You did so much work," he said, amazed by her progress. He removed his overcoat, and Leah took it from him. They were still standing in the foyer.

"I wasn't saving anyone's life." She smiled.

Douglas laughed, privately pleased with what she'd said.

"Is our patient awake?" He addressed her as if she were a nurse.

Leah nodded. She told him how he'd nearly fainted, but he'd managed to drink the orange juice and eat his dinner. There was a lilt of pride in her voice.

Douglas looked up when he heard the footsteps on the staircase. Charles had changed from his sweater into a clean dress shirt. "I didn't realize I had gotten so disgusting," he said, holding the old sweater in his hand. "Thank you so much for everything," he said, looking in Leah's direction, but she couldn't look back at him. "I'm sorry about the house."

"You were sick and alone. There was nothing you could do," Douglas said, studying the way the choir director was observing the deaconess. He felt oddly possessive of her.

Charles walked down the last few steps, holding on to the wood banister. "Can I offer you anything?" Was there any tea or coffee in the house? He had absolutely no idea.

Leah refused, smiling. She checked her watch and rushed to the laundry room to bring over the basket of folded clothes. "I'll take these upstairs."

Charles reached over to take it from her, but Leah wouldn't let him, worried that he might fall. "It's all right," she said. "I like to work, to finish things." She went to put the clothes away.

"You should go back to sleep," Douglas said. "And maybe we can pray for you when the deaconess comes back down."

Charles nodded, thinking he would let them do this.

When Leah returned, they all sat in the living room and prayed for Charles's health and well-being. Douglas asked God to bring about a rapid recovery to the choir director so the church could soon bring greater praise to Him. "To Him be the glory," Douglas said, ending his prayer.

"Ah-men," Leah said, joining the elder's amen. "Ah-men," Charles mumbled softly.

The hospitality committee put on their coats and left the choir director's house. When Charles stood by the open door, Douglas told him to go inside so he wouldn't get cold. For May, it was a brisk evening.

Charles closed the door, and from his front window, he watched the green station wagon drive away. He'd been rescued, but in Deaconess Cho's departure, he felt more alone than he had felt in a long time. He noticed that he was still clutching the dingy sweater. He folded it and saw that it needed badly to be cleaned.

3 | DESIGN

A FEDERAL EXPRESS PACKAGE WITH SAMPLES from a high-end T-shirt manufacturer in Mississippi had been delivered to the store that morning. Although Sabine usually came by on Saturdays, she'd stayed home because of a migraine. Sabine was calling Casey at the hat counter from her salmon-colored bedroom.

"Can you bring them by? Sweet-ie, please?" Sabine took a sip of her frothy *macha*.

"How are you feeling?" Casey asked, trying to sound sympathetic. Lately, Sabine was having headaches more frequently. She hadn't come into the office for two Saturdays in a row.

"Oh, you know. I turn down the shades, and the power naps help. Casey, can't you bring the box over, baby girl?"

Casey could sense from Sabine's petulance that she was bored more than anything else. Her boss wanted amusement. That's why she couldn't just send a messenger to get the package.

"And it would be so nice to see you. You can have dinner here. And Isaac would love to see you, too. I feel so sorry for him when I get these headaches. I'm no fun to be with."

Judith was on break, and Casey was alone at her station. In her salesperson voice, low and courteous, she said to no one, "Yes, miss. May I help you?"

Sabine raised her voice a notch. "Honey, do you want me to call you back?"

It had been a stupid idea. Unless Sabine got her answer, she'd definitely call her back in ten minutes flat.

"Hang on, Sabine." Casey rested the phone on the counter. She leaned her hip against the glass cabinet, her back arching with tension. On the top shelf of the display case, a white camellia hat pin was out of line with its row, and Casey straightened it. Earlier that morning, two English sisters had come by searching for smart New York hats for a wedding in Canterbury. The elder of the two had asked to see the pin. The younger one, about forty years old, had bought a brown cocktail hat with a dotted veil that Casey had made, and her elder sister, the one with a more modern sensibility, picked up a greenish black feathered pillbox. Her commission for the two sales had come to a hundred and eighty dollars. Casey felt guilty at the thought of it, and she put her hand on the phone. If Sabine didn't let her consign her pieces and allow her to keep the full profits, her normal commission would have been sixty bucks.

Casey drew her hand away from the phone. Sabine hadn't invited Unu to dinner. What was he to do on a Saturday night? They were supposed to have spaghetti and rent a video. Poor Unu was still out of work and, as to be expected, not feeling so terrific. But Sabine thought he was a loser and had told Casey as much on more than one occasion. Unu had never once been asked to dinner at Sabine's apartment. Sometimes Casey thought Sabine hated Korean men.

"Casey?... Oh, Casey?"

Casey picked up the receiver. "Hi, sorry about that. A customer."

"No sale?"

"Nope."

"What time is it, honey?" Sabine asked.

Casey looked at her watch. The Rolex stared back at her. "Eleven-twelve."

"Do you have a lot of homework this weekend?"

"I do." An ugly accounting project was due on Tuesday.

"Maybe you can do some during your lunch break. You can use my office."

Casey closed her eyes.

"Dinner won't take long, baby girl. Tell Sabine what you'd like to eat."

And that was that. Casey phoned home, but Unu wasn't there. She left a message on the machine saying she had to go to Sabine's for dinner. Financially, things were rotten for her and Unu. As usual, Casey was perennially in hock, and Unu, who'd spent his severance, was looking for work, trading occasionally on his own account, and mostly gambling to pay the bills. Her mother had taught her that a woman should never make a man feel bad about money. In her experience as a salesgirl, she'd also observed that men across the board were vulnerable about two issues: money and hair loss. Unu was in a bad way at the moment, and she believed that if she said anything about their money situation or his gambling, he'd disintegrate from the shame. She could imagine him vaporizing like a figure in a science fiction movie—Unu breaking up into a billion particles. *Whoosh.* She also had no right to talk when it came to personal finances. Zero.

To cut expenses, she'd stopped taking her classes at FIT. The tuition was negligible compared with what she'd paid at Princeton and NYU Stern, but it was still a month's worth of groceries. She'd also calculated how much it cost to see her friends after class for drinks. Beer and bar snacks added up, not to mention carfare when it got late. The brown cocktail hat was the last one she'd made to sell. At night when she lay in bed with the down comforter pulled up to her chin, Casey found herself praying for one thing—that she hadn't made another incredibly expensive mistake with her life by going back to school. The spot on the summer associate program was, she hoped, the answer to her doubts.

At school, outside of classes, all she ever heard was this distillation of the truth: The whole point of business school for those specializing in finance was to get a summer associate position at an investment bank; at the end of the summer, you were supposed to score an offer to return to the Wall Street firm after graduation; in the beginning of your second year, you could even try to leverage your permanent offer into an upgrade if you were gutsy enough; if all went well, you started the big fat job upon graduation. With those jumbo bonus checks you earned postgraduation, you were supposed to pay off your student loans in two years—the same number it took you to incur the aforesaid debt. Obviously, the only jobs that could help you reduce your debit line with this kind of speed were top investment banks in the only street that mattered. Of all the areas of specialty at Stern, Casey had chosen finance—where the top money went.

Four years had passed since Casey had graduated from college, and this was what she had figured out: She did not want to fail anymore either privately or publicly. More than any other woman Casey had ever known, she admired Sabine, a self-made woman and pioneer in her field. When Casey chose NYU Stern without asking her and Isaac for help to get off the waiting list at Columbia (not that there was any guarantee of her admission, as Sabine periodically implied, merely because Isaac was a trustee or because his help had in fact gotten Jay Currie into Columbia), and when she refused Sabine's offer to pay for school, Casey had bought a kind of autonomy that had a possibly titanic downside—an ocean of humiliation if she didn't land a premium job on her own. And as for her parents, when she deferred away Columbia Law and moved in with a divorced guy who had no intention of marrying her, there was hardly any room for redemption. Her younger sister was married to a nice Korean doctor-to-be and had given birth to a son. No contest. Only this month, she had violated her own sense of propriety and asked Hugh Underhill for help, and now, if she failed to get a permanent offer from the banking program after the summer ended, she would look colossally stupid in front of her friend. She was up to nearly two packs a day and drank a lot of Diet Cokes. She had trouble sleeping at night.

So Casey did what she knew how to do when she woke up involuntarily at three in the morning: She studied. The irony, she had learned, was that there was no point to her lovely transcript if the fancy banks thought so little of NYU Stern and shopped for students only at Harvard, Wharton, Stanford, and even less so, Columbia. In the end, she'd had to call Hugh—a man whose penis she had touched in the backseat of a taxi.

When she had been a student at Princeton, she and her friends were taught that to consider Ivy League schools as being better than non-Ivies was elitist and vulgar. You would never say a Princetonian was superior to a Queens College graduate. Going to NYU (a top ten business school, but not top five) had taught Casey what her father had insisted all along: Designer labels mattered. The very banks that had refused to recruit at Stern had come to interview twenty-year-olds at Princeton for their undergraduate analyst program. When Casey had been turned down by Kearn Davis her senior year in college, she had not understood then that it was because she had been unwilling to play along (the crazy yellow suit, the Nancy Reagan jokes, and her conceit to apply to only one bank—accurately pointed out by Ted Kim), but at least the firm had come by to take a look. She'd had a door open where she could fail or succeed. There had been a door.

Naive. Casey had been that. She had not appreciated the blinding privilege and protections of an Ivy League degree until she went to a school without the cooling shade of its green leaves and silky tendrils. If she had gone to Columbia Law School, she might have been a first-year associate already, and perhaps a third of her loans could have been gone.

When Judith returned, she told Casey to take her lunch break. Casey went to Sabine's office and pulled out her accounting homework, but before she started, she found the FedEx box and dropped it in her tote bag.

Isaac Gottesman opened the door of the penthouse and waited for Casey to come up.

The girl stepped off the elevator with her bare head cast downward, carrying her brown fedora in one hand and a Federal Express package in the other. Casey wore a white schoolboy blouse cinched in the waist with a wide brown belt, a short tweed necktie, wool trousers, and men's-style oxford shoes. Her clothing was comically attention getting, but her expression was dejected.

"Hey, cheer up."

Casey raised her head and grinned, not having expected him. The housekeeper usually let her in. Isaac looked like a tall bear—his towering frame, large open hands at his sides, the faded beige corduroys and camel-colored sweater. It was a relief to see him. Isaac liked her and wanted nothing from her. Jay Currie used to call Sabine her fairy godmother, but it was really Isaac who felt like the godparent, not by what he gave her in terms of things or experiences, but by his acceptance of her. It was a form of wealth bestowed upon you when a good person took you in like that.

But it had been a long week, and she was exhausted. She had left her job as a desk sales assistant precisely because she was too old to run errands like this. Lately, she'd been feeling that her servitude to Sabine had gone on for too long. Even if Sabine handed her the retail empire of Sabine's for a fraction of its market value, the option she would expect in return was a binding indenture enforced by gratitude. How did you quantify that? Would she forever be delivering packages on the weekends, having meals with Sabine when she didn't feel like it, and canceling the wishes of loved ones if Sabine didn't approve of them? Unu would likely have a bowl of cereal tonight if he remembered to eat at all, she thought sadly.

Isaac kissed her cheek and hung up her jacket, but Casey held on to the package. She wouldn't stay for dinner, she decided. She would hand off the package to the queen herself, then beg off.

"She's in her bedroom," he said, looking at her glum face.

"I'm sorry, Isaac. Hey..." She smiled, remembering her manners. "How are you? It's always so nice to see you." He smiled at her warmly, and Casey swallowed, feeling as though she might cry for no reason. There had been three people who had this effect on her just by their kind glances: Mary Ellen Currie, Jay's mom, Ella Shim, and Isaac.

Isaac opened his arms to give her a hug, and Casey allowed herself to be tucked into his big chest.

She could feel his closely shaven chin on her forehead. He smelled wonderful, like cedar chips, musk, and orange peel. No one else smelled like that. Sabine had his aftershave custom-blended by a master perfumer in Paris. The bottles were labeled "I.A.G." for Isaac Antonio Gottesman.

Casey pulled away first, feeling shy and tearful.

Isaac put his hands on her shoulders. She had gotten skinnier, he thought, not in a good way, but as if she weren't getting enough to eat.

"Young lady, did you know that we're giving away a free lamb dinner tonight for the first person who walks in here with a FedEx box?" His eyes shone with amusement. This was his usual shtick, playing Monty Hall on *Let's Make a Deal*. The first time she'd met him, he'd asked her in a serious voice, "Ma'am, if you have a Band-Aid in your purse, I'll give you ten dollars." It had taken her a moment to get that he was joking, but there was another time she'd dug out a safety pin from her cosmetics bag at his request, and he'd given her a fiver on the spot.

"Miss, why, of all the luck! Is that a FedEx package in your hand?"

"Yes, sir," Casey said, keeping it straight.

"That's too crazy! Because tonight we're also giving away a *panna cotta* with chocolate sauce if you have a beautiful smile."

Casey grinned, but in her mind she was still stumbling to find a way to say no to dinner without lying outright.

"Miss, do you have a hat?"

Casey nodded, raising her fedora to his eye level. She felt like a girl joking with her charming uncle.

"Well, tonight we're trading one ladies' hat for a pair of Italian-made shoes and a matching bag!"

She burst out laughing. "Now you're talking."

"Now, that's a real Casey smile. You okay?"

"I'm fine. Don't you worry about me."

"Oh, I don't worry about you, Casey Han. I don't have to. You are good at doing what needs doing," he said. Sometimes saying a thing could make it so.

Casey's eyes filled with tears. "Oh, I don't know, Isaac."

"But I know." He nodded gravely, wanting her to believe him. Isaac regretted not having given his own children this kind of assurance while they were growing up when he'd been too busy chasing deals and skirts. He remembered being around Casey's age, how the world appeared full of possible conquests. It saddened him to think of how his own children had no wish to fight, no larger desire to win. As though they had nothing to prove or could prove nothing even if they tried. Casey had so much fight in her, but she seemed always to want to fight it alone.

"So, where's the boss?" Casey asked. She took a deep inhale.

"In her bedroom."

"Oh yes, you said. She's resting?"

"She's awake. She wants to see you."

"I could just leave this if she's resting." Casey held up the package.

"No, no. Don't be silly. She asked for you to come in. She'd love to see you."

"Oh." Casey put her hat on the bench in the foyer. "Okay."

"You know where, right?" Isaac pointed up the stairs. "Maybe you can get her to join us for dinner. She said I should give you dinner after she spoke to you. You're staying?"

Casey nodded. This was how successful people got what they

wanted, she thought. They just forced outcomes. She gave a small wave to Isaac and went up the stairs.

In college, she had known a boy named John Pringle whose engineer father owned some sort of chemical company. John's dad, the son of a mechanic and a housecleaner and the youngest of six children, had attended Rochester Institute of Technology on full scholarship; and after making his first million dollars, he went on to make several hundred more. At a Cap & Gown party, John Pringle smoked a Dunhill's blunt filled with high-quality grass, and he told Casey and Virginia that his two older half-brothers from his dad's first marriage worked for the old man. John had made air quotes when he said the word *worked*. He also called his brothers Limp-dick I and Limp-dick II. His brothers laughed at their dad's off-color jokes, said nothing when Dad talked too loudly at sporting events, and looked away when Dad habitually stuck his finger in the back of his mouth to clear the food stuck in his molars.

At the party, John was higher than the Empire State Building, and by that time, Casey and Virginia had dried up two bottles of Asti Spumante. Virginia had asked John, "So you"—her words were slurry, her pretty face flushed from the sparkling wine—"and what...what are you going to do with your life?" And John had replied, "I'm gonna fuck around as long as I can, and then take it up the ass like my brothers. Cut my hair, put on a suit, marry a Connecticut blonde with big tits who will bear the fruit of my loins. And I will carry Dad's bags to the airport and laugh at his fart jokes."

That evening, Casey was wasted, which had the effect of making her sleepy and patient, but she had listened carefully to John's family story. And though she'd always thought this thin, freckled boy who lived on the floor above hers during freshman year—the boy who'd gotten into Groton instead of Andover, the one with the handsome roommate whose attention both Casey and Virginia had failed to enlist—was a phony and not terribly interesting, she'd ended up feeling a little sorry for him. He genuinely seemed to believe that he had no choice in life but to follow his brothers' bitter-sounding path. It was nonsense to think that he of all people had no choices in life, but having spent the evening with him, Casey was beginning to understand that what mattered was not what you could do, but what you believed you could do.

But in her Elmhurst apartment building, there had been Sonny Villa, her neighbor. When Sonny finally got his trucker's license, his parents threw him a party because they were going to be rich if Sonny became a Teamsters truck driver. During dessert, as he cut up pieces of a Fudgie the Whale cake from Carvel, Sonny took long sips of Michelob, wiping away the foam from his dark mustache. He swore to everyone there, his lovely black eyes glittering with liquor, that he'd own an eighteen-wheeler by the time he was twenty-five. At such a bold pronouncement, the guests gathered their breath like children before the candles of a birthday cake. Within a year, Sonny got addicted to speed, which he'd started using to stay awake for his late night drives. After two accidents, he lost his job and got a post working security at the Metropolitan Museum of Art.

This was what Casey wanted to know: When life didn't go your way, was it because it wasn't meant to or because you didn't have the faith, or was it that you couldn't make it so by the labors required of you? On Van Kleeck Street, the stories mostly had the same crap endings, and whenever Casey was feeling particularly low, she feared her own conclusion might inevitably be a shitty one.

The high walls of Sabine's bedroom were papered with a chinoiserie pattern—hand-painted hummingbirds and rare flowers on a silvery peach background. With the bedroom lights turned down low and the shades drawn, Sabine looked like a beautiful bird herself, perched on her bed wearing a quilted silk bed jacket, propped up on three square European pillows.

"Helloooooo, darling." When Sabine said "darling," the "r" disappeared, and it had the effect of a forties Hollywood film voice rather than the mispronunciation of an immigrant. "Come here, baby girl, and sit by me."

Casey kissed her hello on both cheeks and sat on the armchair near the standing lamp.

"No," Sabine whined, touching her right temple. "Come sit on the bed. There's lots of room here. Come snuggle with me." She drew Casey in with her sinewy arm.

"I brought you your package," Casey said quietly with her boss holding her close.

"Oh yes." Sabine took it from her and cast it aside by the bed cushions.

"Are you okay?" Casey asked. Close up, Sabine looked exhausted—fine lines fanning around her eyes.

Sabine stared hard at her. "I just have a headache. But you look miserable."

"No, I'm good. Really." Casey tried to sound upbeat. "I just got a summer job at Kearn Davis." She wouldn't take this well, Casey surmised. Sabine had been after her all spring about working for her as a management trainee this summer—just the two of them in an informal program—but Casey had been evading the issue by saying she needed new kinds of business experiences. "For investment banking."

"You used to work there. What's the big deal?" Sabine sat up as though she were getting ready to fight. She took her arm off Casey's shoulder and crossed her arms against her chest.

"I'm not going back as a sales assistant. This is different. I even got turned down for its undergraduate program when I was at Princeton. You can't imagine what the other finance majors at Stern would do for this." Casey couldn't mention how she got the interview.

Sabine closed her eyes dramatically and did her yoga breathing. "I'm sure you know what you're doing," she said finally.

Casey stared at the package that she had carried from the store. How could she explain her desire to flee from the very person who had helped her so much? It seemed so ungrateful, even foolish.

"I was going to take you to Paris, Milan, and Hong Kong this summer if you had come to work with me. Don't you have a little friend in Italy? The one you're always writing to?"

"Why would you take me to those places?" Casey didn't want to talk about Virginia with Sabine. She was jealous of her friends.

"And why do you give me such a hard time?"

"What? Sabine? It's Saturday night, and I took a subway and a crosstown bus to bring you a package. Which you haven't even opened."

Sabine massaged her temples with her index fingers. "Don't raise your voice at me, little girl. I haven't seen you in two weeks. Where have you been?"

"I go to school full-time, and I was at work." Casey's steam was building. "You haven't come in on Saturdays for the past two weeks, and you don't work on Sundays when I do! And when I was working this past Thursday night, you were in a meeting so I didn't bother you." She loaded all her pronouns with as much shrill emphasis as possible. She couldn't believe she was reporting her schedule to her. Her own parents never knew what she was doing, and they no longer even asked. Lately, she spoke to her mother maybe once every six weeks.

Sabine picked up the FedEx box with both hands gingerly and made a show of trying to open it. She had trouble with the tab string, and Casey pulled it for her.

"Here." Casey handed her the open box.

Sabine pulled out the sample of the long-sleeved T-shirt. "This is going to be our store-brand shirt." It was a simple, long-sleeved shirt of very fine jersey cotton. "I'm getting four colors done. It's going to be the most expensive T-shirt in America."

Casey nodded. Sabine didn't look as though she had a headache anymore.

"Why don't you come down for dinner?" Casey said, not wanting to fight anymore. She hated arguing more than anything, and it never made her feel any better afterward. "Isaac looks like he's lost downstairs."

"You told me that Kearn Davis didn't interview at NYU business school." Sabine gazed at Casey; her eyes looked hard and brilliant, like onyx.

Casey blinked. Sabine had a scary memory.

"They don't interview at NYU. My friend Hugh helped me set it up."

"I thought you didn't believe in asking for those back-scratching favors. Isn't that why you never asked Isaac for a letter of recommendation for Columbia? If you had gone there, then you wouldn't have had to ask Hugh. You'd rather have a stranger do a favor for you than a friend."

"Hugh is a friend."

"And I'm not?"

Casey sighed and dropped her head into her hands.

"Life is filled with many complicated tasks, and no one, Casey, no one can do things alone. It's very slow going if you choose that path."

"You did things by yourself." Casey was shouting now.

"You couldn't be more wrong. No one person helped me," Sabine said, more convinced than ever that the girl was too proud.

"Many, many, many people helped me. The bookkeeper who gave me a discount on filing my first returns, the diner owner who let me have free breakfasts when I couldn't pay, manufacturers who gave me credit when I had no right to expect it—so many, many people helped me." Sabine was screaming. "I can't even begin to remember all their names. Why do you think I help people who are having a hard time? It all goes around, little girl. That's the whole point of it, goddammit! Why must you be so stubborn?" Sabine's black pupils disappeared into the darker pools of her irises, filling quickly with tears.

"And why do you act as if poor people shouldn't have any choices? Must I always take what's offered? Must I always be grateful?" Casey brushed the hair away from her face. Her voice was trembling. "Listen, Sabine. I need to try this thing. I need to know if I can make it as an investment banker, make real money, pay back my school loans. I need to see if I can do it on my own. On my terms. And I didn't know that Columbia would make a big difference. All right? I didn't know how the world worked. I was full of shit. You were right. Good for you. For fuck's sake, I'm twenty-six years old, and I don't have it all figured out. I'm not like you."

Sabine pulled back and grew calmer. Her expression was metallic, as though something had gone steely inside her when Casey talked about the poor not having choices.

"I told you that I'd pay for your tuition," Sabine said. "No strings. You didn't even have to pay me back. And it isn't like I'm making you come and work for me afterwards. It's not like the army, you know, I'm not sending you off to war."

Isaac walked in, his face contorted with worry. "Who's going to war?" From the hall, he'd heard both women screaming. The young girl was sobbing and looked a lot worse than when he'd opened the door for her. He smiled at her genially, but Casey just looked at her hands.

"My love, have we offered our guest a drink?" Isaac said to Sabine, raising his eyebrows sternly, all the while smiling at her.

Sabine sighed, softening a little. Casey made her feel crazy sometimes, and she had not, in fact, offered her a drink.

"I better go," Casey said, but Sabine took hold of her hand.

"My darling Casey and I were having a quarrel, but it is all right now. Isn't it?"

Casey said nothing. She imagined John Pringle toadying behind his father, clutching Dad's briefcase, and Sonny Villa boasting about owning a shiny truck one day to anyone who'd be dumb enough to listen. And she recalled Virginia's slurry question to John, "And what are you going to do with your life?"

What had she accomplished, anyway, Casey wondered, with all of her stupid pride?

"Baby girl, if you stay for dinner, I'll even come downstairs," Sabine said, feeling bad for not having thought about the drink.

Isaac chuckled. "Are we trying to make her stay or leave?"

Sabine threw a small pillow at him and clocked him on the head.

"Oh, my head." Isaac acted as if he were stumbling back from the blow.

Sabine still held on to Casey's hand. She would have to stay, Casey realized. If she left now, the damage would be even harder to repair.

The cook had made a delicious dinner with all of Casey's favorites. At the table, the two women tried not to disagree about anything at all. Isaac told stories about indulging his grandchildren, and Casey laughed while Sabine pretended not to find the anecdotes funny. Isaac, who was semiretired, occasionally picked up his grandchildren after school in his chauffeured car and took them to eat French fries, chocolate egg creams, and half-sour pickles at his favorite diners in Brooklyn and Newark. His adult children were not crazy about this, especially all the greasy snacks, but they didn't prohibit him from doing so.

Dessert was served, and Isaac poured tea for the women.

"Casey has an internship with the Kearn Davis banking program," Sabine said confidently.

Casey smiled at Isaac, not knowing what to expect next.

"Congratulations!" Isaac said.

"Thank you." Casey took a tiny sip of her tea.

Isaac knew full well that Sabine wanted Casey to take over the store one day. He liked the girl very much, and in many ways, Sabine's wish made sense to him. She was smart, young, and could do possibly anything. But it was clear that Casey couldn't be pushed. Isaac understood the young girl's wish to work as an analyst at Kearn

Davis. She must've wanted to know what it was like to be a banker, even a junior one, at a white shoe firm. As poor immigrants, her parents had to manage a dry-cleaning store. People like Sabine and him had been forced to start from nowhere to earn their living. Straight out of Hunter College, he wouldn't have dreamed of getting an interview at a single Wall Street firm. As he'd ascended the moneyed heights of New York, there were plenty of folks who believed that real estate was a dirty field, and as successful as Sabine was, she was still a merchant, and that meant she got her paws dirty. Isaac could imagine Princeton as having enough of these line-drawing types, and no doubt they'd done a head scramble to this girl who was never getting a trust fund. He felt sorry for her, because one thing he knew for sure was that you could never wash yourself clean.

His own first job had been to show rentals in the Bronx owned by Mr. and Mrs. Schwartz, formerly of Co-op City. And Sabine had started out selling her handmade handbags and gloves in a two-hundred-square-foot store. Casey could've made a pile of money if she'd paid her dues with Sabine for a dozen years or so, but Isaac understood that she might have wanted to be legitimate right away.

Casey swallowed the last bite of her creamy dessert. She scraped her silver spoon across the wide Bernardaud dessert plate to get at the last bits of chocolate sauce. The handle of the spoon was engraved with the interlocking initials of Sabine and Isaac.

"This is beautiful. I always mean to tell you that," Casey said, holding up the silver spoon.

Sabine winked at her.

Isaac picked up his spoon and looked it over. He and his wife had gone to an antiques and silver shop on Park Avenue to order these. Each piece was hand-forged by some ancient English maker. Sabine had ordered flatware service for sixty people, and each eight-piece setting had cost two thousand dollars. They had used the marrow spoons maybe twice when the cook served osso buco.

"Did you know that my namesake uncle was a silver engraver?"

Sabine glanced up from her teacup, looking at her husband quizzically. No, she did not know that. "Who?"

"Irv. Uncle Irv. You never met him. I never met him. He died. A long time ago. Lungs."

"Oh," Sabine said.

"You mean a person who does these things?" Casey pointed to the monogram on the handle of her spoon.

Isaac nodded, not having thought of Uncle Irv in several decades. His father had told him that the "I" from Isaac was from the "I" from Irving.

"So who is Uncle Irv?" Sabine sat up tall.

"He was the eldest in my father's family. They were maybe fifteen years apart?"

Casey nodded.

"So, all Uncle Irv ever wanted was to become a lawyer. He lived and breathed the idea of being some Clarence Darrow." Isaac raised his hands joyfully toward the clear glass Venini chandelier. "And naturally, my grandparents were delighted. But..." Isaac grew quiet.

"So did he not have the money for school?" Casey asked. Lately, she believed that most of her problems in life could be boiled down to the lack of dollars and cents.

"No. My father's family had no money, but my grandfather had a sister whose husband owned a feather factory in Manhattan, and she, who had only three daughters, had promised to pay for Irv's education."

"Feathers?" Sabine said out loud.

"For trimmings, blankets, and pillows," he said. "Anyway, Irv went to City College, because Columbia turned him down." He raised his eyebrows, amused. Isaac thought everything had some sort of comedy in it.

Casey nodded solemnly. "He's in good company."

"Well, Irv thought Columbia turned him down because he was Jewish and poor." Isaac shrugged. "Whatever. Their loss, right? So, Irv goes to City College. Pre-law. Gets A's. And in one of his classes, he meets a boy who has a very pretty cousin who is very religious. Now, mind you, my grandparents believed that religion was the root of all evil."

Sabine nodded knowingly.

"But Uncle Irv's still sore because he believed that he didn't get into Columbia for being Jewish, but then he figures since he is Jewish, he should get some perks. Like getting to know his friend's pretty cousin Sarah."

Casey smiled at him. Isaac was half Jewish and half Italian-

Catholic. He swore that on his deathbed, he'd ask for a priest and a rabbi ("Maybe heaven has several entrances").

"So his friend, I don't know his name, and his pretty cousin ask Irv to come to *shabbos* dinner. Before you know it, Irv gets involved with some Orthodox community in Brooklyn. When my grandparents get wind of this, they threaten to cut him off, but he keeps seeing the girl and her people anyway."

"And?" Casey asked.

"He decides to join up."

"With who?" Sabine asked.

"With the Jews."

"But he's already Jewish."

"You know what I mean—he wants a bar mitzvah, grows his beard, and all that jazz." Isaac shrugged, because he didn't know much about Judaism and kept himself from it as much as he could. "He wanted to be a practicing Jew. And to marry this Sarah, who will not marry him unless he becomes really Jewish. The funny thing is that Irv got religion, and he started to really believe this stuff. So my grandparents stop speaking to him, but his aunt continues to pay his tuition."

"The Jews and the Koreans..." Sabine shook her head. "So crazy."

Isaac laughed. "Then the girl Sarah asks Irv to write to the head rabbi to get permission for them to get married and to ask if it's okay for Irv to become a lawyer."

Casey tilted her head, fascinated. "Permission?"

"Yeah, I know. Crazy," using his wife's word. "But get this—" He raised his pointer finger.

"Darling, you are giving me a headache," Sabine said.

"I take no responsibility for your headaches." Isaac winked. "The rabbi says yes to the marriage. So Sarah becomes my aunt. Another one who dropped off before I was born, but he says no to Irv on his lifelong wish to become a lawyer."

"What?" Casey and Sabine said at once.

"Lemme finish," he answered, enjoying his hold on the women. "The rabbi says, on reading Irv's letter and recognizing his excessive passion to become a lawyer, he has come to the conclusion that it would be a mistake. If a man loves his job far too much and has a lust for it, he will make that an idol and he would destroy his own life and his family's."

"So, what? Then take a job you hate?" Casey winced in her chair.

"No, he thinks you should take a job, and a job should be a job and not something that you could love more than God." Isaac felt confused himself. "So the rabbi writes to Irv and tells him to be a silver engraver. A job for which Irv would not feel great passion."

"That's so crazy," Sabine said. "I love my job. I feel so much passion for what I do."

"Well, the rabbi would not like that, I guess." Isaac smiled. "But so what? We're not Jewish. And you don't believe in God anyway, so what does it matter? Besides, it's just one rabbi's nutty idea."

Casey didn't know what to say.

Isaac raised his teacup. "He died a happy man, though, my father said. Seven sons and two daughters. He was my father's favorite. My father always snuck around—so my grandparents wouldn't find out—to visit him where he worked. Near the diamond district. But my father never could make sense of the religion stuff. And my mother never liked the church, either. Anyway..." Isaac smiled at them. "Tea?" He looked at the pot.

They both shook their heads no.

"So, you shouldn't find the meaning of your life in your job?" Who would disagree with that? Casey thought, searching for a moral, like a faithful student writing a book report. "So you shouldn't love work more than God."

"Not if you're Irv, anyway. I mean, I guess he was kind of a romantic guy. You know? My father said he knew no one smarter than his brother Irv. He did everything in an intense way. Maybe the rabbi understood that about him. Eh, what do I know?"

Casey couldn't say what a Christian would believe. But a minister would have likely agreed on this point. The Bible was clear that idolatry was a sin, and a person could make anything an idol. Why not a job?

Sabine snorted. "I don't believe that stuff. It's all magic and voodoo, and I think you should just be a good person. And it's crazy to not let a person who wants to be a lawyer be a lawyer. That's a nice job where you could really help people."

It was time to leave. Casey thanked her hosts and excused herself for the evening. "The dinner was delicious," she said.

"You have to come by more," Isaac said.

Sabine said nothing as she and her husband walked Casey to the door. She pulled out Casey's jacket from the closet and helped her put it on. She stood in front of Casey to wrap her thin scarf around her neck, and Casey let Sabine do this. The scarf was tied elegantly— a large square knot, its ends off by an inch of material.

"I want you to be happy, Casey," Sabine said, looking sober. "And I'm—sorry. I'm sorry I never know how to help you in the right way. It's just that I don't know how to love. Without taking over." She started to cry.

A grown-up had never apologized to her before, and Casey didn't know what to say. She was a grown-up, too, but around Sabine and Isaac, she still felt like a girl.

"No, no, Sabine. Please don't cry." She took her friend's hand into her own. And in her mind, Casey was telling her how much she loved her, how complicated it was between them, and how she'd be lost without her. There was a debt, and loyalty, too, and so much affection. But Casey said nothing of how she felt inside. The words just swam inside her head. Isaac put his arm around Casey and reached over to kiss his wife's forehead. Watching the kiss, Casey thought, A blessing must feel like that.

4 | PRICE

*T*HERE WERE TWENTY-ONE BUSINESS SCHOOL STUDENTS in her summer intern class at Kearn Davis, and Casey had a lot to prove. Rumor had it that only sixteen of them would get permanent offers. Hugh Underhill would neither confirm nor deny this (as he was unwilling to ask his buddy Charlie Seedham, who served as Casey's summer boss), but thought that holding an eight-week beauty contest was hilarious and told her so. But Walter Chin, who had joined them for drinks after Casey's first week at work, assured her, "Oh, Casey, you'll make the cut." Regardless, when assignments were passed out, Casey completed whatever was given, then immediately raised her hand for more. Thankfully, Sabine had let her take a leave of absence for the summer, and for the past two weeks, since she'd started her internship, Casey had toiled both weekends at Kearn Davis on the sixth floor, where Jay Currie and Ted Kim had once worked. Her desk was only four desks down from where Jay used to sit when he was an associate.

As to have been expected, her hours were unreasonable, but Unu was trying to be as supportive as possible. On Saturday morning, he made coffee for her before she went to the office.

"I miss seeing you around here, kiddo." Unu handed her a mug of black coffee and sat beside her.

"Oh, baby, I miss you, too," Casey said, and she reached over and kissed him. "How are you?" she asked, feeling as if it had been a long time since she'd carefully thought about him. The frenetic summer program was packed with a wide variety of assignments and after-hours mixers. The first two weeks had zoomed by, leaving her breathless.

"Hey, you know what? I'm going to finish making that book on transportation today for Karyn, so I'll sneak out early and take to-morrow off. If I drop off the assignment on her chair when she's out and hide in the bathroom stall for a bit, I might not get weekend duty." Casey raised her eyebrows and exhaled. "I can't keep up this pace, and besides, I want to go to church on Sunday. Maybe we can have dinner tonight? Even go out. I got paid...." Casey hesitated, not wanting him to feel bad about spending money. He hadn't found work yet.

"Go away with me," he said. "Tonight."

"What?" She smiled in her confusion.

"To Foxwoods. You've never been there. We'll get comped a room, and I'll teach you how to play blackjack. Pack an overnight bag now, and I'll keep it in the car, and we'll drive from your office. It'll be fun. And baby, I want to see you more." Unu looked at her thoughtfully. "I think we need a date." He moved closer and put his hands inside her bathrobe. He put his mouth on her neck, and Casey closed her eyes.

"I have to get to—"

"Shhhh," he whispered.

Joseph McReed stood by the barbershop on Lexington Avenue, shifting his weight between his feet, his hands resting on the alumi-num walker. His bus came, but he let it pass. It was a breezy June morning, and the wind caught the wisps of his white hair and blew it about his face pleasantly. Not that he expected many customers in his bookshop on a Saturday in the summer months, but he pre-ferred to be there rather than at home by himself. He was certain that he would see her today, so when Casey walked briskly toward him a few moments later, he didn't regret his decision to wait.

"You did come. How are you?"

"Were you waiting?" she asked, thinking that it would be lovely to be on a bus with him even for a little while. She looked forward to seeing him on Saturday mornings.

"Not long," he said cheerfully. "How are you, dear?"

"I'm fine. This job is tough, though. I just have to nail that offer."

"I guess you do," he said, smiling. "I brought you something." He lifted up a hatbox. Casey hadn't noticed that he'd been carrying it with the hand that still leaned on the walker.

"Did you bring me a hat? One of Hazel's?"

"Yes, I had to. It's insufferable watching you wear these business-lady clothes. I've no taste for them," he said, laughing. "I don't think you'll ever wear this hat to work, but I did promise to bring you one of Hazel's hats. There are so many of them in the house."

"Thank you. It's so kind of you." Casey felt intensely curious about what might be in the black hatbox, having seen marvelous old hats at FIT that her teachers had brought in as examples.

"This one she bought in London." On the side of the round box, "Lock & Co. Hatters. St. James Street. London" was printed in old-fashioned type.

"May I?" She pointed at the box.

"Of course, you goose."

Casey lifted the lid, and in it was a dove gray hat, like a top hat that a man might have worn to the opera at the turn of the century, but with a shorter crown. The band was a charcoal color. "Oh my. This is the most amazing—amazing thing." Casey held it forth with both hands in wonder. It was a thing of great beauty in its craftsmanship and design.

"I think she wore it only once. It might be something a person wears for riding. My brother-in-law, John, thought it resembled a bridegroom's wedding hat. I'm not sure. But Hazel loved this hat. She always had it out on a stand so she could see it. You know, it was the most costly hat she ever bought, too." Joseph closed his eyes briefly at the memory of his wife in that hat. How pretty she had looked, how full of personality. She had been so girlishly proud to own a hat from the most famous hatmaker in England.

Carefully, Casey put it on her head. She looked at Joseph shyly, awaiting judgment. It was remarkable in its good fit. Head sizes were curious things and difficult to predict.

"Marvelous," Joseph said. "Hazel would have wanted a girl just like you to wear it. I always wish we had girls in the family, there being so many of those hats, but..." He smiled sadly. "I want you to have this. I wish you could have all of them. But I don't know how you'd store them all—"

"Oh, thank you, Joseph. I love it. So much. It's…it's the most wonderful present." Casey hugged the bookstore owner, reaching over his walker, and he hugged her back. His frail body felt small to her, and she wanted to protect him.

The bus came soon after, and they boarded it. Joseph got off first at his stop, and Casey remained until she got to midtown, but she wore the hat on the bus for the rest of the trip, feeling like a queen. As the bus approached her office building, she packed up the hat in its box. Once in the office, she hid the gift beneath her desk.

At the end of the day, Unu came not ten minutes after she phoned him. The old Volvo station wagon whirred as it came to a stop in front of her office building. He was always on time, and it meant a great deal to Casey, who was not very good at waiting. Her overnight bag was in the trunk, and the drive there took less than two hours.

One of the managers, Randy, was a friend of Unu's from back home. He gave them meal vouchers and handed her some tokens for slot machines.

The complimentary suite was enormous but unattractive. There was a gigantic Jacuzzi tub in the bathroom as well as a shower. "I want to take a bath," she said, her eyes brightening at the thought of a long soak. She dashed to her bag to find her toiletries. The hotel shampoo and soap weren't nearly as nice as the things at the Carlyle Hotel. The memory of staying there the night she'd found Jay screwing those girls made her feel funny. It had been four years ago to the month. She hadn't shared a hotel room with anyone but Jay before.

Casey pulled a towel off the rack and looked behind the door for a bathrobe. The rack fell off the door with a crash.

"Leave it," he said. "You silly girl. You don't come to a casino to take a bath. You can take one before going to bed. Let's go eat. I'm starving," he said.

The quantity of food at the buffet was obscene: industrial blocks of cheese, punch bowls full of pasta, platters of red meats and cutlets, horn-of-plenty baskets overflowing with breads and pastries. There was a whole wall dedicated to desserts. The diners piled food on their plates and tucked in quickly. Casey was very tired. She was happy to see Unu as excited as a boy, but she was desperate to go upstairs and rest.

"Blackjack, Casey," he said after their coffee and pie. "Blackjack." He shifted his shoulders comically.

Casey smiled at him and nodded, but she was thinking about Hazel McReed's hat, which she'd left in the trunk of the car. The color and shape had made her curious about Hazel.

Unu took care of the check with the meal vouchers and left a twenty-dollar tip. He was raring to go play cards. For him, the casino must have been the way walking through Bayard Toll was for her, she thought—the stimulation, the temptations, its diverting effects. In life there were so many things you couldn't afford, yet you couldn't bear to go through it without some hope, and you had to at least visit your wishes periodically. For her, she craved beauty and images of another life, and for Unu, he must've fallen under the allure of chance.

The smoking floor was where the better players hung out, Unu explained. But even for a girl with a near two-pack habit, her eyes watered and her throat constricted. Seeing Unu get so excited here disturbed her a little. His physical appearance was markedly different from that of everyone else there—he was tall, youthful, and clean looking. There was no other way to describe him. His skin was so clear, his brown eyes bright with good sleep, and he still wore these prep-school clothes—not much different from the things he'd worn as a boy in private school. All he needed was a blue blazer, and he'd become the nice fraternity brother he'd been at Dartmouth. This was Casey's first time at a casino, and naively, she'd expected something glamorous, like in a gangster movie; instead, the floor was crowded with the beaten faces of paunchy old men, drawn women with marionette lines edging their mouths. There was an obvious sadness about the people there, and if she weren't with her boyfriend, she would've turned around and walked away.

Blackjack sounded like a simple enough game—the object was to accumulate cards with point totals near twenty-one or twenty-one itself. You were bust if you went over twenty-one. Face cards were worth ten points, and aces were worth either one or eleven points. But soon enough, Casey saw there were greater complexities and jargon that would take some schooling, and she was neither alert enough nor sufficiently interested to follow what Unu was teaching.

"Let's play a little," Unu said, and Casey followed along.

The waits were long at the two-dollar tables and nearly empty at the fifty-dollar-minimum tables. Finally, they found a spot at the ten-dollar table. Casey played exactly two hands and lost forty dollars. Unu took her seat.

His change was immediate. He became extremely quiet, smiling at the female dealer only when he wanted a card, and when he did, he'd tap his card once lightly with his index finger. Mostly he appeared to be studying the dealer's quick hand movements. Casey didn't know if he was counting cards—couldn't fathom remembering the sequence and numbers of cards dealt within six decks of cards. She was taken by the grace of the dealer's hands—how she drew the cards from the shoe, the way she swept them up in a single motion when the game was over. The dealer wore two rings on each finger and wore clear polish on her well-tapered fingernails. Unu was winning here and there, but mesmerized by the dealer's dexterity, Casey didn't realize until Unu got up from his seat that he'd been steadily winning over half a dozen hands. He had begun with five hundred dollars and in thirty-two minutes he was ahead by twenty-six hundred dollars.

"What's the matter?" she asked when he stood up, getting ready to go. His pile of chips had multiplied.

"We're going to change tables. I'm feeling my luck return."

Casey didn't believe in luck.

"I think you're my charm," he said, kissing her cheek.

She walked alongside him, feeling nothing like a moll. She was so sleepy that it was hard for her to keep her eyes open, and the smoke in the room had thickened like a gray soup. She had no desire to smoke at all.

At the fifty-dollar table, Unu won again. There were only two men seated there beside him. They had a male dealer with slicked-back hair and an earring. The three players, all experienced, beat the house repeatedly. In fifty-two minutes, Unu was ahead by nine thousand dollars. Watching him win was vexing for Casey, because the colder he grew, the better he played. He displayed signs of neither confidence nor happiness. He was someone else entirely. It had been that way the first time she'd seen Jay Currie play tennis, where he went from being the affable literary boy to a cutthroat athlete. Casey couldn't help being pleased to see him win, but she felt afraid to touch him or to say anything because he was so eerily calm, and she didn't want to disturb his concentration. She was very tired of standing.

When the hand was over and he had won another seven hundred dollars, she tapped his shoulder. "Baby, can we go now? I'm very sleepy."

Unu turned around and faced her. "Open your purse, please," he said, and Casey did as he asked. He put aside ten fifty-dollar chips and poured the rest into her purse. "Can you take these up for me?" he asked. "Let me play just a little longer." For the first time since they'd walked onto the floor of the casino, his eyes betrayed a flicker of worry.

Casey looked at him earnestly, not knowing what would be good for him. "I'll go upstairs and take a bath. You play and I'll wait up. Okay?"

"Yes," he said. "I'll be up very soon."

When Casey woke up the next morning, it was eight-thirty. Unu was lying beside her, dressed in the clothes he'd worn the night before. On the bedside table, there was a large pile of fifty-dollar and hundred-dollar chips. She moved closer to look at him, but the smell of cigarettes in his hair and clothing repelled her. His eyelids quivered ever so slightly, and she wondered what he was dreaming of. Casey got out of bed and pulled the bedspread over his body.

Church services would begin in half an hour. There was no way they'd make it back to the city. Lately, Casey hated missing church. She blamed herself, for it hadn't occurred to her to ask for a wake-up call, which was something she normally did when she traveled for work. But the casino didn't feel like a hotel. This place was geared to make sure you stayed out of your room, and in the morning light, the room appeared even less attractive than when she'd first walked in. It was free, she reminded herself, and obviously Unu had had a good night, and she'd slept a lot. Casey showered, got dressed, and made coffee in the room.

When she checked her overnight bag, she saw that she'd forgotten to bring her Bible and notebook. She felt like kicking something. It had been such a long time since she'd gone away that she didn't realize how routinized it had become for her to read her chapter, to write down her daily verse. She might forget about God for the whole day, and often did, but it had become part of her morning rituals, like her shower, coffee, and teeth brushing. And because she was missing church, too, she felt out of sorts.

There was no newspaper outside the door, either. Her fancy travel style with Kearn Davis had spoiled her for perfectly good and free hotel rooms, and Casey had to laugh at herself. When she'd come out of the shower, the towels had felt scratchy compared with what she used at home and at the five-star lodgings she'd stayed at for work. It was absurd for her to have these princess expectations with a pauper's pocketbook. She drank her coffee from a Styrofoam cup and wondered what was the point of rising in the world if the height was so insecure. Her mother and father had never even stayed at a hotel.

Unu was sleeping soundly. And why did it bother her so much to miss church and her Bible reading? Surely she didn't follow most of the Christian precepts: She was sleeping with a man whom she couldn't marry even if she wanted to; she couldn't stand her parents and had minimal contact with them; she still felt allergic to most Christians and do-gooders; and she wasn't at all sorry about any of this. The Bible was clear: If you believed, you were to turn away from your wickedness. Casey had scarcely shifted. Yet in her resolute irritation and unimproved state, she was looking more for God, if that made any sense at all. She hoped for a clue as to what to do next.

Unu's eyeglasses rested precariously on the nightstand next to the heap of chips. Casey walked toward the table, curious as to how much he'd won. She still had the eight thousand–plus dollars' worth of chips in her purse. There was nearly double that on the nightstand. Was that normal for him to win so much in a night's playing? Who was this man sleeping on the bed so innocently? Casey picked up a hundred-dollar chip. The black chip with gold numbers felt solid in her hand. It must have been something to have this kind of payout. Was it intuition, strategy, or gut feelings? Was it math skills in tandem with good memory? How would he ever walk away from this life? she wondered. There was something sexy about what he could do, but she had seen him lose big, too. This life was too erratic to admire, and Casey recognized that she craved steadiness in a person she loved. He was so different from Jay, whom she had come to love like a relative, and though Unu was the Korean one, he did not feel familiar to her. And she was different now, too. She put down the chip and opened the top drawer of the nightstand, fishing around for hotel stationery. This would be a good time to write Virginia.

There was no stationery. However, there was a copy of a Gideon Bible. Casey sat down to read her chapter in Paul's First Letter to the Corinthians and scribbled down her verse on the memo pad by the phone: "Each one should remain in the situation which he was in when God called him." In that chapter, Paul was talking about what kind of life you had when God called you to have faith and how you should respect it in all its complexities. To be honest, Casey wasn't crazy about the apostle Paul. He was difficult and arrogant, and she didn't think he liked women. There were many things about the Bible and God that confused and irritated her, but Casey couldn't dismiss this faith bizarrely growing inside her like a gangly tree sprouting from a concrete pavement. She often thought about her college professor Willyum Butler and wished she could talk to him, but he was dead. Death. That was upsetting, too.

"Good morning," Unu said, squinting at her. He fumbled around and found his glasses.

"We missed church," she said, disappointed. But she didn't feel angry anymore. "Do you think we can go back to the city now?" She smiled at him. "After you cash in your chips, that is?"

"I'm sorry about last night," he said. "I was doing well, and I wanted to make back the rent."

"The rent?" Casey tried not to look worried.

"I was behind."

"I have my paycheck," Casey said. She hadn't known about the rent. *But how much were you behind?* she wanted to ask him. "You can have whatever I have. I live there, too."

"You gotta pay your debts with it, baby. That was the deal," he said. "Besides, I made eighteen thousand dollars last night. Not including what you took up in your purse."

"Do you win that much...often?" Casey asked. It was more money than she could imagine. It was almost tuition for school.

"It's the most I have ever won. In my life. And I've never needed it more. Now, the problem is cashing it in and walking out."

"Will there be a problem?" She didn't know if he meant that the casino wouldn't let him.

Unu shook his head, as if he were telling himself no. "I'm not going to return to the tables today," he said. "Hey, let's go eat breakfast, then I'll drive you back."

Along the highway, he apologized again about not returning the night before, and Casey told him to forget it. It was really okay, especially seeing him more lighthearted.

"I feel a little bad that we stayed for free, ate for free, and you won all that money."

"Believe me, I've paid my dues," he said, and coughed a little.

Casey nodded, thinking that was probably right.

"Do you have a cigarette?" he asked.

"No," she said after checking her bag.

"Check the glove compartment."

Casey popped it open. There were two packs of Camels and a green sheet of paper. "What's this?" She glanced at it.

Unu was shifting to the left lane and couldn't look her way.

The green paper was a schedule for Gamblers Anonymous. The Wednesday smoking meeting near Fourteenth Street was circled.

"Have you gone?"

"Oh, that." Unu noticed the schedule in her hand, then turned to look at the road. His hair was still wet from the shower, and his sunglasses shielded the discomfort in his eyes. "I went. Once."

"And?"

"Cigarette, please," he said, and Casey lit one for him. "Radio, please."

Casey turned it on, and a Hall and Oates song came on: "Private Eyes."

Unu began to bob his head, his lips pursed, as if he were getting into the music.

"I saw them in concert," he said. "At Foxwoods. Randy, that guy you know from yesterday, gave me a ticket. They opened for Carly Simon."

"I love Carly Simon."

"I didn't know that," he said, smiling. There was so much he didn't know about her. They had never discussed music, for instance.

"There's more room in a broken heart..." she sang.

Unu tapped his chest with his left hand. "Well, don't break mine, baby. There's a warehouse in here already."

Casey folded the schedule and returned it to the glove compartment.

For the remainder of the ride, they talked of where to go for dinner to celebrate his winnings. Casey tried to be enthusiastic about the money but found it difficult. She had grown up without money, and it hadn't occurred to her how she could have it exactly, but gambling felt like a dishonest way to acquire it. She could argue to herself that it wasn't stealing, and clearly it was legal, but the whole thing made her feel uncomfortable. Perhaps it was seeing the faces of the elderly men in gabardine slacks, the fabric shiny in the seat and knees, pulling down the levers of the slot machines, their bold eyes full of cherries. Unu had said to her earlier when he was explaining blackjack, "You can beat the house, and you should beat the house." That made it sound as if you were taking money from a faceless company, but walking through that smoking floor had made Casey see that the house was filled with men and women who were bored, wistful, and full of pipe dreams. It was their foolish money that had built and furnished that edifice.

Unu suggested going to Thirty-second Street for dinner that night. *Kalbi* and *naengmyun*. The works, he said—a real feast. Casey said why not. She turned up the radio and tried to enjoy Unu's happiness.

5 | BLOCK

*C*HARLES HONG DIDN'T HAVE TO SAY ANYTHING. The choir sensed that they were far from good despite the increase in the number of practice hours from four to six. It was the way that the choir director couldn't smile, his lips thinning from exhaustion, and how he'd ask them to repeat the unsatisfactory bars, unwilling to make eye contact nearly. There was a conscious restraint on his part from expressing his unhappiness with their performance, but Charles was more transparent than he thought. After Wednesday evening rehearsals, the men went to eat barbecue and the older women and the ones without young children rushed to New China Hut for *jajangmyun*. At the late dinners, the choir members discussed the director and their failure to be better.

In a curious way, his refusal to affirm any improvement—for there had been some modest gain in his two-and-a-half-month tenure—only fueled their desire to work harder. Their persistence may have originated from their complicated Korean hearts. Also, they were impressed by his intense efforts with no expectation of a larger salary. The chair of the church finance committee, Elder Lee, also a baritone in the men's choir and the owner of six beauty supply shops, signed the choir director's small paychecks himself. If there was no money to be made, then surely, Elder Lee reasoned, this was a man of immense talents who served the Lord alone and not mammon. The choir director of their little Woodside church had a doctorate in music and graduated from Juilliard! Yes, they chided themselves: They must labor to please the new choir director. At the close of these midweek meals, it was generally agreed that in a year or two, under Professor Hong's direction, they would be a superior choir, worthy of touring their sister churches in New Jersey and Pennsylvania.

What stirred in Leah's heart was pride whenever the women in the choir spoke of Professor Hong with reverence. She never said anything in these discussions, despite Kyung-ah's occasional prodding at the professor's favorite soloist, and none of them knew that she'd been to his house twice accompanied by Elder Shim when the choir director had suffered from chicken pox: once when Elder Shim had to leave her to go to the hospital and another time shortly thereafter to bring him groceries. At the store, while she hemmed trousers or sewed loose buttons on shirtsleeves, Leah recalled the afternoon spent alone at his house with vividness. Bits of the day would turn up in her private thoughts: The choir director kept only two pots and one frying pan in his many kitchen cabinets, his socks were navy blue wool or white cotton, his Baekyang undershirts had a V-neck, and he read mostly American newspapers and magazines as well as the *Hankook Ilbo*. In moments of vanity, she wondered if he'd kept his shoes ordered as she had arranged them in his closet, or had he cast them aside in his unused bedroom fireplace as before?

The soloists, both male and female, concurred that Professor Hong's extra work with them after practice had changed their voices for the better. He was a demanding but brilliant voice coach, and the soloists looked forward to their sessions with him. Leah was no different.

Yet she couldn't look at him during practice when Kyung-ah was there, because her blushing became pronounced. To avoid this, whenever he faced her direction, Leah studied her score, making check marks on the margins with a pencil.

On the first Wednesday rehearsal of June, Charles asked Leah to stay behind to practice for Sunday's solo. He dismissed everyone at nine o'clock instead of nine-thirty, but no one was upset by this. The choir members grabbed their light jackets for the cool, springlike evening; they were impatient for their dinner.

Leah rose from her assigned seat and moved to the front of the room. This was what Professor Hong wanted soloists to do. She sat quietly in the first row, awaiting his instruction. She watched the young accompanist pack up her things to go. She had two daughters, too.

Charles waved politely at the accompanist, who bowed on her way out. At the piano, he began to play the first few bars, then stopped to scratch the nape of his neck.

"Damn," he muttered. He began to play again, then stopped abruptly again, shaking his head rapidly like a dog stepping out of a bath.

"Is everything all right?" she asked.

"Yes," he answered, slightly astonished to find her sitting there, as if he had forgotten whom he'd asked to stay behind. "It's still so damn itchy." He rifled through his black knapsack to pull out a tube of liniment that the pharmacist had recommended. He rubbed some on his back but couldn't reach between the shoulder blades. "Goddamn it."

Leah remained seated, wanting to help him but not knowing what to do. She lifted her hand slightly, as if she were reaching toward him, then pulled it back in hesitation.

Charles scratched his neck and back. He trembled as if he were cold.

"Does the cream help?"

"The relief lasts for a little while." He tucked the tube away and searched the bag again. The roll of LifeSavers he'd bought at the newspaper kiosk was nowhere to be found. "Damn, damn, damn."

Leah made a face, feeling sorry for the man. The itching must have been unbearable, and he'd had to control himself during the long rehearsal.

"Would it be better if I came back later?" Perhaps he needed a moment. He had been working without a break.

"No, no. I'm just pissed off because I can't find the candy." Charles laughed then, because it sounded silly.

"I have some cough drops." Leah handed him an economy-size bag of Halls that she kept in her purse.

Charles unwrapped one and put it in his mouth right away. From her seat, she could hear the grumbling in his stomach. "Professor Hong, did...did you eat today?" Having been to his home, she knew he didn't pay attention to things like food.

Charles stared blankly at the back wall with its row of metal wardrobes holding choir gowns. Come to think of it, he hadn't eaten since breakfast. During the day, he'd been so absorbed in his song cycle that he'd forgotten to eat. The song cycle, commissioned by the Lysander Quartet in Boston, was due in two months and would have its world premiere at Berklee College in September. He'd almost been late for rehearsal today because his writing had been going well.

From his lost expression, she realized that he hadn't eaten all day.

"I'll eat after this." Charles faced the hymn music.

"If you want, I can come early on Sunday morning, and you can go have dinner now. You must be starving." She wished she had something else in her purse beside the bag of blue Halls. The grumbling in his stomach grew louder.

"Did you eat dinner?" Charles asked. Suddenly he was ravenous.

Leah shook her head no. For lunch, she'd eaten a navel orange. She rarely ate before practice because she was so nervous. Even now she was nervous just to be sitting in front of him. But she didn't worry about her own hunger. "You have to eat. You're getting over being sick. You must take refreshment." She was talking to him like a child, like one of her brothers, but he didn't seem to mind.

"Ever since I was a boy, I'd forget to eat when I was concentrating on something." When his mother was alive, that was always the first question she'd ask him. "Moon-su *ya*, did you eat today?" Even when he lived in Germany and she spoke to him on the phone, she'd ask him the same thing. It drove his brothers crazy how she'd ship special foods to him from Korea like toasted laver, *custera*, and dried squid from the best shops in Seoul. Up till her death, his mother had worried that he didn't eat enough. The thought of his mother made him feel a kind of ache.

"I am really hungry," he said, surprising himself in the admission. "Is there a place around here where I could buy a sandwich? I could run out, and you could wait for me."

There was no place that was open this late. You'd need a car to get to the nearest diner.

"There's a restaurant about five minutes' drive from here. I could go and get you a sandwich if you want to wait."

"Let's go, then. We can both get something to eat." Charles picked up his bag and sweater.

Leah swallowed. How could she do that? It would be preferable to lend him her car, she reasoned. They could not go to a restaurant together.

"Do you have a license?"

"No. I don't know how to drive."

"Oh."

"Never mind," he said. She was nervous about going with him. She was a married woman, and married Korean women didn't do things like go to restaurants with single men. He'd somehow forgotten that her world was still in the nineteenth century. "We'll practice for a bit, then I'll eat something near my house." He bit down on his cough drop and unwrapped another one.

Leah knew that even if they practiced for thirty minutes, he wouldn't be home for another hour and a half.

"I'll take you." She picked up her purse.

"Okay, then," he said, and followed her out the door.

The hostess asked them how many were in their party, and Charles said two.

"Table or booth?" she asked.

"Booth," Charles answered.

Leah sat in the brown leather booth at the Astaire Diner. She'd understood that they'd get the food to go, but now they were sitting alone at a restaurant. How could she explain this to Joseph?

Charles ordered a hamburger deluxe with onion rings and French fries, a large chocolate shake, and an extra order of half-sour pickles. Leah asked for a cheeseburger and a ginger ale. No one took notice of the Korean couple. Framed photographs of Fred and Ginger dancing lined the orange-colored walls. The restaurant was somewhat crowded, but Leah saw no one from church. The food came quickly, and Charles asked Leah questions between bites.

"When did you come to the States?"

"In 1976," she answered. "And you?" She took a small bite of her burger.

"I'd been coming for visits since I was a boy, but I guess I settled here when I first got married in 1980."

Leah nodded, having heard of his two marriages.

"But I've moved around a lot. Went to school in England and

Germany and here, of course." He felt so much better eating again. "I was starving."

Leah laughed, thinking, How could such a smart man be so foolish? Men were like children. This was what the older women in her town had told her when she was a girl, and it was often the case.

"You must have been very busy to forget to eat."

"I'm working on a song cycle right now."

Leah wrinkled her brow. "A song cycle?"

"A group of songs sung together in a sequence. A common theme or a story unifies them." He shrugged. He hadn't spoken to anyone like this in a while. Sometimes he felt that he wasn't fit for company since he spent so much time alone. That was the thing he missed about marriage, always having someone around that you liked enough to do things with, to talk things over with. The problem was that at the end of his marriages, all he had wanted to do was never be home.

"What is your story about?"

"Well, it's based on a set of poems by Shakespeare. Sonnets."

Leah nodded, trying to imagine what that must be like to sit down and read poems and set them to music. That sounded no different to her from magic or alchemy.

"That must be very rewarding," she said.

What could he say to this? She was idealizing his work. He smiled at her, and Leah flushed deeply.

"It's what I do," he said. "I am a better composer than a singer, a better composer than a choir director."

"Oh no. You're a wonderful choir director," Leah said with great feeling.

Charles dismissed this. He poured ketchup on his plate, salted the ketchup, dipped an onion ring in it, then popped it in his mouth. Leah was amused because this was how her younger daughter ate her onion rings, too.

"It keeps me from having too much salt. I have high blood pressure."

"Oh," she said, embarrassed to be caught staring. "You don't look unhealthy." She blushed again.

Charles nodded. "Looks are deceiving." He'd said this in English, and seeing her confusion, he translated it loosely into Korean, and she nodded. It felt intimate to speak to her in Korean, and it reminded him of how it was with the Korean women he'd slept with before he'd married his white wives, who didn't speak it or have any interest in learning. There were so many things you could say in a native language that made the moment immediately private.

"I make you nervous." He smiled and took another bite of his burger.

Leah picked up her soda glass.

"How old are you?" he asked.

"Forty-three," she said.

"Quite young," he said. They were only five years apart.

"I'm a grandmother," Leah said. "My younger daughter just had a boy." She smiled shyly. They were coming to visit soon. "My grandson—"

"Unbelievable."

Leah didn't know what to say. What was unbelievable about her being a grandmother? She cut her burger in half.

"When is your birthday?" he asked. Charles's second wife had a keen interest in numerology. She'd left him on the day generated by her numerology software.

"February."

"Mine too. Valentine's Day."

"But, that's my birthday," Leah said, surprised. "The fourteenth."

"No, our birthday. We'll have to celebrate it together next year."

He was kidding her, of course. That would be impossible, Leah thought. She couldn't help wondering, however, what they would do to celebrate their common birthday. It felt special to share this day. She took another small bite of her meal.

"Maybe that's why my songs are about love." Charles laughed. "Though I must admit, I know nothing really about love. Or how it lasts."

Leah could hardly breathe.

When the waitress slapped down the check, Charles picked it up.

Leah pulled out her wallet.

"Put that away. I never thanked you properly," he said. "For coming by. I felt like dying that day, and when you and the doctor came, I was so . . . grateful. And you cleaned up my house. Then you brought over the milk and fruit. . . ." He smiled at her. "Thank you. I've been meaning to get you two something, but didn't know what exactly."

Leah shook her head slowly. "Oh no. There's no need for that. I...should thank you for being such a good teacher."

There was such an obvious sweetness in this woman, he thought. She also had some infatuation for him. This happened when you were a teacher. Students fell in love with you. He'd had schoolboy crushes, too, but he was a man now, and there was a lot you could do about a woman if you found her attractive. You could chase her and take her home, or if she was unattainable, you could picture her in your mind as a lovely fantasy. He didn't think Leah got crushes often, and he guessed accurately by her discomfort when they were seated that she had never had dinner with a man alone who wasn't her husband. He wanted to say to her, *You're not doing anything wrong.* It seemed a shame that a woman this beautiful with such talents had this quiet life impoverished of feelings and experiences. She was born to be an artist, but she had to contend with a few solos a year at a small Korean church in Queens. Her stage was too small. He would've bet a thousand dollars that she had slept with only her husband. And more likely that she'd never climaxed.

Charles was a modern man, and the lives of Korean women, in his view, were far too narrowly circumscribed. And religion made it even more so. His own sisters-in-law, very nice women and very wealthy in contrast with Leah, were just grown-up girls. They were hardly women in terms of how they spent their time and what they were allowed to do without penalty. The first married woman he'd slept with had enormous sexual passion. In bed, she would occasionally bite him so hard that skin broke. When Charles ended the relationship, she'd attempted suicide twice without explanation to her husband, who'd almost had her committed to an asylum. Charles had to throw all her letters away because they were too violent. The last he heard, she was doing better after she'd had some children.

"Thank you for dinner," Leah said. She was relieved that it was over. The excitement was too much for her.

"You are a beautiful woman," he said thoughtlessly.

Leah hadn't expected this, and Charles saw that her cheeks stained again in that gorgeous peach color of hers from her forehead to her collarbone, and he wondered if her breasts would be rosy as well.

*　　　*　　　*

When she brought up practice, Charles said never mind. Could she come in an hour before service? he asked. "You don't need as much work as the others." So Leah drove him to the subway station. The green lamps at the station were lit. The darkened streets were empty, and the stores nearby were all closed for the night.

"I should drive you home. I didn't realize you didn't have a car."

"Don't be ridiculous. It would take you an hour each way."

Leah couldn't insist because Joseph might still be awake, waiting up for her. Already she was almost late. He would likely be sleeping in front of the television set.

Leah parked in front of the subway station beneath the elevated platform. A truck drove past and cast a moving shadow across Charles's face. He looked like the actor who played the bad son in a soap opera she used to watch on KBS. She shifted the gear to park. Charles reached for the door handle, and Leah bowed her head to say good-bye. He retreated suddenly and kissed her on the lips.

Her shoulders tensed, and she jerked away. This was her first kiss. Her mouth was closed. She had felt the pressure of his lips against her clenched teeth. It wasn't something romantic like she had seen on television. She and Joseph did not kiss. It didn't seem like something a proper Korean woman might do.

Charles cupped her face with his hands. He kissed her again with greater pressure.

Leah's arms and hands froze in shock. Then in a few moments she came to, as if she were emerging from a cold bath. She pulled back.

"*Uh-muh,*" she gasped.

Charles smiled at her. "You've never kissed, have you?" It was a little mean of him to ask this, but he didn't think she would mind.

Leah moved her head no.

"Hold still...." Charles leaned in and kissed her again. "Do you feel me?" His eyes looked directly into hers.

She'd felt the force of his lips. Was that what he meant? This was absolutely wrong, she thought. "Professor Hong, I have to go home," she said. Tears formed in the corners of her eyes.

"Don't call me that," he said. "I'm Charles. I'm Moon-su." It had been a long time since anyone had called him that.

Leah opened her mouth a bit, but no words would come.

"Relax your face. I won't hurt you." He kissed her and put his tongue in her mouth, and Leah coughed.

"I...I...have to go home now," she said. She was crying.

"I think you are so beautiful." He pushed away the white hair from her face. "Like a goddamn angel," he said in English.

There was no one in the street. It wasn't past ten o'clock, but the streets were bare. The yellow streetlights flickered above them. Charles was the most handsome man she had ever known. He was telling her that he thought she was beautiful. If she weren't married, she would have let him keep kissing her. But what she and her husband did on Friday nights was something that only married people did. Only sexual relations between a husband and wife were sanctioned by God. Leah did not think much about sex, except as something she should do to help her husband, but it crossed her mind that it might be different with Charles. The thoughts filled her with shame. Adultery could be committed in sheer thought alone— that much she knew. The great King David in the Old Testament had killed his trusted friend Uriah when Uriah's wife, Bathsheba, became pregnant with David's child. David, the Lord's anointed shepherd king, had fallen prey to lust. He had murdered his friend to cover his sin. At this moment, what Leah felt was a kind of desire, and the feeling itself was strange. The professor wanted her, too.

Charles stroked her hair, and Leah didn't want that gentleness to stop. When was the last time anyone had touched her hair?

But he had to stop. Leah didn't know how to make him leave the car. Instead, she asked if she could go home.

"Do you want to come to my house?" he asked her.

"I have to get home," she said again. Was he out of his mind?

Charles got out of the car, opened the driver's door, and took her hand. Leah stepped out of the car. Did he want to drive somewhere? But he had no license, she told herself.

He walked around, opened the backseat door, and motioned her to sit in the backseat.

"Let's sit closer," he said.

Leah bit down on her lower lip, not knowing how to make this stop. It felt like a terrifying dream with interludes of comfort mingled with shame.

Charles kissed her and stroked her back as if he were calming a child.

"Professor Hong...please, no." Her shoulders grew rigid.

He kissed her again, and she submitted to the pressure of his tongue.

He put his arm around her waist and pulled her toward him at first, then gently lowered her on her back. He began to massage her breasts.

"I want to see you," he said, unzipping her dress and unhooking her brassiere.

She shook her head. "Please, no," she murmured. "I have to go home," she cried quietly. "Please."

Charles slipped his hands under her panty hose and pulled off her undergarments. He positioned himself squarely above her and lowered himself. "Leah, oh, Leah. My beautiful Leah...."

Leah shut her eyes tight, unable to say a word. She wept, and her jaw trembled. This was her fault. She should not have gone to the restaurant with him alone. He must have known that she found him attractive. That she was in love with him and thought of him at work. He was a man who had been all over the world and known many women. He must have sensed all this, and she couldn't stop him.

When it was over, her face was wet. Charles dried her tears with his hands.

"There's no need to cry. You can come home with me. I will take care of you," he said. "Everything will be all right. I don't care what people think. And you mustn't, either. You are an artist. I can get money. You could leave your husband. We could move away. Anything is possible. I must have been waiting all my life for you." As he said these things, Charles began to believe they were true. It was possible to imagine a future with Leah. He could imagine a happy life with a person like this. She would make an excellent wife for a composer. They could go to his house right now, and he could keep her there. He would make love to her properly on a bed. He didn't want to wake up alone anymore.

Leah looked at him in horror. What was he saying? She licked her lips because they felt so dry. She wiped her eyes with the backs of her hands. "I have to go home," she whispered. She pulled up her panties and hose and hooked her brassiere. She reached behind her to zip up her dress, and Charles helped her. He kissed her forehead again. He felt so happy.

"You mustn't be upset," he said. "We made love tonight. *Yobo*, when can I see you again?"

"I—I don't know," she said, unable to think.

"Come early on Sunday," he said. "As early as you can. You can call me any time you like." She was the purest thing he had ever touched. He loved her. It made sense that she was frightened, but he believed that she loved him, too.

Leah returned to the driver's seat. Charles stood by the car and stuck his head in the car window to kiss her. At the mouth of the subway station, he waved good-bye.

When Leah got home, Joseph was asleep in bed, and she showered. She soaped her breasts and pubes thoroughly. She wanted to forget what had happened. It would have been a relief if someone shot her dead. When she got into the bed, she lay there and said her prayers. In the backseat while the professor was pushing into her, words had blurred in her head like crazy muffled pleas to God to save her. But in that time, whether it was five minutes or less, she couldn't say for sure, no one had passed by or come for her.

6 | MODEL

*H*ER EYES SHUT, Ella could picture the notes seeping into her body. She wanted to rest her head but feared falling asleep—not because she was bored, but because she felt secure and peaceful sitting here. Ensconced in her dark red seat at Carnegie Hall, she put out of her mind the custody hearings, the letters of character reference required by the court-appointed social worker, and the image of her sharp lawyer, who made her feel naive at best and at worst plain stupid. Ella was also tired. At night, she worried about losing Irene, who'd already started to string words together last month. Her baby's favorite breakfast this week was steamed rice, chicken fingers, and apples—Irene called food "bop-bop" and milk "oo-yew." When she was in bed alone, Ella stared at Ted's old pillow. How could she have missed all the obvious things about Ted? How much did a man change after he married? Was she dumb, or had he concealed his true self? What had she done wrong?

But right now she was on a date, sort of, with David Greene. Since he had broken up with his fiancée less than a month ago, they had gone to dinner twice, seen each other at school, and spoken on the phone almost nightly, but they hadn't done much besides. He held her hand during dinners, and they always hugged good-bye. He asked her to go to the movies and parties, but after work, Ella preferred to fix Irene's dinner and give her baths. She didn't like being out during the week. She'd never brought David to her home. He said he understood. Ella was lousy at saying no, but when it came to Irene, she found it easier to do so. But it was Radu Lupu playing Beethoven, he'd insisted earlier that afternoon. You can't miss this, he'd said, his blue eyes darkening. "Call the sitter, please, Ella. You must hear him play. And these are such good tickets."

They were very fine seats. The pianist played sublimely. She and Ted had rarely gone to concerts. He'd preferred films and fancy restaurants. Ted was particular about food. He rarely frequented a restaurant with a Zagat rating below 22. Did Delia know how to cook?

In the past six years of being with Ted, she had forgotten what she preferred. The music that she was listening to now was unquestionably gorgeous. What upset Ella was that she had paid such careful attention to the things that Ted loved (Kurosawa films, Coltrane, lamb curry with naan but not basmati rice, and Relais & Châteaux hotels) and had submitted to all of his preferences. Was that why he'd left? Did he think she was a mindless pushover? Wasn't that what her lawyer thought of her, too? From the few times Casey had answered Ella's questions about Delia (Ella had masochistically begged Casey for scraps of Delia's biography, and Casey had given her the smallest of portions), her husband's soon-to-be second wife had the features of a pistol, a firecracker, a tinderbox. Explosives came to mind. Ella had failed to be stimulating enough to keep her husband at home. And she had gotten fat. Though she had ultimately lost the weight—every pound of it after Ted moved out. She was as thin as she was in college. There were stretch marks and loose skin across her abdomen, but otherwise she had the body of a slender twenty-five-year-old woman.

The piano music ceased, and the orchestra entered the final movement. Ella had played piano until the eighth grade but had stopped because she didn't like her piano teacher, who used to put his arm around her and cuddle when she played well. He had smelled strongly of cloves and wore an old cardigan with holes on the elbows. Her father had let her quit without explanation, and she'd ended up taking more tennis lessons. Ella had liked playing the piano, and she used to love to play tennis, which Ted didn't like as much as golf or skiing. The thought of not having done these things she'd loved made her feel foolish. And it hadn't done her any good. Her husband had cheated on her, and people found her insipid. Ella felt her tears, and she wiped them away before David could see. It would be too difficult to explain them.

The music was done. The audience rose to their feet to applaud. Ella got up instinctively and clapped as hard as she could. There was a debt owed to a person who gave you beauty and feeling. A few dispersed to the exits, while most clapped thunderously for encores.

After two additional songs, David helped her with her raincoat.

"Dinner?" he suggested. Ella might say yes since Irene was already asleep.

Ella glanced at her watch. She felt terribly alert. "Where do you live, exactly?" she asked. All she knew was that he lived on the Upper West Side.

"Seventy-eighth and West End," he said with a puzzled smile.

"Can I see where you live? Is it an apartment?" Ella fixed David's collar and smoothed her hands over his shoulders. The gesture comforted him. "I mean, would that be all right?"

"Yes, of course," he said. Lately she was difficult to predict. Ella hadn't even wanted to come to the concert tonight. He'd had to cajole a little, ask her to call the sitter to stay later; he'd told her that she needed to make room in her life for the beautiful things. And now she wanted to see his house.

On the street, Ella wondered herself what had made her do that. David tried to hail a taxi, but there were none free. Let's take a train, she said, and they took the 1 train to Seventy-ninth and walked. With David, she was allowed to make a suggestion about how to get to places and where to go. It was liberating, but she felt the added responsibility for his happiness. What happened if he didn't want to do what she wanted? It had yet to happen, but it would eventually. It was easier in life, then, to just go along.

As they walked to the house, he talked about his students at the prison. They wanted to publish their poems but feared their ideas might be stolen. David didn't make fun of them, she noticed. "They shouldn't be so suspicious, but isn't it marvelous in a way that they're proud of their creative ideas?" he asked. "That they think of what they made up as something subjectively and objectively valuable? They believe that their poems are good enough to steal." Ella nodded, thinking this was right. What was valuable in her life? If Ted took Irene away, she'd have nothing.

"Are you all right?" David asked.

"Yes," she said. It was unfair to think only about her divorce all the time. "David, your work is amazing. You're making people believe in themselves. You do that for me, too," she said. "Your friendship means so much to me."

David squeezed her hand. "You mean a lot to me."

The house was an orange brick town house in a style Ella couldn't properly name—an arched entryway, a dark-paneled door resembling a chocolate bar, and a sloping roof. Its facade was attractive and evidenced its good maintenance. When David opened the door, Ella was a little taken aback by what she saw.

The living room was beautiful, with old rugs on the floor, a high wall full of books, and heavy mahogany furniture from his family. Paintings that looked like Wyeths hung on the walls.

"Would you like a drink?" he asked, and she said no. "Hungry?" He offered to order dinner from a pizzeria down the street. "I usually have cereal for dinner or a sandwich."

Ella shook her head no again. "I want to see the rest of the house," she said. "It's lovely."

"Okay." David was famished. Or at least he had been at the concert. Now, all he could think about was how to touch Ella, but he was afraid. Under normal circumstances, not that this had happened to him so many times, but if another woman had asked to come over to his house, he might have said no unless he was ready to sleep with her; but when Ella asked, he didn't think it was because she wanted to have sex. There might have been something else, but he didn't know what exactly. But now that she was here, he wanted to touch her, to be close to her.

"I have a record of his."

"Who?" Ella glanced at the sofa. She'd been brazen enough to ask to see his house but felt that she needed his permission to sit down.

"Radu Lupu," he said. "The pianist. From tonight."

"Where's he from?"

"Romania, I think."

Ella shifted her weight slightly from one foot to the other. Feeling increasingly awkward, she finally sat down.

"I'm glad you're here," he said. "It hadn't occurred to me to invite you—"

"I'm sorry." She interrupted him, feeling even more self-conscious. "It was rude. I think I wanted to know how you lived. What you're like outside of where we usually are. I wanted to see your house. I thought—I don't know what I thought." Ella opened her eyes wide, then closed them for a few moments. "Oh, good grief."

"No, no," he protested, smiling at her. It was a good sign, wasn't it? She wanted to know him better. Ever since his confession the day she'd returned from the lawyer's office, he'd been thinking about how things would be between them. He'd hesitated to bring it up. "You don't understand. I'm so glad you're here. Do you want to listen?" he asked.

"Hmm?"

"The record."

"Oh, sure. Yes. I'd love that."

David put the compact disc in the player. It felt good to have something to keep his hands busy.

"Okay, now I'll give you the rest of the tour," he said after adjusting the volume. They went downstairs, and David showed her the kitchen and dining room on the ground floor. There was a small garden outside that needed tending.

He pointed to the staircase and gestured for her to climb ahead of him. On the second floor, there were two large rooms: a guest room and the other, a kind of music room with a large piano and a cello. Two music stands faced each other as if in conversation. Ella sat on the piano bench and placed her hands on the keys. The song she remembered was "Clair de Lune" by Debussy. It had been a difficult piece for her, requiring a lot of practice. She began to play, stumbling in places, but she kept at it, and even in her awkward playing, she felt moved by its sentiment and loveliness. She remembered having to miss *The Brady Bunch* in order to practice her lessons, and her favorite had been Jan, the middle girl with the straight blond hair. She had wanted five siblings, too. Why hadn't her father remarried? She might have had a family, something beyond the life she had tried so hard to create for her father by herself.

"When did you learn that?" he asked.

"A long time ago. I'm full of surprises today." Ella stopped playing and touched her brow. "If I'd known that I'd be playing for you today, I would have practiced more as a girl."

"You play very well," he said. Ella had more feeling in her piano playing than in her words, he thought. She was more careful with the way she said things.

"No, I'm not good. But you know, I enjoyed that. Maybe I'll try to learn again. Irene and I'll take lessons together."

David sat behind his cello and played something she didn't recognize.

"What is that?"

"Debussy, too. Sonata in D minor," he said. "I only played a little of the beginning."

Ella smiled at him. "I never knew."

"I never told," he said, moving his bow away from the strings dramatically. "Okay, only one more flight, unless you want the attic tour to check out my air-conditioning system. But after, I am ordering a large pizza unless you disagree," he said. "Or we could go out and eat something."

Ella didn't reply but followed him up the stairs.

They stood together on the patch of the third-floor landing, and Ella hesitated from entering the rooms, and he didn't move, either. There were three bedrooms: one was the master—large, but almost empty of furniture except for a full-size bed and a single nightstand piled high with books. Another bedroom had been converted into a study. And the third bedroom was another guest room. In the corner window, there were a dozen jade plants in different-size pots.

"They're all jades," she exclaimed. "I have some, too."

"They all came from the same mother," he said proudly.

Ella studied the plants again. There was so much you learned from visiting a person's house.

"It's such a big house. And you take care of it so well." Her own home was also large. That had been very important to Ted. For two people in Manhattan who worked in schools and earned modest salaries, their luxurious housing made no sense. Her own house was paid for by Ted and her father, but now she knew that David must have had family money, too, or investments.

"Did your fiancée live... here?"

"My ex-fiancée," he corrected her.

"Sorry."

"No. She never lived here. That hadn't occurred to me. I'm a nice Catholic boy."

"Oh? It hadn't occurred to you?" Ella said, smiling.

"I'm nice, but I'm not a priest," he said, clearing his throat. He wanted to kiss her. Ella's mouth looked like a small red fruit.

"No, that's not what I meant," she said, her voice faltering. She'd been talking about cohabitation, and he was talking about sex, but she wasn't really talking about that. Was she? They still hadn't left the stairwell. They were both frightened by the idea of sex, but he was trying to say that he thought of her that way. And she was now thinking of how it would be to have sex with David. Then she remembered the herpes and how she had never told him, and perhaps he might never wish to be with her, and how she would, of course, understand.

"I have herpes," she said. Just like that.

"Pardon?"

"Ted. He gave me herpes when he slept with Delia. He told me recently that she didn't have it, but somehow we both do. And if I slept with you, and I had an outbreak, then you might get it. I read a few books about it since. I found out when I was pregnant with Irene. You wouldn't necessarily get it, but you could, and, and... I'm not saying that you want to sleep with me. But since I am being nothing if not presumptuous today, I might as well just say it, because I may never have the nerve again— Oh God." Ella turned around and walked downstairs.

"Wait. Wait. Come back."

Ella turned around.

"Come back, please. Sit with me."

Ella sat on a step. David sat beside her.

"I do want to sleep with you. I want very much to make love to you."

"Herpes," she said, and when she said it again, she didn't know what he thought, because she couldn't even look at his face when she said it. But hearing it from her own lips made it feel less awful. It didn't sound like the plague, which was how she'd felt when the doctor had told her. Reading the books, having Irene be born fine, and David not looking horrified—it wasn't the end, she realized. It was a disease, but it wasn't as if she were going to die, and if he didn't want to be with her anymore, then she would understand. It wouldn't be love. Didn't you go through anything for love? Maybe no one would ever want her.

"Does it hurt?" he asked.

"Not anymore. The first time, it was uncomfortable, but it didn't hurt. And I don't really have outbreaks anymore. I often forget that I have it. And if I don't have an outbreak, then you can't get it. But if I do get an outbreak, and if we"—Ella paused—"made love then, it's possible."

"So you don't feel any pain because of the herpes?" he asked.

"No. It's like a dormant virus that I can't get rid of." How could she explain that she felt contaminated? "I just feel like...there's something gross about me."

"You mustn't feel that way. I'm sorry." David frowned. "You must know that I don't feel that way about you. I could punch Ted for doing this to you, but I'm glad he did what he ultimately did. I should thank him, really."

Ella laughed.

"Ella, I think it's okay."

"No."

"Yes. Yes. I'll do some research. But if I understand it, it's like a tattoo."

"I never thought about it that way," she said.

"But all the research and facts won't tell me how to feel. How would my feelings change because of this?" he said.

Ella looked at him, not knowing what to say. He was so kind.

"I think you should marry me if you love me," he said.

Ella was surprised by his words. "I do love you," she said. The words came out so quickly, and she wasn't sorry.

"After the divorce is final. And the herpes. If I get it, and if it hurts, you'll have to take care of me." David crossed his arms.

"You're serious."

He nodded. "The marriage thing is serious. You don't really have to be nice to me if I get herpes. I was kidding—"

"You really think it's okay?"

"It's not okay. It's awful for you, and it must seem horribly unfair. But illness is like that, isn't it? You don't ask for it." His mother was the gentlest woman, and her cancer was nothing less than brutal. "But doesn't everyone have unfairness? You've had your fair share of that. But herpes—that doesn't matter to us."

"How?" Ella hadn't expected him to say any of this. "Where did you come from?"

David put his arms around her. "Oh, you sweetheart. You sweetheart."

Feeling the stiffness in her body break, Ella moved closer to his chest.

Ted had not expected the news of his father's death, although it had been long in the coming. His father had hypertension and diabetes and had suffered two strokes. For the past ten years, he'd had chronic kidney problems and dialysis three days a week. He had not been well enough to travel to Ted's Harvard College graduation, his Harvard Business School graduation, or his wedding. His sister had just phoned to tell him the news of their father's death, saying that Mom said it was okay if he couldn't make it to the funeral. His mother hadn't spoken to him since she'd found out that Ted had left Ella and the baby. When Ted tried to reach her, she refused to pick up the call or return his messages.

"I don't think I should go," Delia said after he asked her to come with him. "Baby, I do want to be there for you. But you haven't spoken to her yet, and you might want to be alone when you talk to her."

Ted looked miserable sitting there by the beige cordless phone. His sister had been sobbing hysterically on the call, which had made him only stonier. "Do what you want," he said.

The last time Ted and his mother spoke was after she had called the house in August last year and spoken to Ella before her overdose. The next day, his mother had phoned him at the office (this was something she had never done before) and told him that she wouldn't speak to him again until he worked it out with Ella. At the hospital, after Ella had her stomach pumped, Ted had asked her to take him back, but she had refused. Ella had wanted the divorce. Ted told his mother this, but she still blamed him. His mother said that you can't quit a marriage because you got a better offer. "People and promises are not like jobs," she'd said, then hung up on him. He had tried to phone her a few times, but his mother wouldn't relent, and eventually he had gotten tired of trying. His plan had been to take Irene to see his parents for the Fourth of July. But then his father died on him.

Ted took the large green throw pillow from the chair he was sitting on and put it over his gut. He crossed his arms, the pillow wedged between his arms and his torso. All he could picture was his father's charcoal-colored face, the sad yellow eyes and small mouth. His father had loved him in his gruff, quiet way. Ted had been his favorite. Before Ted went to Phillips Academy, his father had taken him to the airport and given him a small white envelope. "Don't let anybody tell you you're nothing just because you're poor and Oriental. They're wrong, Teddy. You're my son. But, Teddy, don't come back to this stupid place. I'll come to see you. I never want to see you living in Alaska." Ted could almost feel the touch of his father's grayish fingers—scarred from scaling fish, the tip of his right pinkie lopped off from a cannery accident. For all these years, he'd kept the yellowing *bong-tu,* after spending the five twenty-dollar bills, framed on his desk, because his father had written "Teddy" on it in his own hand.

"Baby, do you want me to go?" Delia asked, moving toward him.

Ted wanted her to read his mind. Normally, he would have tried to say something optimistic—to make something difficult sound better than it was. But he didn't have the heart for it today.

Delia rubbed his neck. "Let me go with you. I'd like to meet your family."

She then made the hotel reservations for the two of them, ordered the plane tickets and funeral wreaths, and arranged the car service to the airport. She wanted to make sure that Ted wouldn't have to clutter his mind with these mundane details. Delia was determined to prove that she was a good ally. When he had asked her to marry him, he had said to her, "You and I are the same," and Delia had taken that to mean that they had both grown up poor. But that wasn't it. They were the same because they would survive anything. She wouldn't let him survive this alone.

He drove them in the rental car to his parents' house. From the end of the street, he pointed out the modest house covered in beige aluminum siding, no bigger than what Delia had grown up in with her mother and three brothers. Several cars were parked in the front. Ted slowed the car. Delia thought he looked different, as though he were frightened.

Ted had described his summer jobs at the cannery when he was home from prep school, how he used to do his SAT practice exams during his lunch break while the other guys were feeling up ugly girls in the employee locker room. They both had grown up with nothing, but Ted had climbed out of his hole by studying. Delia had hated school. Her dyslexia was diagnosed late in middle school, but she had always thought that she was just stupid. Her senior year, to graduate, she had slept with some of her teachers. She got a 98 in English without ever having gone to class, although she had let Mr. Shert play with her boobs and rubbed him off in his car behind the Benjamin's Hardware store on Friday afternoons whenever he phoned. He was the only one who'd fooled around with her who thought it was wrong to have intercourse with a student, but everything else was okay. The biology teacher had no qualms at all about anything, including anal intercourse, which remained Delia's least favorite sex act, being the most painful.

She had gotten decent grades in art, gym, and drama on the merits. But for all the other classes, it had been easier to barely pass or to put a grown man's hand inside her blouse or to get on her knees rather than write about why Othello killed the woman he loved, when she had difficulty forming the sentences with her pen. Her high school transcript was uneven, but she graduated and did five semesters of college at St. John's before hooking up with a Kearn Davis trader on a commuter train who encouraged her to apply for a sales assistant post. Delia had no wish to ever sleep with another man besides Ted for the rest of her life.

Ted parked the car and came round to open her door. They left their luggage inside the white Ford Taurus.

Mrs. Kim opened the door.

"You came," she said in Korean. She didn't look happy to see him. "But it's right that you came." She smiled weakly.

How odd it was to be home, Ted thought. To hear his mother's Korean, which sounded so different from Ella's father's dialect. A dozen or so church people sat in the plainly furnished living room. A group of women peeped out at him and Delia from the kitchen. He couldn't see his brother or sister.

Ted bowed in the direction of the seated Koreans, who nodded at him. They bowed back. This was Teddy, the son who'd gone to Harvard, made millions of dollars a year, bought his parents and brother and sister homes. He was married to the beautiful Korean girl whose pictures they'd seen. She was a doctor's daughter who called her mother-in-law every Sunday night even when the son was too busy working. They had a baby daughter who must have been over a year old by now. The guests didn't know what to make of the American woman standing next to him.

Mrs. Kim noticed Delia, too. "*Mahp soh sah!* You brought her to your father's funeral?" She couldn't help shaking her head. The girl looked like someone you'd see in a magazine—bright orange hair, shiny blue eyes, and red lipstick. She wore a tight black turtleneck and black pants. The girl had big breasts and a small waist, with none of Ella's quiet loveliness. Teddy had thrown his life away to be with this sexy *mi-gook* girl. Now all three of her children were dating Americans.

"Do you have rocks for brains?"

Ted thought about turning around and leaving. "Mom," he said plaintively.

"Ella sent that." Mrs. Kim pointed to the enormous arrangement of white roses on the coffee table.

"How did she find out?"

"I speak to her every Sunday. She calls to tell me about Irene. I called her to tell her about Daddy."

Ted nodded. He couldn't imagine any soon-to-be ex-wife going to the trouble.

"I told her to come, but she said it wouldn't be right since I hadn't spoken to you yet. But I want to see Ella and the baby. I'm going to go to New York to see them in August."

Ted nodded. It was worse than he had imagined it would be. He hated Ella all of a sudden. It wasn't her intention, but Ella was perennially competing to be the better child, and there was simply no way to beat her. His father used to talk to her every time she phoned them, and he didn't even like talking on the phone.

"I can't believe you brought her here," Mrs. Kim muttered in disbelief.

Delia smiled at Ted's mother, trying to be brave. She didn't know that Ella hadn't told Mrs. Kim anything about them except that Ted had fallen in love with a woman from work and that the marriage was over.

"You brought her to your daddy's funeral. How could you do such a thing to your daddy?"

Ted exhaled. "Can we talk somewhere else? Is my room empty?"

"Your bags?" Mrs. Kim didn't know where Delia would sleep. There was no way she'd allow a married man and a single woman to sleep together in her home. "Where are your suitcases?"

"They're in the car. We're staying at a hotel."

"Ho-tel?" she said in English. Family didn't stay in hotels. Mrs. Kim looked hard at her son.

"Mom, let's talk upstairs." His Korean was awkward. The inflections didn't match his adult voice, and he found that his words were slipping away. What was the word for divorce?

"A ho-tel?" Mrs. Kim asked again. The hotel was like a slap. "What kind of talk is that?"

Ted's back straightened considerably. He didn't feel like apologizing anymore. They were still standing in the entryway, and Delia stood about two feet away from him. He hadn't introduced her yet. She had stopped trying to smile and was staring at the photographs on the wall. There were many of him and Ella. Delia couldn't stop looking at Ella in her wedding dress. Casey had once said long ago, before she knew anything was up, that Ted's wife resembled Gong Li, the Chinese actress, but Delia thought Ella's features were even finer than hers.

Mrs. Kim saw Delia staring at the wedding photographs. Everyone who visited the house looked at them and told her how kind and beautiful Ella looked. How lucky Teddy was. It was too much, Mrs. Kim thought, to lose her husband and to watch her children divorce. Her daughter, Julie, was divorced, and now Teddy was divorcing such a nice girl. Her oldest, Michael, hadn't married yet, and it didn't seem that he ever would.

Mrs. Kim turned around and walked to the kitchen, which was a few steps away from the foyer. At her distraught expression at the new arrivals, the church women who'd been putting away the tea things in the kitchen nodded among themselves and shuffled away wordlessly to the living room, leaving the three of them alone.

Ted turned to Delia. "I'm sorry about this. She doesn't like to speak English, but she understands everything."

"Don't worry about me, Ted," Delia said. She smiled at Mrs. Kim again.

"This is Delia." Ted looked at his mother. "She's my fiancée. We are going to get married as soon as the divorce is over."

Delia extended her hand. "Hello, Mrs. Kim. I'm so sorry about your husband. I wish we could have met under better circumstances." This was what she had rehearsed by herself on the plane.

Mrs. Kim stared at the young woman's face, trying to learn something about her. She didn't like the girl's sharp chin, the way her jawbones jutted out slightly. The girl had a bad *pal-jah*. How would this fate affect her son? Was the girl the fox who'd stolen from the henhouse? Or was she the hen that her Teddy had stolen? Her son was not so innocent. But they were old enough to know that it was wrong to be together when someone was married and the other person wasn't.

Delia took back her unmet hand. She smiled somberly, focusing on the kitchen objects nearest to her: an old-fashioned toaster, the rice cooker, large empty Mason jars just washed and drying on the sink. The smells here were not unpleasant—pungent chili powder, soy sauce, and garlic. Delia didn't cook much, and her kitchen smelled only of the Pine-Sol that she used to wash down her counters.

The church women who'd left the kitchen abruptly hadn't finished clearing up the leftover food. Mrs. Kim picked up the Saran wrap and covered the cakes and doughnuts that hadn't been touched. No one could eat all these things. It seemed like such a waste to throw away all this expensive food.

Mrs. Kim had her back turned to Ted and Delia. She wanted everyone to leave her house, to leave her alone. All her life, she had been a hardworking woman. For over forty years, she had canned salmon and mackerel at Lowry's alongside her good husband. She had raised three children and had dinner made every night. For over ten years, she had taken her husband for his dialysis three nights a week. On Saturdays, she had cleaned the house, done the grocery shopping and the ironing. On Sundays, she had gone to church and made a meat dinner for her family, and now that her children were grown, she cooked for her grandsons. She had never asked anyone for a dollar or tried to do anyone harm. But something had still gone wrong. Michael, who had a steady job at the post office, was always threatening to quit. Her oldest also couldn't keep a girlfriend for longer than a few months. And Julie, who had married that short high school boyfriend Craig Muller who'd beat her after he drank, had finally gotten rid of him but could barely afford to raise her two sons by herself. Craig was often late with the child support. And now Teddy had cheated on Ella, who was better than a daughter to her, and had left her for this person who was standing in her kitchen. Her only comfort was that her husband wasn't alive to see this. Hadn't he suffered enough?

"You left Ella for that girl? For that girl? You must be crazy," Ted's mother muttered to herself in Korean. "What did Ella do to you?"

"Nothing," Ted said. "We just don't love each other anymore."

"No, Teddy. I know Ella loves you. She's a good girl. She doesn't stop loving you just because you did something bad. Nobody just stops loving. That's the stupidest thing to say."

"No, Mom. She doesn't love me anymore. She wants the divorce."

"She wants the divorce because she knows you don't want to be married. If you wanted to be married, she would work things out."

"Well, I don't want to be married to her anymore. All right?" Ted clenched his fists.

"And what will you do when you don't love this one anymore? Will you get rid of her like bad fish and find someone else? Why do people in America care so much about sex? Love isn't sex," she said.

Ted had never heard his mother ever say the word *sex*. She had to say the word in English. He put his arms behind his back the way he did before making a presentation. He towered over Mrs. Kim, who was not even five feet tall. Ted thought to say something, then refrained. He would let her say these things to him, because he could not explain what had happened with Delia. What he felt for her was stronger than what he had ever felt for another person. Delia was like home to him. Ella was the house on the hill he'd dreamed of buying. But he could never relax in her presence. Also, he'd come to see her niceness and mildness as unattractive. She seemed to have no needs or desires of her own. At a Fly Garden party the spring of his senior year, a psych major had said to him, "The wife you choose will be your personal and social mirror. She is how you see yourself," and he had held on to that through the years. When he met Ella, he felt he had to marry her because she was exactly the image he wanted reflected. She was well educated, well bred, and unimpeachably beautiful. But meeting Delia had changed what he wanted from a wife. Delia was a more accurate reflection, he realized. Ted loved her more honestly. He also didn't want to grow old with someone he wasn't in love with—to have a good-looking life with manners covering their lack of romantic feelings. This was what Ted had reasoned out in the time after he'd left his wife. And last, he could afford the divorce. Excluding stock options, his last bonus was close to three million dollars. His new job had a guaranteed contract with far better terms and a bigger upside if there were more deals. There seemed to be no limit on how much he could earn. All this would have been at best difficult to explain to a close friend in English, but it was impossible to say these things in this kitchen. Here, happiness, romance, and love were frivolous and worth sacrificing. So Ted stood there silently. As it had turned out, love was more important to him than he'd thought. He would let his mother yell all she wanted.

"Now Irene has to grow up without a daddy."

Delia raised her head when she heard the baby's name. She had no idea what they were talking about in Korean, but she could recognize some of the names. Mrs. Kim called Ted's daughter "I-lene."

"I'm going to get joint custody of Irene. She will live with us at least half the time," he said.

"What kind of talk is that? How?"

"I just will."

"No, Teddy."

"Where's Michael and Julie?" Ted looked around for his brother and sister. They should have been here.

"How could you do that? I don't understand what's happened to you."

Delia felt sorry for Ted. She wanted to put her hand on his arm or stroke his back. But his mother wouldn't approve.

"Teddy, that is not nice. That's bad." She said this bit in English.

Ted locked his jaw. He exhaled.

"Come on, babe. We're going to the hotel," he said to Delia.

"How could you do that to Ella?" His mother looked upon him with disgust.

"You're supposed to be on my side," Ted said to her. He took hold of Delia's hand and walked out.

Two hundred people attended the funeral. None of the children gave a eulogy, but they sat with their mother in the front row. Mrs.

Kim wailed inconsolably. She leaned against Michael—her body limp and folded like a partially filled potato sack. Julie sobbed through the length of the service.

The trials were over, the minister said. There was comfort in this. Johnny Kim had suffered—his hard life had been filled with difficult physical labor. The body had broken down, but his soul had been perfected. The Lord loved a faithful and humble servant and would give him a fine room in His mansion. Ted could not cry; he felt as though he weren't really there. He wasn't in Anchorage; the heavily powdered body in the casket was not his father; and he didn't know if there was a soul or heaven—though the ideas appealed to him. It was impossible that his father had died without saying good-bye to him. The back of his head hurt, and he pressed his hands against his temples. Delia rubbed his back.

After the service ended, Michael and Ted stood at the back of the church while Mrs. Kim and Julie had to be seated because they could not remain standing. The guests lined up in single file and gave their respects. Michael spoke a great deal more to the guests than did Ted. Delia occupied Julie's two sons, Eric and Shaun, who were seven and four years old, by drawing pictures of Garfield on the back of the service program.

Back at the house, the guests came to the modest reception but didn't linger. Many of the men and women who'd worked at Lowry's told Michael, Julie, and Ted what a good man their father had been. They spoke of how Johnny Kim would spot you with what he had when you came up short on rent and groceries. Ted felt proud of his father, who had been kind to his friends.

For the entire day, Michael and Julie were careful around Ted, as if they were afraid of him. Ted tried to speak to them about their lives, but Michael said almost nothing, and Julie talked on and on but said nothing interesting or new. They knew about his divorce but didn't ask him anything. They promised to talk on the phone when Ted returned to New York, about what to do with their mother. Julie had offered to move in with the kids, but Mrs. Kim made it plain that she would continue to live alone. In the end, Ted and Delia focused on Shaun and Eric, who were lively and bright children. The younger one was smarter than the older one, Ted thought, but the older one was better looking. He would make sure that they were properly educated. When all the guests finally left, Ted decided to go, too. Their flight was at midnight, and they hadn't checked out of the hotel yet.

He went upstairs to get their coats from his brother's old room, which now housed their mother's sewing machine and a foldout bed. He had shared that room with Michael over twenty years ago. This had been his world—the shit neighborhood, the stick furniture, the backward schools, and the uneducated parents who rarely spoke. His old life made no sense to him anymore, and his father had been right to tell him to never come back.

As he walked downstairs with the coats, he saw the crown of his mother's head as she slowly climbed the steps.

"I'm leaving now," he said.

"Already?" she said.

"I'll phone you from New York. I have a lot to do. The custody hearings and—"

"Don't take the baby away from Ella."

"She's my child, too."

"No. Not as much as she is Ella's. If Ella didn't do anything wrong, then she should get the baby. You have Delia. You can have more babies with her."

"She can't have children."

"Makes sense." Mrs. Kim nodded to herself. She had figured that Delia must be over thirty-five, even though she was young looking.

Ted felt cold and put on his overcoat. His mother had always been such a hard woman and full of self-righteousness. Sometimes, growing up, he had hated her. Then it came to him how Delia was almost never self-righteous. Maybe that had come from making mistakes and being judged herself. Ella hadn't been hard, either. The women he'd loved had been much kinder than his mother. They had been more like his dad.

"You cannot take Irene away from Ella. You've already ruined her life. She has to be a divorced person now. How will she survive the shame of the disgrace?"

"Things are different now."

Mrs. Kim grasped the banister. "Your daddy was always so proud of you. You could never make any mistakes. He always said it was okay that you never came home. Even when he was really, really sick, he said, 'Don't bother Teddy because he is working so hard. Don't bother a boy when he is working hard.' He used to tell everyone he knew that his son went to Harvard College and Harvard Business School. You could have been homeless and living under a bridge, but you had done this thing for your father—go to Harvard. Even all the rich people were impressed when he said his son had gone to Harvard. He was so sick that he couldn't go to your graduation or your wedding. But he didn't want you to know how sick he was, because he couldn't worry you. And when you had your baby and you didn't bring her, even then, oh, your daddy was so sad. Your daddy, your daddy said, 'Teddy must be so busy. It's not easy to make millions of dollars a year. He doesn't even take a vacation. He is working hard to take care of his family. Now he has to work harder. Teddy has to take care of one more person, send her to Harvard, too. Teddy is an important man in America.'" Mrs. Kim looked at him with such cold eyes that Ted grew frightened of her. He thought she hated him. "Your daddy, before he died, when he was at the hospital, your daddy said, 'Teddy is a good boy. Don't be mad at Teddy for not coming to see me. I know Teddy is a good boy. America is not easy, and he is successful here. I am so proud of him.' That's what your daddy said."

Ted stared at his feet. He didn't have his shoes on yet. He couldn't speak, and he was unable or unwilling to defend himself against this wrinkled brown woman, her hair a mop of gray wires. He had come from her body and his father's. He didn't know Irene, but he'd thought that if he shared custody of her, he'd get to know her so much better. He vowed to love her even if she messed up. When Ella was pregnant, after she'd been diagnosed with herpes, he had gone to church every single Sunday morning, and he had prayed for one thing: that Irene would not be harmed by the herpes that he'd somehow given Ella. Until this moment, Ted had forgotten to acknowledge that God had answered his prayers. When he was a high school student, he had asked God to let him get into Harvard and make him rich so he could take care of his parents forever. On that deal, he had made good.

"You cannot take Irene away," his mother said. "You should not hurt Ella any more."

"I'll phone you from New York." Ted turned away and walked past her. Everything he had ever done in his life that might have been good was canceled out by his divorce, by his falling in love with Delia while he was married to Ella, and now by wanting joint custody of Irene. His mother thought he was nothing.

But his mother failed to understand. The lawyer had said that if Ella had full custody, she could move far away with Irene without his consent. No one would ever retain the option to take away his child.

"Your daddy—" Mrs. Kim began to sob again.

Ted froze on his step, and when he turned back to face her, she wasn't there. Mrs. Kim had gone into her room and shut the door. The last door he recalled being shut to him was Ella's—the night she'd found out about the herpes. But as soon as it had been opened to him, and he was let in, he had wanted to get out. He didn't knock on his mother's door.

Downstairs, he helped Delia with her coat. They said good-bye to Michael, Julie, and the boys. By morning, they would be in New York.

7 | SCISSORS

*I*T WAS JUST LIKE VIRGINIA TO SEND HER A LETTER via Federal Express. The cardboard envelope hit her desk on Wednesday afternoon.

"Lost the pregnancy. Am okay. Tossed Gio. Am also okay. Desperate for a diversion, dearest Casey. P-rade! P-rade! P-rade! Am flying in on Friday night to JFK, will go to the reunion on Saturday with you, of course, then on Sunday, promised to visit Lady Eugenie in Newport. Am dying to get off Italian reds and switch to tequila. Please meet me at the house on Saturday morning at 7 a.m. I will drive there, and you can drive back. I miss you so much. Four years, Casey. Baby, we are so old. Remember, you promised me one P-rade! xxxxxxxxxxxxs"

Casey had not forgotten. Their senior year, she had promised Virginia during a reunion, where Casey was working as a bartender for some arthritic class of alumni, that she would go to exactly one P-rade with her in exchange for Virginia keeping her company that evening. Casey had no wish to be present at the annual alumni march with its orange-and-black regalia. But you couldn't welsh on a deal.

Jane Craft was awake at the early hour, fussing about what her daughter, Virginia, was wearing to P-rade.

"Casey Han, don't you think that's a touch indecent?" Jane asked as soon as Casey walked into the apartment. Casey could see the source of complaint in the distance from the open door of the kitchen where Virginia stood. She wore an orange-and-black Pucci bikini top, a low-cut sheer shirt, and a pair of black shorts. She was busy attaching a lengthy tiger's tail on her rear. Virginia was still in terrific shape.

"Aaaaaaaaaaaah!" Virginia squealed at the sight of her friend. She clattered toward Casey in her orange mules and hugged her as tight as she could. "You're here! You're here! You always come through. I knew it! I knew you'd come!" Virginia jumped up and down.

Mrs. Craft couldn't help smiling at her irrepressible daughter. She might have been twenty-seven years old, but she had the exact mannerisms of how she'd been at five. Neither she nor her husband, Fritzy, were like Virginia temperamentally, and for that unmitigated liveliness—as she and her husband aged and their lives grew deadly quiet—Jane Craft was increasingly grateful.

Casey hugged Virginia back. It had been too long. In the past four years, she had turned down Virginia's many invitations to Italy, because of money or school or work, and now she wished she'd gone to see Virginia sooner. It felt so good to be with her friend.

Jane turned to Casey, her vexed tone reflecting more resignation than authority. She had always hoped the even-tempered Korean roommate would have a sobering influence on her fanciful daughter. Today, Casey looked older than Virginia, not physically as much as in her expression. Her eyes appeared weary, and she had lost some weight, making her face more vulnerable, her collarbones more pronounced. Less attractive, Jane thought.

"Casey Han, you must put some sense into our Virginia. She cannot possibly walk around campus this way."

Casey had been put in this spot before.

"Mrs. Craft, may I please have a glass of water?" Casey asked brightly, sounding more sixteen than twenty-six.

"Oh, heavens, yes." Jane Craft went to the other side of the kitchen. "Would you like something to eat?"

"No, no, thank you." Casey scowled at Virginia, feeling like a louse for diverting poor Mrs. Craft.

"Nice work, Han," Virginia mouthed, winking. She finished attaching her tail.

Mrs. Craft gave Casey a glass of ice water, and she drank it. When she was done, she walked over to the sink to put away her empty glass. When she got back, her friend grabbed her hand and pulled her toward the kitchen door.

"Mama Jane"—Virginia kissed her mother on both cheeks—"we're off."

Casey waved at Mrs. Craft, appearing helpless. It was rude to dash off this way, but neither had any interest in staying there much longer.

The twenty-fifth reunion class, the leader of P-rade, looked ridiculous but happy in their orange-and-black plaid button-down shirts and Panama hats. They formed the largest group heading out from FitzRandolph Gate, with the oldest classes marching behind, the younger ones following. Streams of old men passed by the crowds wearing tiger-striped jackets and straw boaters with matching hatbands. There were old men waving happily from golf carts and motorized wheelchairs. The spry ones carried jokey placards on wooden sticks bearing messages like SEEN EVERYTHING. DONE EVERYTHING. REMEMBER NOTHING. Wives and grandchildren marched alongside them. Would she ever be so thrilled to march with her friends across campus? Maybe if you were near ninety and doing well enough to attend this, that was something to be joyous about. Casey was twenty-six years old, but she didn't feel anything close to happiness.

Life seemed difficult and uncertain to her, despite the gleeful crowds and the seventy-two-degree cloudless weather. Besides, she'd never seen herself as the proud alumna type. She'd worn a white shirt and white pants, because for the life of her, she couldn't remember where she'd put her orange beer jacket that had been distributed her senior year. Virginia had lost hers, too. Her friend cheered the locomotive at the older classes, and Casey joined along: "Hip! Hip! Rah! Rah! Rah! Tiger! Tiger! Tiger! Sis! Sis! Sis! Boom! Boom! Boom! Bah! Ninety-three! Ninety-three! Ninety-three!" The thirty-fifth reunion class returned the locomotive.

The past classes were overwhelmingly male and white—the decades were reflected in their speckled foreheads, the deep grooves in their jutting brows, the tender wisps of hair left on their pates. They looked like children, Casey thought, very happy children. How could she begrudge them their good days? Somehow, she and these men were connected by this school. Princeton had educated her at their cost. She owed them something, didn't she? Would she make something of her life to give something back to the school? Wasn't that why Princeton had given her a free ride? They must have thought she'd have something to give back one day. If she got the offer at Kearn Davis and one day became a rich banker, she could send them money the way these people probably did and educate another hard-luck kid like herself. But what would happen if she didn't? Or if she blew through her life without much to show for it? Casey bit her lip. Virginia elbowed her to keep cheering, then returned to swinging her tail. After the fifth reunion class marched, Casey and Virginia joined the class of 1993. There were fewer than fifty who'd come back. It was only their fourth year, and in this crowd, Casey tried to act more spirited.

Poe Field was vast, the grass rubbed off in large muddy patches. A tented podium housed the school officials who announced the final arrival of each class and described its time in history back when. Gradually, the throng disassembled from the march peaceably. Everyone was in good humor. Clumps of alumni stood on the field to catch up. Children played on the side with a large beach ball. The parents didn't chase after the children who were running around, but they watched them carelessly from where they had settled down. When she and Tina were growing up, they'd never attended anything like this with their parents. What would that be like to have parents who'd gone to Princeton? Ivy people stopped Virginia to say hello, and Casey pulled back, feeling shy. But she'd agreed to go to Ivy with Virginia after the field because she didn't feel like seeing anyone from Charter, her eating club. Already, she'd talked to a few of her classmates, and what Casey felt was embarrassment. She should never have come back. Not like this. There was nothing glamorous or interesting to report about her life.

In the flock of the class of 1991, Jay Currie was busy introducing his fiancée, Keiko, to his friends. Seeing the new girl, no one asked about Casey. Most of his friends planned to meet up at the barbecue at Terrace, and Keiko was eager to go. She talked to everyone, holding his hand the entire time. His fiancée was a friendly person, far more so than Casey, who could be outgoing when necessary but was more private than he'd wished. Casey had hated dinners at his eating club and felt neutral at best about most of his close friends at Ivy,

Tiger Inn, and Colonial. He was relieved that his fiancée was a so-cial person. But he couldn't help thinking of Casey today. They had been good together, too, and he wondered what had happened in the end. He had loved two women in his life really: Casey and Keiko. They couldn't have been more different.

Casey used to spend a lot of her money on clothes, but she'd also darn her socks, wash her stockings by hand, and make her own hats. She'd always had a part-time job to earn money. Keiko threw away her panty hose after wearing them once. His mother would have had a stroke if she knew. As it was, his mother was polite to the point of being awkward around Keiko and her parents.

Maybe it didn't matter. Keiko made almost as much money as he did as an associate at an investment bank, and her parents paid for all of her clothes. Mr. Uchida was going to buy them a co-op apart-ment on Fifth Avenue for a wedding present. But Jay had grown up with a single mom providing for two boys. He remembered what it was like to split a small piece of beef among the three of them—his mother claiming that she didn't feel like eating meat. He could see no reason why he and Keiko would ever be poor, but he wondered what it would be like if they had very little. He blamed his anxiety on having read too many novels in college about the reversals of fortune in a man's life after marrying, and he couldn't help wanting to save and invest as much as he could. There were other consider-ations, thankfully: Jay had liked having sex with Casey, and he liked having sex with Keiko. That was a major positive, he thought.

Could you love such different people and marry only one? In his two primary love relationships, he found himself comparing what Casey had with what Keiko didn't. This was unfair. He knew this. The two women also shared common qualities: They were both generous and exceedingly thoughtful about his happiness. How were you to merge all the loves and their good qualities into one person? And how were you to accept that this girl didn't exist at all except on the throne of your imagination?

Then he saw her. Casey was standing about ten feet away in her usual pulled-back stance from Virginia and her Ivy crowd, appearing almost forlorn. She used to be afraid of going to parties by herself. He recalled how she'd have to talk herself into speaking to strang-ers at parties and pretend she was good at being social. Her perfor-mance was sufficiently convincing, so no one thought she was shy or insecure. But when she didn't try, she was viewed as aloof. If they went to a party together, and if she disappeared, he'd find her on the roof of wherever they were and she'd be smoking a cigarette, staring up at the night sky. She never made him leave the parties; instead, she'd wait for him on the roof until he was ready to go, as if she knew he had to be social, but he had to understand that she had to be alone.

She looked pretty and young in her white linen shirt and white jeans. She'd gotten thinner than he'd remembered, and her hair was a little longer. She wore her silver cuffs still, and Jay had to smile. He felt the stirring in his heart, and he had to chide himself for being a romantic fool. Keiko was a wonderful person, he told himself, and far more compatible with the life he wanted. She was not ambivalent about success and living a good life. Also, Keiko wanted him, and Casey had not. Yet the terrible truth was that the girl who broke your heart would always have more power than you liked. But she didn't look happy now, and Jay flattered himself a little by thinking that she was thinking about him, that she was sad because they weren't together. He felt an urge to walk over to her and kiss her. *Casey, I'm here,* he'd say, as though he were picking her up at the roof, *let's go now.* He was full of these irrational feelings for her. But he loved Keiko, too. You could love two people at the same time. It just wasn't practical.

Keiko didn't miss the alteration of her fiancé's face at the sight of the tall Asian woman. She felt a pinch of jealousy, but she reminded herself that he had chosen her after all. Keiko believed in love at first sight; their love, she was convinced, was true. She had fallen for him the moment she'd met him in their organizational behavior class. And two weeks later, they had hooked up after their section mixer. Jay had given her her first orgasm.

"Is that her?"

"Who?" he asked blithely. He smiled at Keiko and kissed her on the lips.

"Casey Han," Keiko said loudly. Jay was charming and occasionally full of it.

Casey turned around at hearing her name. It was him. It was really Jay Currie, and he was standing beside an Asian woman who must have been Keiko Uchida, his fiancée. Her name had been burned into her mind ever since she'd read Virginia's letter. Unlike her, Keiko was petite, maybe five two or less. She had a very pretty face, with large eyes and a small nose. Keiko's features were more delicate than hers, and she had thin limbs and narrow feet. She wore a black shirt dress cinched in the middle by an Hermès belt.

Casey walked over to him, and Jay met her partway.

"Hello there." Casey smiled and kissed his cheek.

"Hi, Casey. Hi." Jay smiled broadly, feeling a little crazy inside. "I'm surprised to see you here."

"Me too." Casey laughed. "I'd made a promise to—" She turned to look for Virginia, who was talking with great enthusiasm to Hank Loehman, a hot boy from Ivy—a senior when they were sophomores. She smiled at her friend's vitality. "It's good to see—"

Jay was happy to see her smile. "This…this is Keiko. My fiancée."

"Yes, I'd heard. Congratulations to you." Casey shook Keiko's hand firmly. She was even prettier up close. Keiko had a lovely white throat. She wore large gray Tahitian pearls in her small ears. "Virginia told me that there was a big party for your engagement. I meant to call, but I didn't know—"

"I moved." He nodded, hoping she'd stay and talk for a bit. He could tell she was nervous in the way her jaw seemed fixed even as her eyes were animated. But he was nervous, too. "I'm at Starling Forster now." He rummaged in his pockets for a business card. "Here. Or you can just send me a Bloomberg."

"That's great. Okay…" She smiled and turned to Keiko. "Congratulations. It's lovely to meet you." She looked like a kind person, and though this was hard to take, she felt happy for Jay. She wanted to believe that he'd be happy in the end.

"I heard wonderful things about you," Keiko said. She stood confidently with her shoulders back. "Why don't you guys catch up? I need to run to the lav—" She smiled and gave Jay and Casey a small wave. She walked away briskly, thinking it would be better if they talked now rather than later.

Jay swallowed. It was like Keiko not to be jealous or appear so. She was impressive to him in this regard. She was almost impossible to rattle, whereas Casey was far more fragile than she seemed. He felt happy suddenly at being with Casey alone in the midst of the crowd. It felt right that they got a chance to talk even for a little while.

"How are you?" Casey was the first to ask. She wanted to ask him a dozen things and hoped he would hold nothing back. Jay had always been more emotional than she was—one of the things she liked best about him. She wanted to ask: *Are you happy with her? Are you happy with your life? Do you miss me? Do you love me still? Did our love matter?* She didn't want him back—it wasn't that at all. But he was still attractive to her. It had been three years since they'd broken up. "You haven't changed. Not even a little."

"Neither have you." She was still sexy as hell to him. They had always had that between them.

Casey took a deep breath into her lungs, and she could smell him—the vetiver of his aftershave. A flood of pictures came into her head. But there had never been an image of them being married, of living together forever. Wasn't that why she'd ultimately said no? And she loved Unu, too, who was likely at Foxwoods right now. Last week, he'd turned down an analyst position at a small asset management company because it would have been a step down, he'd said. She looked carefully at Jay's face, as though she wanted to engrave it, his speckled blue eyes, the high bridge of his nose. He had been her best friend in the world. He had taught her to be more affectionate and open—to smile at strangers. There had been bad moments, but she had loved him more than Virginia or Ella and felt closer to him than to her own sister. No one had been as intimate with her as Jay, and it occurred to her that it had been much easier when they had not seen each other. And as she was thinking these things, Jay was remembering what had crystallized the moment he had decided to ask her to marry him—that they were the kids who'd enlarged their lives beyond their circumstances through education, and for sure, no one would understand the other better. No matter where they were—at a McDonald's or on his friend's yacht sailing Nantucket Sound—everything had been interesting to them, because they were learning about the bigness of the world at the same time. Why weren't they together anymore? Oh yes, he recalled painfully. She had not been able to see their future in some cockamamy vision in her mind. But he had. He had seen them growing older together, fucking their brains out till the very end. But she had not wanted him, and he had refused to be her friend. So there had been this three-year break. And here she was.

"My father died this year," he said. Why had he told her this?

"Oh God. I'm sorry. I'm very sorry to hear that." Casey wanted to hold him, and she touched his forearm.

"He was gay. He was living with his second cousin. They were lovers."

"That's why—"

"Mystery solved."

"Oh, I wish I'd known about his death."

He ignored this.

"That's why he checked out and never—" Jay's voice broke. "Case closed."

Casey held his forearm for a moment longer than she should have. She squeezed it, then let go.

"Anyway..." He sighed. "Crazy, huh?"

"Your mother—gosh, how is she?" Casey smiled at the thought of Mary Ellen.

Jay sniffled and wiped his nose. He looked away for a moment, then smiled at her as if everything were okay.

"She sold her book on ED. It's out. She wanted to let you know, but I told her not to contact you, because—"

Casey nodded. "I'll pick it up."

"Because I couldn't handle it, her asking about you. It was really hard when we—"

"It was hard for me, too, Jay. This is hard now."

Jay crossed his arms. It wasn't the same, he wanted to say, to be dumped like that. It was better to be the one who got to go. He got quiet.

"Keiko seems great."

"Yeah. She's great."

"And she's beautiful."

"On the inside, too."

Casey nodded. "You're lucky, then. Everything worked out for the better."

Jay nodded, unable to speak.

She could see the hurt in his face. "Can I say something that is very selfish?"

"Yes, please."

"I missed you, Jay Currie. You were always a good friend to me. And I'm jealous. But I think you will be much happier with her."

"It was selfish of you to say that. And grandiose." He laughed and looked up at the bright sky.

"I'm going to go now. I promised..." Casey rubbed her arms as if she were cold.

"Ivy?" he asked.

"Yup. Terrace?" she asked.

"Yup."

Jay opened his arms, and Casey hugged him.

"You want to come to the wedding?" he asked.

"No. But thank you. You always had a better nature than me. That hasn't changed."

Casey returned to Virginia, who had noticed them talking. She broke away from the guy, Hank Loehman, she'd been chatting with. He was not that interesting after all. She hugged Casey tight and kissed her on the cheek, and Casey smiled at her. Virginia could do things like that. No one else ever did. She loved you without holding back. Later, Casey would tell her everything, but for now they walked off Poe Field together, arms linked like schoolgirls, heading toward Prospect Avenue.

8 | RETURN

$\mathcal{P}$ERHAPS IT WAS PREMATURE TO SAY, but Casey believed that she hated Karyn Glissam and Larry Chirtle, the senior associates who barraged her with assignments. In the past three weeks, on top of the demands of other senior associates, Karyn and Larry had asked Casey to locate the number of tractors in the southern region of China, make up a spreadsheet comparing that number against the number of tractors in Brazil in 1996, and calculate the GDP relationship among Peru, Ecuador, and Honduras relating to canned fruit exports. She had compiled data on soft drink production in India as well as oil wells in Alaska. She had become their go-to girl, because she got the job done, but unlike the brokers at the Asia sales desk, Karyn and Larry, the investment bankers, never said thank you or please. They never asked how she was doing. She told herself to focus on nailing the offer and that niceties shouldn't matter, but they did. They mattered more to Casey than they should have. Maybe what she felt wasn't hatred really, but contempt.

All twenty-one of the interns were housed in a corridorlike office tracked with parallel rows of rolltop desks, and Casey occupied the third desk in from the windowed wall. On the Thursday morning Casey had a visitor, her desk was trashed with research papers, reference books, government pamphlets of consumer data, and charts of LIBOR and the Fed funds rate. Casey had a book to make up for

Karyn due that afternoon, and she was finishing up her index. She was now checking to see if she had organized the last two sections properly when she heard the rap against her desk.

"Hello there."

It was only Hugh.

"God, this is just appalling how they have all these nice young people locked up this way." Hugh Underhill scrutinized the room, and the other interns smiled at him, not knowing who he was. They goggled at the good-looking man, his arms crossed against his broad chest, his face expressing a mock dismay. He was far too relaxed not to be someone important. The interns had no clue as to who'd factor into their futures, so they had no choice but to always be on their best behavior. "And it's a gorgeous day outside. Shouldn't these children be playing in the sunshine? Instead of…" Hugh picked up a pamphlet on her desk and flipped through the charts, turning them upside down and right side up. He pretended to gag.

"Oh, it's you," Casey said. "Do they let brokers up on six? You know, there are no four-star restaurants here or wine bars." She suppressed a smile.

His eyebrows lifted knowingly, and he raised his hand. She slapped him a high five. They both laughed.

"Hello, darling," he said. His smile was headlights dazzling. Most of the interns were still staring at him, and he smiled at them graciously. "Do go back to your tasks, little ones.

"I need a favor, dear girl," he whispered.

"Yes?" Casey eyed him coldly. "And how may I help you?"

"My, such a suspicious look for such a young girl. Hmm, then again, not that young."

"Is this how you get people to grant you favors? I can't imagine that it's very effective."

"Ah, yes. Casey, I need a fourth."

"Pardon?"

"Crane Partners and Kellner Money Management. I'm taking them for a golf outing in Vermont for one of my idea roundtables, and I need a fourth. Walter has three already in his group, I have two, and Kevin is busy. You work for Kearn Davis, so why not? Everyone likes to see a girl golf. It's an idea roundtable for new initiatives on—"

"A bullshit session?" Casey covered her mouth with her hand.

"Oops, I mean, an idea roundtable?" She propped her chin in her hand, her elbow leaning on the desk. "You call yourself a worker?"

"No, darling, I am a genius. You are a common laborer. I am not a laborer. I run idea roundtables. My clients and I will talk about business while we golf. And it would be so very dear of you to join me in this endeavor in your journey to becoming a businesswoman, or should I say business*person?*" Hugh coughed. "Please, Casey. Shall I get on bended knee? Girls like that sort of thing."

"So do boys." She couldn't resist.

"You naughty girl." Hugh grinned and placed his hand on her shoulder lightly. His thumb rubbed across the sharp bit of bone.

Casey turned back to her index. "When?"

"This weekend."

"This weekend? It's Thursday."

"Please."

"I have to work. I had last Saturday off for the reunion."

"I will ask Charlie for a special dispensation," he said very quietly.

"You must owe Charlie quite a lot already," she whispered back, but no one seemed to be listening as far as she could tell.

"No, not at all." Hugh looked serious, and he scribbled on her legal pad in his flowing script: "He gave you the interview as a favor to me, but he wouldn't have given you the spot unless he thought you were qualified. You had the best transcript in this room. Charlie said so."

"You didn't tell me that before," she wrote back.

"Oh, did I not mention that?" Hugh wrote quickly.

"No," she said, then wrote down, "Withholding bastard."

Hugh laughed. "I like that one. That's new."

By then, Karyn had walked into the interns' office and noticed Casey with a man. She approached Casey's desk.

Casey saw her and tucked away the legal pad under her forearm.

Hugh smiled at Karyn. He didn't know who she was, not that he cared. She was some single woman—out of habit, he'd checked her ring finger.

"This is Hugh Underhill," Casey said to Karyn. "And this is Karyn Glissam," she said to Hugh.

They shook hands.

"Karyn, what a pleasure it is to finally meet you. Charlie has said such nice things about...your work." Hugh's face looked composed, but his eyes were smiling, and Karyn couldn't help noticing how attractive he was.

"Oh, are you a friend of Charlie's?" she asked.

"Yes. Good friends." He and Charlie had grown up together in New Canaan, had dated many of the girls in the same neighborhood. Their parents belonged to the same clubs in town and in Manhattan. They had played poker every other Tuesday night since they were in college. But there was no need for this Karyn woman, whom Charlie had actually never spoken of, to know any of this.

"Oh," Karyn said. The senior associate had already figured out that Casey, the twenty-first summer intern to be given a spot in the twenty-student program, must have had an inside track, because Charlie Seedham, the senior banker in charge of the summer program, was almost pleasant to Casey Han. Charlie was customarily indifferent toward the summer kids. It couldn't have been a sexual thing, Karyn reasoned, because Charlie screwed only blondes, and Casey was not pretty enough to get his attention. But now that she met Hugh, she understood the connection perfectly. But then, what was the relationship between this guy and Casey? she wondered. It didn't look romantic. In fact, Karyn thought he was flirting with her instead—especially the way he looked at her in that bedroom way.

Karyn was ignoring Casey completely. Casey wondered if she should excuse herself so they could be alone. Poor Karyn was falling for Hugh the way virtually every naive woman fell for Hugh. On Wall Street, the women might have been savvy about profits and losses, but when it came to boys, they knew as much as middle school girls. It wasn't just that he was handsome and tall and physically fit. He was incredibly attentive—the way he looked at you was exceptional. His focus was absolute. Casey thought it was despicable how he toyed with women. That kind of attention was addictive, and the need would inevitably grow bottomless if you let yourself get hooked. Casey wanted to punish him sometimes, and consequently, she was far meaner to him than he deserved. Although, oddly enough, he had always been very kind to her. He wasn't a bad person—to say that would be unfair. Hugh was just too charming for his own good, and in a way, Casey thought that was irresponsible.

"Casey here used to work at my desk," Hugh said, having anticipated what Karyn was wondering.

Casey nodded once in assent but didn't want to get into it.

"Oh?" Karyn had lost the power of speech. As usual, she was growing quiet around the attractive man.

"No. You look too young...." He spoke as if he doubted himself. "Are you her direct supervisor?" he asked Karyn, feeling his powers grow.

Karyn smiled. "It's not like that, really."

But it was.

"Casey is helping me on a few projects."

"This one is nearly done. I should have it for you in half an hour or less." Casey kept herself from saying, if Hugh went away, maybe ten minutes. Though it was amusing to watch Karyn act like a crushed-out girl. The truth was that under normal circumstances, Hugh wouldn't give Karyn a second glance for romantic reasons. She was too serious and angry—the wire spectacles, the ash blond curls, the flat-chested runner's build, and the one-inch stacked heels with the Ferragamo bows.

"Was there something else you wanted me to do after the book?" Casey asked.

"No," Karyn said. She wouldn't give Casey another assignment in front of Hugh. "But I think Larry might need some support this weekend."

"This weekend?" Casey asked, glancing at Hugh.

Karyn nodded. A gentle smile appeared on her face.

"That would be a shame," Hugh spoke up. "Our desk really needs Casey this weekend in Vermont for a roundtable. A special request from Walter Chin, my colleague. Oh, he also knows Charlie. We play cards. It's a horrible imposition on Casey, but I didn't realize that summer interns worked during the weekends. I hope you don't have to work weekends, too, Karyn."

"No, not every weekend." Karyn smiled shyly. "Have you worked every weekend?" she asked Casey with concern in her voice.

"I had last Saturday off," Casey replied, recalling P-rade. Jay's business card was still in her wallet. "And I had a Sunday off. Two weeks back? It doesn't matter. I can work this weekend. I don't mind."

"Well, I'll talk to Larry, then," Karyn said. "Why don't you do this...roundtable, then? I didn't realize you'd been working so much."

"Karyn, really, I don't mind. I like to work."

Hugh smiled at Casey. If he could've kicked her under her desk, he would have.

"No, no," Karyn said, her voice rich with sisterly kindness. "I'll talk to Larry."

"You are such a darling. To do that for me. Casey is very lucky to work with you," Hugh said, smiling at her with unbroken concentration. "Thank you very much. I do appreciate it."

Karyn smiled anxiously and checked her bare hands. She touched her hair. "Well, bye, then."

She left them, and out of politeness, Hugh turned to watch her walk out. If Karyn decided to turn around, she'd see that he had been attentive to her completely. This was something women seemed to want even as they professed resentment at being treated like pieces of meat. Why else would they swish their hips when they strolled away? They wanted you to check out their ass.

"You big phony bastard," Casey wrote on her legal pad, then drew a smiley face.

"I am big," he scribbled. "And you, Casey Cat, need a weekend in Vermont. It will be beautiful. And you have the best possible golf clubs. Say yes, dear Casey."

Casey yawned and stretched her arms.

"I'll pick you up at 7 o'clock on Friday night. The clients are meeting us there. We'll be teeing off at 8 A.M. the next morning," he wrote.

"You are such a presumptuous bastard," she wrote.

"Thank you, sweetheart. I would kiss you right now if I could," he wrote.

"Ick," she wrote back. Hugh patted her back and left her office.

On Friday morning, Unu watched Casey finish up her packing for her trip to Vermont. She was running late.

"We met at a golf outing," he said with diffidence.

"Yes, we did." Casey smiled to be pleasant. She unzipped the enormous canvas golf bag used for airplane check-in, and Unu lifted her clubs into the bag for her. She tried to imagine walking into the office carrying her golf clubs.

"You haven't golfed in a while."

"No, I haven't. I hope I won't embarrass myself." She felt awkward going to this without him. He hadn't golfed in a while, either.

"Maybe we can go after my internship ends and before school starts again. We can drive out to Jersey. Or at least hit a bucket at Chelsea Piers. Hey, where did I leave my watch?" She looked around the living room. Her watch was next to her keys by the door. "Oh," she said, noticing where it was, then picked up her handbag. "What time is it, honey? Rats, I don't want to be late."

"Let me get your watch." Unu picked up her golf bag and moved it toward the door. He checked her watch. "It's seven forty-six," he said, then passed it to her.

"Thanks, babe." Casey picked up her garment bag. "Oh, damn. Forgot my toiletries. Where is my head?" She ran toward the bathroom and stuffed things into her cosmetics bag.

At the front door, she checked to see if she had everything with her. The thought of getting away made her feel elated.

"I think I have everything."

Unu said nothing, looking more sober than usual.

"Hey. You okay?" she asked. "You miss these silly boondoggles? I can't believe Hugh calls them idea roundtables. Such a crock—"

"I got rid of my car and my watch yesterday."

"What?" Casey put down her keys.

"Yeah. I had to pay Karl, so I gave him the car and the watch."

"Your bookie? Oh, my God. I didn't know."

"How could you? Just happened last night."

"I'm sorry. Do you need money? I have some money. Here." Casey opened her wallet. She pulled out a hundred and twenty dollars in cash. Her bills were under control ever since she'd been getting these large summer intern paychecks. "Do you need more? I'll give you whatever I have."

Unu pressed her money back into her hand. "No. I don't want this. I'm fine."

"You told me that was the watch your dad got you at graduation."

"It's just a thing."

"Well, yeah, but—"

"Don't be late for work," he said, opening the door.

"Unu?" Casey lingered, trying to think of some encouragement.

"You coming back?" he asked her.

"What do you mean?"

"Nothing," he said. "I'll miss you."

"Me too," she said. This wasn't the man who had made her nervous on their first date. She remembered calling Ella after she'd spent time with him in Miami. He'd seemed like the perfect guy: Korean, nice family, good education, and so sweet. Their first date back in New York was at an Italian restaurant near Hell's Kitchen. She was so anxious during dinner that she couldn't eat her angel-hair pasta with clams. Then he'd asked her, "You one of those girls that never eats on dates?" And she'd said, "Is this a date?" He'd said, "Yes, it's a date. And I am trying to impress you." She had slept with him right away, because there was something so sexy about him, so male. He'd been both unfamiliar and familiar to her. Lately, they hadn't been having much sex. Not zero, but certainly not as much as before. What had surprised her was when he had turned down the most recent offer to be an analyst. So what if it was a step down? Wasn't a job better than no job? And the gambling. What could she say about that? His car and his watch? She knew how much he loved that old Volvo station wagon. This was like watching a building fall into pieces.

"Unu. How can I help?"

"I'm okay. I shouldn't have told you like that."

"Do you not want me to go? This weekend?"

"You have to go, Casey. This guy got you your summer job."

"I know, but you're not—" She couldn't say, not doing well.

"I'm fine, Casey. Have a good time. Call me when you can. I should be home."

"Okay," she said. She kissed him good-bye.

Thanks to Hugh's speeding, the drive up to Vermont took half an hour less than expected. As soon as they reached the hotel in Manchester Village, Casey felt like springing out of the car. She was wired from the Big Gulp Diet Coke she'd been drinking, and she was still mulling over what Walter had said. During a rest stop, Walter had asked about Unu, whom he used to cover. "I left a message for Shimkin last week. Thought I might have a lead for him for an analyst position. Not a bad firm, either. But didn't hear. He's probably busy," he'd said, looking at her carefully for a response.

"Oh? He didn't tell me," she said, which was true. Unu hadn't mentioned it at all. Why wouldn't he tell her? And why wouldn't he call Walter back when Walter was great at making introductions for people? It was no small thing to have a person like Walter vouch for you. What was Unu's problem?

When they finished checking in, it was nearly eleven o'clock.

"Drinks at the bar?" Hugh asked her and Walter.

"Yes. I could use a glass of wine," she said.

"I'm turning in, guys. I'll see you at breakfast. Good night," Walter said, and went to his room.

The bar at the lodge was a small paneled room with low ceilings. It was one of the original tavern rooms of the eighteenth-century inn. Hugh found them a sofa in the back of the bar and ordered their drinks.

"Why hasn't he gotten a job yet?" he asked.

"That's none of your goddamn business," she answered, smiling. "Haven't you ever been laid off?" In her tone of voice, she was making it clear that she thought he was an asshole for being so unsympathetic.

"You misunderstand me, Casey Cat. Unu is smart enough to get a job. He doesn't want a job. Why is that?"

"I don't know," Casey replied with a shrug.

"You sound like a disappointed mother," he said. "But you are aging too well to be a mother to a grown man."

"It's often a wonder to me that you are in sales," she said. "Speaking of aging, when do you expect to retire? I mean, no one in your field works in sales after fifty."

"I'm not fifty. Hardly, my dear." Hugh appeared irritated.

"You're hardly thirty, my dear." That was Unu's age exactly. "And you'll be fifty before me. Eleven years before me."

"Ah, well, but what is twenty-six in female years?" He smiled and moved his face closer to hers. "None of us are getting any younger."

"You're crowding me, Hugh." Casey drew back a little and sipped her white wine.

Hugh checked the bar. There were no clients here.

"I think we should leave," he said. "Together. And go somewhere."

Casey looked at his eyes. They were lovely. He had great beauty in his face. She envied him almost. She had never been beautiful the way he was.

"Muddy brown," she said.

"What?"

"The color of your eyes is like mud."

"I think you like me," he said.

"You think everyone likes you. That is a most repulsive quality in a man. I do envy you, however."

"Tell me all about it," he said, reaching for his glass. He was curious as to what she'd say but wanted to appear detached.

"Because you're so free. Your movements, your speech, your appearance. You're not marked as exceptional or different. You're just a tall, good-looking...white guy with solid connections. And you were born like that. What is that like?"

"You envy that?"

"Maybe." Casey hated to admit it. "Yeah, maybe I do. Everyone always likes you. And if you think about it, they really shouldn't. Take Karyn, for example. You don't like her. And she's probably hoping that you'll call her for a date. It's preposterous how much unearned power you have."

"Power? What power? Karyn? That woman you work for? She's...whatever. I'm sure she's nice. I feel nothing for her."

"Exactly. But then why did you flirt so hard with her? You misled her. I hate that about you."

"Are you jealous?"

"Son of a gun." Casey shook her head. "Does Narcissus ever take a holiday?"

"You know, it's true." Hugh spoke gravely, switching his tone. "Perhaps people do like me more than they should. Except you, obviously. But you really should like me because I am quite fond of you."

"Hedge, we're friends. You know that." She hadn't meant to hurt his feelings.

"Close friends." Hugh slid his left hand around her waist and placed his right on her thigh above her skirt.

"What is it with you?" Casey did not push him away but edged back a bit on the sofa. She was awfully curious about what he would say next.

He looked at her squarely, then slipped his right hand under her skirt.

"Excuse me," she said tactfully.

He withdrew his hand. "Unu?" he asked, betting that the boyfriend might be the source of her resistance.

"I don't know," she answered. This was true. That morning, he'd asked, "You coming back?" And she realized she hadn't answered him. Had she done something to make him feel she was leaving him? The thing that kept nagging at her was how he'd turned down that analyst position last week but then had given up his watch and car. He made no sense. "Get the check," she said.

All Hugh had to do was glance at the waiter, who'd been paying attention to the table, and the man brought over the leather folder immediately. He signed his room number, and Casey got up.

The sex was not gentle. They were almost hostile. He did not love her, and she did not love him. But Casey liked the way he moved and admired his lack of self-consciousness. He was excited by her, and she found that its own kind of stimulus. It was hard to tell who was in control, or maybe neither was. When she was done, she put on her clothes to go to her room. Hugh didn't ask her to stay, but before she left, he kissed her for a long time—the only tender moment of the evening.

The next day, she golfed brilliantly, and the clients were both impressed and peeved by the female summer intern's solid game. Walter said, "All right, Han," when he heard that she'd shot a seventy-eight. Even she was surprised by how well it went considering her lack of playing. After the long client dinner, she returned to her room, and not ten minutes later, Hugh came by.

"It's me," he said from outside the door.

Earlier that morning, before going down for breakfast, she had read her Bible, jotted down her verse, and prayed. She had prayed for forgiveness. When she heard Hugh's knock on her hotel room door, she hesitated. Thirty or forty seconds—the extent of her resistance.

Hugh had brought her a bottle of wine, but she refused. She'd already had several glasses at dinner. "I don't need it, either," he said. "It'd be better for us if I didn't." He laughed, then kissed her and removed her blouse. They didn't talk much again but went on to try new things. She was amazed by how much he knew about sex. This was the most monstrous bit she was learning: It was not hard to put Unu out of her mind and to focus merely on the bodies.

Casey looked at Hugh's face after she climaxed. He reminded her of Jay, not because they looked so much alike, but because, like Jay, Hugh seemed perennially amused. They were the kind of men who could laugh at disparate things—in a good way, they faced life with humor; but in a bad way, they appeared to lack humanity at times. She had been with Hugh when he laughed at a homeless man's drunken soft-shoe dance on Eighth Avenue and could recall how Jay would imitate his Indian friend's accent behind his back.

Now, she had done to Unu what Jay had done to her. She had neglected Unu's feelings, although the memory of her own humiliation had not yet gone away—when she saw Jay at the reunion, the image of him with the sorority girls had been helpful. It made their not being together anymore more plausible. Didn't she love Unu enough even as a good friend to not hurt him? Could she have foreseen when Hugh proposed the golf trip that this might occur? She didn't think so. Not completely. And Casey had violated her own morality, however broken and taped up it might have been; she had not believed she could do this.

Casey lay back on the pillow, her body covered loosely with the bedsheet.

"What are you thinking about?" Hugh asked. "You don't look very happy."

"I thought men didn't talk after sex."

"What do you know of men?"

"You got me there."

Casey sat up, then swung her legs off the bed.

"If you wait for a little while, we can go again."

He couldn't see her face, but Casey was frowning. The way he'd said this made her feel bad. She had done plenty of sport fucking in her time before Jay and was amenable to doing more, but somehow, the way Hugh said "go again" bothered her, as if what they had just done were no different from a game of tennis. Unu never said things like that. Their lovemaking had been passionate and erotic, and despite his unwillingness to remarry, she didn't doubt his commitment to her. She felt unworthy of Unu suddenly. He'd be better off with someone else. It wasn't as if Hugh were a stranger. She had known him longer than Unu, but she didn't know if he'd had feelings for her. Maybe it shouldn't have mattered. She didn't love him, either.

Casey lay down, feeling tired and unmotivated to wash up before going to sleep.

She kissed him on the mouth, wanting to test her own feelings. What was this they were doing?

He pressed his lips against hers, and she could feel the weight of his body.

"I don't even like you." She wanted to hurt him.

"I can't stand you," he answered. "But I've wanted to fuck you for quite some time."

"Why?" she asked, trying to appear tough. She pulled her body away from his and propped up her face on bended elbow.

Hugh stroked the curve of her hip bone. "Who can explain it?"

Casey thought he could have said many things. Hugh was a good talker, after all. He was an institutional salesman. He could have said he liked her, her body, that she was pretty, that he liked her smile, her eyes—the crap men said to get sex. He could have delivered the words with some half-felt admiration. But he hadn't. He didn't know why he wanted to fuck her, and he wasn't even going to try to pretend. Maybe she could have been anyone to him.

"You really can't stand me?" This time, Casey was sincere.

"No, silly girl. I like you quite a lot. I couldn't make love to someone I didn't like. Unlike you, my dear, who can."

Casey stared at him, stumped.

"I should go to bed," she said, wanting to be alone. She didn't know what to believe anymore. Was he now being kind, or was he telling the truth? And he wasn't wrong: She had slept with men she didn't like. But she did like Hugh, although now she didn't feel like saying it.

"Will you go back to him?" he asked. Normally, when Hugh conducted an affair, he never brought up the husband or the lover, but he felt that with Casey, it wouldn't work this way. She wasn't someone who pretended not to see things. At worst, she would not say the thing, but she knew what was going on.

Casey turned to him, and he cupped her small breasts in his hands. With his thumbs, he massaged her nipples.

"Cut it out, Hugh," and as she said it, she heard the assonance of the names Unu and Hugh. They both had the long *u* vowel sound. Jay had taught her about assonance, consonance, and other aspects of prosody. It was like being in bed with all three of them. Casey got up finally and put on her robe.

"Do you want me to stay?"

"I'm sleepy," she said.

"Should I go, then?"

"I'll see you tomorrow, Hugh."

"Very well."

The drive back to New York on Sunday felt even shorter. Casey talked to Walter most of the time. Walter noticed the change in the car but didn't say anything. He didn't believe that Hugh would stoop so low as to seduce Casey. That would arguably be sexual harassment, since Casey was a junior employee. When they stopped to fill up the tank near Hugh's parking lot in midtown, they decided to park his car and take taxis back home. Walter lived in Brooklyn, so they gave him the first one they hailed.

"I'll drop you off," Hugh said when the next cab appeared.

Hugh gave the driver instructions, and not a minute later, he began to feel her up.

Casey removed his hand from the inside of her thigh. "No, Hugh. No more of this."

Hugh turned from her and faced forward. "Why?" he asked calmly in his work voice.

"Because I feel like a jerk. I'm such a hypocrite."

And she couldn't tell him that it was Sunday, and all she could think about was how God must think she was a shit, because she was a shit. If God was God, He probably didn't mince words. She was no angel, but this was very low even for her.

"You should leave him."

"What?"

"You could stay at my place for a while. Till you get your bearings."

"You don't live with women."

"I didn't say live with me. You're my friend. You can crash whenever you want."

Casey closed her eyes.

"Unu is a loser. His gambling is no longer normal. You're hooking up with someone who has no future."

"Unu is a good person. He's incredibly honest."

"Yeah, but nice guys—"

"Shut up," she said. "He's a much better person than I'll ever be."

"I'm not asking you to marry me or anything or even to go out. I'm just trying to be a friend to you."

"Thanks." Casey nodded. The only man who'd ever wanted to marry her was Jay, and she had determined that his will was too weak, and now she saw that her will was weak, too. Unu didn't believe in the concept of marriage, so did that mean he just wanted to fuck her on the steady? And to be honest, it wasn't that she wanted to get married now, but every girl felt the insult not to be considered. Wonderful, she thought. She was officially a bad girl—the kind you didn't bring home to Mother. She didn't like to cook or clean, and she wasn't much good at making money on a regular basis. She was able to show up for work, reread classics, and make hats. And as for children, she felt neutral about them at best. What was the point of her being a woman, anyway?

"I don't see what the big deal is. You said he wouldn't marry you."

"He said he didn't believe in marriage. And I don't want to get married, either." Casey didn't know why she bothered to make that distinction except to cover her injured pride. "I couldn't leave him now. He's got no job. No car, no watch even."

"And his girlfriend is screwing another guy," he said, wanting to make her angry.

But it had the opposite effect. Casey grew silent, and whatever good feelings she had left for the day evaporated. She looked out the windshield. It wasn't dark yet.

"Hey, hey, hey," he said. Casey looked irretrievably sad. "I'm an asshole. I mean it."

"That makes two of us," she said. "I'm a horrible person."

"Yeah, but we're all horrible. And occasionally, we're not." Hugh kissed her for a long time, and Casey let this feeling of warmth come over her.

The taxi stopped in front of the building. George, the doorman, approached the car and tapped on the trunk. He saw Casey brushing back her hair with her hands, the man's hand on her breast, and her pulling away slowly.

Casey got out of the car without saying good-bye.

"I'll call you," Hugh said.

She nodded. George had seen them together. Hugh had just

had his hand inside her jeans and the other on her right breast, his tongue in her mouth. She could still smell his aftershave on her skin.

"Hi, George," she said, and looked into his eyes.

George said nothing back, just nodded. He would pretend that he'd seen nothing. That was part of his job. In his work, he had seen more women cheating than men. All the talk about men being dogs seemed like bullshit compared with single girls who fucked a lot of guys at once. Unu's girl was a whore as far as he was concerned. All her nice clothes and fancy talk in that college-girl accent didn't mean a thing to him. George put the golf bag in the elevator for her and asked, "You all right with that?"

"I'm good, thanks." Casey pushed the elevator button to her floor.

9 | SEAM

*J*OSEPH HAN HAD NEVER SPOKEN to the new choir director. Deacon Kim, a whispy mechanic and baritone, had told Joseph that the young man worked hard to support himself even though he came from a *boojah* family and could have easily sponged off his father's wealth. Joseph approved of this. He himself had been born into a rich household but had labored since youth. Occasionally, he wondered what would have happened to him if it hadn't been for the war—would he have gone to the university like his elder brothers or stayed home and loafed as the youngest son? Joseph had not become rich in America, certainly, and didn't have much to show for his life, but he had worked diligently since he was sixteen. He liked the looks of Charles Hong: thin and sober looking. He didn't wear a necktie or a suit. Leah had mentioned that he didn't even own a car.

Joseph had come to the choir rehearsal room this Sunday to talk to Charles Hong, because of Leah, of course. This was the fourth Sunday in a row that she had missed church. She'd been going to work, doing mostly sewing, because she'd lost her voice and couldn't talk to the customers. She'd had a terrible cold the first half of the month, then lately she had been suffering from a stomach virus. This past week, he had made her stay home on Thursday and Friday, because she had been looking wan and feeble. She had lost weight.

If she didn't get better soon, he would get permission to close the store and take her to the doctor himself.

This afternoon, Tina, Chul, and the baby boy, Timothy, were flying into New York, and Casey and Unu were coming to the house. Timothy was finally coming. Ever since Joseph had gone to San Francisco to see his grandson, he had been feeling more hopeful. But oddly, Leah had been worsening. It wasn't like her to go to work and skip church when she wasn't feeling well. In their twenty-six years of marriage, she might've missed church only a handful of times, if that. Even Elder Shim had noted her absence. He had asked about her.

Joseph hadn't always wanted to go to church. It was Leah's faith that had moved him to accept Yesu Christo as his personal savior and redeemer. Joseph's first wife had not been a Christian. But she had been a fine person, and perhaps she might have become a believer. The minister said that the only people who were saved were those who accepted Jesus and turned their lives from sin. Before she had the chance to hear the gospel, she had been taken from him. What happened to her? Joseph had always wanted to ask his minister that but lost his nerve whenever he had the opportunity.

Joseph entered the choir room, and several people greeted him right away. He bowed back at them. Charles was seated in the front part of the room behind a small wooden desk—a rough-hewn thing salvaged from the street.

Charles heard the approaching footsteps and looked up. He could hardly believe whom he saw. The man's serious face appeared pleasant enough. It had been a month nearly since he had last seen Leah—though he'd hardly thought of anything but her since then. In his mind, she had become an imprisoned angel. All this time, he had been trying to figure out how to free her without putting her in danger. He might have thought that her husband could have killed her or taken her away but for the fact that for the past four Sundays, including this one, the soprano Kyung-ah Shin had explained that Leah was sick. It wasn't possible to ask the friend anything beyond if she was all right, and Kyung-ah had volunteered no extra information. In the midst of his frequent reveries, Charles would occasionally come to his senses and recall that she was a long-married woman, someone who'd known nothing of the world except for her husband and two grown daughters. But she was evidently in love with him—Charles felt sure of that. But doubts surfaced inevitably: If she were the kind of woman who'd leave her aging husband after a lifetime of marriage, then would she be the woman Charles would or could love?

When had he fallen in love? Was it when he'd first heard her sing? No, not really. Could you point to a moment, or was it an accretion of impressions? It might have been when she had come to his house with that doctor who was obviously in love with her, too, that he had started to think of her as the woman he had yet to meet. Leah wouldn't have naturally entered into his world. She was of peasant birth, with little formal schooling, and she worked as a tailor at a dry-cleaning store in New York. But she was also a beautiful lark disguised in the body of a woman. The fact that she could read music had been a revelation to him. Some attentive nun had taught her back home. Her existence at all had made him question everything.

Why was Joseph here? Charles tried to calm his thoughts, all jumbled with questions and fear. If Joseph shot him dead, he would have deserved it. Another man's wife was sacred. This was an obvious notion, yet it had never stopped him before. But in his experiences with sleeping with several married women, they had been happy to keep up the affair, to not leave their situations, and the women were pissed off only when he'd wanted to end it. And it was always he who had to walk away. For the first time, he wanted a woman to leave her husband. But she had not called him once. How ridiculous. There was no God, he thought. Only a big joker.

"Elder Han," Charles said, rising from his chair. He clasped his hands behind his back to steady himself.

Joseph bowed his head lightly to acknowledge the younger man. Charles bowed deeper from the waist.

"My wife . . . ," Joseph began.

"Yes?" Charles answered too abruptly. "How is she?"

"She isn't feeling well. Her cough isn't so good. And she's been having some stomach ailments," Joseph said.

"Deaconess Shin has told me that your wife has been suffering with a cold. That she lost her voice. Is it serious?"

"She was very sorry to miss her solo last month."

"Everything worked out," Charles assured him. Kyung-ah had taken over that morning. It had been fine, he'd thought then.

But that morning, he hadn't been able to concentrate on much of anything.

"Her throat is bothering her a great deal. She can't even hum. It's strange not to hear her—" Joseph felt foolish for talking. He didn't know why he had come exactly. She hadn't asked him to. He just knew that the choir was the most important thing to her.

"Has she been to the doctor?"

"She won't go. But she was able to go to work for the first three weeks even though she was sick. She doesn't have to talk to customers so much when she's sewing." Leah had tied a cotton scarf around her neck. For hours, she had worked quietly over her sewing machine without a word. "But this week, I told her to stay home for a few days, because she seemed so tired. And the coughing."

Charles nodded, not knowing what to say. He felt a sharp ache in his chest imagining the silence of her days. He gave a grimace of pain without intending to.

"Is there something I can do? May I call her at home?"

"Oh." Joseph brightened, grateful for the man's kindness. "That would be wonderful. I think she would be honored if you could find the time to—"

"No, no, not at all." Charles waved his hand. "I'd be happy to call. Can she talk on the phone?" He stroked his Adam's apple.

"Oh yes. Probably not long, though. She has a persistent cough. She has been feeling low, I think." Joseph felt relief at confiding this to someone who cared about her. The young man was responsible and warmhearted to be so concerned.

Joseph wrote down his home number on the back of a church program for the choir director. They bowed good-bye.

As he was heading out of the choir room, Kyung-ah Shin called out to him and sprang up from her chair.

Joseph nodded curtly. She came and stood close to him. He jerked back a little. The choir stared at them, then looked away. Charles pretended not to notice and looked over his sheet music.

"Elder Han," Kyung-ah said. "Elder Han," she said again breathlessly. "I was wondering how your wife was doing. This morning when she said she couldn't make it to church again, I was really worried. Is she getting better? She sounded so quiet. I could barely hear her. A cold can turn into pneumonia. Maybe she needs X-rays." She stared boldly into his eyes—his expression was detached and cool.

He didn't like her very much. That was obvious. Kyung-ah's own husband was a shy man who worked hard and stayed out of her way. He was a good father to their children. But he was so dull that she often forgot he was in the room with her. Marriage was a necessary thing, Kyung-ah thought, but unnatural.

"She's resting today. I think she'll go to the doctor next week."

"She said her grandson is coming." Kyung-ah smiled at him. Most men liked her, and it bugged her that he didn't. Clearly, he preferred the white-haired sexless type. "That will cheer her up."

"Yes," he said, smiling quickly before putting on his hat. He had to go to the Korean mart to pick up some feast food that Leah had ordered for lunch.

"You must be busy," she said. He wanted to go, and she was keeping him from it. "You better go home to take care of her. I'll phone her later."

Joseph nodded. He had never understood why his wife even talked to a woman like her. Her lipstick was blood colored so that it looked as though she'd eaten a rat.

Leah was in the kitchen by herself. Before he left, Joseph had made her a pot of ginseng tea, and she had promised that she'd drink some, but the smell of it bothered her so much that when she brought it close to her lips, the few spoonfuls of *bop* she'd had for breakfast almost came up. She was so tired that she could barely stand, and she coughed some more. Her coughing was often so violent that she had to sit down afterward. It felt as if someone were punching her in the chest.

The children were coming today, and she hadn't cooked anything. Joseph had forbidden it. So for the first time in her life, she had ordered prepared food from a store. Kyung-ah had told her that Mrs. Kong's catered meals were perfectly good enough and to forget making lunch. "Don't be a dumdum," her friend had said.

Leah left the kitchen and went to the living room to lie down on the sofa. When she was alone and still, her thoughts drifted to the professor. There were guilty moments when she wished she were sitting with him in that diner, listening to stories about singers he had known, concerts he'd attended. He'd talked passionately about the song cycle commission he was writing, his inexplicable interest in organ music: "Widor is astonishing. You must've heard it. At least the fifth movement of his Organ Symphony number five? The toccata. At weddings, it's often performed." Excited, he had hummed a few bars. Leah didn't know any of it but wanted to. There was so much she didn't know, and being with him had awakened her to the idea that there was something else out there in the world, rhythms she now craved. In her ear, she could hear his voice—when he was stern or excited—and it swam back to her when she was by herself. In the car, he had been so soothing and urgent. She had fallen into his voice despite her terror. At one point during the dinner, he'd pronounced with a kind of finality, "Rachmaninoff is sentimental," as if that were a kind of curse.

It must be something to make judgments like that, to be able to say such things with confidence. It was impossible to imagine a woman being that way. He had said to her, "Your voice is unlike anyone I've ever heard. I'm only sorry we hadn't met when you were a girl." He hadn't said it to be cruel, she thought; it was just a fact that he was a teacher and she was a singer who had missed her chances. That's all. Yet he thought she was a real singer rather than another member of a church choir in Woodside. When she put all that out of her mind, however, she recalled what else had happened in the car. The thing she could never take back. She would be an adulterer forever. The man had entered her body, and when a man and a woman came together to form one body, then everything was different. Sex was the gift a woman gave to one man—her husband. Men needed that like water. Everyone knew that. She had been frightened and stimulated by the recognition that a man as worldly and sophisticated as her teacher could desire her. No, she'd said. Please. She had asked to go home. Yet she must have enticed him. And that was a serious offense against God. The impossible thing was: Leah had never believed that she was capable of seducing a man. No one but Joseph had ever wanted her before, not as far as she knew. In a way, that belief had been her protection. She should never have gone to the diner with him. Leah wanted to die.

The phone rang, and she rose to get it.

"Hello," she said in Korean, and speaking out loud, for she had been alone most of the day, made her cough again.

"Are you alone?" Charles asked.

"*Uh-muh,*" Leah said in shock. It was his voice.

"I can come get you now."

Leah shook her head no. What was he talking about?

"Leah, can you leave? Live with me."

She coughed and coughed.

"You would make me happy."

"I made a mistake. It is my fault. Please pardon my offense. I made a terrible mistake...." Leah began to sob.

"Are you coming next week?" he asked. "Leah?"

"I don't know." She stopped coughing. Tears trickled down her long face. Her nose was runny.

Charles exhaled. He had to return to the choir room. He'd left the choir alone. If he hadn't called now, then her husband might've been there. He was calling from the empty church office. On the wall, there hung a free calendar with tear-away pages from some Bible dealer. The month of June had a quotation from Psalm 23 in Korean. Where is my comfort? Charles wondered. How had he landed up in a church basement reeking of kimchi asking a white-haired woman to leave her husband?

"Please forgive me." She couldn't bear the thought of him being angry with her.

"Maybe it was a mistake," Charles muttered.

Her heart lurched. He had wanted her to come live with him. That was what he had said that night, and he had called to come get her today. Now it was a mistake. *Uh-muh.* A man like this could change his mind so fast. They could never be together—that much she had always understood, and she deserved to die for her sin of wanting him—but a part of her had thought that maybe this was what all the *soh-sul* books and *terebi* programs were about, a kind of pure, impossible love, and she had thought this had been her experience of it. But, no, it couldn't be that if his heart could reverse itself. Was he a *jeh bi*—a smart girl was supposed to guard her soul against a man who'd appear swiftly like the fork-tailed swallow, full of charming songs. A man like that swept into your life, stole the jewels of your faith, then flew away, leaving you blinded and empty.

Leah held the phone close to her ear as she stared at the front door in case her husband walked in. With their lunch. He had been so considerate while she was sick. What would she do if her daughters rang the bell? Did the girls still have their keys? Leah wiped away her tears with the sleeve of her jersey housedress.

"I better go," Charles said. He felt absurd for having called. This past month, he had been preparing himself for her to come to him. He had imagined that she would knock on his door and ask to stay. And of course, he would let her come in. He would marry her. Maybe even take her to Korea. His father would have liked her. He had not liked his two previous wives. The notion seemed childish to him now, no different from his boyhood wish for his dead grandmother to come back to life or how he had yearned for months when he was eight years old for his nanny, who had married a farmer, to return to him—tell him that she'd gone to her village for only a short trip to bring back his favorite *yut* candy. Charles missed his home suddenly, the home of his youth that didn't exist anymore, where his mother was still alive and young, his grandmother was in the drawing room reading her novels, and his favorite nanny, who'd slept at the foot of his bed and brought him yogurt drinks when he did his homework, still lived with them and when his piano playing had pleased these women.

But courtship was a mutual delusion, and once love was captured, things tended to go awry. The divas he had married could never be pleased. It was a mean curse to be married to a woman who refused to be happy. He'd had affairs and stayed away from the house. A wife's pernicious anger gradually amounted to a killing. Extricating himself legally from the divas had been such an enormous waste of time. It was better to be alone. He would never have children.

Leah was still on the phone. "I thought you cared for me," she heard herself saying quietly. "That you wanted me to come and live with you."

Now it was Charles's turn to be silent. He recognized that voice—it was the voice of a hurt woman. Somehow it made him less merciful.

"You have a beautiful voice, Leah. The most beautiful voice I've ever heard." He said this and believed it was true. He had heard Callas, Price, Te Kanawa, and Battle. But this white-haired, middle-aged tailor outshone the divas. If there was a God, Charles thought, his distribution of gifts made no sense. Or was it that God kept the greatest for Himself, for His private pleasure? Just a few moments ago, he had thought of giving her everything he had.

Leah began to cough and couldn't stop.

"You should rest. Your husband was here this morning—"

"He spoke to you?" It felt like a slap to have him mention her husband.

"Yes. He was worried about you."

And you? she wanted to ask but didn't. He did not love her. It was not the love that lasted. There was worry in love, there was sacrifice. There was constancy. In four weeks, he had never tried to contact her. He was someone who could not be counted on, and it embarrassed her that she had even considered Charles as someone to love.

"I should let you go. You must be busy. Thank you for calling." Leah waited for Charles to hang up. She always waited for the other person to hang up before putting down the receiver. That was just her way. But as she waited, she heard no click, only his quiet and measured breath. She remembered the lemony detergent scent of his white undershirts, how she had held it up close to her nose when she had folded his laundry.

Leah put down the receiver. Maybe this was all right. He had let go of her first.

Approaching Van Kleeck Street, Casey fidgeted with the bows of the baby gift. Clothes for Timothy from Baby Gap. She was grateful that Unu had agreed to come with her. On the N train, he had even read out loud passages of *Middlemarch* that she had underlined, speaking in a mock English accent to make her laugh. His being so nice to her made it easier not to return Hugh's charming calls. Casey was excited to see Tina's baby in person but anxious about going back home, her first visit in four years. The photographs of baby Timothy showed a marshmallowy face with a shock of black hair. Unu had called him Don King. Timothy and Tina were reason enough to have boarded the train heading toward Grand Avenue.

The apartment building appeared shorter than she remembered it. She didn't know what Unu would make of the bulletproof glass, the tacky framed posters in the lobby, the roach spray odor in the halls. There was no doorman. "Are you kidding?" she'd replied when he'd asked about one. When she was a kid, she and her sister were afraid to throw out the garbage because a man who lived in the apartment next to the incinerator used to leave his door open while he walked around in his undershirt and shorts. The man was probably harmless, but as girls, they used to run when he'd say hello to them. Unu emphasized that the building was nice, and she laughed at his politeness. The building was a dump; it would never get better, and her parents would never leave it.

Joseph let them in, and to Casey's relief, Unu spoke Korean with her parents, putting them at ease.

She felt awkward standing there in the living room while her father was pouring a Scotch for her boyfriend as well as one for himself. They were sitting on the burgundy sectional from Seaman's, but she didn't feel that she could join them.

"How are your parents?" Joseph asked Unu. He watched the boy curiously.

"They're well," Unu answered. This was true enough. He hadn't heard any bad news, so it was safe to infer that everything was okay in Texas. His siblings were incapable of messing up. When he'd told his mother that he wasn't working, she had said nothing about it. His father had said, "You know what you're doing. I guess." Unu picked up his glass after Casey's father had taken a sip.

Joseph was wondering if the boy would marry his daughter. Unu was divorced, and that fact alone might have at one time dismissed him as a marriage candidate, but with Casey, he wouldn't have raised an objection necessarily. He knew by now that if he said red, she would say blue. So he would say nothing. He asked more questions about the boy's family.

Unu patiently answered Joseph's questions about his parents, two brothers, and a sister. Two Dallas lawyers and a pediatrician. He was the only one in finance and the only one to have left Dallas. Joseph asked a few more things, then told him a little about his own family in Wonsan, details Casey had never mentioned beyond the fact that her father was a war refugee from the North. There was something regal about Casey's father, a kind of courtliness in the way he spoke Korean. He was masculine in his restraint. You couldn't help but be curious about him. He was so evidently proud, and you had to wonder where all that came from. His own father, the owner of a highly successful insurance firm, was someone who made jokes with everyone, tried hard to put people at ease. He used the word *sir* often and insisted on good manners for his children. These seemed to be things Casey's father had little interest in doing. He also had nothing to say to Casey, who had by this time left the living room where the men sat. After seeing to it that he was okay with her dad, she'd gone into the kitchen, where her mother was putting out the food in dishes.

"You're coughing like crazy. What is that?" Casey asked. The walls of the kitchen appeared to have moved in somehow, but that was impossible. They weren't bright white as they had been before. Her mother had been religious about using Fantastik on them. But it wasn't reasonable to expect things to stay the same. "You okay?"

Leah nodded, unable to speak. She took a small sip of the ginseng tea that she had poured out earlier. Then immediately she spat it out in the sink. So bitter. Her stomach felt sour, too.

Casey heard the television go on in the living room. The men would be watching some nature program. Her father could watch those things forever. They weren't talking anymore.

"Is he nice to you?" Leah asked quietly in Korean.

"He's a kind person. Much nicer than me."

"That's good. A man should love more than the woman."

It was such a typical thing for her mother to say.

"Can you bring out some *ahn-ju* for your father?" Leah handed her a wooden bowl filled with dried cuttlefish, and Casey brought it to the men. They were watching a show on PBS on lions. Unu said thanks, and Joseph said nothing. He pushed the bowl toward Unu, who grabbed a handful; then Joseph took some for himself. Both their glasses were full of whiskey.

"More ice," Joseph said, and Casey went to get some.

Her mother sat as she put the prepared food into platters and bowls.

"You don't look right," Casey said to her mother after filling a white Corning bowl with ice cubes. They didn't have a proper ice bucket in the house.

"*Umma* is okay. Don't worry," Leah said, but actually she wanted to die. It would be easier if she were dead—this pain, unbearable. She was ruined forever, soiled. Had he been serious about coming to get her? And what would it be like to live in that house in Brooklyn? Who would take care of her husband, who was no longer young, who had worked all of his life to take such good care of her and their daughters? What would Casey and Tina think?

"How is school?"

"Fine," Casey said. "I have terrific grades, but this summer job is tough as—" She stopped herself from cursing. The word *shit* or *damn* might have knocked her mother over. She looked so frail. Besides, what was the point of explaining her need to get an offer? Her parents didn't understand these things. It was her job to bring home success or not to come home at all. The mechanics of success were her problem. "Maybe you should see a doctor. About the cough."

"*Umma* is okay." Leah folded up the brown paper bags that the food had come in. "How is Unu's work? Is he doing okay?"

"He's not working right now."

"Oh?"

"He's taking some time off. He's trying to figure out what he wants to do."

Wasn't that what her daughter had said after graduation?

"How old is he?"

"Older than me."

Her mother looked at her exhausted.

"He's thirty. Thirty-one in August."

Leah nodded. He was not young anymore.

Casey resented the quiet judgment. She'd always assumed that Unu would get the same job elsewhere. It hadn't dawned on her that it might take him this long to find work. It had been four months. Hardly an eternity, but the way he was looking for a job, or not looking for a job, was disturbing. There were money problems, naturally. That was obvious, but it was mostly from the gambling, not merely the job loss. Hugh had said Unu's problem was serious, distinguishing a kind of gentlemanly betting from a moral failure.

Ted Kim had made it plain on a number of occasions that the way you got a job on Wall Street was through contacts. If you were good, you were contacted. If you were hot shit, everyone in your field monitored your happiness. If things looked a little glum for you, a rival company would swoop into your life, make you an offer impossible to refuse. Get a better life, an upgrade, a bigger piece of the pie. Was this true? Ted was a big talker, but his landing was cushy after what had been his moment of public disgrace. Unu wouldn't have disagreed entirely with Ted's assessment. For Unu's kind of job and at his level, you wouldn't be reading the classifieds. And as for headhunters, the aphorism they followed was: The hired were hired away, the fired would stay that way. If what Hugh said about Unu's gambling was true, did others on the Street think this as well? Could

Hugh have discussed it with Walter? What were the chances that Unu might get hired for a senior position? She'd never before considered what people in the industry thought about her boyfriend. They weren't even married. Her future wasn't tied up with his, she told herself. He would get something. Of course he would.

The baby was here. Swaddled in his yellow-and-blue blanket, Timothy was drowsy from his last feeding, his tiny features peaceful. Joseph was visibly gleeful holding his grandson in his arms. Leah cried from happiness, and Tina held her. Her coughing dissipated some. Leah couldn't hold the baby for fear of getting him sick.

Casey was glad to see Tina and Chul, too. The apartment felt happier with them in it. Her younger sister looked exhausted, but nevertheless pleased to be home. The flight was long, Chul admitted, but the baby had been good. Slept most of the way and was peaceful when awake. Only a little crying at takeoff and landing.

Tina looked older—it might have been the weight gain from the pregnancy, shorter hair, the dark-rimmed eyeglasses she wore for the plane ride. She joked about how large her bosom was: 34DD in her nursing bra. The last time they had all been together was the wedding, but the look of the bride was completely erased. The baby had come so soon, and Tina looked shocked herself that she had a child. "I have a son," she exclaimed.

"It's kinda nutty," Casey said, grinning.

The men went to the living room. Chul chatted with Unu; they were comfortable with each other. Joseph went to the kitchen to get Chul a glass. Soon, they were all drinking whiskey and nibbling on *o-jing-uh.* The nature program was still on, the volume lowered—a lion tore into a hapless wildebeest. From the kitchen, the women could hear the clink of glasses and the calm male voices. Leah was less jumpy with Tina here. For a second, Casey thought, family happiness was completed: the immigrant family with two daughters in graduate school and two Korean boys from nice families, a grandson in tow.

At the dinner table, Chul said grace, and Leah smiled at him. Tina couldn't have brought home a finer husband. Unu came from a better family, but Chul was sincere, still smitten with Tina. Leah tried to put the professor out of her thoughts.

The baby woke up only once to eat and have his diaper changed.

Tina nursed her son in her childhood bedroom. Casey sat with her quietly as she did this. The baby drank greedily, then in a blink fell asleep again.

Tina and Chul gave Unu and Casey a lift to the city. They were going to stay at the Hilton in midtown for the night, even though Leah and Joseph wanted them to stay with them. Chul had to meet some colleagues very early in the morning at Roosevelt Hospital. The men sat in the front seat of the car and talked about the Baltimore Orioles—Chul's hometown team and one of Unu's favorites.

In the car ride, Casey noticed how little Tina spoke. She was utterly absorbed with Timothy. Casey admired the baby. How could you not? The infant was perfect.

"You are so lucky," Casey said wistfully, wanting Tina to notice her. "Hey, Tina, I'm sorry about the baby shower. The finals kicked my ass. And I was freaked out about the school loans and the interviews. The tuition loans are huge. You have them, too, I know." Tina didn't seem worried about her loans, however.

"Oh, showers are stupid. And you sent that crib, Casey. It must have cost—"

"I figured a crib was better for everyone in the long run than the cost of my plane ticket, or flunking out of school. I would've liked to go."

"Look at you. A year of business school and you've gotten all practical." Tina laughed.

"That's a scary thought."

Tina stroked her baby's lovely dark hair. At the baby shower that her girlfriend from school had thrown her, everyone had asked where her mother and sister were. Tina had explained that they were busy with work. Except for her father, who had always made her believe that she could do anything, her mother and sister could not be counted on. They could hardly take care of themselves.

Casey lowered her voice. "I wanted to give you back the money. To pay you back for your loans. This job I have this summer pays really well. If I get hired by them after I graduate, I probably will never have to worry about money again."

Tina shook her head gently. "Forget it, Casey."

"I'll send you a check. I should have brought it."

Timothy stirred, and both held their breath. He was still asleep. The men in front weren't paying any attention to them, either. Tina tucked his blanket into the car seat. Her husband didn't know about Casey's abortion or that she had loaned Casey the money to leave home after graduation. All that seemed minor. Like childhood scrapes from a long time ago. They were supposed to be women now. Tina wanted to think about the future. She'd taken some time off from school, but she'd return in the fall of 1998.

Tina smiled and pointed. "Look at that. You still wear your Wonder Woman cuffs. I love them."

Casey crossed her chest with her forearms, and they laughed. She glanced at the cuffs she'd worn since freshman year in college, one of the first presents Sabine had ever given her. She pulled one off her wrist.

"Here," Casey said. "You take one." She clasped it on her sister's wrist.

"No. I couldn't. They're part of a set. And they're yours. Wonder Woman needs two. You can't break up the pair."

"Then take both," Casey said. "I never give you anything." She removed the other one and put it also on Tina's wrist. "They look great on you."

Tina crossed her chest and giggled. "I couldn't. Sabine gave these to you. And you love them."

Casey touched her bare forearms. "She would understand. I want you to have them."

"Really?" Tina stared at the silver glinting on her wrists.

"You're the real Wonder Woman anyway," Casey said. It was bittersweet to say it, but she did not mind so much.

Tina didn't know how to respond. It was as if Casey were admitting defeat to a rivalry Tina had never felt for her older sister. She had just wanted Casey's love, her attention. There was no contest. Was there? But if she didn't accept the gift, her sister would be hurt.

"You give me lots of things, Casey. The crib from the shower, and just today, the clothes for Timothy."

"I want you to have these." Casey checked the edges of the cuffs, and they were rounded. They wouldn't hurt the baby when Tina was holding him. "Really. I mean it."

"Thank you, Casey."

Casey felt better suddenly. Her wrists were pale where the cuffs had been, the tan lines stark against the white bands of skin stretching over her thin wrist bones.

"I hope Timothy is like you," Tina said.

"Why would you wish such a rotten thing on your beautiful child?" Casey kissed Timothy's forehead.

"Because you're a true person, Casey. You are your own. That's important." Tina's voice was assured. All her life, she had wanted to make decisions not informed by others' needs, wants, and expectations. "No one is like you," Tina said. "In the end, that matters most, I think. And being truthful."

Casey swallowed her breath, trying to contain the good Tina was trying to give her. But it wasn't possible to believe it fully. She touched the baby's soft foot, almost to make sure that he was real.

Chul dropped them off at Unu's apartment. The doorman on duty was Frank, and he waved hello. George was off that weekend.

At home, Unu hung up Casey's raincoat. He pulled out a compact disc wrapped in cellophane from the console drawer in the foyer.

"It's not much," he said.

"What's the occasion?"

"No reason."

It was a Carly Simon anthology with the song "Coming Around Again."

She kissed him on the mouth. "I love it. And I didn't have it. I mean, I used to, but I lost it." She felt terrible.

"I was walking through Tower, and you said you liked that song. A while ago."

"I remember." The day he'd won all that money. Casey sat on the armchair.

"I know things haven't been great. With me lately. I'm trying to figure out the job thing. You've been such a good friend the past few months. I couldn't have made it without you. Things will get better. I should have gotten you jewelry or something like that—"

Casey shook her head. "No. I prefer this."

Unu nodded. He wanted to be with her, and he grew more certain of this as time passed. He'd get his act together. Make the calls he had to make. Quit gambling. You could start again if you had love.

"I slept with Hugh Underhill. In Vermont," Casey blurted out. She covered her mouth with her hands folded.

"What?"

Casey did not repeat herself. The hurt in his eyes was awful, but she couldn't have kept it from him. It needed saying.

"You're unbelievable," he said.

"I'm sorry."

"How could you do that? You read the Bible every fucking day. Go to church every Sunday. Do they make hypocrites as big as you?"

Casey lowered her head. "I'm sorry. Maybe I should go."

"What? Are going to meet Hugh who-fucks-everything-that-moves Underhill? Is that how you got your job?"

"No." She shook her head. "No."

He looked incredulous. "You're a goddamn cliché. The girl who sleeps her way to the top. He doesn't give a rat's ass about you. There are thousands of guys like that on Wall Street. They're no good, Casey. How could you?" Unu felt like he might hit her, and he stepped back.

"That's not what happened."

"Right."

"I'm sorry, Unu. I am sorry. I couldn't not tell you." Casey looked at her hands. She missed her bracelets.

"Get out of here. Get out. Get the fuck out!" he screamed. "And take your shit with you. Get the fuck out!" He sat on the floor, his upper body crumpling. He hated her. He had been right not to marry again. She was worse than his wife. At least his wife had been in love with an old flame. She hadn't spread her legs for a sleazy broker for a job. What kind of person would do that?

"It's not what you think. I can't explain what happened, and it didn't mean anything. I'm sorry."

"Get your shit and go."

Casey hurried into the bedroom and threw some work clothes and shoes into the suitcase she'd used for her trip to Vermont.

When she was done, she stood by the front door with her bag. "I'm sorry, Unu."

"Just go. Please."

Casey left her keys on the console and closed the door gently.

Seventy-second Street was empty of people. Most were gone for the weekend. Frank asked if she needed a cab, and she said no. Casey looked up at the building windows. There were more darkened ones than lit.

10 | ADJUSTMENT

*A*SKING FOR JOINT CUSTODY IS CERTAINLY NOT an unreasonable request," said Chet Stenor. Ted nodded in agreement with his lawyer, unwilling to meet Ella's gaze. She sat at the opposite side of the conference table. Ted focused on the neat stack of papers in front of his lawyer.

"You don't even know what she looks like," Ella mumbled, staring at Ted. She hadn't meant to say this right then, but she couldn't help it. Ronald Coverdale, seated beside her, touched her forearm. She ignored him. "You haven't seen her in weeks. Hardly at all. Why are you asking for half the time, Ted? I don't understand you. You're too busy anyway—" Ronald Coverdale touched her arm again, then picked up his pen.

"What Ella is saying is perfectly reasonable, too. The father has a doubtlessly demanding job. Ella is not criticizing his parenting. That's not it at all. But he may not be able to manage the daily needs of a small child, and in her best interest we should consider—"

"You know that's not true, Ronald," Chet said. "And I trust that you will not be sexist about this. It goes without saying that a father plays a significant role in the healthy development of his child, equal to the mother's role, and should therefore have equal access."

Ella's lawyer stared blankly at opposing counsel. Chet Stenor was a class A prick. Ronald would play the nice card for a little while longer.

"Ted works exceptionally hard at his job, but he is also passionately interested in being involved in his daughter's life. All the studies indicate the essential benefits of having two parents in a child's life, and in Irene's best interest..." Chet paused when he saw Ronald opening his mouth, having anticipated the interruption, but Ella jumped in, beating her lawyer.

"But you don't visit her, Ted. Since she was born, you've seen her maybe half a dozen times. You're just negotiating this because you want to win. Ted, this isn't some game. It's our daughter's life."

"Ella, you're being unfair." Ted finally looked at her face. "I want to know Irene better. I even rented a three-bedroom apartment not five blocks from the house just so I can see her more. I've been settling into my new job at Lally, and—"

"Don't tell me about fair, Ted—"

"Good grief..." Ted sighed, then picked up the coffee carafe and tipped it toward his cup, but the pot was empty. "Is there more?"

Chet nodded. His colleague Kimberly Heath got up and called reception to send up more coffee. Then she handed the crying wife a tissue. Kimberly was a senior associate in her mid-forties who'd gone to law school as a second act after teaching Latin at a private school for a dozen years. She served as a soft touch at these meetings. Chet hated female histrionics. Women cried too damn much, especially if they were ambivalent. From his experience, Chet knew that the judge would take the existing custodial arrangements seriously, but it didn't help the wife's case that she had a full-time job as well, albeit her job was more like 40 hours a week maximum, whereas Ted could work anywhere from 60 to 120 hours a week, especially clocking travel time. But it would be easy to argue that the wife relied on baby-sitting for 60 hours a week, which was likely the case since she'd have to incorporate transit time as well as work time. So it could be easy to establish that there was no full-time parent in either household. Why people who had no time for kids bothered having any was a mystery to him.

Kimberly gave the wife the rest of the tissue box, and the wife blew her nose. The young woman was beautiful in a portrait kind of way, he thought, but the fiancée was definitely hotter. Second wives uniformly were that. Sex was not a negotiable for men who could financially afford a second or third marriage. Chet had advised a prenuptial for Ted, but he had refused. Moron.

Ted took off his glasses. His contacts had been bothering him lately. All three lawyers checked to see if the husband was going to break down, too. It was almost customary to have tears shed in the conference room of a firm specializing in matrimonial law. But the husband wasn't crying; instead, he pinched the bridge of his nose and blinked his eyes rapidly.

"Very dry in this room," Ted said. A gust of cold air came from the wall vents above Ella's lawyer's head.

Ella noticed that Ted was rubbing his face, especially his eyes. Was he crying, too? It had been so long since she'd seen him cry that she felt sorry for him. His father had just died, and Ella imagined that all this must be hard on him, too, though physically he looked no worse for the wear. Like her, he had lost weight. The thinness made their faces gaunt and older. Ted was still a striking man. Today, he looked like a successful art dealer in his titanium eyeglasses, blue jeans, crisp white shirt, and black blazer.

Ted blinked his right eye repeatedly. He swerved his head back and forth and looked at everyone in the room. He picked up the papers in front of him, and with his left eye closed, he tried to read the words but couldn't. His name was written above the word *RESPONDENT* on the top sheet of the pile—he knew that because he could read it with his left eye, but with his right, he couldn't make out his own name. It had to be his name, but it looked like dark, wavy smudges floating on white space. "What in the world?" he said out loud.

"What's the matter? Are you okay?" Ella got up from her seat and walked around to look at his eye, just as if she were examining the scrape of a boy at St. Christopher's. Ted was blinking furiously now, looking up and down at the walls, everyone's faces, then again at the papers. He put a sheet of paper up close to his eye.

"I can't see. In my right eye," he said. "Ella, I can't see."

Ella stood over him and peered into his right eye. "Is it an eyelash? I don't see anything."

Ronald observed his client hovering over her husband's face. Did she still have feelings for this guy? What a mess, he thought. Love was such a fucking toxic waste dump. Women always wanted these divorces because they were hurt and angry, and these men never responded correctly. You shouldn't bluff, he thought. Never bluff in love. If you have to, it's not love. It was like that favorite quote of his grandfather's: "There are only two questions that can't be answered: First, 'How much do you love me?' and second, 'Who's really in control?'" Basically, Ronald believed that a marriage was fundamentally based on these two sphinxlike riddles, but in the end, both parties could get eaten alive giving the wrong answers.

Ella took a tissue and cleaned his glasses, blew away the lint. "Put these on again," she said gravely.

Ted put them on.

"Is it any better?"

"No. I can't make out my own name," he said, apoplectic.

Ella crossed her arms, not knowing if she should return to her spot. Did Ted have some ulterior motive? Lately, she felt almost invulnerable toward surprises or wrong-mindedness. People were not always very good, and she had been naive for a long time. Unu had just told her that Casey had cheated on him with a colleague of hers at Kearn Davis. How could she? After what Jay had done to her? After knowing what it had done to her own marriage? And to Unu, who was such a sweet person? Ella returned to her seat.

"Are you all right?" Chet Stenor spoke up finally. He hadn't wanted to interrupt Ella's efforts. It would have appeared rude.

Ella looked up to see what Ted would say. He didn't say anything but appeared lost. She wanted to help him. "Do you have any drops? Can I get you anything?"

Ted could hear the kindness in Ella's voice, and he felt lousy. He shook his head no, unable to speak. From his left eye, he could see her face perfectly well with his glasses on. He could see the whiteness of her skin in contrast with the navy fabric of her simple dress. It was a knit wool dress that she had bought when they first married. From Saks. It had been expensive, but he had insisted on it, because it made her look so confident and elegant. Had she worn it to upset him? No. Ella wasn't like that. But it did remind him of their happier times. She also wore a pearl necklace that he didn't recognize. Where did she get that? She would never have bought it for herself. Did she have a boyfriend already? The possibility of it rankled him. From his right eye, at best he could manage the outline of a pretty Asian girl—the soft features of an oval face, the dark pink of her lipstick.

Ted looked around the conference room again, his left eye closed, trying to make out the blurry shapes. The edges of the picture frames on the walls were wavy, too. From his right eye, his law-yer's head was the image reflected in a funhouse mirror. No one else spoke while he tried to see them.

"It's like everything is behind a greasy lens. Fuck," he said.

Chet turned aside and put his arm on Ted's shoulder. "Maybe we should stop the meeting here. You need to see a doctor about this," he said, cocking his head to the side, wondering what was really hap-pening to his client. In his twenty-two years of practice, he had wit-nessed one fatal heart attack (a wife, not a husband, surprisingly, and because they were not yet divorced, the husband ended up with a bundle on her life insurance policy, and her family naturally tried to sue), thirty, give or take, physical altercations, and one unloaded pistol-waving incident. Yelling and cursing were par for the course. A client becoming nearly blinded in one eye—this was new. In a perfectly calm voice, he asked, "May we phone your eye doctor for you, Ted?"

"What's his name?" Kimberly asked, nimbly picking up her pen so she could look up his number.

Ted didn't reply, but made a face. He exhaled loudly.

"My father," Ella said. "It's my father. He's Ted's eye doctor."

Kimberly and Chet nodded as though this were not unusual.

Ronald smiled and looked away.

"Do you want me to call him?" Ella asked. Ted had never ap-peared as flummoxed as he was now. He actually looked terrified. She would take him to the hospital immediately.

"I could go to the emergency room. Maybe I should do that. Yeah," he said coolly, accepting that her father was no longer an op-tion. He'd hardly spoken to Dr. Shim since he left Ella.

Ella furrowed her eyebrows, indignant. "Don't be stupid, Ted. My father will see you. He's a doctor."

She phoned her office and explained that she'd be late. Her boss was a saint, as usual. Then she phoned her father's office, and Shar-lene said her dad was in and would love to see her. Ella didn't men-tion that she was bringing Ted. The meeting broke up after Ella's call, and the lawyers shrugged and said all the polite things. Every-one would be in touch.

In the taxi, Ted kept trying to test his vision, but he couldn't make out anything from his right eye except for blurry colors and soft shapes. The light in the taxi was dim.

"I'm sorry, Ella. I'm messing up your day."

"You're messing up my life," she replied.

They were both surprised that she'd said this.

"Right," he said, closing both his eyes. "I'm sorry about that, too."

When the taxi got to Ella's dad's offices, Ted tried to pay the driver, but he couldn't make out the denomination of the money without blinking. Frustrated, he handed his wallet to Ella. "Just take what you need."

It was the black alligator wallet that she'd bought for him from T. Anthony when he'd graduated from HBS. On the left-hand side of the wallet were his initials, stamped in gold leaf. Much of the gold had been rubbed away.

"I gave that to you," she remarked softly.

"I know," he said, his eyes still closed. "I'm sorry, Ella. I am so sorry about everything."

Ella couldn't touch the wallet that he held out in his hands. She opened her handbag and pulled out her change purse, where she kept her ones and fives.

"Do you want the wallet back?" Was he supposed to return all her gifts?

"How could you be so unfeeling?" Ella wiped her eyes.

"I'm sorry, Ella," he said, his left eye open, his right eye shut. She was crying again, and they were about to see her father.

"I gave that to you. I gave you everything you wanted. I did everything you said. But you want to take Irene away—" She sniffled.

The driver was aware of the crying woman and the man with his eyes closed. He shut off the meter, wanting to do something nice for them.

"We have to get out of here." Ella paid the driver and gave him a three-dollar tip. "C'mon." She let him take her arm.

Douglas Shim was reviewing the revised list of residents when Sharlene said his daughter and Ted were here. Ella walked into his office, smiling weakly. Her eye makeup was smudged around the eyes, her lipstick faded. Ted stood next to her, his right eye closed.

"Are you okay?" he asked his daughter, ignoring Ted.

Ella nodded, unable to say why she'd come. His kind look made her tear up again, and she had tried so hard to clean up her face in the elevator before coming to his office.

"Hi, Daddy," she said. "How are you?"

"Ella, Ella," he said, seeing the tears in her eyes. He put his arm around her shoulder, and he stood between her and Ted.

"Oh, Daddy. I'm okay."

"I know. I know you're okay."

Ella tried to gather herself up again. "Ted's eye. He can't see."

Douglas faced the young man.

"*Ah-buh-jee,*" Ted said reflexively. He'd called Ella's dad that since they'd gotten married. "I mean, Doctor—"

Douglas clenched his jaw. Hearing the boy calling him "Father" and then correcting himself was hard. Until the day Douglas's father-in-law passed away, Douglas had called the father of his long-deceased wife *Ah-buh-jee.*

"What's the matter with your eye? Here, have a seat."

Ted sat. "I'm sorry to bother you like this. We were at the lawyers', and talking about something, then suddenly I couldn't see. Out of my right eye. I mean, I can see, but what I see isn't right." He spoke rapidly.

Douglas led Ted by the arm and guided him to the examination room next door. Ella came along.

The examination room was darkened, and a thin bolt of light projected a series of eye charts on the white wall. Douglas asked him to read the first letter on every line on the eye chart, but Ted could hardly make out the largest E on the top row. Douglas put dilating drops in Ted's eyes that stung painfully.

"Wow," Ted said, blinking back tears.

"It'll pass," Douglas said. He'd forgotten the anesthetizing drops prior to dilating him.

Using the ophthalmoscope, Douglas checked behind Ted's eyes, then moved on to the 90-diopter lens for better resolution.

"Central serous retinopathy," he pronounced.

"What's that?" Ella asked her father. She was familiar with many medical terms just from being his daughter, but she hadn't heard that diagnosis before.

"There's a tear in your retinal tissues, and fluid has seeped in, causing a distortion in your vision."

Ted's head jerked back. "How?" he asked.

"There aren't any obvious reasons for this. No one knows for certain. I can guess from what's going on in your life and so can you that there are a lot of dramatic events in it. More men tend to get this than women. It's been correlated with stress. And perhaps from elevated cortisol levels, also related to stress. You know, when you feel out of control. Especially since central serous retinopathy tends to affect type-A personalities." Douglas made a face as though he didn't like saying this, because it sounded too judgmental. "It can recur, and it can also just clear up by itself. I don't see many cases of this. But I have seen a few. All of them were men, and all of them were experiencing great stress in their lives. Also having an objectively high-stress job—like pilots, for example. They apparently get this. Stress." Douglas shrugged, because who didn't feel stress these days?

"But we don't have any stress," Ella said, and laughed. Ted laughed, too.

"I'm glad you find this so amusing," Douglas said.

Ted closed his right eye and focused with his left. His face leaned forward toward Douglas's face. Ella's dad, seated on the other side of the slit lamp, looked nothing like his own father. A soft pile of gray hair crowned his head, and a perennial tan from tennis and golf made him look rested. The crow's-feet around his eyes grew only mildly deeper when he smiled. He wore a jacket and tie with chinos. Almost never a white coat at his offices. The biggest difference was their hands. Ella's dad had medium-size hands with long, tapered fingers. His nails were cut short in a square shape and had small white moons near the cuticles. Ted's hands were more like Ella's father's than his own father's. He had known all along that losing Ella's dad's respect was something quite serious, but it had been easier not to think about it when he hadn't seen him. Ted missed his own father sharply.

"So what do you think I should do?" he asked.

"It'll take a few weeks or a few months to completely clear up. It can fix itself. I've seen that. Or it can get worse. Some people have this in a chronic form. And that is a dangerous thing. We can try to fix it if it gets to that. But it might not necessarily help to operate.

Let's see how you do without any intervention. This is serious, though, Ted. You don't want to lose your vision."

"What?"

"It won't get to that, I hope. I don't think it will. For now, though, you might want to decrease the stress in your life." Douglas had always known that the boy was ferociously competitive, with marked perfectionistic tendencies, but getting central serous retinopathy seemed like the end of a complicated proof: QED.

The boy looked utterly lost.

"Today, you should go home and definitely rest a bit. Your dilated pupils will return to normal in a short while. And tomorrow, figure out how to relax more. Yoga, relaxation techniques. There are also drugs that can treat anxiety. And maybe you might want to consider seeing a counselor or a therapist. To just talk about things in your life. It might help."

"Got it." Ted couldn't imagine talking to a stranger about his problems. Telling the lawyer about the video and the herpes thing had been an ordeal in and of itself. He checked his right eye again, hoping that maybe the vision would return as quickly as it had left him. Everything was still wavy.

"How will you get home?" Douglas asked.

"I'll get him a cab," Ella said.

"Do you want me to do that?" Douglas asked her.

Ella shook her head. "I have to get one anyway to return to the school."

Douglas nodded.

"I'm fine, Daddy," she said, seeing the anxiety in his face. A tiny vein rose on the left side of his forehead when he was upset. Her father had never been anything but good to her, and now she was causing him to worry. "I'll call you as soon as I get to the office." She gave him her big-girl smile.

"Thank you so much," Ted said to Douglas, shaking his hand. "I don't know what to say. Should I give Sharlene my insurance information? Or—"

"Don't be ridiculous. Just try to relax. Go home, Ted."

The doctor watched the two of them leave, and when they were gone, he put his head down on the desk. He then did what he always did whenever something bad happened with Ella. He wondered what his wife would have done, and he hoped to have done that, because she had always known the right thing.

Ella dropped him off at his apartment in her taxi. He thanked her. He had never been wrong about her good character. Ella was capable of being kind to him, even now.

The apartment was empty. Delia was at the office, and he would call her shortly. The doorman had handed him his mail when he walked in; he looked over it and could barely make out the lettering because his eyes were still dilated, but he spotted a flimsy three-by-five envelope that his father liked to use. Could his father have sent him something before he died? But the handwriting was more like his mother's. It was hard to tell right now.

In the envelope was the check for a thousand dollars that he had sent to his parents last month. Since graduation from HBS, he had sent his parents a check each month and larger gifts on holidays. Ted closed his right eye and held the letter as far off as he could and made out some of his mother's writing. She was returning his check, and she asked him not to send money anymore. She didn't want to take his money. She didn't have any real expenses. At the bottom of the page, she wrote: "I hope you are kind to Ella. She has always been so kind to your parents. Be a good boy, Teddy," and she signed the letter as she always had: "*Umma.*"

On Tuesday after the Fourth of July weekend, Ronald Coverdale phoned Ella at school. The ring echoed in the empty headmaster's office. The building felt ghostly with all the children gone for the summer. Soon, the administrative staff would also leave the building for six weeks.

The lawyer's hello sounded cheerful. She almost didn't recognize him.

Ted had decided not to pursue joint custody with an equal time split. And if she could buy out his share, Ted would let her keep the house. Ella would get full custody of Irene, but he asked for weekend visiting rights and shared holidays.

She was speechless for a moment. "Oh, thank God. But why?"

"Didn't say. Maybe he wants to get this over with. Chet said he'd rush with the paperwork. Don't ask why. This is very nice, you know. You two can get on to the next stage of your lives."

"Yes, yes, of course. It's what I wanted. Thank you, Ronald. Thank you so much." Ella felt overcome with emotion.

"I can't take credit for this."

"And neither can I," she said, ending the happy call.

Ella ran out of the office to tell David.

Casey let herself into the Gottesmans' apartment with the key Sabine had given her the night she'd come from Unu's.

She slipped off her high heels and tiptoed to the guest room where she'd made camp. When she opened the door to her room, a light was on, and Sabine was asleep on the chaise longue with an open book about Modigliani on her lap.

Casey hung her handbag on the doorknob.

Sabine stirred from sleep. "Hello," she said, pushing the bangs off her face. "What time is it?"

Casey checked her watch. "One-twelve."

"You coming from work?"

"Where else?" she replied. Why was Sabine sleeping in her room? If she didn't want to sleep with Isaac, there were two other empty bedrooms in the apartment. "Is everything okay?"

Sabine sat upright, her body forming a right angle. She was fully alert. "And how is work?"

"It's work." Casey wouldn't complain, refusing to provide ammunition for Sabine's case against Kearn Davis.

"It's very late, Casey."

"I'm sorry, Sabine. I hope my stay hasn't been too disruptive. It's incredibly kind of you and Isaac to let me sleep here. I'm trying to figure out what to do about an apartment. I just haven't had the time to—"

"No, no, sweetie. It was my idea for you to stay here till school starts. And you can stay on as long as you like. It's just that we hardly see you. I thought I'd see you far more. I saw you once this past week—for like ten minutes in the kitchen before you went off to the office. What's wrong with those people there? It's inhumane how they make you work like that. And the idea of not giving every person who deserves an offer an offer. That's no way to run a business. How about if every person who's working with you is good? Then what? They create this situation where you have to cut people?" Sabine was on a tear. "And you hardly eat anything. You look terrible."

The more she talked, the less Casey had to say. It was that way between them. And now she was a guest in Sabine's house. Casey stowed away her shoes in the closet, taking care to be neat about it. She wanted to change out of her clothes but felt shy about undressing. Would Sabine leave her room soon? In the closet, beside her own clothes hung half a dozen suits Sabine no longer wore and had loaned her to wear to work. She was wearing one of Sabine's sleeveless blouses at the moment with a gray skirt she'd bought years ago when she'd first moved out of her parents' apartment. Casey had lost a few pounds and was able to wear Sabine's things, but her arms were too long for Sabine's jackets.

"Casey? What's the matter, honey?" Sabine sounded concerned. "Are you okay?"

"I'm fine. I'm just tired."

"You missing that guy? That gambler?"

"No," Casey replied instantly. That wasn't true, but she couldn't tell Sabine that. She thought about him a lot. Worse, she felt awful about what she had done—the cheating and then the confession. On a week's reflection, she'd concluded that both actions were heartless. That morning, she'd picked up the phone but couldn't actually call him. All her things were still in his place, but asking about that now seemed cold. Sabine was dead-on: She missed him. As soon as she got an apartment, she'd contact him, she told herself. By September, he might hate her less, and she might have more nerve.

Casey stepped into the guest bathroom. She left the door ajar; Sabine was obviously percolating with more things to say. She changed into one of the two guest bathrobes Sabine had placed in there—the kind you covet at a fancy hotel. Her host wasn't making any move to leave the room.

Casey began to wash her face. When she heard Sabine's voice, she turned off the faucet.

"You cheated on him because you were angry at him."

Casey frowned. Sabine had theories about everything. Casey wiped away the residual soap from her face with a towel and sat on her bed—arms folded, her back slouching. She smoothed down the Italian bedspread. The blue quilted fabric was beautiful.

"And why was I angry with him?" she asked.

"It's obvious. He lost his job, wouldn't get a new one, has a serious gambling addiction, and he doesn't want to marry you."

"I didn't want to get married," Casey said, unable to refute much else.

"That's not the point, and you know it. He wasn't thinking about the future, and you didn't respect him for it."

"Wow, a free room and free advice. Thank you." Casey didn't feel like being polite anymore. It was so damn late, and she wanted to sleep. She had to get up in a few hours. Karyn had given her a monster assignment that afternoon. "May I go to sleep now?"

"Cheaters always have a reason."

"Okay, I'll bite." Casey wriggled her toes. "Then why did Jay—"

"Because you wouldn't introduce him to your parents. He was angry with you because you were ashamed of him."

"An answer for everything. And quick, too." Casey smiled, appearing unfazed. In fact, she was taken aback by this insight. "How do you know so much about this?"

"Because Isaac cheats on me."

"That can't be. He adores you."

"I know he does. And he's not leaving me. He can't live without me."

"Well, I'm glad you're not suffering silently from low self-esteem."

"I can't prevent it. He is just a cheater. I sensed it when I married him. He thinks I don't know, but I know. I can't meet all of his emotional needs, and he can't fix himself of whatever childhood injuries doled—"

Casey was starting to tune out. It was always this babble with Sabine when it came to sex or love. For Sabine, everything could be boiled down to psychological motivations, as if cake were just flour, milk, sugar, and eggs. Casey found it unattractive and ultimately unpersuasive. Maybe Sabine was not entirely wrong, but it seemed to take the heat out of the recipe—the romance. Unu would've found Sabine ridiculous. They'd never met, however.

Sabine closed her art book and leaned her head back against the chair.

Casey hadn't known about Isaac's infidelity. That must have hurt.

"Why do you stay with him?" she asked.

"Because we're very good together. I respect him enormously as a businessman. He's also very kind. That's not as common as you'd think. Also, he leaves me alone. So I can do my thing."

"How about love?"

"Love is respect, Casey. You don't respect Unu."

"Yes, I do," she said. "He's very smart. Unu is an original thinker. I admire that more than most—"

"How could you respect a man who—"

"You don't respect Unu. But I do. He's going through something hard. You're allowed to make mistakes. I don't care if he doesn't make lots of money. That's not my thing."

"Yes, it is. How else do you explain Kearn Davis, then?"

"I'm trying to get rid of my debts, Sabine. I have to pay for school—"

"And you have to do it all by yourself?"

"Well, obviously not, since you're housing me right now, and I owe you—"

"Oh, stop it. Who cares about this? Your pride is simply ridiculous."

"Thank you." Casey wanted to smoke. There was a fresh pack in her purse. Isaac didn't like the smell of cigarette smoke in the house, but she could have one on the terrace by the living room.

"I love you, Casey," Sabine said, wanting Casey to look at her.

"I love you, too, Sabine," Casey said, her voice disgruntled and resigned.

"And I respect you," Sabine said.

"Ditto."

"But you are ignoring the obvious in your life," Sabine said.

"Clue, please."

"Stop ignoring your feelings."

"Okay, I'll think about that."

"You are angry with me right now," Sabine said. It had taken her a decade of therapy to figure out this invaluable lesson: Your truest feelings led you to greater and greater success in life. She had accomplished nearly impossible goals by recognizing her finest and ugliest feelings and everything in between. "You're furious."

"No, I'm not."

"Yes, you are."

"No, I'm not." Casey made her face go blank. "I'm grateful that you are such a good friend."

"You can be grateful and angry. Such feelings can coexist."

Casey sighed. "I'm so tired, Sabine. I should go to bed."

"Okay." Sabine got up from the chaise. "Unu is a lousy choice. A man is supposed to help you."

"Thank you. I'll try to remember that."

Sabine came by her side and put her hand over Casey's brow. "My dear Casey. You don't know who you are. Try to—"

"Sabine..." Casey was seething. "I am doing the best I can."

"No one ever doubts that of you. You should perhaps do less." Sabine smiled. "I shall let you go to bed now."

"Okay," Casey said.

"Good night, baby. And drink that detoxification tea I bought for you. It's on the counter next to the espresso machine."

She nodded, letting Sabine kiss her on the cheek good night. As soon as Sabine closed the door, Casey climbed out of bed and grabbed her purse. She opened the window as far as it would go and lit a cigarette. Unu would be asleep, she thought. He always slept on his left side, facing the middle of the bed, his left arm tucked in by his shoulder, his hand beneath his cheek. When she came home late and he'd been sleeping, he'd open his eyes and murmur, "Hey, babe, you're home. Come to bed." Sometimes he'd continue snoring quietly. Casey stubbed out her cigarette on the window ledge and lit another.

11 | BASTE

THE SILVER CUFFS SHE COULDN'T POSSIBLY WEAR lay on top of
the dresser. Tina fingered the extravagant gift Sabine had
made to her sister and that her sister had later made to her. There
was no way Tina could have refused them, but the gift only rein-
forced in her mind that her sister was out of touch. It was a kind
gesture, surely, but what did she need a pair of matching bracelets
from Tiffany's for? Where was she going with a two-month-old that
would require her to wear Wonder Woman cuffs? As it was, she and
Chul barely had money for groceries, diapers, and the occasional
video rental. They took the BART everywhere because they couldn't
afford to keep Chul's Toyota in San Francisco. Besides, even if the
edges were smooth, the hard metal would bother Timothy when
Tina was feeding or bathing him or changing his diapers. That night
in New York, right after Tina and Chul had dropped Casey and Unu
off at their apartment on the Upper East Side, Tina had slipped off
the cuffs and dropped them into her diaper bag.

In forty minutes, Timothy would wake from his nap and need to
nurse again. Hopefully his last feeding for the night. Chul was still
studying at the library. He was taking summer classes to accelerate
graduation. She'd made tuna salad for dinner, but he'd called to say
that he'd grab a burrito before he got home. She had spent another
day alone in the apartment with the baby. Tina craved her books,

her classes. Seeing adults. It was Friday night. But it could have been any other.

What was her sister doing right now? Tina wondered. In their last brief phone conversation, Casey had dismissed any possible worries about their mother's health. She was thoroughly anxious about getting a permanent offer from Kearn Davis. Tina had thought of reassuring her, but it wasn't easy to do with Casey. You never really knew if she was listening. Also, Casey was single again. She had screwed some guy she used to work with on some out-of-town business trip, then confessed. "But I felt like such an asshole for not telling him." Tina had kept from saying, *Well, now he probably thinks you were an asshole for sleeping with another guy.* For now, Casey was staying with Sabine and Isaac until she got her shit in order. Nice life, Tina thought. Nice landing.

Tina dialed her parents' number to make her Friday night call, and Leah picked up.

"*Yuh-bo-seh-yoh.*"

"Mom, it's me."

"Ti-na. How is the baby?" Leah asked. She remembered Timothy's softness, the round black eyes beneath the ruffle of his dark lashes.

"He's good. He's sleeping now."

"And eating well?"

"I'm nursing constantly. Some days it's like twelve or thirteen times." Tina blew the overgrown bangs away from her face. Whenever the baby wasn't nursing, it felt as though Chul were trying to slip his hands beneath her shirt. She still had thirty pounds left to lose, but Chul didn't seem to mind. Her engorged breasts made him horny, he said. Her boobs had become communal property. Had her mother ever felt like that?

"How are you?" Tina asked.

"*Umma* is okay."

"But Daddy said you missed church again."

"*Umma* is okay. Have you heard from Casey?"

"Last week." Why didn't her mother just pick up the phone and call Casey?

"I thought Ella's cousin was nice," Leah said.

"They broke up," Tina blurted out.

Before her mother could ask any more, she said brusquely, "Let me talk to Daddy now."

"But they seemed happy," Leah said, her voice cracking.

"It didn't work out, I guess," Tina said, trying to skip the details. She hated being the messenger.

"Where is she living then? I don't have her phone number."

"She's staying with Sabine Gottesman. Until she finds a place."

"Oh," Leah took a breath. "I'd hoped that they would…"

Leah nodded. Tina wouldn't tell her any more than that. The nice young man was gone. It wasn't that she believed that if her daughter was married, then everything would be all right. But she wanted her child to be stable. And why didn't she come home if she needed a place to stay? Maybe Casey was right to look up to a person like Sabine, who was a success in America.

Was God punishing her? Was she losing Casey to Sabine because of what had happened between her and the professor? No, Leah argued with herself. God wasn't like that. You didn't always get what you deserved. Thankfully. Job was a good man, and he had suffered. Christ was the son of God, and all he did was suffer. But Leah had sinned. King David lost his baby after taking his friend's wife and killing his friend. Her daughters did not respect her. They didn't like her.

"*Yobo,*" Leah shouted over the noise of the television coming from the living room.

Joseph folded his newspaper and dropped it on the seat of his chair. He muted the television and picked up the phone.

Leah held on to the receiver. She could hear the happiness in her husband's voice. First, Joseph asked to speak to the baby, but he was asleep. Then he asked Tina how she was. Tina told him how tired she was, how much she missed school.

Leah put down the receiver.

Tina heard the click. Her mother had sounded awful. And there was little she could do for her so far away. After graduation, she and Chul intended to go back east.

"Daddy, can't you and Mom come for a visit?"

"The store. One of us has to be here. You know that."

Tina nodded. The store. They had never been on a family vacation. Her parents had never asked Mr. Kang for the time off, and the owner had never offered. But even if her father had gotten permission to close the store for a few days, Tina didn't believe that her mother would have gotten on a plane for California.

"Why hasn't *Umma* been to the doctor?"

"You know she doesn't like to go. I told her, but she said she's doing better. It sounds like a cold. Maybe the flu."

"Daddy, a cold shouldn't take this long."

"If she doesn't go to church on Sunday, Elder Shim is coming by with the hospitality committee. He's a doctor. Maybe he can talk to her."

"He's an eye doctor."

"Okay, okay. When will you bring Timothy to New York?"

"We were just there, Daddy. You should come here."

"Okay, okay."

"I better go," she said, getting ready to say good-bye.

"Take care of my grandson."

"I will," Tina replied. She wanted to keep talking to her father; she wished he'd ask her more questions. Was it possible to tell him that she felt lonely ever since she had the baby and that Chul had no idea what her life was like now, to lose school and friends? He just wanted to have sex regularly and get good grades.

"Daddy..."

"Hmm..." Joseph cleared his throat, unable to say how much he missed her. He could tell she was tired, and he was embarrassed that he couldn't send her a maid. That was what a rich man would have done back home—send his daughter a nanny so she wouldn't have to work so hard.

"Good night," she said.

"I know you will do a good job with everything," he said before hanging up.

Tina got off the phone, then went to check on the baby.

The following day, Leah went to work, came home, and made dinner, then went to sleep at eight o'clock. On Sunday morning, she could hardly move her body out of bed. The weight of it over-whelmed her. Joseph made her stay home and went to church by himself. That afternoon, whether she liked it or not, the hospitality committee would come.

Douglas Shim, Elder Kim, and Deaconess Jun rang the buzzer at exactly three-fifteen. After being let in, they marched inside with-out much of a greeting, sat on the sofa, and prayed silently. Doug-las finished praying first, Elder Kim second, and Deaconess Jun prayed vigorously for another three minutes. Joseph led them to the bedroom.

Everyone bowed and smiled at one another.

Leah felt shy about being in bed in her nightgown and robe in front of the elders. She offered them coffee. A little while before, she had boiled water and put out a fresh jar of Taster's Choice and Coffee-Mate on a tray with three clean mugs so Joseph could fix the coffee in case the committee wanted some refreshment. There were no biscuits at home, and she was embarrassed by this, but she hadn't had company in a long time. But the committee explained that this was their third visit of the day and they couldn't drink another drop of coffee or tea. They had brought her twelve cans of orange juice and a box of eclairs from Le Paris bakery.

Joseph brought three kitchen chairs into the bedroom.

The committee sat down and prayed for her quick recovery.

"Your husband said that you had a cold," Douglas said, concerned that she might have something more serious, but he didn't want to frighten her. He had tried to visit earlier, but Joseph had put him off, saying that Leah couldn't manage having visitors. After nearly two months of Leah missing church, Douglas had insisted, and Joseph could no longer say no. The last time they spoke about the committee visiting, Douglas had sensed that Joseph might even welcome a little help. "How are you feeling?"

"Much better. I had some stomach problems which have gone away, but I'm so sleepy. And there's been a lot of work at the store."

Deaconess Jun nodded, understanding perfectly. She worked in a dry-cleaning store that her mother-in-law owned on the Upper West Side. She did the alterations when she wasn't working as the cashier. With two little boys at school and work, she felt as though she never had enough sleep. If it wasn't for her *midum* in Yesu Christo, she could hardly bear her angry mother-in-law and her feckless husband, who could never take her side.

"Have you seen a doctor?" Douglas asked.

"I told her to go, but...," Joseph interrupted. Douglas nodded and waited for Leah to add something.

"I really am much better," Leah reassured them. She made her voice a bit stronger. "It was good of you to come by. But I really am okay. I hope to go to church next Sunday."

"You've lost some weight," Douglas remarked.

"Have I?"

"You didn't have anything to lose. Aren't you eating better now? After the stomach problems?"

Leah nodded. She wasn't being truthful but couldn't take any more of this attention.

She wasn't really sick. At least, she didn't think so. And lately, it had been getting better.

"I was worried that you had chicken pox," he said with a smile, re-calling their visit together to the choir director's house. "But you'd said that you had it as a child."

"Nothing so serious. Maybe I'm just tired because I'm getting older." She smiled, pointing to her brilliant white hair.

"Don't be silly," Elder Kim chided. She couldn't have been more than forty-five. The woman who sat up in bed in her pajamas had the face of a pretty girl from the country. The accountant felt sad for her. Many of the women at church labored sixty to seventy hours a week in small businesses without pay or breaks. When home, they faced chores and took care of their children besides. His wife helped him out at his office during tax season, but she stayed home mostly with their two sons.

"No doubt you've been working too hard," Elder Kim said.

Joseph bit the inside of his cheek.

"Maybe it's good that you rest on the Sabbath and miss those bor-ing sermons." Douglas winked. "I'm sure God would understand."

Both Elder Kim and Deaconess Jun laughed. Today's sermon on tithing and the necessity of sacrificial giving had felt unusually long.

"Are you anemic?" Douglas asked.

"No. When I was pregnant with Tina, the doctor did say some-thing about eating more meat and spinach."

She needed to get her bloodwork done, he said. He knew of an excellent internist not far from her store. Maybe she could walk over during her lunch break. Leah thanked him but said it would be all right. She'd been feeling well enough that she planned on going to church next week, she said. The committee clapped their hands at this. Deaconess Jun exclaimed, "Ah-men." The elders and the deaconess got up from their chairs. They bowed their heads and prayed for her healing in the name of their savior and redeemer Yesu Christo.

After the hospitality committee left, Joseph went out to buy seasoned *bulgogi* meat from the Korean market. At home, he washed the rice, turned on the cooker, and heated the frying pan.

The garlicky smell of the meat frying soon filled the apartment. From the bedroom, Leah could smell the ginger and sesame oil of the marinade. She tried to get up, but the pull of her own weight fought her. She took a deep breath and willed herself out of bed, her bare feet thudding against the floor. In the kitchen, she saw Joseph's squat back. He was putting out kimchi in a bowl. The kitchen table was already set with two place settings. He had done this. She pulled out a chair to sit, and at the noise, he turned to her, proud of the Sunday dinner he'd fixed.

The smell of the meat grew stronger; a cloud of steam wafted above the pan. Leah tried to get up to open the window. There was no air conditioner in the kitchen. It was as if she were submerged underwater wearing a heavy coat.

There was a hard smack. Sharp pain—such sharp pain in the center of her face—radiated across her cheeks and brow. Her nose hurt. So much. Tears sprang to her eyes, their warmth trickling down her cheeks and nose. Joseph's slippered footsteps rushed toward her. *"Yobo, yobo, yobo!"* he cried. Her head had planted straight down on the table. The meat sizzled in the pan, and all Leah could think of was that the stove was still on and the meat would burn. It would be such a waste of money. How could she turn off the stove? But she had lost her words. A thin trail of blood streamed across the white table. Everything darkened with smoke.

Douglas Shim hovered over her. "Deaconess, Deaconess…"

Somehow she was in bed, the bib of her nightgown covered in blood. She remembered the kitchen. She had fallen, hadn't she?

"Is this okay?" she asked Elder Shim. It hurt to talk.

"Your husband called my pager. I was only a few blocks away at Elder Chung's." He smiled knowingly at her. Elder Chung was ninety-three years old and bedridden. He lived with his childless son and daughter-in-law in Maspeth. The visits were more social than spiritual. Elder Chung loved to talk more than anything, and the hospitality committee always visited him last, because he might cry at short visits. "You saved me, actually. He was about to tell the one about the freckled Japanese soldier who had fallen in love with his sister. You know that one."

Leah nodded. "He's okay?"

"Of course. Elder Chung's doing much better than you."

Douglas was talking mostly to see how clear Leah was. Her nose might've been broken.

"I'm sorry to be so much trouble." Elder Shim was staring at her nose. Leah touched it. She winced in pain.

"Don't do that."

Leah folded her hands together and laid them above her stomach.

"Maybe you wanted me to come back because you felt like singing."

Leah smiled. How long had it been since someone had teased her? Chul-ho *opa* used to call her Nightingale. Her dead brother, the second oldest, had given her this pet name when she was little, and she had forgotten about it till now. Nightingale. Was she going to die, too? Would she see her two dead brothers again in heaven? What would they look like? And her mother. Oh God, oh God...Leah wanted to see her mother again. Death would mean nothing if she could see her mother again. God could take her now, and it wouldn't be anything but relief. But who would care for Joseph? She had to get better so she could take care of him. Her husband was standing in the corner of the bedroom looking impassive, but she could sense that he was frightened. He must have been—to call Elder Shim on his pager.

Douglas came closer, raising his hands gently as if he were asking for permission. He touched her cheeks first, then her nose as gently as possible. Leah kept herself from flinching at his touch. It hurt so much.

"I think you broke it," Douglas declared. He stepped back two paces, then studied her face again, trying to remember the shape of her nose. "But I don't think it's misaligned. Maybe just a hairline fracture. You could still be on television."

Leah stifled a laugh because it would cause pain. She touched her nose again lightly. There was a tiny bit of swelling on the bridge.

"Joseph was cooking..." Her eyes crinkled in confusion.

"You fainted and fell facefirst onto the table. Joseph carried you here. He called me. Now it's time for you to sing."

Joseph smiled. He had always disliked the elder's joking, but he appreciated how it lightened things for others. He could see how the doctor relaxed his wife, let her talk.

Douglas motioned to Joseph and asked him for a few cubes of ice wrapped in a dish towel. Joseph went to the kitchen.

"How old are you?"

"Forty-three."

"When was your last period?"

"I don't remember. I don't get it every month," she said, unable to look him in the eye. These were things she didn't discuss with anyone. She'd gotten her period at fourteen, later than most, she found out later, and her periods didn't come every month as they did with other girls. Sometimes she got them every two months and they lasted for ten days or more. Except for when she was pregnant, she hadn't seen a gynecologist. There had never been any real problems as far as she could tell. Tina was always telling her to get tests, but where was there time for those things? It also cost so much money.

"Maybe several weeks ago?" Leah tried to recall, but it wasn't clear. More than two months ago.

"So you're not pregnant," Douglas said calmly.

"Oh no," Leah said, dismissing the impossible.

Joseph walked in carrying a large bundle of ice. Douglas removed all but three pieces of ice in the towel. He showed Leah how to hold it against her face.

"So you're not a father again." Douglas smiled at Joseph, thinking that the man was far too serious for his own good.

"I had a vasectomy after Tina was born. The doctors said Leah shouldn't get pregnant again. I didn't want her to take drugs."

Douglas nodded vigorously, having lost his wife in childbirth. "It is one of the most effective methods of birth control. Probably ninety-nine percent." That a man of his generation and background had cared enough about his wife to have such a surgery was quite remarkable. But he felt a shot of envy toward Joseph for having an attractive wife. It made Douglas wonder where his desire for sex had gone—it was as if that part of him had gone to sleep.

"I want you to see an internist. For some simple tests. And you should see an ENT for your nose. He won't do anything, probably not even X-ray unless you're going to sue your husband for cooking for you. Do you have health insurance?"

Leah shook her head no.

"We can pay. We have money to pay doctors," Joseph said.

Douglas nodded. "Yes, of course." He would make the calls tomorrow.

Leah looked at the men helplessly, not knowing how to fight this.

Douglas had to leave. He promised to call her the next day.

The following week, Leah went to the ENT because his office was three blocks from the store. The nose was broken, the doctor said. There was minimal swelling on the bridge. A bright blue spot was her only bruise. There was nothing to do, he said. The internist couldn't see her till the following week, but Leah thought she might cancel the appointment because she had been feeling much better. She tried to eat more regularly, preferring to eat more bagels and rice rather than the expensive roast beef sandwiches Joseph bought for her lunch from the corner deli. On Sunday, the blue spot was smaller, and she decided to go to church. It had been too long since she had been in God's house. Leah had been praying unceasingly for forgiveness. No matter what she did, she had come to believe that He would be merciful to her. For God was good.

Leah walked into the choir practice room quietly and sat in her assigned chair. The choir director had not yet arrived. At her arrival, the choir members gasped and greeted her warmly. Kyung-ah shrieked with happiness. She hugged her.

"I tried to visit. But your bear of a husband said you needed to sleep," Kyung-ah whined, stroking Leah's hair. "*Uh-muh,* what happened? What's that?" She pointed to the blue shadow on the bridge of Leah's nose.

"I fainted and fell on the table. It's broken."

Looks of worry flashed across the choir members' faces.

"No, just a little line break, the doctor said. I'm fine. Not serious. I can still sing." Leah smiled to reassure them. Then she thanked them for the ficus tree they had sent her while she was away.

The members looked at the doorway. Charles had come in. Leah's stomach clenched. He saw her, the crowd gathering round her chair. Kyung-ah smiled at him, then turned away, catching herself. Charles, his mouth slightly agape as if he meant to say something, went to the front of the room. He put down his bag on his desk and removed his jacket.

He tried to compose himself. She was here. Despite everything, a part of him was pulling at him, wanting to take her by the hand, walk out, and never return. They could be happy. But she'd said it was a mistake. She hadn't tried to reach him. Even after the call, he had waited for her to change her mind, but no. She had not come back even to church. Never called him at home. He checked now to see her again. Several people were talking to her still. There was a pale bruise on her nose. Had he hit her? Maybe she couldn't leave the old man. Charles grimaced. He had been thinking about quitting this job, just taking on more voice work. His father would've happily sent him more money if he'd explain that he wanted to work on his song cycle commission. That choir directing was a waste of his time. After all, the world premiere was less than two months away. But there was a new reason to stay. For a little while longer, anyway. Kyung-ah had come to him last week after practice. And yesterday she had come by the house. There was something delicious about her abandon. And it had been too long since he had been with a woman in a real way. Making love was much better when meetings were frequent. And she wanted something regular, too. But interestingly, she didn't want to be his mother, wife, or girlfriend. "We're not friends," she'd said, laughing. Kyung-ah was not interested in romance. She was in heat, no different from a bitch, she'd said herself. Yesterday, she hadn't even wanted to have a cup of coffee with him. She'd left his house at five o'clock to finish up her bookkeeping and to lock up the store. He'd meet her again tonight after rehearsal if she could get away.

Charles handed the choir secretary, Mrs. Noh, the new score for next week.

"I thought on Sunday, we'd try this arrangement of 'How Great Thou Art.' There will be two duets—a male and female pair."

The Kim brothers were very pleased when their names were announced.

"Deaconess Cho, you have returned to us," Charles said, his voice flat.

Leah nodded, her jaws clamped down.

"And how are you feeling?"

The choir members looked at her kindly, waiting for her reply.

"I...can sing," she said.

"Good. You and Mrs. Shim will do the duet together," Charles said to her quickly, then faced Mrs. Shim, a young mother of two and a mezzo-soprano.

Kyung-ah whispered, "I did two solos this month already since you were gone." She giggled, remembering how Charles had held her by the waist possessively before she'd left his house yesterday. Men were ridiculous, but they were good for a few things.

Mrs. Shim turned to Leah and smiled shyly at her. They'd never sung together as a pair.

Charles asked the accompanist to play today's first selection. The rehearsal began.

After services ended, Leah grabbed a cup of tea and followed the choir to the room for next week's rehearsal. She hadn't anticipated singing in a duet next week. Last night, she had not slept well thinking of all the possible things she would say to the professor. How were they supposed to work together after what had happened? She had pledged to God to be a good choir member, to practice more, and to always be careful around him. It had been a careless and foolish indulgence to have romantic feelings for him. That night had been a sin for which she would always be guilty. The memory of it made her want to die. But she had reasoned that suicide was a greater sin. She had to live to take care of Joseph. But it was so confusing. God would want her to respect her superiors, and the professor was her superior. God must have wanted her to be under the professor's instruction, and Leah intended to obey his teaching. In her shameful heart, though, she'd imagined being alone with him again, talking about music and his life. After he had called her house, she had found his phone number through information and had picked up the phone numerous times when she was home by herself. But she had envisioned him hanging up angrily at her. *You said it was a mistake,* he would say. *You made a mockery of our love.* He could have said all those things, and he would have been right. What Leah had felt for him, she had never felt before for another human being. But she had never intended to be an adulteress. What God had made—her sacred marriage bonds to Joseph—she could not possibly break. Her love for the professor would be her sacrifice for God. She would place it on the altar of her heart. Christ, the one without sin, gave up everything, including the communion with his Father, for her sake, for her sins. Forsaking the girlish feelings she had for the professor seemed paltry indeed. Last night, Leah justified herself with these thoughts as she lay awake in her bed, dreaming of the sound of the professor's voice. I will give him up, she'd told herself, and I will serve God by singing faithfully to Him alone.

When the rehearsal for the choir ended, everyone left except for the Kim brothers, Mrs. Shim, the professor, and her. He hardly looked her way except for when it was to give her an instruction. Leah wondered where the feelings between them had gone. Perhaps she had imagined all of it. She gathered her music when they'd finished the duets' rehearsal. Everyone said good night to the professor, and he did not give her even a quick glance. There was this heavy push inside her chest. God was with her in this. Somehow, this was what she deserved. What God would want for her. She was a married woman, and her husband was a good man.

In the parking lot, Leah waved good-bye at the Kim brothers, two large men who had little to say for themselves and smiled uneasily at women, and at Mrs. Shim, who was sweet and wouldn't stop bowing. Leah got into the car, knowing that the professor was still inside the church building. She belted herself into her seat and turned on the ignition. You must not go inside, she told herself. She drove home slowly, wiping her face at the intersections along the way.

12 | LINING

*I*T'S DAMN, DAMN HOT," Kyung-ah muttered to Leah, tugging at her white sateen collar. "I hate this polyester crap." The reversible V-neck shifted askew over the sky blue choir robe. The soprano was also tired of Elder Ahn, who droned on with her prayer. "Jesus did not have that much to say."

A few of the basses and tenors seated behind Kyung-ah snickered. Leah patted Kyung-ah on the thigh as if she were calming a fidgety child. She was hot, too. This morning, she had put on her good blue dress—a summer-weight wool with sleeves that reached to her elbows—that should've been cool enough for the end of July, but the pale blue lining she'd sewn in herself stuck to her clammy back. Parched and uncomfortable, she forced herself to pay attention to Elder Ahn's long petition to their Father in heaven.

Elder Ahn's beseeching grew louder and faster, and in her watery Kyung-sang-do accent, she panted to her dear *Ah-buh-jee* in heaven. One of the tenors clocked her at twelve minutes forty-three seconds on his gold Rolex Perpetual. The service was only half over, and the choir had to remain seated in their white partitioned pews, their black-haired heads bobbing just above the wainscoted church walls. The choir was only a few feet away from the lectern. The sermon was up next. Though it was only seventy degrees outside, in the sanctuary it felt like eighty-five. The air conditioner hadn't worked all summer. Naturally, jokes had been made about how this must be a foretaste of hell. The Kim brothers pulled on their neckties. Their duet with Deaconess Cho and Mrs. Shim was already sung. They were dreaming of cold beer. There was no amen in sight.

The strong morning sun streamed in through the tall windows— wide blocks of light fried the unlucky parishioners seated beneath them. Elder Ahn was now praying for those named in the prayer request cards dropped in the offering plate the previous week. The seventy-four-year-old female elder who'd sold boiled corn on the streets of Seoul for three decades to send her children to school, but now lived in her own fully-paid-for brick house near Corona Boulevard, paid careful attention to each ailing parishioner needing a communal prayer, not failing to embellish the specific ailment with words of urgency. It was the least she could do, she felt, for her fellow brothers and sisters in Christ. "Have mercy on Deaconess Sohn, who has been suffering with agonizing arthritis pain in her hands and legs. Have mercy on her, dear Father in heaven...oh, my Lord, my God, have mercy on your daughter." The chubby alto, his hair darkened with Grecian Formula, seated beside Kyung-ah tried to amuse her by counting the requests thus far: twelve.

Kyung-ah was now making a rapid spooling gesture with her hands, not entirely hidden in the wide blue sleeves of her robe. But nothing would disturb Elder Ahn, who was reaching an ecstatic pitch. Tears flowed. Several congregants were evidently moved by her passion. Only twelve women were installed as elders in the congregation numbering five hundred; each gave one prayer per year. This was not a privilege Elder Ahn took lightly. Both her daughters and her one son, none of whom attended the Woodside services regularly, had come today at their mother's request. Kyung-ah widened her eyes and pinched Leah jokingly. Thankfully, Kyung-ah and Leah were sandwiched in the middle of the three rows, so the congregation could not see Kyung-ah's antics. Leah's father used to say whenever her brothers teased the pious grandmothers of their church, "One day, you too will be very old, and only God will matter." Leah glanced reprovingly at her friend, yet this had no effect. Kyung-ah smiled prettily and fanned herself with the program.

Charles sat with the congregation in the first row, on the seat nearest the aisle. He looked particularly attractive today, Kyung-ah thought: well shaven, the white linen shirt and dark cotton pants coolly refreshing compared with the others wearing dark suits and cheap ties. Kyung-ah raised her sable-colored eyebrows at him suggestively. After the evening rehearsal, she was supposed to meet him at an Italian restaurant on Mulberry Street. No one they knew would spot them there. In making their plans for tonight, he'd asked her to sleep over, and she'd said casually, "We'll see." But yesterday she'd gone to Macy's and purchased a three-hundred-dollar Natori peignoir set in champagne-colored lace. Her husband thought she was staying at her sister's.

At last, Elder Ahn cradled her head with her knotty brown fingers. She was rapturous—her grief consoled—certain that her prayers were heard by God. She stepped down from the lectern, grasping her gray metal cane that had been leaning beside her all that time. On cue, Miss Chun, the summer organist, played the beginning bars of "When Morning Gilds the Skies."

Leah stood up with the choir, air filled her lungs, and she opened her mouth to praise God with her song. The first two lines of the hymn were gorgeous. The rise of the music almost lifted her bodily. This was why she had gotten dressed that morning, though she had felt the pull of her bed, the weight of her shame at having to face the professor again, the leaden lump of sin in her chest. What else was music but a miracle? What she could never say in speech, she could sing in verse, expressing the depth of her passion for her Maker. She'd never be capable of praying like Elder Ahn or be as eloquent as Reverend Lim, the best preacher of the ministry staff. "My heart a-waking cries, May Jesus Christ be praised! A-like at work and prayer, To Jesus I repair; May Jesus Christ be praised!" Leah closed her eyes, her head lilting with the tune. But a thrust of nausea clutched her stomach violently. Liquid gushed out of her, drenching her L'eggs panty hose. Had she peed? Her ankles were dark red, as were the edges of her robe. A large puddle of blood spread across the floor. The blood had reached even Kyung-ah's shoes and those of Miss Oh, who sat next to her. Leah gasped, then fell down. Kyung-ah shrieked out loud, "Call an ambulance!" Charles bolted out of the sanctuary to get to the church office phone.

Once they were at Elmhurst General Hospital, the doctors and nurses deferred to Douglas as a matter of professional courtesy. Douglas told the staff that he was Leah's brother, and they didn't question him. Joseph held Leah's dry, lifeless palm while Douglas filled out the paperwork. Joseph answered Douglas's questions when the doctor didn't know the answers. He handed Douglas a credit card that he had used perhaps twice in his life. He signed whatever Douglas told him to. How should he contact Casey? Douglas asked. Joseph didn't know. When the doctors took Leah away and directed Joseph to the waiting area, Douglas phoned his daughter and asked her to find Casey. Leah had had a spontaneous miscarriage.

It was Sabine who finally gave Ella the Kearn Davis number. Casey was surprised to hear Ella's voice on the phone and stunned to hear the news.

"Oh, thank you so much for calling. I...I don't know what to say. Oh, my God. What should I do?" Casey mumbled to herself. She had a research project due in a few hours, but she had to leave. Offer decisions came out in two weeks. How would she get out now?

"Your parents need you there now," Ella said sternly, surprised that Casey didn't immediately offer to go.

Casey felt the reproach. Did Ella really think that she wouldn't go right away? What did Unu say to her? After thanking Ella, Casey got off the phone, saying, "Take care," with the precise intonation she'd use to indicate that the conversation between them was over. She called a car service and requested a driver to take her to Elmhurst General Hospital.

When Casey arrived, Dr. Shim explained everything to her. He had to go. He was late for a dinner with a board member from his hospital.

"You'll take care of your mom?" Douglas said. He felt better now that Casey was here.

"Yes, of course. Thank you, Dr. Shim. Thank you for everything you did today. Please thank Ella for finding me."

"It's nothing. I wish I didn't have to go to this dinner. But I really have to. I'll call later. Okay?" He looked at her fondly. "I'm sure you have all this under control."

Casey nodded. "We're going to be okay. Thank you, though."

Douglas smiled and hugged her before leaving her alone with her father.

Her father was staring at the beige hospital floor, unable to look her in the eye. The thought of her parents having sex was not awful, but surprising. Her mother had been pregnant. She and Tina could have had another sibling. How crazy.

"How is she? Have you seen her since?"

"She's still in there." Joseph pointed to the area behind the swinging doors. "They're cleaning out..." He couldn't say any more. Did his daughters know? That he'd had a vasectomy after Tina was born? In all these years, she had not gotten pregnant. Not as far as he knew. Could she have kept that from him? Elder Shim had said sometimes women miscarry and don't even know it. It could appear to be a heavy menses. His wife never talked about her periods or things like that. "Ella's dad said vasectomies are not a hundred percent."

"What are you talking about?" she asked.

Her father looked alarmed, as if she were learning something she wasn't supposed to know. "Oh sure," Casey said quickly. "I read that somewhere. That you can get pregnant even if a man has a vasectomy." She had never read that anywhere, but her father's relief was palpable. Her father had a vasectomy? Casey knew nothing more than the average person about contraception. She'd had an abortion, for crying out loud, having gotten pregnant while on the pill. Shit happened. She fought the urge to phone Tina right then. To ask if a vasectomy was foolproof.

Joseph sat down. He rubbed his temples with his hands. His headache was worsening. Casey sat beside him, her body parallel to his. From the corner of his eyes, he could see her in profile. Her eyes were dark brown with short black lashes. She was so close to him that he could make out the layer of black mascara coating her eyelashes. Her eyes were small, different in shape from his wife's, far more like his own. She had his mother's nose, and her lips were like his, taking after his side of the family. This was something he had always known, had been pointed out to him, but he had not liked this about her, and he felt sorry that he had always favored the younger one. But he had. The younger one had been easier to love. She had been more like a child, mild in nature and obedient.

Casey was wearing something that looked like a short necktie with a white shirt and white trousers. How odd. He was wearing a tie, but he was a man, and he had just come straight from church services. She looked strange in her getup. Not bad, but weird. She had always dressed so bizarrely. She had come from her office; routinely worked on the weekends, she'd said to Elder Shim. Why couldn't she dress like normal people? And in her hand she held a straw fedora with an orange ribbon band. Like a man's hat, too. Was his daughter a lesbian? No. She'd had boyfriends. Who knew? Tina was *yam-jun-heh,* ladylike, in comparison, though it was Casey who had loved skirts and wearing beaded necklaces as a little girl—the one who had fooled around with their mother's lipstick. Tina was reserved, did better at most things without having to be reminded, helped out her mother. Casey had been more trouble. Not so much at school, but in all things, she'd wanted to do things her own way without anyone's help. His girls were so different. Casey had the temperament of a boy. She had acted like a rebellious son. Before the war, he had been that way.

Joseph had not counted on it, but she had come to help. Suddenly, it seemed natural for him to pat her on the back, the way he patted Tina when she sat close by him at dinner. At first Casey stiffened at his touch, then she relaxed. She started to cry, but Joseph did not know why exactly.

A middle-aged Filipina nurse in white pants and a loud-patterned shirt, oversize for her petite frame, approached them. Her ID read "Eva Bulosan, R.N." Everything was okay.

"She needs to rest for a while, but she'll be able to go home tonight."

Joseph sighed, then lowered his head into his hands. Casey could hear him praising God in Korean.

"Nurse Bulosan, my mother...," Casey said, grateful for the nurse's smile. Her oval-shaped face was beautiful. "Can I see her?"

The nurse swiveled her body slightly, as if to give Joseph some privacy. She gazed at the daughter's face intently.

"Yes. Her room is the third door to your left, past the swinging doors. She'll be groggy, but that's normal. She might also be more emotional than her usual self. That's understandable, of course." The nurse stayed to answer questions, then left. Her step was light, and she was gone quickly.

Joseph finished praying.

"Did you want me to phone Tina now?" Casey asked.

"No. I'll phone her," Joseph replied. "You go ahead."

"Don't you want to see Mom?"

"I'll be there soon. Go. Go check," Joseph said, and got up. He wanted to have a cigarette, though it had been a long while since he'd last had one. He could buy one for a dollar from any of the smokers in front of the hospital. There would be phones on the main floor.

The anesthesia had pretty much worn off. The procedure hadn't taken long. What Leah remembered was counting backward in English at the doctor's instruction. She was still lying on the gurney. The hospital bed wasn't ready for her yet. She was in a shared room, but no one was in the other bed, so she was here alone. She looked down at her stomach. A dark pool of blood surrounded her narrow hips. The blue plastic sheets clung to the backs of her thighs. Where was Joseph? He must know that she was pregnant. The door opened slowly. Leah strained to see Casey entering the room.

"*Umma,* are you all right?" Casey asked.

"How did you find *Umma?*"

"Ella found me at the office."

Leah nodded.

Casey stood close by the gurney. A clump of her mother's long hair partially covered her right eye. She pushed her mother's hair away from her brow. Her mother looked tired, but otherwise she looked okay. Fragile, mostly. "God, I was so worried," she blurted out in relief.

"*Umma* is okay. Where is Daddy?"

"Phoning Tina."

"Oh."

How the hell did her mother have a miscarriage when her father had a vasectomy? Casey wondered. She took a breath.

"Did you have sex with someone else besides Daddy?" Casey asked. Had she actually formed those words in her brain, then uttered them out loud?

"Yes," Leah answered.

Casey looked up at the ceiling.

Leah did not feel any better from unburdening this truth to her daughter. Her wish to die only resurfaced.

"I sinned against God."

Casey shook her head. "He got you pregnant, then."

"I didn't know I was—"

"How could you not know?"

"My periods don't come every month."

"Daddy said he had a vasectomy."

"He told you?"

"He thought I knew."

"I deserve to die."

Casey paused a little before speaking and made sure to speak as calmly as possible.

"I don't care who you fuck exactly. I'm just a little surprised, that's all."

Leah closed her eyes. Her sin had to be punished. Her husband would leave her. Perhaps he had left her already. Everyone should know what a horrible person she was.

Casey turned to check the door. It remained closed.

"Daddy thinks it might have been his baby. Dr. Shim told him that vasectomies are not a hundred percent."

"I sinned. Against God. Against my husband. Against myself."

"Do you still love this other guy? Are you still seeing him?"

"No, no. But I sinned."

"Cut the sin talk. Just tell me what happened and how it happened. Explain very carefully."

Leah told her about the professor. The chicken pox, the choir rehearsal, the diner, and the sex in the car parked by the subway station.

"Wait a second. The choir director? Mr. Jun?" Casey made a face.

"No. Professor Hong, he's new. Mr. Jun retired. The professor is also a voice coach. And he is a composer. He's writing a song cycle that will have a world premiere at a famous music school." Leah rattled off the impressive things she knew about the choir director. "He's coached opera singers from the Metropolitan—"

"Okay. Whatever. Why did you get in the backseat with him?"

"I didn't know he wanted to have sex."

"Did you think he wanted to hold hands and sing you songs?"

Leah sobbed, and Casey grew silent.

"But I must have made him have this desire for me. I didn't know how to make it stop. I told him no, but he said I didn't understand. He said he loved me."

"You said no?"

Leah nodded. "I asked him to please. Please, no. I begged him. To please…but he couldn't. A man can't stop when he's excited.

I knew that. Everyone had told me that when I was a girl. I should have—"

"You said no." Casey rolled her eyes. She inhaled deeply. "But he did it anyway. Men are not all the same. Some men can stop and will stop. You know nothing about men." She said it quietly, without any harshness in her voice. "Nothing. You've slept with one man in your life. No, technically two, but I think you were date-raped, so just one." But her mother didn't know what that meant.

"It wasn't some sin for you to take him to a diner. He was hungry, and you had a car. You would have never let anyone be hungry. He was your choir director, and you had a crush on him. Big fucking deal. He knew you were having a crush on him, because he's been around, and he took advantage of you. He's an asshole."

He'd said she was beautiful. That he wanted her to come live with him. It had given her pleasure to think about running away, even though she'd felt awful about that, too.

"What happened between you and the choir director was hardly consensual. Did you want to sleep with him?"

"No. I...," Leah stammered. "You have to believe me. I wanted him to be interested in me. I took him to the restaurant. I really enjoyed myself during the dinner."

"You're allowed to have dinner with someone you like. That's not the same thing as letting a man fuck you afterwards just because he wants to."

"I want to die. Please let me die!" Leah began to scream.

"Stop it! Stop it. Calm down."

Leah opened her eyes wide. She became silent.

"I'm very sorry this happened to you. I really am. But you're not going to die. You can't."

"Suicide is a sin," Leah said softly. "I can't kill myself."

"I'm glad you feel that way."

Leah was still crying.

"Listen. You can't tell Daddy. You're not going to tell him what happened. There's no point. Trust me. It would kill him, and why? So you can have a clear conscience? You had a crush. And you were raped. It's not your fault. I'm not mad at you. I'm not. I don't think less of you." Casey stroked her mother's white hair, feeling the awkwardness of having to comfort her mother. "It's going to be okay." Her mother was less experienced than most American teenage girls. Didn't she talk to her friends in her *geh* about sex? About men? Didn't they at least complain about husbands? Couldn't sex have come up?

By having slept with nearly a dozen men, Casey had developed theories about sex; she had her own sexual point of view. She was interested in making love, in being a good lover, sometimes just fucking. Sex was often bracketed by both humiliation and flattery; awkwardness and beauty were found in the spaces between. She had learned that her body had value to herself and others. Jay had been someone she had trusted with her body. Unu was someone who had deserved that trust, and she had blown it by fucking Hugh. Hugh had been an irrational lay. She had not loved him, and he had not loved her. It was questionable if Hugh was capable of loving someone for a sustained period. Experience was a funny thing: The downside of knowing things intimately was that she had also, in the process, degraded sex. She was still lost. What was sex for? She'd had good sex, bad sex, losses, and conquests. Stretches without. But more importantly, if she were to take off her clothes again and agree to another round, why? And whom would she love?

Her own mother had gotten pregnant after she had been with the choir director. If it wasn't rape, it was certainly some kind of molesting—Casey hesitated at the words, because they made her forty-three-year-old mother sound dumb.

"It was my fault," Leah burbled through her tears. "It was my fault. I have to confess my sin. Repent," she cried.

Casey checked the door again.

"Please don't do that. Please don't hurt my father." She touched her mother's head. "I have never asked you for anything like this."

Leah continued to sob. No one came to the door.

Tina offered to come to New York right away, but Joseph said it was okay. He explained that she'd had a spontaneous miscarriage, but the D&C had gone fine. The nurse said so.

"*Umma* can come home tonight. It was just a big shock for all of us. And Casey is here."

"Casey is there?"

"Yes. She came a while ago. It's easier for her to take care of *Umma* because she's in New York. You have to think about Timothy and your husband. Don't worry. And Chul needs you to be there while he has finals. You said his grades are really important."

"Yes, but if *Umma* is sick..." It would be wildly expensive for her to take the baby and go to New York again. Their budget was tight as it was. "I could try—"

"She's okay, Tina. Elder Shim said that she'll heal very soon from something like this. It's not something very serious. You should stay in California."

"But, Daddy—"

"Tina, you don't have to do everything. I know how hard you're working at home. Casey can help out, and I'll take care of *Umma*, too. You don't have to do everything, Tina. I'll tell *Umma* that you wanted to come. She knows that."

Tina nodded. He was trying to make sure that she didn't feel bad about not being able to come. "I'll call her at home, then. Later."

"Okay, okay."

"Bye, Daddy. Thank you for calling. Take care of yourself."

"Okay, okay. You take care of yourself, too, Tina. Good care. You can't get sick. Your family depends on you."

As he approached Leah's hospital room, Joseph saw the large group of women by her closed door. It took a minute for him to realize that the group was made up of some of the female elders and deaconesses from the hospitality committee and many of the female choir members. The professor was not there.

At the sight of Elder Han, the women flipped through their hymnals to find the right page of "Our God, Our Help in Ages Past." They bowed.

"*Waaah,*" he exclaimed, astonished by the large number. There were at least twenty-five women.

"Is she all right?" asked Mrs. Noh, the choir secretary.

"Yes. She had a miscarriage. She'll be able to go home today."

The women clicked their tongues. It was always a heartbreak to have a miscarriage. Many of them had experienced it themselves. Of course, it was not an illness, but it was terrible just the same.

"We didn't want to knock on the door. In case she was sleeping."

"Have you been waiting here all this time?"

"Just a few minutes. Maybe you can knock for us," a choir member suggested.

Joseph nodded and knocked on the door himself. Casey called out to him, "Come in."

He opened the door, and at that moment, the choir burst into song. A hush fell at the sound. People leaned out of open doors to listen, and the doctors and nurses stopped moving for a moment. Nurse Bulosan, who'd spoken to them earlier, stood still to sing along. She crossed herself.

The music filled the hall, and Leah began to sing. The church had come to her. It was Sunday night, when the choir members should have been with their families. How did the girls leave behind their children and husbands, with dinners unmade, houses left to clean, all to come and sing for her, a sinner?

Casey helped her mother to sit up a little. Leah sang through her tears: "Under the shadow of Thy throne, Thy saints have dwelt secure; sufficient is Thine arm alone, and our defense is sure."

Leah turned her head and saw her husband standing by the door. His concern for her was so clear. He smiled at her, and she reached her hand toward his direction.

13 | GIFT

On Saturday morning, Unu caught the Metro-North to New Haven, then took a bus to Foxwoods with a hundred bucks of gambling money. Following his bookie's advice, he'd taken no credit cards or ATM card with him, because the temptation to borrow on cash advances would be too great. By nighttime, he returned with exactly a hundred and thirty-two dollars in his money clip. The transit cost and a Subway sandwich had neatly erased his thirty-two percent gain. Six hours of travel time door-to-door, five hours of gambling, with net zero in the margins—finally, Unu was standing in front of his apartment door.

The key wouldn't fit. There were only two keys on the metal ring with its yellow plastic fob from Lucky Bastard Lounge off I-95: one for his apartment and another for the mailbox. His bookie already had the Volvo key. Unu kept at the lock, but nothing doing. The Medeco dead bolt wouldn't budge. Was he on the right floor? His door? At his feet, near the pile of newspapers he'd neglected to bring in earlier, a squiggly length of masking tape affixed a thick envelope to the hallway brown carpet. From the city marshal's office. His name typed in blurry carbon. In it, he recognized the photocopies of the notice of eviction papers he'd been served several weeks before. Unu tossed the envelope on the floor with his keys.

*   *   *

George Ortiz was tying up stacks of magazines with twine in the basement. The regular weekday porter left the monthly recycling jobs for George, who did not mind organizing-type work. Tidy cinder blocks of glossy periodicals formed a low wall along the corridor connecting the laundry room to the back-door exit—the harvest of an evening's labor. The elevator dinged its arrival. George's handsome round face contorted with worry. He nodded hey to his friend.

"The city marshal came by. Hernando changed the locks," George told him, volunteering all that he knew. "You okay?"

Unu nodded, more lost than angry.

"I didn't know where you were. I didn't know how to call you, man."

George's pool buddy, the only resident of the ninety-four-unit building who had ever invited him to hang out, had aged this past year—thin lines fanned around his dark eyes, a patch of gray had formed smack dab in the heart of his right part. Usually these Oriental guys looked ten years younger than white guys, but Unu looked older than his age. George had worried about his friend, so much so that he'd mentioned it to his wife, Kathleen, and she'd said in her usual patient manner, "George, honey bear. You are not responsible for everyone. He'll tell you when he's ready." But in all this time, Unu had not mentioned why he didn't have a job, why that girl Casey left without taking most of her stuff or coming back for it, or why he hadn't paid rent in three months so that the management company had to throw his ass out. The super had told him this before working on the locks.

"I asked Hernando, and he didn't know, either...how to reach you."

"No, of course not. That's all right," Unu said. No one was responsible for this but himself.

George liked Unu's reserved manner. The Korean was someone who'd be tagged as a quiet brother in George's neighborhood in Spanish Harlem. It wasn't as though Unu were shy, because the *hermano* talked, but it was obvious that he was preoccupied with some deep shit, and when you hung out with him, he'd ask you thoughtful questions about stuff you knew. He listened carefully to your opinions on landfills, salsa, and Catholicism. Unu believed in labor unions, while George called Unu naive about those organized thugs. You'd shoot a couple of games with him at Westside Billiards, drink a few bottles of beer, and it wouldn't hit you until you were on your way home that you'd done all the talking while the two of you were together, and that no one so smart had ever listened to you so respectfully, and that time and attention were a kind of present that you couldn't buy. Yeah, Unu was a brother who liked his privacy, but George did not mind that.

"You have a lawyer or something?"

Unu shook his head no. He brushed his right hand through his hair, long overdue for a cut.

"You got a place to stay?"

Again, Unu did not answer. Because he didn't know.

George felt terrible for him. But this guy had gone to college. Besides, weren't Koreans rich compared with the people from Puerto Rico? They owned all those giant bodegas with neat-ass piles of oranges, and they hired Mexicans and Guatemalans to peel potatoes for their salad bars and break down the endless stream of boxes in the smelly basements. Their women owned nail salons and wore diamond rings the size of your eye. Frankly, he couldn't remember who owned all those dry cleaners before the Koreans came and took over that job. And it had happened so fast. They had taken over—fast. The folks from P.R. were doing all right, but they weren't like the Cubans, who were more successful like the Koreans. What was the matter with him? The brother was a real nice guy. But he didn't have a single friend who could take him in for the night? I mean, really, c'mon now. If Kathleen threw his ass out, he could call up half a dozen buddies or ask his sister if he could sleep on her sofa. But no matter, the *hermano* was not talking. He looked as if someone had hit him, but there was no blood.

"I mean..." George hesitated. *"No le hagas a otros lo que no quieres que te hagan a ti."* His *abuela* Liliana had taught him that as a boy. He could see his grandmother standing by the counter, chopping onions for her *asopao*—her deep-set brown eyes watery behind a pair of bifocals strung on a rope chain, her brown cheeks drooping with age for as long as he had known her, the small mouth that expressed her every feeling. When she spoke to you about something serious, she'd finger the rosaries blessed by the pope kept in the pocket of her yellow apron, as if she were trying to keep God in her hands. If George had nowhere to go, he'd hope that Unu wouldn't turn him out. "You can stay at my house. Kathleen would be cool with that."

Unu tried to smile.

"I'll call her. Right now. You know, get the boss's permission." George chuckled.

"No, George, that's okay. I'm fine. I'll…I'll call someone. I have a place to stay." Unu tried to smile with assurance, as though he had people waiting for his call.

But there was no one. Especially at this hour. He couldn't even imagine dialing up his bookie or any of his frat brothers, who'd surely have put him up. How could he explain this? If he called his parents, it would kill his father, and worse, his mother would fly in from Texas on the next flight and bail him out. Probably make him return to Dallas. He was divorced, unemployed, in hock, and evicted.

The doubt streaking across his face was hardly lost on George.

"It's late, man, you know? To call people. Kathleen would understand. I don't have to call her. She'll be asleep anyway. You can even go in the morning if you feel more comfortable." He knew Unu was fronting like he had places to go and money in his pocket. Like I was fucking born yesterday, he thought.

The truth was that the offer was tempting for Unu. But for some reason, he didn't want George's wife—a second-grade teacher from Far Rockaway, a woman George worshiped—to think poorly of him, even though he had never met Kathleen Leary Ortiz. When George talked about his smart wife, Unu felt wishful for a Kathleen of his own who might rescue him from his troubles, too.

George pulled up a metal folding chair splattered with dried paint. He pointed at it with his chin. Unu sat down.

"Thank you." Unu covered his mouth with his hands and opened his eyes to wake himself up.

The scent of detergent and fabric softener drifted toward the two men from the building's laundry room, somewhat masking the odor of the garbage bags. George continued to tie up the magazines, keeping an eye on his friend, who remained sitting.

The bright basement, lit by rows of naked white lightbulbs, felt cool and light. There had been many different climates in one day: the hot August morning, the air-conditioned train and bus ride, the seasonless casino with its make-believe daylight and filtered cold air, the muggy city evening, and now, a silent cool basement. Unu shivered a little in his black polo shirt and chinos.

Everything he owned was behind a strange lock: the closetful of suits he'd bought from all over—custom-made suits from Itaewon tailors from the time he was married, several from Century 21 that Casey had selected, a couple from Brooks Brothers that his mother had gotten for him after his first job in the city. His suit size hadn't changed in a dozen years. He tried to catalog his possessions, but he could hardly recall what he owned. All of his furniture had been rented. He'd never wear those suits again. It was difficult to imagine returning to a finance job, putting on a tie—all to convince a money manager that his stock call was right—for a six-figure bonus that had never meant very much to him.

And there was that pile of laundry. He'd washed a large load of whites two nights before. After drying them, he'd dumped the snowy pile onto his rented sofa. He'd meant to fold the wash since then, but for some reason, the sight of it had comforted him—the cleanness of it; or perhaps because he'd done something that needed doing, some evidence of labor for the day—so he'd left it alone. When he'd gotten dressed the previous mornings, he'd plucked out his white boxers and Hanes T-shirt from the pile, its size hardly diminishing. He would never see that load of wash again. Oddly, Unu felt its loss. Why was he able to remember that his boxers were Fruit of the Loom bought from Kmart or that there had been four white bath sheets, six washcloths, a set of queen sheets from Macy's? He yearned to put his nose into a warm towel fresh from the dryer smelling of Tide. When he gave up his Rolex or his car, he had not minded very much, far less than he'd have thought he would. Unu had never wanted a fancy watch for his college graduation. It had been his father's idea—a thing a Dartmouth graduate who worked on Wall Street would wear. His father was a kind man who had only wanted his son to have an emblem of arrival and belonging—some talisman of protection. But the watch had not been that.

"*¿Oye, tienes hambre?*" George had finished with the magazines and had moved aside the glass bottles. "Man, I'm starving. You know."

Unu got up and helped George transfer the bundles of magazines to the other side of the wall. George didn't stop him from helping. Kathleen always let her shy dinner guests work in the kitchen. She'd tell them to wash the lettuce or slice the tomatoes, no different from instructing her second graders; it was good to keep busy, important to feel useful—she'd say. They finished moving the bundles in a few minutes.

"I got meat loaf sandwiches in my cooler. I don't know why she complains about this"—George patted the curve of his belly rising above his brown workman belt—"when she'll go on and pack me like three sandwiches to eat in the middle of the night. Makes no sense, right? Women." He checked to see if Unu was smiling. He wasn't. The *hermano* was very low, but it wasn't like he had no reason. "C'mon, man, you should have dinner with me. Keep me company. What, Mr. College too good to hang out with the porter?" He winked at Unu.

"The porter is too good to hang out with a bum like me."

"Man, you are feeling like shit." George looked at Unu tenderly, put out his fist, and hit him lightly on the shoulder. "It's gonna be okay. You'll work it out. You will work it out."

Unu nodded to be polite.

"So you want a sandwich or what?"

"No, George. But thank you, though. I really...really appreciate it." Unu swallowed. "That's very kind of you."

George reached into his back pocket. He had at least two hundred in twenties and fifties and a thick packet of singles in his front pocket from the tips he'd made from the residents of 178 East Seventy-second St. "You got money?"

"I'm flush." A hundred bucks wouldn't cover a cheap motel in Manhattan.

"You sure?" George looked Unu square in the eye.

"Yeah."

"What happened, man? I mean, I don't mean to be nosy. You know, I respect your privacy, man, but—"

"It's complicated, George," he said, but it wasn't really, was it? He'd gambled and lost a lot of money. And losses led to more.

"Was it that girl?" George believed that Unu had been doing well until he'd met that girl. In the beginning, she was okay, and he'd seemed happy, but then George saw her in that taxi with that Anglo. A woman cheating could fuck a man up. A few years back, a quiet guy from the neighborhood set himself on fire when his girlfriend slept with his best friend. "That stuck-up tall girl. Casey what's-her-name."

"Nothing to tell, George. Nothing to tell." Unu closed the folding chair and returned it to the spot where George had taken it from. He turned back to his friend and raised his hand. The men slapped their open palms first, then shook hands heartily. George reached out his left hand and tapped Unu's right arm.

"You going?"

Unu nodded. "You're a good man, George. I got some calls to make."

Unu walked away without turning back. Mercifully, the elevator car was still waiting so he wouldn't have to stay in the basement a moment longer. His friend's mentioning of Casey had cut him unexpectedly. It was near midnight.

David Greene answered the door. His feet were bare, but he was dressed in a white button-down shirt and jeans.

"Hey, it's good to see you," David said.

"I'm really sorry to bother you," Unu said. There was no sign of his cousin in the living room. "But Ella said that it would be okay if I dropped by—"

"She's coming right out. She was putting something in the oven right after you called."

Unu's large hands swung uncomfortably from side to side. The fingers on his right hand would occasionally tap against his right thigh like a keyboard. David had seen this before. In fact, from his prison writing students. He almost wished he had a cigarette to offer a man who did not know what to do with his hands. "Come on in. Please. I was just about to leave, but—"

"I ruined your night."

"No. We just had some dinner, and we were both wide awake. Talking about the wedding...."

Unu nodded. "Right. Right. I'm really happy for you."

"Thanks," David said. The man looked as though his heart were shattered.

Ella came out of the kitchen carrying a wooden tray bearing a teapot, blue striped mugs, and a plate of corn muffins she'd recovered from the freezer and heated through. She set the tray on the coffee table, then sat close to her cousin.

"Unu." Ella embraced him immediately. She looked directly at his face, her eyes full of worry. "I'm so glad to see you. So glad. You know, we don't see enough of each other. Why is that? It's been, what, a month? I should have called you. Hey, hey—"

Unu's lips trembled. Even as a little girl, she'd had this goodness.

As children, they'd play during family vacations and she'd fix him snacks or get him cold compresses if he got hurt. Despite their five-year difference, she had always seemed like the older one. He had never wanted to look bad before her, but Ella would accept you. She'd never cast you out.

Ella moved closer to him to rub his back. She smoothed his hair, permitting him to sit in his anguish privately but not be alone. David remained seated in the armchair, not knowing if he should stay or go. It would be wrong to rush out, to draw attention to himself right now. His fiancée was so lovely, caring for her cousin in this way. Her heart was so big. David couldn't look away, to not observe this moment. Unu was sobbing violently, almost unable to breathe. His hands, however, had stopped their fidgeting. David leaned his body forward; he'd say nothing, wait for Ella to indicate what he should do.

"Honey, whatever it is, it will look different tomorrow. It's always worse at night. You need to rest." Ella knew this was true. The awful could be different the next day. A social worker at the hospital had told her after she had taken too many of the codeine pills that every day the pain would alter a little and somehow you'd manage just a bit better. "I promise, Unu. There isn't anything you can't face."

"I was evicted today. I lost everything."

Ella tried to contain her surprise. David nodded solemnly.

"Then you'll stay here. You'll tell me everything in the morning. I'll go make your room right now." She pulled away from him so she could see his face better. She kept her arm around his shoulders. He looked so exhausted. "Do you want to sleep?"

Unu shook his head no. He wouldn't be able to sleep like this. Without having explained. So he told them about the gambling. He spoke rapidly, hardly slowing down to give sufficient details, as if he'd lose his nerve if he took too many breaths. In his telling, he could hear the pattern himself: The gambling had started in Korea after his wife left—the occasional game of blackjack at Walker Hill; then, when he returned to the States, he'd placed a few bets on NCAA games through his frat brother, and then he found himself driving to Foxwoods on the weekends to stifle the boredom of his job. Things had gotten better when he was with Casey but got worse after he was fired. When she left, it had gone to hell.

Ella's mouth was slightly open. A long time ago, Casey had mentioned something about Unu going to Foxwoods now and then. She had never mentioned that it was a problem. But it wasn't like Casey to criticize others. When people were wrong or unkind, Casey tended not to talk about it. In all the time Ella was married to Ted, Casey had not said anything bad about him, though Ted had often been awful to her. How had she lived with Unu's gambling? Especially if Casey had always worried about money. This didn't justify her sleeping with her former colleague, but Ella couldn't think any more that her cousin had been entirely innocent. Their breakup must have been more complicated than that. Ella should have thought about that, too. Her own divorce was baffling at best. She barely understood what had happened to her and Ted even now. Where had she gone wrong? Where had he?

Unu stopped crying. His face was calm, his eyes drained of the terror that had been there when he had first walked into the house.

"Did Casey—" Ella stopped herself. All she knew about their breakup was that Casey had slept with Hugh Underhill. Unu had said he had ended it because of that. Naturally, Ella had thought that was right. And Casey had not called her after moving out, and Ella had spoken to her only once—about her mom—and that call had gone poorly. "I mean, how did she..."

Unu paused before speaking. What did Ella want to know?

"I threw her out because she fucked Hugh. Maybe she fucked him because she was angry at me. Maybe she fucked Hugh because she thought I was a bum. Maybe she fucked him because she felt like fucking him. Maybe she fucked him because I wouldn't marry her. Who the fuck knows?" Unu laughed. Suddenly he felt ridiculous. All this time, he had done everything he could to stop thinking about her. She had cheated on him even though she had known what his ex-wife had already done. He'd thought it was love—what they had, or at least on his side, anyway. Could he have read her wrong? The market calls he'd made—buy the growth and hold on long—Unu had been a true believer, not some damn hedger. The Street seemed to function on the slash and burn—live for this crop cycle and forget next year. Then whatever, he'd thought, he'd gamble it all, because what was the point of accumulating everything anyway or building something up? But inside, he'd been fighting to cling to some old notions of love. He had loved her. He had wanted it to work out. All along, he'd hoped that she was a true believer, too. Had she loved

Hugh Underhill? No, it couldn't have been that, he told himself. But they had never spoken about what had happened. Not really. He had made her leave because it had hurt too much to see her.

Unu sighed, then looked at Ella, his eyes confused and sad.

"We'll think about Casey later, sorry," Ella said slowly. "But right now, we have to get you to bed. Tomorrow we'll look into getting help for you." She glanced at David.

"There's a lot of things we can do about gambling," David said. There were programs for addiction that the inmates he'd taught had gone to in the city when they got out. He would call some people he knew.

"I have a list of meetings for Gamblers Anonymous. But it's in my apartment." Unu chuckled, remembering the green sheet of paper he'd saved from the glove compartment before giving up his car. "The landlord will get it. Like everything else in the place." He shook his head in disbelief. It was all gone, he realized. Everything.

"Can't we get your things back?" she asked.

Unu didn't say anything. He didn't have all the back rent, penalties, and lawyer's fees—the things described in the eviction notice. More than that, he didn't have the stamina to claim them.

"How much is owed?" David asked, surprised to hear the sound of his own voice.

"No. I don't want anyone to bail me out. Everything is gone. I did this."

Ella was sure that Unu would not change his mind.

"I'll take you to the meeting tomorrow. We'll find another schedule," Ella said. David nodded encouragingly.

"I don't want to be like this, Ella," Unu said. "I don't want to be a loser."

Ella winced, hearing Ted's word. "There are no winners or losers, Unu. That's all..." She twisted her mouth a little before saying, "That's just bullshit."

Unu had to laugh, never having heard Ella swear before.

She took his hands into hers. "May I pray with you? I mean, can we try?"

She had never done this either.

"Come, David," she said, and he moved toward them. The three of them held hands.

Ella tried to think of what she'd say. Speaking was not something she wanted to do, but she was scared for Unu, and she didn't know what else might help.

"Dear God..." She took a breath, her eyes shut tight. "Please let Unu feel Your love. Please never let him go. In Him we pray, amen."

Unu opened his eyes and smiled at his cousin. David kissed Ella on the cheek.

"I am sorry, Ella. To bring this to you," Unu said, choking up, and he looked at David, feeling ashamed about everything.

"Oh, Unu. Don't you know? There's nothing you could ever do that would—" She tightened her grasp of his hands.

"You will figure out what to do," David said. "You have friends."

"Yes," Ella chimed in. She squeezed his hand again before running upstairs to make up the guest room.

Casey phoned the church office from her desk at Kearn Davis. She identified herself as Leah Han's daughter, saying that she wanted to ask the choir director for advice about some choral recordings for her mother. A surprise to cheer her up. "My mom loves hymns, you know."

Of course, Mrs. Kong, the church secretary, knew that Deaconess Cho had suffered a miscarriage. The congregation had prayed for her during Wednesday Night Alive services. How nice of the daughter to get a present for her mother.

"And if I could have his address, I can send him a thank-you note for his help."

Mrs. Kong took the time to spell out the choir director's street address in Brooklyn and read out loud his home phone number twice.

"I'm sure the professor will want to know how your mother is doing."

"Yes. I think so." Casey thanked Mrs. Kong.

The church secretary wished her mother a blessed recovery.

14 | CROWN

*T*HE COPIERS SHUT OFF AUTOMATICALLY AT NIGHT, so Casey had to turn one back on to make two copies of her memo for Karyn and Larry. Anticipating that it would take a few minutes to start up again, she'd brought along the day's paper. It was two in the morning, and she was at the office waiting for Xerox to cooperate. If she weren't so tired, she'd find it funny that a copy machine by its design got a chance to rest but that interns didn't. Her life was privileged, absurd, or shit, depending on how you looked at it, but this was the final week of the Kearn Davis banking summer intern program. The offer decisions would come out on Friday. Till then, Casey would do whatever Karyn and Larry wanted her to do.

Two of her office mates had already finished the crossword expertly, so Casey flipped to the movie section for new releases. In the middle of the right-hand column of the arts section, there was a black-bordered memorial notice from Icarus Publishers: "Joseph McReed, a true lover of books. 1913–1997. You are missed already."

The green copy button lit up. The machine whirred steadily. Casey placed her forty-page memo on top of the feeder and pressed "copy." She sat on the nearest chair and cried.

By eight in the morning, Casey was showered and dressed in a black suit. Sabine and Isaac had been long awake and were drinking their wheatgrass shakes in the Gottesmans' marble-tiled kitchen. Melon wedges, yogurt, and toast had been put out on the counter.

"Have something to eat," Isaac said.

"And the green stuff." Sabine lifted her glass, grimacing. "Mmm."

"Good morning," Casey said, politely waving away the offers. She poured herself a cup of black coffee. If she could smoke in Sabine's apartment, life would be a lot better. She had to move before school started.

"How are you?" Sabine was scanning the front page of the *Times*. She pulled down her reading glasses. "You look awful. When did you get in last night?"

"Three. Another great party at the office. Ha, ha." Casey was disgusted with her lack of sleep. After she'd dropped off the memos on Larry's and Karyn's chairs, she'd worked for another twenty minutes, then finally taken a black car home.

"Poor baby," Sabine murmured. It was pointless to tell Casey to quit now.

"They don't pay you enough to work like that," Isaac declared.

"Joseph McReed died," Casey said. She leaned her hip against the island counter and sipped her coffee.

"The old guy with the bookstore?" Sabine frowned, noticing Casey's melancholy expression.

"Who?" Isaac asked. He was snipping wheatgrass to make Casey a double shot.

"This book dealer that Casey took the bus with on Seventy-second Street," Sabine explained, then turned to Casey. "Oh, how sad. He was your friend. And he gave you that incredible vintage hat from Lock & Co. You know, I called them in London after you showed me that hat. But they weren't interested in distributing through us. I had this amazing idea of doing our windows with their things. You know, an Ascot theme!" Sabine raised her open palms like a showgirl. Her rose-colored manicure twinkled. "I phoned our window guy, Jolien, and he thought—"

"I hadn't seen Joseph since I moved out of Unu's. Because now I take the bus on Fifth. And I hadn't checked in with him because I was busy, and—" Her stomach gurgled. She took another sip of coffee.

Isaac came forward and put his arm around her. Sabine moved closer to huddle with them.

"His memorial service is in an hour. At the Society Library."

"You can make it?" Isaac asked. "Those bastards are going to let you go? Ah, then again, who cares. Go anyway."

"Speaking of those bastards, I have to call Bastard One," Casey said.

"Have fun." Sabine shuddered and returned to her paper.

Isaac handed Casey a glass of wheatgrass juice. "For courage."

She downed it, then ate a bite of toast. After taking a deep breath, she picked up the kitchen phone. Isaac pinched his nose with one hand and waved away the air with the other, as if there were a foul odor. Sabine burst out laughing.

"Larry Chirtle speaking."

Casey zipped her lips in the direction of Isaac and Sabine. "Good morning, Larry. It's Casey Han."

"Hey, Casey," Larry said brightly. "Got the memo. Did you get a chance to look up the numbers for Drane—?"

"I should have it for you this afternoon."

"Not this morning?"

"I have to go to a memorial service."

"Someone die?"

"Yes. A friend."

"That's too bad."

"He was a good friend," she said, sensing his disapproval.

"Will you get a chance to finish the project this afternoon? I don't mean to be a jerk about it, but if you can't, I'll hand it over to someone else."

"No need, Larry. I said I would. But I have to go to the memorial."

"Yeah, yeah. Of course."

"Thanks."

"O-kay." He hung up the phone.

Isaac uncrossed his arms. "That's a stupid business. And that's no way to talk to another human being. He's going to make a terrible banker."

"Well, he's my boss for now." Charlie Seedham, the real boss, had charm to spare, but he reserved it for important people, not interns. Even Larry could be perfectly human if you didn't work for him.

"You should go to the service. Good people who are kind are not common. Larry is common," Isaac said.

Casey finished her coffee and put on her shoes.

The Members' Room of the Society Library was mostly filled. Casey sat near the back row. She recognized no one. The eulogies were brief, but there were many of them. The speakers were introduced by John Griswold, Hazel's younger brother and Joseph's closest friend. It turned out that Joseph had suffered for years from arterial sclerosis—a heart attack came in the end. He'd been visiting John and his wife, Lucy, for the weekend at their house in Lakeville. When he didn't come down for dinner, Lucy had knocked on the door. She'd discovered his body slumped over on the sofa, an Auden biography in his lap. The man who wrote the biography, a friend, was in attendance, and he spoke, too, making a joke about how boring his prose must have been to send poor Joseph to his final rest.

There were other things Casey learned about Joseph McReed: He was a sailor; he possessed an enviable collection of Trollope; he had played the oboe for sixty years. He'd had a drinking problem, which he'd controlled through abstinence. He and Hazel had loved to dance. A tall, elderly woman with ginger hair joked that Joseph was a terrible shopkeeper, because he didn't actually like selling his beautiful old books. Knowing guffaws erupted at that remark. It was Hazel who'd had the head for business. After she had died, many of the speakers suggested that Joseph hadn't much spirit left to carry on.

There were funny stories about book parties that had turned into dance parties, the kind where men knew how to lead and women knew how to dress up. Writers had come from all parts of the city to talk about Joseph and Hazel. Two of the poets were the best speakers. One recited Auden and Dylan Thomas. The other had made up a funny limerick yet burst into tears after saying it. The last memorial service she'd attended was for Willyum Butler, her professor at Princeton. Casey didn't know if Joseph was religious or not. No one mentioned God.

When it was over, John Griswold invited everyone to the house for sandwiches. His wife stood in the back of the room handing out printed cards with directions for their place in Turtle Bay. Casey would miss the reception. It was already eleven o'clock. The bastards would have her head.

On her way out, Lucy Griswold stopped her. "You must be Casey."

Casey looked about the room. There could be no mistake. She was the only minority person there.

"Yes. I'm Casey. Hello."

"I'm Lucy Griswold." She looked up and waved her husband over. "She's here."

John moved through the crowd toward them.

"Joseph told us about you. And I'm glad you're here, because it would have been difficult to find you. It occurred to us to stand by the bus stop on a Saturday morning on Seventy-second Street to honor his wishes, but, anyway..."

Casey stared at the couple quizzically. "I don't understand."

"Joseph said to us several times that he wanted you to have Hazel's hats. I think he might have mentioned my sister's hats." John smiled. "There are more than a hundred."

Lucy nodded gravely. "I hope you have a huge place."

Casey tried to keep it together. Her eye makeup was already undoubtedly a mess. As it was, she had been looking for a restroom where she could tidy up before heading back to the office.

"I can't believe he even mentioned me."

"Oh yes. He looked forward to seeing you at the bus stop. He'd tell us how much Hazel would have loved you. You bought *Jane Eyre* from him. I can't believe he let it go."

"Yes." Casey found an old paper napkin in her purse to mop up her face. "I didn't know him long. But he was always so nice to me. He'd make suggestions of what I should read and didn't tease me for rereading the same books over and over."

"I thought you'd be wearing a hat," Lucy said. "We heard you always wear a hat."

"I'm working in a bank right now, and—"

"Oh?" John said. "Where?"

"Kearn Davis. I'm an intern for the investment banking program."

"Do you like it?" he asked.

Casey nodded.

He'd caught her neutral expression, however. "Ah, the world hardly needs another investment banker."

"Oh, John—" Lucy elbowed him. "Mr. Sensitivity."

"They're not so bad," Casey said halfheartedly.

"Oh, they're awful. I used to be an investment banker before I retired. And my father was one, too. So was Lucy's dad."

"Can you come to the house? Chicken salad sandwiches and iced coffee. Chocolate cake. That was Joseph's favorite lunch."

"I wish I could. But I have to get back to work. Offers come out this week. I wasn't supposed to be here even." She didn't know why she was telling them all this. "But I happened to see the memorial in the *Times* this morning, and I wanted to say good-bye—" Casey stopped talking. Lucy patted her back.

"Here's the directions for our house. Our number is on the bottom. You call us when you want the hats. They're in the attic at Joseph's place in Litchfield. We can hold them for a while. But why don't you call us. And give us your number, too."

Casey wrote out Sabine's number and gave it to Lucy.

"Joseph said you were a born designer," she said.

John nodded, having heard the same.

"That's funny."

"He said you made beautiful hats and wore the prettiest dresses he ever saw," she said.

Casey looked over her black suit—a Sabine hand-me-down, the fake Chanel slingbacks, the Kearn Davis tote bag. Her outfit felt like a disguise.

"He was kind to say those things," she said.

"The old flirt. Gosh, I miss him." Lucy smiled. She peered at the tall girl. The dark circles under her eyes showed through her concealer. Crying had made her small eyes puffier. "Do call on us, Casey. To get the hats, but come over when you like."

"Thank you so much," she said, leaving the Griswolds to attend to the other guests.

It was a glorious August day outside, and Casey dreaded returning to the office. It would have been wonderful to take a long walk in the park to shake off some of this sadness. But she hailed a taxi. After giving the driver her address, she stared at the park on her right as the car moved down Fifth.

On her desk, there were three messages from Karyn and two from Larry. The other interns looked as exhausted as she did, and she felt a little sorry for everyone, including herself. Five of the twenty-one wouldn't get a spot. There was talk that they might make fewer than sixteen offers. Casey put down her things and immediately returned to Larry's project. After she finished her assignment, she'd take thirty minutes to pay her personal bills. It was a good feeling to have money in the bank to pay them. The tuition invoice sat on top of the pile, but that would have to wait until the loan check arrived. Including living expenses, she'd borrow almost fifty thousand dollars for her second year of school.

By nine p.m., more than half the interns still remained at their desks. Casey had finished Larry's project and had another day to work on Karyn's. She hadn't eaten dinner yet but couldn't fathom the idea of more greasy take-out or pizza. The endless stream of coffee and Diet Cokes kept her wired and anxious; sleep would not come easily. All day, she'd been pushing back the idea of asking Unu if it would be all right for her to pick up some of her things. Sabine had been lending Casey skirts and blouses that didn't fit her anymore, but it would have been nicer to have her own things. If Unu left the key with the doorman, she could get her clothes, the *Jane Eyre*, Hazel's hat. The rest, she'd pick up when she found her own place—that being the next item on her to-do list. Of course, she'd understand if he didn't want to see her.

Casey picked up the phone. After three rings, a recording came on. The line had been disconnected. No forwarding number. She put down the phone and went to the empty conference room that she used occasionally to work in the evenings. No one noticed her leaving the shared office.

It was quiet here, and she was finally alone. She sat at the head of the conference table. Unu was gone. The truth was that she had no right to know where he was. She couldn't very well phone Ella, who'd certainly know how to reach him. People like Ella knew how to get in touch with others; no one was ever mad at them. She wasn't stupid enough to torch bridges. But the last time they'd spoken, Casey had heard the judgment in her voice. Ella must've heard about Hugh, and though Casey could have imagined it, it sounded as if Ella doubted that she'd even bother to show up at her own mother's hospital bedside. Whatever good opinion Ella might've once had of her had been lost.

She drummed her fingers on the polished conference table. On the credenza beside the wall sat a tray of glasses and a stainless carafe of ice water, stacks of fresh notepads, and two phones with video-conferencing capabilities. The door closed, she felt safe, private. Just a few yards away, more than a dozen interns in the shared office toiled, seeking to edge out the inferiors in the pack. At least five, if not more, would have to go back to school with no offer letter in hand. The people Casey had worked with in the past eight weeks had been perfectly nice, bright, and interesting. They had been uniformly attractive people. They were also out to beat her, so she them—it wasn't personal.

Casey poured herself a glass of water, then dialed Hugh's number.

"I was wondering who was calling me from the New York office," he said, studying the caller ID box near his phone. "Hello, Casey Cat. I had given up on you. Almost."

"What's up?" she asked.

"Come on over and have a drink with me." He didn't expect her to say yes. But it was always better to make the suggestions. Surprises happened.

"I'll be there in fifteen minutes."

He offered her a drink, but she turned it down. She walked around his spacious white apartment, noticing everything. She felt exceptionally alert. The modern Italian furniture, the black-and-white art photographs of clippers with billowing white sails, the tall fireplace in the west wall. She'd expected more clutter, more books, or old carpets. More men's club. Or at least dishes in the sink. But nothing was out of place. When she commented on how clean it was, he only said, "I have someone who comes in to do those things."

"How nice for you."

"You look...somber," he said casually.

"My, you are observant. A friend died. I went to his memorial service today."

"Oh, baby, I'm sorry. Come here," he said, and put his arms around her.

Casey froze and drew her arms closer to her body, but he held her anyway.

Hugh was humored by her visit. It was unexpected, but she was here now, her feet parallel, her back as straight as a post. Her nerves like live wire. Even more so than usual. He was happy to see her. She was young, slightly neurotic—it turned him on. She was frightened to be here. But he wouldn't hurt her—he wasn't the hurting kind.

"May I sit down?"

"Yes, by all means." He laughed at her severe tone. "I feel like I'm in trouble."

"How are you?"

"Fine, and you?" Hugh sat by her. He would play along.

He wore a blue shirt, his sleeves rolled up to his elbows, a pair of light-colored slacks, loafers, no socks. He smelled wonderful, citrusy yet dark.

Hugh looked at her square in the face, focusing on her eyes. He removed her jacket, and she didn't resist. He kissed her collarbone as he unbuttoned her sleeveless white blouse. They didn't speak anymore, and they did what they had done before. His expertise was a relief to her, the sex enthralling. But she wouldn't confuse this for love. Seen in the finest light, it was affection; it was comfort—a salve for loneliness. There could be no expectations from Hugh. A woman would get hurt only if she wanted more. Hugh would always disappoint—this would serve as a reliable mantra. He couldn't help falling short. His emotional stamina was lacking. That was what she had learned from being his friend all this time. When the sex ended, she felt sad again. They didn't talk much after, but he brought her a glass of ice water. He had a sweetness, so you could not be mad at him.

He asked her to stay the night, but she had to work the next day. It was only Tuesday.

"Offers are announced on Friday," she said. The worries had returned after all.

"I know something you don't." Hugh smiled.

"What?" she asked, thinking his beauty was almost wasted.

"You're in the top five. Charlie told me. It's yours to lose."

"How did you find out?"

"I asked him last week. During the game."

Casey nodded, not believing fully what she'd heard. "Why didn't you tell me before?"

"I thought I could get some sex out of this. And look, I did. Ta-dah."

Casey slapped his arm. The sound of it surprised her. A pink mark flashed on his skin.

"Wow. That was very unkind." He stroked his arm. "I can't believe you did that."

"I did not sleep with you today or at any other time to get an offer, asshole."

"I was kidding. A little sensitive, Ms. Han. I could never have gotten you a permanent offer despite all of your bedroom gifts. Rest assured, you got this because you are a stubborn and hardworking girl. Good for you. Now, don't hit me again."

Casey got up from the bed. She picked up her brassiere at the foot of it and put it on.

"Come here, I like angry women."

Casey went back to the bed and settled down. She should not have hit him. Her violence embarrassed her. His hand entered her immediately, and, aroused by his touch, she turned to him. He pushed down her brassiere cup to put his mouth on her breast. She climaxed quickly, far quicker than she'd thought possible. Hugh placed his hand on her head, guiding her downward toward his hips. "Can you finish me off?" he asked her quietly.

The pressure from the back of his hand against her hair had startled her. She tried to be efficient, letting her mind wander. After he came, she wiped her mouth with a corner of the sheet. It was almost eleven o'clock.

When she came out of the shower, Hugh was dressed in his shirt and trousers, watching David Letterman.

"I thought you'd be sleeping," she said.

"Ice cream," he said. "You want ice cream?"

"Game," she said, smiling. Ice cream sounded perfect.

"I will do an ice-cream run. Flavor?"

"Rum raisin."

"I approve," he said.

"Shall I go with you?"

"You stay."

"But I should get back—" But her mind had altered somewhat

after he'd told her about the offer. Could it be true? But why would Hugh lie? He was a playboy, but he'd never lied to her. She could work at Kearn Davis after graduation. Never worry about money again. It would take only a couple of years to pay off the school loans, then she could buy an apartment, help out her folks.

Hugh promised to return in fifteen minutes, tops.

Casey was still in a towel. Her suit jacket on the sofa was crumpled, as was the blouse. From Hugh's closet, she pulled out a white dress shirt. She'd looked for an older one, something with a blown-out collar or frayed sleeves, but they were all in beautiful condition. She put it on. He had loads of them. His closet was immense, filled with very fine clothing, and above the closet rod, there was a deep shelf lined with cashmere sweaters. Near the sweaters, there was a cache of videos stacked neatly in three rows, and she laughed. "Oh, Hugh," she said out loud.

She pulled out the first stack using both hands. She spread them out on the bed to read the titles. They seemed innocent enough, blond college coeds, husky men with mullets. More *Playboy* than *Hustler*. She looked over the other two stacks. One of the two dozen or so had an Asian woman on the cover—titled *Pearl Necklace*. Casey made a face. The two white men on the video box were unattractive, and the woman looked too old to be doing this kind of thing.

The television and videocassette recorder were set up right opposite the bed. Casey popped the video in the recorder. What would Hugh say if he found her watching his porn? He would laugh his head off.

In less than two minutes, the story became explicit: The Asian woman, who looked even less attractive in the film than on the touched-up video box, enters an office. She wears a red Adolfo-copy suit, long black hair with bangs, crimson lipstick, black patent-leather stilettos. Naturally, she wears a string of gumball-size pearls around her throat. The woman Pearl is the secretary for four men who work in an accounting firm. Two of the men head home after a long day. She stays behind at the request of the other two, Craig and Kip. Without much dialogue, she takes off her red suit, keeping on her black bustier, revealing the tops of her impressive breast implants, a wasplike waist, and short, thin legs in garters and black fishnet stockings. She leans one hand against the wall, leaving space on both sides for the men to sandwich her. One enters her vaginally, then the other joins her from behind. She moans and cries out continuously. Casey reddened with shame. Nausea brewed in her stomach.

After Pearl has a series of orgasms, Craig, the tall one who'd been with her from the front, says nicely, "Can you finish me off?" Pearl gets on her knees and performs fellatio hungrily. His necktie swings with her thrusts.

Casey stopped the video there. There was at least another half an hour to go, but she saw no point to it.

Less than an hour ago, Hugh had said to her, "Can you finish me off?" That was what he'd said. Was he aware that was a line from this film? Casey hadn't given much thought to pornography before; it hadn't touched her life directly. Jay had found it vulgar and not romantic. Unu didn't own any. A few guys at Charter used to watch it on Saturdays, and girls trying to be cool would watch along with them, but Casey had never been interested in it. The image of the middle-aged woman between the two ugly men burned in her mind. What could Hugh find sexy about this? Could he have watched it so many times that he had unconsciously memorized a line like that? Would he have said it to any other woman? Or did he think that it was okay to say it to her? She rewound the video and put it back on the shelf with all the others.

Casey put his shirt back on the hanger. She dressed in her clothes. Should she leave a note? she wondered. Was this the way he saw her? How could she ever know what he really thought of her? Was that his fantasy? Was that why he had once said to her that he had wanted to fuck her for a long time? The girl looked nothing like her, but Casey used to own a red suit, and Hugh had complimented her on it. But he had often complimented her on what she wore. That was the way he talked to women. Feeling the lurch in her gut, Casey ran to the bathroom and threw up. After, she rubbed toothpaste on her teeth with her finger, then gargled repeatedly.

In the hallway, she met Hugh, who was stepping off the elevator.

"Hey, I got ice cream. And they had Mallomars."

"I have to go."

"Where?"

"This was a terrible mistake."

"What are you talking about? It was great. Where are you going?

Come back in. I have rum raisin and vanilla Swiss almond. Don't be silly, Casey Cat."

"I saw *Pearl Necklace*. The thing in your closet. I thought it would be funny to watch it with you. I'm sorry. I shouldn't have. I had no business doing that. I went to get a shirt to wear. You said the same thing that...guy says to the girl. 'Can you finish me off?' "

"What are you talking about?" He looked incredulous.

"I can't talk about this."

"So I watch porn. I never thought of you like that girl. She's like a hundred. I use it to jerk off, I don't actually follow the story." Hugh looked at her incredulously. "Why are we having this discussion in the hallway? Come back inside."

She shook her head slowly, unable to move from her spot. "I'm sorry. Never mind. You're not a bad guy, Hugh. I shouldn't have called. I just will never forget...that picture. You know? I'll always think of it when I'm with you." Casey had never felt so viscerally revolted before. It wasn't Hugh's fault, was it? This was something he had every right to do, but she couldn't imagine him ever touching her without thinking of that woman in her fake pearls making those over-the-top sex groans.

"Casey. C'mon, Casey. Don't be ridiculous. We can talk about this." He unlocked his door. With his free hand, he gestured for her to come to him. His brow wrinkled with concern. "Casey—"

"I know you're not like that, that's not what I'm saying." Casey closed her eyes, trying to forget what she'd seen, but she couldn't. The image only seemed to burn brighter. Men had these fetishes, she knew that, but she'd never imagined it would be so ugly.

"Casey. I don't see you that way. You're my friend. You must know that." Her disbelief was apparent, however.

"We are friends, Hugh. I know. I'm sorry about this evening."

"Okay," he said. Casey was now pushing the button for the elevator. "I'm sorry, too."

"I have to go. Bye." The elevator door opened, and she disappeared into it.

In front of Hugh's place, there were many cabs, but Casey walked back to the Gottesmans', moving briskly through the clammy air.

15 | SKETCH

CHARLES HONG DID NOT KNOW WHO SHE WAS. The only reason he answered the door at this hour in the morning was that he'd seen from the window that it was a young Korean woman.

"I'm Casey," she said, wondering if he'd let her in. "May I?" She peeped into his living room. His house was enormous.

"I'm sorry, I don't think we've met." Charles was getting annoyed. Was she a former student from Juilliard? "And this isn't a good time. Maybe you can come by tomorrow. I'm home on Saturdays." He checked his watch: 7:10 on the dot.

"I'm Leah Han's daughter. You know, Deaconess Cho? She sings in your choir. I realize that it's very early, but I have to get to my office, and this was the only time I—"

"Oh." Charles opened the door wider. "Is she all right?"

Casey walked into the living room. She didn't sit down but stood by the grand piano near the front window. On top of the dusty piano was a thick pile of handwritten sheet music.

"My mother told me that you're a composer. Besides directing the choir."

"Yes. Yes, I am."

"This? Did you write this?" Casey smiled at him almost flirtatiously, touching the papers on the piano. The markings were beautiful.

Charles smiled at the young woman. She was attractive, but she didn't look anything like Leah. Maybe her open brow and the fair coloring. The height threw him off.

"It's a song cycle. The world premiere is in—"

"Where are you?" Kyung-ah called out, descending the stairs. "Professor—" She laughed.

It was her mother's friend, Kyung-ah *ahjumma*. She was wearing a tight black skirt, a rose-colored lace brassiere, and no panty hose. Her toenails were dark pink against her powdery white skin. Casey had never realized how beautiful Kyung-ah *ahjumma* was. Dishabille, she was ravishing in a dangerous sort of way. The choir director's teeth were clenched, as if he were trying to lock up his mouth. In contrast, he was fully dressed: jeans, white shirt, and navy socks.

"Are you fucking her, too?" Casey asked him, wide-eyed, pouting her lips.

Kyung-ah coughed, then turned around. She'd never suspected that he might be involved with Leah's daughter. The girl must have been twenty-six or -seven at most. It had dawned on her long ago that he might have girlfriends. They had never discussed such things. After all, she had a husband and children. That morning when she had showered, she had bent over and stared at the faint bumps behind her thighs in her closet mirror. She had worried about meeting him in the mornings, though it was the best time for her to get away (no one would miss her then, because her sister could open the store for her), mainly because she feared the unflattering lighting of daytime. But their screwing had been so great that she'd figured it wasn't important that she had some crow's-feet, a little fat behind her thighs.

Her mother's friend covered her chest with her left arm, her body rigid at the top of the stairs.

"*Ahjumma*," Casey cried out. Her voice sounded almost cheerful. "Where are you going?"

"*Uh-muh*..." Kyung-ah's left leg wouldn't budge. This girl could ruin her life.

"No, don't go," Casey said. The amusement hadn't left her expression, but her tone grew far more serious. "You should know something. He fucked my mother. Probably raped her, then he moved right on to you. Who knows who else he did in that choir." Casey tidied the pile of sheet music on top of the dusty piano.

"What?" Kyung-ah exclaimed. She had misunderstood. "Was that your baby?" The blood from Leah's miscarriage had covered her shoes. Kyung-ah had had to throw them out.

"You know, I wondered about that, too. My mother thinks it might have been. She thinks she should die because this son of a bitch date-raped her."

"I didn't...I didn't do that."

Casey stared hard at him. His mouth quivered almost unnoticeably. He was afraid. No matter what, she would hold this gaze. Her father had taught her this—to not look away—the intensity was worse than the pain that would surely come.

"Did she say I raped her?"

"No, worse. She thinks it's all her fault. But you know what? She did tell me what happened, motherfucker." Casey had lowered her voice, then laughed coldly, because that's what he was. "Did you hear her say no? Did you ever hear her say no to you in that fucking car?" She wanted to shake him. "Did you hear the word *no*?"

His memory was perfect: Leah had hesitated; she'd said no, had asked him to please. That was the word she kept using—please. But she had responded to his kissing. And when he went inside her, she had been ready for him. Their connection had been beautiful and passionate. He would never have called it rape. And neither did she. They had made love; they had felt passion for each other.

"Did she say no?"

Charles nodded once. He had slept with married women before. He was an artist, and he possessed his own morality—a higher standard from that of the rest of the world. If any of the husbands had ever asked him if he was screwing their wives, Charles wouldn't have denied it. But none of them ever did. Leah had hesitated and pushed him back a little, but she had come willingly to the backseat of the car with him—there had been no force, and he had accepted her pliant body like a sacrifice, a gift expressing her love, and he had reciprocated with his true desire. He would have taken her into his life. She could have left her husband, and he would have never abandoned her. All Kyung-ah wanted was a good, steady lay. This suited them both. Had he taken advantage of Leah? He had never thought of it that way. He had loved her. He cared for her still. It was out of respect that he was keeping his distance.

"So she said no, but you did it anyway. God in heaven, you are such a shit. She thinks that she deserves nothing short of death because of you." She paused to breathe.

"This is what I want: You will quit that job. Go do whatever the hell you want, but you better never enter that church again. You will not take the choir away from her. And you stay away. Don't test me, Charles." Her arms stiffened against her body. If he'd come near her, she would have hit him.

Kyung-ah watched Casey silently from the stairs. Had the girl been in the third or fourth grade the first time she'd met Leah? The older daughter had always been so tall and flat-chested, with those long feet. Like Olive Oyl.

Casey faced her then, her chin lifting a little. "And I hope you know what you're getting into."

Charles would not defend himself. He knew what was true, but he would quit. It was what he had thought to do anyway.

Kyung-ah climbed the stairs slowly, her joints wooden. She wanted her clothes and shoes. There was nothing she could say to the girl. So he had slept with Leah. How impossible.

Charles rushed up the stairs. He wanted to explain. She couldn't leave now.

Casey watched them vanish behind the closed bedroom door. She stared at the pile of music in front of her. The score was one long sheet of paper, folded up like an accordion. There were several long sheets in the thick stack. In her hands, it felt like holding the insides of a book without its cover. Beneath her fingertips, she could feel the impression of the notes he'd made with his black pen. Casey picked up the entire stack and stuffed it into her tote bag. She shut the front door behind her quietly and went to work.

She was the last to arrive at the office on the morning of the offers. Starting at ten o'clock, each intern would be called in privately to speak with Charlie Seedham and whoever their senior associates were. When it was Casey's turn, she marched into the conference room unblinkingly. Hugh was either right or wrong; there was little she could do about it now.

"How did you enjoy your summer, Casey?" Charlie asked her. He smiled pleasantly.

"It was great." She laughed.

Karyn and Larry smiled at her, too.

"Baloney," Charlie said, still smiling. "You were worked like a dog."

"Yes, I was." She winked in the direction of Karyn and Larry. Fuck 'em, she thought, then added, "But I did learn an awful lot about banking."

"Good attitude," Charlie said.

"She has a terrific capacity to work," Karyn said. "Learns very quickly."

Casey smiled at her. Karyn made her sound like an obedient mule or a fast computer.

"We'd love to have you join us when you graduate," Charlie said. "The quality of your work was tremendous. Everyone agreed."

"Oh," she exclaimed.

"Congratulations," Charlie said. She didn't appear much different upon hearing the news.

"Thank you," she replied, then sat up straighter.

"And when you come back—that is, if you come back..." Charlie paused, expecting to be interrupted. "You'd work with Karyn and Larry, most likely. A few other people, and me occasionally if you're put on my team. Karyn is likely to get promoted this winter, as is Larry."

"Oh, how great. Congratulations to you," Casey said to them.

Charlie glanced down at his clipboard. "Well, good news always takes less time. I'll see you at the lunch later?"

"Thank you so much. To all of you." She made a point of making eye contact with each person.

"You are accepting?" Charlie asked as a matter of courtesy. It was fairly normal to accept on the spot. But she had not said yes immediately.

"Oh, am I supposed to say now?"

"No." Charlie smiled. "You don't have to do anything."

"When do you need to know?"

Karyn and Larry looked at each other. Was she for real?

"A week? How's that?" Charlie almost admired her detachment. The girl who had come through the back door would get a week to think it over.

"I'll let you know sooner than that. Again, thank you for the summer. I learned a great deal, and that's very important to me. Thank you." Casey smiled at them. Their words had come as a surprise, oddly, though it was true that she had worked harder than she had ever worked. In the seventh week, she'd thought she was getting ill from lack of sleep. A part of her had never believed the offer was possible. There was an offer, she told herself, still doubting it inside. They'd said they wanted her to join them after graduation. Casey smoothed her skirt and got up.

Charlie flashed a quick grin, then asked her to send in the next person awaiting his fate in the hall.

The door closed behind her, and Casey did not know what to do. She made herself go back to the office. Hugh had been right after all. She was relieved somewhat, only a little less anxious. In a morbid way, she'd half expected him to be wrong. There was also a part of her that had wondered if Hugh might push Charlie not to give her the offer. But she couldn't imagine Hugh doing that. It was too mean, and Hugh was not that.

Back in her office, the happy faces outnumbered the upset ones. It was obscene that it had to be this way. Why couldn't losing be a private affair? At least two of the ones who didn't get offers were men who had worked alongside her nearly every weekend. One of them had a baby. What was he going to do? She could hardly face them. Would they have worried about her, however, if she'd been booted? The world was cruel with its rations. Who didn't know that? A disappointment—that's what it was, but it was hardly the end, right? None of them would ever starve, her refugee father would've said quickly. Americans were goddamn lucky. The United States was a rich country. You had to work, but at the very least, you would eat. Here, they fed you even if you didn't work, he'd say. A professional failure was zilch compared with your family lost behind the 38th parallel. Casey peeked at Scott, the guy who'd just had the baby. He was trying to be brave—be a good fucking sport about it. Her father was wrong, she thought. Suffering was that—it sucked not to get what you want. No one wanted to fail publicly, and tragedies came in an assortment of sizes.

From under her desk, Casey pulled out her bag. Beside her wallet was the sheaf of music. With the fat pile tucked under her arm, she left the room. The enormous shredder hummed peacefully near the bank of copier machines. The whole business took about two minutes. She phoned her mother and checked to see how she was. Her parents were fine.

Lucy Griswold drove them up to Litchfield in her blue Saab. She'd welcome the company while going through Joseph's things, Lucy had said when Casey phoned on Friday afternoon. The drive was not quite two hours, and Casey kept up the chatter by asking questions. They listened to NPR. Lucy said she liked Bill Clinton's voice.

Joseph McReed's sister-in-law was a nice-looking woman, trim, past her sixties, who talked intelligently about most everything. There was an authority in her voice; she would never suffer fools. She read two books a week, she said—mostly biographies and histories. A member of the Cos club, the mother of one grown son—a marine biologist who lived in California; she was a docent at the Frick. "You haven't seen the Fragonards?" she'd remarked with disappointment, as though Casey had been born missing a finger. Her intentions were always good, though. That was obvious. A girl from the Manhattan School of Music gave her cello lessons on Tuesdays.

There were only three houses on Joseph's street. His house, the one in the middle, was a two-story clapboard with a remarkable porch painted cream white. The shutters were a French blue like Joseph's glasses and his watchband. The rooms smelled fresher than expected, but it was warm today, so they opened all the windows. There was no air-conditioning, but Lucy said the house had been winterized in the eighties. John was thinking of selling it in the spring, but it made him sad to think of doing so. Besides, the market was slow right now. A lady came to clean the house still; the plants had been watered. Lucy took the bills and circulars from the hall desk and dropped them into her net grocery bag. You died, but you still got mail. There were some hats in the second-floor bedroom, more in the attic, and the remainder in the guest room on the main floor.

"Take a look," Lucy said. "They're yours."

Casey felt awkward, but this was what she had wanted to do today. She had phoned the Griswolds yesterday after the offers were announced, and Lucy had been so charming on the phone.

"I never understood their appeal, really. I mean, for me, anyway. I look funny in them," Lucy said.

"I doubt that," Casey said. Lilly Daché, the famous milliner, had written that every woman looked better in a hat. She just had to find the right one. Daché believed that wonderful things could happen to a woman wearing a hat—get kissed, meet a new friend, at the minimum, avoid freckles. Casey had worn a plain broad-brimmed straw today with a white T-shirt and chinos, tennis shoes. "Here, try mine. No, better, I'll find one of Hazel's." How strange it was to say her name.

"Oh no," Lucy protested. "Trust me, I know two things about me and fashion: I look lousy in hats and in the color green. My skin becomes lizardly."

"C'mon. You're silly. I don't see that at all." Casey shook her head dismissively. It could take a long time to convince a woman that she looked fine. Occasionally, you had to repeat the script of assurance till you were tired. But she was in no mood. Her fatigue from the summer internship had been compounding like interest, hitting her exceptionally hard this morning, but she'd rushed out of the apartment unwilling to yield to it.

Lucy continued to open cabinets and shut them as though she were searching for something in particular.

There were photographs of Hazel everywhere. In every image, even the color ones taken not long ago, she was wearing a hat. She was maybe five two, medium build. Friendly looking but not beautiful. Her clothes were simple but with dramatic lines, like Dior's New Look. When she and Joseph were photographed together, he stood a head taller, his arm encircling her thickening waist. Her eyes were more green than blue. Near the end, her hair was white and puffy.

"She was very funny," Lucy said. "She could tell a dirty joke. And loyal. No one was loyal like Hazel. Hated to cook meals, but baked on Sundays. Joseph liked a nice cake with his coffee." In front of the heavy mahogany sideboard, Lucy unbuttoned her shirtsleeves and cuffed them.

Casey held up a photograph framed in marquetry wood of the two of them in front of the shop. They were almost strangers to her; she had never even met Hazel, but to be in this house so soon after Joseph's death, they felt like kin.

Lucy took a deep breath, as if she were bracing herself for the task ahead. John had gone sailing today, and it was just as well. He would have taken things out of closets and cupboards without deciding what to do with them.

"Casey, the guest room is in the back," she said cheerfully, pulling out the silver-and-ivory-handled tea set from the sideboard. For as long as she'd been married to John, she had admired her mother-in-law's silver, which had gone to Hazel and not John. Now it would go to their son, Michael, but would he even want such things in his bungalow in Sausalito? "Past the bathroom and linen closet," she said when Casey appeared confused.

Casey went to the rear of the house, opening the wrong door first, then discovered the large spare room beside the laundry room. There must have been fifty or sixty hatboxes stacked up like towers—a landscape of striped paper, floral fabric, and squat leather cylinders. The windowed room with white cabbage rose curtains smelled of a dry, forgotten closet, and the scent of perfumed sachets lingered; someone had kept up with the mothballs. It would be impossible to take these back to Sabine's. Casey opened the box nearest her and the one next to it, soon realizing that each box contained at least two hats. Some had more. They were sublime, but they were old hats nonetheless and for all intents and purposes unwearable. Not worth money, either.

She put on a pigeon-gray feathered hat shaped like a small oval plate. The feathers curved a little toward the face teasingly and were held up with two tortoiseshell combs and elastic. You'd wear your hair up, the hat cocked slightly over one eye. With a charcoal suit or maybe a pink one. Another was a luncheon hat with a bird's nest cradling three blue eggs on a slender branch. The extravagance in design made Casey marvel. An ordinary woman could not pull this off. Surprisingly, the hat stayed put with only an elastic band worn beneath the nape of the neck. She checked the mirror near the door. How could she not smile? She dashed out to show Lucy.

"That was for a garden party in Wilton. Hazel had so much fun making that one. Those are real robin's eggs," Lucy said. Hazel's hair was still brown then, she recalled. Her sister-in-law had worn a tailored sage-colored suit—something out of *The Sound of Music* with a nest on her head. Hazel was a wonder.

"One second," Casey said. She ran back to the room and brought out a hat with a bisque-colored fan perched on top of a small brown pillbox. "You try."

Lucy made a face. "No, no. You're just like Hazel. She'd always make me do silly things."

"Please," Casey said.

Lucy's pretty eyes lurked skeptically beneath the sober brow. She didn't say anything. She was holding a pair of ice spoons in flannel bags.

Casey sensed acquiescence. "Oh, goody." She deftly tucked the hat elastic over the back of Lucy's head and moved the fan portion down closer to the forehead. "You look beautiful." Casey smiled, because she took your breath away.

Lucy shook her head in denial, preparing to shed the thing herself, but she was admittedly curious.

"Go look." Casey pointed to the Chippendale-style mirror in the foyer.

Lucy remained standing there, however, clutching the slotted spoons.

Casey removed the silver from her grasp and took her by the hand. "Come."

Lucy cringed in the mirror reflexively. She felt self-conscious and ridiculous. "I don't look good in these things." When Hazel wore a hat, her neck had been as upright as a stalk of wheat.

"Nonsense. Look at yourself. It's all right. It's all right to look at yourself," Casey said softly, only a little puzzled by the woman's reluctance to admire herself. Excessive modesty being vanity's sister, after all.

Casey studied Lucy for a moment, her hand covering her mouth in mild hesitation. "You look knowing," she said.

Lucy glanced at the mirror and chuckled. The smile softened the straight line of her jaw. She raised her hands to remove the hat, but Casey wouldn't have it. "Keep it on for five more minutes. Please."

Casey headed to the attic, climbing the steps two at a time. She felt excited to see more.

When Lucy heard the attic door open, she shuffled quietly to the foyer mirror. Her image was so different. The hat hid the ash blond pageboy—the hairstyle she'd maintained since the seventies. Knowing. That was the right word. Lucy smiled shyly at herself and did not remove the hat until Casey came down much later.

Until evening, Casey went through each box in all three rooms until her hands were sooty and her hair covered in dust. Lucy drove her back to the city. A collapsible silk top hat rested in her lap for the ride back.

*   *   *

On Sunday morning, Casey sewed the trim on a new summer hat. It was a finely woven straw with a wide brim that had been blocked for her professionally at Manny's Millinery. She'd found the vintage green-and-white ribbon for its band at Tinsel Trading. In the past year, she'd scrawled names for her hats on the brown hatboxes— mostly after her favorite book women: Charlotte, Becky, Valerie, Lily, Edith, Jane, Anna. This one, though, was Hazel. When she had knotted her last stitch, there was no one to show it to. Sabine and Isaac were away at Fishers Island visiting friends, and the big apartment felt dead without Sabine's high heels clacking across the ebonized floors. The housekeeper and cook were off this week.

Casey wore her new hat to church. The regular minister was away for the summer, and the visiting minister spoke beautifully, but she didn't feel much of anything. After the sermon, she tried praying for once, but she couldn't quiet her mind well enough to think of much to say, beyond thank you—maybe everything would be all right. When she opened her eyes, she saw the others who were deep in prayer, and she wondered how they did that. Was it like turning on a switch for an invisible microphone? Did they really believe that God heard them? Was it just wishfulness? What comfort they must have, she thought, not without a little envy. At the end of the service, she walked down the crowded aisle by herself. There was a light touch on her upper arm, and Casey figured that she'd been bumped along the way.

"Hi," Ella said.

"Oh, hello," Casey said. By Ella's side stood a white guy with wavy brown hair and dark blue eyes. He was tall, well over six feet. He wore a white shirt and faded seersucker trousers. Ella wore a simple sundress in a blue chalcedony color that Casey had never seen before. She looked lovely.

"Casey, this is David. David Greene. My fiancé."

His eyes held a kind expression. David was a good-looking man. Something about his demeanor made you want his approval.

"I know who you are," Casey said, slightly amused. "Ella works with you." She shook his hand.

Ella turned to David. "If it wasn't for Casey, I wouldn't have called you. To get my job back. She even picked out what to wear that day." She laughed at herself. How nervous she had been; how nice he was.

The crowds milled past them, and Casey inched closer to Ella's side of the aisle to get out of the way.

Ella opened her arms to embrace Casey. "I've missed you."

Casey didn't know what to say in return, but she hugged her back. She could feel Ella's thin shoulder blades beneath her hands.

"How are your parents?"

"Good," Casey answered. "I saw them last week at their store. And spoke to them Friday. My father's thinking about buying another building. Elder Kong found a smaller one for him. You know the other one burned down. The cost of this one is much lower, and—" She stopped abruptly. David was nodding encouragingly, but Casey remembered the primary rule about talking about money in front of people like David Greene. You shouldn't. Money was alluded to in where you spent your holidays or your hobbies, but never in dollars and cents. She had learned all this in college. "Anyway, they're both well."

"Your mom?"

"She's good. She even went to church today."

"Irene would love to see you."

"Oh, how is Irene?" Casey asked. "I have hats for her. I made her two for the summer. A canvas beach hat in white and a linen in a tangerine color. But summer has ended almost—"

"Oh, that's so sweet of you." Ella felt happy. "Are you free for lunch? Can you come by? I wanted to call you and talk to you about the wedding. Can you come? I made a frittata last night, and we have this very good brioche from... Casey, please."

The organ music of the postlude swelled about them. Ella slipped her arm through Casey's and led her out of the church.

Irene ran into Casey's arms. She showed off her sock monkey Grover. Casey made funny voices behind Grover. Irene considered the monkey seriously, understanding that the voice came from Casey, yet she talked to Grover anyway. David made Casey a Bloody Mary that was delicious.

The dining table had already been set with four places, with white roses for centerpieces. Ella set another place.

"Who else is coming?" Casey asked.

"I have a confession," Ella said. "But I didn't tell you before because I was afraid you wouldn't come."

Casey laughed. "Ella Shim is now conducting subterfuge? I am impressed. Divorce has been good for you." Casey's drink was half-gone already. She took a bite of the celery. Irene made a face when she was offered some.

"Grover—" Irene stuck the sock monkey near the stalk.

"Mmmm," Casey said, pretending to be the monkey eating the celery. "Crunch, crunch."

Ella smiled, afraid to break the good feeling. "Unu is here."

"What?"

"I mean, he's not here right now, but he's staying here with me. He's had some troubles. David helped him get a job at St. Christopher's, and he's starting next month. Teaching statistics and pre-cal."

"Is he all right?" Casey asked. "He's living here?"

Ella nodded. "He's much better now. I mean, he's doing great, actually. But the gambling, Casey. You never told me. That it was serious."

"It wasn't your business," Casey snapped.

"No, Casey, I didn't mean that you had to tell me. I think you were respecting his privacy. I understand that. I do. I think you were right not to tell me. It wasn't my business."

Casey stirred her drink with the celery stalk. What would he say when he saw her? That's why his phone was no longer in service. He must have moved out of the apartment.

"Where is he now?"

"He went to a Gamblers Anonymous meeting. He'll be back any minute. I didn't want you to be surprised."

"Why are you telling me all this? It's none of my business."

Casey had offered to take him to those meetings, but he had not gone. But now that he was at Ella's, he was going. How did Ella get him to quit gambling and to get a job?

"Maybe I should go."

Irene pulled at Casey's shirt, pushing Grover into her hand. "Talk," she said. "Make Grover talk."

Casey picked up Grover. "Hi, Irene. Can we eat banana cake for lunch? Yum yum yum." She made Grover kiss Irene's cheek.

Irene laughed, but Casey's mood had darkened considerably. She wanted to go back to the Gottesmans'. She'd been trying to figure out what to do with her living situation in the fall. Now both she and Unu were living in other people's houses. It was so pathetic.

Casey picked up her handbag.

"I do wish you would stay," David said. "I've heard so much about you. All wonderful things. I wanted to hear about your hats. Did you make the one you were wearing today?"

"Yes," she replied.

"It's beautiful. Ella wore the one you made for her to my mother's birthday party. She looked marvelous in it."

"Oh," Casey said. "That's nice."

"Everyone said I should wear the hat all the time," Ella said.

Irene raised her arms, and Casey put down her drink to pick up the child. She kissed her on both cheeks, then put her down.

Casey tapped her jacket pocket. "May I?" But she remembered her friend's allergies. "I mean, never mind. I'll step outside for a minute." She didn't want to smoke in front of Irene anyway. "I won't be long."

In the backyard, Casey lit her cigarette and inhaled. White roses climbed the green trellised wall. They had faded a bit, but the smell was glorious. Irene's toys were strewn about, and Casey felt comfortable seated on the Chinese ceramic stool. She would leave after her cigarette. Ella couldn't really expect her to stay. What was the point of it?

She heard the sliding glass door opening.

"Wonder Woman, where are your cuffs?"

Casey smiled at him. A patch of gray streaked Unu's forelock. He looked good to her, less tired than before. He smiled at her, too.

"I had planned on leaving after this cigarette."

"Am I so awful that you'd run away?"

She shook her head no. "I'm sorry that I'm here. I didn't know. I didn't mean to—"

"Sit, please. Ella sent me out here to convince you to stay for lunch. She misses you terribly."

"You don't mind?"

"Do you?"

"We're ridiculous."

"Yes," he said. "How was your summer?"

"I got the offer."

"Are you going to take it?"

"Why did you ask me that?" she asked. No one else had asked her that except for Charlie Seedham.

"Because you hate it there."

"I don't hate it."

"Okay, you don't like it."

"I don't like it," she said calmly.

"In a way, it's tragic when you can do something you don't like," he said.

"Will you like teaching?" She felt like arguing with him.

"I don't know. But I will try it."

"Fair enough." Casey hesitated for a moment before saying, "I wanted to ask you about my things."

"I was evicted. Your things are gone." He had been practicing this statement in his mind for some time, not knowing exactly when he'd have to recite it. "The landlord took them and probably sold them. I'm sorry. I will pay you back." This was one of the steps from GA—making amends or something like that.

"Everything?" Casey put her hand to her mouth.

"Everything."

"Oh. My."

There were no more cigarettes left in her pack. Her purse was inside the house.

"Wow," she said.

"If you make a list of what you had and tell me how much it was—"

"No." She closed her eyes. "I guess we're even."

"No. We're not, Casey."

She opened her eyes and blinked, hurt by what he'd said. "I am sorry about what I did. I do regret that."

"And I'm sorry that I didn't—"

Casey shook her head. She didn't want any apologies.

"Hey, I have missed you."

Casey nodded, but she couldn't face him. She clasped her hands together. "I don't think I'm going to take the offer."

"Good."

"I don't think I'm going back to business school." The words just came out. She could never keep anything from him, though she hadn't known this last thing herself. Unu had seen her act a fool, yet in all the time he'd known her, he hadn't judged. Then she'd hurt him. It had meant a lot to have his respect. His company. His friendship. "I don't think I can, Unu."

"Even better." Unu reached over, his large hand enveloping hers.

She pulled her hand away gently. There was a plastic tub of street chalk on Irene's child-size picnic table. With yellow and green chalk, Casey drew a row of tulips on the slate-paved ground. The heads of the tall flowers resembled giant soft-boiled eggs with their shell tops cut off, their edges crimped simply.

"Grown-up life is harder than I thought," he said.

"You're not kidding." They both chuckled.

"Why don't you make hats?" he said.

She almost laughed. "There's no money in that."

"Since when did you want money?"

She stopped herself from calling him "private-school boy."

"Are you really not going to finish business school?" he asked.

It sounded so much worse to hear the word *finish*, as if she were leaving something undone. She put down the chalk and dusted off her hands, then sat down again.

"I just can't see it." She tried to imagine herself as a milliner; that was not impossible. "And the loans—"

"It would be stupid to get into more debt if you don't need the degree."

"My life has become stupid."

Unu moved closer to her and kissed her.

He pulled away first.

"Casey, you lack nothing."

"I am living in someone else's guest room, and I can put all of my possessions in one suitcase. And so can you."

Unu didn't flinch. "It's temporary. I'm not ashamed of that. I've helped others."

"Yes." She bit her lip. "You helped me."

"Casey, I wouldn't want you to become one of those hard people." He placed his hands beneath her wrists and held them gently. "They're so bare without them."

Casey studied the underside of her pale wrists. Loose braids of thin blue veins ran up her arms.

From the kitchen, Irene tapped on the glass door, despite her mother having forbidden her to disturb Uncle Unu and Aunt Casey outside. They turned to see her and waved. Irene tapped some more, smiling.

Unu picked up a piece of purple chalk. Hunching over, he drew long stalks of grass framing her flowers.

She fell softly on her knees and began to color in the petals, and Unu joined her on the ground and began to draw a tree.

ACKNOWLEDGMENTS

I want to thank my superb agent Bill Clegg, who is both wise and kind. I feel fortunate to have his keen insights and steady counsel. I am grateful to Suzanne Gluck for her faith and passion, and to Matt Hudson, Matt Lewis, Alicia Gordon, Cathryn Summerhayes, Caroline Michel, Shana Kelly, Tracy Fisher, and Raffaella De Angelis for their tireless efforts on my behalf. I owe an enormous debt to my incomparable editor Amy Einhorn, whose intelligence and care shine throughout this book. I am grateful to Jamie Raab and to the marvelous Emily Griffin, who patiently answers all of my many questions. I would like to acknowledge the inspired work of Tanisha Christie and Anne Twomey. Much thanks to Chris Barba, Emi Battaglia, Judy DeBerry, Kim Dower, Linda Duggins, Randy Hickernell, Mindy Im, John Leary, Kelly Leonard, Jill Lichtenstadter, Tom McIntyre, Tareth Mitch, Martha Otis, Bruce Paonessa, Miriam Parker, Les Pockell, Jennifer Romanello, Judy Rosenblatt, Roger Saginario, Renee Supriano, William Tierney, Karen Torres, and Sona Vogel.

A number of kindhearted and patient individuals agreed to be interviewed for a work of fiction—no small act of trust—and gave of their time to explain many difficult things to me. Thanks to Linda Ashton, Ana Bolivar, James Calver, Ben Cosgrove, Lacy Crawford, Christopher Duffy, Alexa du Pont, Stuart Ellman, Chris Gaito, Shinhee Han, Alex Hungate, Brian Kelly, Lisa Kevorkian, Alex Kinmont,

Hali Lee, Jin Lee, Dr. John Mastrobattista, Christopher Mansfield, Anthony Perna, Dr. Mary Rivera-Casamento, Catherine Salisbury, and Ginee Seo.

I am deeply grateful for the friendship of Lynn Ahrens, Jonathan Angles, Harold Augenbraum, Shawn Behlen, Susan Berger Ellman, Ayesha Bulchandani-Mathrani, Kitty Burke, Lauren Cerand, Alison and Peter Davies, Steven Fetherhuff, Sam George, Susan Guerrero, Sarah Glazer and Fred Khedouri, Wendi Kaufman, Henry Kellerman, Robin Kelly, Wendy Lamb, Diane Middlebrook, Nancy Miller, Tony and Sue O'Connor, David and Michael Ouimette, Kyongsoo Paik, Jennifer Peck, Lois Perelson-Gross, Peter Petre, Sharon Pomerantz, Iris San Guiliano, Angella Son, Sally Steenland, Lauren Kunkler Tang, Jeannette Watson Sanger, Kamy Wicoff, and Donna and Neil Wilcox.

I'd like to thank Speer Morgan and Evelyn Somers of *The Missouri Review,* Carol Edgarian and Tom Jenks of *Narrative Magazine,* Quang Bao of the Asian American Writers Workshop, and the New York Foundation for the Arts for their invaluable support.

I am indebted to Elizabeth Cuthrell for her intelligence, encouragement, and goodness. Robin Marantz Henig has taught me much about literary excellence and artistic community through her work and life. Elizabeth and Robin gave me a book when I didn't have one. Bob Ouimette has offered solace in the writing of this work and continually teaches me about the meaning of friendship. Thanks to Rosey Grandison, whose love and labor permitted me to write. It was Dionne Bennett who saw this book first and whose love and insights have been indispensable to me since we were girls. Dionne, you made me believe that it was possible. Thanks to my family for their love, sacrifice, and faithfulness.

And finally, my darling Christopher and Sam: You are my sunshine.

READING GROUP GUIDE

DISCUSSION QUESTIONS

1. Lee has said elsewhere that she believes everyone is a kind of millionaire because each person possesses innate gifts or talents that make him or her wealthy. What do you think of this idea? What inherent gifts or talents do Casey, Ella, and Ted have? Are they aware of their own gifts?

2. Why did Ella and Ted marry? How does adultery affect their relationship? Is sexual betrayal the reason why they end the marriage? Why is Ted drawn to Delia? Why is Delia drawn to Ted?

3. Does Leah love her husband, Joseph? Does she love the choir director, Charles Hong? How are these feelings different and similar?

4. How does an Ivy League education affect Casey's development as a young woman?

5. What does Joseph want for his daughters and why? Why does he drink? How does he change by the book's end?

6. Casey often makes unpopular choices. Why does she make them? With which choices do you agree, and with which do you disagree?

7. The novel is divided into three sections entitled Works, Plans, and Grace, respectively. What do these title names mean to you, and why do you think Lee organizes her book this way?

8. How does immigration affect Casey's characterization and her goals? How might this book be changed if she were not an immigrant? If she were not Korean? If she had not grown up working class?

9. Casey and Ella have known each other since they were little girls in Sunday school. How does their relationship change throughout the novel? What does Ella want from Casey, and what does Casey want from Ella?

10. When Casey meets Jay again at the Princeton reunion, how do they feel about each other (Book III, Chapter 7)?

11. The book has many scenes that take place in a Korean-American church in Queens. What role does the church serve for the Han and Shim families?

12. How does Sabine's relationship with Casey compare with Leah's relationship with Casey?

13. The bond between Casey and Tina is a strong one, but how do they get along as sisters? What does Tina want from her life? How does she change in the novel?

14. There is a scene where the Han family exchanges wedding presents with the bridegroom's family (Book II, Chapter 9). Why does Leah spend so much money on the gifts? How does this Korean practice differ from American wedding rites?

15. What do you think Casey and Unu will do with their lives? What would you like them to do? In the final image of the book, why do they draw a tree and flowers?

QUESTION AND ANSWER
WITH THE AUTHOR

How did you choose Casey Han's name?

I began this novel shortly after September 11, 2001. And until August, 2007 I lived in downtown New York, not ten blocks from the World Trade Center.

After the attack, the *New York Times* published a series of brief obituaries with photographs of all those who had died. I could hardly read them, but now and then I tried. One day, I opened the section and saw a young Asian woman's face. Her first name was Casey. She was pretty, with a beguiling expression—like someone you'd look forward to seeing at work. She had a Korean surname, and I'd never met a Korean with the given name Casey before. I don't know anything about her except for what was on that brief obituary, but I named my character after this woman who died so close to where I lived.

As for Casey's surname, I have been told that there is only one Han family line in Korea, whereas there may be many branches of Kim, Lee, or Cho. The word *han* can be loosely translated as a uniquely Korean sentiment of lament—an inexpressible anguish or suffering of a people from a divided nation whose national history is one of humiliation and loss. The meaning of *han* is considered by some to be a national cultural trait, reflecting historical oppression and isolation. That a young woman growing up in America with such enormous freedom and advantages could somehow carry with her this unconscious sense of historical suffering was something I considered throughout the writing of this book.

Casey Han and her traditional Korean father have a pretty violent opening scene. It might be helpful for readers to get his perspective on the events taking place. Is there anything you'd like to add about this scene and why it's happening?

This scene was difficult to write, because domestic violence is prevalent yet hidden in patriarchal cultures, and to write about it seemed like a betrayal. It was essential to write this scene in an omniscient voice because I wanted to dramatize and personalize the experience of violence for each character in the room. In this scene, the father is the perpetrator of the violence, while Casey is the victim; the mother is present but helpless and the sister keeps to herself. Each character acts out all that he or she cannot express. I think about children who do not have language and who have to hit, bite, or cry. I love the phrase you say to preschoolers: "Use your words." But grown-ups don't always have the words either, yet they, too, have all this feeling. I wanted to show that kind of emotional illiteracy and frustration sympathetically in this scene. The fight between the father and daughter was unfair, but to me it was Casey, the one who was hit, who was in some measure stronger because she had greater power of expression and awareness.

Where did you find the inspiration for the book?

A friend told me a story about the free lunches given at investment banks after a deal ends. For example, if an investment bank closed a bond offering for a Chinese telecom company, there might be a free dim sum lunch for some of the employees of that investment bank. My friend told me that where he worked, sometimes the wealthiest employees were the first in line to grab a lot of food. I thought this was ironic and funny: free food for millionaires. I had intended to write a short story, but my best friend, Dionne Bennett, a professor at Loyola, said it would make a great novel because I am familiar with this world of Wall Street and New York's complicated class structure. I started this book in 2001 and finished it in 2006.

How did you decide to write about Casey and Ella?

I quit being a lawyer in 1995 to write fiction. For about five years, there was no relief to the number of rejections I received. It was then I began a short story called "Bread and Butter." It became my first published story, and I was thirty-two years old. The story was about two young women who become friends by accident and about how failure affects each one and their feelings for each other and themselves. They were both Korean American and newly married— one was wealthy, beautiful, and depressed and the central character was poor and unattractive, but possessed enormous confidence and even larger dreams that she could not fulfill. It was really that story and how it was received that gave me the courage to write about friendship—permitting me to render Casey and Ella's dynamic. I have also met the Ellas of this world, who romanticize poverty, and those who escape it. It felt true to me that Ella was drawn to Casey for her energy and desires in the same way she is drawn to Ted and his exuberant ambition. Everyone always talks about how the poor want to be rich, and there is that, of course, but I've also seen the opposite to be true.

Do you have any favorite male characters?

There are the obvious good guys like Isaac Gottesman or Dr. Shim. I love them for their kindness and wisdom. I adore the rake Hugh Underhill because there is something sexy about his carelessness regarding his beauty and privilege. Nevertheless, I think my favorite male character might be Ted, because his desires were so strong. He may be repellent to some, but I think we all know a variation of Ted in our lives, and whatever they are doing, we want to watch them compulsively. I wanted to see how the son of uneducated cannery workers goes to Phillips Exeter Academy, Harvard College, then Harvard Business School, marries a beautiful doctor's daughter, an heiress's. What would it be like to give him what he wanted and worked for? What would he want next? I found his behavior on the page interesting, because what I learned was that he craved to feel at ease, though it looked as if he was winning every battle smoothly. The person who made him feel this way was Delia, the office "slut." How bizarre, but to me, very true. I believe that Ted could not and would not have chosen Delia unless he had actually lived and experienced the fulfillment of his primary wishes and goals.

You've chosen to write this book showing many points of view. Is there a reason why?

More than anything, I wanted to try to write novels in the style of the ones I loved. I have always loved nineteenth-century literature from England and Europe, and early twentieth-century literature from America. The books I reread for pleasure almost always employ an omniscient narrator—either a fictive person who knows everyone's thoughts and how the story will be told or the author himself who knows how the story ends and why. There is a godlike quality to omniscience, and it is that I am vainly approaching in storytelling.

Also, I think I loved Tolstoy, Dostoyevsky, Turgenev, Thackeray, Flaubert, George Eliot, Balzac, Edith Wharton, Maugham, Dickens, the Brontes . . . because they reveal marginal characters as well as the central characters. Perhaps this is important to me because of my own background in which I have felt both marginal and central at different times. Obviously, none of those books featured anyone biographically like me. It's very difficult to share what you learn and speculate only through one point of view. The omniscient point of view lends itself to far greater flexibility and spaciousness.

Though omniscient narration is an unpopular way of storytelling for modern writers, it can reveal how everyone in the room is thinking about the issues and each other and themselves, rather than what they are actually doing and saying. Even the people of the finest character don't speak truthfully or act honestly all the time. It is only in fiction that all the dimensions of personality and behavior may be witnessed. I wanted to have a go at taking it all down.

Who are your favorite authors, and which are your favorite books?

George Eliot: *Middlemarch*
Charlotte Bronte: *Jane Eyre*
William Makepeace Thackeray: *Vanity Fair*
Sinclair Lewis: *Main Street*
Thomas Hardy: *Jude the Obscure*
Honore de Balzac: *Cousin Bette, Lost Illusions*

Leo Tolstoy: *Anna Karenina*
Toni Morrison: *The Bluest Eye*
Theodore Dreiser: *Sister Carrie*
Zora Neale Hurston: *Their Eyes Were Watching God*
Edith Wharton: *The House of Mirth*
Gustave Flaubert: *Madame Bovary*
Junichiro Tanizaki: *The Makioka Sisters*

What's the best piece of advice you ever received? How have you applied it to your writing career?

I heard in a sermon once that the definition of self-control was to choose the important over the urgent. I think as a writer, it is difficult but necessary to defer gratification and to do the work and to keep doing the work regardless of its prospects. I think John Gardner's advice to writers was very good—basically, not to expect that writing would provide for your needs, but to write anyway if you must. Often, I've wished that I could've had quicker success, greater financial security, more respect, et cetera, as a writer. For nearly twelve years now since leaving the law, I have often felt ashamed for wanting to be a writer and doubtful of my talents. What helped in these moments was to consider what was important, rather than the urgent feelings of embarrassment and helplessness. What was important is still important now: to learn to write better in order to better complete the vision one holds in one's head and to enjoy the writing, because the work has to be the best part.

What will your next novel be?

I am working on a novel called *Pachinko*. It is set in Tokyo and its central characters are ethnic Koreans, Japanese, and expatriate Americans. I started this book in pieces long before *Free Food for Millionaires*, and a story excerpted from the manuscript was published in *The Missouri Review* a few years ago. The story, "Motherland," features Etsuko Nagatomi, an important character from the book, but the novel's main character is the boy Solomon in the story, who appears mostly as a young man in the novel. Solomon Choi is an ethnic Korean whose father owns lucrative pachinko parlors in Tokyo and Kyoto. Solomon is sent to international schools in Tokyo, educated at universities abroad, then finds work as a trader in an investment bank. Solomon is a romantic character and a highly seductive person.

I have been curious about the ethnic Korean population in Japan and their history since college. For me, fiction usually starts with a personal question or actual event, then I try to see the people and how they behave under their circumstances. I am most interested in what people want and what they do in relation to their desires. I have recently moved to Tokyo with my family, so it should be a rich environment for my next work.

On Writing

FREE FOOD FOR MILLIONAIRES

My parents, sisters, and I immigrated to Queens, New York, in March of 1976. My family was sponsored by my uncle John, a computer programmer at IBM. I was seven years old—two years older than my main character, Casey. Also, like her, I grew up in Elmhurst in a blue-collar neighborhood. We lived in a series of shabby rented apartments for the first five years, and then my parents bought a small three-family house in Maspeth and rented out the other two floors while we lived on the second floor. I learned how to speak English and to read and write in the public schools of Elmhurst and Maspeth, Queens. My sisters and I were latchkey kids. Our summers were spent working in our parents' wholesale jewelry store and hanging out at the Elmhurst Public Library.

I could not have articulated it in this way then, but my childhood was continually informed by immigration, class, race, and gender. This book features first- and second-generation immigrant characters, and therefore, I believe that it satisfies the definition of an American story because unlike any other country in this world, America has this generative quality due to its immigration policies and early colonial history. With the exception of Native Americans and descendants of slaves, in the United States everyone's biography is ultimately connected to an immigrant's journey.

I was a history major in college, and my senior essay was about the colonization of the eighteenth-century American mind. Quite a mouthful. My argument then was that original American colonists from England and the generations that followed felt profoundly inferior intellectually and culturally to Europeans and those back home in their motherland. That idea has affected how I see my own challenges in America as an immigrant. I am not legally colonized—far from it—but an immigrant is like an early colonist (a word currently out of favor), that is, a person who has come from somewhere else, who learns to adapt to her new land with all its attendant complexities with an overall wish to acquire new "territory." It is an interesting position to consider since I am venturing to make culture—my crayon drawings of what I see and notice—in the form of fiction. I can be critical of how this country works, but I also respect its ideals of rugged individualism, the Protestant work ethic, and the American entrepreneurial spirit. It is easy to criticize America, but from a global perspective this is an amazing country with tremendous openness. This comment has been made before, elsewhere, by many pundits, and I think it is worth considering: Many who criticize America would still prefer to live here rather than anywhere else. Carlos Buloson, the Filipino American author, titled his rich novel *America Is in the Heart.* To me—another immigrant from a later time—I, too, possess a complex America in my heart.

Having said that, if you honestly love any object or subject, you will ultimately need to admit to its flaws in the hopes of some idealized love. We recall America's checkered backstory: the near-annihilation of Native Americans, enslavement of African Americans, Jim Crow legislation, gender inequality, immigration quotas for people from southern Europe, the Chinese Exclusion Act, the internment of Japanese Americans, America's reluctance to entering World War II, Hiroshima, McCarthyism, Vietnam, and the list continues. And thus, we recognize with both shock and compassion how with every generation, America has transferred its set of insecurities and anxieties to the newcomer.

With all this in mind, I wanted to chronicle the personalities and issues that abound in my village of New York in the form of a novel, because I wanted to reveal these images and thoughts to myself and, hopefully, to my reader. I was profoundly affected by nineteenth-century European novels when I was growing up, and in college, I had the opportunity to read American novelists like Sinclair Lewis, Ernest Hemingway, James Baldwin, F. Scott Fitzgerald, Theodore

Dreiser, John Dos Passos, and Edith Wharton, among others, who made me realize that what you saw and wondered about should be reflected in a literary work with an eye toward integrating emotion, history, insight, and narrative shape.

There are many kinds of immigrants. When I was growing up in Queens, the immigrants were German, Polish, Irish, Greek, Italian, and Hungarian, as well as Chinese, Korean, and Indian. One of the interesting and perhaps obvious aspects of being a non-white immigrant is that an Asian American cannot "pass" as a member of the majority group as long as his or her phenotypical features remain racialized. Simply put, if your eye shape, nose, hair texture, or your physical body type reflect a distinctiveness compared to the ones belonging to the majority group—for good or for bad—full assimilation may not be possible. This can cause all sorts of interesting problems to crop up even in an open place like America. Some have argued persuasively that racial minorities may always be immiscible with the majority. Naturally, this theory may cause consternation to many who wish to be a member of the majority culture with all its privileges and responsibilities. In this book, I handed my characters all sorts of gifts: education, good appearances, talents, strong family structures . . . and I wanted to see what they would do with their ambitions. They also received trials and caused some troubles of their own. Would race, class, immigration, and gender politics affect them? Or you might ask, how could they not? I wanted to know very much what would happen, too.

I believe that the dearth of accurate representations of Asian Americans in the media and in the arts has led to a misrepresentation of Asian Americans. Very often Asian Americans are perceived as highly competent, hardworking, and non-belligerent—that being the "positive" image—or they are represented as devious, inscrutable, and megalomaniacal. Whichever way it is done, these images do not fully represent the Asian Americans I know. If an Asian American, or anyone for that matter, is not given a voice and language with clear expression and evidence of feeling, his humanity is denied. What separates us as humans from machines or animals is our ability to feel, to express, to wonder, to yearn, to regret . . . I believe that the absence of accurate reflections is effectively a kind of social erasure with grave psychological consequences. The difficulty, however, is in discussing that which is not seen. In my attempt at the community novel, I wanted very much to reveal the complicated individuals who make up the Korean Americans I know. As a writer, I wanted to place the same demands on my non-Korean-American characters as well.

Forgive me for stating what may be to many of you the obvious: A Korean-American man can be romantic, passionate, loving, funny, and he can be troubled, sad, and frustrated. He can be all those things and so much more. A Korean-American woman can have existential questions about her world. He can be afraid. She can be heartbroken. It was extremely important to me that the Korean-American men and women I know and love in my life were given a fair shake in terms of their complexity. I have known Korean men who listen to opera, write poems, worry about losing their hair, and would give every cent in their pockets to their friends. I have seen Korean women ruin their lives through too much sacrifice or self-sabotage. I wanted men and women like that in my story. It is an ever-present concern for me that in our collective wish to succeed and assimilate, we, as Korean Americans, will not make trouble or not say what we think or feel. That silence or deferral until the time is safe permits others to interpret our characters and lives for us. I cannot speak accurately for all Korean Americans. This book is clearly one person's limited point of view. Nevertheless, I love being Korean American, and I love my family, my communities, and my history. This love was a kind of filter and a kind of bias. I wanted to honor what I know by telling it as truthfully as possible—with all its flaws and with all its beauty. My goals for this novel were embarrassingly lofty, but at the minimum I wanted the characters to be imperfect and to be gifted, too, because I believe that is how we are all made.

Lastly—but I think, for me as a fiction writer, most importantly— I want to share with you that for all of my life, for as long as I can remember, I have loved to read. A writer is always a reader first. Throughout my life, what has consistently given me great consolation was being able to read. When I studied how to write fiction better, my models were always the books I wanted to read again and again.

I hope this book pleases you. Thank you for reading this. It means a great deal to me to have your attention and time.

M.J.L.
Tokyo, Japan, 2007

ABOUT THE AUTHOR

MIN JIN LEE went to Yale, where she was awarded both the Wright Prize for Nonfiction and the Veech Prize for Fiction. She has received the New York Foundation for the Arts Fellowship for Fiction, the Peden Prize from the *Missouri Review* for Best Story, and the Narrative Prize for New and Emerging Writer. Her work has also been featured on NPR's Selected Shorts and anthologized in *To Be Real* (Doubleday, 1995) and *Breeder* (Seal Press, 2001). She lives in New York with her husband and son.